PART 35

BOOKS BY JOHN NICHOLAS IANNUZZI

FICTION

Condemned
J.T.
Courthouse
Sicilian Defense
Part 35
What's Happening?

NON-FICTION

Handbook of Trial Strategies
Handbook of Cross Examination
Trial: Strategy and Psychology
Cross Examination: The Mosaic Art

PART 35

A NOVEL

JOHN NICHOLAS IANNUZZI

A MADCAN BOOK

All rights reserved, including without limitation the right to reproduce this book or any portion thereof in any form or by any means, whether electronic or mechanical, now known or hereinafter invented, without the express written permission of the publisher.

This is a work of fiction. Names, characters, places, events, and incidents either are the product of the author's imagination or are used fictitiously. Any resemblance to actual persons, living or dead, businesses, companies, events, or locales is entirely coincidental.

Copyright © 1970 by John Nicholas Iannuzzi

ISBN 978-1-4804-7687-5

Cover image, *New York Cityscape*, by Kurt Schumann

Cover design by Neil Alexander Heacox

Distributed by Open Road Distribution
345 Hudson Street
New York, NY 10014
www.openroadmedia.com

for
Nicholas P. Iannuzzi, Esq.,
my partner, my friend, my father

PART 35

BOOK ONE

CHAPTER I

PATROLMEN ROGER SNIDER AND FORTUNE LAURIA stood in the rubbish-strewn rear yards of the tenements of Stanton Street, blinking skyward into spiraling rain. It was heavy, humid rain, and it had been falling all day, and now summer wasn't hot or sunny anymore; it just stank of rubbery raincoat, of perspiration, of grease, of squalor, of rotting wood, of wet cardboard.

The wooden plankings of the fences that separated the rear yards of the buildings on Stanton Street from those on Rivington Street were a leaning, disintegrating patchwork. They enclosed refuse, abandoned, rotting junk—a bicycle fender, a worn-down broom, bags of garbage thrown from windows, rusted toys, broken bottles, a mattress, rubble, cardboard boxes used by kids for sleds in winter and forts In summer. A gangling pole, shorn, tilting at the over-cast sky, was pulled in a dozen directions by a myriad of clotheslines.

Raindrops rolled down the cheeks of the two policemen as they scanned the building tops. They had responded to a telephone report of a prowler on one of the roofs.

It was 2:27 P.M.

"What a filthy hole," said Snider. He was the taller of the two, well-built, strong. "What the hell is there to steal in these dumps?"

"Junkies'd sell their sisters for a fix. What filth these spics live in," replied Lauria. He was shorter, thin.

"I can't wait for this tour to end," said Snider, his eyes still searching. "At four o'clock I take off for the country. Fresh, clean country, where I don't have to smell this stinking precinct for four days."

"Nice. You get a four-day vacation, and I get an eight-to-four tour for the holiday. Who do you know?" Lauria bitched.

A back window on the first floor of 152 Rivington Street slid open. A woman motioned frantically with her arm, pointing toward one of the roofs.

"Up there. Up on the fire escape," the woman called.

Lauria twirled. Overhead he caught sight of a Negro clambering up the steps of a top-floor fire escape toward the roof. He was carrying something.

"Up there, Roger," Lauria called sharply, pointing. "Take the stairs, quick."

"Okay, but you take it slow."

It was 2:28 P.M.

Snider ran, cutting through an alley to the street. He drew his revolver as he ran. Lauria looked for a way up. The building, 153 Stanton Street, had a one-story extension with a vertical ladder on the side. Lauria climbed the ladder to the roof of the extension. From there he jumped and grabbed the bottom rung of the fire-escape ladder, pulling himself in a half-kip up to the first-floor platform. He vaulted the rail and began grinding up the metal steps. He unsheathed his service revolver as he edged sideways along one of the fire escape landings.

Anilda Rodriguez stopping mopping. Through her rear window she watched Lauria mount the last steps to the roof.

In Apartment 5A, the front apartment just below the roof, Gloria Mae Winston was frozen by fear as she listened to feet thundering overhead.

In the building's stairwell, Snider made a running grab at the banister as he started up the last flight of steps to the roof.

PART 35

A violent, shattering fusillade of gunfire assaulted the stagnant, rotting tenements.

It was 2:30 P.M.

Carmen Salerno, who had seen Patrolman Lauria running past her window on his way to the roof, edged back until she could feel the wall against her shoulder blades.

Tomas Echevaria, sitting at his cobbler's workbench at the front of his shop, paused. Kids, he thought, with firecrackers. In the rain? he wondered, as he continued hammering.

Josefina Ramirez, walking along the sidewalk in front of her house, bringing her small daughter, Dorida, home from the day-care center, heard something. The woman who owned the *bodega* also heard the noise, looked out through the window and saw Josefina. They shrugged at each other, then smiled. The woman waved at Dorida.

"Open the door, somebody. This is the police," screamed Patrolman Snider as he tore down the stairs, his face blanched.

Rafaela Santos, who lived in Apartment IB, gathered her child in her arms and ran to the superintendent's apartment. She heard the cop screaming overhead.

Alma Soto, the tenant in Apartment 5B, the rear apartment just beneath the roof, was three blocks away, having lunch at her mother's apartment.

"A cop's been shot on the roof. Open up. Hurry!" Snider pounded on the door of 5A. Gloria Mae Winston didn't move. She heard the footsteps race down. Someone on the floor below opened a door.

"You got a phone—a phone?" Snider demanded. Amy Hollander, the old woman who had lived in Apartment 4A for the last thirty-five years, pointed to a table by the couch. Snider grabbed the phone and dialed. His knuckles turned white on the receiver as he waited for an answer. "Sergeant? Snider. Lauria's been shot! Yes, shot! Lauria. I don't know. Nobody was there when I got there. On the roof. One fifty-three Stanton Street. He's bleeding bad. Right! Right! Okay. Hurry!" He slammed down the phone and dashed into the hallway again. "Anybody—any men in this building?" he shouted, leaning across the banister, searching the stairwell below. "You. Yeah. Hurry up, up here! Come on." He spun about and dashed up toward the roof again. Sweat poured from under his cap. He glared at Gloria Mae Winston, now standing at the slight opening of her chained door. His eyes were glazed as he ran past her and up the stairs.

The time was 2:37 P.M. It was Monday, July 3rd, 1967.

CHAPTER II

ALESSANDRO LUCA, LAWYER, thirty-one years old, wearing a double-breasted tan suit custom-tailored by Scagliatti, and black ostrich shoes handmade in Florence, stepped from the elevator at the thirteenth floor. He had dark hair and dark eyes, weighed 165 pounds, and stood five feet, ten inches tall, although his records in the Air Force Advocate General's Office conceded him no more than five feet nine. He was American-born, of Italian-born parents, fatherless since the age of eight. He had been graduated from the Spring Hills (Connecticut) Military Preparatory School and Princeton University, and had been fourth in the class of '60 at Columbia University's School of Law. He liked an occasional Jamaican cigar, cognac, and tall women. He was unmarried, although he seldom lived alone.

Sandro entered his office. His secretary was not at her desk. He walked through the passageway leading to his private office. She was just emerging from the file room at the rear.

"Good morning, Mr. Luca," she smiled. "Your messages are on your desk."

"Good morning, Elizabeth. What's happening?"

"The clerk from the Supreme Court called. You've been assigned a murder case. A policeman was killed. Two men were arrested. Your defendant's name is Alvarado. I have the indictment number and the name of your co-counsel on my desk. And Judge Porta called. He asked that you call back before ten if you can."

"Get the judge on the wire for me, please."

The intercom buzzed, and Sandro picked up the phone.

"Hello, Sandro," the judge said in his gravelly voice. "I'm glad you got back to me before I got on the bench."

"Good morning, Judge."

"How's Mama? All right?" Sandro could almost see the smile on the judge's solid face—eyes, mouth, everything beneath the thin gray hair, smiled.

"She's fine, Judge. I spoke to her last night. Same as ever, independent, always Mama."

"Good, good. Don't forget to tell her her old sweetheart was asking for her." Eleven years on the Supreme Court bench had not dulled the effervescent politician in Mr. Justice Porta. Rough-hewn, skeptical, learned, he was a product of the city, its streets, its schools, its politics, and its courts.

"Listen, the reason I called," the judge continued, "is that I was able to assign you a murder case sooner than I thought. You'll probably get a call from downstairs today or tomorrow."

"We already received a phone call this morning, Judge."

"So soon? That kind of fast work can give bureaucracy a bad name." The judge laughed. Sandro joined him. "I put you in with Sam Bemer. You know Sam?"

"I know him from around the courthouse. I don't know him too well personally."

"Well, he's an old firehorse on homicide cases. He was an assistant D.A. in Brooklyn years back. I put you with him so he can teach you the ropes. Just remember what I told you: this is no game. This case is a cop-killing. Your man can get the chair."

"Judge, I won't let you down."

"Me? Hell! Don't let the defendant down. I'd tell you a story about my own first murder case, but I have to get on the bench. Good luck, Sandro. And don't let Uncle Jim down either."

PART 35

Sandro started to reply, but the judge was already gone. It was only two weeks since he had visited the judge in his chambers, Sandro thought.

"I don't want to have this sound like soap opera or anything like that, Judge," Sandro had said then, "but I've been thinking that I'm about ready to contribute some time to defendants who can't afford their own lawyer, some of the people who get a fast shuffle through our courts."

"Legal Aid does a pretty good job representing the indigent, Sandro."

"I know, Judge. When I first started to practice, I was impressed. But the more experience I get, the more I see cases handled as if they were on an assembly line. And a lot of times, there are cases where it seems that just a little something more could make the difference. I'm not running Legal Aid down. It's just that they have so many cases that it's impossible to devote enough personal attention to each. I think I might do somebody some good, sort of like a doctor doing clinic work."

"Well, Sandro, you know Legal Aid handles everything except for murder in the first degree. That's what it would have to be."

Sandro nodded.

"Murder cases are a great responsibility," the judge cautioned.

"They're work—real, serious work."

"I realize that, Judge."

The judge grew distant for a moment. Sandro waited respectfully. "You know, seeing you sitting there, Sandro, I can't help thinking of your Uncle Jim at your age. Handsome, and the way he carried himself, imposing. That was just about the time when he was getting so well known—or should I say, infamous?—that it wasn't healthy for a young politician to be seen in his company. He knew it, too. He knew it and stayed clear of me for more than thirty years. I didn't see him from the time I first ran for alderman from the old neighborhood until my children gave us a Mediterranean cruise for our fortieth anniversary, 1961. That must have been about a year before Uncle Jim died."

"The spring of '62," Sandro supplied.

"The ship stopped at Naples, and I looked him up. He got to be an old man in those thirty years." The judge laughed self-mockingly. "I guess I didn't look like a spring chicken, either. But I remembered him when he was a power, a force not to be defied."

Sandro said nothing, nodding or smiling occasionally, well aware that Judge Porta's ramblings eventually revealed a destination.

"We talked about when we were kids together and how we used to drop five-pound paper bags filled with water from the roof of the very building you were born in on Mulberry Street." There was mischief in the smile that warmed the judge's face.

Sandro found it difficult to visualize Uncle Jim, the notorious Don Vincenzo Tagliagambe, better known in the tabloids as Jimmie Pearl, throwing water bombs off a roof. Sandro's own earliest recollections of Uncle Jim barely predated his father's death, when Don Vincenzo, childless himself, became a second father to his sister's son.

"I think Uncle Jim felt he had to keep away from the people he loved," said Sandro. "Perhaps he felt they'd be smeared with the tarred brush the newspapers used on him."

The judge fell silent momentarily.

It had not been long after his father's death, Sandro thought, before Don Vincenzo exiled him to that pristine fortress of propriety, the Spring Hills Military Prep School—and at first it was an exile for Sandro, away from his friends, his family, the old neighborhood, and the old ways: Sandro had been abandoned in a world that he never knew existed and Don Vincenzo had only heard about. Those first months were lonely. But the boy's street instinct served him well; he was wary, close-mouthed, and never spoke to anyone about his background or about how his education was being paid for. As Don Vincenzo had instructed him very carefully, it was nobody's business that he was Jimmie Pearl's nephew.

The future that lay ahead of Sandro, according to Don Vincenzo, was to be great. He was going to be a gentleman, and a lawyer, the best, the toughest that ever lived.

"Your Uncle Jim did very well by you, Sandro, very well indeed, but he wasn't really a pillar of that community you want to devote your time and mind to," the judge now said. He was apparently getting closer to his point.

PART 35

"I've always thought he was a basically good man," Sandro replied, "underneath all that copy in the newspapers."

"Sure, he was a good man. To you, to your mama, to his family, to me, to his friends. But what about the other people he didn't love, that he terrorized?"

"I'm not able to tell you about that, Judge. You know, Uncle Jim kept me totally in the dark about what he did. There aren't even many people who know that I'm his nephew."

The judge shrugged over the long-distant past. "He was always trying to help people in his strange way. He thought—*Buon Anitna*, may his soul rest—that I didn't know when I first ran for alderman that his people were going around to all the polling places casting ballots for dead voters whose names were still on the rolls." The judge was smiling. "Fortunately, I won by more than the number of dead voters, so I don't feel so bad about it."

"The only thing I feel bad about, Judge, is that he had to die so far away from everyone, deported. I know he was involved in a lot of things, but I've never believed he was mixed up with narcotics. He thought that drugs were vile."

"Sandro," the judge cut him short. "That's a subject I won't discuss. He was a man whose principles I vowed to fight with my last drop of blood. He was your uncle, my boyhood chum, but he was convicted by a jury of being a racketeer, a hoodlum. He had his appeal, he lost, and the case is closed. The community is better off without him. I'm sorry to say that."

"Could he help the conditions in which he was born?" Sandro defended. "The poverty, the violence…"

"Hey, Sandro, don't tell me a hard-luck story. He and I grew up together. I went through it too. I'm here. Where did he end up? An old man, alone, back where he started, with no one near him to help him spend his money. That's all he could talk about that day in Naples." The judge studied Sandro. "He also talked a lot about you. He knew he was finished. But you were just starting. He told me you were going to be— the phrase struck me—a beautiful lawyer. That's what I was getting at before I got sidetracked by my own stories."

"Sidetracked, Judge, but never derailed."

"No," the judge laughed. "Your coming here today is fate working itself out, Sandro. Through you, your Uncle Jim will make his reparation. You will pay back for him. You know what I mean?"

Sandro did.

He buzzed Elizabeth on the intercom. "Give me the name of the defendant again."

"It's Luis Alvarado."

"Okay. Now get Sam Bemer for me, please."

She buzzed shortly, and Sandro picked up the phone.

"Hi, Sam, how're you?"

"Never better, m'lad. How's yourself?" Sam Bemer's hearty voice was an essential part of his benchside manner. It seemed fitting for a thick stocky man with thick curly hair and a thick black cigar—for such Sam Bemer was.

"Very well," Sandro answered. "I understand that I have been assigned the distinct privilege of being cocounsel in a murder case with the legendary Sam Bemer."

"You're much too kind. I received the same word myself this morning. I'm delighted we'll be working together."

"I hope it'll be a delight. I'm sort of in the dark about murder cases," said Sandro. "Where do we start on this?"

"Well, the first thing we want to do is to talk to our client and hear his story. Then we'll talk to the D.A. to see what we're faced with. Of course, with a cop-killer, it's tough to do very much except try the case. The D.A. doesn't usually entertain any plea to a lesser charge for a cop-killer. You go over to the court and get out the file. See whatever there is to be seen. Then we can meet and go to the Tombs to see this Alvarez."

"I think it's Alvarado."

"Whatever. His being a spic is just another strike against him."

"Another?"

"I read about this one in the newspapers when it happened. Some guys read stocks, sports. I read crimes. I think our guy is a junky besides. And he's a colored Puerto Rican. And he's got a record. And he's charged with killing a cop. And besides all that, I think he confessed to the cops. This case is like walking into a furnace."

There was a pause as Sandro digested these words.

"When shall we get together?" he finally asked.

"Let's see. How about tomorrow, say eleven, at the Tombs?" Bemer suggested.

"My calendar is open."

"Fine. Oh, it might not be a bad idea if you could pick up copies of all the newspapers that carried the story. The reporters get a lot of off-the-cuff stuff from the cops. You never know how helpful it might be."

"Right."

"Don't be glum," said Bemer. "In a case like this, where there's nothing to lose, we can take the long shots, pull out all the stops. The experience'll be good for you."

"I hope it's good for our client."

"He's lucky already; don't worry about him."

"How is he lucky?" asked Sandro.

"The cops didn't kill him in the station house."

CHAPTER III

AS SANDRO TURNED THE CORNER from Centre Street into White Street, he could see Sam Bemer standing atop the four-step entrance to the Tombs. Officially it is the Manhattan House of Detention for Men. But everyone calls it the Tombs. It is probably the busiest prison in the world, housing every person detained for trial in Manhattan and Staten Island, as well as all those who have been arrested in other boroughs and are arraigned in night court. There is a turnover of at least six hundred men a day in the Tombs, three to four hundred new inmates received, three to four hundred released or bailed, each with papers, physical examinations, photographs, files, cards, and a host of other records.

Sam saw Sandro and started to nod his head, a smile spreading from either side of the cigar in the center of his mouth.

"Hi, Sam."

"Sandro," Sam responded, removing the cigar, still smiling, nodding his head in tight, muscular movements. Sandro shook Sam's large hand.

"Waiting long?" Sandro asked, as they turned to enter the vestibule.

"Not more than two or three minutes. You certainly look prosperous."

PART 35

"Well, I'm keeping busy, not doing too badly."

"That's fine—fine."

Ahead was a huge door made of a grid of steel bars over thick glass with a frame of brass-faced steel. In the top part of the door a hinged glass panel, called a Judas eye, opened, and a wizened face appeared.

"Morning, Counselor," said the front-door guard.

"Morning, Joe," said Sam. Joe turned a large key in one of the door's locks, and the huge door swung open. Sam and Sandro entered the reception area. There were offices to the right and left. Those on the right were enclosed within five-foot-high half-glass panels. In them, men in the blue uniform of the Department of Correction were sifting through files, answering phones, writing. On the left were the executive offices. Straight ahead was an entire wall of bars with a gate in the center. On the other side of that was a lawyers' waiting area, and twenty feet beyond that was still another wall, with its own steel and glass door. The lawyers' waiting area gave the appearance of a cage. Inside it, a uniformed Negro sat at a desk. There were also a few chairs and oil paintings on the walls.

"Want to sign the book, Counselors?" said Joe, directing them to a desk to the left of the entrance. Sam wrote the name of the prisoner Alvarado, his own name, and Sandro's name. Sam also filled out a slip of paper with the prisoner's name on it.

"You know what floor he's on, Counselor?" asked Joe, taking the slip.

"No. This is the first time with this fellow, Joe," said Sam.

"I'll get it for you," said Joe, handing the slip over to one of the uniformed men, who fingered through a file of orange cards, wrote something on the slip of paper, and handed it back to Joe.

"He's on the seventh floor, Counselor." Joe handed the slip of paper through the bars to the guard at the desk inside the waiting area. He stood, selected a key from a ring of large keys, and opened the barred gate.

Sandro and Sam stepped into the cage and sat while the guard crossed the room to the door in the far wall. He handed Sam's slip of paper through the Judas eye to an unseen guard within.

Sandro got up to inspect the paintings. They were the work of men awaiting trial. One depicted the Four Horsemen of the Apocalypse against a gray background. The horses were elongated; the artist was probably a better burglar than painter. There was another of President Kennedy, one of Pope John XXIII, a clipper ship at sea, flowers. A few were quite well done. Perhaps some painters got arrested, too.

"Did you have a chance to get any of those newspapers I suggested?" Sam asked.

"Yes, they're in my bag. I read them."

"Well, what's the story?"

"From the newspaper accounts, these two were burglarizing an apartment in the Delancey area, on Stanton Street. Someone called the cops. Two cops arrived. One of them ran to the roof, became involved in a struggle, and was shot in the back with his own gun. By the time the other cop got up to the roof, the killer was gone. They picked up one of these guys at the scene. He lived a few doors away. He confessed and named the fellow we represent, who was picked up at his home several hours later, about one A.M., and subsequently confessed."

"Both Puerto Rican? Both junkies?"

"Yes. You were right. Alvarado is Negro, too. Very dark. Now there's a question for you. Is he Negro or Puerto Rican or both?"

"Negro, Puerto Rican, junky, a police record, a cop killed, and he's supposed to have confessed. Well, let's see what this fellow has to say for himself. You can't always trust these newspaper accounts. Sometimes you have to wonder how the hell anyone could have invented some of the stuff they write."

Sandro didn't speak. He sat watching Sam and then the Negro guard, who continually thrust his keys into the gate or the door, maintaining a flow of traffic. Presently, a slip of paper was passed through the Judas eye in the door in the far wall. The guard took it and read. "Alvarado?"

"Yes," said Sam. They walked to the door on the right, which the guard unlocked for them. It led into a large room with frosted windows covered by steel bars. Doorless cubicles, each furnished with a small table and two chairs, lined both side walls. There was a bench against the wall at the end of the room. On it, a short, trim

PART 35

Negro with a pencil-thin moustache sat studying the two lawyers as they entered. A guard sat in one of the rear cubicles, reading a newspaper.

"Alvarado?" asked Sam.

"I'm him," said the man on the bench, rising, walking toward them. He was about five feet six. He had short hair and was quite dark. His features were Caucasian. He wore chino pants and a white T-shirt, no belt, and laceless scuff slippers; most prisoners held for serious crimes are never allowed laces and belts, in order to discourage suicide attempts.

"I'm Mr. Bemer, this is Mr. Luca." Sam motioned toward an empty cubicle. "Grab another chair, will you, Sandro?" said Sam. Sandro took a chair from another cubicle, and the three men surrounded one of the small tables. They looked at each other silently. The adventure of life and death was about to begin.

"As you probably already know, Mr. Alvarado," Sam plunged in, "we've been appointed by the court to defend you on the charge of murder in the first degree. We don't know anything about what happened, or what this is about. We can only go by what you'll tell us. Now, what's the story?"

Alvarado had not stopped studying them. His eyes went from one to the other, watching. He listened attentively as Sam spoke, his tongue just poised on the edge of his bottom lip.

Now he shrugged, his two hands shrugging too. "I know little as you," he said with a Spanish clip to his English. "These guys arrest me, beat my ass, and I here. They keep sayin', 'You know, man, you know what happen on that roof.' And then one of these gentlemens, a big fuck, a baldie, he do like that"—Alvarado gave a short, violent straight punch to the air—"and they get me right here." Alvarado placed his fist at the center of his chest, just beneath his breastbone. "They gave me a lot of punches. I told them nothing. They gave me more. Then I go out."

"You went out where?" Sam queried.

"On d'floor. An' I gasps for breath. But I couldn't get none."

"When you say you went out, you mean unconscious?" Sandro suggested.

"Unconscious, yeah," Alvarado nodded, looking at Sandro.

"Wait a minute," said Sam. "Let me get some facts from the beginning. Where do you live?"

"I was have a room on South Ninth Street, Brooklyn."

Sam took out a pad, wrote July 26, 1967, on the top, and then began to make detailed notes of everything Alvarado said.

"Married or single?"

"I got a wife in Puerto Rico, but I ain't living with her for years." His word *years*, Spanish-clipped, sounded like *jeers*. "I living with a woman here for a while though."

"Children?"

"Sure. Two in Puerto Rico, and four here."

Sam looked at him. "Four children with this other woman?"

"Yeah. I got two other childrens with some other woman, but I don't see her for a long time."

"Eight children all together. Any more?" Sam was noting everything.

"I don't know any more if they are," he smiled briefly, looking to both lawyers. They didn't smile. Alvarado wiped his hand across the smile, quickly removing it from his face. He twisted sideways in his chair, leaning his back against the wall. He looked out through the glass partition to see where the guard was.

"You got a match for me?" he asked, keeping his eye on the guard. He took a crushed package of Pall Mall from a trouser pocket. Sam slid a book of matches across the table.

"Now, what do you know about this crime, about the cop on the roof?" asked Sam.

"Like I said, I know nothing. The cops gotta get somebody, so they get me, but I don't know enough as them how it happen." Alvarado saw the guard's attention distracted. He struck a match and took a long drag. He palmed the cigarette, fanning the air constantly to distribute the smoke. He slid the matches back to Sam.

"Look, we have to know the truth if we're going to be able to help you in any way," said Sam. "So don't bullshit us. I'll lay it right on the line, bullshit won't do you any good with us."

"I know it. I know it. I swear to you, I don't know what these men are sayin'." He took another drag, then continued the sweeping motions, which dispersed the smoke. "I went home and I stopped to see the super. Jorge is the super. I went into his apartment."

"When was this?"

"The night the cops got me, July, I think third. Yeah, July third, late night, like one A.M. No Independence Day for me, believe me. Three cops were waiting upstairs. They been there all along, but I wasn't home, so they waiting, and when I go to his apartment, Jorge says, 'Luis, did you kill a copy?' An' I look at Jorge. I say, 'Jorge, you crazy? Why you ask a thing like that to me, Jorge?' And he tell me, 'The cops are here, waiting upstairs, three detectives.' I looked at him, you know. I say, 'Jorge, is this a joke?' and he said, 'No, Luis, three guys are waiting.' I say to Jorge, 'Come on. I got nothin' to hide. Let's see these cops.'

"I turned and Jorge walked with me outside, and when I start up the stairs outside—the stoop—these three cops got their guns pointin' at my brains. I ask them, 'What's this about?' And one of them says to me, 'You'll find out.' I had a paper with me and in there was the story about the cop being shot, and I said, 'You're not bringing me in for this?' And I pointed to the paper, cause there in the subway I read about the cop killed. And it said there the cops were looking for a tall Negro, five nine or five ten, so I know it couldn't be me. And the cop tells me, 'You'll find out at the station house. You'll tell us about the roof.'

"Then they take me to the station house, you know. And I walk in, and the place is full with peoples. And they sayin' to me, 'Hello Luis, hi, Luis,' and I don't know any of these peoples, and I thinkin', how they know me? One cop, I don't know his name, a baldie, but red hair like fire on the sides, takes me up the stairs, and we go up to this room, all the way up, on the third floor, and there are these... these"—Alvarado motioned a rectangle with his hands—"closets, little ones, of 'eye-ron,' metal."

"Lockers?" suggested Sandro.

"That's it, lockers rooms. And they put my hands in my back with handcuffs, you know, like this." He demonstrated. "And they asked me I know Chaco? I says, I know someone called Chaco."

"Who's this Chaco?" asked Sam.

"That's Hernandez, the other guy the cops bring here."

"He's the one who told the police your name, the one who lived on the block where the cop was killed?" asked Sam.

"Must be he tol' that to them," Alvarado answered.

"Then what happened?" prodded Sam.

"About seven, eight other cops, without uniforms, I think off duty, come in, and they get around me like a circle, and one of them, the big baldie guy, give me punches here." He again demonstrated with his fist in the center of his chest. "And they ask me, 'What happen on that roof?' And I tell them, 'I don't know nothin' about that roof, cause I wasn't there.' Then this baldie starts working on me some more. Then I go out, like I said before. And one cop, an old guy with red face, says, 'You ain't out yet, spic,' and two guys pull me up and hold me, and this big baldie keeps punch-in' me, and I keep tellin' him I don't know what happen, I wasn't there."

"How long did this go on?"

Alvarado studied the air for a moment. "I can't tell you that, but I believe it was a long time they was beatin' me. Maybe one hour." Alvarado took a long drag, then stepped on the tip of the half-finished smoke, and preserved it carefully in his pocket.

"Go on."

"They keep it up more. Once somebody was comin' up the stairs, so they listen at the door, and one guy puts his hand on my chest and listen to my heart, and he put his fist in my face and told me keep quiet. And then somebody who came go away, and they start again with punches, askin' about the roof. And I told them, 'You gonna kill me here, cause I don't know what happened.'

"Then I went out a couple times more. I don't know for how long. I remember next they pick me up, and told me I was going to tell them about the roof, cause Chaco already told them about me. And I told them that if he already told them, they didn't have to ask me. And this big guy make his teeth show and he hit me. I was ascared of this guy. He was big, and he was like crazy. And he smell like whiskey, you know."

They watched Alvarado as he spoke, Sam looking down intermittently to make notes. Alvarado was calm and unhurried.

"Then another cop says, 'Don't hit that man again.' And they stop the punches, but they keep askin' these questions about the cop and the roof, and all. I tell them I wasn't the guy, and if they want to kill me, okay, but I wasn't the guy."

"Then they pick me up in the air. One guy picks up one leg and holds it behind me, and the other guy pulls my other leg to the front. You know, they holding me up in the air by my legs wide open, and one of them says, 'Okay, kick him in the balls.' And I scream and beg them and tell them I got a operation there and a kick will kill me. They let me down and keep workin' punches on my chest. Later, they tell me wash up cause the district attorney was coming and I was going to speak to the D.A. They bring me downstairs again and I wash my hands, my face, and they puts handcuffs behind me, in my back, on a chair, and they say, if I tell the D.A. about what happen, you know, beating me, I don't know what a beating is yet. And I waiting for the D.A., and they clean my nails, take some stuff from my nails. And another cop puts some toilet paper on my hand."

"Toilet paper?"

"That's what it look like, toilet paper, you know, long, and they put it here, on my palms. That's what it's call, right?"

"For traces of gunpowder," Sandro interpreted.

"No," Sam corrected. "They haven't done that for twenty years. It must have been for palm prints."

Sandro nodded.

"Then while I'm waiting, the cops bring in a radio, a TV, and they showed me fingerprints on them, you know, with white powder on them, and one guy says: 'You better talk. We got your prints all over this stuff.' And I told him, 'Maybe you take prints, but you don't read good, cause those can't be mine.'"

"Look," Sam interrupted, "I told you, no bullshit. I'm your lawyer, not the D.A."

"I know I got to tell you. I'm sayin' the truth. I got no reason to say a lie." He was not excited.

"Well if you didn't confess to the cops, what the hell was the D.A. coming for?" Sam asked sharply. "The cops don't send for the D.A. just to waste time, not in New York County. They send for him when they've got something for him to listen to. Now, you were waiting for the D.A. What for, if you didn't confess?"

"I don't know. I was jus' there, and they say to wash, the D.A. is coming. And they tell me if I say anything to the D.A. about what happen in the lockers room, they'll show me what a beating is. Maybe the guy coming wasn't the D.A. I don't know why they tell me that."

"Maybe you confessed to this crime. You know, I'll find out."

"I know this. That's why I'm tellin' the truth. Maybe they got the D.A. to talk to Hernandez. He was there, too."

"In the room with you upstairs on the third floor?"

"No, they take me down, and I was sitting in this room with the detectives, and Hernandez was in this cage, you know, waiting, too. Then the D.A. arrive, this guy they say was D.A. and he talk to Hernandez for a while in another room. Then they bring me to see the D.A."

"What happened?" Sam asked.

"He ask me questions, too."

"What questions?"

"I don't know. He say, I'm so-and-so from the D.A.'s, and this is so-and-so, the guy with the little machine."

"The stenotypist?"

"Yeah. And the D.A. ask me questions. I told him I don't know about that roof, cause I wasn't there."

"Did he advise you of your rights, about being silent, about having a lawyer?"

"Sure. But I tol' him, I didn't do nothin'. Why be silent, you know?"

"You sure you told the D.A. that you didn't commit this crime," Sam pressed.

"I'm sure I say that."

"Did the cops advise you of your rights when they questioned you?"

"The only thing they do is hit me right in my chests," he replied quickly.

"The D.A. ask you anything else? You tell him anything else?"

"The D.A. told me Hernandez already told him I did it. And I told him Hernandez was *loco*, crazy, that I didn't."

"Then one of the cops was behind the D.A., and he motion to me with his fist, you know? And then I told the D.A., 'Yes, I did it.'"

"You told the D.A. what?" Sam looked up from his notes.

"I told the D.A., 'Yes, I did it.' And the D.A. asks me, 'You know what you're saying?' And I says, 'Yes, but I don't really kill nobody, but I am being threatened by a detectives unless I says yes, I did it.'"

"Did a stenographer take this down on the machine?" asked Sandro.

"I know he was there, but he was behind me. I couldn't see his hands."

"What did the D.A. do then?"

"He asks me about one or two more question. I told him I don't know nothing. Then I show him my wrist. See my wrist." Alvarado showed the inside of his right wrist to the lawyers. There was a long thin scab across it. "That's from the cuffs the cops put on me."

"The D.A. see that?" asked Sam.

"I show him. He got to see it. Maybe they got that in the pictures with no clothes on."

"The what?" Sam asked.

"They make me take pictures with no clothes."

"That's a new one to me," said Sam. "Okay, tell me about that burglary. If your fingerprints are on the goods from that job, you haven't got a prayer. You know that, don't you?"

"I know that, Mr. Bemer. But I wasn't there. My prints can't be there, unless these cops can put them there. I know when a cop is killed, they can do anything. I don't even know the block where it happen."

"One fifty-three Stanton Street," Sandro supplied.

"That's the block where Hernandez lives, but I don't know that block. I wasn't there. I read that Hernandez car was double-park there and a woman, I think she's a whore, you know—and she does the womans' operations—she told the cops the car belong to Hernandez."

"What do you mean, operations?" asked Sam.

"When they got a kid, you know?"

"Abortions?"

"Yeah. She live on that block in Hernandez house. She told the cops the double-park car belong to Hernandez cause she knows Hernandez robs apartments and she thinks he hit her apartment once. I think she tell them she see me too."

"How do you know these things?" Sam queried.

"Cause they bring people when I waiting for the D.A., and the people, mostly womans, are on the other side of a glass, a mirror…"

"A two-way mirror?" Sam asked.

"That's right. They could look at me, but I don't see them. But I hear them, I know people are there, lookin', and I'm bendin', sideways."

"You don't know who was there?" Sandro asked.

"No. Only the one I say, the whore, cause I heard the cops on the other side talkin', thinkin' I can't hear, like they know this one. Asunta, that's her name."

Sam made a note. "Anybody else you know was there?"

"No, that's the only one. They were others there. Womans. But I don't know their name."

"Okay, then, if you didn't commit this crime," said Sam, "where were you?"

"I got up late. I seen some guy. I do a couple things. I eat. In the afternoon, I go to my room. I go downstairs to see Jorge, the super."

"The same Jorge you spoke to when you came home?" queried Sandro.

"Right, that's the same guy. And I had this whiskey, and I ask him, 'Jorge, you want to buy this?' And he says, 'How much?' So I told him, two bucks, and he says, 'Okay.' Then I stayed and talked to him for a while, and then I went down the block, and after, I took the subway over to Times Square."

"Where were you going?"

"I was going to Times Square, to the movies."

"Who was with you?" Sandro asked hopefully.

"I was by myself."

"Go ahead," Sam suggested.

"That's all." He lifted his hands in a gesture of finality.

"What are these marks?" asked Sandro, pointing to a small cluster of pinhole marks on the inside of Alvarado's arm near the elbow. "Are these fix marks?"

"No. They from a scab when I failed down in the station house, when these guys are beating me."

"You are a junky?" Sam said rather than asked.

"Yes, sir. I have no fix now since I'm here, three weeks, so I'm pretty clean."

"Before, you were using the stuff?"

"Yes."

"Heroin?"

Alvarado nodded.

"How about pushing the stuff?" Sam continued.

"I was hustling in the street. I wasn't pushing, but sometimes a guy needed something, and he didn't know where to get it. I help him out, deliver it. Stuff like that."

"You serve any time for it?"

"Yeah, I got busted three times."

"When."

"Once in '60, I did ninety days. Another time in '62, I did ninety days. And another in, I don't know, I guess that was '62, too. I got one year, nine months, to three-six in Sing Sing."

"How much time did you serve?"

"I did two year and a half."

"Listen, you know what the score is then," said Sam. "If you're giving me a story, and we go into court and get buried, it's your hide that's going to burn, you understand that?"

"Yes, sir, I understand."

"What movie did you go to?" prodded Sandro.

"I think it was something called *It Happened at the World's Fair*, with Elvis Presley. And there was another picture with Steve Reeves, *The Son of Spartacus*, something like that."

"How much time did it take to see the movie?"

"I don't know, a few hours. I was nodding in the show."

"What time did you go into the show?" asked Sam.

"About six."

"You left Jorge about what time?"

"About three twenty, three thirty," Alvarado replied.

"Okay, three thirty. How did you go to Times Square?"

"I took the subway. At Marcy Avenue. I change at Delancey Street and get the express to Times Square."

"How long did that take?" Sam pressed.

"I don't know, forty minutes, forty-five minutes."

"That makes it about four fifteen when you got to Times Square. What happened to the other hour and forty-five minutes?"

"When I got to the Times Square I walked, you know. I look in some windows. I look at things. I bought a cigarette lighter. I look at the pictures in the theaters. I ate a hot dog." He was more calm than Sam at this point.

"Then you went inside and saw the pictures?"

"Right."

"Two pictures?" asked Sandro.

"Yes, sir."

"And you arrived home about one in the morning?"

"That's what time the cops got me, about one. They took the ticket from the movies, too. I had the little ticket, you know, that they give back to you. A cop took it from me."

"Did you get it back?"

"No, and my money. They took my things. Maybe the ticket is with my things."

"Make a note of that, Sandro. We'll have to check that stub out."

"Did you take a fix in the movie?" asked Sandro.

"Yeah. While I was there, I had my fix. That's why I was nodding, you know."

"Where did you get the works to take the fix?"

"I had it with me."

"Then when the cops arrested you, you had the works with you?" asked Sandro, trying to shake his calm.

"No. When Jorge told me the cops were waiting for me, I threw the stuff in a garbage can. They didn't see me."

"Listen, Sandro. I have to get going," said Sam. "I have another appointment back at my office. You can stay. Or we can come back and continue this in a couple of days."

"I have to get going, too," said Sandro.

"Okay, Mr. Alvarado, we'll be back. Meanwhile, try to remember everything that happened. There may be something you haven't told us. Okay?" Sam stood.

"Okay. When you coming back?" Alvarado stood.

"In a few days. We have to scout up some facts in addition to what you tell us. Meanwhile, I want you to remember everything you possibly can about what happened."

"Okay, sir. I remember." He smiled and shook hands with both lawyers.

Sam and Sandro walked to the door. Sam took out a coin and tapped on one of the thick glass panels. The guard in the lawyers' waiting area unlocked it and let them out. As gates and doors were being locked and unlocked for them, Sandro thought of Judge Porta's words. In the abstract, a murder case was dramatic, exciting. But now, faced with an actual corpse, tangible death and violence, holding a man's life in the palm of his hand, Sandro felt the weight of the responsibility. At this moment, Sandro wasn't as much concerned with living up to Don Vincenzo's ideal of a beautiful lawyer as he was with getting out into the fresh air.

"What do you think of that story?" he asked as they reached the street. He wondered if Sam was uneasy, too.

"It stinks. At least if there was somebody with him in the movies or something."

"Even so," added Sandro cautiously, "the killing took place sometime in the early afternoon, about two thirty, according to the newspapers. All these details about Jorge and the whiskey bottle and the movies took place after three and have nothing to do with the killing at all. He could have killed the cop, gone home, then taken the subway to the movies."

"Sure, he went to Times Square to get lost in the crowd for a while. This son of a bitch did it, all right. He was cool as a cucumber, too cool for a man under indictment for murdering a cop. He sat and talked about it like it was happening to someone else. He's guilty, this bastard."

"We do have little as hell to work with. What kind of a defense can we devise?" Sandro paused, then continued, struck by another thought. "But didn't he say that he saw some guy and went someplace when he got up, before he saw Jorge later in the afternoon? Maybe those other things happened about the time of the killing?"

"I don't remember him saying that," Sam replied. "I'll look at my notes later. Or ask him next time."

The morning sun was hot as they turned the corner into Centre Street, walking past the huge doors of the Criminal Courts Building.

"He said the cops didn't advise him of his rights. We could get them right there, couldn't we, Sam?"

"Doesn't mean a thing, Sandro. Not a thing. People griped like hyenas when the Supreme Court required the cops to give admonitions. And what'd it do? The cops just have to change their testimony. You think if they can lie about beating a defendant, that lying about an admonition is a big deal?"

"I guess not," Sandro admitted.

"You know, Sandro. I've been thinking of something else. Judge Phillips'll be sitting in the arraignment part when Alvarado pleads. A more liberal, lenient judge never sat on a bench. He's a defendant's man if there ever was one. Maybe the best thing we could do for our guy is to plead him guilty to something in front of Phillips."

"What kind of a plea do you think the D.A.'d give us in this case?"

"Maybe murder in the second degree. He wouldn't give us anything less than that. He might not even budge from murder one. Suppose we plead to the indictment, to murder one—the D.A. can't stop you from pleading to what you're indicted for, can he?"

"No, I guess not."

"And with Judge Phillips up there, this Alvarez—"

"Alvarado."

"Okay, Alvarado. Phillips'd never send him to the chair on a plea. He'd give him life sure. Otherwise, we'll have to try the case and end up with a conviction after five or six weeks. This guy is a sure fry in front of a jury."

Sandro quickly chased from his mind a picture of Alvarado being strapped into the electric chair. "You've handled these cases before, Sam. I'll listen to you on that."

"Let me sleep on it, and I'll give you a call. You take the arraignment, will you, Sandro?"

"Okay. I'll be able to check out those other places with Alvarado then, anyway."

CHAPTER IV

SANDRO BROUGHT THE SMALL CONVERTIBLE to the curb at Lexington Avenue between 120th and 121st streets. He sat and looked around him. The sky above the tenements was seared with the setting sun. The wilting heat was releasing its victim's throat, and the city was beginning to crawl into the night to revive. In many of the windows of the surrounding buildings, Puerto Rican men and women were propped motionlessly on pillows set on window-sills. Children in soiled pants and ripped shirts ran and screamed and climbed stoops or hop-scotched across chalked sidewalks.

In a nearby storefront hung a sign, proclaiming MEMBERS ONLY. This was the entrance to the Friendship Social Club, domino champions of the United States and Puerto Rico. Sandro slid across the front seat. As club attorney and honorary member, he was the only non-Puerto Rican allowed inside. The front room had a desk and a phone. On the wall were pictures of the members, the flags of the United States and Puerto Rico crossed, membership lists, and newspaper clippings which described club victories in domino tournaments. The back rooms were filled with card tables and chairs. A clattering fan shifted the humid air where a dozen men were bent over the tables studying their dominoes. Some held cans of cold beer. Sandro walked to the back.

"Hey, Sandro, how are you?" smiled Juan, the president and moving force of the club.

"Hi, Juan, com'esta usted?" replied Sandro, shaking Juan's strong hand.

"*Muy bueno*," Juan laughed, calling to one of the men to bring a cold *cerveza* for the *abogado*.

The members looked up and acknowledged the lawyer with smiles and greetings. He pulled a chair up next to Juan, once again engrossed in the game. Juan held a small wooden shield in his lap, containing custom-made mother-of-pearl dominoes with red spots.

"So, what's news?" asked Juan.

"I'm waiting for Mike. We're going down to Delancey tonight to see the building where a cop was killed, and try to talk to some of the people."

Delancey is a neighborhood on Manhattan's Lower East Side in the shadow of the Williamsburg Bridge, sometimes called the Delancey Street Bridge. Just like the club's neighborhood, El Barrio—known to the rest of New York as Spanish Harlem—Delancey is a low-rent area that gets handed down from one wave of immigrants to the next. The Puerto Ricans were the latest, and it was they who had taken to calling it Delancey.

Mike Rivera was a member of the Friendship Social Club. He was also a private investigator, whom Sandro had helped to obtain his license. It was through Mike that Sandro had become the club's lawyer.

"Mike should be here very soon, then." Juan moved one of the dominoes from the shield in his lap onto the table. "You see these boys I play with here," Juan taunted Jesus, his opponent, with mock sternness.

Jesus smiled. He had a prominent gold tooth. He nodded toward Juan. "When I'm finish with you, Juan, you be sorry you not gone, too, with Sandro."

They exchanged moves on the table, frowning as they studied their remaining dominoes.

"You don't want to have put that one down, my boy," Juan said to

PART 35

Jesus. "You don't, I'm telling you." He added a piece decisively to the arrangement on the table. "Ah hah," he crowed. "I tol' you. I think I am the champ now. Don't you think, Sandro?"

"*El campeon*," Sandro allowed. "That is, until you play me, Juan."

"Okay, I do that, too. I play you and Jesus at one time." He laughed as he rose.

"*Un otro mas*" said Jesus.

"*Un otro? Tu eres loco*" Juan said, sitting again and starting to turn the pieces face down.

A Puerto Rican in his late thirties, shorter than Sandro, stocky, with dark short-cropped hair, entered the room. His clothes were good. He walked toward Sandro.

"Hi, Mike," Sandro greeted.

"Hello, Counselor." Mike smiled as they shook hands. "What's your pleasure?"

"Well, I didn't want to go into all of it on the phone. What I want to do is talk to some of the people who live down where the cop was killed. Sam Bemer is talking about pleading Alvarado—that's our man—guilty. I'd like to get some idea for myself whether this is really the guy who did it."

"And if he is?"

"Well, I'll have given him the very least I owe him as his lawyer. I couldn't just plead him without checking out some of the facts."

"Then let's get going before it gets too late," Mike said with enthusiasm, as they left the club.

Sandro let Mike drive. They headed out into traffic, through the streets alive with people and noise, turning onto the East River Drive. They emerged at Houston Street, into streets equally throbbing. Mike parked a few doors from 153 Stanton Street. They sat in the car for a moment, looking around to get their bearings. It was a typical Lower East Side street, with old buildings, their facades seeming to be as much fire escape as brick, their windows open, unwashed, an astonishing variety of window shades behind them, and people leaning out. Children ran and screamed back and forth across the sidewalks, dodging between cars, throwing beer cans at one another. Their parents and other adults, white, black, Latin, mixed, were also out, sitting on the stoops, sitting on milk boxes on the sidewalk, sitting on the sidewalk, propped against the sides of buildings, standing in the lighted doorways of *bodegas* and candy stores that were blaring music, drinking from beer cans, singing, throbbing to Spanish songs over blaring radios. Four children had already begun to rest on the trunk of Sandro's car.

In the middle of the block, a fire hydrant had been turned on, water gushing, and the kids were diverting the water skyward with a topless and bottomless barrel. A crowd of them stood in the falling, cooling spray.

"That must be the house up there, with the stoop," Mike pointed. One fifty-three Stanton Street was a brick-faced building of five stories, with a fire escape entwining the length of its face and a short stoop leading into its entrance. On one side was a tenement of the same height, on the other side one that was two stories taller. On the street level, to one side of the stoop, was a shoe-repair shop, now closed for the night. On the other side was a *bodega*, a Spanish grocery. Two women lounged on the stoop.

"Let's go," said Sandro, opening the car door.

As they approached the building, they passed a small group on the sidewalk. In the center was a short Puerto Rican dancing. He was naked to the waist, wearing only a pair of gray slacks, sandals, and a panama hat. His neck was encircled with a fine gold chain, from which a small crucifix hung. In one hand he held a can of beer, and with his arms keeping rhythm to the music he danced a slow circle around a heavy woman, who was smiling patiently, amusedly. A protruding belly bulged her thin dress.

Perspiration welled from Sandro's face. In this heat, a suit and tie became instruments of torture. His eyelids were pressing shut. He felt droplets rolling down his back. He had debated with himself whether to dress casually and pass as just a friend of Alvarado's or to dress as Alvarado's lawyer. The latter, he decided, so people would respond to his pointed queries. A friend could not command the respect or get the answers Sandro needed. Besides, no one would respect an *abogado* who couldn't afford a suit. Now he was afloat within that suit.

The two women on the stoop were machine-gunning Spanish at

PART 35

each other. Sandro and Mike started up the stoop. They stopped and eyed Sandro. His suit, his tie, his briefcase made him obviously an outsider, perhaps an enemy.

Sandro stopped as he reached them. "Do you know where the superintendent lives?"

One of the women was young, her hair pulled tight into a ponytail. Her face was etched around the eyes and mouth with lines of hard work and struggle, lines that tenement women get when they have to yell at the super to collect the garbage, to send up hot water, to clean the halls. The other woman was older, heavy. She had the same look of weariness and mistrust.

"Down 'da hall. Apartment 1A," surrendered the younger woman.

Sandro and Mike entered the building. Apartment 1A was immediately to their left. Sandro knocked on the door. An old woman opened it and peered out cautiously. Her face looked kindly; her gray hair was gathered in a bun on the back of her head. "Yes? What is?" she asked. She must be from the old days, Sandro thought, when the neighborhood was predominantly Jewish and Slovak.

"My name is Luca. I'm a lawyer." The old woman's eyes were curious on Sandro; then they moved to something at his left. Sandro turned to see the young woman from the stoop now at his elbow. He had been too curious a spectacle for her to resist. "I'm the lawyer appointed by the court to defend the man accused of killing the policeman on the roof." Sandro pointed ceilingward for emphasis. "Luis Alvarado. He's the one the police took to jail."

The old woman nodded. Her face was now creased with uneasiness. "I know nothing. I was in a hospital. My husband, he was sick. I was in a hospital." She seemed pleased to plead ignorance about the day of the murder. Sandro made a mental note to check out the hospitals in the area.

"That punk," the young woman at Sandro's left sneered. "You his lawyer?"

"That's right. You know something about what happened that day? Sandro turned to her.

"I know they oughta put that punk in the electric chair. He killed the cop."

"Did you see what happened here that day?"

"Nah. I didn't see nothin'. But he did it, that punk. I know that."

"How do you know if you didn't see it? I'm appointed by the court, not by the man. I want the facts, too. If you know something about it, I'd like to know. It's going to be difficult enough for this fellow to have a fair trial. He's Puerto Rican, and a cop was killed. The district attorney isn't going to be giving him any breaks. He's one of your own, isn't he?"

"Don't hand me that. I don't know nothin' about him. 'Cept he's a no good punk. He oughta be put right in the chair and burned."

"Miss, if you were in his place, you'd want a fair trial and a lawyer. All I'm trying to do is find the truth. If he's guilty—"

"*If* he's guilty?" She was incredulous. "He did it!"

Sandro nodded slowly, turning toward the superintendent's wife again. "You weren't here, is that right?"

The super's wife smiled her uneasy smile again. "No. I was in a hospital. My husband."

"Do you know if there is anybody in the building who saw anything that day? Anybody who saw the crime, saw the policeman on the roof? I'd like to talk to them."

"No, I don't know," she shook her head.

"How about you, miss? Anyone in the building who might know what happened that day?"

"We know what happened that day. He killed the cop." She shifted stiffly from one foot to the other, crossing her arms.

"Thanks," said Sandro, turning back to the superintendent. "Whose apartment was it that was broken into?"

"Soto," she replied. "Top, in the back."

"Thank you."

Sandro and Mike turned, watched silently by the women. The hallway was narrow and dark. The stairway was on the right side of the hallway. On the left, along the side of the stairs and behind the superintendent's apartment, was a corridor leading to a rear apartment. There was a toilet closet under the stairs, its door next to the rear apartment.

"That's a sweetheart, that young one," said Mike as they ascended. "If it was up to her, you'd be sunk."

PART 35

"You're not just kidding. Listen, Mike, you've got to talk to these people in Spanish. When you talk to this fellow Soto, make sure you tell him about Alvarado being Puerto Rican, and that if he doesn't help his own people, the cops and the district attorney sure aren't going to give Alvarado a break. Not when a cop's been killed. They'll throw Alvarado in the chair like so much dirt. That's probably what they think of him anyway. Understand? Tell him in Spanish as if I don't understand what you're saying."

"Okay, Sandro. I'll tell him."

As they climbed, they saw that there were two apartments on each floor. The front apartments were marked by the floor number and the letter A; the rear apartments had the letter B. They reached the top floor and walked to apartment 5B. Mike knocked on the frosted glass panel that was the top half of the door.

"Who?" The sound came muffled through the door.

"Tony!" Mike replied. Everyone knew someone called Tony.

The door opened. A naked fat-bellied child burst through the doorway, scampering quickly. A tall, thin young Puerto Rican man with a moustache snared and restrained the little boy. He eased the door shut to a small opening; only his eye appeared to search the callers. Within, Sandro could see two other naked children climbing over a soiled couch. A television set was playing loudly.

"Señor Soto," Mike inquired.

"Mr. Soto," the man corrected.

"You speak English, Mr. Soto?" Sandro asked, stepping forward.

"Sure. Of course."

"My name is Luca. I'm an attorney. I represent Luis Alvarado, the man who is accused of killing a policeman on the roof several weeks ago. I believe he was supposed to have burglarized your apartment too."

"Yes, that's right."

"I'd like to talk to you," said Sandro.

"Can I put some clothes on first?" Soto asked.

"Sure. Go ahead. Why don't you meet us on the roof?" Sandro suggested.

"All right. I'll come right up."

"We might as well get a look at it, Mike," Sandro said as he led the way up. At the top of the steps was a door. They stepped out and found themselves at about the middle of the roof, halfway between the street side and the rear-yard side. The roof, with its tarred surface, was long and narrow, drab and unimportant, like thousands of other roofs in New York, except that here a man had been shot to death, protecting the pitiful possessions of people he never even knew. This was no place to make the leap to Eternity, Sandro thought. Nobody would ever pick it for a movie set.

Sandro and Mike stood looking toward the street side, almost unaware of being drawn to the noises and glow of light coming from there. On their right was the tenement of the same height. The two buildings were separated at the front by a brick wall taller than a man, at the center by a huge airshaft, and at the rear by a smaller wall, perhaps four feet high. On their left was the taller building, rising two stories of unbroken brick into the summer sky.

Sandro and Mike walked toward the street side of the roof, but could not look over because of the coping, which rose away from them at a forty-five-degree angle to a height of about seven feet. They went back to the rear of the roof. There was a low wall, and they could look down into the rear yards. The fire escape came up to the roof level here.

While waiting, Sandro drew a diagram for his records. Presently, Soto came up. He was smiling and friendly.

"What I'm trying to do, Mr. Soto, is get the facts about this case. If Alvarado is guilty, I want to know about it myself. If he's not, I don't want to see an innocent man convicted just because he's Puerto Rican."

"No, that's not right. Even if he's not Puerto Rican," Soto replied.

"That's true," agreed Sandro. "I didn't say that because the district attorney is against Puerto Ricans, or we should save him just because he's Puerto Rican. But with a cop dead, Alvarado is going to have a difficult time showing he's not guilty—not only because he's Puerto Rican, but also because he's colored, and he's a junky."

"Oh, yeah, that's right, he's a junky," Soto repeated.

"You know Alvarado?" Mike asked.

PART 35

"Which one is Alvarado, the dark guy or the guy who lives over here?" asked Soto, turning to point east across the rooftops.

"Alvarado is the dark one."

"No, I don't know him. I seen him at the station house that night, that's all."

Sandro's eyes widened as the words floated into the night from Soto's lips. "You were at the station house the night this happened, when Alvarado was there?" His eyes scrutinized every movement of Soto's eyes.

"Alvarado is the dark guy, right?" Soto inquired again.

"Yes."

"Yeah, I went to the station house and was sittin' there, you know, when they brought him in. They wanted me to identify the things that was taken from my apartment."

"And who else was there?" Sandro hoped he sounded casual. "Was there a woman there, someone who saw what happened?"

"Let's see. I was there first, then a couple of minutes later my wife came over with her mother"—he was raising a finger for each—"the girl from down the block, Asunta, and an Italian girl. Five I know of."

"This Asunta, is she an abortionist, Puerto Rican?" Sandro probed.

"I don't know what she does. She lives down the street. She was the one who told the cops that the other guy, the guy who lived down the street, he owned the car, you know, the one double-parked, that he lived upstairs."

"Did she say anything about one of them coming out of the building?"

"I don't know."

"Did you talk to her, to Asunta, since this happened?"

"After that night, you mean? No."

"Is that all the people who were there?" Sandro asked.

"That's all when I was there. I don't know about before me or later. There was lots of people going in and out."

"You weren't home at the time of the shooting, were you?" Sandro knew he hadn't been.

"No, I was at work. I didn't know anything until I got home that night, and then I seen all the police in the street."

"Did you speak to the police or any other people in the neighborhood since this happened, besides in the police station?"

"I spoke to a lot of police and a lot of people." He was very proud.

"What did you hear?"

"Well, I didn't take it down or nothin', you know?"

"Just tell me whatever you remember hearing."

"These guys was robbing my apartment, and this Italian girl saw them on the fire escape and told the police. And then the cop went up to the roof, and the dark guy had a fight with the cop. Then this dark guy—that's your guy, right?"

"Yes," Sandro replied with restraint.

"Well, he shot the cop in the back, and ran down one of the other buildings."

Sandro's face remained calm; the rest of him was jolted. "Were there witnesses who actually saw this happen?"

"Gee, I don't know. Like.I said, I wasn't paying too much attention, if you know what I mean. To tell the truth, I was a little scared, you know."

"Mr. Soto," Sandro said, "you might be able to help save a man's life. It's quite possible that Alvarado didn't do this thing. If the police come around to see you again, if you see the other people in the neighborhood, perhaps you could lend us a hand, talking to them, asking questions."

Sandro handed Soto his business card. "We need to know who these witnesses are, where they live. Like that Italian girl you mentioned."

"Okay. I'll keep my eyes open."

"What's your phone number?"

"We don't have a phone, but you can call at work. I work at the Perfect Printing Shop. The phone number is Murray Hill 4..." He took out his wallet and studied a piece of paper. "7302."

Sandro wrote it down. "Fine. I'll be in touch with you shortly. Maybe you'll have dug up something more by then. It's very important. Okay?"

"Yes, okay." Soto smiled. Sandro extended his hand. Soto, nonplussed by such formality, gave Sandro a hand that felt like a dead

PART 35

fish. Sandro and Mike went downstairs, and Soto returned to his apartment.

Sandro turned to Mike. "We've got to check on the superintendent's wife. Find out what hospital the super was in that day. You take care of that, okay, Mike?"

"Sure. Maybe she didn't even visit him."

"Right. Check the visitors' lists. And we'll have to come back and see the other witnesses. This Asunta. Alvarado told me he thought she identified him as the man leaving the building."

"Okay. We can canvass the area and check it out."

Sandro turned to Mike, shrugging. "Of course, if we plead guilty, we won't have to do any of this."

CHAPTER V

SANDRO SWIVELED IN HIS CHAIR, peering over the top of the newspaper as Elizabeth entered his office with the morning mail.

"What time is it?" he asked.

"Nine thirty."

"Remind me at nine forty-five that I have to get over to the arraignment in the Alvarado case."

"Yes, sir."

Sandro's attention poured back into the newspaper accounts of the murder.

The Daily News, dated July 4th, 1967, blazed the headline: QUESTION ADDICT IN COP-KILLING. On the front page were pictures of Lauria and of the police hunting out the killer. The story said that a "good suspect" was nabbed about 5 P.M. as he tried to enter a green and white automobile double-parked near the murder site. He was believed to be the driver of the getaway car. The *News* story indicated that a police all-points alarm went out about 11 P.M. for another man wanted for the homicide. The suspected triggerman was described as a dark-skinned Negro, twenty-eight to thirty years old, about five feet ten, with a moustache, a long thin face, a wide forehead. The

PART 35

suspect was described as wearing a gray short-sleeved sports shirt and black trousers.

Well, thought Sandro, Alvarado was right about the story in the papers and the Negro suspect being described as five ten. Alvarado is only about five feet six.

Sandro picked up *The New York Times* for July 4th. The story was on page 36 and bore the headline SUSPECT IS HELD IN POLICE SLAYING. In its story, *The Times* added one important piece of information: "As Patrolman Lauria lay dying on the roof, he gasped out a description of his assailant as a thin, dark Negro, about thirty years old, five feet nine or five feet ten inches tall, wearing a gray outfit."

Both newspapers reported that Lauria had been shot several times in the back with his own gun. If anything could have made a cop-killing worse, thought Sandro, that was it.

In *The News* for July 5th, 1967, the lead story's headline was CAPTURE! On page 3, Alvarado was pictured with Ramon Hernandez, the first arrested suspect, whom the newspaper had originally referred to as the driver of the double-parked car. The suspects were shown closely guarded by policemen.

The News stated firmly, "Both men confessed to the police and the district attorney."

This case is impossible, Sandro thought to himself. This is open-and-shut murder in the first degree. He hoped that Sam was right about the leniency of Judge Phillips.

The New York Post dated July 5th, 1967, was the clincher. Its lead story said: "Lauria's partner, Patrolman Roger Snider, was on the stairs, headed toward the roof. He heard a fusillade of shots as he neared the second floor. Lauria lay dying in a pool of his own blood when Snider reached the roof. The killers were gone. Hernandez confessed to the police that Alvarado had jumped the cop from behind, took the cop's gun, and began to shoot, once, twice, three times, more."

Hernandez's words placed Alvarado at the scene and even put the gun in Alvarado's hands. The intercom interrupted Sandro's thoughts.

"Yes?" asked Sandro.

"Mr. Bemer on the wire for you."

"Hi, Sam, how are you?"

"Fine, Sandro. You're going to handle that arraignment today, aren't you?"

"Yes, I'm leaving in a couple of minutes. I was just rereading the newspaper accounts."

"Yes, and . . . ?"

"We've got quite a mess here."

"Now tell me something I don't know. We've got a rotten bastard on our hands who shot a cop. I really think we should get out of this fast. I'm sure the D.A. won't take a plea to a lesser charge at any time. He wants to fry Alvarado. If we wait five or six months just to plead to the full indictment, we won't have Judge Phillips, and this guy won't get any breaks."

"Have you been talking to the D.A.?" Sandro asked.

"Yeah, yesterday. I was speaking to Ellis. He's going to handle the case. He said there was no lesser plea available. He gave one good reason, and I'd do the same in his spot. They have an outright confession. We'll have to cop to the full indictment to plead to this one."

"You know, I was just reading about those confessions," said Sandro. "Alvarado tells us he's innocent and that he wasn't involved, and here he confesses to the police and the D.A. Unless this is just a newspaper story to sell copies."

"Well, the cops and the D.A. aren't interested in newspaper circulation, and they both say they got one. Of course, Alvarado was telling us they beat him. He wants us to knock the confession out by denying that it was a voluntary confession. I've heard that a thousand times before. It doesn't mean beans."

"I haven't read anything about witnesses to the crime," Sandro added. "Just Hernandez, who was kind enough to implicate Alvarado, and then put the gun in his hands."

"They could have a lot of witnesses they're not revealing now. But I didn't give you the biggest piece of news." Sam paused. "If we don't cop out on this, Hernandez is probably going to be a state's witness against us. Ellis told me he'll probably move for a severance in the indictment, try us separately, and use Hernandez as the chief witness against us. Then they'll give Hernandez a plea to a lesser charge."

PART 35

"Only thing to make it worse now would be fingerprints. Are there any?" asked Sandro.

"Hey, Sandro, this guy doesn't have to shoot the cop again right in the courtroom to convince a jury. If they get Hernandez to cop out and testify, we can warm up the hot seat. The confession, at least we have a talking point, it was beaten out of him. But Hernandez! And fingerprints too..."

Sandro's intercom buzzer sounded again. "Hold it, Sam." Elizabeth reminded Sandro that it was time to leave for court.

"Sam, I've got to get going over to court now. What shall I do?"

"I say, see if he'll plead out."

"You *really* think so?" asked Sandro again.

"You got a better idea?"

"Well, maybe..."

"Maybe what? The evidence'll go away?"

"No."

"No is right. If we can get him a life term, he's lucky. See if you can get him to plead today, Sandro."

Sandro's office was near City Hall. He started across Chambers Street toward the Municipal Building, which houses part of the vast government of the City of New York. The Municipal Building is twenty-eight stories high and straddles Chambers Street, so that automobiles pass through a giant arch cut out of the building's base.

On the left as one approaches the Municipal Building is the venerable Hall of Records, where the last wills of the world's elite are processed and records of deeds and real estate dating from the beginnings of the city are maintained. The Hall of Records is a magnificent edifice, containing a scaled-down version of the staircase of the Paris Opéra, mosaics, and carved marble fireplaces.

Across the street from the Hall of Records is the Tweed courthouse, a remarkable example of brickwork, domes, and balconies, for which the Tweed cronies went to prison, because it had not cost as much to build as they said it had.

Just behind the Municipal Building, the Brooklyn Bridge stretches its sinews toward Brooklyn Heights and Atlantic Avenue.

Sandro turned through Foley Square, upon which the Federal

Court House and the State Supreme Court front, and walked down through Centre Street to the Criminal Courts Building.

This is a community unto itself, the legal community, and for a lawyer, a walk along the street disposes of many social and professional calls.

Sandro entered the Criminal Courts Building and took the automatic elevator to the eleventh floor. He walked to Part Thirty, where Alvarado would be arraigned. Judge Phillips was already on the bench. A defendant was at the dock being arraigned. Sandro walked to the first row of benches. David S. Ellis, the assistant D.A. in charge of prosecuting Alvarado, was sitting within the bar, a folder on his lap.

Sandro walked along the rail that separates the spectators from the dock and the court. Turning to the right, he went through a door in the paneled wall and entered the "bullpen." The bullpen is the detention area to which a prisoner is brought from the Tombs on the day his case is to be called before the judge. At the end of the morning and afternoon sessions, prisoners are marched back to the twelfth floor of the Criminal Courts Building, a floor inaccessible to the public—the courthouse has a thirteenth floor, but no twelfth floor—and back to the Tombs.

Unlike the court, the bullpen is neither solemn, nor wood-paneled, nor polished; it stinks. The bullpen reeks of unwashed bodies, of urine, musty clothes, fear, defiance, and resignation.

In an open area between the two bullpen cells sat a guard at a wooden desk. Inside the cells, some men stood or squatted against the walls because the single bench was filled. The prisoners looked out at Sandro as he entered the bullpen.

"Morning, Counselor," said the guard. "Who you got this morning?"

"Alvarado, Luis Alvarado."

The guard's finger skimmed down a handwritten list in a book on the desk. "He's still upstairs, Counselor. Go ahead up."

Sandro ascended a steel staircase next to one of the cells until he came to another barred gate, which was locked. This was now the twelfth floor, with its honeycomb of passages, cells, and gates, designed to maintain a constant, secure stream of prisoners from the Tombs to the courthouse.

PART 35

"Gate," Sandro called out.

Sandro heard a rustle of metal keys. A guard emerged from a small room. "Hello, Counselor. Who you looking for?"

"Alvarado."

"All the way around."

Sandro walked through a corridor flanked on the left by cells, on the right by windows overlooking a park where Chinese kids were playing softball. The prisoners watched Sandro as he walked past the cells.

"Hey, man," a prisoner called to him. "Open the window a little, hanh?" Sandro swung one of the windows across from the cell open a bit farther.

"That's a tough suit you got, Counselor," the prisoner remarked, smiling.

"Thanks." Sandro continued until he saw Alvarado in a large cell. One of the other prisoners was standing, using the open urinal. He, too, was watching Sandro. Alvarado saw Sandro and walked to the bars.

"Good morning, Counselor," he said. He smiled.

"Morning," Sandro whispered, to keep the guards or the other prisoners from overhearing. "I've been reading about this case in the newspapers."

"I read the newspaper, too," Alvarado whispered.

"Well, then you know what I'm worried about. They say many times that you confessed. Did you confess to this crime?"

"Maybe they say Chaco confess. I confess to nobody. They full of chit. I don't confess. I wasn't there."

"What about Hernandez? According to the papers he said you were there."

"Ah," he waved his hand in dismissal. "The cops hit that son of a bitch, and he'd tolds them his whole life. He said to me, over here, 'I no tell them, Luis, I no tell,' but I know he did that. Those cops were at my house so soon as they pick up that punk. He says, "You know, Luis, they beat me for hours. I had to tell them some-sing. I couldn't think of another colored guy. Forgive me.' He's fulla chit. They hit him once to start him talking, then twenty times more to make him shut up."

47

Sandro laughed. A tall, thin prisoner walked over. From the newspaper photographs Sandro recognized him as Ramon Hernandez, Chaco.

"Hey, hi, what you think, hanh?" Hernandez asked.

Sandro looked to Alvarado.

"This guy is Hernandez," said Alvarado.

"I want to talk to my client right now," said Sandro.

Hernandez didn't understand. Alvarado spoke to him in Spanish. Hernandez seemed hurt. He walked back into the crowd in the cell.

"Don't mind him, Counselor. He's just a dummy," said Alvarado.

"Is he going to be a witness against us?" asked Sandro.

"I don't know. I got a book here, you know." He handed the book to Sandro. It was a copy of the penal laws of the State of New York. "I been readin'. Can you get me a pad of paper? I don't got money to buy any paper here."

"What's this for?"

"I want to be able to check on the law, you know. Can he be witness on my case?"

"He could be. Look, Luis, I went to the house where the cop was killed. It doesn't look good at all."

"Mr. Luca, you got to believe me. You the only one I got in this whole country who can help me. I didn't do this thing. Please believe me."

Sandro felt himself wavering.

"Another thing that bothers us is the possibility of fingerprints, Luis. If they have your fingerprints, that's the end. You know that?"

"I know, but you don't have to worry about that. They can't have my prints, I know that. Unless they can put them there themself. I couldn't put my prints in a place, I wasn't there."

"Still, Luis, I have to tell you it looks pretty bad for you. Mr. Bemer and I have been discussing the possibility of your pleading guilty to save you from the electric chair."

"Cop out? I coppin' out to nothin'. Why you want me to cop to somethin' I didn't do?"

"No one said to plead to something you didn't do. But if we're facing a sure conviction—and it looks like it from here—a plea might be best."

PART 35

"If they give me spitting on the streets, I ain't pleading. I didn't do it, Mr. Luca. If I do this thing, then I say, maybe, get me a good plea, maybe good time, somesing. I didn't do this thing. No plea." He was studying Sandro intently.

"I must have the truth, Luis. You'll pay, not us, if we build your defense on sand and it crumbles beneath us. Don't let me make a bad decision now only for you to regret it later."

"I won't bullchitting you. I tell you the truth. I wasn't there."

An inmate from the prison maintenance crew wheeled a steel cart around the corner toward the cell. He stuffed waxed-paper-wrapped jelly sandwiches through the bars, counting two sandwiches for each man as he went. He also passed a paper container of tea for each into the cells.

The guard entered the cellblock. "Alvarado, Hernandez," he called out. "You want to go outside, Counselor, while I bring the prisoners down?"

Sandro descended and walked out to the courtroom.

"Hello, David," he said to the assistant district attorney, walking back toward a bench.

"Hello, Sandro, how are you?" Ellis rose as Sandro motioned with his hand. They walked toward the back of the courtroom and out to the corridor.

"Well, you've got a tough one here. I know you have a good man, Sam Bemer, with you, but I think this case is beyond help."

Ellis was shorter than Sandro. He was about fifty, his black hair thinning on top. His eyes were a faded blue.

"David, I know you don't have to come through on this point—but it might help us in disposing of the matter, and it's been done in other cases. Can you sec your way clear here to fill me in on whether there are actually confessions in this case?"

"Oh, there are confessions, all right. This guy of yours confessed to the whole thing, in detail."

"No doubt about it?"

"None at all."

"Would you let me read the confession. I think it might be to our mutual advantage if defense counsel knew the score. It might eliminate the necessity for a trial."

49

"I can't show you the confession."

"You can't, or you won't?"

"Have it your way; I won't. I've got a case to prepare, and I'm not going around giving out the evidence."

"I'm not asking you to give out the evidence, David. We're basically on the same side, the side of law and order, I mean, I'm court-assigned counsel, not a defendant. If these men are guilty, and you can show me where they said so to you, what's the point of a trial?" Sandro didn't believe that. He would fight the confession, if he thought for a minute that it had been beaten out of Alvarado. But he wanted to flush Ellis out.

"I'm sorry, Sandro. I can't."

They walked back into the courtroom.

"Luis Alvarado," called the clerk. Alvarado, escorted by a guard, stepped forward. "Are you Luis Alvarado?"

"Yes."

"And are Alessandro Luca and Samuel J. Bemer, represented here by Alessandro Luca, your lawyers?"

"Yes."

"You are charged with murder in the first degree and in that, on the third of July, 1967, you did willfully, feloniously, and of malice aforethought shoot and kill one Fortune Lauria with a pistol. How do you plead to that charge?"

Alvarado looked to Sandro. "You my only man, Mr. Luca." Sandro shrugged. "Not guilty," he whispered.

"Not guilty," Alvarado repeated aloud.

"You are further charged with the crime of burglary in the third degree in that on or about the third of July, 1967, with intent to commit therein the crime of larceny, you broke and entered the dwelling house of one Robert Soto at One fifty-three Stanton Street, County of New York. How do you plead?"

"Not guilty."

CHAPTER VI

SANDRO WALKED THROUGH THE NARROW STREETS of Little Italy, only a few blocks west of where Lauria was killed. Mott Street, Mulberry Street, where for a century Italian has been as much the native tongue as English, perhaps more. It was hedged on the south by an area where, for the same length of time, Chinese has been more the native tongue than English. Traces of Spanish spiced Little Italy now, as Puerto Ricans reflected the insertion of a new bottom rung on the New York social ladder.

As he walked, Sandro saw the provisions stores with cheeses and *prosciutti* hanging in the window, the *pasticcerias* with their trays of *cannoli* and *pasticciotti* and the strong aroma of espresso and anise wafting out. After he finished his business, he thought, he might go see Mama, whom dynamite could not dislodge from the old neighborhood, and have some beautiful food.

Sandro walked down two steps and opened the front door of the Two Steps Down Inn. As he entered, several men, sitting at a table near the front door, studied him. They were rough-looking men, and they looked at Sandro roughly. Their eyes slowly returned to their conversation, conscious of Sandro but not looking at him. In the rear, at a side table, half-hidden by a divider screen, he saw Sal Angeletti sitting, facing the front door. At Sal's back was the rear wall. This was the seat Don Vincenzo always occupied when he was alive. It was now Sal's as heir to Don Vincenzo's power.

Sal looked up as Sandro entered, squinted, looked doubtful a moment, finally smiled and waved to him. Sandro waved back, making his way toward the rear. The eyes of one of the men at the front, a huge, hulking man, slid from Sandro to Sal. He was satisfied that the intruder was no threat, and the conversation at his table relaxed again.

"Sandro, hello," said Sal as Sandro approached. There were two other men sitting at the table with him. One looked like a businessman, definitely not someone who was part of Sal's power structure. The other was one of Sal's "boys," perhaps the "good fellow" to whom the businessman went for help in some unorthodox difficulty. "I'll be finished here in a minute, okay, Sandro? Joey, get a drink for the counselor," Sal called to the waiter, who moved gingerly toward Sandro to show him to a table.

In another age, an age more pioneering, demanding, rawer, when nothing was fed into a computer, and when bugs were only insects and had not invaded the electronic world, when Little Italy was bursting with the energy of men bold enough to come to a strange land where they would be considered "wops," something akin to monkeys, who spoke the "divil's" tongue and who never took charity, the Two Steps Down Inn was the hangout for the toughs, the hotheads, the ones later to be known by romantic, melodramatic titles.

Nowadays, old-timers meet there, but now they meet to drink wine and eat steak sandwiches and talk, and watch television depict how it was not, and to listen to stories of the past, and to remember. It borders on the ludicrous to look at these old-timers, walking slowly with age, grayed and stooped and benign, taking pills, and to think that these are the men whose names are bandied about by the news media and in the Congress, that these are the men of the fabled Mafia. That old man who limps with gout and who can't hear and has trouble digesting a steak sandwich is a man known in some officially compiled dossier as a vicious killer. The tall man whose hands shake, who looks like anybody's grandfather, if your grandfather's

PART 35

hands shake, is supposed to be a kingpin racketeer. To anyone who had not heard of the infamous reputations of some of the customers of the Two Steps Down Inn, the restaurant would seem a reunion of the Italian Club, Class of '05, happy, harmless old men, reminiscing, chatting, not really interested in pillaging New York this week. Of course, there were younger men in the restaurant, but they were not infamous, not notorious—not yet. And perhaps they never would be. Some of these Young Turks were impatient and hungry, lacking in respect for the elders of the family, and as a result they were filling the jails quickly.

As Sandro sat alone in the cool, dimly lighted restaurant, watching Sal and the two others leaning toward one another in quiet conversation, seeing again the table of Sal's boys near the front entrance, he thought of Don Vincenzo Tagliagambe. Don Vincenzo had not allowed Sandro into this restaurant often when he was alive, but Sandro could remember vividly Don Vincenzo sitting in that chair of authority where Sal was now sitting—somehow the title *Don* fit Vincenzo Tagliagambe better than it did Sal—and he could almost see himself early one evening years before, bursting furiously through the door. Two of Don Vincenzo's boys, at the front table, rose to the ready the instant Sandro made his sudden move.

"Hello, Sandro," Don Vincenzo had said loudly from the back of the room. The moving toward Sandro were stayed by their master's voice. Sandro moved quickly to the back. Don Vincenzo sat at his table calmly eating his supper alone.

"Sit down, and don't talk loud," Don Vincenzo suggested. "I been expecting you."

"Jesus Christ, Uncle Jim," Sandro said, sitting down next to him. "Do you know what two of those meatheads you have working for you did this morning?"

"You mean about your girl friend?" Don Vincenzo spoke in a very precise English, so well controlled that it was not to be classified as broken English, merely colored, warmed with an accent.

"That's exactly what I mean. Taking *my* girl out of *my* apartment and to a gynecologist! You told them to do it, didn't you?"

"Of course. You don't think they usually go taking girls to doctors.

We're not running no Red Cross here. Joey, bring a plate for the young man."

"I'm not hungry."

"Have a drink, then."

"Goddamn it, Uncle Jim . . ."

"Not loud. Don't yell in here." Don Vincenzo looked toward the front where the boys were sitting, watching. "They wouldn't understand why a strange young kid can come in here and start being fresh to me." Don Vincenzo smiled warmly. "They don't know you're my son." There were still many in the neighborhood who knew Sandro as the child of Don Vincenzo's early widowed sister, despite all of Jimmy Pearl's efforts to keep the connection from possibly damaging his nephew. But what Don Vincenzo said his people didn't know, they hastened to become ignorant about.

"Then what the hell are you trying to do to your *son*? The girl called me from the apartment, crying, upset. You shouldn't have done that. It wasn't necessary."

"How do you know? You going to be a lawyer or a doctor? I only had her go to the doctor, to see she was clean, that's all. You want her living with you, okay. That's your business. But I'm not going to let her give you something that'll ruin your life."

"But she's not some bimbo off the street," Sandro complained. "She's a real nice girl, the Park Avenue type you want me to meet, and here you have two of these meatheads, one on each side, take her to the doctor."

"Hey, he's a high-class doctor, Park Avenue. I didn't send her to no quack."

"But you just don't take nice girls to doctors to have them checked like a used car."

"I don't? I already did."

"I know, that's why I'm here. She's crying and all upset, wondering what kind of person I am to do such a thing. She thinks I did it."

"You tell her your father did it. She don't have to know who I am. Tell her it's all right, just a doctor, a real doctor, give her examination. What's the difficulty? She's clean, and now you know it, and you don't got to worry no more. What's so wrong with that?"

PART 35

Sando shook his head as much in exasperation as in frustration. "I'm old enough to have something to say about my own life, Uncle Jim."

Don Vincenzo smiled. "You're a good boy, Sandro. When you get angry, you're beautiful. You're gonna be dynamite. But you're not so smart yet in street ways, Sandro. I been around, and I know the street, and I know a lot of fancy people who are degenerate bastards. They lie, they cheat; they come in here and want us to bust somebody's head. Why couldn't they have some disease, too? You think them fancy-looking girls can't have disease?

"Listen," Don Vincenzo said, continuing to eat, "she's a nice girl. Now everything is okay. And who was hurt? Buy her something nice, a jewelry, something, anything you say. Whatever it costs, I pay. Tell her you got a silly old man for a father, and he apologizes, and give her the present. If it shines enough, she'll be quiet real soon. Now come on, have something to eat, something to drink."

"I'll have a light Scotch and water," Sandro said to Joey.

"How's school?" Don Vincenzo asked. "That's more important. Your exams'll be coming soon. You ready?"

"Sure. Sure."

"Sure, you're ready. You'll pass them eyes closed. And then law school. Sandro, I pray only that I live long enough to see you a lawyer."

"You won't die. Who'd want you? Not even the devil." Sandro smiled.

So did Don Vincenzo. He squeezed Sandro's cheek affectionately.

"I been in court a lot, Sandro. I never got a conviction, but I got arrested enough times. I seen a lot of lawyers. I would have liked to be a lawyer, but I couldn't go to law school, cause I had no education. I was too busy hustling to stay alive. I would have been some lawyer. I'd wipe up the courtroom with the D.A. I'd destroy him, and when he was down, I'd kick him. That's what you're going to do. And you'll have respect. Me, I have respect, but it's because of this"—he raised his solid fist—"and because of them"—he pointed his chin at the men at the front table—"But you, just with your mouth, your words, you'll do more things, have more respect. If you can do that with just words, you'll be more powerful than me. Understand?"

"I understand."

"If only I live that long, Sandro. I want to see you wipe up the district attorney. You're going to be a beautiful lawyer."

"I'll try, Uncle Jim."

"What try? You're my family, you got the same blood in you I have. You got guts, and you got brains. You think I'm going to let some little girl you want to go out with this week mess all that up?"

"Let's not go into that again, Uncle Jim."

Joey set the drink on Sandro's table, a twelve-year-old Scotch on the rocks, more potent than the drink of that early evening years ago, when he was a student and Don Vincenzo was alive. "You want something to eat, Counselor?"

"No, Joey." He looked over to Don Vincenzo's chair and watched Sal finish his business. As Sandro lifted the glass to his lips, he could almost hear Don Vincenzo say, "Drink hearty."

"Sandro, how are you?" Sal said, smiling, standing in his place as the two men left his table. Sal was tall and thin, stooped now and gray. He was about seventy-three years old, a couple of years younger than Don Vincenzo would have been.

He took the cigar from his mouth with his left hand, shaking Sandro's hand with the right. He studied Sandro for a moment. "Jesus, you lookin' like a million bucks, Sandro, real class."

"Thanks, Sal, how've you been?" They sat at the table.

Sal stuck his cigar back in one side of his mouth. "Ah, what's the use of kickin'? *Vecchiai ena carogna, ma non ciarriva, ena vergogna.* You understand?—it's a bitch to get old, but it's even worse if you don't." He lifted his eyebrows and his head in a shrug of resignation. "That lousy bastard doctor. If it was up to him, I'd be in a wheelchair. Pills for this, pills for that. He don't even want me smoking cigars. Who the hell wants to be so healthy anyway?" Sal waved his hand through the air. "One of these days I oughta have that doctor hit in the head," he laughed. "But what brings you around anyway, Sandro? I ain't seen you since six, seven years. You got trouble?" Sal studied Sandro carefully.

"No, no trouble, Sal," Sandro assured him. "I've got a heavy case over on the East Side, over by Stanton Street, I'm defending a fellow accused of killing a cop."

PART 35

"Good for him. That's one less rat." Sal shifted his cigar. "But what can I do for you? You know, anything, anything you want, you name it."

"I really just wanted to know if you know anybody who's still over in Stanton Street, somebody who might have a finger in things there."

"Naw, that neighborhood's all changed now, crummy. Used to be Jews, but now it's all full of crazy spics. It stinks there now. Most of my friends aren't over there any more."

"I thought maybe somebody taking bets or numbers. I want to get a friendly introduction to the neighborhood, see if I can find anyone who knows anything about this case."

"I'll send somebody to look around. Maybe I can find somebody over there for you. I doubt it, but . . . Can I buy you a drink?"

"I just finished one, thanks. Shall I call you in a couple of days?"

"Better you come around," Sal said. "You never know some bastard is tapping on the phone. Especially with you—*Buon Anima* Jimmy would come down to hit me in the head if I let you get in trouble." He slapped Sandro on the back.

"Oh, by the way," said Sandro as he rose to leave, "it was somebody who used to live around here who assigned me to this case—Judge Porta."

"No kidding? Tommy Porta! How is he?" Sal thought for a moment. His head began to nod slightly. "I ain't seen him neither since maybe thirty years. Not since he became a big-shot politician. He hangs around with me, he's in trouble," Sal laughed.

"Okay, Sal, and thanks," Sandro said, laughing also. "I'll drop back to see you next week or so."

Sandro walked toward the door. As he passed the front table, the men looked up, nodded, a hint of a smile coloring their lips.

CHAPTER VII

IT WAS NOW MID-AUGUST. The dog days, held down by humidity, hung around the city's neck like a steamed towel. The huge doors were swung open to allow Sandro into the Tombs. He sat beneath the misery of the Four Horsemen of the Apocalypse.

"Alvarado?" the guard asked, holding a slip of paper.

"Here," said Sandro, rising. He found Alvarado sitting at the far end of the bench with other prisoners. He smiled, rose, and shuffled toward Sandro in floppy slippers.

"Say, Mr. Luca," said Alvarado, sitting, "when you come here next time can you bring me a bar of soap?"

"Soap?"

"Yeah. The stuff they got here makes me itch. They only got one soap here. If you could bring me some Dial, I be okay."

"All right, if I remember it, I'll bring it. It's as hot as blazes in this place." Sandro looked for a window to open. There were none. "You have air conditioning upstairs?"

Alvarado snorted. "Air conditioning? You kidding? You see that little hole up at the top of this windows?" He turned and

PART 35

pointed toward the window, thick translucent glass barred from the sill to the top of the frame. At the top were two small louvered openings through which air passed. During the winter these openings were covered with a metal plate. "That's our air conditioning."

"You mean that's all the air that gets into your cell?"

"That's it. But I got a good system. I take my blanket, they give us a blanket upstairs, I soak it in the sink until it's soaking wet and then I put it on the cot and I sleep on that."

"You'll get arthritis. Does it keep you cool?"

"It keep you soggy but not too bad. It helps."

"Listen, Luis, I wanted to talk to you alone today because I want to get to the bottom of this story of yours. Once and for all."

"Okay, Mr. Luca. What you want to know?" Alvarado pulled a single cigarette from his shirt pocket. It was a Pall Mall again. Filter cigarettes aren't allowed in prison—supposedly because prisoners can do funny things with filters, make something to get high. Pall Mall, as the original king-size cigarette, has never relinquished its popularity in prisons, where smoking is a luxury to be prolonged. It outsells all other brands there two to one.

"First, let me explain this to you," said Sandro. "I want you to tell me the truth. No phony story. Understand?"

"I tol' you, I got no reason to lie to you, Mr. Luca," Alvarado said firmly, looking directly at Sandro. "I know you trying to help me."

"That's right. And we told you that if you give us a story that's not true and we accept it and build your defense on it, and it blows in our face, it's your hide. Understand? Your hide's going to find itself in jeopardy, not ours."

"I understand."

"So what I'm suggesting," Sandro said very carefully and slowly, leaning toward Alvarado, "is that you don't know the law, and if you want to make up a story or alibi, at least you should make up a story that's right, that'll help. I know the law." Sandro was hoping to lead Alvarado into the truth through the back door. "We can work out the story together. At least, if it's going to be manufactured, it will be

59

manufactured right." Sandro didn't intend to manufacture the story, or suborn perjury, but he did want the truth.

"I already telling you the truth. I know it's no good for my case to hide anything from you," replied Alvarado.

"All right. Tell me again all that happened."

"Like I told you. I was in the house. Oh wait, I remember something I didn't tell you and Mr. Sam Bemer last time. About a quarter after two, two thirty, before I went home to get a shower and then go in the subway, I took a haircut on Roebling Street."

"A haircut. You got a haircut about two fifteen or two thirty?"

"Yes, I didn't tol' you last time you was here. I remember being out of the house and being near Broadway and Roebling Street. I did some things, killed time, and then I went to take a haircut. After, I wented home and taking a shower and dressed and talking to Jorge. Then I went to Times Square."

"Are you sure about the time at the barber shop?" Sandro studied Alvarado closely.

"Sure."

"Where is this barber shop?"

"It's on"—he studied the ceiling, his eyes zeroing in on the barber shop—"I think between Broadway and South Ninth on Roebling Street on this side of the street." His hand motioned toward his left.

"What side of the street is that? Is it the east side or the west side of the street?"

"I think it's the . . . well, when you looking from Broadway to South Ninth Street it's on the left side. What side is that?"

"East. It's on the east side of the street between Broadway and South Ninth Street?"

"Yes."

"Do you know who the barber was or what he looked like?"

"A short guy with a moustache. Young." It sounded like "jung."

"Was he Puerto Rican?"

"Yes."

"And he gave you a haircut around *two fifteen or two thirty* on the afternoon of the day the cop was killed?"

"Yes, sir. I remember it was about that time and there was another

PART 35

guy with me, Eugene," Alvarado explained. "I gave a guy a dollar to let me go ahead of him."

"How long did this haircut take?"

"I don't know. How long a haircut take?"

"Fifteen, twenty minutes?" Sandro suggested.

"Somesing like that, I guess."

"And then what happened?"

"Then home, like I told, took a shower, talk to Jorge, then got in the subway and wented down Times Square."

"And when you were in Times Square you went to the movies?"

"Yes, sir. First I look aroun' for a while."

"And what time did you get out of the movies?"

"I guess about twelve midnight, twelve fifteen, somesing like that."

"And then?"

"And then I go home, and walking up the street I see Jorge's lights on. I go in Jorge's, and Jorge says, 'Hey, Luis, you kill a cop?' And I say, 'What's the matter, you crazy?' And then he says, 'No cause there're three cops upstairs waiting for you.' I walked to go up, and then the cops come jumping out the door."

"And when you were at the station house, they questioned you?"

"Question me?" Alvarado gave off a bitter chuckle. His eyes grew wide, the black pupils round and hard. "They didn't question me, they told me—with punches. They beating me and saying 'We know you up there, Luis, make it easy on yourself.' and I told them I can't make it easy cause I was not there and I kill nobody. And they bring these things in, you know, a radio and a TV and they say, 'Your fingerprints are all over these things.' And I say, 'You better go back to school to learn to read prints, cause they can't be mine.'

"And then this big red-hair baldie guy gives me a couple of punches in the stomach again. And then there was a skinny cop that stopped them from beating me. And he was sitting there with me. Last time I didn't say to you what he told me. He sits down with me and he says, 'Hey, Luis, you're thirty-five, like me. Luis, he says, 'you know when we arrest a guy we afraid too. Just we carry a gun, a badge, doesn't mean we're not ascared sometimes. Tell the D.A. you were on the roof and you got panicky, you know. You saw the cop and you fought with him and you got the gun and you were ascared and you fired the gun. You wind up with manslaughter.'

"'You're okay,' I tell the guy, 'but killing a cop is death,' I tol' him. 'I didn't do it. I not goin' to say nothin'.' An' then this skinny detective says, 'Well, it's up to you, you know.' And then there was the other detective behind the door. The guy who liked to beating me, and he comes out, he's angry, you know, and he's all red in the face. Even his baldie head was red. I smell whiskey on his breath. And he was listening, and he says, 'You think you're goin' to beat this case, hanh Luis?' And I said, 'I think so. I don't know, cause I wasn't there.' And he says, 'Listen, Luis, we goin' bury you. And I says, 'Well maybe, if you frame me up. Sometimes I read books what open up my mind.'"

"You said what about books?" Sandro asked.

"I says that sometimes I read books what open up my mind and I can understand things, and this cop says, 'Books don't mean chit. You can be sure we're going to bury you.' And I said, 'I know you can frame up your own mother just to get an arrest.'"

"Are those fingerprints yours, Luis?"

"I told you they can't be mine cause I wasn't there."

"I know I repeat a lot of these questions, and I know you give me the answers, but I want you to understand that I must have the absolute truth. Do you understand? If your fingerprints are there, we're in tough shape, and I want to know what shape we're in before we walk into court."

"I know that. But you can believe me. Those are not my fingerprints there."

"All right."

"Listen, did you check who was the womans who look at me through the glass at the police station?"

"I told you we got some information, but no names yet. I have the fellow whose apartment was burglarized finding out for us. You have no idea what any of the women looked like? Or if they identified you?"

"No. I know some witnesses came, cause they had me standing in this room, you know. And there was two police, and there was a door between them with a mirror like. And they made me stand on one side, and I had to bend down and twist around this way and up and down. I know it was womans. I could hear. I think they was Puerto Rican, on the other side, but I don't know who."

"Can you describe any of them?" Sandro pressed.

"I don't know cause I couldn't see through the mirror. But Hernandez's wife was downstairs. I saw her downstairs. Maybe she saw this woman come in, and then you could find out from her."

Sandro made a note. "Did you know Hernandez before this?"

"Well, I use to see him around Delancey around Essex Street, Rivington Street. He use to hang around there. And I would see him from time to time, you know, with a bag or something, but I never hang around with him."

"Where does Jorge, this superintendent, live?"

"In the same building where I live. Sixty-four South Ninth Street."

"Have any visitors come to see you here?"

"No, nobody. Not yet."

"Do you have any relatives in New York?"

"I have a brother. But he don't come. I have a mother, too, in Puerto Rico, but she's very sick. I have my wife and kids."

"Is this the woman you married in church?"

Alvarado looked at Sandro and shrugged slightly. "No, this is another one. This is the woman I really love, Tina. But she's away now."

"Away?"

"Yeah, she's with the authorities for a while, but I wrote to her, and she is going to write to me."

Sandro shrugged slightly.

"This is a very tough case, Luis. I don't want you to think any other thing while you're here. I don't know what's going to happen, and I can't promise anything. I'll fight to the last drop of blood, if necessary, if you're right. But remember, if you are lying, it is you and not me who is going to suffer. You understand?"

"I understand, believe me. And believe me, I didn't do this thing."

"Okay. Keep thinking, and write down anything new you remember."

CHAPTER VIII

SANDRO WALKED UP THE STONE STEPS and entered the Seventh Precinct station house. Just inside, to the left, was a long counter and desk. A sergeant sat behind it, writing. A shortwave radio squawked somewhere. A patrolman, routing calls, manned a switchboard to the side of the sergeant. The noises of a typewriter clacking and a large fan moving the warm air around filled the background. Everything was painted light green—old, dusty, light green. Paint peels clung to the walls. There were many posters and announcements. The wooden floor was similar to hundreds of wooden floors in New York's old public schools, the cracks between the old boards routed with age, the nails shiny from being polished by generations of feet. The only difference was that in the schools you could always dig your pencil into the cracks and come up with some old lead points, broken in action long before, to throw at your classmates. Here, everything was business. Patrolmen walked about in their uniform trousers and short-sleeved, dark-blue shirts, no ties. Some had sodas or snacks. Some were reading bulletins on the walls.

"Can I help you?" the desk sergeant asked.

"I wanted to go up to the squad."

PART 35

The sergeant nodded, jerking his thumb over his left shoulder.

The squad was the designation for the detectives, to distinguish them from the uniformed force. Without variation, the squad office was at the top of the first flight of steps in the old station houses. Sandro made his way to the end of the long counter and saw the stairs, with their polished brass handrails. Just to the rear of the stairs, a number of patrolmen sat in a large room skylarking, sipping coffee or Cokes.

At the top of the first flight he saw a sign with a hand pointing to a doorway—SQUAD OFFICE. AS he entered, he came up to a waist-high rail that kept visitors at bay. Within the large room, many desks, some with typewriters, some with phones, all with papers and files atop, stood vigil, a long vigil from the looks of them, having been manned constantly for more than thirty or forty years, twenty-four hours a day, having the histories of pain, anguish, and joy, too, thrust upon and into them, handled and abused by hundreds of men in that time, all wearing badges, all carrying guns, listening to bizarre accusations, justifications, confessions. To the side of the large rooms, two small offices, with doors ajar, housed the squad commander, usually a lieutenant, and the squad clerical office. Between them was a two-way mirror for witnesses to observe suspects without fear that the suspects could see their accusers and perhaps retaliate. These offices were also painted light green; they were drab, old, dusty, with the same wooden floors. In one corner was a cage, called a detention cell. A man was lying quietly on the floor there, his back to Sandro. On one wall was a fingerprint board.

"Can I help you?" asked one of the detectives. He was in shirt-sleeves. A Chief Special .38 was strapped to his belt on the right side.

"Tom Mullaly?" Sandro inquired. He had checked, and learned that Lieutenant Garcia was the commander of the Seventh Squad detectives and that Detective Mullaly was in charge of the Alvarado case.

"Mullaly," the detective called out.

A tall, powerfully built man with thinning red hair looked up from typing. His face was smooth, wide, his lips thin.

"Yeah?" He rose and walked over to where Sandro stood. He was about six feet three inches. Sandro gauged him for 225 pounds. There was a .38 on his hip. He looked like a cop—like the cop Alvarado had described. Whether men who look like Mullaly are more attracted to the job, or whether the job, with its daily crises and dangers, carves its own inimitable visage on the men who hold it, is hard to know. Mullaly looked at Sandro, somewhat hostile, skeptical.

"My name is Luca, Alessandro Luca. I'm one of the lawyers in that Alvarado case you're carrying."

Mullaly's face was blank and didn't change. He was, however, quickly assessing his adversary.

"What can I do for you, Counselor?" Mullaly's words slipped out between motionless lips. He had sized up Sandro and apparently decided he was a pushover kid. He seemed to like that idea.

"Since you're carrying the case, I thought I might come over and chat with you," said Sandro. "See if there's anything I could pick up to expedite the case, you know."

"There's not much to *chat* about," Mullaly said. He obviously thought the word *chat* was just grand. "You appointed counsel?"

"Right."

"They stiffed you this time. A real loser."

"How's that? What's it look like? I don't want your investigation, just maybe some of the official entries, you know, arrest record, blotter."

"Hey, Counselor. You think I was made with a finger last night? You can't get those things, and you know it. If you don't, you better go back to law school." Sandro hadn't really expected to get the records, but it was worth a try, particularly because he also wanted to make sure of the physical layout of the station house.

"It'd save time if I got some of them now."

"Maybe your time, not mine. Draw yourself a subpoena when we go to court."

"Yes, I know the procedure."

"It doesn't sound like it. Get the records? These punks are vicious. They shot five holes in a cop. They're gonna burn, Counselor, burn. You got it. There's only two ways to get the chair these days, and one is a cop-killer, and that's what we got here."

"You in on the investigation?"

"Hey, Counselor, don't be too cute, you know. I'm not going to get sucked into a conversation. I was here from beginning to end. I got the call Lauria was shot right here, on that phone. I was right here when these punks confessed, both of them. And I'll be there when they burn. Anything else, talk to the D.A."

"They actually confessed?"

"You can read the newspapers, can't you, Counselor? They're still requiring reading for law school, aren't they?"

"I think you may have the wrong man," Sandro said calmly.

"Yeah, that's great. You keep thinking that." But Mullaly's eyes showed interest. "I suppose you got it all figured already. It was the butler." He laughed, looking over his shoulder. The other detectives were listening.

"I'm not sure yet. But I've got some good leads."

"For instance?"

"I wasn't made with a finger either, Detective. But I'll tell you this from what I know so far, some of the investigation in this case doesn't add up."

"What doesn't add up?" Mullaly's voice was streaked with impatient sarcasm.

"I think I'll save that for the jury."

"Yeah, well, we'll see you in court, Counselor. I'm awful busy. Okay? See you around."

"Thanks." Sandro turned and left the squad office. He stood outside, looking up the stairs to the third floor where Alvarado said the *lockers* room was supposed to be. Perhaps he could just walk up there quickly to get a look around. He hesitated....

"Anything else, Counselor?" Mullaly was at the door of the squad room. The other detectives were watching.

"No, I was just thinking if there was anything else."

"To *chat* about?" He really liked that word.

"No, nothing. Thanks." Sandro started down the stairs.

Mullaly stood at the top. Sandro could almost feel the sneer that followed him.

CHAPTER IX

"HELLO, MR. LUCA?" Robert Soto said into the phone diffidently.

"Yes, hello. I hope you're calling with good news for me."

"Well, I've been doing what you asked me. I been talkin' around to a lot of people, and I have some information you might want."

"That's great, Robert. When can we meet you?"

"Whenever you're ready. I got the information whenever you're ready."

"I'd better do it this week. This weekend is Labor Day, and I'll be away for four days. How about tonight?"

"Sure, okay. Where'll we meet?"

"I'll come over to your place. About eight thirty?"

"Okay. So long now." Soto hung up. Sandro was already dialing Mike Rivera.

"Mike, can you pick me up at the office at about six thirty? We'll grab a bite to eat and then go over to Soto's apartment. He's got something for us."

"Do I have to wear my chauffeur's cap?"

"No, just a fake beard. Which reminds me—did you ever snoop out that story about the super's wife and the hospital?"

"Oh, yeah, I meant to tell you. I found her on the book at Gouverneur Hospital. She used the visitors' pass on July third from two to four."

"Okay, we can scratch her as a witness."

"Right. See you later."

The skies were filled with the maximum number of stars visible through New York's polluted air on a cloudless night, as the three men walked onto the roof. They walked toward the street end and leaned against the wall on the left.

"Well, what have you been able to dig up?" Mike asked.

"I found out about that woman, Asunta," said Soto. "She was the one who told the police that the guy who owned the double-parked car was a junky who lived upstairs in one sixty-three. I think also that she saw the dark guy, your guy, coming out of the building afterward. That was after the cops were there and everything, you know."

"She tell you this?" Sandro asked.

"No, but I've been talking around to a lot of people like you told me and checking things out."

"And what else have you found out. Did anybody else say they saw Alvarado?"

"I found out a lot, Mr. Luca, a lot. You know, these guys are real losers. Especially your guy, the dark guy."

"What makes you say that?" asked Mike.

"Just from the things I heard, that's all."

"You want to start at the beginning and tell me what you know, what you heard about what happened that day," Sandro suggested.

"Okay. It was raining, you know, like all day. I went to work early. My wife went out about eleven thirty to go to her mother's house. About one thirty this car comes into the block, and there are these two guys in there. The guy who lives down the street and a dark guy. Then the guy who lives down the street gets out of the car. The car is double-parked across the street, down from the factory. And the guy who lives down the street goes over to his own house, a few houses over on the same side as we are, and he goes to the roof of One sixty-three and crosses over to here. The other guy, the dark guy, he's sitting there."

"Go ahead."

"Well, then this guy in the car, the dark guy, gets out, you know, and goes around to the back here and up the fire escape. He's checking apartments to see if anyone's home, you know. Then they come down from the roof, and they jimmy open my door. And then they take my television, my radio, all the other stuff to the roof."

Mike wrote in his notebook as Soto spoke. He wanted a rough outline of people to be interrogated and places to be investigated.

"And then?" Sandro prodded.

"Well, the Italian lady—I found out she lives across the yard." Soto pointed over his shoulder.

"Show me where she lives," said Sandro, walking toward the rear of the roof. Soto stood at his side, gazing down to the rear yard.

"She lives over there, in that building." Soto pointed to a building directly behind them. There was a large yard between the two buildings, the Stanton and Rivington Street sides bisected by the rotting fence. Soto pointed out windows on the first level, approximately eight feet from the ground. There were four windows. The middle two shared a fire escape.

"In which apartment, the one on the right or on the left of the fire escape?" asked Sandro.

"I think the one on the left."

"What does this woman look like?"

"She's Italian, short, a little heavy, nice-looking, you know."

"What color hair?"

"Sort of light, blonde, brown, something like that."

"Go ahead. What did she do?"

"Well, she called the cops when she seen the guy on the roof. So she stayed by the window, waiting, you know? And then seen the dark guy in the window. Alvarado, right?"

"Right, you have it now," Sandro agreed wryly.

"Well, then they took the stuff up to the roof. Then she seen the dark guy go down the fire escape and fool around with the window. Then the cops come to the backyard, and she yelled to the cops and one cop runs up the fire escape, and the other cop, she saw him run down the alley to the front of the building.

"Then the dark guy ran and hid behind the stairs," Soto continued, "over there." He pointed to the small bulkhead shed which covered the top of the stairway. Mike was standing near the doorway in the side of it. He was holding the door open with his foot, using the light from the inside to see his notebook. Soto walked to the shed and crouched beside it. "Like this. And the cop came up the fire escape and across the roof, and he sees the guy from down the street on the roof, up in the front. So he put up his gun and he says, 'I'll fire, stop,' and he walks to the guy. He didn't see the dark guy behind the wall here. And when he's just walking past, his gun in the air, the dark guy hits his arm with a pipe. Then they struggle, you know, wrestle, and the dark guy got the cop's gun and shot him a lot of times.

"The other cop got on the roof after they all ran," Soto continued. He was pleased to have such undivided interest. "The two guys ran across the roof and down into the other guy's house. The cop that was shot was on the roof, bleedin' and all. He wasn't dead."

"He wasn't?" asked Mike.

"No. And he told the other cop that a Negro, not too tall, jumped him."

"Who told you that?" Sandro asked.

"I don't know. I spoke to so many people."

"Go ahead."

"Later, when the other guy, from down the block, went down to get his car, the cops grabbed him. I think cause that Asunta told them on him." Soto looked from Sandro to Mike to see if there were any questions.

"And you think this Asunta said she saw Alvarado walking out of the building?" asked Sandro.

"I think she did. I didn't talk to her. But I heard, you know, that she saw the dark guy, Alvarado, walking out of her building after the cop was shot. She saw him escaping."

Sandro nodded gravely. Alvarado's fears were confirmed.

"She knows a lot about this case," Soto added.

"Oh? You think Asunta may know more about the killing than she's telling?" Sandro asked.

"Yeah, she knows everything that goes on in the neighborhood. I mean, she always has people in and out of her apartment, like maybe she knows what jobs are being pulled and all."

Mike made a note. "Maybe she's a fence," he said to Sandro.

"You know what you said about your guy maybe not doing it, not killing the cop," Soto said, moving to new ground. "I think I know who did do it."

"You do? Who?"

"There's a guy I think he's a junky, who lives on the second floor," explained Soto, "an Italian guy, and him and me, we were never friendly or nothing, you know. I never talked to him before. And his wife and my wife don't know each other neither. But after this happened, this guy starts talking to me when he sees me in the street, and he wants to kid around, be friends, trade comic books, you know."

"Did you say, trade comic books?"

"Yeah, and he wanted to buy me a ice cream one night by the Good Humor. And there he asked me about what the cops said, and about if I got the television set back and all. And his wife, she invites my wife to this party, a Avon party, or something, when they buy lipsticks and everything. So I think, how come this guy is so interested, you know? So I been watching him. A lot of guys come to his apartment, all a' time, and they stay, and then some of them have packages. And I know that he's been getting rifles and guns, and he keeps them in his house. And then there's something else."

"What's that?"

Soto thought for a moment. "Oh yeah. After he talks to me a couple times, one night he comes up to me and asks me about if I got everything back. I figure I'd fool him. I say I got everything except the money. I told him they stole my wife's pocketbook, you know. There was really only five dollars gone, but I told him that there was three hundred dollars in there missing, and he told me I was a liar. You know, he told *me* I was a liar, and it was *my wife's* pocketbook. I mean, you know what I mean? It sounded kind of funny that he would say something like that."

"It sure is," said Mike. "This guy who collects guns seems to know a lot."

"What's this fellow's name?" Sandro asked.

PART 35

"Salerno. Tony Salerno," Soto replied.

Mike made a note.

"Well, try and keep an eye on him. Remember what he tells you. And don't get reckless. If this man is really involved, he might be dangerous. Have you heard anything about anyone else who might have seen something that happened on the roof?"

"No, nobody. Only the ones I already told you, you know, the Italian lady who lives across the yard, and the other ones I told you about."

"Well, this is terrific, Robert. It helps a great deal. I'm proud of you."

"I like to help. This is my country, too, you know?" Soto smiled. They started down the stairs and said good night to Soto at his apartment.

"You know, Sandro, this is great, about this Salerno guy," Mike said, as he followed Sandro down the stairs.

"It's peculiar, anyway," Sandro allowed.

"Sure. If Alvarado didn't do it, somebody had to. Now, here's a guy who could have killed the cop, run across the roof to another building, and walked out into the street and not even be noticed. Everybody knows he lives over here, so seeing him on the street wouldn't even be remembered."

"It's a possibility," said Sandro. "But there's nothing else to point to him. No witnesses, no evidence, nothing."

"It won't hurt to check it out."

"Yeah, you're right. We have to check out everything. A regular San Juan Sherlock Holmes I've got."

CHAPTER X

"HIYA, COUNSELOR," said Joe, swinging back the huge door to the Tombs. "How was the weekend?"

"Fine, Joe, fine."

"Back to work now, hanh?"

"Yeah, I guess so." Sandro was beginning to feel as if he lived here, and the idea appalled him.

The guard in the lawyers' waiting area admitted Sandro in turn. While he sat, he watched the guard pace constantly from the wall of bars to the far wall, back and forth, like a polar bear spending the summer at the zoo. Was the guard, Sandro wondered, less imprisoned than Alvarado? This man spent his main waking, living, breathing time, eight hours a day, forty hours a week, two thousand hours a year, behind bars. By the time he retired, with time off for good behavior, that would be equivalent to serving a seven-year sentence.

Sandro looked at the other guards, the men behind the desks, the deputy wardens passing through the room. They were all prisoners.

"Alvarado," the guard intoned, accepting a slip of paper passed through the Judas eye of the door in the far wall. Sandro stood and entered the interview room. The guard locked the great door behind

PART 35

him. Across the room, Alvarado sat on the bench with several other Negro and Puerto Rican inmates. As Sandro came into view, Alvarado nudged the man seated next to him, smiling proudly, and pointed to Sandro. In prison, when there is still hope, lawyers are talked about, admired, bragged about, fawned over in place of pinups and cheesecake. Lawyers, after all, are more useful to imprisoned men than pinups. Alvarado rose as Sandro pointed to an interview booth.

"Hello, Mr. Luca."

"Hello, Luis. How are you today?" Sandro noticed that Alvarado was putting on weight.

"All right. Good. How's my case?"

"Coming along. I was over to Stanton Street again last week."

"Oh? Listen, Mr. Luca. I was talking to a guy in church who was talking to Hernandez, and he said that Hernandez is going to court next Wednesday. Are we going to court next Wednesday?"

Sandro thought for a moment. All he could conjecture was a severance for a separate trial, to allow Hernandez to plead to a lesser crime in exchange for testifying against Alvarado. "I'm not aware of any court appearance. I'll check with Mr. Bemer. I doubt it very much."

"How come that rat is going to court? He's going to be witness against me?"

"I don't know. I'll find out. I was speaking to Robert Soto," Sandro went on, "The fellow whose apartment was broken into. He told me who the woman was who saw you in the station house that night. And he told me about that Asunta, who might say she saw you coming out of the building, just as you told me."

"Them peoples don't know what they talking," Alvarado flared. Sandro had never seen his client angry before. It was reassuring.

"The witnesses may not, Luis. But understand this. There are two worlds, one on the outside, the real world, and the other inside the courtroom. It doesn't matter what really happened outside."

"I don't get that, Mr. Luca. If I didn't do this thing, they ain't got no witnesses that says I did."

"Maybe you can understand it this way. Last year I was handling a burglary, and the woman whose apartment was burglarized came in and testified. I told the defendant she was going to identify him. He looked at me as if I were crazy. Said what you just said—she couldn't testify to that, she wasn't even in the apartment till he was two flights down the fire escape. Well, she testified that she saw him face to face in the apartment. The jury bought it, and he was convicted. If witnesses tell the jury you were there—even if you weren't—and the jury believes them, then you were there. What really happened doesn't matter."

"The witnesses can't say those things," Alvarado protested.

"Oh, they can. They may be mistaken, but the jury doesn't know that. I know I asked you this before, but I must ask you again. Were you there?"

"I wasn't. I really wasn't." Alvarado was looking straight at Sandro, his eyes pleading.

Sandro knew perfectly well how many times he had repeated these questions. But very often the criminal, in hopes of arousing the sympathy and fighting confidence of his attorney, lies about his involvement in the crime. And the lawyer, borrowing a technique from the police, goes over the same ground again and again, searching for possible inconsistencies.

"Is there anything new that you remember since the last time we spoke?"

"I told you everything. Oh yes, I remember that when they were beating me, the cops, they brought Hernandez into the room. I didn't tell you this. Well, I told you, but this is just more. They was beating on me and told me Hernandez said that I was the one from the roof. And I tolds them to bring Hernandez here. And they bringing him in and I look at him and say, 'Chaco,' I espeak Spanish to him. I say, 'Chaco, why did you tell to these people what you tell them?' And Chaco, he wink at me and say, 'Yes, this is the man.' You know, he wink at me like he was just telling them that. And they taked him outside and they were beating on me again. I know I was bleeding inside because when I come here one night I was bleeding in the mouth and in the ass, and they had to bring a doctor and bring me to Bellevue."

Sandro was thunderstruck. "You went to Bellevue Hospital? After you were brought here to jail?"

"Yes, one night in my cell. I was bleeding in the mouth and the ass. And I had a lot of pain in the stomach. I lied down on my cot.

PART 35

The guard call the doctor, and they put a mask over my face with air in it, and I stayed there because I couldn't breathe. I was lying on my bunk, and my chest, you know, from where they were beating me, was tremendous pains. The doctor come and send me over there to the Bellevue. You see I'm not telling a lie to you because these things happen to me when I was here. And they know. You can know they happen, too, because my medical card says that, and the doctor knows that, and my cellmate knows that it happen. I am not lie to you."

"You were sent to Bellevue from the Tombs?"

"That's right, in a ambulance. They mark the papers, internal bleeding."

If Alvarado wasn't concocting a fairy tale, he was innocent. Hospital records were objective facts, easier to check and more reliable than witnesses' stories.

"Is there anything else I should know? You keep remembering more things each time I come. Can't you think of them all and tell me at once to save time?"

"I try, but sometimes I don't remember. Remember I told you I was having a haircut when all this happened and then I went to the movies?"

"Yes."

"Well, before I had the haircut, I met this friend of mine, this guy named Eugene, and together we wented to a five-and-tens, and I changed a hundred-dollar bill. In the five-and-tens store on Broadway near Roebling Street."

Sandro was confused. "A hundred-dollar bill? You changed a hundred-dollar bill?"

"Yes. I changed a hundred-dollar bill with this colored girl. She was at the counter in the five-and-tens store, a big fat-face she was, like she got peaches pits in each cheek. I don't know what her name is. And she changed the bill for me, and I remember we was kidding cause she changed a hundred-dollar bill a couple days before for me, and she says to me, 'What are you, making these things?' And I says, 'Yeah,' and then she changed the bill for me."

"Was Eugene in the store with you?"

"No. I didn't want a big crowd, you know. Maybe they think we rob somebody."

"Where were you getting these hundred-dollar bills?"

"No stealing. Believe me. Some guy on the street give me three hundred dollars—three hundred-dollar bills—to buy some stuff for him. You know, junk, and I was suppose to buy stuff for him, but I never did. And I have this money in my pocket, and I need some money, so I spend it."

It would be far better to be tried for hustling narcotics or stealing three hundred dollars than for murdering a policeman, Sandro reasoned.

"And you're sure you changed one of these hundred-dollar bills the day the policeman was killed?"

"Yes. Before I went to take the haircut, and I was talking with Eugene. I walk in and change a hundred-dollar bill. And I think she can remembers me because we were talking and kidding."

"What time was it?"

Alvarado studied the ceiling. "Maybe one thirty, a little later. Somesing like that."

"Where was this five-and-ten?"

"On Broadway near Roebling Street. It's a big store right on the side of the street there, a little bit from the corner."

"And it was a colored salesgirl?"

"Yes. She works there because I see her there before, you know. As soon as you walking back, about two of them stands where they sell things, right in the middle."

"I'll check it out. Is there anything else?"

Alvarado studied the ceiling for a minute and, looking back to Sandro, shook his head. "I can't think of anything."

"While I follow up on these leads, you keep thinking, and write down anything you remember that you haven't told me, and tell me next time." Sandro stood. "Are you getting any visitors while you're here?"

"No. My wife is away up in Westfield. They say I could write to her. I have a brother named José. But he is angry. You know, someone called him for me when all this happened, and he got all angry when

PART 35

this person call. I guess he's, you know, he don't want to be bothered. He's a big citizen or something. He works in the Department of Sanitation, and he doesn't want to know no trouble."

"He hasn't come around to see you at all?"

"No, he doesn't- come here. When you get in trouble, peoples leave you alone: That's why, Mr. Luca, I got all my hope in you, because you are the only one in this country that I have going for me. I didn't do it, even, Mr. Luca."

"I'll do what I can," said Sandro. "I'll see you again shortly." He walked toward the barred door to get out, wondering what a Negro woman eating peaches' pits looked like.

CHAPTER XI

MIKE RIVERA BACKED THE CAR INTO A PARKING SPOT on Broadway in the Williamsburg section of Brooklyn. Sandro got out, and Mike joined him. They walked to the corner of Roebling Street and Broadway.

"Now the barber shop is supposed to be on the east side of the street, between Broadway and South Ninth. That's this way," said Sandro, turning left. He walked to the curb to scan the storefronts across the block, a myriad of colors and painted signs.

"There it is, Sandro. The Imperial Barber Shop," Mike exclaimed.

"Right. Now we'll know very quickly if there's anything in all this," said Sandro.

"I hope the same barbers are still here," said Mike.

It was a small, three-chair shop. The linoleum on the floor was worn, with nailheads pressing upward from beneath. The mirrors were framed in wood that squinted through strokes of cheap paint. There were tattered girlie magazines strewn on the wooden chairs provided for waiting customers. No one was waiting. Two barbers were clipping their way around two Puerto Rican men. All the men, barbers and customers, watched the intruding reflection of Sandro and Mike in the mirrors. Their eyes lingered on the gringo.

PART 35

Mike spoke Spanish to the barber at the first chair. He was portly, middle-aged. Sandro caught a few words—*abogado, policia,* muerto. The eyes of all the men shifted to Sandro's image watching more intensely.

Sandro handed the newspaper clippings about the murder to Mike, who continued speaking to the older barber. He turned to Sandro.

"He says he wasn't working that day. This other guy was," said Mike, walking down toward the third chair. The other barber was young, with a moustache. Mike spoke to him. Sandro could only catch an occasional word. The young barber nodded. Mike spoke to him at length. The barber stopped cutting hair and just listened to Mike. The customer forgot his haircut, watching the conversation.

Sandro looked from Mike to the barber to Mike and back, feeling as if he were at a tennis match.

Mike showed the news clippings with Alvarado's picture to the barber. The young barber studied the papers.

"*Si.*" He nodded. Then the barber walked across the floor to the wall opposite the mirrors, where the unoccupied chairs stood. He pointed at one chair with his scissors, speaking Spanish all the while. He walked back to the middle barber chair and pointed to it.

"What the hell is he saying?" Sandro urged impatiently.

"He says he did give Alvarado a haircut that day," Mike explained. "Alvarado was waiting over here, and then he got a haircut in this second chair."

The young barber added something more.

"And his moustache got trimmed," Mike translated.

Sandro looked at Mike, then the barber. Could it be so easy? Maybe it was a put-up job!

"Ask him if he knew Alvarado before this, if he was a friend of his."

Mike asked. The barber answered. "He says he didn't know him. He still doesn't even know his name except for the newspapers. But he remembered the face, and he remembered the man being here. The morning after the murder, when these pictures were in the papers, he saw them, and he remembered that Alvarado was here the afternoon before. The only way he knows Alvarado's name is he read it under the pictures in the paper."

"Is there any question in his mind about Alvarado? Is he sure that this man was here having his hair cut on July third?"

The barber took the pictures in his hand. The other men all got up and crowded behind him, studying the pictures. The young barber spoke.

"He says that that's the man who was here that day. He remembers him coming in, having a haircut and his moustache trimmed."

"Does he remember what time it was when Alvarado came in?" Mike asked again. "He says he can't say for sure, but it was in the afternoon, after lunch."

"Get an approximate time," Sandro urged. Life and death hung on the answer.

Mike asked.

"He says he was here around two thirty, two forty-five," he translated the answer.

Sandro studied the crowd of Puerto Ricans for a moment. He studied the barber, the barber shop. Life and death, murder and innocence were so unhistoric, so matter-of-fact, everyday.

"Was that the time Alvarado came in or left?" Sandro pressed.

Mike asked the barber.

"He says he must have come in around two twenty-five or so, *mas o meno*, more or less."

"How does he know?" asked Sandro, wanting to anticipate Ellis. "Did he have a watch, or look at a clock in here?" Sandro looked around. There was no clock on the wall. The young barber was not wearing a watch.

"He has a friend," said Mike, after the usual preface in Spanish, "who works in a day-care center and playground near here. Every day this friend comes here about four, after the playground is closed. On this day, July third, because the next day was a holiday, the friend got off from work early, and he came here early. They kidded about it, the barber and his friend. You know, like 'Hey, only half a day today?' That sort of thing. While this friend from the playground was here, Alvarado came in with another guy."

"Who is the fellow from the playground?"

"He says the guy's name is Julio. But he hasn't seen him for a while. He moved."

PART 35

"Does he know this other fellow with whom Alvarado came in?" Sandro directed to Mike. Mike translated.

"He knows the other guy from seeing him around the neighborhood. His name's Eugene. But he hasn't seen him today," Mike replied for the barber.

"Was there anyone else in the shop when Alvarado came in?" he asked.

"There was Alvarado, this guy, Eugene, this barber, another barber, and the friend from the playground, Julio," Mike interpreted.

"There was another barber here?" asked Sandro. "Does he still work here?"

"No. The other barber works in another shop. But this barber sees him once in a while."

"All right. What's this barber's name anyway?"

"Francisco Moreno."

Sandro smiled. He shook Francisco Moreno's hand firmly. "Maybe you'll save someone's life. You understand what I say?" In case he didn't, Mike gave a running translation. The barber smiled and shrugged, because it had not been really challenging to recount what had happened on a rainy afternoon in a barber shop on Roebling Street.

"Take Mr. Moreno's story down so that we can have a signed statement for our file," Sandro instructed. Just in case, Sandro thought. The first thing he had learned in preparing cases for trial was to obtain signed statements. It might act as a reminder. It could also be used against the witness if he decided to change his story and help the opposition.

Mike took a pad of yellow paper. Again, he spoke to Francisco Moreno about the afternoon of July 3rd, writing as he listened. Sandro added comments and occasional instructions. Mike wrote first in Spanish, and then, on the same paper, wrote a translation in English:

> My name is Francisco Moreno. I am 26 years of age. I live in 136 South Fourth Street, in Brooklyn, Apartment 2C. I have no telephone. I work at the Imperial Barber Shop, 319 Roebling Street, Brooklyn. The 3rd of July, I was working in the barber shop and between the hours of 2:30 or 3, and about that time

Luis Alvarado was in my shop. He seated himself in my chair, and I cut his hair. I remember that Mr. Alvarado was calm and he was not excited. He was wearing a sweater. I cut his hair and moustache and he left the store. I noticed that Mr. Alvarado was well dressed; that his clothing was dry and did not give me the impression of having taken part in any fight.

(Signed) Francisco Moreno,
September 6, 1967

When they had finished, Sandro asked Mike to instruct Moreno not to talk to anyone about the case. He handed Moreno his card. Mike wrote his home telephone number on the back of the card so that Moreno could call in case of any new developments or trouble. Sandro had Mike ask Moreno to look for the other barber, for Alvarado's friend Eugene, and for Julio, his friend who worked in the playground.

The barber smiled and nodded. They all shook hands again.

The five-and-ten was typical, with open counter upon open counter of merchandise, each with little price cards in front of the .bins.

"Alvarado said about two counters down from the door in the center, we'd see the counter where the girl works," Sandro said as they entered. They stood at the front counter, looking back. There were no girls at any counter. Off to the side, about two counters back, some customers had just made a purchase. They turned from an employee who was placing merchandise in a bag. When the customers moved, Sandro beheld an apparition. A Negro girl, young, with nice, fat, puffy cheeks, as if there were peach pits in them. Sandro looked at Mike, who returned his look. They smiled.

"Pardon me," said Sandro. "My name is Luca. I'm an attorney. I represent a man named Alvarado who is being charged with a crime. At the time it happened, he says he was here and you were serving him."

She shrugged and smiled. Her smile was extraordinarily bright, delightful. "I wait on a lot of people, mister." Her voice had a southern sound. She wasn't Puerto Rican. "I don't know all them who comes in. What's his name?"

PART 35

"Alvarado."

"That Spanish?" she asked.

"Yes. He's Spanish, but he's colored too. You know, very dark."

"I don't know nobody by that name. When was he supposed to be here?"

"July third," Sandro said.

"Mister, that's two months ago. I couldn't tell you one guy from another."

"Well, you might have remembered his face. This is his picture." Sandro handed her the newspaper clippings.

She looked at the picture. Then she looked at Sandro.

"He changed some money, I believe," Sandro said.

"A hundred-dollar bill?"

"Yes," he said, trying to sound calm.

"I 'member him. I 'member him now," she said, her face bright. "He changed another one before that, too, another day. I 'member when he come in again, cause I kidded with him, you know."

"Any trouble here, gentlemen?" asked a young white man with a little badge pinned to his shirt that identified him as the assistant store manager. "Any trouble, Annie?"

"No, Phil. This here is the lawyer for that fellow—I showed you the paper and told you about the one-hundred-dollar bill I changed, and the guy's picture was in the paper about killin' a policeman?"

"Yes, the one-hundred-dollar bill. I remember that. You're his lawyer? That's a murder case, isn't it?"

"That's right. A policeman was killed."

"On a roof, right?" asked the assistant manager, pleased with his memory.

"That's right. You remember the fellow with the one-hundred-dollar bill being here?" asked Sandro.

"No. I didn't see him. I do remember Annie telling me about the one-hundred-dollar bill."

"You okayed it cause I had to get somebody to okay changing the bill," Annie said to him. She turned to Sandro. "I can't change no more than a twenty without gettin' it okayed by the assistant manager or the manager."

"Did I, kid?" the assistant manager questioned the girl. "If you say so. I'm not sure. I do remember you telling me about it the very next day. What day was it?"

"The policeman was killed on Monday, July third. You were probably closed the next day, Independence Day. The picture wasn't in the paper until Independence Day. July fifth was a Wednesday," Sandro explained.

"That's when I showed it to you. Wednesday, when I came in," Annie said. "His picture was all over, in the newspapers, on TV. I knew him soon's I seen the pictures. I said to my husband, 'That man was in the store yesterday.'"

"Is there any question that this is the man who was here?" Sandro asked.

She looked at the picture again, then up at Sandro. "That's the man all right. I know I seen him here that day. Cause I seen him on television the next day. I was off. That was the day all right."

"Did you know him? Was he a friend of yours before that day?"

"Except he changed another hundred-dollar bill here, a few days before, I never seen that man before in my life."

"Now, what time was he here that day?"

She studied the floor for a moment, her left hand to her chin. "Well, I just finished my break. I work ten till three. Only part time. And about one, one fifteen I have a break. I got back from my break that day, and then I seen him and changed the bill."

"Could it have been before one o'clock?" asked Sandro.

"No. Had to be after one. Maybe a little later. One fifteen, one twenty. Something like that."

"I want to have Mr. Rivera write down these facts. So I'll have a record for my file and I won't have to inconvenience you again."

"I won't go to no court," she said firmly.

"No, no. I just want this statement for my records. Let's face it, you know the police aren't going to give a Negro a soft time, especially when a cop was killed. I'd appreciate your cooperation."

"He's not Negro," Annie said flatly.

Sandro looked at her. Alvarado was darker by far than she was.

He turned to Mike. "Start writing," he whispered.

"What good is a statement if she won't go to court?" Mike whispered back, taking out his pad.

"Just take the statement. We get that now, and I'll worry about court later." Her reluctance to help Alvarado was more comforting than eagerness would have been.

Mike started writing. He handed the finished statement to Sandro:

My name is Annie Mae Cooper. I am 34 years old. I live at 346 Havemeyer Street, Brooklyn. Married, my husband's name Johnny. I am employed at Associated Five & Ten store at Broadway and Roebling Street, Brooklyn.

In regards to Mr. Luis Alvarado and July 3rd, 1967, I remember that Mr. Alvarado was in the store that I work in on that day because he had come into the store and had asked me to change a one-hundred-dollar bill. On that day it was raining and I was off from work the next day. I had returned from my lunch that day about 1:15 P.M., a few minutes more or less, and a few minutes later Mr. Alvarado came and we kidded about him changing the hundred-dollar bill. I changed the bill and he left the store. I would say this was around 1:20 P.M.

Sandro nodded. He handed the statement to Mrs. Cooper. She read it and signed it.

Sandro and Mike walked back to the car. Sandro felt more at ease now. Not that he was sure beyond doubt. It was possible that these people were friends of Alvarado and lying to him. But it was a good start.

When he arrived back at his office, Sandro photostatted the two statements and placed the originals in a sealed envelope in his safe. He wasn't leaving anything to chance or police snooping.

The intercom buzzed. "Dr. Travers from Bellevue is on the wire," said Elizabeth.

"Hi, George, how're you?" Sandro was ready to jump on the desk and dance if the Bellevue records had been found.

"Fine, Sandro. I called in reference to that Alvarado thing you asked me about. There are four or five ways of checking when Alvarado was here and where he was treated, and obtaining his hospital chart. I've checked just about every one of them so far, and none of them checks out. There are a couple more things I could try, but so far it doesn't look promising."

"All right, George. Just cover every possibility there is. A man's life is at stake, and I have to have the answer. From what he says, he was there about July tenth."

"Well, unless somebody has removed his record and is looking at it, I don't know where it could be. But I'll keep at it and get back to you as soon as I can."

"George, you're a prince. Thank you." Sandro hung up the phone. The day seemed suddenly gloomy.

CHAPTER XII

SAM AND SANDRO SAT NEXT TO EACH OTHER in adjoining jury-box seats. This was the favorite roost of defense counsel while waiting to have cases called for disposition or trial. An assistant D.A. and another lawyer were sitting in the second row at the other end. A defendant was being arraigned. He had been charged with assault in the first degree, and, after a conference at the bench with the judge and D.A., defense counsel announced that the defendant was willing to plead guilty to assault in the third degree, a misdemeanor, to satisfy the entire indictment. The D.A. recommended the acceptance of the plea. The court accepted it.

"The D.A. must have had a weak case," said Sam.

"The hell with that case. What do you think about the barber shop and the hundred-dollar bill?"

"It sounds great—if it's true. Even if we get some people to testify, it doesn't mean they're telling the truth. They might be friends of Alvarado's, trying to help him."

"I thought of that, too," Sandro said.

"You'd better check them out with a lie detector. I mean, what the hell kind of bullshit is this? Every time you go to the Tombs, Alvarado's got a new story for you. He must have people in the street working for him, getting him witnesses, telling him what to say."

"But he doesn't have any visitors."

"He doesn't need them. There are so many Puerto Ricans, junkies, going in and out of the Tombs every day, he's got his own private messenger service."

"You think his story is a phony, then?" Sandro asked.

"How the hell do I know? It sounds great, perfect. But how about those witnesses Soto told you about. Why would the people who live on the block where the cop was killed say they saw this guy Alvarado that day? They have no reason to lie. They're independent witnesses. That's what the jury'll believe, anyway. They'll think this barber and salesgirl are friends of Alvarado, people he knew from before."

"I may be getting sucked in," said Sandro, "but I believe Alvarado."

"That's fine. But it's what the jury believes that counts," Sam cautioned. "I've handled too many murder cases to get hopped up about the statement of some witness or other. They'll come in later and change their story, or you'll find their story full of holes, or they'll be horrible witnesses whom the D.A. destroys on cross-examination. Look, this is good experience for you. You'll be an even better lawyer after getting a case like this under your belt. But I don't want to see you getting yourself all tied up in knots over one case for some lousy junky."

"I just want to see the case through and see it through right."

"Okay, but don't set all your hopes on these people. They sound great. But you can't trust these spics—any witnesses for that matter. They're treacherous. Especially junkies. They tell you anything, just for a fix, for a few bucks. They have no conscience."

"Well, the barber and the salesgirl aren't junkies, and she's not even Puerto Rican."

"Okay, you got a Puerto Rican and a nigger. I doubt it makes much difference in front of the jury."

Sandro shrugged. Sam was cynical, he thought, but he might also be right.

"I've seen too many of these things go wrong to get all excited or go *shlepping* all around those neighborhoods, maybe get stabbed,"

PART 35

Sam went on. "We'll see what else you discover. By the way, I saw Ellis in the corridor before. He was talking, and I was listening."

"What did he have to say?"

"Nothing much, just talked about this and that. He's pretty smug about it. I'll bet he really has a confession from this son of a bitch Alvarado. What do you think of that?"

"Alvarado said he was in Brooklyn at the time of the killing. And now we have witnesses who agree that he was in Brooklyn."

"Not enough. You've also got independent eyewitnesses who saw him in Manhattan. Let me tell you where it's at. In Bellevue! If he went to Bellevue bleeding, then the rest of the stuff—the beating, the alibi—fits together. If we've got that going for us, the jury'll take all the rest along with it, everything. Without it, you've got a bunch of bullshit."

"I've got a doctor by the name of Travers on the staff over there checking out the story. He's a brother of someone I went to law school with. But he hasn't come up with any record so far."

"If it ever existed! And even if it did, the cops may have already destroyed it anyway."

"You think they could do something like that?"

"Could they beat a guy and lie about it? Could they lie about having warned him of his rights? Why couldn't they throw away a couple of sheets of hospital records? You keep forgetting, a cop was killed here. You think letting a couple of pieces of paper disappear from a city hospital is a big deal? The same city that the cops work for? Don't put anything past these people. If they want you, they can get you."

"Alvarado's cellmate saw him bleeding and being sent to the hospital. He can testify."

"A con! Who the hell will the jury believe, a con or a cop? Listen, I know and you know that a cop is only a man, and he can lie like anyone else. But the jury thinks that all cops are good guys. Juries go in and jerk around, and nobody knows what the hell they talk about. Maybe they play cards. And they throw a man's life up in the air, and come out and send him to the electric chair not because he did it but because they think spics can't tell the truth or junkies are no good."

"You think the jury won't believe the cops beat Alvarado?"

"They'll think that's the usual story some wise-guy lawyer made up."

"But if the guy was bleeding?"

"They'll think—or the D.A.'ll make them think—he did it to himself," said Sam. "The jury'll stretch their imagination to any length to believe the cops. And the cops'll go to any length to sink a cop-killer. I know what the cops can do. I was a D.A. myself for fifteen years. Listen, I remember Judge Chapansky, now on the bench in Brooklyn, when he was a D.A. He went to a station house one night to get a statement, and just as he approached the station house he heard this horrible scream. He went inside and asked what happened, who screamed? And the cops looked at him like he was crazy, like they heard nothing. Then he went to see this guy who was supposed to give the statement. The guy was as white as a ghost. He looked like death. Judge Chapansky told the cops he wouldn't take the statement. That if they thought that he'd take a statement from a man in that condition, they were nuts.

"You know, years later," Sam continued, "when I was a D.A., I had to go to Sing Sing one night. I spoke to an orderly there, and when he heard I was a D.A. from Brooklyn, he was my slave. He confirmed Judge Chapansky's story. He was the guy from that station house. He was up for something else when I saw him, but he told me the same story the judge told me. And he told me that they had pierced his back with something. It was his liver they got, he later found out. He screamed like a stuck pig and they told him they'd kill him if he didn't talk to the D.A. Fortunately, there was a man like Chapansky there that night. Most D.A.'s wouldn't give a damn. They stick with the cops and take the statement." Sam fingered one of the cigars in his breast pocket momentarily.

"I remember another instance. Where a D.A. from Brooklyn went out to take a statement with a new stenotypist. You know these stenos are supposed to take down everything they see and hear in the station house. So this night they go to a station house and they're taking a statement. In the middle of the statement, the prisoner starts to falter, and one cop gives him a roundhouse right to the chest. The steno put down in the statement a description 'At this juncture, Detective Dolan delivers a forceful blow to the chest of the prisoner.' When the steno got back to the office and typed the statement up, the D.A. called him in and he says, 'Are you out of your fucking mind?' And the steno tells him that he took an oath to report everything he saw and heard, and that's all he was doing.

"You know, usually the experienced steno knows when to take his hands off the keys, while the witness falters or blurts things out which'll tend to confuse the confession," Sam said. "This steno put everything in. He was civil service, so he stayed on the job, but he never rode felony again. They made him a clerk in the office. That's why I don't get too excited about any case, especially when a cop is killed. The cops got us over a barrel, and we can't tell what'll happen."

"But we have an alibi, witnesses."

"And what do you think the cops'll do to those witnesses when they get their names and addresses?"

"We won't give them to them." Sandro was angry now.

"Listen, the law says—look at the Code of Criminal Procedure when you get back to the office, I forget the section numbers—but it says the D.A. can move for a bill of particulars about an alibi up to eight days before the trial. And we have to give him full disclosure of the names and addresses of all the alibi witnesses so that he won't be surprised at the trial. If we don't give them the names, we can't use the witnesses. Practically speaking, if we do give the names, the cops'll be up to see these people in ten minutes."

"They wouldn't do anything to innocent citizens, would they?"

"Oh, they wouldn't touch them, no. But what is a barber going to say, or a salesgirl, when a cop from the neighborhood comes in and talks to them. They got their livelihood to think of. These cops are around all the time. They need the cops for protection. Alvarado is just a flash in the pan. Do you know what a pain in the ass these cops can be to these people? And they don't have to make the people say they didn't see Alvardo, lie outright. All it has to be is, well, Alvarado looks like the guy, but they're *not absolutely sure*. If they're not absolutely sure of Alvarado, their testimony is worthless to us. So the cops confuse them a little. How can they be absolutely sure it was Alvarado? And that's the end of your alibi. The cops aren't going to let some spic barber or a nigger salesgirl foul up this case."

"The sons of bitches!"

"Well, they got a job to do. I'm not sure I would do it any different. We need a hell of a lot to overcome what the D.A. most probably has in his file. You have to remember, Sandro, Ellis has been an assistant D.A. a long time. And he's not going to come into court to make a fool of himself with a case that doesn't hold water. I'm not going into court to make a fool out of myself either. I've got a living to make and a reputation that helps me make it. If I go out on a limb and get it sawed out from under me, I get hurt where it hurts. I'd rather run to fight another day."

"But, Sam, what if you run to fight another day, and the next time after that you run, and the next time? Hell! You may be sending a lot of guys to jail for no reason. What the hell service is that to an innocent man?"

"Look at the service I am to the guilty when I get them lesser pleas, light sentences. Ninety-nine percent of the defendants are guilty. Besides, clients want successful lawyers to represent them. Not losing crusaders. I have an office to run, a secretary to pay."

"If you see what has to be done, if you know you could do more, but you don't, what the hell are you?"

"You're making a living."

Sandro studied Sam.

"Well, I believe Alvarado," Sandro said with finality. "And I've got statements, written, signed statements."

"Let's just hope they don't turn around and say that you made them sign the statements, or gave them money to sign, or something like that."

"Are you crazy? Why would I do that?"

"After the cops finish talking to your witnesses, you can't tell what they'll say. Particularly if the cops know you're breaking your head to get this guy off. Manny Weiss was indicted when a people's witness said he forced him into making a certain statement. Sure, he was acquitted, but look what an indictment did to his practice. No. You're not getting this old bag of bones to poke around with you."

"I know we're on the right track," Sandro assured Sam.

"I hope so. I'll be delighted if we are."

PART 35

"The only thing that really worries me, Sam, is Hernandez. If he turns state's evidence for a break on his sentence, that'd kill us but good."

"What a case you want me to get excited about! I'd have to have a hole in my head to waste time on this. But it's good experience for you. I just hope they don't throw us in jail for trying to defend this guy."

"Joseph Devlin," the clerk intoned, calling a case.

"That's mine," said Sandro, rising. "I'm going to stay on this, Sam. Follow it wherever it leads."

"Sandro, you're a good kid. Crazy, but good. Find the Bellevue records if you find anything."

Sandro walked to the counsel table to represent his client. As he stood before the bench of justice, he wondered if disillusionment was too high a price to pay for a practical education in the law.

CHAPTER XIII

SANDRO SAT AT THE TABLE in his mother's spotless kitchen; the room was filled with the rich aromas of her cooking. From outside came the almost Arabian, lilting, wailing quality of a true Neapolitan singer floating from the loudspeakers on the bandstand of the *Festa di San Gennaro*, the annual celebration for the patron saint of Naples held in New York's Little Italy in the middle of September. Police barricades kept out traffic, and carts and stands lined the sidewalks, while the streets were thronged with people who came to eat sausage and pepper sandwiches on Italian bread and to watch *zeppoli* and *calzone* being dropped into boiling oil. Sometimes the young men from the neighborhood would try to climb a greased pole, and always there were Italian singers and music, and the parade where the men would carry the statue of San Gennaro, and money was pinned to the statue or collected by the officials of the festa.

"I gotta good fettucini for you. Your favorite," Sandro's mother said, turning from the stove, her wooden cooking spoon in her hand. Sandro was always amazed that that selfsame instrument of childhood punishment could be the helpmate of delicious food. Mama was old now, gray, her hair gathered in a bun at the back of her head;

PART 35

she smiled warmly, pleased to have her Sandro home again, even for one meal.

"It smells great, Mama. I can't wait."

"You not eat good, Sandro. You thin." Her eagle eye assessed him.

Sandro wasn't about to tell Mama that the reason he was getting thin was that his roommate for the last few months, a blonde model named Claudia, was no longer cooking for him—or anything else for him, for that matter. She had gone by mutual agreement. Besides, Mama would never have approved of Claudia. She couldn't even pronounce *osso buco*, or *spaghetti carbonara*, or *linguine con vongole*, much less cook them.

"And then some veal *piccata*, just like you like. *E ensalata rugola*" her eyes lit up for Sandro as she said it. She knew what his favorites were.

"Stop, Mama. Stop talking about it. Just bring them out one at a time, and I'll eat my way through them." He was happy now. How many meals like this he had had to miss as part of the price for his wonderful education!

As he was eating, he wondered, just for a moment, what Alvarado had eaten for dinner this night.

"It was great, Mama, great," Sandro said as he sat back in the big stuffed chair in her living room, his feet up on a hassock. Her apartment was three rooms—a bedroom, living room, and kitchen. Not much different, in size, from the apartments on Stanton Street, except that Mama was on her hands and knees everyday scrubbing everything, including the public hallway outside.

Her eyes were warmed by the very sight of Sandro as she pretended to watch television. "Take a little nap, Sandro, rest. You work too hard on these case."

"I can't, Mama. I have to see a fellow called Frankie Sausages."

"Who? Frankie what?" She laughed. "Sausige?" She pronounced it *saw-zeach*.

"He's a fellow who has one of the sausage stands down at the feast," Sandro laughed with her. "He's a fellow Sal Angeletti told me to talk to. He might be able to help me with one of my cases."

"With a name like Sausige, I should know he's a friend of Sal. And his wife is Peperone, no? They make a good combination."

Sandro laughed with her. "Where's that sugar bowl of yours, Mama?" he asked, rising.

"Never mind. Leave the sugar bowl alone." She moved protectively toward the kitchen, where the sugar bowl stood on the sideboard. Sandro was faster. He snared it and quickly slipped a fifty-dollar bill in with the money she kept there. It was all right if he could get the money into the sugar bowl, which was her bank, but she wouldn't accept money outright. He put on his jacket and made his way to the front door.

"Call me."

"Okay, Mama. Every couple of days."

They kissed, and he descended the two flights. He was immediately swallowed up in the crowds swelling Mulberry Street like a river coursing to the sea. He started moving in the direction of Spring Street. He felt his senses gorged with the pungent smells of cooking sausages and peppers and onions, the hot oils, the pastry, the coffee, the smoke filling the air, the yelling kids, the gawking tourists, the pushing humanity, the people at the booths shouting their wares, the games where you had to throw quoits onto sticks, PingPong balls into fish bowls, pennies onto small numbered circles, the spinning wheels, and the floating, lilting, Neapolitan singing. He reached the stand where he had been told he would find Frankie Sausages.

"Yeah, how many?" a young, curly haired man cooking sausage on an open grill asked Sandro, ready to stuff the meat into a quarter loaf of bread.

"I want to talk to Frankie," Sandro said.

"Frankie who?" the man asked, shrugging his shoulders and shaking his head.

"Frankie Sausages," Sandro said reluctantly.

"Who's 'e want?" asked a second man, in an apron, pointing his chin at Sandro.

"Somebody named Sausage." The curly haired man's face wrinkled into a question and another shrug. "You know anybody named Sausage?"

"Yeah, right here," his colleague answered, spearing a sausage with

PART 35

a fork and lifting it, "*u-sausige nabolitan* and all his brothers. You want a sangwich, fella?" They were both smirking.

"Sal Angeletti sent me over here to talk to Frankie," Sandro said finally.

Their faces suddenly went blank.

"Frankie's in the store," one of them said quickly. "We didn't know who you were."

"I know. Which store?"

"Right here, the pork store," the first man said, pointing to a store on the ground floor of the building directly behind the sausage stand. Sandro entered. A red-headed man was stuffing meat into a sausage machine with one hand, grinding with the other. The ground meat was being forced into a skin, which was winding itself into one large sausage on the counter.

"Frankie?"

The man just looked at Sandro. He stopped grinding, cut the skin from the machine, and started to tie a cord deftly around the long sausage every few inches, making neat joints.

"What d'ya want him for?"

"I'm a lawyer. My name's Sandro Luca. Sal Angeletti told me you might be able to help me."

The man wiped his hands on his apron, extending the right one to Sandro.

"Hello, Counselor." They shook hands. "I'm Frankie. What can I do for you?"

"Sal thought you might know some people over on Stanton Street, near Suffolk, Norfolk."

"Nah, not any more. We useta operate over there, you know, bets, numbers. But no more. Now they got them spics over there. We gave it up. It don't pay no more to bother with them dirty bas-tids. What'a ya need? Maybe I can help ya anyway?"

"I'm representing a fellow who's supposed to have killed a cop over on Stanton Street."

"You mean that one about two, three months ago?"

"Yes."

"Nah, I don't know no people over there no more. But I know that cop that was the dead cop's partner that day. I read about it in the papers."

"Snider? You know Snider?" Sandro asked with surprise.

"Yeah. He was around that section a long time. He was in narcotics, but we didn't have no bother with him, you know? We don't fool with that stuff. He was plainclothes, but I knew he was a cop."

"Snider was in the narcotics squad?" Sandro asked.

"Yeah. That was maybe five years now, maybe six. Before even he was in the precinct. I tink he got hisself a beef, and they put him back poundin' a beat."

"Other than that, Frankie, do you think you could help me out, introduce me to anyone who'd still be over in the neighborhood?"

"I hate to say no, Counselor, but I couldn't help ya. That useta be some sweet neighborhood, too. Ahhh," he sighed. "If I can help ya wit anything else, just let me know, okay? Ya want some sausage, Counselor? I just made it fresh."

"No thanks, Frankie. Next time."

"So long."

Sandro walked back into the surging crowd. The two men at the sausage stand waved to him as he made his way toward the side street where his car was parked.

CHAPTER XIV

AS HE WALKED TOWARD THE COURTROOM, Sandro was absorbed with thoughts of the arguments he was about to present to Judge Conboy to support his application for a bill of particulars in the Alvarado case.

Sandro entered the courtroom and sat in the back. He reread his motion papers in which he requested the time of the killing, the exact place, the type of gun used, the wounds inflicted, witnesses' names, statements, photos of the scene of the crime. Ellis, of course, was opposed to revealing any such information. Sandro felt someone reading over his shoulder. He turned.

"Nicholas Siakos, how are you?"

"Hi, Sandro, how are you?" Siakos, Hernandez's lawyer, spoke with a slight Greek overtone to his English. Having handled many Spanish clients, he also spoke Spanish, or at least, Puerto Rican Spanish, that too with a Greek overtone. He was about Sandro's height, but thickset, stockier. He had a thick neck, square jaw, and heavy black hair.

"I'm just fine. How are you doing with the Hernandez situation?" Sandro asked.

"All right. Actually, I haven't had much time to get at it yet, but I think we have a situation here which could prove very interesting. We may have a little bomb on our hands." Siakos nodded and narrowed his eyes for emphasis.

"Are you going to trial with this case or are you going to see if you can get a plea?" Sandro fished.

"Oh, I don't know." Siakos smiled slightly, pleased at an opportunity to be sly and noncommittal. "My man tells me he feels very bad about getting your man involved. He says the only way your man got into all this is because of him, and he wants to fight to save your man. But I don't know." Siakos obviously wanted Hernandez to plead guilty to a charge less than first-degree murder, even at Alvarado's expense.

"What are your plans?" Sandro asked. "I'd like some idea, so we can prepare our defense."

"As it stands now, I have to try the case—my man refuses to plead. I don't know what's going to develop later on, but my man insists that he wasn't there and your man wasn't there either."

"Do you have a defense, any evidence to prove your man wasn't involved? Does he have an alibi?"

"Oh, there'll be a defense," Siakos assured Sandro. He jutted his lower lip and nodded forcefully. "Hernandez has mentioned some places where he says he actually was. I have to go to these places soon. Maybe somebody at those places will remember him. He told his wife all about it. I'll have to get in touch with her and have her explain where Hernandez was. Then I'll have something to start on."

Sandro studied Siakos's wide, smiling face. A man's life in his hands, and he hadn't done a thing about it. He was going to get organized next week. Fate curses those without money, even in the courthouse. A poor man gets into trouble because he is poor; and then can't pay for enough legal help to get him out of it—again, because he is poor.

True, the state was paying Siakos and Sandro a thousand dollars each to defend these men, but what is one lawyer and a thousand dollars against a district attorney's staff of hundreds, a police force of thousands, and the public's fear of a criminal world known only through the blood and guts of newsprint.

"I'd like to talk to your man's wife," said Sandro. "She might have some information that could be helpful." Sandro didn't mention that he wanted to know more about where Hernandez claimed to be at the time of the killing. If Hernandez had a good alibi, he would be worthless to the D.A. "Would you mind if I asked her some questions about that?"

"Oh, sure, sure. As soon as I talk to her, I'll tell her you want to talk to her, and maybe we can make a date in your office or my office."

"That'll be fine," said Sandro. "I'll call you tomorrow to confirm the appointment. Okay?"

"Yes, okay. Perhaps tomorrow is too soon, though. Let me set things up and then we can all get together."

"Sure." Stalled, thought Sandro. "I have to read these papers now, Nick. I made a motion for a bill of particulars in this case."

"Oh good, good. I intended to make that motion. I'm glad you did. That saves me work." Siakos laughed. "Will you give me a copy of the bill of particulars when you get it, so I can read it? Maybe I won't have to make my motion."

"Sure." Sandro forced himself to smile. "I want to cooperate with you on this case. Even though we represent different interests, I'm sure we can work something out between us to help both men."

"Sure, sure. I'm sure of it." Siakos smiled widely. "Okay, I'll talk to you in a few days then. Let me know what happens about the bill of particulars."

Sandro peered up at the bench. A prisoner was being arraigned before the judge, a court officer standing on either side of him. Sandro saw Ellis sitting at the D.A.'s counsel table. He was not handling the case before the judge. Sandro walked forward and sat in the first bench of the spectators' section of the courtroom. Ellis turned and nodded toward Sandro. Sandro moved forward to the railing.

"They call the motion calendar yet?" Sandro whispered.

"No." Ellis was a crafty fighter who worked slowly, precisely, with deadly intensity, whose face never revealed emotion or gave away any unnecessary information. He had two facial expressions; one, blank, the second just a few wrinkles added to the bridge of his nose.

"Let's go outside for a smoke, David," Sandro suggested.

Ellis nodded. They walked out of the courtroom and stood in the corridor.

"What's on your mind, Sandro?" He studied Sandro's face. Ellis, like so many D.A.'s, policemen, law-enforcement officials, was a bloodhound by profession, by dedication, by imprisonment. He was a prisoner of the system to which he had sworn allegiance. His role as prosecutor had become his life, and his tolerance for mere mortals was limited. Having seen and prosecuted so many criminals, men like Ellis sometimes delude themselves into believing that everyone except the sworn minions of the law are out to topple the system. Not only do they lose their perspective but, in direct proportion, their humor, as well.

"I wanted to see how you stood on this motion for a bill of particulars. Are you going to oppose it?" Sandro asked for openers.

"Certainly. I'm not going to give you all the information you asked for in that demand of yours."

"What's the difference if I know the exact time the crime was committed, or where it was committed, or what injuries the man has sustained, and by what pistol?"

"Look, Sandro, you know as well as I do that you're not entitled to some of that information. I don't make the laws; I just follow them. Besides, I don't see why we have to give you a preview of every piece of information that the police uncovered and we're going to use in the trial."

"But the physical evidence, David, the dead body in the position it was found, the burglarized apartment—they no longer exist. Certainly, I can't change the pictures of them, nor does my knowing about them hurt your case. What there was, there was. I just want to prepare my case on facts, not what I have to conjecture."

"You want me to open my file to you, is that it?"

"I'm not asking for a full disclosure, but it would be nice to know something about what Alvarado is charged with besides the wording of the indictment, 'did cause the death of Lauria with a pistol.' At least let me begin the race from the same starting line. Didn't Judge Botein suggest a trial should be a more informed search for the truth?"

"We'll see what this judge has to say." Ellis didn't intend to argue, knowing the judge would probably agree with him.

"David, I understand there are certain witnesses involved in this case," Sandro probed. "Are you willing at least to let me have a copy of their statements, or must I make another motion?" Sandro said straight-faced, wanting to get a rise out of Ellis.

"Are you kidding?" Ellis was stunned. "You think I'm going to give you witness statements in this case?"

"Well, the Court of Appeals has indicated I'm entitled to the statements of witnesses," Sandro continued, knowing he was stretching the Court of Appeals decisions.

"In what decisions?" Ellis looked at Sandro, his somber eyes curious.

"All of the cases which follow *People v. Rosario*," Sandro replied. "They indicate that I'm entitled to witness statements."

"But not now," Ellis emphasized hurriedly. "When the witness is on the stand and you cross-examine, maybe then you can get them. You think I've gone crazy, that I'm going to give you witness statements in advance? Defendants are getting away with murder these days, and you defense counsel always want more. Soon we won't be able to put anybody in jail."

"Come on, Dave, you're kidding me, aren't you?"

"No, I'm not kidding." He wasn't. "With the decisions that are coming down from those clean-handed judges in Washington these days, in a short time it's going to be impossible for the district attorney to put anybody in jail."

"You've got such an advantage over a defendant and defense attorney now, particularly in a case like this, where I'm assigned by the court, that you can win hands down," Sandro said. "To begin with, you have thirty thousand policemen working with you. All I have is myself and maybe, maybe, a couple of fellows whom I have to persuade to help me out, and then I have to pay them from my own pocket, hoping the court will reimburse me. Besides, you're the district attorney. You have the badge to show people. They have to cooperate with you or you subpoena them to the grand jury, and if they refuse to testify you can have them put in jail for contempt."

"What's wrong with that? We have to investigate, or don't you want us to do that either?"

"I have to beg witnesses to talk to me, and if they don't feel like getting involved, don't want to run afoul of the cops because this is a cop-killing, they can thumb their noses at me, and I can't do a damn thing about it. A lot of people won't even talk to me just so they don't get involved with the cop on the beat."

"I wouldn't know. I never have too much trouble getting a witness." Ellis smiled. "I just call one of the detectives, and they bring the witness down to my office."

"Thanks for the salt. You just have them brought down! And then you have the grand jury to hear the evidence and indict a defendant. As secret a proceeding as Henry the Eighth's Court of Star Chamber—and just as antiquated. Can we get the grand jury minutes, find out who was there, what they said? Sure. At the trial, when the witness takes the stand. Always too late. You get the case prepared in advance, and we have to juggle on the run, catch as catch can, after the trial is in full motion. If we have something that we discover during the trial, we have to go out at night and investigate it ourselves. You go to sleep and have a detective do it for you."

"You think I have slaves to carry me home, too," Ellis said curtly.

"No. You have a case to prepare for the next day, as a lawyer should. But we have to prepare *and* investigate. We can do one or the other, but we can't do both well and sleep too."

"I can't help that."

"Then you have the fingerprint bureau and the police lab and the engineers and architects and the ballistics men, every sort of expert, all of them working for you, figuring things out, giving you expert opinions on everything from shoelaces to baby powder. Do I have any of that? Can I afford to utilize anything like it for a guy like Alvarado, who had to sign a pauper's oath to get a lawyer?"

"No, you only have the Supreme Court of the United States telling us we have to warn a defendant of his rights before we can even let him confess to us. And we can't detain people, or search them, or anything else. You must be kidding with all of that."

"Because others in the past didn't get the rights they deserved, does that mean we should continue to deny defendants their rights to the end of time? Everybody's rights have to be protected, not just the ones that you think deserve it. For Christ's sake, David. The only difference between the old days of anything goes and now is that the cops have

PART 35

to add a couple of words to their testimony that they advised a defendant of his rights, that they were suspicious of a defendant before they searched him."

Ellis stared at Sandro. "You're not going to stand there and tell me that every cop is a liar and gets on the stand and commits perjury?" Ellis's back was stiffening visibly.

"No. But I am saying that the advantages you say defendants now have are easily canceled out by testimony. The advantages over a defendant that you have are practically insurmountable."

"I think you're exaggerating a great deal. This state isn't run for the benefit of criminals."

"No, for the citizens. Defendants weren't born with numbers under their chins. I don't even know, and I won't know until the trial, what the hell this crime is all about. I only know Lauria was shot. They refused a preliminary hearing down in the lower court in this case because it was going to the grand jury. How would you like to prepare a case totally in the dark?"

"Look, Sandro, I'm only doing my job. I'm not the district attorney, only one of his assistants. Take this up with him—or with the chaplain."

Sandro checked himself from mentioning also that Ellis had the power to demand a bill of particulars setting forth the names, addresses, and places of employment of all alibi witnesses. He had gone to the Code of Criminal Procedure as Sam had advised. Failure to provide any of that information, he soon realized, would get his witnesses disqualified.

"You have all of that going for you," continued Sandro, ignoring Ellis's taunt, "and you're going to oppose even my request to know of what wounds the cop died, at what time? For crying out loud, David, you have a ninety-nine to one shot to win any case you come up against. No, thirty thousand to one."

"You've got subpoena power. Subpoena the information you want," Ellis suggested.

"That's only at the time of trial and relates to police records and the like. What about witness statements?"

"I don't make the law, Sandro, I just apply it." He shrugged. "I'm not going to give you the witness statements, that's for sure. You can even make a motion. You can do whatever you want. I'm not going to give you witness statements."

"I was sure of that, David."

"Look, it's not that I don't want to help you. It's just that I have my job to do. I know this is a tough case. I don't think you should feel bad when you lose, if you lose, because it's a tough case."

"Thanks, David. I'll keep that in mind. I wouldn't want you to feel bad either if you lose."

Ellis studied Sandro as he held the door open. The two adversaries re-entered the courtroom.

CHAPTER XV

SANDRO WALKED ALONG THE DIM, empty corridor of Bellevue Hospital with Dr. Travers and Jerry Ball. Ball was a professional photographer who sometimes worked with Sandro, more for friendship's sake than money. Their footsteps echoed within the green-tiled and green-painted walls.

"By then, I had checked every possibility except one," George Travers was saying. "I checked and double-checked the hospital entry records, the X-rays, the admission lists, everything for a Luis Alvarado who was here sometime in mid-July. The ambulance records were the very last possibility I could think of. At first it didn't sink in when you said he must have come here by ambulance from the prison. But that's exactly where I found the only record I could find. An ambulance call to the detention prison in the ambulance-dispatch book."

"Name, date, and all?"

"Right." The doctor took a small piece of handwritten paper from the pocket of his white jacket. He read from it. "He came here July ninth, 1967, about ten P.M. and was released about two thirty on the morning of July tenth. He was returned to the prison in ambulance number twenty-one. The driver was J. Lacqua, and the attendant was Winston Smylen."

"Did the ambulance book indicate any diagnosis?" Sandro asked.

"No," replied the doctor. "There was just the transportation notation. But now that we know what day he was here, we can check upstairs in the prison-ward log. I was really just lucky to find this notation in the dispatch book. No one has access to it except the dispatcher. I took a chance and looked at it today while I was passing. I still can't find any hospital record, the actual diagnostic record. Did you try and get it through official channels?"

"No, George," Sandro replied. "I want to have a copy in my hands first. Then I'll order it through official channels just to cover us. I don't want to alert anyone and have the records destroyed before I get a copy of it. Besides, if I can produce a copy, it'll make destruction of the record look even worse."

"You think they'd really destroy such a record?" asked Dr. Travers.

"I don't know. I'm not about to take a chance on it though. That's why Jerry came along tonight with his camera."

Jerry, tall and lean, lifted his equipment bag forward so the doctor could see it.

"All right. We'll go over there. I'll get the book somehow, bring it to the office, and you can photograph it in my office. Then we can go to the prison ward."

The three men walked past the cafeteria to the ambulance entrance. An ambulance pulled up, and through the double doors, half-glass, half-wood, they saw the attendant jump from the back of the ambulance, moving toward a stretcher on wheels.

"This one's really a mess," the attendant announced to other drivers sitting near the dispatch office, awaiting assignment. One of the attendants who had been sitting near the ambulance entrance helped to push the stretcher to the ambulance. Within was a man lying on a pallet. His head was swathed in bandages oozing blood. His hair was matted with dirt and blood. His clothes were old, soiled, ripped, bound on with cords and string. The two attendants eased the body onto the rolling stretcher and moved him through the double doors and turned right into the emergency ward.

PART 35

Sandro and Jerry watched with fascination. Dr. Travers hardly noticed.

"Wait here for a minute," said the doctor. "I'll go to the dispatch office. If the book is there, I'll get it now." Dr. Travers walked quickly down the corridor.

Sandro and Jerry were standing outside the emergency room entrance. Within were people sitting on chairs, sitting on tables, lying on tables, propped against the wall, waiting for treatment, hoping for relief. Some were in wheelchairs. All looked uncomfortable, poor, pained, afraid. A wheelchair with a heavy woman in a nightdress, gasping for air, was being pushed down the hall by a thin, effeminate Negro attendant. A large man with gray hair and purpled cheeks was lying on his side in the emergency waiting room. Except for the blood-lines etched on his cheeks, his face was ashen. His eyes stared numbly at a wall. He did not stir, except for an occasional soft inhalation. A Puerto Rican man carrying a child, wrapped in an adult's jacket, entered the emergency room; a frantic woman and two small children trailed behind.

The waiting room of the emergency clinic was just a long corridor leading into a room outfitted for emergency care. The corridor was filled with a line of sufferers, looking neglected and forlorn, waiting, while some bled, some died, all suffered. And as they waited, more people continued to stream into emergency, to be herded into line to wait their turn.

"This place is fantastic," commented Jerry as he stood next to Sandro.

"One look at this and you don't want ever to get sick," replied Sandro.

A man with one leg was wheeled down a corridor in a wheelchair. The stub seemed to be seeping fresh blood.

Another man carrying a child in his arms came through the doors into the hospital. The child was awake, her eyes opened but motionless. She was resigned, content in that fortress of her father's arms where nothing could harm her. The father looked around hopelessly, frantically.

"You want emergency? *Emergencia?*" Sandro inquired.

The man nodded quickly, the slightest hint of a smile of thanks seeping through his strained face.

"This way," said Sandro, pointing. An attendant was passing. "This man needs emergency," said Sandro, pointing to the father and child.

"Right in the emergency room. We'll get to him as soon as we can," replied the attendant, with weariness and apathy.

Sandro shrugged and pointed to the waiting room. The man gave that slight hint of a smile again and walked in to stand at the end of the line with the child in his arms.

"Here's the doctor," said Jerry as Travers returned, walking quickly, carrying a large ledger book under his arm. He walked past Sandro and Jerry without stopping or turning his head their way.

"Come on," he whispered as he passed.

Sandro and Jerry looked at each other, hesitated, then began to follow the doctor at a distance which would eliminate any suspicion of their being together. The doctor stopped in front of the huge elevator door in the hospital's A Building. Sandro and Jerry sauntered up and stood beside him. Sandro looked around to be sure they were alone and could not be overheard.

"Is that the dispatch book from that night?" Sandro asked.

"Yes. I'll show it to you when we get upstairs."

The door slid open, and the three men entered the elevator. At the fourth floor, they alighted.

"It's at this end of the hall," said the doctor, walking to his right. Jerry and Sandro followed. They entered a small office at the end of the corridor. There was a room for secretaries, a working office for the doctor, and a door marked LIBRARY, which the doctor walked through, Sandro and Jerry following him. "Here it is, Sandro. In this book, I found Alvarado's name as having been brought here July Ninth, 1967, and having been brought back to the prison on the tenth. Now let me find the exact page," the doctor thumbed through. "Here it is."

Sandro moved closer, his eyes scanning the lines until he saw *Alvarado, Luis*. And there it was, the dispatch record indicating Alvarado had been returned to the Tombs from the Bellevue prison ward at 2:30 A.M. on July 10th, 1967.

"This is tremendous," Sandro exclaimed. "This can't be denied. No one would ever have thought of looking for this to destroy it. Jerry, can you get pictures of this?"

Jerry, who had been looking over Sandro's shoulder, unbuckled his

PART 35

equipment bag. He took out a camera with flashgun and started to focus several times.

"You know, I feel like Shapiro the spy or something, taking these pictures," Jerry grinned. He focused again, and the camera flashed. "Okay, I've got pictures of these two pages. Any more?"

"No, that's fine," said Sandro, closing the book.

"I've got to get this book downstairs before anybody realizes it's gone. You sure you have everything you need from it?" Travers asked, putting the book under his arm.

"Yes, sure. Jerry'll develop the pictures. We don't even have to write anything."

"Okay, fine. Wait for me here." The doctor went out. Sandro slouched down into a big leather chair. Jerry took out a medical journal and leafed through it. In a few minutes, the doctor returned without the book.

"I'd rather just you came Sandro. Not that I don't like you, Jerry," he grinned. "It's just that the less conspicuous we are, the better. Jerry can wait right here for us. Nobody will bother you. If anybody comes in, just say you're waiting for me."

Dr. Travers led Sandro along the corridor into and through another corridor which led to an adjoining building of the Bellevue compound. They continued through long, dismal, tiled corridors, which were occasionally stirred by moans, into another building, and finally ascended several flights of stairs. They approached an iron-bars-over-sheet-steel door. There was a bell at the side of the door.

"Yes?" asked the policeman, who peered through the Judas eye in the steel door.

"I'm Dr. Travers. I want to come in to see one of the doctors inside."

"Who's he, Doctor?" the officer pointed his chin at Sandro.

"This is one of my associates. We're just here to check the records, not to go into the ward."

"All right, Doctor." The officer unlocked the door and allowed Sandro and the doctor to enter. The room was used as a clerical office, doctors' station, and police office. Opposite the steel door, through which they had come, was a wall of bars separating the office from the prisoners. Beyond, under constant scrutiny, was a roomful of prisoner-patients in blue prison-ward pajamas. Some of the prisoners were in beds lined against the wall on the sides of the ward; some were in wheelchairs; others sat on chairs, talking among themselves.

Dr. Travers approached the nurse and spoke with her. She led him to a large ledger book on the desk. The doctor opened it and began searching its papers. He motioned to Sandro to help him. The doctor's attention was drawn suddenly to one of the pages.

"Look at this, Sandro," said Travers, pointing to a line in the book under the date July 9th, 1967. It was the name *Luis Alvarado*. The entry indicated that Alvarado arrived at 10 P.M., July 9th, and was sent for X-rays and examination. Under the column marked *Diagnosis* was the notation *RO internal bleeding*.

"What does this 'RO internal bleeding' mean?" Sandro asked.

"It would seem there was some reason to make the doctor on duty believe that Alvarado might be having internal bleeding, and he sent him for X-rays and to make sure whether there actually was internal bleeding. RO means Rule-out, a medical abbreviation—check for internal bleeding and rule it out or affirm it as the diagnosis."

"Well? What happened? Did they find internal bleeding?"

"I don't know. There's no further information here. Let me ask the nurse." Travers motioned to the nurse. "Miss Dawson," he said, addressing her by the name-badge pinned to her uniform, at the tip of her left breast. "Is there any record here, other than this book, which would indicate the diagnosis or the treatment the patient received?"

"Well, I don't know," she said in a soft southern accent. "I only know that they mark everything down here and that's all."

"Well, doesn't the doctor make out a diagnosis sheet or some report after the examination?" Sandro asked.

"There is a sheet, just a single sheet of paper that the doctor fills out, I guess when he examines the patient," she replied.

"Where is it in this case?" Sandro pressed, pointing to Alvarado's name. "Do you have it on file?"

"The doctor sends that back to the prison when the prisoner is returned," the nurse explained. "That's where it probably is now, so the prison doctors can treat the prisoner."

"Damn. If it's at the prison it will be inaccessible until I subpoena

PART 35

it at trial," Sandro said. He turned back to the nurse. "Is there any way of knowing the name of the doctor who treated or examined Alvarado that night?"

She studied the ledger. "Dr. Waxman's signature? Yes, this is Dr. Waxman's signature. He probably examined the patient."

"Is he here? Is he still at Bellevue, Nurse?" the doctor asked.

"No, sir. I think he's at New York University Hospital now."

"Thank you." He shrugged at Sandro. "Guard, will you let us out now?" Travers asked.

The steel door shut with a heavy thud as Sandro and the doctor retraced their footsteps toward the library.

"Is there anything else you want to do here, Sandro?"

"I don't think so. I'll have to talk to this Dr. Waxman. Can you set up some sort of appointment with him, George?"

"I can't right now. I have to get back to the clinic. I'll give him a call as soon as I'm free and try to arrange a meeting."

Jerry Ball and Sandro lounged in the back of the cab as it drove across town. "The weather's getting nippy. Let's have a couple of drinks to celebrate and warm up at the same time," Sandro suggested.

"Hey! I'm going to like this job."

"This is the greatest thing in the case so far."

"But even if you find that this guy of yours was bleeding, how do you prove that whatever he had to go to the hospital for was a result of the cops?"

"I don't have to prove it was a beating. They have to prove it wasn't."

"I don't follow you," Jerry said.

"In order to prove beyond a reasonable doubt that the confession is voluntary, they have to account for his physical condition. That is, he was healthy when he went into the police station. They have to account for any physical disability that might have developed in there and show that it was not the result of a beating. If they can't, then there goes their case."

"That makes sense. You think you have enough to make them start worrying?"

"Not yet. But we're closing the gaps."

CHAPTER XVI

DESPITE THE COLD, RAINY, OCTOBER WEATHER, Sandro was still cheerful as he walked into Sam's office. This was his first stop of the morning. The secretary buzzed Sam on the intercom and showed Sandro into his office.

"I've got it, I've got it, Sam," Sandro announced victoriously. "Dr. Travers found the goddamn record that shows that Alvarado was in Bellevue on the ninth of July. There's your acid proof."

"Jesus, Sandro," Sam exclaimed. He stood to shake Sandro's hand. "That's powerful stuff. Where is it?"

"A photographer, Jerry Ball, took pictures. I'll have them in a couple of days. Well?"

Sam sat smiling. "They may have denied most of our motion for a bill of particulars, but we don't need it now. Now Ellis has to prove beyond a reasonable doubt that Alvarado wasn't beaten. That's the Barbato case. That was my case in the Court of Appeals."

"You think they can justify his condition, Sam?"

"What did the diagnosis say?"

"I couldn't get the diagnosis chart. It was sent back to the Tombs with him. But he went up there for internal bleeding."

"Goddamn, you got them cold. How can they account for internal bleeding. I mean, Alvarado hasn't got an ulcer, for Christ's sake."

"We'll destroy them," Sandro heard himself say. The words sounded familiar, like what Don Vincenzo had said about destroying the D.A. and finishing him off. "Taking some guy walking home from the movies and beating him to get a confession," he went on. "And now they want to talk him into the electric chair. The merciless bastards."

"Bullshit. That's pure bullshit, Sandro," Sam said dryly.

"What do you mean? You think these cops should get away with it?"

"Look, Sandro, I've been on both sides of the fence. So I've got the benefit of a little experience you don't have."

"And that makes what I said bullshit?"

"No, but I know what I'm talking about. Don't lay all the blame on the cops. Just think about it for a minute. You've got a guy like Lauria, getting paid how much? Nine thousand bucks a year. And for that, every day, day in, day out, he had to be ready to go get his ass shot at, to go into dark apartments with madmen inside, armed madmen. Or maybe jump in the river to save nuts who want to kill themselves, or maybe deliver babies, catch thieves and junkies, a million and one other things full of danger. How much would you want, Sandro, to run into a hail of bullets from a killer or burglar? Would you do it for nine thousand per?"

"I wouldn't do it for anything," Sandro replied.

"Damn right. Me neither."

"Does that make busting a guy's head to get a confession out of him right?"

"Of course not, Sandro. There are other things though." Sam puffed his cigar. "How many cops are there in New York City?"

"About thirty thousand."

"Okay, thirty thousand, and there are eight million people, maybe more, plus millions of visitors. And all the cops aren't on the street all the time; two, three thousand at one time at most? You know how many people each cop's got to cope with. Thousands. One cop. One guy that bleeds like you and me. A guy that gets scared, too. And he gets paid a lousy nine thousand. Who the hell do you expect to take that kind of job, atom scientists, Nobel Prize winners? You get just ordinary, everyday guys, kids. And they do a goddamn good job keeping your ass and my ass safe while we're sleeping."

"Climb off the soapbox, Sam—"

"No, let me finish, because I want to be objective about this trial. I've watched you getting more and more hot under the collar with every piece of evidence. Now you've got what you wanted. Okay. But don't go off half-cocked."

Sandro watched Sam, waiting for him to continue.

"When you give an inadequate force inadequate pay to do an impossible job, there's something wrong with it. You pay for what you get, and you get what you pay for in this life, Sandro. The people want to pay nothing, and get everything. So the cops do the job the best they can, and then the people complain they don't like the methods."

"You're the one who knows what it's like. You're the one who told me the stories. Do you think that's right?"

"You think you're kidding. That's not such a bad idea. The moon. That's good, Sandro. All the criminals'd be in one place, the court like it was a turnstile? All these professional bleeding-hearts, they want to love everybody. They haven't been in the street, they don't know they're dealing with animals who want to be loved only long enough to get your purse or your wallet. When there's a knife at your throat, it's too late to know you were wrong."

"That's very nice, in the abstract, Sam. Let's take specifics, take Alvarado. He had three convictions. You want to lock him away for being picked up by mistake, grind him into a wall because he's a junky? That piece of human debris is reading, trying to dope out the law in his cell, so he can understand his own case. Maybe it's too late for him to make it on the outside, but Christ, he's only a couple of generations behind our people, *yours* and mine. Would you want to be treated like that? I've still got people over on Mott Street. I had an uncle with balls and brains enough to be President of the United States if he had had the chances I have. What do you want to do, give the cops a free hand to break people's heads because they come from some shitty neighborhood?"

PART 35

"Tell that to the goddamn judges, the sociologists, the liberals. Tell that to Lauria's mother." They stared at each other. "When a guy does something, let him pay for it, let him stand up and pay for it like a goddamn man."

"Lock a guy away as if he were an animal, throw away the key? What good is that doing him? What good is that doing society?"

"No good. Our system of penology is so out of date we ought to be ashamed of ourselves. You don't want to hurt the dear boys? Well, with all the money this country is spending getting to the moon, we could spend some money to let the scientists devise some new system, some escape-proof place where criminals can be alone, in their own society, to farm, to kill, to do whatever they want. What's more humane than that. No bars, no incarceration. Just a life among their own kind."

"When do they get back?"

"There could be a system of evaluation. They could return when they're not hostile, bellicose."

"With all your talents, Sam, I never suspected you were a crackpot visionary. I'd like to see how your evaluators could go in to find out who isn't hostile or bellicose anymore. Maybe we could send all the criminals to the moon. No one could escape that."

"Listen, you think it's right that cops keep picking up the same crumbs, time after time, because the judges let them go through nice people in another. Then the cops could devote more kid-glove time to defendants."

"Let's get back to this case. Are you telling me I should forget all about this evidence that the cops beat Alvarado?"

"I guess I didn't make myself clear. Knock them on their ass with it. That's okay. That's the way it should be. Just remember, they're doing a job, same as we are. They don't really give a personal damn about the defendants. They didn't invent the system. They're stuck with it, just as we are. And part of that system is, don't expect cops to be geniuses or saints. Part of the system is that the judges are too merciful; the people too cheap; the politicians too political; the criminals too criminal. Blame everybody for just being human, imperfect. It's not just cops. They're the frontline troops, they're the first to get hit with shit. But we're all responsible for the system. If it stinks, it's not the cops' fault. That's a popular cop-out, if you don't mind a pun. You understand? When we reach the millennium, it'll be better." Sam paused. "Now, I think we can really kick the shit out of them with this Bellevue stuff."

"I'm glad we could get together on something."

Sam smiled. So did Sandro.

CHAPTER XVII

"I TOL' YOU I WAS IN BELLEVUE, Mr. Luca, I tol' you." Alvarado was triumphant.

"I believe you, Luis. I saw the record with my own eyes."

"And you saw the barber and the colored girl with the peaches pits, and they remembered me? She remembered me changing the hundred dollar?"

"Yes. I didn't even have to ask the girl about you. She told me. She knew all about it. I was glad of that. She made your story more true. You know what I mean?"

"Yes." He nodded and smiled.

Alvarado and Sandro watched each other's eyes. An understanding and confidence passed between them. For Sandro the understanding was belief in the man he defended; for Alvarado, it was confidence in the man defending him.

"I spoken to him, Hernandez," Alvarado said. "They got him on a different floor from me. In church the other night, I talk a little bit to him. Wait a minute, though. Before I tell you that, you know the barber shop I was to? Before I went to that barber shop, you know, I went to a restaurant. It was after I change the hundred-dollar bill."

"Now wait a minute yourself, Luis. Every time I come here you tell me more places you were at that day. It's like you sit up nights, making this stuff up."

"But what I telling you, it's truth, Mr. Luca. You know that. You checking it out yourself."

"But if all these things happened the day the cop was killed, and it's so important to you, what the hell is taking you so long to tell it to me all at one time."

"How can I tell you that? I sit in that cell there, and then I remember somesing. I cannot say to my head, remember more things for Mr. Luca. When it remembers things, I tell you right away. I only been to the fifth grades, Mr. Luca."

"I can't argue with that, Luis. When you remember, you tell me. But think hard, try and bring it all back to mind."

"I tryin', Mr. Luca, believe me that thing. I tryin'. I been in the death house, cookin', Mr. Luca. It ain't nice there. I don't want to go back there to be cooked."

"You were in the death house?"

"Once in a while, you know, they have a Spanish guy there, an' they ast him what he want for the last meal, you know. So they have to get a guy which can cook Spanish food for the guy. I cooked for two, three guys up there before when I was doin' time for drugs. They don't eat nothin' though, you know? They always talk about a guy's last meal goin' to the chair. These guys can't eat nothin', Mr. Luca. You neither when they gonna fry you in a few minutes."

"What do you cook for them then?"

"The guy gonna be executed asts the others guys in the death house what they like. You know, the food is chit in prisons. Excuse my language. This way the guy orders all kinds of things they don't serve for the other guys. It's like a big treat to the other guys, you know. He can't eat anyway, but might as well let them have some good food."

"Just try to remember whatever you can, Luis," Sandro said, changing the subject. "Now what about this restaurant you were at?"

"I remembered that later, since I speak with you. I ate somesing in the restaurant after I change the hundred dollar. When I have my money in my pocket I went and eat somesing. Eugene came with me.

PART 35

I ask, 'Eugene, you want somesing,' and he didn't, and I went inside by myself, into the restaurant. After, then I went to the barber's. It's a long shots, but maybe the person in the restaurant will remember and can say somesing for me."

"Where is this restaurant?" Sandro took out his pen.

"On the street with the barber's, Roebling Street, down from the barber shop. It's a Spanish restaurant you know, it's got Spanish food there. I don't know the name."

"Do you remember who served you."

"No. Only a man."

Sandro added this information to the long and ever-growing list of things to investigate before the trial. There was even Hernandez's alibi to be substantiated.

"What about Hernandez? You said you were talking to Hernandez in church. What did he say?"

"He told me a couple of things. One was crazy, you know? He tell me about his wife."

"What about her?"

"I think the cops, you got to excuse my saying these words to you, Mr. Luca, but the cops was doin' wrong things to her, you know?"

"What things?"

"Remember, I telling you I seen her? In the station house?"

"Yes."

"Well, Hernandez tol' me the cops takes her to her apartments, and they was two cars. She was in one with two cops, and the other fulled with cops followed down the block. When they get her in that apartments, these guys were still crazy angry, and they ripped her clothes right off her. She's standing, her beautiful ass and tits in the wind. Forgive my words, but man, she's some womans!"

Alvarado shook his head admiringly.

"Anyways, the cops lifting her and put her on the kitchen table."

"What happened?"

"They got her down, no clothes, one guy on one side, another on the other, holding her down, touching her, you know. Two of these rats are holding her legs. Oh, man . . ."

"Okay, okay. And what did they do?"

"No, Mr. Luca. Just when this guy is going to do her, another cop knocks on the door and stops them. He's yelling and angry and cursing, and they all getting out."

"I don't believe it, Luis," Sandro said flatly. "Hernandez is telling you a lot of crap. Did he say his wife told him this?"

"I don't know, Mr. Luca. He tell me he know this thing from some guy who come in from the street. I only telling you what he tol' me."

"It's idiotic. Especially that part about another cop breaking in to stop it. Somebody's putting Hernandez on, and he's even more stupid to be repeating the story."

"I don't know. I try to think of this thing myself, but I don't know. I know if someone should teach that Hernandez a lesson by doin' this thing to his wife, it should be me. Oh, man . . ."

"Luis, I'm not interested in your going loco over a woman. Do that upstairs. I don't believe that story about the cops. Besides, whether it's true or not doesn't help you on this murder charge. Did he tell you anything else? Anything we can use?"

"Not about that. But he said he was in some pawnshops that day, you know. He had somesing to pawn, and he went to a pawnshops before he went home to his house. He pawned a radio."

"Did you find out where the pawnshop was?"

"On Bowery Street near Grand Street. It's on the corner there, you know."

"Which corner, do you know?" Sandro slid a piece of paper toward Alvarado. "Draw a picture and show me."

"Here, on the corner of Bowery." Alvarado sketched a corner. "It's a couple of doors from the corner on Bowery. He doesn't remember no name, but it's on the side toward Essex Street."

"That's the east side of the street," Sandro suggested.

"Yes, the east side. And he use the name Antonio Cruz."

"He used the name Antonio Cruz when he pawned the radio?" asked Sandro.

"Yes, and he make a mistake when he spell it, so he have to spell it again. He used a little 'c,' you know, not a capital, when he spell Cruz, and the guy make him to write again cause you have to use a big 'C cause the first letter is a big one."

PART 35

"Did Hernandez say anything else? Did he say whether or not he was going to testify against you or what he was going to do?"

"He say we fight this thing together cause he got me into this thing. He says it was that they were beatings him and everything and that he would make sure to help me because it was him that got me here. Then you know he was telling me that they were beatings him for a long time and he had to tell somesing or they don't stop beatings him, and I was the only one he could think of. I said okay and I listen. He got no guts, that bastard."

"Did he say anything about testifying?" Sandro asked. "Did the district attorney offer him a plea?"

"He says only he's going to fight it, he's not going to cop out because he was innocent, and he wouldn't do this thing. He says also somesing about a job he pulled that day, and he done a lot of things but he didn't do this murder."

"He pulled what job? On the day of the murder?" Sandro grabbed Alvarado by the shoulder.

"I don't know. We couldn't talk too good in the church, cause they don't want us to talkin' together. Maybe he did pull a job that day."

"Find out. That's very important. I don't care if he did or didn't, but I want to try and build up his alibi, too. Talk to him again. Ask him about it."

"Okay, Mr. Luca, I try."

"I'll go to this pawnshop where he said he was, and I'll talk to his wife. So that, even if he tries to be a witness against us, we'll have his alibi to jam down his throat."

"That's good. You a smart guy, Mr. Luca. That's a real smart idea." Alvarado smiled, very pleased.

"Is there anything else now that you remember that may be helpful to us?" Sandro pressed.

"Nothing. But I'm thinking every day. I have nothing else to do. Also, I still looking up the law. See this." He slid some pages out from under his shirt and across the table.

"What are these?" Sandro asked.

"I'm writing these things so I can learn the law. See, I'm reading this section about witnesses and about an accomplice being a witness. Hernandez is an accomplice, right?"

"Yes. If he testified, his testimony could only be accepted as a co-conspirator or accomplice. The testimony can't be used unless corroborated with other independent evidence."

"That's what I reading here," said Alvarado. "Unless they have some extra evidence, he be no good anyway to the police. They got anything else?"

"As far as I know and have been able to find out, they don't have anything," Sandro replied. "But since they don't have to give us any information until we walk into court, we'll have to wait to find out when we get there. They might have information, fingerprints. They might have a lot of witnesses."

"Don't worry about fingerprints. My prints can't be there. I didn't do it, Mr. Luca," Alvarado insisted.

"I believe that, Luis. I'm on your side." Sandro smiled and rose. "And I'm glad you're on my side. At least with you and all the law you're learning I won't get caught short."

Alvarado smiled, pleased. "I'll keep my eyes open, Mr. Luca. If I hear anything, I'll have the operator get a message to you." He rose and walked with Sandro toward the doors at the end of the room. Sandro turned left to the door that led to the outside; Alvarado right, to the one that led to the cellblock.

CHAPTER XVIII

MIKE RIVERA KNOCKED ON MRS. HERNANDEZ'S DOOR. Sandro, standing beside him, had decided to interview Mrs. Hernandez without approval from Siakos, who seemed to be waiting for the eve of trial to prepare his case.

Feet shuffled within the apartment. "Who?" A boy's voice.

Mike explained through the door in Spanish that it was a lawyer, a friend of Hernandez. There was silence inside.

"Who?"

Mike explained again. The door opened slightly, a boy's eye appearing. Mike conversed with him in Spanish.

"This is Hernandez's son. He says his mother's not back from work yet. She goes to the prison Tuesday and Thursday after work, and she's not home yet."

"When is she going to be here?" Sandro asked Mike.

"He says she'll be here about eight thirty. In about a half hour. What do you want me to tell him?"

"Tell him we'll be back." Sandro turned and started down the stairs.

Mike spoke to the boy again, then started after Sandro.

"Let's go downstairs and measure the distance from that Italian woman's building to the one where Lauria was shot," Sandro suggested.

"For Christ's sake," exclaimed Mike, "not only is it dark out there, it's cold. And besides, someone'll send out the midnight mail, and we'll get hit in the head with flying garbage."

"I never heard anyone make up three excuses so fast. Come on, we'll dodge the flying garbage and just get a quick idea of the distance the Italian woman would have had to see across the yard."

Mrs. Hernandez was a tall, striking woman, with deep olive skin and long, black hair pulled tight. She had sparkling eyes and a full, taut figure. She was, as Alvarado said, some woman, even more striking, Sandro thought, in contrast to the wreck of a building she lived in. Her apartment was clean and neat.

Sandro and Mike sat at a porcelain-topped kitchen table as Mrs. Hernandez took down some dishes for her evening meal. She spoke almost no English, so they conversed with Mike translating, as she fried some food on the stove. She offered Mike and Sandro a cup of coffee.

"Mike, be delicate on this," Sandro cautioned. "Ask her if she was bothered by anyone the night of her husband's arrest. Tell her we have reason to think that perhaps she was."

Mike asked her in Spanish. Her eyes studied Mike as he spoke. She shook her head slowly as he spoke.

"She says no. The police brought her home, but there was no difficulty. What kind of difficulty do I mean?"

"Tell her we had heard that some of the policemen might have been, I don't know, fresh is a good enough word."

"What the hell are we talking about?"

"Alvarado told me that Hernandez said that the cops tried to rape her when they brought her home."

"They what?"

"That was my reaction, too. But ask her anyway." Mike asked.

"She says that they brought her home to search the apartment and then took her back to the station house, but that there was no trouble."

Mrs. Hernandez watched Sandro as he received the news. She said something else in Spanish.

PART 35

"She says that the detective was careful that he didn't wake up the boy."

"Have the cops been around or bothering her since?"

Mrs. Hernandez was sitting stiffly as they spoke.

"She says they've left her alone, but once or twice she saw Detective Mullaly around the neighborhood."

"Okay. Ask her if she saw her husband tonight."

Mrs. Hernandez watched as Sandro spoke. Her eyes turned to Mike. Mike explained in Spanish.

"She says she did."

"Has she spoken to him about where he was the day that all happened?"

"She said she did. He explained everything to her. He wrote it down for her in a letter that she is supposed to give to Siakos."

"Did she give it to Siakos yet?"

"No. She hasn't seen him. She says she thinks he's not working too hard on the case, because she hasn't seen him or spoken to him in a couple of months. She has the letter here."

"I want to look at it." Sandro watched Mike speak to Mrs. Hernandez. His eyes were distracted by a roach crawling slowly up the wall directly behind Mike.

In another room, next to the kitchen, the son was watching television. Beyond that was a bedroom overlooking the rear of the building.

Mrs. Hernandez rose and walked through the living room into the bedroom. Sandro could see her opening a dresser drawer and rummaging through it. On the dresser, a candle in a votive glass flicked its red glow at a picture of the Sacred Heart. She returned to the kitchen carrying a piece of paper, which she handed to Mike. Mike handed it to Sandro.

"Why are you giving this to me? I can't read Spanish." Sandro handed it back to Mike.

Mike studied it. "There are censor marks on it. At the top, it says page one. And it starts: '*Esta es mi historia del dia—*'"

"In English, if you don't mind."

"'This is my story of the third day of July, 1967. I was in the house in the morning with my wife around eight thirty. And I drove her up to the factory where she works. After I left her, I went to do a robbery in El Barrio—'"

"Where was that?" Sandro asked quickly.

"'I went to do a robbery in El Barrio.'"

"Does it say where in El Barrio?"

"No. That's all it says."

"Go ahead."

"'And after I finished the robbery, I went back to the factory to see her, my wife, and have lunch in the diner. That was from about twelve fifteen to one. Then she gave me a dollar for gasoline, and then I went and got gasoline in the car, and I went on the highway down to Seventy-third Street. I drove to Second Avenue. I drove down Second Avenue to Houston Street, where I turned to Allen Street. On Delancey near Allen Street, I went into a pawnshop.' He says *casa empeño*, that's a pawnshop."

"Go ahead."

"'I went to this pawnshop,'" Mike continued, "'and I pawned two suits for fifteen dollars. Then I went to another pawnshop on Delancey closer to Essex Street. I couldn't pawn a radio there because they knew me by my name Hernandez, and I was pawning this radio as Antonio Cruz. I got in the car and went to another pawnshop at Grand Street and Bowery.'"

"That must be the one he told Alvarado about."

"I guess so. He says here he pawned a radio there for twelve dollars under the name of Antonio Cruz."

"Right. Go ahead."

"'I finished in the *casa empeño*, the pawnshop, around two fifteen, more or less. Then I went to Essex Street and I bought...' I can't read some of this stuff," said Mike. "This guy writes like an infant. 'I bought some two shots of...' looks like 'heroin,' I guess 'for nine fifty, and then I went to my house on Stanton Street. When I entered the block, there were many, many cars of the police in the middle of the street and hospital cars too, and I couldn't pass or back up. I needed a shot of stuff very much, very much, so I left the car double-parked in the street.'"

"He says the ambulances and cops were already in the street when he got there?"

PART 35

"That's what it says," replied Mike.

"Go ahead."

"'I ran up to my apartment. I passed some guy on the way up, and I asked him what was all the commotion. He said that somebody robbed an apartment and that the cop shot the robber. I went up to my apartment and injected myself. Then I made a sandwich, and I ate the sandwich and had some peach juice. The police came to my door soon. I answered the door. They asked me if my car was downstairs, and I said it was, and then they took me out of the house. They wanted me to go downstairs. I told them I had not been out all day, that someone else parked the car. I had the suitcase and stuff from the El Barrio job in the trunk, and I didn't want trouble. When I find they're interested in a cop-killing, I told them that I had been at a pawnshop. They called the pawnshop and the man told them that I had just been there, and then they asked me about the car what was double-parked in the middle of the street. Then they took me to the police house. They hit me and kicked me, and hurt me very much. I did not do it, but, so they would not kill me, I said I did. I didn't kill nobody. Luis didn't either.'"

"Anything else?" asked Sandro.

"That's it," replied Mike.

"Ask her if we can take it to photostat. We'll give it back by return mail," Sandro suggested. He took the letter from Mike's hand and looked at the signature. This statement, in Hernandez's own hand, would destroy Hernandez if he ever tried to testify against Alvarado.

"She said it's okay. Just bring it back soon."

Sandro smiled at her as he folded the letter and put it in his pocket. She smiled back, widely and brightly.

"Why do you think she told us the cops didn't bother her?" Mike asked as they descended.

"Maybe because it didn't happen. It sounded incredible to me anyway."

"Then why would Hernandez have told such a story?"

"How should I know? Prisons are fantasy mills. Guys in jails make things up, pass them on. The next guy embroiders on the story. I don't know."

"I don't believe it. I mean about somebody making it up. If the riverbed makes noise, there's water running in it. That's a Spanish proverb."

"Have it your own way, Mike. Why believe Hernandez—Alvarado thinks he's some kind of meathead—and not his wife? Besides, what the hell difference does it make to the case even if the cops did give her a tough time?"

"To the case, it doesn't make any difference. Hernandez could've killed the cop, and they still could have given it to her."

"Exactly, so why not drop it now? Anyway, keep your own fantasies straight. Alvarado said the gang rape didn't come off. Another cop is supposed to have come in and broken it up."

Mike shrugged. They reached the street and got into the car.

CHAPTER XIX

THE SHORT, THICKSET PUERTO RICAN standing behind the restaurant counter eyed Sandro and Mike. He said nothing as he contemplated their inquiry. He was clearly uncomfortable at the very thought of a police-killing. He bent, picked up a wet rag, and began to trace wet circles on the counter.

"What day you say this happened?" he asked.

"July third, a Monday," Sandro replied.

"I don't think I was workin' here then," he said with relief.

"I thought you owned this place," Sandro remarked, wanting to cut away any pretense.

"My brother-in-law, he own this place, but he's down in Puerto Rico now. I'm here just to take care of it. But in July . . ." He searched the front window, which was steamed by the cold winds outside and the warm cooking inside. He shook his head. "Nope, I was in Miami then. You know, I don't know too much about the restaurants. I work in electronics, and I was working in Miami in electronics company. I was the foreman. I had forty men working for me," he announced proudly, looking directly at Sandro, the *abogado*. "I'm just taking care while my brother-in-law's away. He was here in July."

"This man accused of the crime was here that day," said Sandro. "And it is very important that we see whoever served him or saw him. He's in a tough position, especially because he's Puerto Rican. You know how the people in the court think about Puerto Ricans. We have to find the people who were here that day, because if anybody is going to help a Puerto Rican it's another Puerto Rican. Do you understand?"

He nodded knowingly. "Yes, I understand." That appeal seemed to hit home. "I think my brother-in-law said something about this thing that you are talking about. I don't remember, but he said something. But he's in Puerto Rico now."

"Well, do you know if he said he saw this man? Did your brother-in-law say he served him?" Sandro pressed.

"I don't remember what he said. I know he said something, but I don't remember."

"Can I get in touch with him? Do you have his address in Puerto Rico?"

"I don't have his address, but my wife has it. She's home. I can call her. Maybe then you can write him a letter."

"When is he going to be back?" Sandro asked.

"Maybe three or four months."

"Will you call and find out his address?"

"Okay. I'll see what I can do." The man stuck his stubby hands into the pockets of his pants, which encircled his waist just beneath a plump belly. He took out a dime and stepped around the counter and into the public phone booth. "Hey Pablo, Pablo," he called over his shoulder before dropping the dime into the telephone. A short, red-headed Puerto Rican with fair skin and a red moustache came out from the kitchen. "Take care of the counter for a while, will you, Pablo? I want to make a phone call." The dime chimed, and he began dialing. He listened silently. After many seconds he turned, the earpiece still at his ear, and shrugged. "Maybe nobody's home." He listened longer, then hung up. "Nobody's home."

"Two cups of coffee," Mike said to Pablo. Pablo turned the spigot on the coffee urn and filled two cups. The steam table, next to the coffee urn, was heaped high with all sorts of exotic yellow and brown

PART 35

edibles: saffron-colored rice, pork parts, chicken legs, meats floating in richly steaming gravies.

"How about Pablo?" Mike suggested. "Should I see if he was here in July?"

Sandro nodded as he sipped his coffee.

Mike spoke to Pablo in Spanish. Pablo watched Mike's mouth utter words. He nodded, and Mike continued. Mike turned to Sandro.

"Give me the newspapers and let me show them to him."

Sandro handed Mike the clippings. Pablo studied the clippings, then looked up at Mike, speaking in Spanish. Mike listened carefully.

"He said he can't read the newspapers because they're in English," Mike translated. "But he recognizes the pictures of Alvarado. He said he remembers Alvarado being here and remembers reading the story about the policemen and Alvarado in the Spanish newspaper."

"Does he remember Alvarado being here on the day of the killing?"

Mike spoke. Pablo responded. "He says he remembers because he read about it, and he saw Alvarado's picture, and he told the boss that he had served the guy that day. Alvarado came in here with another guy, a real dark Puerto Rican, and he served Alvarado something to eat. The other guy didn't want to eat. He went outside and waited."

"Is he sure it was July third, the day of the killing?"

Mike asked and Pablo replied in Spanish. "It was the same day the policeman was killed," Mike translated. "He doesn't remember the date, but knows that it was the same day that the policeman was killed because he remembers seeing Alvarado's picture in the paper the next day."

"Was Alvarado a friend of his?" Sandro asked.

"He says he didn't know him, although he saw him once before in the restaurant," Mike replied.

"Mike, does he know what time it was that he served Alvarado?"

"He doesn't remember what time it was, but he remembers definitely that it was that day."

"Ask him to try hard to remember. It's important. Was it in the morning, when there wasn't too much of a crowd here, or was it in the rush hour, when a crowd was here? Or was it after the rush hour? See if you can tie him down that way," Sandro suggested.

Mike and Pablo spoke back and forth.

"He says it wasn't crowded when he served him. It was not in the morning, but around after the lunch rush. He doesn't know exactly what time it was."

"Don't put words in his mouth, see if he can tell you about what time. Approximately."

"He says it must've been a little before two, something like that, after the lunch rush, because it wasn't so crowded."

"Ask more questions to make sure he knows what he's talking about. Make sure this is the right man, this is the right face in the papers," Sandro insisted.

Mike spoke with Pablo for several minutes, then turned to Sandro. "He says this is definitely the man. He remembers him. He knows it was the same day that the cop was killed. But he can't say exactly what time Alvarado was here. He knows it was after the regular lunch, a little before two."

"Take a statement from him," said Sandro. "Don't tell him anything about court or anything like that. You'll scare him. Just tell him that I want to keep a record, and we have to have it written down."

Mike spoke to Pablo and, while speaking, took out his yellow pad and put it on the counter. He asked Pablo questions and began writing. Mike wrote the entire story as Pablo repeated it. Pablo watched Mike write each word. Mike finished and handed the page to Sandro.

"Will you stop handing me things written in Spanish!" Sandro handed it to Pablo.

He read it through, then read it again, with painful slowness. His eyes moved across the lines, recoursing their path several times each line to make sure he understood every word. Then he signed it.

"Ask him if the police have come around here to talk to him or if he has spoken to anybody about this," Sandro said.

"He says the police haven't been here, and he hasn't spoken to anybody about it," Mike replied. "He forgot about it until just now, when we brought the newspapers in."

"Tell him not to talk to anybody about it, and if anybody questions him, he should contact us right away." Sandro handed his card to Pablo, then shook hands with him. "*Muchos gracias.*" Sandro also

PART 35

shook hands with the owner's brother-in-law, who was now standing at the far end of the counter. Mike shook hands with both men, and followed Sandro out of the restaurant.

"Let's go see the barber," Sandro suggested. "We can make sure he hasn't changed his mind or someone hasn't changed it for him."

Francisco Moreno was cutting a customer's hair. He saw Sandro and Mike, smiled, and walked over to them.

"Has anybody been here to talk to you about the case?" Sandro asked.

"No. I talk to not anyone."

"Make sure he understands what I asked him."

Mike explained to the barber. Moreno nodded his head.

"I no talk to anyone." He looked directly at Sandro to show that he had some understanding of English. "Hey!" he exclaimed, snapping his fingers. He turned to Mike and spoke rapidly in Spanish.

Mike translated. "He says that he's seen that guy Eugene who was with Alvarado the day he had a haircut. As a matter of fact, he saw him walk past here a little while ago. He didn't know we were coming, or he would have stopped him."

"Does he know where he went?" asked Sandro.

"He says he doesn't know."

The barber walked outside and stood in front of the shop, looking up and down the block. He walked back in, shaking his head, speaking Spanish.

"He hangs out on the corner here," Mike continued to translate. "Maybe he's walking around the block or something."

"Let's get the car, Mike. Ask Francisco if he'll come with us while we drive around."

Mike spoke to Moreno. He nodded and walked over to his customer and spoke in Spanish for a minute. The man in the chair was content to read the girlie magazines for a few minutes. Moreno, Sandro, and Mike got into the car and drove around the block. The barber sat staring at the faces they passed.

"Hey, hey," Moreno exclaimed, pointing to a Negro standing on a stoop. "That's the guy."

Mike pulled the car to the sidewalk.

137

"Let Francisco get out alone and talk to him," Mike suggested. "We'll stay here."

Moreno left the car and walked over to the Negro, who looked almost the twin of Alvarado.

"Maybe this guy pulled the job," Mike joked.

"Maybe so." Sandro studied Eugene. "You know, we may be able to use his picture or bring him into court or something to confuse the witnesses who are supposed to identify Alvarado."

"Hey, that's a great idea. How about getting a few, maybe five other guys, all real dark, with moustaches, and put them side by side in the back of the courtroom, and let this Italian woman see if she can identify them. If they all look like this guy, she'd never be able to pick Alvarado out."

"That sounds good," said Sandro.

Moreno returned to the car and spoke to Mike.

"He says he'll meet us in the barber shop in a minute. He's got a little business to finish." Moreno got in, and they drove back. The barber returned to his customer. Presently, Eugene walked in. He looked around, his eyes resting on Sandro. Moreno nodded.

"You da lawyer? You da lawyer for Luis, man?" he spoke the junky's singsong, hip talk.

"That's right. I understand you know a little bit about what happened."

"That depends, you know? I don't know nothin' about it really, man. All I know, I was here that day and Luis was with me."

"Tell me about it," Sandro suggested.

"Well I went over to his pad to see Luis about maybe one o'clock or something, y'know, and we sittin' aroun' his pad, you know, and then he got dress and we come down and walked aroun', you know." His head was nodding easily, his eyes were fluttering closed occasionally.

"I'd like Mike to write all this down while you tell us. Okay?"

"That's okay, man, that's okay. I want to help Luis, cause I know that cat was with me and couldn't a killed no cop."

Mike started writing:

My name is Eugene Mercader, age 29. I live at 173 South Third Street, Apartment 2D. I am living here since 1959. I have no

PART 35

phone. I am not employed now. This is my statement. On July 3rd 1967, at about 1 P.M. I went to Luis Alvarado's house at 64 South Ninth Street. This is a rooming house, and he lives on the second floor. I woke Luis up and waited for him to wash up and get dressed. Then we came downstairs together. We went to the five and ten store on Broadway off the corner of Roebling Street, where Luis changed a hundred-dollar bill. That was between 1 and 2 in the afternoon. We stopped and talked with a man for a moment, then we went to Velez Restaurant on Roebling Street between Broadway and South Ninth Street. Luis had a steak, and I waited for him because I had already eaten. When we left the restaurant it was about 2 or 2:15 P.M. Then we went to the Imperial Barber Shop on Roebling Street on the same block as the restaurant. Luis got a haircut, and I waited for him in the block on the sidewalk. It was close to 3 P.M. when he was finished. We left together, and we split up around 3:30. Then I went home. I did not see him any more.

(Signed) Eugene Mercader
November 20, 1967

"Now I'd like you to sign that so I can have it for my files," said Sandro. Eugene read the statement and signed it.

"If there's anything else I need, can I get in touch with you at this address?" Sandro asked.

"Yeah. That's my old lady's place."

"Your mother or your wife?" asked Mike.

"My mother. I was away for a while. I was inside on a bit, but I'm out now. You can get in touch with me anytime."

"You've got a record?" Sandro inquired.

"Yeah, I got a little sheet, man," Eugene said, his head nodding. Sandro looked at Mike.

"Anything besides drugs?" asked Mike.

"Nothing much, man. Ya know, I got a petty larceny and an assault, third degree. But mostly, man, it's for drugs, you know?"

"Yeah," Mike said, as Sandro motioned to him slightly. "Excuse me a minute." He and Sandro moved away from the others.

"With friends like this," Mike muttered, "your guy doesn't need any enemies."

"We can't use him as a witness. Wouldn't Ellis just love to get him on the stand and tear him apart, make us look lousy. It's just too risky."

"Yeah, right. What about other colored guys? You know, all lined up in the back of the court?"

Sandro shook his head. "Too hard to control, now that I think about it. We'd have to control clothes, color, size, too many things."

"How about photographs?"

"Maybe we could still do that. Let's hold him on the side, but tell him we may need him again." Sandro suggested. He handed his card to Eugene. "If anything comes up, anybody questions you, get in touch."

"I'll do anything you say, man, I mean, mister. You just get in touch with me. If I know anything, I'll tell you."

"Fine. Mike, tell Francisco if he sees the fellow from the playground who was in here July third when Alvarado was here he should get in touch with us right away."

Mike told him, said good-bye to both men, and walked out of the shop with Sandro.

"Everything falls into place so beautifully," said Sandro. "I can't believe it, but here it is. What a rotten deal for Alvarado, though, if we're right."

They reached the car and got in.

"Where to?" asked Mike.

"Well, we've seen the fellow in the restaurant. We have the barber. We have Eugene for whatever he's worth. We have the girl and the manager from the five-and-ten. Let's start on Hernandez's alibi. We'll see if we can find somebody at the pawnshop on the Bowery near Grand Street."

"Okay." Mike started the car and turned across the Williamsburg Bridge. Tugs were gliding toward the sea, pulling garbage scows. They drove through areas where new project buildings loomed up from the midst of the old tenements, where people had hung out of the windows and where ripped paper shades had let the sun in upon the

PART 35

squalor, where kids had run up and down the stoop, and broken beer bottles had been strewn all over the street. Soon the people would hang out of the new windows, and the kids would be running over broken glass into the new buildings, because the people weren't being changed; their income was the same, and so too were their ignorance, hunger, and need.

"If we go right across Delancey to the Bowery, we should be a block from this pawnshop," said Sandro.

"Right." Mike drove across Delancey Street to the Bowery and swung left. "There's no pawnshop on the corner," said Mike as they neared Grand Street.

"There," Sandro announced. "A couple of doors in. Sid Goodman's."

Mike parked. They got out of the car, and walked toward the pawnshop. Behind the front window, trays of imitation gold and silver watches and rings abounded, as well as binoculars and knives, radios and cameras, bugles, banjos, guitars, tools, suits, shoes. Mike and Sandro entered. All around the interior were steel gates atop counters and showcases. Behind the cages were all sorts of packages and pawned items. Sandro stepped to one of the counters and waited while a clerk filled out some papers and handed a customer fourteen dollars for a suit. The man pledging the suit made a dissatisfied face as he gathered the money. He counted it, raised a resigned eyebrow, and pocketed the money. Sandro moved up to the window to talk to the clerk.

"My name is Luca," said Sandro. "I'm an attorney." Sandro handed him a card. The clerk, a Puerto Rican with a moustache and glasses, stopped working and listened. "I'm the lawyer for a fellow accused of a crime, a murder, on Stanton Street." The clerk was visibly uneasy now. "Another fellow, also accused of the crime, was in here the day of the killing, pawning some goods." Sandro took the newspaper clippings out of his briefcase. "I'd like a little help if you can give it. "Were you here that day, July third, or would you have the pledge book from that day so we can check to see if this other fellow was here?" Sandro put the clippings on the counter. He pointed at Hernandez's picture. "This is the fellow. He was supposed to be here on July third pawning a radio or something. He used the name Antonio Cruz."

The clerk studied the picture. He looked up at Sandro.

"Yeah, he was here." He was quite positive. "The police already asking me about this."

"When was this?"

"Oh, they were here, I don't know, a few months ago. When it happened, this thing. They come over and show me some pawn ticket, and they want the stuff this guy here pawned." The clerk tapped Hernandez's picture. "I showed the stuff, it was a detective, I think, and they put a stop on it."

"You sure this fellow was here on July third?" Sandro repeated.

"Sure. I got his name in the book. I seen him before. His name is different there in the paper, but he came in before and put down in the book Antonio Cruz. I showed the cops. I'll show you." The clerk walked around to another counter where large ledgers were kept.

"What's the trouble, Willie?" asked a thin, nervous-looking man who came out of the front office. He was obviously Sid Goodman or Sid Goodman's successor.

"No trouble," replied Willie. "This is about that radio that some guy pawned over here and the cops came in and put a stop on it. Remember? I think you have the slip up there on the cash register."

"Oh, yes, yes. I think I remember that," Goodman answered cautiously. "What's the difficulty?"

"No difficulty," Sandro answered. "I am an attorney and represent one of the people involved in that case." Sandro handed Goodman a card. He studied it. "I understand one of these men was here pawning things," Sandro continued. "I need some information. If this fellow was here pawning something, he couldn't also be at the scene of a crime."

"Well, I don't know what time he was here or even if he was here," said Goodman curtly. "Do you know anything about this, Willie?" His tone intimated that Willie didn't either.

Willie had carried a large ledger to the counter where Goodman stood facing Sandro. He opened the book to "July 3, 1967." "Here, you see his name here," Willie pointed. "Antonio Cruz. That's the name he use. Antonio Cruz was the same guy in the papers there," he pointed to Hernandez. "Only I didn't know his real name. You have the signature card on the cash register," Willie said to Goodman.

PART 35

Goodman shrugged and walked to the cash register and searched through a pile of papers. Willie went over and took up the search. Goodman watched, somewhat nervous. Willie selected a slip of paper and brought it back to Sandro. "Here, see. See where the cops wrote on it, and they said to hold the radio and not let the goods out. That's why I remember, because the cops made us keep the goods."

"And did he sign that book there?" Sandro asked.

"Yes, here. See." Willie twisted the book around so Sandro could see it. At line number 43 on the page was written *Antonio Cruz, Radio, $12.00*.

"It's Hernandez's handwriting, all right," Mike observed. "Like a small kid's."

Sandro nodded. "Could you tell me what time Cruz was in here that day?"

"Well, I don't know 'zactly," said Willie, studying the list of names.

"Well, it's pretty far down the list," Goodman contributed, warming up. "I would say, from my experience around here, that it must've been sometime in the afternoon. I couldn't tell you exactly what time though."

"Yes. It must have been sometime in the afternoon," Willie agreed. "I can't tell you 'zactly, but I know this Antonio Cruz, whose name is here, is that guy who was in the newspaper. I seen him in the papers the next day, and I seen him here before."

"Is there any question in your mind that this fellow in the papers was in here that afternoon on July third?" Sandro pressed.

Willie studied the picture and shook his head. "He was here, okay."

"What did he pawn?"

"A radio. I have it still upstairs." Willie left and went up a stairway at the back of the shop. He returned with a package wrapped in brown paper. "This is the radio. See, it says here *Hold* on it. The cops made us hold this thing and wouldn't let us do anything with it."

"Do you know which policemen that was?" Sandro asked.

"It says here Detective Mullaly," Willie read. "And it got his phone number here. He was the one."

Willie opened the package and showed Sandro a portable radio in a brown leather case.

"I'd like to write down some of the facts for my own records, so that I'll remember all the things that happened," said Sandro, taking out a pad.

"Well, I don't know anything about it," said Goodman, backing off again. "If you want to, Willie, it's all right with me. But I don't know how you're going to tell them exactly what time this fellow was in here."

"I don't know what time, but I know he was here in the afternoon," said Willie.

"You know that for a fact?" Goodman asked Willie suspiciously.

"Yeah. See his name on the list, number forty-three out of seventy-six people all that day. And the morning is always slow. And here's the cutoff at sixty-nine. We draw a line when we go to the bank at four o'clock, and that's after sixty-nine that day. So he must've been here in the afternoon," Willie explained. "Besides, it was after my lunch for sure."

Goodman picked up the book with its various markings, looked at Willie, pursed his lips, and as if having some confusion on the point, studied the pages. He shrugged, looked at Willie again, then at Sandro, and handed the book back to Willie.

"You say you saw this fellow in the shop before?" Sandro inquired as he wrote.

"Yes. He use the name Antonio Cruz, but I have seen him before in this shop."

"And you're sure this fellow in the newspaper whose name is Hernandez is the same fellow who came in and used the name Cruz?" Sandro watched Willie's face.

"Yes. I'm sure about that." Willie was. "The police came in and spoke to me about the radio a couple of days after I saw this in the paper. When I first saw it in the papers, the day after the police was shot, I remembered this man from the shop on the same day the police was kill. I say to myself, my God, you know, I wait on this guy the same day the papers say he kills somebody. It was funny, you know? I remember when the police were here. And that makes me remember now."

"And what time was it. Can you approximate it?" asked Sandro.

"In the afternoon."

"About what time?"

Willie studied the book again. He shrugged. "I know it was after my lunch."

"What time do you eat?"

"Sometime between one and two."

"Is that every day?" Sandro asked.

"Every day!"

"So this fellow came in after two on July third?"

"Probably earlier. A little after I got back."

"You sure about that, Willie?" Sandro pressed.

"Sure."

Sandro wrote quickly.

"Is this the number on the radio?" Sandro inquired, writing all the details on his pad. Willie nodded. Now if only he could tie this radio up with Hernandez's July 3rd burglary in El Barrio, Sandro thought. "And do you have a piece of paper that you say Hernandez signed when he came in?" Sandro asked.

"You have that signature card, Mr. Goodman," Willie said.

"I do? Oh, you mean this one," said Goodman, pushing the signature card across the counter.

"Are you sure that this is the same fellow, Willie?" Goodman asked.

"Yes, that's the fellow. The same fellow Hernandez as in this picture," replied Willie, pointing to the clipping.

"How can you be sure, Willie? I mean, so many people come in here." Goodman studied Willie's face, obviously impressed by his conviction.

"Because this is the same fellow who sign and pawn a radio, and he's Hernandez. And I remember because the police made us put this signature card to the side. Remember when the detective was here?" Willie looked at Goodman.

"No. No, I don't remember too well," answered Goodman. "But if it was up on the cash register, then it must be there for a reason. I guess the police did tell us to put it there. If you remember, Willie, that's what happened."

"May I have this signature card? I don't mean to keep it. I'd just like to take it to get a photostat of it," Sandro requested.

"Well, the police told us not to misplace it, to take care of it," cautioned Goodman.

"Mr. Goodman, a man's life is at stake," Sandro said acidly. "The state wants to put somebody in the electric chair for a crime that he couldn't possibly have committed. The man was here in your store at the time he was supposed to be committing the crime. Willie saw him! And yet the police say he was on Stanton Street, about ten blocks from here at the same time. If you were accused, Mr. Goodman, would you want someone to help you if you were innocent?"

Goodman looked sheepish.

"I'm not going to destroy this signature card," said Sandro. "I'm just going to make a photostatic copy of it. You'll have it back within a half-hour from the time I take it."

"Well, I don't know. I mean, I don't want to get involved with this at all," said Goodman.

"Mr. Goodman, you won't become any more involved than you are now," Sandro assured him, letting a threat seep into his voice. "I'll have to subpoena these papers and books to court anyway when the trial begins. So what's the difference if you let me have them now? It'll be back here in half an hour. No one will be hurt, and you'll have done a service to humanity."

Goodman studied Sandro. He wasn't too concerned with humanity, but the price was right. He didn't have to do anything.

"Well, if you get it right back to me. I want you to give me a receipt for that. Give me your card and I'll write a little something on it, and you can sign it. At least I'll know who took it, you know. I won't get in trouble."

Sandro handed him a business card. Goodman scrawled words of receipt on it and handed it back. Sandro signed his name.

"I'll have this back to you within a half-hour," said Sandro, as he and Mike left the store.

"This is terrific," said Mike, excited at having found Willie. "Every piece is falling into place."

"Yes, but the police know about these things. Yet they still have a case; they're still prosecuting Alvarado. They've got to have something we're not figuring on," said Sandro.

"Yeah, well, we've got some stuff they aren't figuring on, like that guy with the guns in Soto's building, Salerno."

"I'm waiting to talk to a cop I know in the narcotics squad about him. He's been tied up lately."

"We can forget the whole case if we get the goods on this guy Salerno," Mike said.

"Meanwhile, we can't forget the Italian woman and Asunta," Sandro cautioned. "They're pretty sure to be state's witnesses. I wish we could interview them without running the risk of getting into a bind. Well, hell with that now. We've done enough today."

CHAPTER XX

IT WAS DECEMBER NOW, and the street outside the building where Lauria had been killed was not filled with kids or people dancing or noise. It was filled with people moving quickly to keep warm. The only thing that escaped the mouths of the moving people was steam. Gone was the music, the cold *cerveza*.

Robert Soto had moved from 153 Stanton Street to 161 Stanton Street. The front door to Soto's new apartment was covered by a sheet of metal. Sheet metal was used to cover the old wooden doors in these tenements so burglars could not punch a hole in the wood panel and open the lock by slipping a hand inside. The only chink in Soto's armor was made by the two small circles that were the cylinders for the door locks. Mike stood to the side of Sandro. Within, they heard shuffling.

"Who is it?" floated a voice through the metal.

"Mr. Luca, the lawyer," Sandro replied.

A clunk of metal resounded as the steel bar wedged diagonally against the inside of the door was lifted. The people in these houses know how near terror and violence are. Their entire worldly fortune may consist of a television set bought on the installment plan and second-rate furniture also sold to them on time payments by some

PART 35

sharp trader on 14th Street, which furniture shall not endure so long as the payments. But they live within cages, locked inside with dead locks, double locks that require two keys, by barred, locked gates on their windows, and sheets of metal strapped to the front door. It is the poor, those who breed the core of the criminal world, that are hounded by the criminal, much more than those in the luxury neighborhoods filled with wealth and valuables.

"Come in, come in," said Soto, succeeding in loosing all the locks on the door. He stood shoeless, in black chino pants and a wrinkled T-shirt. He was hastily donning a sweater, which was a mass of wrinkles and creases and looked as if it had been stored in a ball on the floor in a corner. Within, two of his children sat on a couch covered with worn material, watching cartoons on television. A third child, wearing only a diaper, was dragging himself across the linoleum floor. The walls were painted a washed-out pink. The paper window shade was pulled down across the otherwise barren steel-gated window. There was a lone, naked bulb in the ceiling, and the walls were bare. The other furniture in the room consisted of a small, free-form, Formica table—it couldn't be considered a cocktail table: the Sotos didn't drink cocktails—and an upholstered chair occupied by a pile of unironed clothes, blankets, sheets, shirts, diapers, sweaters.

"Sit down, sit down," said Soto, pointing to the couch. "Go inside now," he commanded the children. He snapped off the cartoons. The children started howling. One of them attempted to turn the television on again. Soto stopped him. The child hit him in the leg. Finally, the children were repulsed and turned to another room, where they began to fight among themselves.

Sandro and Mike sat. Soto sat on the radiator just beneath the window with the paper shade pulled down.

"How've you been?" asked Sandro.

"Oh, okay." He smiled a little.

"I see you've moved since the last time I saw you."

"Yeah. We're just fixing this place up, you know?"

"Yes? Have you seen any policemen or people who know about the case since I saw you last?" Sandro inquired.

"I see Mullaly all the time, you know. He comes around to see me when I get home from work, to say hello. And I talk to him about the case, you know. I try to see if he'll tell me something I don't know yet, or something. He trusts me, you know. I'm not like them other people around here who don't care." Sandro studied Soto's face. "I said I'd help him, and anything I find out I'll tell him. So he tells me everything. We sort of sit and talk about it. He can talk to me. I learn good English."

"Has he told you anything that you haven't told me?" Sandro pressed.

"No. There's that Italian woman across the rear yard. Did I tell you about the ladies in the factory? He told me that there were some ladies on the top floor of the factory doing their work and they saw this guy, the dark guy, running across the roof after the cop was shot."

Sandro felt a wince proceed directly up his back.

"Do you know who these women are?" asked Mike.

"No." He shrugged.

"Were they the women at the police station the night you went there after the murder?" Sandro asked.

"No. I never saw any of them."

Sandro turned to Mike. "I guess we'll just have to canvass every woman in the factory." Mike looked unhappy. "Okay, anyone else?" Sandro asked, returning to Soto.

"No. That's all I know so far. But if Mullaly tells me anything more, I'll let you know. I want to help if I can, cause I know what you say is so, about nobody's going to help this guy. I mean, if he didn't do it, I don't think he should go to jail for that."

"That's right. And that's what we're trying to do, help this fellow," added Mike.

"This Italian woman you spoke about. She saw this Negro on the fire escape?" Sandro asked.

"Yeah, that's right. She seen this dark guy inside the apartment, looking out the window, you know? So she watched. Soon she seen him again. He was coming down the fire escape from the roof. He goes to the window and bends down and opens the window. Then she seen him go back up to the roof. And then she seen the other guy taking some stuff out of my apartment."

PART 35

Sandro walked over to the window overlooking the rear yard. He peered through the crisscrossed folding iron gates at the apartment where the Italian woman lived. As he stood there, Sandro noticed that in addition to the swivel lock ordinarily found on windows, Soto had a screw-type safety lock attached to each one. It was like a long screw with a rubber head on the end of it. If you tightened the screw, the rubber head was pressed into the window, which could then not be lifted.

"Did you have this kind of lock and gate on the windows in the other house?" Sandro asked.

"Sure. I always put them on."

"When you went to work the day the cop was killed was everything locked?"

"I don't remember. But my wife would know, because she was home after I went to work."

"Where is she now?" Sandro asked.

"Why do you want her?"

"Don't worry. She's not going to court or anything, Robert. She won't get involved."

"Yeah, I know, but she's a woman, you know. I mean, I don't want her to get involved in this thing, you know. She only knows what other people told her, a couple of people like Asunta and the Italian lady across the way."

"I just want to talk to her," Sandro said calmingly.

"She'll be here soon. She just went to her mother's a couple of minutes before you got here. She just went for a minute. She'll be here right away."

"I'd like to talk to her a little. Just to see what she remembers. She was the last one in the apartment before the burglary, right?"

"That's right."

Sandro and Mike returned to the living room and sat on the couch until Mrs. Soto returned. Alma Soto could not have been older than twenty-two, but her face bore the marks and lines of a woman much older. She was dressed in clothing that hung about her like a sack. Soto explained that Sandro wanted to talk to her. She moved the clothing from the chair and placed it on the floor. She sat and watched Sandro.

"Alma, the day the policeman was killed, you were still in the apartment when Robert went to work, weren't you?"

"Yes. I was there until I went out about eleven thirty. I went to my mother's." She watched Sandro intently.

"When you went out, did you lock the windows?"

She nodded. "I always lock the windows before I go out."

"And the safety locks, were they screwed tight?"

"Always. Before I go out, I make sure all the locks on the windows are locked. There are a lot of robberies in the building, you know? So I make sure I lock all the windows."

"And you're sure they were locked before you went out that day?"

"Positive. When I finally got back in at night, you know, about eight o'clock the cops let us back in, the locks were open and the gates were still shut. But I know the locks were shut tight too before I went out."

"Okay," Sandro said, slightly puzzled but going on. "You went to the police station that night, didn't you, Alma?"

"Yes. I met Robert there, me and my mother."

"Robert was there before you, right?"

"Yes. I didn't want my mother to worry. So I went to her house first. Robert went ahead."

"Did your mother see or have anything to do with this?"

"No. She just came with me, you know. I was scared."

"You speak English well. Do you read English?" Sandro wanted to know if her statement would have to be taken in English or Spanish.

"Living with Robert you have to know English. I don't think in all the time I know him, he said two words to me or my mother in Spanish. He won't even let me speak Spanish to the children. English. They have to learn English."

Soto smiled. Mike studied him, as if trying to figure Soto out.

"Did you see anyone else there, at the police station? Did you see Asunta there?"

"She was leavin' the station house when I was goin' in," Mrs. Soto announced. "Her and the girl from downstairs in our old building."

"Which girl from downstairs?" Sandro asked.

"You know, that guy's wife who's collectin' guns," Soto added. "They musta had everybody from the block down there that night."

PART 35

"Have you talked to that fellow any more?" Sandro asked Soto.

"No. I've been careful, like you told me, keeping away from him."

Sandro returned to Mrs. Soto.

"Have you spoken to Asunta since then?"

"About this case?" she asked. She shook her head.

"How about the woman who lives across the yard?" Sandro asked. "Was she at the station house when you were there?"

"Yes, I was sitting next to her."

"Did you speak to her while you were there?" Sandro asked.

"Sure. You know we were all talking about it, about what happened. And I was talking to her. And me and Robert talked about her."

"At the station house?"

"No. Since then we talk about her."

"Did she tell you what she saw that day."

"She said she saw a colored guy on the fire escape. She was sitting sewing, and she looked up and saw this guy."

"Did she say it was Alvarado, the man I represent? The man who was at the station house?"

"I didn't ask her that. I don't know. Let's see. I think she was just saying that she saw this colored guy lookin' out. I don't know if she knows it was that guy or not."

"Looking out?"

"Looking out the window. Didn't she say that, Robert, or did you tell me that?"

"She said that," Soto agreed.

"And later," Mrs. Soto went on, "she saw him come down the fire escape, and she didn't think nothing of it, you know. She thought it was the person who lived in the apartment. Then she seen him try to open the window, but he couldn't get it open, so he went back to the roof."

"Did she identify Alvarado?"

"I don't know. We looked separate through the window at the police station."

"Did she tell you anything else?"

Mrs. Soto thought a moment, then shook her head.

"Do you remember seeing a car double-parked in the street that day?"

"When I came home and I couldn't get into the house because of the police, I saw a car double-parked across the street, over by One sixty, down from the factory."

"Alma, for my records, Mike will write down what you said, so I'll have it and I won't have to bother you for it. Okay?"

She shrugged. "Okay."

Mike wrote the statement. Mrs. Soto signed the pages. Mike and Sandro bid the Sotos good-bye and left their apartment.

"Let's get going. I've got something to do this afternoon, for my wife," said Mike as they walked down the stairs. "Saturday is her day."

"Let's just walk over to the factory. I want to see where these women were who saw the man running along the roof."

They walked to the front of 153 Stanton Street. Across from it was a three-story building with large doors and platforms at the street level for trucks to back into.

"You see what I see?" asked Sandro.

"The factory, you mean?"

"Yes, but look at how many floors in that factory building!"

"One, two, three. How many on this building?" Mike turned and looked up at the facade of the building where Lauria had been killed. "This one has five."

"I know." Sandro smiled.

"How the hell could they see someone running on the back of a roof two stories above them?"

"That I don't know! I don't think they could. And look at the windows on the factory. All of them are frosted, except for some where there are air-conditioners. Some windows aren't frosted but have steel screens across them. That means even if someone was standing at those windows, they couldn't put their head out far enough to see a car double-parked down near One sixty. That'd be down there," said Sandro, pointing.

"That's about a hundred feet from the factory," Mike gauged.

"About. And on the day of the murder, it was raining heavily. Therefore, most of the windows must have been closed. Now all we have to worry about is if the women could see someone running on the roof. Come on," said Sandro, crossing the street. They stopped at the factory and looked back and upward.

"Anybody who could see anything on that roof'd have to have eyeballs two stories high," said Mike.

"Or an imagination the same height. Let's go up to the roof for a minute." They crossed again, entered 153, and walked up to the roof.

"Look at that front coping," said Sandro. "Anything that went on on this roof happened behind that front wall. A person in the factory couldn't see a thing up here because this is two stories higher, and there's a seven-foot wall between. Mike, damn it, I have to hand it to you. You did it."

"Yeah, terrific, hanh?" Mike smiled widely.

"Now we've eliminated the factory as a possible haven for witnesses—and also eliminated the necessity for a canvass. We're going to need some pictures of all this, just in case those women show up in court."

"Okay." They started down. "But why would these women say they saw things that they couldn't have?"

"There are lots of people who talk a lot about things after everything is over. Maybe someone from the factory was just running off at the mouth," Sandro replied.

"Maybe Soto is giving us a snow job."

"He's not that bright," Sandro replied. "He's just a silly guy who's trying hard to be helpful."

"How come we took his wife's statement and not his?" asked Mike.

"He doesn't know anything firsthand," Sandro replied. "He was at work, right?"

"Yeah."

"So what he tells us gives us leads, but he can't give any evidence. His information is all hearsay. His wife can testify about being locked from the inside when she went out may be very valuable."

"How do you mean?"

"Remember that she said the Italian woman across the yard told her that the man on the fire escape was in the apartment first? Then, later, he couldn't open the windows when he was on the fire escape?"

"Yeah."

"Well, if she's going to testify to that, we can create a lot of doubt with Mrs. Soto's statement about the locks. If the guy had been inside first he'd know whether he had opened the locks or not. He wouldn't have to wait until he came down the fire escape to find out. It just wouldn't make any sense."

Mike's eyes narrowed as he studied Sandro. "But then how come the locks were open when Mrs. Soto came home?"

"That's easy, Sam Spade. What time did she get home?"

"She said about eight o'clock. And there were cops all over, in and out of there after the murder, right?" Mike figured out for himself.

"Exactly. The cops must have opened and closed those windows a million times for fingerprints, pictures, all kinds of things."

"Where to now?"

"Me, I'm going to my apartment, a nice warm bath, a warm drink, and who knows what else warm."

"That's a nice way for a nice Italian boy to talk. Santa Claus won't come down *your* chimney."

"Did you know that Santa Claus was Italian?" Sandro asked.

"Come on," Mike scoffed. "He was Puerto Rican, from Ponce, I knew his sister."

CHAPTER XXI

SANTA CLAUS HAD COME AND GONE, and Alvarado had been in the Tombs just half a year. Sandro drew his overcoat about him more snugly as he walked up the few steps to the Criminal Courts Building. The sky was overcast, and it looked as if the first snow of the new year would be coming soon. As Sandro walked the long entranceway to the front doors, he saw a swarthy man with dark glasses and a beard standing just within. He was dressed like someone who hung out on corners pushing junk.

"Hello, Charlie," Sandro said to him.

"Hey, Sandro. How's it going? I haven't seen you for a while."

"I've been pretty tied up with some cases. I'm glad you could get over here. Where are you assigned now?"

"Over in the Delancey area. Been there for about six months." Out of costume and role, Charlie D'Andrea was a New York City policeman. He was assigned to the narcotics squad and was one of the undercover agents who patrol the high-density drug areas, making friends of junkies, learning their buying and selling habits, ultimately arresting drug users and pushers, and all the rest of the procurers, prostitutes, and thieves on the edges of their world.

These undercover agents look like, talk like, dress like rundown junkies.

"That's exactly the section I wanted to talk to you about," Sandro said. "But first I have to adjourn a case in One-D. You going up?"

"No, I just finished. I'll meet you over in Happy's," D'Andrea suggested. Happy's is a bar behind the courthouse frequented by policemen, D.A.'s, and lawyers on recess from the court.

When Sandro entered Happy's, he saw Charlie D'Andrea sitting on a stool at the bar talking to one of the detectives on the D.A.'s squad. He walked over.

"Hi, Sandro," said the other detective.

"Hello, Frank, how are you?"

"Keeping busy, what else?"

"I'll have some cognac, Louie," Sandro said. "See what Frank and Charlie want." Louie poured drinks all around. "Cheers," said D'Andrea, raising his glass. They all raised their glasses and drank.

"What's up, Sandro?" D'Andrea now asked.

"Since you've been in Delancey, have you come across a junky by the name of Salerno from Stanton Street?" Sandro inquired.

"Salerno, Salerno. That sounds familiar. Where on Stanton does he live?"

"Stanton near Suffolk."

"Yeah, I know that guy. He's sort of a nut. Not really a nut, just a dumb kid. He's really like a kid. What do you need?"

"Whatever you can tell me about him," Sandro replied.

"Is it important?" D'Andrea asked.

"Yes."

"Wait a minute, then." D'Andrea got up and walked to the telephone booth. He closed the door. Sandro saw him dial a number.

Frank, the detective from the D.A.'s squad, was now talking to someone on his other side. At the booths around the room, many discussions of cases pending that day in court were going on simultaneously. Some detectives were explaining how they were being cross-examined by defense counsel, some defense counsel were telling other defense counsel how liberally the judge was handing out sentences this morning. Laughter exploded from the end of the bar near the front door.

PART 35

D'Andrea opened the door of the phone booth and returned to the bar. "His yellow sheet reads like a junky tour guide. Mostly all drugs." The yellow sheet is the record maintained in the police department's Bureau of Criminal Identification for each person arrested in New York City. Each new arrest or conviction or sentence goes on it, making the yellow sheet an up-to-date criminal history. It is always printed on yellow paper. "His last arrest was 1966. He was sentenced to a year at Riker's. He did nine months and was released last July fifteenth."

"What date did you say?"

"July fifteenth."

"You mean he was in jail on July third, 1967?"

"Yeah, why? What's so important?"

"Nothing much. Somebody thought he might be a witness against me in some case, but I guess he can't be. The crime took place on July third."

If Salerno was in jail on July third—and the nine months preceding Lauria's death—he couldn't have killed Lauria; he couldn't even have been part of the job. Sandro absently traced wet circles on the top of the bar. Why was Salerno acting so suspiciously? Perhaps, Sandro decided, he should go and see Salerno. If Salerno was in jail, he couldn't be a people's witness, and Sandro ran no risk of compromising himself. This story about Salerno didn't make any more sense than the story about the gang-bang.

"Let me buy you a drink," D'Andrea said, breaking into Sandro's thoughts.

"No, this is on me. Louie, the same again, on my tab," Sandro called to the bartender.

"Here's a happy New Year, Sandro," said Charlie.

"That's right. Happy New Year, Charlie." Sandro raised his glass. "Charlie, do you figure a bunch of cops would gang-rape a woman? Let's say they were all full of piss and vinegar, worked up about something like a cop-shooting, and the woman was the wife of a defendant."

"That depends," Charlie answered slowly, studying Sandro's eyes.

"Depends? On what?"

Charlie smiled. "On whether she's a good-looking broad or not." He shrugged.

"What can I expect from a wise-ass cop?"

"What do you want? I answered your question," Charlie smiled.

"One other thing, while I've got you here. Do you know a guy named Snider who was in narco a few years ago? Had some kind of trouble."

"No. I know the guy you mean. I heard about it, you know? But I never met him. He left before I got in the squad."

"What kind of trouble was it?"

"I don't know. A lot of guys were involved. A big shake-up. I think some guys were on the take. I don't know about Snider."

"I've got to run now, Charlie. Want another drink?"

"No, I got to go to court this afternoon. I don't want the jury to sniff an alcoholic cop."

"Thanks a lot, Charlie. I'll talk to you soon. Louie, here's some money, keep the change. Take care now, Charlie," Sandro said, moving out into the street. The cold felt good, but he still had lots of questions, and not too many answers.

CHAPTER XXII

"I CAN'T FIGURE THAT OUT AT ALL," Mike said with annoyance, as they drove toward Stanton Street. Sandro had just finished repeating what Charlie D'Andrea had told him.

"Sorry. I know how you liked that idea."

"Okay, so Salerno was in jail. What's all this suspicious stuff, then, if the guy was in jail?"

"Maybe he's just one of those people who go around confessing to different crimes for kicks, you know?"

"C'mon, Sandro, for Christ's sake. I'm serious."

"So am I. How else can I explain it. Unless he wasn't in jail. Maybe D'Andrea made a mistake."

Mike turned into Stanton Street and looked for a parking space.

"Unless he's in with some other people who weren't in the can," Sandro suggested.

Mike turned in the middle of maneuvering into a tight space. "That's a possibility."

Sandro knocked on the door of Apartment 2B. They could hear a radio playing inside and a baby crying.

"Yeah, who is it?" demanded a female voice from inside.

"Mr. Salerno home?" Sandro inquired.

"Who is it?" the female voice demanded again. The radio had been turned down, and the baby had stopped crying.

"Mr. Luca, a lawyer," Sandro answered.

The door opened a crack. Sandro saw an eye peer out. It was a short woman with her hair pulled tight in a ponytail. As the door opened more fully, Sandro recognized her as the young woman who had been so venomous the first night he had been in this building, the one who wanted to put Alvarado into the electric chair without a trial.

"I'm sorry," Sandro said abruptly. "I was looking for the Salerno apartment."

"You found it." She was as cold and defensive as before. Mike looked at Sandro, confused.

"Is this where Salerno, I mean, Mr. Salerno, lives?"

"That's right. What can I do for you?"

"Is he home?"

"Who is it, Carmen?" said a thin, dark-haired young man, coming to the door. He was in need of a shave and about twenty good meals.

"This is the lawyer for that guy who killed the cop on the roof," she said coldly.

Salerno looked at Sandro, then Mike. "You want something?"

"I'd like to talk to you for a minute," said Sandro.

"About what?" the woman demanded.

"Are you, do you live here, too?" Sandro asked her.

"I'm Mrs. Salerno."

"Oh? Fine. Can we come in for a minute?"

Mrs. Salerno shrugged.

"Yeah, yeah," said Salerno. He smiled. "Come on in. Let the lawyer come in, honey."

Mrs. Salerno moved to the side of the doorway to allow Sandro and Mike to enter. She closed the door and leaned against it, her arms folded across her bosom, watching the two strangers.

"Mr. Salerno, we'll make it brief. I represent, as Mrs. Salerno told you, the man accused of killing the cop on the roof here in July."

"Which one do you represent, the guy from this block or the other one?"

PART 35

"The other one, Alvarado. And I'm trying to interview all the possible witnesses. I'm trying to eliminate people, really. When I talk to someone who doesn't know anything about the case, then I can forget about them."

"Right. What can I do for you so you'll forget about me?"

"Well, I already spoke to your wife. She told me she wasn't here that day, didn't know anything about it." Salerno looked at his wife. She was busy watching Sandro. "I just wanted to check all the people in the building. Were you here that day?"

"No, I wasn't here," he said. He smiled with the inoffensive smile of a junky. He didn't want any enemies; he had enough. "I was at the hotel, if you know what I mean."

"How long were you away?" Mike asked.

"About nine months, yeah, nine months," he recollected.

Mrs. Salerno was tapping her foot lightly now as she watched.

"You couldn't know much about the crime then if you were away," said Sandro.

"Right." He smiled again briefly. "Not only couldn't. Don't want to, you know?" He nodded knowingly to Sandro. "I don't want no more trouble. I was away for nine months. Before that I was in Lexington. I don't even know my own wife. We only been married two years, and I been away almost two years."

"When were you in Lexington?" Mike asked.

"Just before I got busted the last time. I guess I didn't get so clean down there, you know?" Salerno had nothing inside him, he was washed out and washed up, and he couldn't have passed twenty-five long ago. "I can't help you, honest."

"Do you know Robert Soto, the fellow whose apartment was broken into that day?" Sandro asked.

"Nah, not really. He moved in while I was away. I think I seen him once since I been home, maybe said hello, but that's it."

"Do you know Asunta?" Mike asked.

"I know who she is. I see her around. That's about it. I got enough trouble, you know." His wife walked over to him, now carrying the baby, who looked to be less than a year old. He slipped his arm around her waist.

163

"Just one more thing," Sandro said. "Have the police come around to speak to you about this killing?"

"Yeah," Mrs. Salerno answered for both of them. "They come snoopin' around here, too." She glared at Sandro pointedly. "That Detective Mullaly is over in this neighborhood as much as you."

"I guess that's it, then. Thank you," Sandro said as they walked out into the hall. The door closed quickly behind them.

"She's as sweet as usual," Mike said, as they descended. "The winter really agrees with her."

"The hell with her. This whole thing is still up in the air, Mike. He says he was in jail. Okay. He says he doesn't know anything. Now where the hell are we? What's going on?"

"Yeah. Soto tells you this guy is asking all kinds of questions, and Salerno tells you he hardly even knows Soto. It doesn't make sense. None. Somebody is snowing us."

"You know who I trust more?" Sandro evaluated. "Soto. He's been cooperating with us right along. We don't even know this guy, except he's a junky."

CHAPTER XXIII

MIKE AND SANDRO ASCENDED THE CREAKING WOODEN STAIRCASE leading to the second floor of the rooming house where Alvarado had been living when he was arrested. The building had a drab interior, painted a flat, continuous white, its monotony of dull walls unbroken by pictures, colors, artifacts, or diversions. A bare bulb lit the top of the landing. At the rear of the hall, a door stood ajar. It was the common bathroom. Mike knocked on one door after another. Only a woman who lived in the rearmost room was at home. She peered through the space of her chained door. Mike spoke to her in Spanish. She shook her head. Sandro and Mike walked down the stairs and out into the street.

"She's only lived there four weeks," said Mike. "She knows nothing."

"Let's see if we can find that superintendent, Jorge," Sandro suggested. "He was the one who was here with Alvarado during the day, and the one who told Alvarado about the detectives waiting for him."

"Maybe he lives down here," said Mike, descending three stone steps, which led to an iron gate beneath the stoop. He rang the bell. No answer. He rang again, turning to look at Sandro.

"Who are you looking for?" asked an attractive, dark-haired young woman standing at the top of the stoop of the next building.

"Jorge."

"Jorge who?" She studied them suspiciously.

"The super. I don't know his last name. His first name is Jorge. He's the superintendent of this building."

The girl descended the stoop and stood on the sidewalk. She knew something; her face was trying hard to conceal it.

"I'm a lawyer. I represent a fellow named Alvarado. He lived here, and last July he was arrested here, charged with killing a policeman," said Sandro. "Jorge was with him that day and knows that Alvarado couldn't have done it."

"I don't know anything about that. I don't know if Jorge knows anything about that." She still studied Sandro.

"I'm not the police. I'm trying to save Alvarado from the police. He's charged with killing a policeman, and because he's Puerto Rican, the district attorney and the cops are going to give him the works. He's in a very tough position. That's why I need Jorge. If the Puerto Ricans refuse to help their own kind when they get in trouble, what kind of help can you expect from the people downtown, who think every Puerto Rican is a no-good junky."

"Jorge isn't here. I don't know where he is," she said sincerely. She was afraid of something.

"What's your name?" Sandro asked.

"I'm Jenny. Jorge is my brother."

"Well, Jenny, you can see how important it is that I talk to your brother. He was here with Alvarado when the cop was supposed to have been killed. He knows Alvarado didn't do it. I just want to talk to him. I'm not going to get him in trouble."

"I don't know where he is right now."

"Well, when will he be back?"

"I don't know. He's in Puerto Rico."

"What's his address? I'll write to him," said Sandro.

"I don't have his address. My father might. I'd have to talk to my father."

"Look, Jenny, I don't want to get Jorge in trouble. I only want to

PART 35

talk to him, write to him, if necessary. You call him, have him call me. I don't even want to know his phone number."

"I don't know where he is to call him."

"Well, talk to your father. I'll talk to your father," Sandro suggested. "If Jorge is out of town, let me write a letter to him. You can address it so I don't even know where it's going. I don't want Jorge. I only want to talk to him. A man's life is at stake, Jenny. It's important. It's a matter of life or death, frankly."

"I understand. But I really don't know where he is."

"When will he be back?" Sandro pressed.

"I don't know."

"Does his wife know? Is he married?"

"Yeah, he's married. His wife is with him, though. I don't know where they are."

"Let me talk to your father then. Is he here?"

"No, he's not here. I'll have to talk to him. If there's anything I can do, maybe I can call you. You got a phone?"

Sandro handed her his card. "Do you have a phone here where I can call you?"

"No, I don't have a phone."

"Is there one in the hall where I can get you?" Sandro asked.

"No. Look, I'm not trying to make it tough for you. I can't help it right now, you know." She pleaded with her eyes.

"Yes, I know. I understand. But you have to understand, make your father understand, that this is a man's life at stake. Tell your father I don't even want to know where Jorge is. You get in touch with him for me. I must talk to him or write to him."

"All right. I'll tell my father. I'll call you and let you know. Okay?"

"It'll have to be okay, won't it?" Sandro replied. He smiled. She returned his smile.

"Okay. I'll let you know." She stood watching Sandro and Mike walk toward Roebling Street.

"I wonder what the hell Jorge is on the lam for?" Mike said to Sandro.

"Damn, if that doesn't beat all. Alvarado's friends are all in trouble with the law. What the hell kind of witness would Jorge make anyway?

They'd probably arrest him on the witness stand. Well, we'll see after we talk to him."

"Okay, Sandro. Say, you want to stop off and see the barber and the others, see if they're still okay, if the cops have been bothering them?" Mike asked.

"Might as well as long as we're here."

They walked to Roebling Street and turned toward the barber shop. There, they found Francisco Moreno. They all said hello, smiled, talked for a few minutes. Sandro checked if Francisco's recollection of Alvarado on July 3rd still stood. It did. They spoke to the other witnesses in the neighborhood—Annie Mae Cooper in the five-and-ten, Pablo Torres in the restaurant. All stood firm. And the police had not been around to talk with anyone.

"As we're driving into New York, stop on Stanton Street," Sandro directed Mike. "This time I want to go take a really good look at that backyard. That woman across the yard had an awfully long view of whatever she says she saw. I want to see what her windows look like again, too."

"Okay."

The rotting fences that separated the rear yards of the Stanton Street buildings from the rear yards of the Rivington Street buildings were broken through here and there to form a no-man's-land of weeds and concrete. The Stanton Street yards were approximately fifteen feet deep and had no fences separating them. They served as an alley that extended to Suffolk Street. Near Suffolk Street, there had once been a fence to block the way, as evidenced by remnants of wire mesh and cement, but it was long since gone.

The yard behind 153 Stanton Street was really the top of the one-story extension on the building. A ladder was bolted to the wall of the extension. This was the ladder Lauria had climbed on the way to his death.

Mike and Sandro walked through the alley from Suffolk Street, climbed over some rubble where the fence was broken, and stopped directly beneath the Italian woman's windows. These were on the first level above the yard, starting approximately nine feet from the ground. There were two windows. One opened onto a fire escape. An air-conditioner protruded from the bottom half of the other.

PART 35

"You see that air-conditioner?" Sandro was whispering so that their presence would not attract attention.

"Yes." Mike whispered.

"And look at the fire escape at the other window. Both windows have some kind of obstruction. And look at the fire escape up by Soto's old apartment," Sandro turned full around.

The tall, narrow building loomed five stories above the one-story extension in its rear yard.

"Look at the bottom of the fire escape outside Soto's apartment. From down here at this angle you have to look right through the steel slats on the bottom of that fire escape to see Soto's windows," said Sandro.

"Yeah. That's a tough view to get a good look at a dark-colored guy on a rainy day," agreed Mike.

"Especially if you've never seen him before. She'd have to look through the railing of her own fire escape, or through the window where the air-conditioner is . . ." Sandro turned to look at the air-conditioner in the Italian woman's apartment again. "Look at that! In order to install the air-conditioner, the windows had to be raised at the bottom, right?"

"Right."

"And the window above the air-conditioner is then a double window, right? The top half plus the raised bottom half."

"That's right," said Mike, studying the window.

"And to seal the room so the hot air doesn't come in, the windows are locked in position and some insulation is placed between them."

"Yeah, some kind of rubber or foam stuff," Mike added.

"Right. And that's a sort of permanent installation with almost a sealed vacuum between the windows. And except for inside the apartment, the windows never get washed because they're locked and sealed. Look at those windows. They're kind of grimy and hard to see through." Sandro was smiling.

"You're right. It's like black and sooty between the windows."

"Right! And that's at the very height that a person would have to look to see the Sotos' fire escape."

"In other words, it'd be real tough to see through that sooty window, through the dark and the rain, through the fire-escape slats up there, and recognize a colored guy, especially a real dark guy like Alvarado, if you never saw him before in your life."

"Exactly," agreed Sandro. "And if she looked through her other window, she'd have to look through the railing of her own fire escape. And there are stairs that come down from the apartment above hers. Look at them."

"They come down right by her window."

"Exactly. That's another obstacle in her way. Now, if she only wears glasses or something. I have to get pictures of these windows. Maybe also some motion pictures of that fire escape."

"Motion pictures? What for?"

"I want motion pictures to time how long it takes to go up and down that fire escape. It may be that she only saw all of this for a bare few seconds. I've got an old client who looks like Alvarado. I'll get him for the motion pictures. Then I'll bring the photos and the motion pictures into court to cross-examine this woman. She's the crux of their case. If we break her, we break their case. What do you think?"

"I think we're going strong now."

"Drive me back to the office, will you, Mike? I want to make some phone calls. Arrange for photographs so we can get ready for this Italian woman."

CHAPTER XXIV

THE EARLY-MORNING JANUARY SUN WAS BRIGHT. The sky was blue and clear. The fire escapes loomed dark and ugly above. Sandro turned to Mike.

"Go up to the old Soto apartment, see if anybody is in there. If anybody's there, tell them you're the insurance man and you want to inspect the fire escapes."

"And then what do you want me to do?"

"Then you just stand on the fire escape looking down toward the Italian woman's apartment, while Jerry takes some pictures. But don't go up right away, because I want Jerry to be able to get some shots of the building without you in them."

"Okay," said Mike.

Jerry began to assemble his camera equipment. Mike walked across the rear yard and turned to make his way to the street through the refuse-strewn passage between the buildings. These passages, actually airshafts, provided air and light for the interior apartments.

"Rehearse me in my lines," said Jerry. "What do I say if anybody asks what we're doing?"

"Tell them we're from the insurance company. Somebody is buying the buildings, and we have to take pictures to evaluate them for coverage estimates," Sandro replied.

"I sure hope you know what the hell you're doing," Jerry grunted as he picked up his camera bag. "I'm glad you asked me to bring this movie camera along."

"Sorry. That guy I wanted just couldn't make it today."

They walked across the rear yards beneath the Italian woman's windows.

"*Are* we trespassing?"

"Don't worry about it," Sandro assured Jerry. "The cops who'll respond when somebody reports prowlers will be from the same precinct as the dead cop. They'll be friendly as hell when they find out I'm Alvarado's attorney."

"Oh? Well, that's makes me feel a little better anyway." Jerry laughed and shook his head. They squeezed through a broken part of the fence and, walking noiselessly, approached a spot beneath the Italian woman's windows. Sandro looked around. No one was to be seen yet.

"Start getting pictures of that fire escape," whispered Sandro. "Get some the full length of the building, and then some close-ups of that fire escape. When Mike gets out on the fire escape, get his picture looking down here. Then get some shots while he's standing on the fire-escape platform at the roof, and some while he's standing on the roof."

Jerry aimed his camera and started snapping. Shortly, Mike looked out from the window of Soto's old apartment. Apparently Mike had been a convincing insurance man. Sandro waved to him, signaling he should not yet come out onto the fire escape. When Jerry had taken all the pictures of the empty fire escape, Sandro whistled. Mike climbed out and began feigning an inspection of the building and the fire escape. Jerry snapped rapidly.

"Now, Jerry, get a few pictures of this apartment right here. It's the apartment of the Italian woman who may be the people's chief witness."

Jerry crossed the yard and snapped several pictures while Sandro stood next to him. As he did, a window opened in the building next to the Italian woman's, and two women peered out.

PART 35

"What yez doin'?" asked the younger of the women. She was heavy-set, dark-haired.

"We're just taking some pictures," Sandro replied. "Some people are buying the buildings across the yard, and they want pictures for the insurance company." Sandro smiled disarmingly.

"Who's buyin'?"

"Don't know. Must be some big outfit," said Sandro. "Maybe they're going to build a big new building here or something."

"Yeah? I'm the super here. Maybe they want to buy this building, too?" the woman suggested.

"Maybe they do. I'll ask them."

"Maybe you should take a picture of this one and show it to them," said the woman.

"Sure. Maybe they'll be interested." Sandro turned to Jerry and winked. "Point your camera at them and make believe you're taking their picture," he whispered.

Jerry pointed the camera at them and focused.

"Take a good picture now," the younger woman called. She fluffed her hair with one hand. A smile flickered onto and off her face. She wasn't sure a smile was necessary in a business transaction.

"Okay, all done," Sandro called. "Maybe they'll do something." The women nodded and smiled.

Mike crossed the yard to rejoin Sandro and Jerry.

"We're all set down here," said Sandro.

"How'd I do?" Mike asked.

"Great, Mike, great. Jerry said he'd never seen such poise in front of a camera before."

"That's right, Mike," Jerry added. "You ought to try getting a modeling job. You'd go over great." They started out toward the street.

"Don't forget to show them that picture," the younger woman called after them.

"Okay. We will," Sandro called back.

"Who the hell is that?" asked Mike.

"She's going into the modeling business with you. She's another natural talent. You'll make a great pair."

Mike looked back at the two women. "Thanks a load."

"Jerry, you need a lift?"

"No, I'm fine. I followed Mike in my car."

"Listen, Jerry, before you go, how about going into the street and taking the front view of this building," Sandro said.

"And don't forget the factory building," Mike added.

"I guess the best thing is to get pictures of the fronts of the buildings on both sides of the street. Then we'll be prepared for everyone."

"How about the roof?" Mike suggested.

"Jerry, take pictures of everything."

"Okay. When do you need all of this by?" he asked.

"As soon as you have them. When will they be ready?"

"Say Tuesday. Is that time enough?"

"That'll be fine," said Sandro. "Mike can pick them up at your place, okay?"

"Fine, Sandro. I'll see you. So long, Mike."

"So long, Jerry. Where are we headed?" Mike asked Sandro.

"Let's try some pawnshops on Delancey Street. Hernandez mentioned something in his letter about trying to pawn two suits on Delancey Street near Essex. Let's find the place."

"You still think he might testify against us?"

"To save his own skin? He might. He's already gotten us into this for no reason. Why not save his skin now by getting our guy the chair?"

Mike started the car. They drove along Suffolk Street to Delancey Street. "Which way?" asked Mike.

"Turn right, Mike. Didn't Hernandez say between Allen Street and Essex Street somewhere?" Mike drove along Delancey Street to where it was crossed by Allen Street, then circled back. "I saw a couple of them. How about you, Sandro?"

"The same. Let's go back to Essex. We'll walk our way along the street."

They studied the windows of the first pawnshop west of Essex Street. It was the typical pawnshop—cutlery and banjos and cornets and guitars and binoculars and cameras proliferating in the window. Sandro entered first. A small, gray-haired man was sitting on a high accountant's stool behind a caged window. A clerk was sorting items in a showcase.

"Can I help you?" The man on the stool chewed into his cigar.

Sandro walked to the back. "My name is Luca. I'm an attorney."

PART 35

The old man's eyes studied Sandro more closely. He flickered a glance to Mike, then back to Sandro.

"I'm investigating a case involving a fellow named Antonio Cruz, who's charged with a crime last July third," Sandro continued. "He says that at that very time he was pawning some things right here. I'm just trying to find out if it's so."

"Listen, I couldn't tell ya. There's so many people . . ." The old man shrugged.

"I know you don't remember everybody who walks in, but his name would be in your pledge book, wouldn't it? And, after all, you don't want a man to go to jail for something he didn't do."

The man studied Sandro a bit longer. He turned to the clerk. "Angel, get me the book for—what day you say?"

"July third."

"July third. Bring it."

Angel, a young Puerto Rican, walked behind a counter and carried a large ledger book to the old man. The old man opened the book, licked his thumb, and leafed through the pages. When he reached July third, he turned the book so Sandro might read it.

"What's his name? If it's there, he was here. If not, maybe he's a liar too," the old man said flatly.

"Or perhaps he was in a different pawnshop," added Sandro.

The old man shrugged. "Why should I say no?"

Sandro's finger quickly descended the list of names before him. There was no Antonio Cruz nor Ramon Hernandez listed. He went through the names again. There was a Santiago Cruz, but no Antonio Cruz.

"This is the only book you have for that day?" Sandro asked.

"That's it. Your fellow's not there?"

"I don't see him."

The old man shrugged again. "Maybe another pawnshop. Good luck." He closed the book and handed it back to Angel.

"Thanks very much," said Sandro.

"For what? You didn't find nothin'."

"Because you're a nice fellow. You let us look at the books."

"When I'm going to jail someday, maybe I'll need a lawyer. You'll do me a favor, charge me not so much."

"It's a deal." Sandro smiled. "*Sei mir gesunt.*"

The old man's eyes twinkled. "*Sei mir gesunt.*"

Sandro walked out behind Mike. "What did you say to him?" asked Mike.

"That was Yiddish. I told him, 'Watch out for Puerto Ricans!'" Sandro and Mike laughed. "And the old man said, 'Watch out for the sneaky one behind you.'"

Closer to Allen Street, they found another pawnshop. Sandro talked to the proprietor, traced through the names listed in another pledge book. Antonio Cruz's name was not there.

"Well, what do you think?" asked Mike. "That's Allen Street."

"There's a pawnshop on the next block. Maybe Hernandez can't tell one street from another."

Mike studied the private detective badges in a showcase as Sandro spoke to the proprietor of the next pawnshop. The tall, slick-haired man behind the counter went to the back and picked up the pledge book. Sandro ran his finger down the list. A little more than halfway through the list was the name Antonio Cruz, and sure enough, it was written in Hernandez's scrawl. There was also a pledge number, 57, and the item pawned: one suit. Beneath that entry was a ditto mark for a pledge of another suit.

"This is it," Sandro announced, smiling. Mike walked over. The proprietor turned the book toward himself and studied the entry.

"Do you know who entered that pledge?" asked Sandro.

"Look, kid, all I know is that there are two suits here with this name. I don't know who brought them in here months ago. I mean, we got a lot of people coming in here, a lot of people."

A young clerk who was listening and watching walked over, looked at the book and then at Sandro.

"I think the police came in about this pledge a while ago," the clerk announced.

"Did they take the suits?" asked Sandro.

"No, the suits are right here, in the back. They just put a hold on them."

Mullaly again, thought Sandro. "Can I see the suits?"

The clerk looked at the proprietor.

PART 35

"Show him the suits." The clerk walked to the back. "Listen," said the proprietor, "you can look at the suits, but I don't know anything about the guy who brought them in here. It could be you for all I could remember."

"Who was on duty here that day? Do you know?" Sandro asked.

"I was, but I don't remember. The clerk wasn't. That kid wasn't," he said, pointing toward another young Puerto Rican polishing bugles. "It must'a been me, but I don't remember this name, especially the guy, what he looked like."

"Mike, would you hand me my briefcase."

Sandro took out the newspaper clippings with Hernandez's picture. "Start copying the information out of that pledge book while I talk to this guy," Sandro murmured as he feigned rummaging further through the briefcase. "Get the pledge numbers, the items pawned, the amounts, even get the brand names out of the suits. Don't let him see you. We're going to have trouble with this guy."

"This is a photograph of the fellow," Sandro said aloud, turning to hand the clippings to the proprietor. "What's the name of this shop, anyway?"

"Excelsior Pawn Brokers," the man said, studying the photos. "A cop got killed? Is that the case? A cop got killed?" The man looked apprehensive.

"Yes, that's the case. But if one of these fellows was here pledging something at the very moment he's charged with killing the cop, he couldn't have killed the cop."

"I don't know nothing about it, I'm telling you. Nothing!" He pushed the clippings back across the counter.

"What's your name? May I know your name?"

"What's the difference?" He looked blankly at Sandro.

The clerk came over with the suits. Out of the corner of his eye, Sandro saw Mike writing intently, copying the information from the pledge book, opening the suit jackets and writing down the brand names of the suits. The proprietor noticed Mike writing and abruptly closed the pledge book.

"Listen, I don't know this guy," said the proprietor. "I don't remember the pledge, nothing. I took the suits in, and that's all I know. If they're stolen, I don't know it. A cop!"

"Can I see the signature card this fellow signed?" asked Sandro.

"Listen, I can't show you a thing. I'm not supposed to even show the pledge book. The cops are tough on pawnshops. I'm not going to get involved, commit a crime besides. I might be liable or something."

"Mister, a man's life is at stake. Besides, I'm only interested in seeing the book. I'm not going to ask you to let me have it," Sandro explained.

"Look, I showed the book, you saw the suits, that's it. I can't help it if a guy brings in stolen stuff. A lot of people come in here. You think I can remember everything? I'm a little busy right now, so if you don't mind." He picked up the book and walked behind the counter toward the back of the store.

"The son of a bitch," muttered Mike.

"Don't worry about it. You get the information?"

"Sure. I got the whole bit."

"That's all. He can't destroy the book, the suits. He's got to keep them here. When I need them, I'll subpoena the book, the suits, everything, even the guy. Thanks," Sandro called to the proprietor as he followed Mike out of the store.

"What a bastard!"

"Forget it. Be happy," said Sandro. "The case is sewed up now, back to front. We've an alibi for Alvarado; we have an alibi for Hernandez. I'll take care of the pawnshops when we need them. I'd like to find the man who fits in those suits, the man whose place Hernandez burglarized that morning in El Barrio."

"Where we going to find him?"

"I don't know. Maybe Hernandez can tell us. We're going to have quite a story to tell that jury." Sandro felt good as they walked back to the car.

Mike was muttering to himself, "Find a guy who fits into a suit we don't even have! We haven't finished some of the easy work yet, like Asunta for instance."

"I know, I know. There's also the Italian woman. And I need a doctor."

"If it's for one of your girls, maybe Asunta can help you out."

"Very funny. I need a narcotics doctor."

CHAPTER XXV

MIKE STOOD AT SANDRO'S SIDE, studying the photographs spread out on the conference table.

"These are great shots," said Sandro. "We've got every house, every store, every roof. No matter what any witness talks about, we'll have a picture of it. Come on into my office, and let's go over what we still need."

Mike sat across from Sandro. Elizabeth brought in the second mail. Sandro's eye was caught by one of the envelopes. It had the district attorney's return address on it.

Sandro shook his head slowly as he read.

"What's up?" Mike asked.

"This is a copy of the D.A.'s motion papers to have a special panel sent over for the Alvarado case."

"Does that mean we'll be going right to trial?"

"Not immediately, I don't think. This has the county clerk send over two hundred jurors instead of, say, fifty. Because it's a capital case. A lot of jurors don't want to get involved with the electric chair."

"So what does it mean? When do we go?"

"Soon. I'd better call Sam and ask him." Sandro swiveled and buzzed Elizabeth.

"Yes, sir?"

"Would you get Sam Bemer for me?" Sandro asked. "Mike, do you know Sam?"

"No."

"Why don't you get on the extension in the conference room, and I'll introduce you."

"Okay." Mike left the door between the two rooms open. He was clearly in sight at the conference table. The phone buzzed.

"Mr. Bemer on seventy-five."

"Sam? How are you?"

"Okay, Sandro. How are you?"

"Tired."

"Well, with your other practice and the way you've been working on this Alvarado case, you should be. If that guy Alvarado had a million bucks, he couldn't have a better defense than we're giving him."

"*We* sure are, Sam."

"Well, you know I've been tied up. But I'll be with you on the trial."

"There's still a lot more to do, Sam. Sometimes I feel overwhelmed, working alone."

Mike pulled a large handkerchief from his pocket and began to dab at his eyes. Sandro smiled.

"Sam, I've got someone on the other phone I'd like you to say hello to. Mike Rivera. He's been working with me on the investigation."

"Hi," Sam said, "I've been hearing about you."

"Well, you can't believe that stuff." Mike was smiling.

"No, no. The pleasure is all mine."

"Sam," Sandro said, "we received a motion for a special panel of jurors this morning."

"We did? Oh, oh. That means we'll be coming on for trial. Are we ready to go?"

"If we have a few more weeks, yes. Do we?"

"Sure. They're just starting to prepare. That's the first thing out of the way. We should go to trial around three or four weeks from now, around the middle of March, maybe even the beginning of April."

"What do you want to do with this motion then?" Sandro said, feeling relieved.

"We'll have to get answering papers together," said Sam. "When is the motion on?"

"The twenty-sixth of February."

"Let me look at my calendar. February twenty-sixth, February twenty-sixth. Damn! I've got to be in Queens that day on a burglary case. You'll have to handle the motion. Is that okay? You won't have to go to court, no sense going in to argue. They'll grant this anyway."

"Okay. You draw the papers. I'll submit it."

"Well, my secretary is out this week. I haven't a girl."

"Sam, you're getting paid as much as I am for this assignment. Try and do a little bit, will you?"

"Don't take it like that, kid."

"Okay, I won't. But draw the opposing papers for the motion, Sam."

"Okay, Sandro."

"And we'll finish up this investigation. I want to go over it with you as soon as we're finished. I think you'll be pleased by some of the evidence we have."

"I'm sure I will. Okay, Sandro, Mike, I'll talk to you."

"Yeah. See you in court," Mike said. They all hung up.

Sandro swiveled in the chair and buzzed Elizabeth.

"Yes, sir?"

"Dr. Travers gave us the name of a Dr. Waxman who was on duty in the prison ward the night Alvarado went there from the Tombs. Call him and arrange an appointment at his earliest convenience."

"Yes, sir."

"And send to the weather bureau and get a copy of the weather report for last July third. I know it was raining that day, but I'll need the official weather report for court."

"Yes, sir."

"And remind me in about two days that Sam Bemer has to send over some answering papers on the motion for a special panel."

"Yes, sir. Do you want some tea?"

"No, we're going to the Athletic Club to get a massage. If you need me, call me there. After that we'll be investigating over in Delancey."

"You have the Joseph Train case on in Part Thirty in the morning."

"I'll handle that before I come to the office." It was a burglary case.

"Yes, sir."

Sandro turned back to his desk.

"I don't know why the hell I'm taking you to an athletic club," said Sandro.

"I hope they have boxing gloves there," said Mike. "I'll paste that fine Roman schnoz of yours all over your face." They laughed as Sandro started a quick glance through the papers on his desk. The intercom buzzed again.

"Yes?"

"It's Robert Soto on seventy-four, sir."

"Soto," Sandro said to Mike. "Get on the other phone. When I count three, we both pick up." Mike went back to his post.

"Ready?"

"Yeah," Mike answered, nodding.

"One, two, three." They raised the receivers.

"Hello?" said Sandro.

"Hello, Mr. Luca. I'm at work, a phone booth outside. I wanted to call you because I think I know a girl who lived in the same building where the cop was killed. She moved now, but she's a friend of my wife. And she was talking to my wife, and she said she knows something about this case."

"You know that fellow Salerno you told me about," Sandro interjected. "He was in jail the day the cop was killed."

There was no sound on the other end. "I'm just trying to help," Soto explained. "I can't help a guy acts funny. I'm just trying to tell you everything I hear. I didn't know."

"Okay. Who is this other woman? What's her name?"

"I think she's called Concepcion. She's a friend of my wife," Soto repeated.

"Was she at the station house that night?"

"I didn't see her when I was there."

"Do you know where she lives?"

"I'm going to find out for you. I thought if you could come over to my house, I'd get the information, and I'd go with you to her house."

"Fine. Let's see when I can make it." Sandro looked at his appointment book.

PART 35

"And then, remember," Soto added, "you said once that maybe you and me, we'd go speak to some of the witnesses so that I could translate for you, or something?"

Sandro thought for a moment. He could remember no such conversation. "Yes?" he said tentatively. He glanced in to Mike. Mike shrugged, shaking his head.

"Well, maybe we could do that, too, when you come here," said Soto. "I've got some time. I could go with you."

Sandro still remembered no such conversation. "Perhaps we could do that," he said, stalling. Mike was riffling through a small notebook he had pulled from his pocket and was now gesturing to Sandro.

"We could, ah, maybe talk to some, I don't know, witnesses, something like that, you said. Can you come over to my house tonight? About eight o'clock?"

"Can you hold it just one minute, Robert. I've got another call coming in. I'll just tell them I'll call back." Sandro pushed the Hold button, and Mike hung up.

"Do you know what the hell he's talking about?" Sandro asked.

"There's nothing in my notes about that," Mike answered. "There's something fishy. I don't trust this guy."

"I can't figure him out." Suddenly, Sandro felt a flush of anger. "I'll be a son of a bitch!"

"What?" Mike asked.

"I'll lay my life on a bet that this little bastard in his dumb way is trying to pump *me* for information."

"How come?"

"I don't know, but he's fishing for something. Let's not keep him waiting too long."

They picked up their phones.

"Now, where were we?" Sandro asked calmly. "Oh, yes, about getting together to do that investigating. I'm not sure I can make it tonight, Robert. I'm all tied up."

"Well, er, maybe you can make it tomorrow night?"

Sandro's mind was working logically again. If it's information he wants, Sandro thought, that's just what he'll get. "I'll have to call you on it, Robert. You see, I'm so jammed up with work trying to get some kind of defense for Alvarado that I can't even see straight. I'm trying to find an alibi for him, find some people who might know where he was the day of the killing. But I can't find a single person, not a single one, to testify for him."

He looked over to Mike. Mike nodded approvingly.

"You see," Sandro belabored it as much as he dared, "I haven't been able to find one person who can testify where Alvarado was the day of the killing. I'm very worried, and I'm trying desperately to find some kind of story I can tell the court when we have the trial. Right now it looks impossible. I haven't any alibi. But I need your help, too. You've been terrific till now. I'll call you the minute I get a break. Then I'll come over, and we can see this woman you're talking about, okay?"

"I guess so. When do you think you can make it?"

"I'll call you, Robert. Perhaps the beginning of next week. Meanwhile, if you hear anything else, please let me know right away, okay? It's very important to Alvarado."

"Okay." They hung up.

"I never liked that little fink," Mike said.

"What would you say if I told you that's Mullaly's work?" Sandro asked quietly.

Mike took that in. "Sure," he said at last.

"Soto's working both sides of the street. No wonder he acted funny when we wanted to take a statement from his wife. Did you notice that?" Sandro asked.

"Yeah. That fink, spic bastard."

At another time Sandro would have laughed.

"I thought he was just worried about her being involved. He was afraid she'd let something slip." Sandro sat in his chair, staring at Mike.

"That's the explanation for that crazy Salerno story!" Mike exclaimed. "How about the rest of it?"

"Mullaly. Feeding us bullshit. Every time we see Soto, he runs and tells Mullaly."

"Son of a bitch," Mike said. "That Mullaly has been screwing us good."

"That's his job. He's not dedicated to making our life easier."

"Listen, Sandro, I know cops, and he's doing a job all right. On us.

PART 35

Every rock we look under, he crawls out. All the pawnshops. He put a hold on all the stolen goods, the signature cards. You didn't see him take that stuff to headquarters for evidence. He's just leaving it there to rot. He's screwing around with this case."

"If he really wanted to screw around, he could take the evidence and destroy it."

"But then it'd look worse if anyone found out," Mike countered. "And he knows Hernandez's alibi, knows he wasn't on Stanton Street when Lauria was killed. And these false leads he's throwing us."

"He's outmaneuvered us, that's all. We'll have to try harder."

"No. I don't buy it. Mullaly's trying too hard, you know? He's over there all the time—Soto told us and Mrs. Salerno and even Hernandez's wife—talking, investigating. It's not the only case he's got."

"It's probably the only cop-killing."

Mike looked at Sandro with exasperation. "Will you stop, already? He's breaking his stones for some reason, and it's not his job."

"Let me see your notes from the first night we spoke to Soto," Sandro said abruptly. Mike handed him the notebook.

"There. That's what I'm looking for," Sandro said, sliding the book to Mike. Mike read where Sandro pointed.

"I wrote here that an Italian girl was at the station house, and she said she saw Alvarado on the fire escape."

"That's right. That was before Mullaly got into the fantasy game and started filling Soto's head."

"How do you know when Mullaly got into this game?"

"We saw Soto the first time about three days before the arraignment. See, the date on the notes is August second. About two weeks later, I went to the station house and told Mullaly I was going to knock some holes in this case. Now look at the date for the next time we saw Soto. August thirty-first! He called to say he'd been going around gathering information for us. And he even told us he had been talking to Mullaly."

"So, what's that prove?"

"Come on, Mike. You're my Sherlock. Part of Soto's story still stands up. The first part he told us. Mullaly just shoveled bullshit on top of it. So we've still got to cover the Italian woman, and Asunta, and all the rest, just like it's all for real. Nothing has changed, except we'll be a little more careful." Mike didn't look mollified.

"At least Soto is still working for us," Sandro said.

"He's what?"

"Passing on information. If he runs to Mullaly with the story that we still haven't got an alibi, we've hurt them more than they've hurt us. Cheer up, things could be worse."

"Yeah, so he cheered up. And, sure enough, they got worse."

CHAPTER XXVI

FOOTSTEPS ECHOED DOWN A CORRIDOR. They stopped. There was the sound of knocking on a door.

"*Quién es?*" The voice sounded muffled. It was coming through the door.

"Rivera."

"*Quién?*"

"Rivera."

After a few seconds, a squeaking noise, as if the door were opening.

"And then this little, skinny, dark-skinned broad in her late twenties is staring at me," Mike said. He sat with Sandro in the car parked around the corner from Stanton Street. They were listening to the small tape recorder Mike had hidden in his briefcase play back his visit to Asunta. "You should have been there to see it. I thought I was going to be killed."

"I thought you had been," said Sandro. "You were gone twenty-five minutes. Another five minutes, and I would have been knocking on that door, even if it would have screwed up everything. What the hell is all that howling?" Sandro asked as the tape continued. The voices in the background varied from a single, rapid-fire Spanish to a howling, screaming, mass confusion.

"Asunta had her sister—she's about the size and color of a gorilla—and some guy and some other dumb broads there. Man, as soon as they knew who I was, they began screaming, yelling. They told me I was okay, but you were a pain in the ass and a fuck."

"They said that, just like that?"

"That's not all they said," added Mike.

"Why me?"

"Cause you're always nosing around the neighborhood. You're an intruder. As bad as that cop Mullaly." Mike winked. "Listen, here's the important stuff, now. She said here that she didn't know anything about the killing of Lauria."

"She said she didn't know anything?"

"That's right. She said she was at her sister's apartment. The fat gargantua was her sister. Here, that's her sister screaming. She had some mouth on her," Mike chuckled. He translated her remarks for emphasis. "Now she's saying Asunta was at her house on Norfolk Street when the cop was killed. She came back to her apartment only after the cop was already shot."

"You sure they said that?"

"Sure. I had them repeat the story a couple of times. Don't worry, it's there on the tape. Nobody could mistake it."

"What about identifying Hernandez's car to the police? Did you ask her about that?"

"That she did. She was standing down in the street in front of her house watching the ambulances. The cops started thinking it was funny that a car was double-parked with the window open. It was raining, right? So they asked if anybody knew whose car it was. She said she told them it was Hernandez's. That's all."

"Was she down at the station house that night?"

"Yeah, I asked her that," said Mike. "She said she went down there. Soto was there only the last minute or so before she left. She left with that Salerno broad—some combination!—and Alma Soto came in as they were going out. Asunta said she told the cops she never saw the colored guy before in her life. She told me she was

PART 35

telling them the truth. She doesn't know Alvarado from a hole in the wall."

"I guess Alvarado just had his witnesses confused," said Sandro. "He couldn't see who was on the other side of that mirror."

"And we just about told that bastard Soto that we were worrying if Asunta identified Alvarado. He passed it on to Mullaly, and Mullaly must have told him to play it up."

"Well, it eliminates a witness for us. That helps," said Sandro. "Won't she be surprised to hear her own voice making her a liar if she *is* a witness at the trial. Let's go. It's just about time for Dr. Schwartzman to be in his clinic." He glanced at the clock in the lighted window of a *bodega*. "It's already ten o'clock. You know, we ought to get Sam Bemer out here doing some of this leg work. Keep him in shape."

"Yeah, what about that guy? What the hell is he doing on this case?" Mike started driving again.

"He's waiting for us to bring him the stuff. What the hell, he's letting me have a free hand. I can't complain about that. I hope I know what I'm doing."

"What street does Dr. Schwartzman have his office on?"

"I think it's Catherine Street near the river," replied Sandro.

After a short drive, Mike stopped the car in front of a tenement-type building. Sandro stood on the sidewalk. He could smell the river spicing the air. A short stoop led into the building. To one side was a storefront with great panes of glass painted dark from the inside. A group of people huddled about the entrance to the store.

Sandro and Mike made their way through. Eyes in the crowd viewed them suspiciously. On the door was a small sign, ARNOLD SCHWARTZMAN, M.D. Sandro knocked. A narrow strip of light appeared as a girl opened the door only enough to see who was knocking.

"I'm Alessandro Luca. I've an appointment with Dr. Schwartzman for ten."

"Just a minute." She shut the door. Sandro turned to see the eyes watching every move. In a few moments, the door opened wide. "Come in, please." The voices of the throng behind Sandro stirred into activity for an instant, dying as the door was closed again. Mike and Sandro were ushered into a small office.

189

The man sitting behind the desk was talking on the telephone. He was about thirty-five, with thinning black hair. There was an unusual, pale, bluish quality about his lips. His face was trim.

"You're clean now? That's swell, great," the doctor said. "See what you can do if you really try? Now I want you to keep working." He motioned Sandro and Mike to sit. "And if you have any difficulty at all, I want you to call me. I don't care what time it is. I'm always available to you. You feel good? That's swell. I just want you to stay that way. Okay. Let me hear from you right away if anything starts going wrong. Okay?"

The doctor hung the phone back on the cradle. He looked at Sandro. "That was a fourteen-year-old kid who got hooked, and now we're getting her off the stuff. Her old man came in here one night to the clinic crying, actually crying about the kid. And now we've got her clean for three weeks, and working, and the old man is ecstatic."

"Fourteen years old? That's a little young, isn't it?" asked Sandro.

"It sure is, as years go. But to become a junky, they're never too young. They've just got to be pushed enough, cramped enough, and then they break and they need some stuff, and there's always some punk around to give them a fix or so."

"Well, you're doing a fine job, Doctor. I've seen you on television, discoursing on narcotics, about what it does, about what the city hospitals aren't doing for addicts," said Sandro.

"I've been on television a lot. Matter of fact, on Lew Reston's network show twice. He's going to be at my dinner as M.C. We're trying to raise six hundred thou' to build a hospital for addicts here in New York. Instead of treating them like criminals, they've got to be treated like patients. Addicts have just given in to human weakness, but instead of being addicted to gambling, whiskey, cigarettes even—some escape—they're addicted to narcotics. It's different, sure. But junkies are junkies for the same reasons some people drink too much and others even eat too much. They need relief from pressures around them."

"You mean to say fat people are junkies?" Mike asked.

"Sure. Food-junkies. But it's not different—not the reason they start. The ones who get involved with this stuff, most of the time, Puerto Ricans, Negroes, they got nothin' going for them in life. Junk gives them kicks, you know?" The doctor spoke the street argot easily.

PART 35

"And you run this entire project yourself?" Sandro asked.

"You're not kidding. I've got my regular practice, and then I've got this clinic every night from ten to three in the morning. I've got one of the only ambulatory addict clinics in the U.S. of A., and I put up all the bread to keep this joint going. Fortunately, we're getting a lot of people interested in the project."

"I know. I see your name all over these days."

"We're going to have a terrific dinner on the twenty-fifth of April. You can buy a couple of tickets if you want," he urged. "Twenty bucks a throw."

"Maybe we can do that," said Sandro.

"Mary. Bring in some of the folders you're sending out, will you?" Dr. Schwartzman called to a secretary in the other room. The girl who entered was not the same girl who had let them into the clinic. "Here's some of our literature." He handed the leaflets to Sandro. Sandro handed some to Mike. They described the history and purpose of the clinic, and there were pictures of the doctor in clinics, pictures of the doctor with television personalities or celebrities, as well as abstracts from magazine articles written about the doctor.

"I don't want to waste too much of your time, Doctor," said Sandro. "I'm here, as I told you over the phone, because I've been assigned to represent an addict charged with murdering a cop on a rooftop over on Stanton Street last July."

"Yeah. I know the case. I remember it. The guys that come here were all talking about it after it happened."

"I need your help, Doctor. You're one of the only ones in New York, it seems, who knows what this junk stuff is about and how it affects people. My man says he was beaten and he never confessed. The other fellow says he was beaten and named my man when he couldn't think of anybody else. I want to find out how debilitating the habit is. If a guy on the stuff gets a beating, can he withstand any punishment, or is it torture in itself just to stand around and wait until he needs a fix?"

"These guys all give the same bullshit," the doctor exclaimed.

Mike looked at Sandro.

"You know, I don't like to get involved with these guys," the doctor continued. "They go in, do whatever they do, and then want to blame it on junk. You know, when a guy is on the stuff, he still knows goddamn A that he's pulling a trigger. So don't let them give you that shit that they didn't know what they were doing."

"That's not the case here, Doctor," Sandro explained. "My man indicates he was beaten. The other fellow, too. My man isn't claiming he didn't know what he was doing. He wasn't even there. I can prove that to you. And now the cops say these fellows confessed to something. I'm concerned with the capacity of a junky to resist a beating. In other words, whether or not a beating to a junky is more violent because he has less power of resistance."

"Yeah, they all give that bullshit about beatings. I had a guy here, swore he was beaten, swore he wasn't near the scene, had all kinds of people swear the same thing. And the son of a bitch did it, and the D.A. proved it. I got in that case, and I messed myself up with the people at City Hall."

"How's that, Doctor?" asked Sandro.

"I'm trying to get a hospital going, trying to raise money, get approval from City Hall and all that. When I go into a case, and I'm the expert on narcotics, and I screw up the people's case, I get a black eye with the city, if you know what I mean. I mean, I need their help, and they say 'screw you' when I go in and mess up one of their cases. I don't like to get involved."

"But, Doctor, if you don't help an addict, you who are supposed to be the one who understands addiction as a medical and not a penal problem, who *is* going to help them? You know once the cops discover a prisoner is a junky, anything goes, and any crime conceivable is blamed on them."

"Yeah, I've heard that. But don't bullshit me about confessions, will ya, fellas. I know that story from way back."

"Doctor, I don't know which story you're talking about," said Sandro. He was trying to keep from being curt. "All I want to know is the truth. I'm not telling, I'm asking."

"Sure it could be. A lot of things could be. I'd have to know more about the facts, more about the fellow, how long he's been on it, what he's been taking."

"Let me give you the information, then make up your mind. Doctor, I'm trying to save a man's life. And that's what you're devoted to, isn't it? Especially here, Doctor. I'm asking you to help an addict."

"I'm telling you, I don't want to get involved in a case where I'm going to throw a monkey wrench when the guy is guilty and he's trying to cop out of it by saying it was the junk that made him do it, or something like that. I'm trying to help thousands, and I can't jeopardize it on one case."

"Doctor, this man is headed for the electric chair, and you want to sacrifice him for some people who may come into the picture sometime in the future. This man is for real, and right now."

"Who said he didn't do it?" the doctor asked. "Don't let them bullshit you. I told you about the other case I was in where everybody swore the guy didn't do it, and the lousy bastard did it. You know these junkies can bullshit you to death. They can do anything, say anything, fake anything, just for some junk. Besides, the word is out that these are the guys who did it."

"Which word is that, Doctor?"

"The boys that come into the clinic. This is a small community, these addicts. They all know each other. And right after it happened, some of the guys who know these guys were here and said that these were the guys."

"You must be kidding me, Doctor," Sandro remarked. "You just told me you can't believe junkies, and now you're telling me my man is guilty based on what a junky told you."

The doctor looked at Sandro closely. A thin smile wrinkled his face. He called to his nurse to tell the people waiting that he wouldn't be much longer. He turned back to Sandro. "I told you, you've got to know them to tell. I can tell, just talking to them, when they're being straight and when they're not."

"Look, Doctor, I don't know of any other doctor who has your inside knowledge of this narcotic stuff. I need your help. How about talking to my man," Sandro suggested. "I'll get you into prison. I'll even bring the witnesses who know he wasn't at the scene of the crime here to talk to you. Will you help us then?"

"When is this trial coming up?" He was stuck now.

"In about two or three weeks, I believe," replied Sandro.

"Don't you know yet?"

"No. The D.A. likes to keep defense counsel as much in the dark as possible."

"Well, I got this dinner coming up. I won't, under any circumstances, come to court before the dinner. I'm trying to get all the judges and D.A.'s to come to the dinner, trying to get their help. I can't go into court and screw them up before the dinner."

"But you will testify after the dinner?"

"I'm not saying that," the doctor replied, standing, stretching onto his tiptoes, flexing his chest. He shook his head vigorously. "Boy, I'm tired. And I've still got the clinic all night."

"You look like you're in good shape, Doctor," Mike remarked.

He smiled, pleased. "You're not kidding, boy." He leaned forward, bending his arm and extending the flexed muscle toward Sandro. Sandro touched the arm and looked impressed. Mike too.

"You really keep in shape?" said Mike.

"Every day." He flexed his chest again. "I've got to stay in shape, otherwise I wouldn't be able to keep up this pace."

"Okay, now that we've got you where you'll testify after the dinner," said Sandro.

"Wait a minute, I didn't say that. I said I'd consider it. You've got to show me first."

"Right. I'll get back to you with the proof. All I want to know is that you will testify, if I can satisfy you that this is a case where the man is worth helping. Right?"

"You come on back, and we'll talk about it." He was playing cute. "I still think your man is the man who did it. I mean I got the word already, right after it happened. Not just now, but right after it happened."

Sandro restrained his impatience. "I appreciate your time and your cooperation." He rose and extended his hand and waited for the crush the doctor would put on his hand. The doctor's hand met Sandro's and pressed it hard. Sandro tightened his grip on the doctor's hand equally hard, returning the doctor's stare.

"You're not the only one who knows where the gym is, Doctor," said Sandro.

PART 35

The doctor laughed. Mike and Sandro left his office, walked out past the painted glass door, through the crowd of junkies milling in the night, waiting to get in. They walked to the car.

"Well, what do you think, Sandro?" asked Mike.

"I think that guy is a phony."

"I think he hates junkies," Mike added. "He thinks they're all no-good liars and bums. He doesn't give a damn about junkies."

"You know, you're right. I didn't think about it exactly like that, but I think you're right. He's only interested in the grand, glorious spectacle of himself that he creates by being a crusader in this field. A hospital! He wants a hospital! I think he really just wants to be seen, have his name at the top of some list. And that muscle bit goes right along with his personality. The junkies are just poor saps, a means to an end."

"What a lousy shame, what a rotten crime," said Mike.

"What's that?"

"This creep is one of the only ones in the city who knows enough about this stuff to help Alvarado, and he's just interested in bullshit. He'd let the guy die."

"But think of what a shame it is for the dumb junkies in this world. He's the only one who wants to help them right now, and even he doesn't care. Well, we'll find someone else. Some other doctor. I wouldn't even talk to that creep again."

As they drove from the curb, they passed the painted glass windows and the crowd huddled hopefully outside.

CHAPTER XXVII

IT WAS LATE AFTERNOON, and Nick Siakos sat at Sandro's conference table, totally absorbed in Willie Morales's statement, which confirmed that Hernandez pawned a radio at Sid Goodman's Pawnshop in the early afternoon of July 3rd.

"This is terrific, Sandro," Siakos exclaimed. "You know, I think we have a once-in-a-lifetime case. These fellows may actually be innocent, and the cops might actually have the wrong guys."

"Nick, from all I've uncovered so far, these men *are* actually innocent."

"They may be innocent, you know that," Siakos mused aloud, not having heard Sandro. "Maybe we'll pull these cats out of the bag. What a coup it will be. These statements you have are terrific! This proves Hernandez pulled that job uptown in El Barrio, and pawned the stuff. He couldn't be two places at once."

"Not only do I have that statement, Nick, but I have the pledge books from the other shop he went to. I've seen his signature; I know what he pawned; I know how much he got for it. I've got your whole alibi for you."

"And you know, Sandro, these statements throw the lie to that confession Hernandez was supposed to have made naming Alvarado. The confession says he met Alvarado and they were in Brooklyn in the morning, then went driving around, and things like that, then killed the cop."

"You saw the confession?" Sandro asked with surprise.

"Sure. I was at Ellis's office one day. He showed me the confession, wanted me to talk to Hernandez about being a witness against Alvarado. They offered me manslaughter in the first if he testified," Siakos said.

"Are you going to do it?"

"I told Hernandez about it. This is murder one, I told him. Maybe the chair. Manslaughter one the maximum is twenty years. But he says that he will fight." Siakos seemed disappointed. "More so because he got your man into this. He wants to testify and tell what really happened, about the beating. He says he didn't do it, he wasn't near Alvarado all day."

"Did you see Alvarado's statement there?" Sandro pressed.

"I read it, yes, but I can't remember it too well. I remember that I don't think he did confess to the D.A. As I remember, he didn't admit anything to the D.A."

"Don't you remember what it said?"

"I can't." Siakos shrugged and shook his head. Sandro was fighting his anger. "I really can't. You know, I have some people who work with Mrs. Hernandez at the factory, and they tell me that Hernandez was at the factory with his wife at a Hundred-and-tenth Street and First Avenue, the morning of the crime."

"Do you have statements?" Sandro asked.

"Some. These people saw him drive her to work in the morning. And I have another fellow who saw Hernandez come back there to meet her at lunch hour, around twelve fifteen. After Hernandez pulled the job in El Barrio, he went back to lunch with his wife or something, and this fellow who works in the same building saw them together."

"Do you know his name?" Sandro asked.

"Ortega. German Ortega. Better than that, I've got his signed statement that he saw them together in El Barrio around lunchtime."

"Was Alvarado with him?"

"No. German just said he saw the two of them, Hernandez and his wife."

"That's fine. Another link in your alibi, Nick. Has Ellis asked you for the names of your alibi witnesses in this case?" Sandro wondered.

"No. Has he asked you?"

"No. I'm hoping that he doesn't. We'll be able to stuff this case right down his throat if he doesn't."

Siakos relished that with a high-pitched laugh. "Will you give me a copy of that statement you took from Morales, from the pawnshop?" Siakos asked.

"Surely," Sandro agreed. He had been pondering how to get Ortega's statement from Siakos. "I'll give you a copy of this, and you give me a copy of the statement you got from Ortega."

"Fine. I've got it right here." Siakos leafed through his briefcase and brought out a sheet of yellow paper. Sandro read the statement. Sandro gave both statements to Elizabeth to photocopy.

"Well, Sandro. I have to get going," Siakos announced, putting his papers in his briefcase. "I have a closing on a luncheonette this evening. I have to get out to Brooklyn."

"Okay, fine. Let me know what you're doing, so we can work together from here on in," suggested Sandro. "The trial is too close to work separately now."

Elizabeth handed the Ortega statement and a copy of the Morales statement to Siakos.

"Fine, I'll talk to you, Sandro." Siakos rose. Sandro walked with him to the door. Siakos bade a profuse, courtly good evening to Elizabeth and left. Sandro turned.

"Elizabeth, get Sam Bemer on the phone for me." He walked inside to his office.

"Hi, Sandro," Sam said as he picked up the phone.

"Hello, Sam. I was just talking to Siakos. I told you that we were trying to put together an alibi for Hernandez to stuff down his throat if he testified against us."

"Right."

"Well, now we've got it. Back to front, solid. We know where he was, at what time, and we have people who will testify to his whereabouts on July third. And none of it has to do with Alvarado or even the scene of the crime. We can establish he wasn't anywhere near it."

"Okay, kid. That's great."

"Now that we've done it, Sam, instead of being worried about a severance from Hernandez because he'd testify against us, maybe we ought to move for one ourselves and be tried without having Hernandez or his confession as a stone around our necks."

"That's not a bad idea, Sandro. Not bad at all. Because even though the judge'll instruct the jury that whatever Hernandez might have confessed, including accusing Alvarado, can't be considered evidence against us, the jurors would have to be goddamn atom scientists to handle all that in their heads."

"I think we're in pretty good shape," said Sandro. "Why let Hernandez's confession stink up the trial?"

"Good thinking, Sandro. Really good. You want me to draw up the papers?"

"I'd love you forever if you do."

"Goddamn. I can't pass that up. I'll send you a copy of the papers. When do you want to get together on the other stuff, Sandro?"

"I'll call you in a couple of days, Sam."

CHAPTER XXVIII

THE MORNINGS NOW WERE WARMED with a promise of spring. Those who awoke before the daily traffic rolled and rumbled could even hear birds.

"Who is the colored guy up there?" asked Jerry Ball, standing with Sandro and Mike in the rear yard of 153 Stanton Street.

"A client of mine named Shorts. He's working off the fee he owes me."

Mike stood next to Sandro, hands stashed in his pockets, eyes bleary from lack of sleep. Sandro gave a signal. The Negro on the roof stepped onto the fire escape and started down. Jerry's motion-picture camera began to whirr, following the moving figure. Shorts walked down one flight, moved behind the steps, bent down at the window, and climbed back to the top again. He followed the routine twice more, as Jerry filmed it.

"Now, I want you to take still pictures of this guy standing up there, looking down here." Sandro gave the man on the fire escape another signal.

"Okay."

"Take the pictures from directly beneath these windows," Sandro whispered, pointing toward the Italian woman's windows.

PART 35

Jerry moved into position and began to assemble his still camera. A window just above their heads slid open. *The Italian woman's window*!

"Keep taking your pictures, Jerry," Sandro whispered quickly. "Don't worry about a thing. Just keep snapping." Sandro turned and looked up.

"What you do?" inquired an old woman.

"We're from the insurance company," answered Sandro. He heard Jerry's camera clicking. "We're just taking some pictures of that building."

She looked up at the man on the fire escape, back to Sandro, shrugged, and shut the window.

"Must have been the Italian woman's mother," said Sandro. "Finished yet, Jerry?"

"In a minute, Sandro." He continued focusing his lens on the buildings.

"Mike, go and give Shorts five bucks so he'll be happy." Sandro handed Mike the bill. "Tell him thanks for going up on the fire escape for us."

When Jerry finished, he packed his cameras, and he and Sandro started out of the yard. Sandro turned to look at the Italian woman's apartment. No one was at the windows. They walked through the litter-strewn alley that ran the length of the block behind the buildings. Someone had had a fire in one of the apartments and had thrown the burned furniture out the windows to add to the debris. When they got to the car on Suffolk Street, Mike was nowhere to be seen.

"Where's Mike?" Sandro wondered.

"Maybe he's having coffee."

Sandro looked into a *bodega*. Mike was not there. "Might as well put our equipment in the car, Jerry."

"Right."

Jerry and Sandro sat in the car and waited. In a short while, Sandro spied Mike turning the corner from Rivington Street. Mike waved and smiled broadly.

"Where the hell did you go?"

"I went to talk to that old Italian lady," Mike explained.

"You did what? I told you we had to be careful about people's witnesses."

"You didn't see her; *I* did. I spoke to her."

"Great." Sandro smiled. "What did she have to say?"

Mike smiled broadly. "Nothing. She said she knew what we were doing. Her daughter was the one who saw the guy, but she said the daughter can't say what the guy looks like. She didn't see his face." Mike studied Sandro.

"Are you kidding?"

"Sandro, would I kid about that?"

"Is the daughter at home now?"

"No."

"But the old lady told you the daughter definitely didn't see the guy's face?" Sandro repeated.

"That's right."

"Did you ask if the daughter saw the guy looking out of Soto's window?"

"She said she didn't see the guy's face at all. So what's the difference where she saw him?"

"Did you get the old lady to sign a statement?"

"She doesn't read English. But she said to come over later, and her daughter would be home. We can get one from the daughter."

"Jesus Christ!" Sandro exclaimed. "Jesus Christ! That's fabulous."

They were both happy and smiling.

"You mind if I get out of here before you guys start kissing?" Jerry said.

"Listen, Mike. You go back there later when we're finished and get the daughter's statement in writing, including the bit about the window. That's fabulous!"

"That's their case you hear crashing, baby. That's their whole case," Mike exclaimed happily.

"We've only eliminated this one," Sandro said, suddenly cautious.

"Wait just a minute, you guys," Jerry interjected. "Does this mean that I've been taking all these pictures and films for nothing?"

"No, not for nothing, Jerry. We need pictures of the rear anyway. As well as the roof and the front of the building. We've been planning

PART 35

around witnesses we know of, or at least think we know of. They may have some, however, that we don't expect. This way we're prepared for anything they throw at us. And now, Miguel," Sandro said, turning to Mike. He smiled mischievously.

"No. Whatever it is, no!"

"Come on, Mike. This is easy. All I want you to do is run up the fire escape."

Mike looked blankly from Sandro to Jerry. "Are you kidding me?"

"No. I'm serious. I've got a stopwatch. I want to time you running."

"What the hell for?"

"I'm just following up on something I've got in my head. Now run up the fire escape, will you?"

"It's in *your* head? Then you run up, and I'll time *you*."

"No. You're about the same age and condition Lauria must have been in. I'm too young, too good condition."

Leaning over the back edge of the roof, Sandro watched Mike run, climb the ladder onto the one-story extension behind the building, jump for the bottom rung of the fire-escape ladder, and start up the fire escape. Mike began banging up the steel steps. Sandro watched the face of the stopwatch: *fifteen seconds.* Mike twisted around the steps, edged sideways along the landing, and ran the second flight in short, jerky, side-to-side motions as his feet hit each step: *thirty seconds.* Sandro moved back approximately fifteen feet from the rear edge of the roof to await Mike's arrival. Mike clambered up the last flight of steps and jumped to the roof.

"Run to this spot, to here," Sandro called, pointing. Mike ran to the spot. Sandro pressed the stop button.

"Sixty-five seconds," said Sandro. "That's not much time at all."

"How long should it have taken?" asked Mike, slightly winded.

"I don't know, but it didn't take too long. Okay, Mike, old buddy, we're almost finished," Sandro announced.

"Whatever it is, screw you," said Mike.

"Come on, Mike, you're doing great. This is the most important part now."

"What now, jump off the roof?"

"No, just run up again," said Sandro. "This time up the stairs inside the building from the same spot in the yard."

"Now I get it," said Mike. "The way I just ran up was the way Lauria ran up. Snider ran up inside the building and didn't get to the roof until after Lauria was shot and the killer was gone. You're checking out Snider's time."

"That's right. Now, go back down, run through the alley to the street, and up the inside stairs to this same spot."

"Well, here goes nothing." Mike started for the steps. He turned to Jerry. "You know, I must be crazy doing these things."

Mike turned and disappeared. When he was down on ground level again, beside the extension, Sandro gave him a signal. Mike was off. Sandro walked back to the finish line. Soon Mike's feet could be distinctly heard pounding on the landings. His steps were getting closer and closer. The timer passed thirty-five seconds. Mike burst through the door and ran to the spot.

"Forty-seven seconds," Sandro announced. "*Only forty-seven seconds!*"

Mike was gasping for breath. Sandro and Jerry grabbed him under the arms and began to walk him in a circle. The blood was drained from his face.

"And Snider didn't have to run up the stairs twice," Mike gasped out.

"That means he could have gotten here even quicker than forty-seven seconds," said Jerry.

"Exactly. Lauria's time would have been about the same as Mike's. But Snider's time would have been even faster. So where the hell was Snider? That's what's been banging around in my head. *Where was Snider?*"

"You should feel my heart banging around in my chest, you bastard," Mike rasped. They continued to hold Mike up as they walked him around in a circle.

"You were great, just great, Mike," Sandro said absently as they walked. "How could Lauria beat Snider up to the roof, get in a fight, have his gun taken away, and get shot five times, with enough time for the killer to escape, before Snider even reached the roof?"

"The son of a bitch killed Lauria, that's how," Mike gasped out.

"The run damaged his brain," said Jerry.

"That's too incredible, even for you, Mike," said Sandro.

PART 35

"Why?" Mike's breathing was slowing to near normal as he warmed to the theory. "Let's just suppose Snider shot his partner."

Both men watched Mike.

"It's possible. Who had an easier shot? No one around. While Lauria is struggling with some burglar, Snider gets the idea this is the way to be rid of him. Maybe Lauria was going to spill the beans on some racket Snider had going. You told me he had his ass in trouble before, didn't you? Thrown out of the narcotics squad?" Mike was sitting on the rear wall now. Sandro and Jerry stood listening.

"Mike, you're off your head."

"Then explain where Snider was if, after I was all pooped out, I could have beaten Lauria up here by twenty seconds." Mike's chest was still heaving.

Sandro and Jerry just stared at Mike, unable to answer. Mike nodded, smiling. "See what I mean? It's more than just crazy ideas. And I'll bet Mullaly knows it too. And that's why that bastard's been doing so many suspicious things, screwing us up, ignoring evidence that might save our guys. He's covering up for a cop! Snider!"

"That's horseshit," said Jerry flatly.

Sandro studied Mike. "It's hard to buy. But, still, where was Snider?"

They stared at one another silently. Sandro shrugged and started for the stairway. Jerry and Mike followed.

"Listen, Sandro," said Mike. Sandro turned. "This guy, Alvarado. He burns before I run up or down anything again."

CHAPTER XXIX

THE STEEL DOOR CLANGED SHUT behind Sandro and Siakos. In front of them, sitting side by side on the wooden bench were Alvarado and Hernandez.

"Over here," Sandro motioned to Alvarado. Siakos nodded to his man to come to the same place, and Sandro let them precede him into one of the interview cubicles.

"Say, Mr. Luca," said Alvarado, stopping short before they too entered. "How come we're together today?"

"I want to interview Hernandez to see if he can remember anything about the apartment he burglarized that day. I want to find the fellow he burglarized and bring him to court to prove that Hernandez was in El Barrio, pulling a job. Listen to everything he says so you can tell me."

"Okay. Listen, I just remembered something else. When I was over on Roebling Street that day, the day the cop got killed, I went to another store to buy a belt."

"What? When were you going to tell me about this other store, after the trial?"

"I just remembered."

PART 35

"Where is the store?"

"Right across from the barber's store on Roebling Street."

"What's the name?"

"Of the store? I don't remember that," said Alvarado, shaking his head. "But it's a Spanish guy there. Two Spanish guys, one tall, one short. I bought a belt, a black belt."

"When did you go there?"

"Musta been before I eat."

"I'll check out the store. On Roebling, across from the barber, right?"

"Yeah."

"Okay, now come on," said Sandro, "and listen to everything Hernandez says about El Barrio."

Sandro and Alvarado walked into the cubicle. Sandro took a chair next to Siakos. There were no other chairs. The two prisoners stood facing the two lawyers.

Siakos spoke to Hernandez in Spanish, and Hernandez answered. Sandro just listened as Siakos made notes. Occasionally, Alvarado, who was listening intently, snickered.

"What's the matter?" Sandro asked Alvarado.

"This fool doesn't remember anything," said Alvarado. Alvarado turned and spoke sharply to Hernandex in Spanish. The harangue between Siakos and Hernandez continued. Hernandez attempted to gesture, to show the shapes of buildings, the position of a tall building.

"What's he saying?" Sandro asked.

"He says there was a church, the color of limestone or something like that, white, on the same street where the house was that he burglarized," Siakos replied.

Siakos continued at Hernandez in Spanish. Alvarado assisted, trying to clarify an occasional point for Hernandez.

"He says he parked his car in the parking lot of a housing project," Siakos said to Sandro. "He doesn't remember which project it was."

Sandro was angered by Hernandez's ignorance. He had caused the entire difficulty, and now he was almost useless in clearing it up.

Siakos asked further questions. Hernandez answered, but when his replies were translated, he didn't know, couldn't say, even if he were above or below 116th Street, east or west of Lexington Avenue. His face seemed to indicate that the existence of compass points was a revelation to him. Siakos kept after him, with Alvarado still adding to the interrogation from time to time. Sandro added questions for translation.

Hernandez kept screwing his face into a knot, kept gesturing, talking rapidly, but he didn't know anything except that he pulled a *robo* at about noontime on the third of July. He knew he was near a housing project at the time, but did not know which project or how far from the project he walked after parking his car. He knew there was some sort of edifice, a church or something similar, nearby. He knew that when he left that street, which was in El Barrio, he went to meet his wife.

Sandro was disappointed. Finding the right limestone church or school in El Barrio was going to be nearly impossible without more information.

Hernandez told of how, after he pulled the job, his wife gave him a dollar for gasoline. He got the gasoline, drove downtown to the pawnshops and pawned the suits and a radio. He said he finished the pawnshops about 2:15 P.M., and then he drove to a place on Allen Street and bought some heroin from a pusher. Then he drove home. When he got back to Stanton Street, the street was alive with policemen, ambulances, and the like. Patrol cars were blocking the street.

Hernandez said that at that time he was going through the torture of need for heroin, and with total unconcern for a ticket, unable to move the car, he left it in the middle of the street and went upstairs to take his fix. Shortly after he got to his apartment, the police arrived and asked questions. He said to them he was not the one who left the car there, he had not been out all day. He didn't realize they were after a murderer, and he wasn't about to tell them of the burglary he had just committed or the remaining stolen goods still in the trunk of the car. The police felt his coat. It was wet. They took him downstairs to the double-parked car. The wet jacket and the double-parked car were enough to make his story suspicious. The police took him down to the station house to ask a few gentle questions.

Other than the repetition of that story, which Sandro was pleased

PART 35

to hear directly from Hernandez, Sandro had gained nothing. Hernandez couldn't remember where that burglarized house was to save his life. And that's exactly what he had to do.

Sandro called Mike the moment he left the Tombs, and they drove across the bridge to Williamsburg to look for a haberdashery on Roebling Street.

"This is crazy, you know that?" Mike suggested. "This guy Alvarado gives birth to his information like an elephant. One piece every two years."

"I know. But it's all been true, so far."

The Del Gato Haberdashery was the only haberdashery on the block. It was directly across from the Imperial Barber Shop. Sandro went ahead as Mike locked the car. Glass counters filled with clothes were spotted about the store. A tall young man emerged through curtains separating the store proper from the back.

"Can I help you?" he asked Sandro. He was a light-skinned Puerto Rican with dark-rimmed glasses. His face was expressionless behind them.

"My name is Luca. I'm an attorney. I represent a man accused of a crime. But he tells me that about the time he was supposed to be committing the crime, he was in here buying a belt." Mike entered the store and walked toward Sandro. The young man watched Mike, his eyes following him until he stood next to Sandro.

"I don't know anything about a crime," the young man said slowly. His slowness seemed to come more from dullness than wariness. "I can't remember everybody who comes in here."

"Let me show you his picture," suggested Sandro. He removed the clippings from his briefcase and spread them on the counter. The young man took a long time to plod through the text.

"This is it, the guy who killed the cop?" he asked finally.

"That's right. He told me he was here the day of the crime, and bought a belt. I represent the colored one, by the way. Do you remember him?"

"I don't." He looked at Sandro and Mike. His eyes spoke things he did not say; he wouldn't remember even if he could. He eyed them with distrust.

"It's very important. A man's life may be at stake, and if you remember, it's most important that you tell us," Sandro urged.

"I know, but I can't help you. I don't remember that guy. I never saw him before."

"Were you working that day?" Mike asked in Spanish.

"What day was that?" he asked. Someone walked into the store. "Excuse me," the salesman said, with evident relief. The new customer was a soldier who had a date that evening and was looking for accessories for his mufti. He wanted a gray shirt and gray socks to match. The young man took some boxes from the back. As he passed Sandro and Mike, he stopped.

"I'm very busy. I was working that day, but I still don't remember that guy. If I did, I'd tell you. You can be sure of that." He started to move away.

"Who else was working that day? Someone shorter than yourself?" Sandro asked.

"My uncle. But he's not here now."

"When will he be here?"

"I don't know," he called from across the store as he unboxed socks to match the gray shirt the soldier was admiring. "He's in Puerto Rico now."

Mike looked at Sandro. "Son of a bitch," he whispered.

"Okay, thanks anyway," Sandro said curtly. "If you happen to recall, or if you hear from your uncle, will you get in touch with me?" Sandro handed the young man a card.

"Sure, sure."

Mike and Sandro walked back to the car.

"I'll bet that bastard knows," said Mike.

"I happen to agree with you. But there's nothing we can do about it. He says he doesn't remember. We haven't got a grand jury to summon him to, nor a subpoena to require him to talk under oath like the district attorney has. We're stuck with it." Sandro got into the car and slammed the door shut.

CHAPTER XXX

THE MOTION-PICTURE IMAGE moving across the screen in Sandro's office was climbing back up the fire escape. It disappeared onto the roof of the tenement.

"Let's watch the entire sequence again," said Sandro, reversing the film. Mike was sitting on the couch. Sandro started the film again. On the screen the image of Shorts started to move from the roof of 153 Stanton Street onto the fire-escape platform, descending from right to left. At the bottom of the steps, the figure on the screen turned away from the camera and toward the building, then walked sideways along the platform to the window of Apartment 5B.

Sandro clicked the stopwatch in his hand. "It took four seconds from the time Shorts stepped from the roof until he reached the bottom of the steps," Sandro announced. "Then he turned toward the building—his back to the yards—in order to walk on the fire escape, behind the steps. He bent to open the window."

"I could only see his face as he walked down the steps," said Mike. "For four seconds."

"Right. And on the way down, he turned away from the camera. On the way up, he turned toward it," said Sandro.

"All together, then," Mike paused, adding, "his face was visible for about ten seconds."

"No." Sandro shook his head.

"What do you mean no? We just counted it."

Sandro again reversed the film. "Watch." Once again Shorts started from the roof onto the platform. Sandro stopped the film. "See how his face is obscured by the handrail?"

"Hey, you're right," said Mike. "I didn't even notice those bars across the face before."

"Okay," Sandro smiled. "Now pay attention. As Shorts went up and down the steps, his face was visible *only* in profile."

"Right," Mike said.

"Behind the steps, of course," Sandro pointed out, "he couldn't be seen at all."

"Then, actually, there's only about two seconds when the guy could have been seen full face. At the bottom of the stairs and partially at the top."

"Exactly," Sandro agreed.

The intercom buzzed. Sandro turned on the lights and picked up the phone.

"Mr. Bemer is here," Elizabeth announced.

"Send him right in."

Sam came in and shook hands with Mike, then turned to Sandro.

"What brings you here, Sam?" Sandro asked.

"I just saw Ellis in court. He said he's ready, wants to start the Huntley hearing and then the picking of the Alvarado jury the beginning of next week."

"What's a Huntley hearing?" Mike asked.

"That's where the judge hears evidence about the confessions they're supposed to have," Sam replied. "If Ellis can prove they were voluntary, they'll be admitted into evidence for the trial."

"What about that severance?" Sandro asked. "We don't even know whether we can have a trial separate from Hernandez."

"That's why I'm here. Ellis told me the decision against us is in the mail this morning. I called my office, and it wasn't there. So I came here."

"I didn't get it either."

"It just came in the second mail. I asked your girl, and she said she just got it." Sam handed Sandro an envelope.

Sandro slit it open. It contained the court order denying their motion.

"So now there's nothing to stop us from starting a full trial next week," said Sam. "Are we ready?"

"You tell me, Sam. Mike and I were just looking at some films we took in the rear yard. Let's finish them, and then we can talk it over."

Sandro turned off the light and turned on the projector. Once again, Shorts stepped from the roof onto the fire escape. Sandro went through the timing with Sam.

"Only problem with the film," said Sandro, turning the light on again, "is that the famous Italian woman isn't going to testify. After we shot this, Mike got a statement from her saying that she can't identify the man on the fire escape."

"Maybe we can enter it in the New York Film Festival as neorealism," Mike suggested.

"We may need it anyway," said Sam, nodding, puffing his cigar. "Keep it."

"What for?" Sandro asked.

"Right now, nothing. But when you investigate a case like this, just gather as much information as possible, and store it away like a squirrel stores nuts for the winter. You never know what the D.A. is going to turn up, and you may have saved just what you need for counterattack. For instance, Ellis's got to have a case here. I'm sure I've said it before, he may not be fireworks or fancy footwork, but if you step into his bear trap, brother, you'll never walk again. And neither will Alvarado."

"What do you figure he has, Sam?" asked Mike.

"We won't find out until the trial. That's why you should follow every lead, even if it leads to a blind alley. You never know when that blind alley opens up."

"As for any other possible eyewitnesses," said Sandro, "they can only come from the rear yard."

"What about the front of the building, the roof?" asked Sam.

"The roof can't be seen from the buildings across the street in front.

On one side of it is a blank brick wall. And the killer ran over the other side to escape. I'm sure nobody was standing there."

"He'd be dead meat," Sam said. "The interior should be no problem. Being inside a building isn't a crime, unless someone can connect you directly to the shooting. And if the D.A. has someone who can connect you directly to the shooting, why worry about someone who just saw you in the building?"

"Right, Sam. That's why we only have to worry about the rear. Now here's something else. We've been talking about getting large still photographs of guys who look like Alvarado. I was thinking we could use them in the back of the courtroom to test a witness's powers of observation. What do you think?"

Sam was just chomping off a straggly end of his cigar. He lifted it off his tongue with the tip of an index finger.

"Dangerous," he said, putting the strand of tobacco in the ashtray.

"How are they dangerous?"

"Identifying this guy through the dirty windows, the fire escape, across the yard, in the rain, all that, sounds impossible. Anybody who testifies to a positive identification through all that, the jury'll look a little funny at them. Now, supposing you put up these pictures in the back of the court. And the witness can't really tell Alvarado from a hole in the wall. But he has to point out one of the pictures. He can't just sit there. So he points, like he's aiming a dart at a telephone book. And he points at the right one. By mistake. At that point, Alvarado's dead. If the witness just happens, just happens, to be right, you've helped buttress his original identification. Why take the chance?"

"No contest, Sam," Sandro agreed. "You're right."

"The only thing the D.A. seems to have," Mike said, "are those confessions."

"Do you think we can knock them out at the Huntley hearing, Sam?"

"All we can do is play them by ear," said Sam. "The confessions rise or fall on the cross-examination."

"But Alvarado says he was beaten," said Mike.

"Okay, we have a shot with the medical stuff when we put it

together. But don't kid yourself, when a cop testifies you confessed, that's real trouble, whether you did or not."

"If a guy didn't actually confess, what the hell difference does it make what a cop says?" asked Mike.

"All the difference in the world." Sam paused to puff at his cigar. "The cop says he heard the defendant confess. The defendant says he didn't. Now, who's the jury going to believe?"

"The cop, I guess." Mike nodded reluctantly.

"You bet your ass," Sam assured him. "It's hard to prove someone didn't hear something. Hearing can't be measured, weighed. I say I heard something. How can you say I didn't?"

Mike didn't seem to like that.

"Jurors are just ordinary people," Sam continued. "They hear a cop say one thing, the defendant say another. And if they have to decide, they'll go for the cop every time. Thank God, most cops have some decency in them."

"Yeah," Mike scoffed.

"More important are our alibi witnesses, Sandro. Will they stand up?"

"They'll hold up, Sam. We'll prepare them to stand up to the juggernaut," said Sandro. "I just hope we can get them all to court."

"And when they do get there, we have to hope they don't get slaughtered by Ellis," added Sam. "Let's go through the alibi, Sandro."

"Okay. First we have Annie Mae Cooper. She says Alvarado was in the Associated Five & Ten about, say, one fifteen, one twenty, the afternoon of July third."

"Okay," acknowledged Sam.

"The assistant manager of the store, Phil Gruberger, supports her story. He remembers okaying her changing the hundred-dollar bill, and he remembers her coming to talk to him the day after July fourth and showing him Alvarado's picture in the paper."

"Then what?" asked Sam.

"After he left the store, Alvarado bought a belt. But the guy in the store won't help us. We should be okay without him though."

"Next," said Sam.

"Next, we have Pablo Torres from the Velez Restaurant who says

Alvarado ate there. He says Alvarado came in about one forty-five, somewhere after the lunch crowd, and before two. Alvarado took about twenty minutes to eat."

"That means he left about two ten, two fifteen, at the very latest," Mike said.

"These people have to be sure about these times," Sam said.

"We'll have them prepared. We'll go over it with them," Sandro assured him.

"Okay. I'll rely on you for that."

"You getting skeptical of me in your old age, Sam?"

"No," Sam smiled. "I just want to remind you."

"Okay. The last alibi witness is the barber, Francisco Moreno. He says Alvarado came into his shop about two twenty-five, two thirty. He gave him a haircut and trimmed his moustache. Alvarado left about two fifty."

"I don't know how Ellis'll get around that if the witnesses stand up," said Sam. He was nodding appreciatively.

"I wish there was some real evidence we could use to prove the haircut, bolster the barber's story," said Sandro.

"Don't need it. I'd like to have motion pictures of Alvarado getting a haircut too," said Sam, "but we can be satisfied with what we have. It's enough."

"That's it," exclaimed Mike, snapping his fingers. "We *can* get motion pictures. Everyone we talked to saw this thing on TV the next day. The TV stations have pictures of Alvarado a couple of hours after he was arrested."

"He's right, Sam. What the hell have we been thinking about? We can subpoena the newsreel film from the TV stations."

"Fabulous," said Sam. He was smiling, shaking his head admiringly. "You fellows are really working on this. Of course, they might have tossed out that film by this time. Let's not get too carried away until we check it out. But even if they don't have them, we've still got a great case. Does that about wrap it up?"

"Sam," Sandro began, "Mike has come up with a theory about the killing. Perhaps we can prove someone else actually shot the cop."

"Let's hear," said Sam, studying them both.

PART 35

"Well, in our investigation we came up with all sorts of strange things—like Mullaly trying to pump us for information."

"You should be glad he did," replied Sam. "I never heard of a D.A. getting so sucked in that he didn't move to have you reveal your alibi. That's the best thing we've got going for us."

"Well, this guy Mullaly was, as Mike puts it, under every rock we turned over."

"What's this theory,"asked Sam, "if Mullaly's been doing his job, and trying to screw us up? That isn't against the law, by the way."

"We timed the routes of the two cops, Lauria and Snider, with a stopwatch," said Sandro. "Mike ran their routes to the roof consecutively."

"Bastard," complained Mike.

Sandro laughed. "He ran Lauria's route first. And even though he was pooped, he still ran Snider's route twenty seconds faster."

Sam's eyes narrowed.

"I figure Snider shot Lauria," Mike said boldly. "Either by mistake, or maybe even intentionally. This guy Snider got himself in trouble with narcotics several years ago. Was thrown off the narcotics squad. Maybe he was still involved in something and Lauria was going to turn him in."

"We don't know what he was thrown off for," Sandro corrected.

"Okay, but we know he was thrown off," said Mike. "And this guy Mullaly has been going around covering up the trail so the dirty finger won't point to a fellow cop."

Sam just listened, looking from Sandro to Mike.

"We can bring this stuff out at the trial, Sam. We can show the time sequences, show that Snider was on the roof before Lauria was shot. It'll look awfully suspicious to the jury."

"Sandro, let me ask you a serious question. Are you a lawyer in this case, or a detective?"

"Come on, Sam . . ."

"No, I'm serious. Answer the question. Which are you?"

"I'm a lawyer, all right?"

"Well, remember it. We're supposed to defend Alvarado, not figure out who did it, if Alvarado didn't."

"Would it hurt if we did both?" Sandro asked.

"No. But you won't do it with that evidence. You said yourself it's just suspicions. Can you prove Snider did it? Can you prove that he was actually on the roof before Lauria was shot?"

"No."

"Do you have witnesses, anything besides supposition pieced together with speculation because of some time discrepancy?"

"No," Mike answered.

"Now, I'm not saying it couldn't happen. Don't get me wrong. But this won't do a damn thing except hurt Alvarado. The jury'll think here's some son-of-a-bitch lawyers who'll stop at nothing, even accusing a cop of murder, to get their lousy goddamn client off. They may resent it. If you had more, it'd be all right. But just to throw bare suspicion out might ruin our chances of showing the jury our alibi, showing that Alvarado was in Brooklyn. We've got a great case going for us now. Why screw it up with wild ideas we can't prove?"

"Maybe we can get more," said Mike.

"Get it. Then we'll talk."

Sandro nodded. "I guess you're right, Sam. We really can't prove anything with what we have."

"But we can do our job with what we have. I just hope we didn't miss anything. Well, we'll see next week."

"What Part is Ellis moving the case in, Sam?" asked Sandro.

"Thirty-five."

"Who's sitting there?"

"Judge Porta."

"Judge Porta?" Sandro had never even considered the possibility. "He appointed us."

"He's also trying the case. He's a good trial man," Sam said, "right down the middle. See you on Monday."

BOOK TWO

CHAPTER I

SANDRO AND SAM walked toward the courthouse. The day was clear, crisp, and sunny. Spring would be arriving soon. Green buds had begun to appear at the tips of tree branches and on shrubs.

"Well, he sure as hell gave Ellis an edge," Sandro was saying.

"Look, Porta had to pick the lesser of two evils—he could either give Ellis another bite at the apple in front of the jury or give us the entire case before it even got to the jury. I'm not saying this is always what happens. But, speaking practically, in this case the Huntley hearing had more to do with tactics than with deciding if the confessions were voluntary."

"But even so," Sandro said stubbornly, "that's exactly what the Huntley does have to decide. Ellis didn't even produce medical evidence to explain away Alvarado's trip to Bellevue. So how could the judge be convinced beyond a reasonable doubt that the confession wasn't beaten out of Alvarado?"

"He wasn't. All he had to do was *say* that he was convinced. Now, instead of crippling the D.A.'s case—maybe killing it—by tossing out the confessions, he drops the whole bundle into the jurors' laps. Let them hear all the evidence and decide it. Why should Porta go out on a limb to make a tough decision he doesn't have to make?"

"Okay, from a practical standpoint, that makes sense. But then why have the Huntley hearing at all?"

"Because the United States Supreme Court said so. What's the big deal? We'll have a chance to go through the whole thing again when we have a voir dire on the confessions in front of the jury. And then we'll tear them apart with our medical stuff."

"Sam, don't you think it's a bit ludicrous to go into a voir dire in front of the jury when the judge is automatically going to deny our motions to suppress the confession again?"

"But this time he's going to let the jury decide it as a question of fact—if they believe our evidence they can throw it out, if they believe the police they can consider it as evidence. That's the way the Supreme Court figured it'd be fairer to the defendants."

"If the jurors are aware people, they'll know the judge has already decided it was voluntary beyond a reasonable doubt. And if they're not aware, why the hell do we want them on our jury?"

"Porta decided it, practically speaking, as a question of law. The jury will decide it as just some more facts in the case. That's the system, Sandro. I told you, come the millennium, it'll all be perfect."

They entered the building and took the elevator up to the eleventh floor. As they entered Part Thirty-five, they saw the spectators' seats in the large courtroom filled. There were more than two hundred people there, men and women, young, old, black, white, and all variations between, well dressed and not so well dressed. This was a random sampling of New Yorkers, making up the panel from which the jury would be selected. Ellis was already seated at the prosecution's counsel table. Sam and Sandro put their briefcases on the defense table and sat down. Siakos hadn't arrived yet.

"We have to break these jurors in, Sandro. There are a couple of things they'll have to live with if they're going to sit on this jury—Alvarado's record, cop-killing, confessions that were beaten out—"

"How about the narcotics?"

"Right. Whatever Ellis'll throw at us during the trial. I'd rather shake up prospective jurors that we can challenge than sworn jurors that we're stuck with during the trial."

Siakos arrived and joined them at the counsel table.

PART 35

The court clerk went into the judge's chambers. Shortly, thereafter the door opened again, and a court officer, who had been with the judge, came out. He looked about the courtroom and then pounded the door twice. Judge Porta swept into the courtroom, trailing his long black robes and the court clerk behind him. He ascended the bench. The clerk returned to his desk.

"All rise. Hear ye, hear ye. All persons having business in Part Thirty-five of the Supreme Court of the State of New York, in and for the County of New York, draw near, give your attention, and ye shall be heard. The Honorable Gaetano S. Porta presiding," the officer announced.

"Bring out the prisoners," the judge instructed another court officer.

A door next to the judge's bench opened, and Hernandez and Alvarado entered the courtroom. Hernandez was in a gray suit. Alvarado was wearing a Madras jacket two sizes too big. He must have borrowed it from another prisoner, and could not be too choosy about fit, style, or season. They sat at the defense table. A guard sat behind each of them.

"You may proceed, Mr. Ellis," said the judge.

Ellis rose and faced the entire panel sitting in the spectators' area.

"Ladies and gentlemen, my name is David Ellis. I'm the assistant district attorney in charge of the prosecution of this case. The name of the case is People of the State of New York against Ramon Hernandez and Luis Alvarado. Mr. Nicholas Siakos is the counsel for the defendant Hernandez. And Mr. Samuel J. Bemer and Mr. Alessandro Luca are the attorneys for the defendant Alvarado. Now this is a trial for murder in the first degree, the defendants being charged with the death of one Fortune Lauria, who, it will be revealed in evidence, was a policeman of the City of New York."

Many heads in the panel turned, and a slight murmur rose in the room.

"I am making this preliminary statement so that you will understand the type of case on which you are going to be asked to serve, and so you get to know the names of the defendants and their attorneys. This is a case which might involve capital punishment. But that does not come into play in the first part of the trial. Only if the defendants are convicted. However, you should know that, too, in the event that you may wish now to make any application to be excused from this trial. To save time, rather than asking individually, I'll ask any persons who have moral scruples against capital punishment in the proper case—and I emphasize that, in the proper case, where the defendant may be proven guilty beyond a reasonable doubt—any persons who have such scruples, please rise so that you may be brought to the judge's bench to see about being excused."

About sixty percent of the panel rose and began to line up before the judge's bench. Ellis sat at his table while the judge began to excuse the jurors who had risen.

"Looks like not too many people are for execution these days," said Sam. "That's a good example for the rest of them, makes them feel bloodthirsty."

Finally, the first prospective juror was asked to sit in the witness chair. Two others were brought up to sit closer, so that there would be no delays in the flow of traffic. Ellis rose.

"Now, Mr. Randell," Ellis said, looking at a card the clerk had handed him, "I see that you're a real estate broker."

"Yes, sir."

"Have you ever been a juror before?"

"A few years ago. On a civil case."

"And did you get an opportunity to go into the jury room to deliberate with your fellow jurors in that case?"

"No, it was settled."

"You know, of course, Mr. Randell, and if I'm speaking too loudly, it's because I want everyone in the room to hear the questions." Ellis turned. "I'll ask everyone in the room to listen to the questions being asked, so that if there is anything that comes to mind as a result of questions asked of another prospective juror, when you come up on the witness chair, you can save us time by just mentioning it. Now, Mr. Randell," Ellis continued, turning back, "you know that the jury in a civil case does not have to agree unanimously. You need only five sixths or ten out of twelve members of a civil jury to reach a verdict."

"Yes, sir."

"But in a criminal case, unanimous verdicts are necessary. You do understand that?"

"Yes, sir."

"Now, there may be some things about the law that you may not like, may be surprised at, but if the judge tells you what the law is, will you follow His Honor to the letter of that law?"

"If the judge says so, sure."

"Have you ever been the victim of a crime?"

"No, sir."

"Have you any friends or relatives who are on the police force, or are in any fashion connected with law enforcement?"

"I have a couple of friends who are policemen."

"Do you feel that this friendship will interfere with your giving an objective verdict in this case?"

"Not at all, not at all," he smiled.

"He's too willing to please the D.A.," Sam whispered to Sandro.

"Do you feel that you could deliberate with your fellow jurors in this case, and reach a verdict, if a verdict is at all possible?"

"Sure."

"The fact that this is a crime of violence wouldn't deter you from making a decision, even if that decision might have serious implications for the defendants?"

"Not at all."

"You realize that you are not to be at all involved with questions of punishment?"

"Yes, sir."

"That's the function of the judge."

"Yes, sir."

"And sympathy has no place in your verdict either, you understand?"

"Yes, sir."

"I don't like this guy either," said Sandro.

"Okay. Always follow your feelings when you pick a jury. There's not too much else to go on, and the defendant's life is at stake."

"And you feel that you could be fair, both to the defendants and the people?" Ellis continued.

"Yes, sir."

"No challenge for cause," Ellis announced.

"I'll take him," Sam said, rising. "Mr. Randell, would you accept the word of a policeman just because he's a policeman, or would you give him the same test of credibility you would give any witness, that is, watch his demeanor on the stand, listen to what he says, weigh it in your mind as to veracity and accuracy?"

"Well, that's hard to say. A policeman is a policeman, after all. He should know."

"Mr. Randell," Sam continued, "would you feel that if a policeman gets on the stand and testifies, that he's telling the truth because he is a policeman, and policemen don't lie?"

"I'd have to be shown that he lied. I'd go along with the policeman unless somebody showed me he was lying."

"And if someone not a policeman was on the witness stand and testified that a policeman beat the defendants in this case, in order to cause them to confess to a crime, would you, in all honesty, have a tendency to disbelieve that, or would you be able to listen to such evidence objectively and make up your mind after you heard all the evidence?"

"I'd have to have it proven to me, that a policeman'd do that. I find that kind of hard to believe. Sort of television and movie stuff."

"Do you start out believing, then, Mr. Randell, that policemen do not beat defendants, and that a defendant would have to prove to you that he was beaten?"

"My feelings would be with the police."

"I challenge this juror for cause, if Your Honor please," said Sam.

"Overruled. I don't think sufficient cause has been shown," said the judge. "Continue."

"Mr. Randell, you are saying that you would believe policemen, merely because they are policemen, and you'd stick with those feelings, giving the policemen the edge, the benefit of the doubt?"

"Yes. After all, if we can't believe our policemen—"

"I press my objection," said Sam.

"I don't think there's been any showing of cause, Your Honor," Ellis said, rising.

PART 35

"I'll excuse the juror," the judge said. "Thank you. You're excused, Mr. Randell." The juror rose and walked back. One of the two prospective jurors who had been brought closer took the witness stand, and another came up to take his vacated chair.

The man in the witness chair, a Negro, gave his name as Ralph Sanders. Before Ellis had a chance to ask more, Sanders leaned over and whispered something to the judge. The judge called all counsel to the bench, where the prospective juror repeated that he had been the victim of a crime of violence, and he didn't feel that he would be able to be objective. The judge excused him with the thanks of the court.

A postal clerk named Alan Stern was next. He had never been on a jury before, he answered Ellis. He was not a friend of any police or enforcement official, he would accept the court's view of the law, and he felt that he would be objective and fair both to the people and to the defendants. Ellis had no challenge for cause.

"You question this fellow, Sandro," said Sam.

Sandro rose.

"You understand, Mr. Stern, that any effective verdict in this court must be unanimous."

"Yes."

"So, you understand that your vote would be *the* important vote on this jury, for without your vote there could be no verdict here?"

"I guess that's so. Yes, I do understand that."

"Mr. Stern, do you understand the concept that the defendants are presumed to be totally innocent of the charges of which they are accused?"

"Yes, sir."

"Do you understand that to mean that as he sits here in this court, my client is presumed to be as innocent of this crime as you are, or I am, or Mr. Ellis is?"

"Yes, sir. That's his Constitutional right."

Sandro had mixed feelings about Stern's answer. It was good, because it meant Stern had brains in his head, he might understand the legal complexities of the case; it was bad because Ellis probably did not like Stern's reference to the Constitution.

"And do you understand further that the defendant does not have to prove anything in this court?"

"Yes, sir."

"That he can just sit here, and if the district attorney doesn't, all by himself, convince you beyond a reasonable doubt of the defendant's guilt, you would be required to acquit the defendant?"

"Yes, sir, I understand that."

"You don't find that too burdensome a requirement for the district attorney, do you? You don't resent it, so that you'd give the D.A. a little edge in this trial, do you?"

"Not at all."

"Would you promise that if you were picked as a juror in this case, you would hold the district attorney to that burden of proof, that is, make him prove the defendant's guilt to you beyond a reasonable doubt?"

"Yes, sir."

"Now in so holding the D.A. to his burden of proof, do you further understand that there are several elements to the crime charged here, and that you have to be convinced of the defendant's guilt beyond a reasonable doubt regarding each and every one of those elements before you can vote for conviction?"

"Yes."

"Mr. Stern, should you be convinced beyond a reasonable doubt that the defendant is guilty of say four elements of a crime, but there were five elements, and after deliberating you were not convinced about the fifth element beyond a reasonable doubt, would you hesitate to acquit?"

Stern studied Sandro for a moment. "No, sir."

"Do you understand that at the end of the case you do not have to be convinced of the defendant's innocence beyond a reasonable doubt?"

Stern was hesitant. "I'm not sure I get you."

"In other words, you may be convinced about certain elements of the crime beyond a reasonable doubt, and there may be others about which you haven't been convinced beyond a reasonable doubt. At that point, you would be convinced, perhaps fifty-fifty, that the defendant was guilty, and the same percentage that he was innocent. At that point you wouldn't be convinced beyond a reasonable doubt he was guilty, right?"

"Right."

"Do you understand that you would then have to vote to acquit under your oath as a juror?"

"I got it. Right."

"Do you have any quarrel with that concept?"

"None."

"In other words, Mr. Stern, anything short of being convinced of guilt beyond a reasonable doubt requires an acquittal. Do you accept that?"

"Right."

"Would the fact that the defendant might have been in trouble before in his life, might have been convicted of using narcotics, would that make him in your judgment a totally useless person, capable of every sort of crime? Do you think a person could get in trouble with drugs and yet not be a murderer?"

"I accept that as a possibility, that the fellow needn't be a murderer."

Sandro walked back to the counsel table. "Do you think I should go further into the narcotics bit?"

"No. I'd keep this guy," Sam said, "but I don't think Ellis will."

"I have no challenge for cause," Sandro announced, sitting down.

Siakos stood and asked Stern about testimony by policemen. Stern said he would not accept a policeman's word merely because he was a policeman. He believed a policeman could make mistakes, even lie. Siakos had no challenge for cause. He sat.

Ellis half-rose in place. "The people excuse the witness, Your Honor."

"That's one peremptory challenge for Ellis," said Sam, marking it in his notes. "Twenty-nine to go."

The next prospective juror was a woman named Edna Santangelo, a retired secretary. She was about sixty-five years old, from Sam's guess.

"I don't like her," said Sam as Ellis was questioning. "She lives alone and is probably scared to death of crimes of violence. She'd vote everybody guilty just to get them off the street."

"You want to challenge without wasting time?" Sandro asked.

"No, you can't do that. The rest of the jurors might take offense that you cut her short without giving her a fair chance. Question her, Sandro, drive home the bits about not having to be convinced beyond a reasonable doubt of innocence in order to acquit. If no one gets her for cause, we'll challenge her peremptorily."

Sandro questioned Miss Santangelo at some length. After he sat, Siakos questioned her. Ellis said she was satisfactory to the people. The defense challenged, and she was excused.

The judge took a luncheon break at this time, telling the panel to return to the courtroom at two fifteen.

The first prospective juror after lunch was an electrical engineer named Howard Munchen. Ellis found him without challenge for cause.

Sandro rose and asked the usual questions about the burden of proof and reasonable doubt. Munchen's answers were satisfactory.

"Mr. Munchen, I assume you've heard, read about, probably seen on television some things relating to narcotics and narcotics addiction."

"I haven't made a study of it. I've some familiarity with it."

"And do you find a person who may be addicted to narcotics loathsome per se, or would you put him in the same category as anyone else who has given in to a temptation of the flesh, such as someone addicted to alcohol, or someone addicted to gambling?"

"I would imagine they all have their start in the same place, some kind of weakness."

"Can you accept as a possibility that a person might be addicted to narcotics, just as others might be addicted to alcohol or gambling, and still hold a job, earn money?"

"Yes, I'm sure there must be people like that."

"And, Mr. Munchen, can you accept the idea that an addict might be employed, might have sufficient money to afford to buy narcotics, and not have a propensity to commit crimes?"

"I'm sure that's also possible."

"So that, Mr. Munchen, you would accept the concept that it is not addiction to narcotics, but the need for funds to buy narcotics, that might cause a person to commit a crime?"

"Yes, surely."

Sandro was pleased with Munchen's answers. He was going to use him as a sounding board to hammer home the idea for the other prospective jurors.

"And also, Mr. Munchen, that a person *not* addicted to narcotics or anything else, might have a need for funds—to buy a car, to pay for his wife's operation, to impress a new girl friend—and might commit a crime to obtain money?"

"Sure."

"Would you accept the idea that a person might have been convicted of a crime relating to narcotics at one time in his life and still not be a murderer?"

"Yes."

"And would you be able to hold off judgment of such a person until all the evidence was presented, and if you were not convinced beyond a reasonable doubt, would you have any hesitation to acquit?"

"None."

"I have no challenge for cause, if Your Honor please." Sandro walked back to the counsel table, as Siakos stood to examine.

"What do you think of him, Sam?" Sandro asked.

"I like him. He's a professional man, he's educated, he's an engineer, he can handle figures, make sure everything is supported, stands up properly. He's outspoken. I like him. What about you?"

"I agree."

"What about you, Luis?" Sam asked Alvarado.

Alvarado shrugged. "It's up to you. You know more about those things than me."

"Do you have any particular dislike of him. Is he all right?"

"He sounds okay to me. I leave it to you."

Siakos finished with his questioning. He had no challenge for cause.

Ellis rose. "The people will excuse the witness."

"You're excused. Thank you," said the judge. "Next."

"That's two for Ellis," said Sam, making another notation.

By the end of the first day they had examined nine prospective jurors and selected none.

The next morning an attorney from the police department legal bureau was in court with a copy of Sandro's subpoena of police documents. The subpoena was three pages long and covered every imaginable piece of paper and record in the file. The police attorney argued that the range of the subpoena was far too broad. Judge Porta disagreed. This was, he said, a capital case, and he wanted to permit the defendants every possible opportunity to uncover the truth and defend themselves. The police attorney countered that the material would take at least three days to assemble because it was widely scattered.

"At the rate we're picking jurors here, you can have five days if you want," the judge told him.

Jury selection resumed. Prospective jurors continued to walk up to and away from the witness chair. Not one was selected that morning either. By lunchtime, each side had used three more of its thirty peremptory challenges.

During that afternoon, an advertising agency account executive in his late thirties named Richard Haverly took the stand. He seemed to be fair and objective. Sam kept questioning him, giving him much the same treatment he would have given to a prospective juror he thoroughly detested.

After Siakos finished questioning, it was the consensus that Haverly was acceptable. He was sworn in as the foreman of the jury and took his place in the jury box.

No other juror was selected during the remainder of that day.

Haverly, as a member of the jury, was segregated from the rest of the panel still sitting in the spectators' section. He went to the jury room during cigarette breaks, and was admonished upon leaving court at the end of the day not to talk to anyone concerning any aspect of the case.

In the middle of the third morning of questioning, after four more prospective jurors had been examined and refused, a Negro cashier with the city's housing authority, who spoke proudly of having sent his three children to college, was selected as juror number two. His name was Roscoe Anderson.

Toward the end of the afternoon, a widow of about fifty-five, whose

PART 35

husband had worked for the New York Central Railroad, was selected. Sam seemed to regard women jurors with deep misgivings. Nevertheless, she had answered all the questions objectively and seemed otherwise to be a fine selection. Sandro thought she looked motherly, a little overweight, inclined to mirth and goodwill.

"At this rate, Sam," Sandro said at the end of the third day, "it'll take us two and a half weeks just to impanel a jury."

"You haven't counted the four alternates, in case some of the regulars get sick," Sam corrected. "That makes it a smidge better than three weeks."

On the fourth day, they picked three more jurors. The number four juror was an older man, short, chubby. His name was George Simkin. He was a salesman for a shoe company. He had been active in civil rights and mentioned having been in the march on Washington with the Reverend Dr. Martin Luther King, Jr. The number five juror was a telephone repairman named Arthur Youngerman. He had just married, after returning from army service in Vietnam. The number six juror was a man in his forties, bald on top, named Anthony Fresci. He was an insurance salesman, who at one time had been a prizefighter.

In the middle of the morning of the fifth day, Sandro was questioning a young bookkeeper who seemed a good prospect. Sandro was sure Ellis would challenge him peremptorily, and he decided to try the tactic Sam had used for getting Haverly, the foreman, through. Sandro kept asking questions, looking dissatisfied with the prospective juror, as if probing for some flaw that only he knew was there. To his amazement, he found one. The man was fair and objective about everything, but he refused to consider the possibility that a narcotics addict could perhaps not be a dangerous criminal.

The judge refused to excuse the juror for cause.

Sandro walked back to the counsel table and sat down. "Christ, I was sure that guy was going to be number seven. If he just hadn't answered that question like that."

"What lies beyond what is, is not," murmured Sam. "Forget it, and challenge him when you get the chance."

Sandro didn't have to. Ellis did.

By the end of the fifth day, there were ten jurors. Number seven was a bearded man named Nicholas Spoda, who taught music in a city high school. He was unmarried. Sam thought he would be sympathetic because the popular imagination arbitrarily links musicians and drugs. Number eight was a retired executive buyer for Saks Fifth Avenue named Dora Kleinsinger. Number nine, Harry Magnusson, was vice-president of a large company that exported and imported home furnishings. Number ten was a Negro letter carrier named Clarence Noble.

The judge, before dismissing the jury for the night, admonished all the jurors not to discuss the case with anyone. He then asked the court clerk to send for a new panel, because there was no one left of the original two hundred.

By the end of the sixth day, the final two regular jurors had been selected. Morris Apfel was number eleven. He was in textiles and was a grandfather of six. Charles Hanrahan was number twelve. He was a retired rewrite man on the foreign desk of the Associated Press.

During the morning of the seventh day, the jury-picking stalled again, with the alternates not yet chosen. Among those excused was a man who identified himself as an equine podiatrist. The score of peremptory challenges used by now was seventeen for Ellis, twenty-three for the defense.

That afternoon, the four alternates were picked. Solomon Roth, a fur salesman in his forties, was the first of them. The second was Michael Sobiestz, a baker. The third was Arthur Kovinsky, a time salesman for an advertising agency. He did not know Richard Haverly. The last alternate was named Philip Littick. He was a negative-opaquer for an offset printing plant.

"Gentlemen and ladies of the jury," the judge said after the entire jury box was filled with sworn jurors and alternate jurors. "It is now three thirty on a Friday afternoon. Although it is still early for court work, I think that the foreman and the other jurors who were picked first need a little rest, as do the lawyers, as does everyone, before we begin what may be a long trial. So, I'm going to excuse you until Monday morning at ten A.M. Please be prompt, as we want to get started on time. Do not discuss this case with anyone, and do not let anyone discuss it near you. Good afternoon." The judge turned toward the lawyers. "Counsel, please be prompt. You shall open to the jury at ten A.M."

"Well, Sandro, this is it," said Sam. "Don't worry. If we're not prepared, no one ever was."

They walked out of court together.

CHAPTER II

SANDRO ENTERED JUDGE PORTA'S CHAMBERS on the seventeenth floor of the Criminal Courts Building.

The woman behind the desk looked up from her typewriter and smiled. "Yes, may I help you?"

"I'm Alessandro Luca. The judge said defense counsel might come up to look at some records we subpoenaed from the police department and the Department of Correction."

"Oh, yes, Mr. Luca. I'm sorry I didn't recognize you. I was all involved in typing one of the judge's opinions. The judge is not in, but he did tell me to expect you. Are the other lawyers coming?"

"Perhaps Mr. Siakos. I'm not sure."

"Well, I've set everything up in this office," the woman said. She rose and led Sandro to a small cubicle. There was a desk, and on it were several thick envelopes. "The judge said you could stay as long as you like." She smiled sweetly, quickly, and left Sandro alone.

Two of the envelopes were filled with pages of photostatted police reports and DD5's—printed supplementary report forms filled out and signed by police force members who participate in an investigation. Sandro set about sorting out the records. He read each page carefully and, when finished, placed it on a pile according to subject matter, so that he could find what he would need during the trial when this material would be officially turned over to him.

One thick pile was for the DD5's that described interviews with the tenants of all the buildings in and around 153 Stanton Street on July 3rd, 1967. Many officers had been involved in this aspect of the investigation. Each building was reported on a separate DD5, with entries for each tenant by apartment number or name. All results were negative. No one had seen anything.

Sandro was surprised to find a DD5 concerning an interview of Mrs. Salerno. She told the police she saw a man moving on the fire escape, a very dark Negro, but she didn't see his face. She told me she didn't see anything, Sandro thought. No matter, not seeing the face was just as good.

A second pile was for DD5's which verified the ownership of every car that was parked on Stanton Street, Suffolk Street, or Norfolk Street on July 3rd.

Sandro also separated the DD5's recording interviews with every store owner on Stanton Street. These, too, had been negative.

There were miscellaneous DD5's, some relating to telephone calls that were traced in the search for the person who had made the phone call about prowlers on the roof; also negative. Some related to the factory across from 153 Stanton Street. No one had seen anything.

In another pile were the DD5's filled out by the officers who had arrested or interrogated Hernandez and Alvarado—Tracy, Mullaly, Johnson, Jablonsky. These DD5's were terse, indicating only that the defendants had been arrested, that statements had been taken, that the case should still be marked active. There was no hint, however, about what had been said in those statements.

Sandro was pleased to find a DD5 made out by Mullaly on July 9th, 1967, that reported an interview the big Irishman had had at the station house with two men named Quinones and Arce. They lived in an apartment on 119th Street in El Barrio, which had been burglarized the morning of July 3rd, 1967. They had identified as their own the property in the valise taken from Hernandez's car, as well as the goods Hernandez had pawned.

Sandro next separated the reports from the police department laboratory. Here it comes, he thought. He read them quickly, then, incredulous, read them again. The lab investigation showed that there had been no fingerprints belonging to Alvarado in the Sotos' apartment. All the prints belonged to Soto or his family. There were also none of Alvarado's on the stolen property or in Hernandez's car. Only a fragment of a fingerprint had been found on the patrolman's gun, and that fragment could not be identified.

The lab reports also stated that the door of Soto's apartment had been opened by a force other than a jimmy, probably a kick-in.

Sandro finished the police reports and returned them to their envelope. He searched through the Department of Correction records, and drew out the medical diagnosis report that had been sent back to the Tombs from Bellevue on July 10th, 1967. It contained the findings of a Dr. Edward Maish who was on duty at the Tombs late on the evening of July 9th. The report indicated that Alvarado had been found on the floor of his cell in the throes of a clonic seizure. That was a new one, Sandro thought. All he had had to go on before was a possibility of internal bleeding.

Dr. Maish's report stated that he had found Alvarado in "an apparent clonic seizure, with Cheyne-Stokes breathing, all his extremities spasmodically shaking, with tachycardia, guarding and rigidity in the abdomen, and exquisite tenderness in the epigastrium. In lucid moments, the inmate claims to have been beaten at the police station prior to being brought to Manhattan House of Detention for Men." Dr. Maish had sent for an ambulance and had Alvarado transferred to Bellevue so that the hospital might "rule out internal bleeding." At the bottom of the diagnostic report, Dr. Waxman from Bellevue had written that there were no signs of internal bleeding.

With all these other symptoms, Sandro thought, the internal bleeding was now only a minor factor.

Hernandez's medical records were also there. They indicated that Hernandez had been suffering from traumatic pleuradynia when he entered the Tombs. His chest was then strapped, and he was given some medication. These records are a gold mine, Sandro thought.

PART 35

He put all the reports and DD5's back in the envelopes, and put his notes in his briefcase, glad that he had been so hard-nosed about getting these documents. They were going to be very useful—and Ellis couldn't say the source was tainted.

CHAPTER III

Monday, April 1st, 1968

FOURTEEN SOMBER MEN and two somber women filed out of the jury room, into the courtroom, and entered the jurors' box, glancing furtively at the lawyers and defendants. The four alternates sat farthest from the judge's bench. Alvarado was wearing the oversize Madras jacket again. Hernandez watched the jury settle in. Sandro read some notes on the yellow pad before him. Ellis filled a paper cup with water. The clerk polled the jury. The stenographer recorded their names. A court officer pounded the door of the judge's robing room just as it swung open before the judge. All rose.

"Hear ye, hear ye, all who have business with Trial Term, Part Thirty-five of the Supreme Court, draw near, give your attention and you shall be heard. The Honorable Gaetano S. Porta now presiding," announced the officer.

The judge strode to the top of the steps leading to his bench, nodded to the jury and to counsel, and sat. He gathered his robes about him and gazed down at the district attorney. "Mr. Ellis, you may open to the jury." The judge swiveled in his chair, until he was three quarters turned away from the jury, staring straight ahead, his mind at the ready.

PART 35

Ellis rose. He walked slowly toward the center of the jury box and placed his notes on a shelf hinged outside it. He turned to the bench and wrinkled his face into one of its two basic positions.

"May it please this Honorable Court, gentlemen for the defense, Mr. foreman, gentlemen and ladies of the jury:

"At this point in the trial, the law imposes upon me, as assistant district attorney charged with the prosecution of this case, the duty of making what is known as an opening statement.

"Now, the purpose of this opening is merely to preview the evidence you are about to hear or see, so that you may follow that evidence with more facility and understanding.

"In all fairness, I should point out that what I am about to say to you is certainly not evidence. You will get the evidence from the witnesses who appear here to testify."

Sandro watched the back of Ellis's head. Ocasionally, he jotted notes on the pad before him. Ellis rested his hands flat on the jury-box shelf.

"Now, the evidence will show that these two defendants, Hernandez and Alvarado, were friends. They met on the morning of July third, 1967, in the vicinity of Stanton and Allen streets. During a conversation, they decided between themselves to burglarize an apartment, steal some property, sell it, and obtain some money.

"Thereafter, the defendants entered a car, driven by Hernandez, a Chevrolet, bearing Connecticut plates. They proceeded uptown to east Harlem—or, as it is called, El Barrio—where they spent some time. Then, in the early afternoon, they returned to Stanton Street between Norfolk and Suffolk streets.

"Hernandez lived in that block at that time. They double-parked this Chevrolet on the north side of the street near number One sixty Stanton Street. According to a prearranged plan, Alvarado ascended the rear fire escape, and, as he climbed, he looked into each apartment to see if anybody was home. When he got to the roof, he again met Hernandez.

"Now someone saw Alvarado climb that fire escape, and that someone called the Seventh Precinct. A radio car was dispatched to investigate a prowler on the roof of One fifty-five or One fifty-seven, not, mind you, One fifty-three. In that radio car were Patrolmen Roger Snider and the now deceased Fortune Lauria, both in full uniform.

"The evidence will further show that the defendants went down the interior stairs to the top-floor landing, and, by use of a jimmy, they broke and entered the rear apartment, 5B, leased by Mr. and Mrs. Robert Soto."

Sandro made a note about the jimmy, the police lab report still fresh in his mind.

"Meanwhile, the police arrived in the street and proceeded to the rear yard. While there, a back window in a building on Rivington Street opened, and a woman directed the policemen's attention to the roof of One fifty-three.

"Patrolman Lauria went up the fire escape, while Patrolman Snider went back through the courtyard to the street and started up the front stairs of One fifty-three."

Ellis moved down toward the jury foreman.

"Now, the two defendants, in the meantime, carried from the apartment a television set, a radio, and a woman's purse containing a sum of money. They deposited this property on the rooftop. Then Alvarado went down the fire escape, to re-enter the apartment from the window to get whatever else he could find. When he got to the window, Alvarado was unable to raise it because there were screw locks and a metal gate on the inside."

Sandro wrote another note. Apparently they were going to stick with this story about a burglar so inept that he went into the apartment first and then had to climb down the fire escape to discover that the window was locked from the inside. He wondered why.

Ellis, still speaking, moved down to the alternates' end of the jury box. "They began to carry the stolen property over the roof. Alvarado heard noises on the fire escape. He went to the edge of the roof and saw Patrolman Lauria coming up. Alvarado told Hernandez the cops were coming. Then Alvarado hid behind the bulkhead that housed the stairway leading up from the top floor. Patrolman Lauria reached the roof, his revolver in hand. He pointed it at Hernandez, who was standing by the stolen property.

"At this point, Alvarado jumped from behind the bulkhead onto

Lauria's back. He hooked his arm around the patrolman's neck and wrestled the revolver from his hand. Lauria, knocked off balance, fell to his hands and knees. Alvarado stepped back and fired five shots into the back of Patrolman Lauria."

Ellis was silent, letting the effect sink in. He walked back to the jury-box center. Juror number five, the young Vietnam veteran, stared at Alvarado. The foreman just looked ahead, his jaw set.

"Hernandez ran to his apartment," Ellis continued. "Alvarado, still carrying the patrolman's gun, ran across the roof and down the stairs of building number One sixty-one. When he got to the ground floor, he went to the rear of the building, where he dropped the gun near the bottom of the stairs, then he went out the back entrance, and hid in the rear yard for some time. Later he made his way back through the building onto Stanton Street and escaped in the crowd."

Sandro envisioned the rear yards, through which he had walked directly to Suffolk Street several times.

Ellis moved back to the foreman. "Snider found his partner, Patrolman Lauria, lying in a pool of his own blood." He hesitated, letting the blood soak in. Juror number four, the mild-looking shoe salesman who had marched to Washington, stared at Alvarado.

"Patrolman Snider immediately summoned help." Only the eyes of the jurors moved as they followed Ellis.

"Within a very short time, an ambulance arrived, and detectives were swarming all over the place. They removed the body to the fifth-floor landing to get it out of the rain. The detectives carefully removed the stolen property from the roof. A short time thereafter, a doctor pronounced the patrolman dead.

"Now the evidence will show that the detectives began an investigation of these tragic events. Their attention was called to the double-parked car on Stanton Street. One of the detectives, as a result of conversation with people in the vicinity, went to the apartment of Hernandez. Hernandez was questioned. You will hear the various and conflicting stories he gave in connection with the double-parked car. Hernandez was then taken to the Seventh Precinct where he was questioned further. And you will hear all the details of this questioning.

"No one saw the patrolman shot. Hernandez himself supplied the details that I am reciting to you about the circumstances of this crime. As a result of Hernandez's information, Alvarado was apprehended outside his apartment in Brooklyn about one A.M. the next morning.

"Alvarado was brought to the station house, and he, in turn, was questioned. And he supplied the main details about the events on the roof. You will hear testimony as to how he described the manner in which he shot and killed Patrolman Lauria.

"The evidence will show that Patrolman Lauria's gun was found at about ten to four that same afternoon, where Alvarado had dropped it.

"On the morning of July fourth, an autopsy was performed on the body of Patrolman Lauria, and you will hear the assistant medical examiner who performed the autopsy disclose that Patrolman Lauria died as a result of five bullet wounds that entered his back.

"The defendants were booked on the morning of July fourth, and were subsequently indicted for murder in the first degree and burglary in the third degree. The defendants have pleaded not guilty, thereby creating an issue for you, as judges of the facts, to decide.

"Now, before I conclude my statement, there is one thing I want to make crystal clear, and that is the theory of the people's case. These two defendants, while perpetrating a burglary, while in possession of stolen goods, by the actions of Alvarado, shot and killed Patrolman Lauria. This is what is known as felony murder. The people contend this murder took place during the perpetration of a burglary and that both defendants are equally guilty, regardless of which of them fired the fatal shots. I ask you only to listen to the judge when he lays down the law on this point at the proper time.

"I ask you, in the interests of justice, to keep your minds open until you have heard all the evidence in the case and have had the law explained to you by the court. After that, and in the interests of justice again, I will ask you to find both of these defendants guilty of murder in the first degree and burglary in the third degree. I thank you."

Ellis turned, wrinkled his face toward the judge, and sat at his table. He stared at the papers in front of him.

"The defendant Hernandez," announced Siakos, standing to face the judge, "waives his right to make an opening statement, Your Honor."

PART 35

"Very well. Counselor?" The judge looked toward Sam Bemer.

Sam nodded, rose, and walked toward the jury box. He turned toward the judge. "May it please Your Honor, Mr. Ellis, Mr. foreman, gentlemen and ladies. The opening, this preview, as you have been informed by Mr. Ellis, is in no way evidence. It is merely a synopsis of what is to come, and it is our task to show that the people's proof is wanting in many respects, even as outlined by Mr. Ellis.

"We are going to show you that at the time this alleged burglary on Stanton Street was committed, neither Ramon Hernandez nor Luis Alvarado was on those premises or even near them.

"We will show that Luis Alvarado, the man Mr. Luca and I have been assigned by the State of New York to defend, was a very considerable distance away from Stanton Street at the time the burglary and shooting were perpetrated.

"We are going to prove that any admissions Luis Alvarado allegedly made were coerced out of him by the police, that he was supplied and fed certain details by the police, who, in their haste to solve this crime, put a patch-quilt story together and fastened the blame on the wrong men.

"All we ask is that you pay strict attention to the evidence. We ask you to keep your eyes and ears and minds open. When the case is finally submitted to you, we shall have an opportunity to speak to you again."

Sam turned and walked back to the counsel table. "Okay?" he whispered to Sandro as he sat.

"Sure."

"Your first witness, please," requested the judge, looking down toward Ellis. He was facing forward now, impassive, stolid, ready for action. There was no sign of a twinkle in his eyes.

Sam Bemer rose again. The judge looked at him. "Your Honor, I respectfully move that any and all persons who shall be witnesses for either side during this trial be excluded from the courtroom during the entire trial."

"I have no objection, Your Honor," said Ellis, half-rising.

The judge nodded. "Very well. I direct the clerk of the court to enter an order of exclusion of all witnesses," said the judge. "Post a notice on the door."

"The people's first witness is James Loughlin," said Ellis. A court officer opened a door in the side of the courtroom near where the spectators sat. It led to the witness room. The witness room is used exclusively for the people's witnesses. It has chairs and a table, and even an extension of the district attorney's telephone. Defense witnesses are relegated to the public corridors outside the courtroom, where they huddle on windowsills or against the walls. Sometimes they wait in other courtrooms, spectators at other trials. Ellis moved two large diagrams from beneath his table, careful to keep them facing away from the jurors.

Loughlin, a tall man with glasses, walked onto the witness stand, raised his right hand, and was sworn. He testified that he was a civil engineer employed by the district attorney's office. He went to the scenes of crime to measure and thereafter draw scale-model diagrams of the physical layout to aid the jury. He said he had gone to 153 Stanton Street and took measurements there. Ellis showed Loughlin the two diagrams. Loughlin identified them as diagrams of the scene as he saw it on July 10th, 1967. One diagram depicted the rooftop of 153 and several adjoining rooftops, as well as the street in front. The other showed the hallway where Lauria's gun was found and the backyards. Ellis introduced the diagrams into evidence without objection from defense counsel. They were marked people's exhibits 1 and 2. Loughlin described the scene on the diagrams and his markings. They were drawn on a scale of one-quarter inch to the foot. Ellis turned the witness over to the defense.

Siakos rose and said he had no questions.

"We don't want anything from this witness, do we?" Sam whispered, leaning toward Sandro.

"Why not get the exact dimensions for the roofs and yards instead of making the jury figure one foot to a quarter inch. Distance is important for the identification," Sandro replied.

"That's good. You take him; he's an easy witness. And while you have him up there, get him to identify your pictures of the scene. The more he identifies, the less trouble we'll have getting them in later."

"Mr. Bemer?" Judge Porta looked to Sam.

"Mr. Luca will question the witness," Sam announced, half-rising.

PART 35

"Very well." The judge swiveled toward the witness and jury.

Sandro walked to the far end of the jury box. He asked Loughlin to give the measurements of the roofs in feet, and to indicate the physical features of the roof of 153. Ninety-nine feet, Loughlin said, separated the eastern edge of the roof of 153 from the stairway of 161, the building in which Ellis had said the gun was found. Loughlin described how the roof of 153 was separated from the adjoining roof—the brick wall at the front, seven feet high, the airshaft at the center, creating a space nine feet wide, and the four-foot wall stretching back from there.

Sandro walked to the counsel table and zipped open a large leather portfolio in which he had Jerry Ball's photographs. One by one, he handed Loughlin seven photographs of the roof, the rear of the building, the front of the building. Loughlin studied his notes and acknowledged each to be a fair representation of the buildings he had inspected.

"Will you be much longer, Mr. Luca?" the judge inquired.

"I have several more photographs, Your Honor."

"I think, then, that we'll recess for lunch. Members of the jury, do not discuss this case amongst yourselves or with anyone else." The judge rose and retired to the robing chambers. The jury filed out. The defendants were accompanied by court officers back to the bullpen.

"And so it begins," said Sam, as he and Sandro gathered their papers.

"Sam, you have your notes. Didn't Ellis say that Alvarado hid in the rear yard? Then went back through the building and got lost in the crowd on Stanton Street?"

"That's what he said, all right," said Sam. "Here it is, right here." He pointed to his notes.

"Look at this picture, Sam. One of the ones I introduced through Loughlin." Sam took the picture in his hands. He sat on the edge of the counsel table.

"I'm glad you told me about putting the pictures in through Loughlin. Look, from this angle you can see straight through from behind One fifty-three to Suffolk Street. No fences, no obstructions, nothing."

"That's right. A straight alley right behind the buildings." Sam nodded. "Why would anybody hide when he could walk out the back way?" He smiled, slapping Sandro's back. "Now let's eat. My treat today. Tomorrow, we'll eat fancy. It's your treat."

After lunch, the clerk polled the jury, saw that all lawyers were present, and sent word to the judge. The judge entered and assumed his bench.

"Have you any further questions?" the judge inquired, looking steadily down at Sandro. He was barely tolerant of the length of the cross-examination. Usually lawyers accepted Loughlin's diagrams and measurements without question.

"Yes, Your Honor." Sandro rose and walked up to people's exhibit 2.

"Mr. Loughlin, when looking across these yards, does this space behind the buildings extend unobstructed all the way to Suffolk Street?" Sandro pointed to the diagram.

"I don't know."

Sandro handed Loughlin defendant's exhibit C in evidence.

"Now, Mr. Loughlin, you identified defendant's exhibit C as a fair representation of the back of the building, including the rear yards, did you not? And that was as of July tenth, 1967. Approximately one week after the shooting?"

"Yes." Loughlin was obviously uncomfortable testifying about things not drawn to a scale of a quarter of an inch.

"Now, sir, I ask you to look at defendant's exhibit C. From behind building number One fifty-three, which you see there, is there any structure or obstruction all the way through to where you see cars parked, in the background of that picture?"

"No."

"And, sir, do you know what street or thoroughfare that is where the cars are parked?"

"That's west." He consulted his notes. "That should be Suffolk Street."

"So that there is no obstruction from the rear of One fifty-three Stanton Street to Suffolk Street?"

"Well, I don't know when the picture was taken. I have nothing in my notes to show that when I was there I could see to Suffolk Street." Loughlin was easing away from the answers Sandro wanted.

"Is there anything in your notes indicating there were any obstruc-

PART 35

tions when you were there on July tenth, 1967, seven days after this event?"

"I have nothing in my notes. I don't recollect any obstruction there."

"I have no further questions, Your Honor."

Ellis looked at Sandro, then Loughlin. "I have no further questions."

Ellis next called for Henry Thomas. Thomas was with the police department's photographic unit. He testified that he visited 153 Stanton Street on the very afternoon of the crime, about four o'clock. He testified that he had photographed the Soto apartment in its ransacked condition; the roof with the stolen articles still on the wall where they had been found by Patrolman Snider; the street with the double-parked car still in place; and the interior of 161 Stanton Street. Ellis offered the photos into evidence.

"Show them to counsel," said the judge.

The defense attorneys studied Ellis's eight-by-ten pictures and asked permission to approach the bench so the jury couldn't hear. Sam objected to a picture of a revolver under a stairway on the grounds that no evidence relating to a revolver had yet been offered, nor to whom it had belonged, nor when it had been found or by whom or under what circumstances. The judge nodded and excluded that photo.

"Off," the judge said to the stenographer, who was recording even these "sidebar" proceedings. The stenographer's fingers lifted from the keys of the machine. "Sam, you know I usually don't interfere," said Judge Porta. "But are you going to let in that picture of the body?"

Sam surprised, took the photos again quickly and studied them. He studied them all again. A mischievous twinkle danced in the judge's eyes. "Just want to see if you're alert, Sam," he whispered. "All right, any other questions of this witness, Mr. Ellis?" he said aloud.

"None, Your Honor."

"Any cross questions?" The judge looked about. "None? Step down. Thank you, sir. Your next witness."

"Rafaela Santos," Ellis called.

Sandro turned to watch the door to the witness room.

"Who the hell is Rafaela Santos?" Sam whispered.

"I wish I knew," replied Sandro. They masked their surprise from the jury.

A thin, young Pueno Rican woman with a pimply, olive complexion entered the courtroom.

"What is she going to testify to?" Sam whispered.

"I never saw her before," said Sandro. He took out his pen.

Rafaela Santos testified that at the time of the shooting she lived in Apartment 1B of 153 Stanton Street, although she had since moved. She testified that she had been five months pregnant on the afternoon of the shooting. She said she had walked out of her apartment to the front door, looking for a friend in the street. It was raining. While standing in the doorway, she said she saw a 1961 Chevrolet double-parked across the street.

"Was anyone in that car?" Ellis asked.

"I saw him in the car." She pointed at Hernandez.

The jurors' eyes swiveled in unison to Hernandez.

"I think you'd better stand up, Mrs. Santos, and come down and show us," Ellis suggested.

She stepped down from the witness chair and walked to within four feet of Hernandez. She pointed right at his nose, then returned to the witness chair.

"May the record show she pointed out the defendant Hernandez," said Ellis.

"It shall be so noted," the judge replied.

"Was he alone or with someone else?" Ellis continued.

"He was with another man."

"Now, this other man, do you see him in this courtroom?"

"Yes." She aimed her finger at Alvarado.

Sam continued looking down at his notebook, writing nonchalantly. Sandro watched in silence.

"Step down, please," said the judge. Mrs. Santos walked over to Alvarado and pointed directly at him. Alvarado's eyes were glazed with a kind of wonder and terror. The witness started back to her witness chair.

Alvarado leaned over and whispered to Sandro, "She a goddamn liar."

"Shh. Don't get excited. Let's hear what else she has to say."

Mrs. Santos continued to tell how the two men she saw were just sitting in the car, conversing. As she was turning to go back to her apartment, she noticed the men start to alight from the car. She walked to the rear of the hallway and entered the toilet closet just outside her apartment. Shortly, as she was opening the door to leave, she heard a noise.

"And when you came out of that toilet, did you see anybody?"

"Yes."

"Who did you see?"

"He was going up the stairs." She pointed at Hernandez again.

They weren't following Soto's story, Sandro thought, and then wondered at himself for even thinking they would.

"What part of the stairs was he on when you saw him?"

"He was on the second step going up."

Mrs. Santos testified she then returned to her apartment. Her son, whom she had left watching television, had fallen asleep on the couch. She put the boy in his bed and returned to the living room, where she began to watch television. She said she heard a noise from the fire escape outside her son's window.

"Did you look out the window in your son's room?"

"Yes."

"And when you looked out the window of your son's room, did you see anybody?"

"Yes."

"Who did you see?"

"He was going up." She pointed across at Alvarado.

"May the record show, Your Honor, that she pointed to Alvarado," said Ellis.

"Do you acknowledge that?" the judge asked.

"Yes, she pointed to Alvarado," Sam affirmed.

Ellis continued. Occasionally, Mrs. Santos hesitated, seeming to have difficulty understanding the questions. The judge ordered the woman who had been assigned as interpreter for Hernandez and was sitting next to him to come up to assist the witness.

"Before we continue," said the judge, "let's have a short recess." He walked to his robing chambers.

"What do you make of her?" Sam asked after the jury had retired.

"She's a liar," Sandro retorted. "I've been in that hallway many times, and from where she said she was standing, she couldn't see anyone on the stairs. And standing on that stoop, on a rainy day, if she could see the faces of two men sitting inside a car eighty or ninety feet away, especially a dark Negro, she's got X-ray vision."

"I think you should cross-examine her," Sam suggested. "I'll take the cops." They walked outside so Sam could light his cigar.

"You got a tough one this time, Counselor," said an old woman with glasses and close-cropped gray hair. She was one of the courtroom buffs, the professional jurors on pensions or disability who hang around the courts to listen to the more sensational criminal trials.

"It's too early to tell much," replied Sam.

"I want Siakos to question her long enough to take us through the end of the day," Sandro said as they paced the corridor. "If I'm to examine her, I want to go to Stanton Street and get some more pictures this evening. Nick, Nick," Sandro called to Siakos. "Can you carry Mrs. Santos until the end of the day? Do you have enough cross-examination to do that?"

"Sure, okay," Siakos said, nodding slowly. "This woman has a motive for coming here, you know? There must be a reason for her coming here and lying for the D.A."

"Case on trial," called the court officer from the door to the courtroom. The lawyers and spectators filed back.

Through the interpreter now, the witness resumed testifying that she saw Alvarado on the fire escape.

"Where was he in relation to your apartment?" asked Ellis.

"He was facing to my window."

"And in what position was he when you saw him facing your window?"

"Face to face." Her hand raised flat, palm down, she made a parallel motion.

Alvarado, according to Mrs. Santos, then ascended the fire escape. She went back to watch television in the living room. In about a half-hour, she heard many shots from the roof.

"Your witness." Ellis sat.

Siakos stood and walked toward the jury box. He wheeled.

"Mrs. Santos, are you married?"
"Yes."
"Legally married?"
"Yes."

Siakos studied her. He asked if she had any prior acquaintance with Hernandez. Although he lived on the same block, she said, she didn't know him personally. She had seen him before, however.

"Are you pregnant now?"
"No."
"Did you have another child?"
"I was pregnant, but I lost it."

Siakos nodded stiffly. His manner was haughty, caused more by nearsightedness than by arrogance. He studied the floor.

"And how many months were you pregnant at the time of this crime, at the time you saw the two men?" He was digging, hoping to come up with something.

"Five months."
"While you were on the stoop, Mrs. Santos, did you see the car?"
"Yes."
"Where was it as exactly as you can tell us?"
"It was at One fifty-nine or something. I don't know the exact numbers of the building. I lived in One fifty-three."
"Was the car across the street from you, or was it on the same side as your home?"
"They was on the same side."

Sandro took one of the photographs that Ellis had introduced into evidence. In it, the double-parked car was pictured on the side of the street opposite 153, approximately in front of 160. Sandro slid the picture unobtrusively across the counsel table toward Sam. Sam studied it and looked up at the witness. He inclined his head toward Sandro.

"Does Siakos know this?" he whispered.

Sandro nodded.

"Same side of you as your house, right?" Siakos inquired.
"Yes."
"In other words, it was parked in front of One sixty-one?"

"Something like that. I can't tell you the exact number of the building," the interpreter said.

"But it was in front of a building that lies on the same side as your house, right?"

"Yes."

Siakos turned away from the witness and consulted his notes. When he turned back, he asked Mrs. Santos what the men were doing in the car. Mrs. Santos, almost unblinking, with dark, round eyes, was watching every move of Siakos, answering his questions without hesitation.

Sandro looked up at the clock. It was only five after four. Siakos had to have another fifty-five minutes of questions to last out the day. Siakos continued, asking her what time it was when she went out to look for her friend and saw the car instead.

"More or less, it was after one thirty when I went out."

"Would you say that this double-parked car was in front of the *bodega*, the grocery store?"

"Yes."

"And the grocery store is on the same side of the street as your building. Correct?"

"Yes."

Siakos turned away from the jury and winked at Sam. He turned back and asked about the previous occasions when she had seen Hernandez.

Sandro looked at the time. Four fifteen.

Siakos asked Mrs. Santos about the time she went into the toilet closet in the hall. She said she had been there only a minute and she came out immediately upon hearing a noise.

"And what did you see?"

"He was going up the steps." She pointed at Hernandez again.

"This gentleman was going up?"

"Yes."

"Where was he when you saw him? Was it in the hallway?"

"He was on the staircase, going up."

Sandro looked at the time. Four twenty. He knew Siakos had little more to question. The judge wouldn't let him be repetitious or ask

PART 35

questions about what she saw on the fire escape because that didn't pertain to his client. Siakos hadn't dented her story in the slightest. Sandro stood and walked toward him. Siakos moved away from the jury and inclined his head to Sandro.

"Stretch it. We need until the end of the day," Sandro urged, pointing to his notes as if offering Siakos an important reminder.

"I'll see if I can. I don't have too much more," Siakos whispered. He looked quickly at the clock, then returned and questioned Mrs. Santos about the length of time she saw Hernandez and how much of him she saw. She said she saw him for about a second or two, from the waist up, as he ascended. Siakos then returned to questions about her son, his TV program, and whether or not it was a cowboy picture.

The judge was becoming restless. The jury began to look at the spectators.

"Are you almost finished, Mr. Siakos?" Judge Porta asked, shifting in his seat.

"Not quite, Your Honor. A few more minutes."

"We'll adjourn for the day. Remember, gentlemen and ladies of the jury, do not discuss this case amongst yourselves or with anyone else. Ten A.M. tomorrow morning."

Sandro looked at the clock. Four forty-seven. He winked at Siakos.

The jury and the judge filed out. The prisoners were escorted back to the Tombs.

"He didn't touch her. Not a bit," Sam said. "She's hurting us bad right now."

"She couldn't have seen what she said. I know that hall," replied Sandro. "There's a wall there, obstructing the view into and out of the rear part."

"You've got to knock her brains out, Sandro."

"I'm going to call Jerry Ball. I hope he's still at his studio." Sandro moved quickly toward the corridor. "I think you ought to go up with us, Sam, to get a view of the place."

Sam took his briefcase and walked to the corridor sighing.

"Okay. Okay. You're finally going to get me over to that lousy neighborhood."

255

CHAPTER IV

IT WAS 6:45 P.M. when Mike Rivera ascended the stoop at 153 Stanton Street. Jerry Ball followed. Behind them were Sam Bemer and Sandro. They entered the first-floor hallway. The stairs lay directly ahead. As they reached them, the rear portion of the hallway became visible. It was on the left beside the stairs. They walked down it toward Apartment 1B, whose door faced them at the end of the hallway.

"So this is it?" said Sam, looking around with displeasure.

"That's the wall I was telling you about," Sandro said, pointing back the way they had come. If the rear part of the hallway had not been visible from the front, the front door could not be seen from where they now stood.

"I guess this is Mrs. Santos's old apartment. This must be the common toilet she went to." Sam opened a door on the right, under the stairway. The toilet had a pull-chain mechanism.

"Let's get cracking," said Sandro. "Jerry has to get back to his studio to develop and enlarge these pictures if we want to have them for tomorrow morning."

"What pictures do you want?" Jerry asked. He put his camera bag down and assembled the flash unit.

PART 35

"Take some looking down here from the front of the hall so we get a view of Mrs. Santos's apartment. Then I want some from the back here, right where Mrs. Santos said she was standing when she came out of the toilet closet and saw Hernandez. Let's see where she was. Mike, stand on the second step, please."

"Okay."

Sandro entered the tiny cubicle. He turned and stepped back into the hallway. "She must have been standing right here." Without moving, Sandro looked toward the front hall and the stairs. On his left he could see the wall supporting the stairs, the wall into which the toilet closet was set. He could also see the banister and the banister post. Sandro twisted and moved, trying to get a view of the stairs. But as long as he remained near the door of the toilet closet, he could see no part of Mike, no part of the front hall beyond.

"That lying bitch," Sandro said. "Sam, come here and look at this."

Sam walked to the spot where Sandro was standing. "You're right, absolutely right. You can't see a goddamn thing from here."

"Take some right from here, Jerry. Get as close as you can to the wall opposite the toilet closet. I want to give her the benefit of every doubt." Sandro and Sam returned to the front of the hallway as Jerry moved his equipment to the back.

"I'll stand by the foot of the steps," Sam suggested.

"Right. Don't even stand on the second step," Sandro added. "And put your hand on the banister post. Lean right against it so we can get you in the picture."

Sam got in position, leaning against the banister, his hand on the post.

"Jerry, take this shot while Sam stands near the steps, so we can get exactly what she said she saw."

"Okay, Sandro, just let me finish with this flashgun," Jerry said absently as he bent over his bag and wound the film into his camera. He stood.

"And when you finish that, let's get a shot of the inside of that toilet closet. And then get a picture of the hall with the closet door open, so we have a picture of which way it opens."

"Okay, Sandro. Is this where you want me to stand to take the shot of the stairs?"

Sandro looked back. "Get back a little, so you can get that closet door in the foreground as a point of reference. Wait until I move out of the way. I don't want to be in the picture." Sandro stepped back. "Can you see me here, Jerry?"

"No. The angle in the wall here by the stairs blocks the whole front hall."

"Okay, take your shots."

"Hey, Sandro, don't you want Sam standing at the stairway when I take this picture?" Jerry called as he sighted his camera.

"Jerry, Sam *is* standing there. Right at the stairway. His hand is on the banister." Sandro looked at Sam.

"Jesus Christ, you know I didn't even see him there," Jerry exclaimed, walking forward to the stairs and looking left to see Sam. "I couldn't see a goddamn thing from back there."

Sam snorted. "Well, I know some broad who said *she* could."

"Not after we get finished with her tomorrow," said Sandro. "Let's shoot the pictures, Jerry."

Jerry returned to his post. The flashgun flared in the dim hallway again and again. Sandro, Sam, and Mike stood motionless as Jerry moved about them.

"Okay, I got them," he announced.

"Great," said Sandro. "I guess you'd better get back right away to develop these things and enlarge them. I want Sam to look around a bit as long as he's here."

"Usual, it takes a veek," Jerry mugged, "but for *you*—"

Sandro smiled.

"Do you want Mike to give you a lift to where you can catch a cab?"

"I think it'd be a good idea. I don't like walking around this neighborhood with all this equipment."

"Mike, could you come back for us? Sam and I are just going to look around a bit," said Sandro.

"And hurry up," said Sam, the unwilling tourist.

Mike and Jerry walked out to the street. Sam and Sandro started for the stairs.

"Soto's apartment is on the top floor," Sandro said as they ascended.

PART 35

"How about these other apartments? Did anyone see anything that day?" Sam asked.

"We canvassed them. So did the police. No one saw anything. Hey!" Sandro exclaimed.

"What?"

"The police canvass on the day of the shooting must have included Mrs. Santos. We probably have a DD5 that includes her in it."

"You're probably right," Sam said. "We can use it on her in the morning. Now we're making some progress, I feel a litttle better about Mrs. Santos."

They reached the top floor. "This was Soto's apartment," said Sandro.

"It doesn't look any different from the others." Sam studied the hall, fixing it in his mind.

"And up here is the roof," Sandro said, walking up. Sam followed. Sandro opened the door, throwing sudden light into the darkness. Startled figures moved through it. There was a sound of running footsteps. Sandro stopped short, and Sam bumped into him from behind.

"Camarones, camarones," someone yelled.

There was a thud as a young Puerto Rican fell, sprawled out, into the light. He rose quickly to his knees, his eyes fixed on Sandro and Sam. The sweat on his face shone in the light. One sleeve of his shirt was rolled up to the elbow. His eyes were wide and wild. His mouth twitched. He reached into his pocket as he got to his feet, his eyes still fixed on the men in the doorway. The light suddenly caught the silver flash of a knife blade.

"Jesus Christ!" Sam moved backward.

The young Puerto Rican, his knees bent, his body poised to spring, held the knife in front of him, underhand, moving it slightly from side to side.

"*No policía, chico,*" Sandro said quickly, summoning up fragments of street Spanish mixed with Italian. "*Yo soy abogado—para un hombre puertorriqueño. No problema, chico. No problema. Va! Va!*"

The young Puerto Rican's eyes shifted from Sandro to Sam. He wheeled and disappeared into the black shadows. His footsteps echoed across the roof. In a moment there came the sound of another roof door several buildings away being opened. The light shone from within, momentarily, before the door banged shut. The night enveloped them again in silence. Sam sat on the top step and opened his tie and top shirt button.

"Sandro. Sandro." The words sounded choked.

"Okay, Sam, it's over."

"So's our goddamn visit. Bullshit . . ." Sam stood abruptly and started down the stairs. He stopped in midflight and turned, spluttering.

Sandro was laughing now. Sam was looking up, pointing a finger at him, apparently unable to say anything. Sandro came down and put an arm around the older man's shoulders, turning him back around. They both descended.

"Screw you and this whole place," Sam said finally.

Sandro laughed. But he didn't think it was funny.

CHAPTER V

Tuesday, April 2nd, 1968

THE COAL-BLACK CIRCLES of Mrs. Santos's eyes stared down from the witness chair at Siakos. He was groping for her motive again, with questions about her husband. Sandro was restive. He had prepared a cross-examination the night before after the visit to Stanton Street; he had Jerry Ball's pictures. He wanted to get at her before Siakos put the jury to sleep.

Siakos turned his inquiry to the stairway on which she said she saw Hernandez. She testified that the stairway was ahead and on the left as she would look from the door of her apartment, that the toilet closet was also on the left, and that opposite its door, on the right, was a blank wall.

Siakos nodded and walked back to the counsel table. "Let me borrow those pictures you showed me this morning, Sandro," he whispered.

Sandro looked at Sam. The jury was watching.

"Better give them to him," Sam said, shielding his annoyance from the jury.

Siakos took the photos, and walked back to the witness. He handed her the picture Jerry had taken in front of the toilet closet. Mrs. Santos identified it as the hallway outside her old apartment.

"Would you say that this photograph fairly represents the way it looked on July third, 1967, with the exception of what appears to be a hand on this stanchion there?" Siakos pointed out the banister post and Sam's hand to her.

"Yes, it looks like it, yes."

Sandro leaned over to look at Sam's notes. "The stupid son of a bitch."

Sam kept writing, not looking up. "All right, forget it. Just listen and see if you can pick up the pieces."

Siakos offered the picture into evidence. Ellis studied it and had no objection. Siakos also offered a picture of the interior of the toilet closet.

"Show it to the district attorney," the judge advised.

Ellis studied the picture. "May I approach the bench, Your Honor?"

Judge Porta nodded. All the lawyers huddled at the sidebar away from the jury. The stenographer slipped in beside the judge.

"Your Honor, for the life of me, I can't see the materiality of a toilet bowl and a pull-chain," said Ellis. "I object."

"May I see the picture, please." A court officer handed the photo to the judge. The judge studied it. From his position in the huddle, Sandro could see Alvarado sitting in the folds of the huge Madras jacket. Alvarado winked his right eye, the one on the side away from the jury. The guard behind Alvarado had his shoes off and was massaging the sole of his foot on the rung of Alvarado's chair.

"What is the purpose of this photograph?" the judge asked in a whisper. "What bearing does this toilet bowl have on the case?" The reporter's fingers recorded the proceedings. The corners of the judge's eyes crinkled.

"Your Honor," Sandro began.

"Let Mr. Siakos speak first."

Sandro turned to let Siakos move closer to the reporter. "Position of the witness," Sandro whispered to him.

"I want to show the position of a person in this little room, and therefore what position that person would have to take in order to exit from it. The exit from this toilet is most germane and relevant," Siakos explained.

PART 35

"You're certainly out in left field with your pants down on this," the judge commented, starting to laugh. The lawyers began to laugh. "Objection sustained," the judge said, resuming his chair at the top of the bench.

Siakos returned to face Mrs. Santos. She testified that the door of the toilet closet opened from right to left as one exited from it.

"That would be toward the front door," Sandro whispered to Sam. "The door would have blocked her view."

In answer to another Siakos question, Mrs. Santos insisted she saw Hernandez on the second step as she came out of the toilet closet. Siakos turned toward the counsel table. "I have no further questions."

Sam nudged Sandro with his knee. "She's all yours, kid," he whispered.

Sandro rose. Mrs. Santos eyed the new enemy warily. She leaned forward, her hands folded in her lap.

Sandro began slowly. He started with her past, her schools, the names of the streets on which she lived in Puerto Rico, the place where she first lived when she came to New York, the date of her marriage. Her memory was average, and he made no great discoveries. Mrs. Santos had relaxed, however.

The judge called a short recess.

When the session resumed, Sandro questioned Mrs. Santos about the toilet closet and the way the door opened. Again she said it opened from the rear of the hallway toward the front. Sandro didn't want the jury to think he was trying to trap the witness, perhaps take advantage of the language difficulty. He showed her a picture of the door; the hinges were on the left as one faced it, making it quite clear that the door could only open from the front of the hallway toward the rear. Judge Porta leaned over to see the picture. He asked Mrs. Santos to look at it carefully. She did, and still insisted the door opened from the rear toward the front.

Sandro looked at the judge. The judge looked back blankly.

"May I show this picture to the jury, Your Honor?"

The judge nodded.

One by one the jurors looked at the picture. Some nodded. They seemed to get the idea.

It was a very little stick, thought Sandro, but the little sticks counted, too.

Sandro continued. Mrs. Santos testified that it had been a short time after noon when she was on the stoop and saw the two men in the car.

Sandro introduced a picture of the front of the building, showing the stoop. Mrs. Santos said she had been bent over from the waist, looking toward the *bodega*, where she thought her friend might be. At that time, she saw the car double-parked in front of the store.

"May I see counsel for a moment," asked the judge. They approached the bench. "How much longer will you be, Sandro? I understand that Mrs. Santos has a sick child at home. Is that right, David?"

"Yes, Your Honor," said Ellis. "She'd like to get home as soon as we can finish. I think the baby has a fever."

"We'll be as brief as we can, Your Honor," said Sam.

"How long do you think, Sandro? If you can finish now, let's do it. Otherwise, if it's going to take too long, we'll take lunch recess now."

"I still have to go through her testimony about seeing Hernandez in the hall and Alvarado on the fire escape. I'll be a bit longer."

"Members of the jury, at this time we will recess until two twenty. Do not discuss this case amongst yourselves or with anyone else." The jurors filed out. Sam and Sandro walked out to the public corridor.

"You keep her up there as long as you want," said Sam. "Let her get nervous and upset about the sick kid. That's tough. She's lying, and we've got to break her one way or another. This is Alvarado's life."

"Okay. I'll give her my Chinese water-torture examination."

When lunch ended, Mrs. Santos resumed the witness chair, eyeing Sandro like some startled, frightened deer.

Sandro walked toward the jury box carrying a pad and a police DD5 filed by a Patrolman Edward Dunleavy. It reported the canvass of all the tenants of 153 Stanton Street on the day of the shooting. The notation next to Mrs. Santos's name was *results negative.*

"Your Honor, I would like to offer this DD5 supplied to me by the police department into evidence as a record kept in the regular course of police business," said Sandro.

"The man who made this out should be on the stand when you

introduce this, Mr. Luca," said the judge. "If Mr. Ellis, however, does not produce the officer who made it out, I'll reconsider my decision. Proceed."

"When for the first time did you speak to the police on July third, 1967?" Sandro asked Mrs. Santos.

"I don't know the exact time," the interpreter translated.

"At the time you first saw them, did they write down anything that you said?"

"I didn't see them writing anything."

"Do you mean they had no paper and no pencil and they were not writing?" the interpreter asked her.

"They had it," was the answer, "but I didn't see them write anything."

"Did they write your name?"

"Yes. Just my name. That is all."

"Did you read it to see what they wrote?"

"No."

"Did you tell them that you saw something in the street that day?"

"No."

"Did you tell them that you had seen something in the hallway?"

"No."

"Did you tell them you had seen something on the fire escape?"

"No. I was too nervous to tell them anything. They asked me. I wasn't able to speak, I was so nervous."

"Did you see the police the next day?"

"Yes. Many days."

"Did you tell them when they came to your house on July fourth?"

"No."

"On July fifth, when the police came, did you tell them what you had seen?"

"No, I don't tell that to nobody."

"You never told what you saw to any policeman?"

"No."

"When for the first time did you know you were to be a witness here in court?"

"A couple of days ago. Detective Mullaly came to my house."

"Detective Mullaly came to your new house? Not in the old place where the policeman was killed?"

"Yes."

"And he told you that you were to testify in court?"

"Yes."

"Did he help you with the answers you were to give in court?"

"No!" Her eyes darkened still more in anger.

"You mean, Detective Mullaly came to your new apartment and said he just wanted you to testify about things you had seen on July third?"

"Yeah, only the things I saw."

"But you never told anyone what you saw, did you?" Sandro asked softly.

Ellis rose. "I object, Your Honor, as argumentative."

"Sustained."

But the jury had already heard it. Sandro walked to the end of the jury box and leaned against it. He wanted the doubt to sink in.

"This car you say you saw in the street, you identified as a Chevrolet?"

"Yes," the interpreter said.

"And you said it was a '61 or '62 Chevrolet?"

"Yes."

"Will you describe a 1961 Oldsmobile?"

"Oldsmobile?" the interpreter asked in turn.

"Yes." said Sandro.

"That is a silly question," the interpreter translated.

"I'm sorry it's a silly question. But I would like an answer anyway."

"No, I don't know how to."

"Will you describe a 1961 Cadillac?"

"You have me confused making all these questions."

"I'm sorry I'm confusing you," Sandro said softly, sincerely. "I will try to be more simple. Please describe a Cadillac of the same year as the Chevrolet you say you saw."

"I know it was more or less that year, because the husband of my—"

"I'm going to object to this answer as far as it has gone, Your Honor. It is not responsive to my question."

"Sustained. Strike it out."

PART 35

"Will you describe a 1961 Cadillac?"

"I can't."

Sandro watched Mrs. Santos silently. The courtroom was silent. Mrs. Santos took a sip of water. Sandro walked to people's exhibit 1, Loughlin's diagram of roofs and street, and asked that Mrs. Santos step off the witness stand. He had her mark the spot on the diagram where she thought the car was double-parked. She put her initials at a spot across the street from her house. She resumed the witness stand. Sandro walked back to the end of the jury box.

Siakos stood and walked to Sandro. "Yesterday she said it was on the same side as her house," he whispered.

"I know. I'll get that right now." Sandro picked up the minutes of Mrs. Santos's previous testimony.

"Mrs. Santos, you recall being here and testifying yesterday?"

"Yes."

"I'm going to ask you if you remember certain questions and answers from yesterday. Don't answer until I read both the question and answer." Sandro thumbed through the transcript. "Page ninety-seven, Mr. Ellis," Sandro announced. "This was the question: 'Was the car across the street from you, or was it on the same side as your home?' And you answered: 'They was on the same side.' Do you remember that?"

"He confused me."

"Just answer the question," said the judge, before Sandro had a chance to object.

"Do you remember making that answer?" Sandro asked.

"Yes."

"And do you recall this next question: 'Same side of you as your house, right?' And your answer was: 'Yes.' Do you recall that?"

"Yes." She was glaring at him.

"And do you also recall this question: 'But it was in front of a building that lies on the same side as your house, right?' And you answered: 'Yes.' Do you remember that question and that answer?"

"He had me confused."

"I'm asking you whether you were asked those questions and whether you gave those answers?"

"Yes." She spat the answer out.

"And when you gave those answers to those questions, were those answers true?" Sandro kept his tone calm.

"He had me confused."

"Just answer the question," the judge instructed. "Were they correct? Were they truthful?"

"No."

"So that when you gave those answers yesterday, they were not true."

"I forgot."

"You forgot the facts in this case?"

The interpreter, standing by her side, put the question to her in Spanish. The witness said something to the interpreter. The interpreter, without interpreting Mrs. Santos's statement, said something else in Spanish.

Siakos rose. "I object to this colloquy. I believe the interpreter should just tell the jury all that the witness says."

"Yes, quite right. Do not have conversations," the judge admonished. "Just answer the question, Mrs. Santos. Madame interpreter, just translate. Did you forget the facts in this case yesterday, Mrs. Santos?"

She stared at Sandro. "Si."

"Yes," said the interpreter.

Sandro walked over to Sam and bent close to his ear. "I just want her to dangle over there," he said. "I'll bet her eyes are cutting holes in my back."

"You're not just kidding," Sam whispered.

Sandro turned and walked back.

"Can you estimate how far away from you this car was?"

"No."

"Well, can you pick out in this courtroom and point to a distance similar to the distance this car was from you? Will you translate that for her please," Sandro said to the interpreter.

"I don't know."

"I'm not asking you to be exact. I am asking merely if you can give us an approximation, more or less."

"I can't say, even approximately."

Sandro measured the distance on the diagram between the stoop and the spot she had pointed out. "The diagram indicates the car was more than eighty feet away."

"If you say so."

"Can you tell me now far away from you I am?"

"I don't know."

"And you say you recognized this man," Sandro pointed to Alvarado, "sitting in that car?"

"Yes."

"Had you ever seen him before that day?"

"Yes."

"When?"

"I don't remember when."

"Well, how many times had you seen him before July third?"

"I don't know. I don't go around counting how many times I see a person."

"Members of the jury," intoned the judge, "at this time we'll have a recess for a few minutes. You may step into the jury room. Do not discuss this case."

Sandro walked to the counsel table. "Well, what do you think?"

"She's getting punchy," replied Sam. "Her answers are getting sloppy."

"Say, Sandro, how much longer are you going to be at this?" asked Ellis, walking over to the defense table.

"A few more minutes, David."

Ellis turned and followed Mrs. Santos through the door to the witness room.

When recess ended, Mrs. Santos again sat in the witness chair, staring at Sandro.

"When you saw Mr. Alvarado, before July third, was he alone or with someone?"

"He was always with others."

"With whom?"

"I don't know. I didn't pay attention."

"Do you remember what he was wearing any other time?"

"Of course not."

"How tall is Mr. Alvarado?"

"I don't know."

"Well, is he taller than I am?"

"I don't know. I don't even know how tall I am myself."

"Well, look at me. Now, is he as tall as I am, or is he taller?"

"Something like that. I don't know. I never set out to measure either."

Sandro didn't interrupt.

"Was it raining when you saw these men in the car?"

"Yes."

"Were the windshield wipers going?"

She shrugged. "I don't think so."

"Did you see a moustache on the face of that Negro in the car?"

"You could see it."

"Were the lights on inside the car?"

"Lights? Not that I remember."

"Were the men in the car drinking?"

"I didn't see them drinking."

"Were they moving, or were they sitting still?"

"I don't know. They were seated like talking."

"Were they facing each other?"

"I don't remember if they were facing each other."

"Were they looking straight ahead?"

"I don't remember."

"Which way were their faces turned?"

"Fronting." She indicated, by hand, straight ahead.

"You said a moment ago you didn't know where they were looking. Now you say you do. Do you or don't you know where they were looking?"

"I don't know. I saw them looking, but I didn't know whether they were looking at the building or where they were looking."

"As you sit here now, you really don't know where they were looking, do you?"

"Well, they were looking, but I don't know where. They did not have their eyes closed."

"You could see inside a car more than eighty feet away, in the rain, that their eyes were open?"

PART 35

"Yes."

"Could you see the whites of their eyes?"

Some of the courtroom spectators snickered.

"No, but I know they were open."

"Could you see the pupils of their eyes, the black dots in the center."

"Can you see mine?"

"Yes, very well."

"Well, the pupils I couldn't see, but I saw they had their eyes open." She leaned back in her chair, then turned to the interpreter and said somethng in Spanish.

"The witness wishes to be excused, Your Honor," said the interpreter.

The judge looked up at the clock in the rear of the court. "We'll have a short recess. Don't discuss this case."

The jury filed out. The judge went into his chambers. The interpreter spoke to a court officer, and Mrs. Santos was led into a room to the side of the bench where the court officers had an office.

Shortly, the interpreter came out. "She's vomiting," the interpreter said, looking at Sandro and shaking her head.

"Lies are difficult to digest," Sandro replied.

The interpreter went to see the judge. The judge reconvened the court and said that the session was adjourned until the morning. After the jury had gone into the jury room and the judge left the bench, Mrs. Santos came out of the room. She was pale and angry. She looked at Sandro once as she walked, aided by a court officer, then continued out of the courtroom.

CHAPTER VI

Wednesday, April rd, 1968

AFTER THE JURY WAS POLLED, the judge entered the courtroom. Mrs. Santos came in through the side entrance and resumed the witness stand.

Sandro rose, carrying Jerry Ball's photograph of the hallway and the banister with Sam's hand on the banister post. He put the picture on the jury-box shelf and looked through his notes.

In response to Sandro's questions, Mrs. Santos testified that when the men were starting to get out of the car, she went back into the building to the toilet closet. She was just leaving when she heard a noise outside in the hallway. She opened the door, she said, and saw Hernandez on the second step of the stairs, going up. She placed an "X" on the photograph at the place where she said she had been standing when she saw Hernandez. The "X" was just outside the bathroom, right where Jerry Ball had stood to take the photo.

"Now, Mrs. Santos, will you tell me who the person is who is standing in that picture, whose hand appears on the banister post?"

"Your Honor, I object," said Ellis, rising. "How can the witness possibly answer a question like that."

"Exactly," said Sandro.

"Sustained."

"Do you see a hand in that picture?"

"I object to this line of questioning," said Ellis.

"Sustained."

"May I show this picture to the jury, Your Honor?" asked Sandro.

"You may, sir."

"Your Honor," said Sandro, "might it be germane if I pointed out the hand in the photograph?" He waited for Ellis's objection.

"I object, Your Honor."

"Sustained. Strike out counsel's remark."

A court officer handed the picture to the jurors. They passed it around. Each one looked at the hand on the post.

Mrs. Santos testified that she then went back to her apartment. Her son was asleep. She lifted the boy and put him to bed, returning to the living room to watch television. She soon heard a noise on the fire escape. She went to the window in her son's bedroom and looked out. There, she said, she saw Alvarado on the fire escape.

"Was he standing on the fire escape?"

"Yes."

"And when you answered Mr. Ellis's questions two days ago, you said you saw him face to face?" Sandro made a motion with his flat hand at eye height, parallel to the floor, indicating from face to face.

"Yes."

"In a straight line?"

"Yes."

"When you saw him face to face was he standing still, or was he moving?"

"I don't remember if he was moving, but I know I saw him. He was going up."

"You say he was going up? Was he moving?"

"I don't remember."

"Was he standing still."

"He was standing there."

"He wasn't moving, then? He was standing still?"

"Afterward I went to my room."

"I object, Your Honor," said Sandro. "I ask that the answer be stricken as not responsive to my question."

"Strike it out."

"Was he moving to go up?"

"I didn't see, because I went into my room."

"So you didn't see if he was moving or standing still?"

"No."

"And you don't know what position he was in?"

"He must have been frontward, because I saw his face."

"When you say, 'He must have been,' you don't know that as a matter of fact. You're just guessing?"

"I saw him. I only saw him," she insisted angrily.

"How long did you see him."

"One minute."

"Was it quick?"

"Yes."

"It wasn't a minute. It was like that?" He snapped his fingers.

"Yes." She nodded. "Fast."

"And then you went to the other room to see from another window. And he was on the stairs then?"

"Yes."

"And his back was to you then as he went up?"

"Yes."

"You saw his face then, didn't you?"

"No."

"You only saw his face from your son's room?"

"Yes."

"How high from the floor is the windowsill in your son's room?"

"I don't know."

"Is it right at the floor?"

"No."

"It's up a little bit?"

"Yes."

"Would it be up here?" Sandro asked, indicating his hips. "At approximately the hip bones?"

"It could be."

PART 35

"It's much lower than the hips, isn't it?"

"No."

She distrusted him enough now to give answers opposite to anything she thought he might want to hear.

"The windowsill was at the hips then?"

"Yes, at the hips."

Sandro showed Mrs. Santos the police picture of the room which had been ransacked in Soto's apartment on the top floor. She said her windowsill was approximately the same height from the floor.

"Now, this fire escape that was outside your son's window. Was its floor right outside at the level of the windowsill?"

"I don't know. I moved from there."

"Well, look at this picture of your old fire escape." Sandro showed her one of Jerry's pictures of the rear of the building, which he had introduced through Loughlin. "The fire escape is right at the level of the windowsill, isn't it?" Sandro held the picture for her to view. She looked at it, but did not answer.

"Is the fire escape platform at the level of the windowsill or not?"

Still she did not answer.

"I'll let you see it a little closer." He walked directly up to the witness. "Does it start at the windowsill, is the question."

"Do you understand the question?" the judge asked.

"It looks enough like it."

"When you saw this man, you were in your apartment, standing on the floor at the window, right?"

"Yes."

"And this man was standing outside, on the fire escape?"

"Right."

"And while he was standing on the fire escape, you were face-to-face level with him?"

"I turned my head to look outside and saw him."

"Face-to-face level, you saw him?"

She nodded. "I saw him."

"No, the question is: were you face-to-face level?" Sandro indicated a parallel line from his eyes outward. "As you were standing inside, looking from that window at the man outside?"

"I saw him. I saw him."

"No, the question is: were you face-to-face level as you stood at the window?"

"Your Honor, I object," said Ellis.

"She has not responded to the question," said the judge.

"I object to counsel's position. He looks like he's ready to pounce on the witness."

Sandro became aware that he was leaning toward the witness, his eyes fixed on her.

"Sorry, Your Honor," he said, backing toward the jury box again.

"Mrs. Santos," said the judge, "the lawyer wants to know, when you saw this man on the fire escape, if your face was on the same level as his."

"Not at the same level, no," the interpreter said for her.

"Wasn't it at a level, face to face, when you first saw him?" Sandro again made the level motion of his hand moving from his eyes.

"I don't remember."

"Two days ago for Mr. Ellis, and five minutes ago, when I first asked you about that fire escape, you said the man was face-to-face level. A moment ago you said you were not at the same level. Now you say you don't remember. Which of your three answers is true? Was he face-to-face level, wasn't he, or don't you remember?"

Mrs. Santos was glaring at Sandro now. She bit her lip. "I was a little lower."

"It was just an inch, wasn't it?"

"No."

"You weren't more than five inches lower though, were you?"

"Yes, I was."

"Fifteen inches lower?"

"I don't know."

"Were you four feet lower?"

"I don't know."

"Were you ten feet lower?"

She didn't answer.

"I have no further questions." Sandro returned to the counsel table.

Sam was drawing figure eights in his notebook. "You destroyed her," he whispered, not looking up from his doodling.

Alvarado slid his hand over and squeezed Sandra's arm. "You my man."

Ellis got up and directed some additional questions at Mrs. Santos in an attempt to clarify some of the discrepancies. He asked a few questions and sat down.

Siakos rose. Sandro watched apprehensively.

"Mrs. Santos, the baby you were pregnant with when you saw these men as you say, did you have the baby?"

"No."

"You lost it?"

"Yes."

"When?"

"In the end of July."

"And you think the men who shot the policeman, whoever they are, are responsible, don't you?"

"No."

"No further questions."

The judge recessed the court for lunch.

"Your Honor," said Sam, "before you leave the bench, may counsel approach?"

"Yes, come up."

They moved close to keep out of range of the jury's hearing.

"Your Honor," Sam said, "based on the developments in this witness's testimony, I feel it might be advisable for us to go with the jury up to the scene of this crime and let them see firsthand what the hallway looks like."

"I go along with that application, Your Honor," said Siakos.

The judge turned to Ellis.

"I don't think there's too much necessity for all that, Your Honor. We do have photographs, particularly all these pictures Mr. Luca has. We've also had the engineer describe the scene."

"Yes," agreed the judge, "and we have the engineer's diagrams. I don't think there's any necessity for taking the whole jury over there. Motion denied." The judge rose and left the bench.

Mike Rivera had arrived and accompanied Sam and Sandro back into the courtroom after the lunch recess. Ellis recalled to the stand

Loughlin the engineer. Loughlin testified that he measured the distance from the windowsill of Apartment 2B in the rear of the building at 153 Stanton Street to the railing of the fire escape of 5B, Soto's apartment. The distance was thirty feet. Loughlin drew a line on a photograph the D.A. handed him and marked it thirty feet. Ellis had no further questions.

"Can that be for the Italian woman?" Sam whispered.

"No. She's not going to testify. Besides, Two-B is the junky's apartment."

Defense counsel had no questions for the engineer.

"Call your next witness," the judge said.

"Carmen Salerno," Ellis called.

"I thought we weren't having the Italian woman." Sam said.

Through the side door came Mrs. Salerno, wearing her ponytail, without makeup. She jiggled keys as her heels scuffed in a sort of strut. "That's not the Italian woman. That's the junky's wife. She's Puerto Rican."

"Well, she's got an Italian name. What's she going to testify about?"

"She told me she didn't know anything. I found a DD5 where she said she saw someone on the fire escape. She wasn't able to identify his face, however."

Mrs. Salerno was sworn by the clerk. Her face was like a mask as she waited for Ellis to question her. She didn't look at Sandro.

Ellis questioned Mrs. Salerno. She testified that she had been in her apartment on the day of the shooting, watching her own child and two children of a friend. Early in the afternoon she heard a squeak of the fire-escape ladder. She did not pay any attention to it at the time. A little later, she heard another sound, like someone climbing the fire escape. She went to her window, the one next to, but not on the fire escape, opened it, and looked down. There was no one below. She looked up and saw a man standing on the fire escape outside the Soto apartment, three stories above. She said the man was standing facing the window. She testified he turned and leaned over the rail, looking down in her direction. She testified she saw his face.

"Do you recognize anyone in this courtroom?" Ellis asked.

PART 35

"Him." She pointed at Alvarado.

"Let her step down," said the judge.

"Walk over to the man you say you recognize, Mrs. Salerno," said Ellis.

She scuffed her heels toward the counsel table and pointed directly at Alvarado.

"Let the record reflect the witness pointed to the defendant Alvarado," said the judge. "All right, Mrs. Salerno, return to the witness chair."

"Here it is," Sandro whispered to Sam. He slipped a sheet of paper between the pages of a yellow pad, and slid the pad to Sam. It was a copy of the DD5 Sandro had been quietly searching for, recording an interview with Mrs. Salerno on July 3rd, 1967, by Detective Anthony Panetta. She told the detective that she had seen a very dark Negro, in a shabby mustard-colored jacket and black pants, moving on the fire escape. She did *not* see his face.

Sam read the document and nodded.

"We should be able to get at her with this," said Sandro.

Sam shrugged. "Ellis has all the DD5's too. He'll probably have her admit this, say she was frightened, like Mrs. Santos. Then you have no discrepancy, and you can't use this to show she's lying."

Ellis asked Mrs. Salerno what happened after she saw the man on the fire escape. She testified she saw one of the policemen as he climbed the fire escape in the rear. He went up to the roof. She heard the shots, Mrs. Salerno testified, and then she stayed in the house with the children.

Sandro was puzzled as Siakos rose to cross-examine. She hadn't even mentioned Hernandez.

She testified that she had never appeared before the grand jury in this case, but she did speak to the police and to the district attorney at the police station the evening of the shooting. Sure, Sandro remembered now, hadn't Alma Soto seen her coming out with Asunta? Soto must have seen her too then, he thought, because he was there before his wife came in. But he hadn't mentioned her, only Asunta and the Italian woman. Something wrong there, Sandro thought.

Siakos was now asking for any statement by this witness or notes concerning her that the district attorney had in his possession. Ellis gave Siakos two handwritten yellow sheets.

"Perhaps the other counsel can read the pages at the same time, so that we may proceed without too much delay," the judge suggested.

Siakos walked over to Sandro and Sam. They laid the sheets out on the table. The notes were made by Assistant District Attorney Brennan, who went to the police station the evening the defendants were arrested. The notes indicated that Mrs. Salerno was on relief, lived with her husband and baby son. She told D.A. Brennan that she had heard a noise in the rear of the building, looked out and saw someone above on the fire escape standing and bending. He had ripple-sole shoes, black pants, and a short yellowish jacket. He was a very dark Negro. She said the man she saw in the station house that night looked very much like the man on the fire escape.

"This identification in the station house is a hell of a lot less positive than the one she gave just now," said Sam.

"Sure, that night he just *looked* like him," Siakos added.

"You see this bit about her being on relief?" Sandro pointed. "And also her husband's a junky. He just got back from doing nine months. He was in Lexington for a year before that."

"How'd they have the baby, then?" Siakos wondered.

"Anyway," Sandro said, "she's probably an easy mark for police persuasion."

"Sure," said Siakos. "She cooperates or they'll bust her husband again. Maybe she wants a big family." Siakos smiled momentarily. He stood and walked back toward the jury box. He put Brennan's notes on the shelf and looked up at Mrs. Salerno. If ever a witness was hostile, it was she. She huddled in the chair like an animal ready to spring.

Siakos asked about her husband and her home. Her husband, she testified, was not employed. He was being given clinic care for narcotics addicts. She said she was on relief. She denied that any policeman or detective had threatened to arrest her husband and send him back to jail if she didn't cooperate. Siakos questioned her about the first noise she said she had heard. He asked if she had seen Hernandez. She testified she hadn't. He had no further questions.

Sandro walked over and faced the witness. He questioned her

PART 35

about the weather on the day of the shooting. She testified that it had been cloudy, but that the sun had come out once in a while.

Sandro introduced the official United States Weather Bureau report for July 3rd, 1967. There was no sunshine whatever, and the sky had been covered by maximum clouds the entire day. It had rained constantly from 11:30 A.M. until 3:45 P.M.

Sandro looked up at the clock. It was now 3:40. He walked toward Sam at the counsel table. "Sam. In a few minutes, why don't you ask the judge for an early adjournment today. I want to go over to Stanton Street and get some pictures of the fire escape while there's still light."

"Okay. Keep at it until about four, then I'll ask him."

Sandro walked back to the jury box. He started on a tangent, asking Mrs. Salerno how she arrived at court that day. She said Detective Mullay drove her. She said she did not know that she was to be a witness in this case until a few days ago. Detective Mullay was the one who had come to her apartment and taken her to the D.A.'s office.

"May I see all counsel for a minute," requested the judge. They approached the bench. "Come on, Sandro. You're fishing around with nothing. She said she saw your man. That's the real point, isn't it? Don't waste time with this stuff."

"Your Honor, Sandro's not trying to waste your time. You know us better than that. We have to defend our client though. It's his life," said Sam.

"I know it, I know it, and I love you like a brother," Judge Porta said playfully, "but for justice's sake, let's get going. If you have some point, I'm not going to stop your questioning. You can question her until doomsday. But when I see you going nowhere, I've got to cut you short."

"Your Honor," said Sam, "we have some investigation to complete today. Do you think we can adjourn now? The investigation pertains to this witness."

"Well, we're not accomplishing anything this way. Are you prepared to cut out this baloney and move along tomorrow?"

"Scout's honor, Judge." Sam raised a three-fingered salute just high enough for the judge to see it, but shielded from the jury.

The judge looked at Sam skeptically.

Sam renewed his shielded three-finger salute.

"Sam, if this young whippersnapper doesn't get down to business tomorrow, you'll both be put on my sentencing calendar for the following morning."

"I have a wife and family," Sam protested.

"Six months of jail for you'll do them good." The judge turned to the jury. "Ladies and gentlemen, the attorneys have requested an adjournment at this time to finish some work relating to the case on trial. I am inclined to grant their application. Tomorrow morning at ten, promptly. Do not discuss the case. Good afternoon." The judge retired to his robing room.

Mike walked up to the counsel table.

"Mike," Sandro said as he collected his papers, "do you remember if Soto said anything about Mrs. Salerno being at the station house?"

"He only said he saw the Italian girl and Asunta."

"You mean the Italian woman."

"No," Mike said, taking his notebook from his pocket. "Here. He said Italian *girl*." Mike handed the opened book to Sandro.

"Son of a gun! He *did* say Italian girl. And then it was Italian woman every time after that, after Mullaly straightened him out."

"So?"

"So Mrs. Salerno is the Italian woman we should have been worrying about all along, the one who looked at Alvarado through the two-way mirror."

"But she's Puerto Rican, Sandro," Sam broke in. "Didn't you tell me that?"

"You're right, Sam. But she's Italian to Soto, just as she was to you. He kept calling her husband the Italian guy downstairs."

"Sure," Mike said. "And Mullaly was faking us out of our jocks about the woman across the yard. He got Soto to keep us worrying about her and not even thinking of Salerno's wife. I hope the next time I run into Soto, I'm in my car."

"Now's your chance. We're going to Stanton Street for some pictures of that fire escape. Sam is going to pose."

"To quote Mike," Sam snorted, "this guy'll burn before I go back to that lousy neighborhood."

CHAPTER VII

SANDRO HAD CALLED JERRY BALL'S STUDIO and found that he was out shooting and was not expected back before 5:30; by then, there would be too little daylight to take photographs in the rear yard. Sandro was holding his own camera as Mike Rivera knocked on the door of Apartment 1B, where Mrs. Santos used to live. It was also the apartment directly under the Salernos'. Sandro wanted to get out on the fire escape to take pictures of the view above.

The door eased open an inch. A man's eyes, watery and red, peered through the opening. Behind him, the apartment was black. Mike addressed the eyes in Spanish. There was a curt reply, and the door shut quickly.

"What did he say?" asked Sandro.

"He didn't want us to go in. He said if we wanted to go on the fire escape we could, but to go through the yard."

"Wonder what's happening in there," Sandro said.

Mike shrugged. "Something. Who cares? Let's go."

Sandro climbed the ladder at the side of the one-story extension in the rear. He stepped carefully onto its roof. His eye level was now about five feet below Mrs. Salerno's window. He looked up to study the Soto fire escape and the steel slats that formed its platform. They were approximately two inches wide, with three-quarter-inch spaces between.

"If someone had been standing up there," Sandro called softly down to Mike, "Mrs. Salerno would have had to look up at him through the bottom of the fire escape, through the steel slats."

"She wouldn't even be able to see his face that way," Mike gauged.

"Right. That's why Ellis had to have her testify that the man leaned over to look down at her."

"That's great. Except if a burglar is looking down, sees her looking straight up at him, and then she disappears, would he stick around to wonder was she maybe calling the cops?"

"Of course not. It's illogical," Sandro replied. "The story she told the cops the day of the shooting makes more sense. She saw the burglar, he didn't see her, and she didn't see his face."

"Yeah, but how're you going to get around her saying that she did see this guy leaning over?" Mike asked.

Sandro studied the fire escape overhead. "You know, Mike, I'll bet that even if a man did look over the rail of that fire escape, the way Salerno said he did, she couldn't have recognized his face. Especially a very dark Negro."

"Why not? It doesn't look that far away."

"It's not. But from where you're standing, the angle is different. From here, looking straight up, there'd be nothing as a background but the sky. He'd be silhouetted. Like someone on a stage where all the light is in back of him."

"Yeah," Mike exclaimed, smiling. "How can you recognize a very dark Negro in silhouette?"

"Mike, go up to Soto's fire escape. Let's take some pictures before all the light is gone. First, I'll take you standing straight on the fire escape, through the slats. Then you bend over the rail and look right down into the camera. If we can't see your face, how could we see the face of a very dark Negro?"

Mike walked back to the alley and disappeared. Sandro waited, camera in hand, standing on the shed. He wondered what was going on inside the Santos apartment. Perhaps another crime was brewing,

PART 35

another defense would be needed. Mike whistled from above. He was on the fire escape.

As they drove uptown, Sandro wound the film and removed the exposed roll so that Jerry Ball could develop and enlarge the pictures for the morning.

"What street does Dr. Waxman live on?" Mike asked.

"Eighteenth. Three-oh-eight east."

"He's expecting us, isn't he?"

"Yes," Sandro replied, "he said this was about the only time he could see me."

"Well, it's more than my wife can say. She doesn't get to see me at all. Which isn't so bad, now that I think of it."

Mike drove to 18th Street and parked the car. They walked to the doctor's house, and Sandro rang the bell. A young man with a blond crew cut answered the door.

"Dr. Waxman?" Sandro asked.

The young man nodded. "You Mr. Luca? Come on in."

The furniture was sparse, and there were many paperback books.

"Doctor, here's the medical report you made out at Bellevue in the early hours of July tenth, 1967." Sandro handed the single sheet to Dr. Waxman. "Do you remember Alvarado? Can you tell me about that night—what Alvarado looked like, if he had any signs of a beating?"

The doctor shook his head. "There are so many cases in Bellevue. I don't remember this." He read his report. "Apparently, I checked out what he was sent for, and I didn't find any bleeding or signs of bleeding."

"How about the other things that were in Dr. Maish's original diagnosis? Clonic seizure, Cheyne-Stokes breathing, all the rest. Do they have anything to do with.internal bleeding?"

"No."

"Did you check anything about his head, Doctor, any head X-rays, or EEG?"

"No, apparently not. We just checked out the internal bleeding. We were only for consultation. The doctor in the prison was in charge of the case."

285

"In other words, the clonic seizure could exist, as it apparently did, even though there was no internal bleeding?" asked Sandro.

"Sure. The clonic movement or seizure has to do with a brain dysfunction. It hasn't anything to do with internal bleeding. It's like an epileptic fit. Lots of people have them and don't bleed."

"And you didn't rule out the possibility that a physical beating caused the clonic movements and Cheyne-Stokes and whatever else there was?"

"I didn't get involved in that. I checked if he was bleeding internally. He wasn't. I couldn't tell you what caused the other things."

"Let me ask it this way, Doctor: if you were called by the district attorney, could you say that the clonic movements and the rest were *not* caused by a beating?"

"I didn't get involved in that. I examined him specifically for one thing. That's all."

"Fine. I guess I need a neurologist to give an expert opinion," said Sandro.

"Can you wait about four years?" asked Dr. Waxman.

"In a word, no." Sandro replied, smiling.

"Neither can I," laughed Waxman.

CHAPTER VIII

Thursday, April 4th, 1968

"AND IN ORDER FOR YOU TO SEE THIS MAN," asked Sandro, "the one you saw standing on the fire escape, Mrs. Salerno, you had to look up through the steel slats. Isn't that right?"

The defiant dark eyes bored into Sandro. "That's right," she released through unmoving lips.

"I show you this photograph and ask you if you recognize what it depicts." Sandro handed Mrs. Salerno the photograph of the Soto fire escape viewed from just below her window. "At the bottom of the picture is the window you were looking from, and in the background, at the top, is the fire escape you say the man was standing on, isn't that correct?"

She studied the picture carefully. "Yeah." She didn't like giving Sandro yes answers.

"And it looks the same as the day when the man was there, doesn't it?"

"Well, those things weren't on the fire escape," she said, pointing to the dark, round mass which appeared through the slats of steel.

"Well, other than these things being on the fire escape then, is this what it looked like?"

"Yeah."

"I offer this into evidence, Your Honor," said Sandro.

"Show it to Mr. Ellis."

Ellis studied the photograph. "Your Honor, I have no objection to this being received in evidence, provided it is understood that whatever these things are that appear up on the fire escape, they were not present at the time."

"On July third?" the judge inquired.

"Yes, sir."

"May I see it, please?" the judge requested.

A court officer carried the picture to the judge. "Those dark objects which appear on the fire escape will be deemed deleted from the exhibit. Otherwise the district attorney has no objection. Received in evidence."

"Defendants' exhibit G in evidence," said the clerk.

The court stenographer marked the photograph and handed it back to Sandro. He walked to the end of the jury box and turned. Mrs. Salerno's eyes had never left him. It was as if she thought he would pounce on her if she let him out of her sight. Mrs. Santos must have told her of cruel tortures at the hands of the cross-examiners.

"Now, Mrs. Salerno, these things, these objects that you see on this photograph which weren't there on July third, can't you tell me what they are?" Sandro handed her the photograph.

"No, I can't," she said with relish.

"If I told you the objects were the feet of a man standing on the fire escape, would you disagree with that?"

She looked at the photograph again. "That's what it looks like to me—a man."

"Mrs. Salerno, didn't you testify a moment ago that you couldn't tell what the objects were up there."

"I thought it was a man, but I didn't—"

"I move the answer, as far as it's gone, be stricken as not responsive, Your Honor," Sandro said, turning to the bench.

"Strike it out."

"Mrs. Salerno, didn't you say a moment ago you didn't know what these *things* were?"

"Yes, but I didn't say what was inside, you know."

"I move the answer be stricken as not responsive, Your Honor."

"Strike out everything except 'yes.' Proceed."

"May I show this photograph to the jury, Your Honor?"

"You may, sir."

A court officer handed the photograph to the foreman. The jurors studied it minutely.

Mrs. Salerno, in answer to Sandro's further questions, testified that on July 3rd, 1967, she didn't know who lived in the Soto apartment, and that as far as she knew, the man on the fire escape could have been the tenant of Apartment 5B.

Mrs. Salerno testified that she had to lean far out of the window and twist to her left to see upward. She testified that it was not raining at the time she looked up, and no rain went into her eyes as she watched the man above.

"And while you were leaning way out, your head twisted to the left, you saw the face of a very dark Negro looking down?"

"I saw him, sure."

"Did he have a moustache?"

"I didn't say I saw that."

"So you don't know if the dark Negro looking down had a moustache or not?"

"I saw him, but…"

Sandro watched her sip a glass of water. He now picked up the photograph of Mike Rivera standing on the fire escape, leaning over the rail, looking directly down at the camera. Mike's face appeared ninety percent shadow, the ten percent being the side of his face away from the building, lit by the late afternoon sun of the day before. He was unrecognizable.

"Can you recognize this?" Sandro asked, handing her the photograph.

"This is a man."

"The same view as you saw from the window on July third?"

"Yes."

Sandro offered it into evidence, and it was accepted without objection. The officer handed the photograph back to Sandro. He held it in both hands and studied it momentarily. He wanted to pique the jury's curiosity. Sandro looked up to the witness.

"Now, on the day that you viewed this *dark* Negro on the fire escape, his head was outlined against the sky as in this picture, wasn't it?"

"Yes."

"In other words, the *dark* Negro's face was silhouetted against the sky, wasn't it?"

Her eyes narrowed slightly. "I don't know what you mean by that."

"There were shadows on the dark Negro's face, weren't there?"

"What do you mean by shadows."

"You know what a shadow is, don't you, Mrs. Salerno?"

"Yes."

"Was the man's face covered with shadows?"

"I don't know exactly what you mean by shadows."

Sandro looked again at the photograph in his hands.

"The dark Negro's face had about the same amount of light on it as the face in this photograph. Isn't that right?"

"About the same."

"His face was covered with shadows when he was looking down, wasn't it?"

"I don't know exactly what you mean."

"May I show this photograph, exhibit H, to the jury, Your Honor?"

"You may, sir."

The jury grabbed it up. Sandro walked to the counsel table and sat. He and Sam watched the jurors devour the photograph.

When they had all viewed the photo, Sandro continued to question Mrs. Salerno. She testified that when the police came, the man had long disappeared. She testified that the man she had seen, as far as she knew, might have even descended the fire escape and walked away through the yard before Lauria made his fateful climb.

Mrs. Salerno testified that she saw the police in the building after the shooting, and went to the station house that night. There, she viewed Alvarado through a two-way mirror.

Sam signaled him. Sandro walked over to the counsel table. Sam handed him the notes that the assistant D.A., Brennan, had taken at

PART 35

Mrs. Salerno's interview. He leaned toward Sandro and whispered, "That sure as hell is your Italian woman. Here's your chance to get her."

Sandro introduced Brennan's notes into evidence.

"You were not as positive in the station house, when you spoke to the D.A., as you are here at this trial, were you?"

"I don't understand. You better say that again."

"On July third, you said the man you saw in the station house only looked like the man on the fire escape."

"I had my reasons for it."

"You had special reasons for not telling the district attorney what you knew about this case?"

"Sure, I had my reasons."

"Do you have special reasons for telling the jury what you're telling them?"

"No, only then."

Sandro studied her, as if to contemplate her reasons. The jury watched him.

"Do you remember talking to me in the hallway of One fifty-three Stanton Street early in August, 1967, Mrs. Salerno?"

"Yeah."

"And do you remember telling me you knew nothing about this case?"

"Yeah."

"That was a lie, wasn't it?"

"Yeah."

"You had a reason for that lie though, didn't you?"

"That's right."

Sandro took a DD5 out from between the pages of his yellow pad and read it to himself slowly as he stood before the jury. Mrs. Salerno watched him.

"You remember speaking to the police in the very building where all this took place, on the very day it took place?" Sandro still studied the DD5.

"That's right."

"And they took notes of what you told them?"

"Yeah."

"And did you tell the police"—Sandro read from the DD5 as he questioned—"that you saw a man on the fire escape?"

"Yes." She stared at the paper Sandro was reading.

"And did you describe what he was wearing?"

"I don't remember that. It was a long time ago."

"I'll let you read this and see if this refreshes your recollection." Sandro walked forward and handed the DD5 to Mrs. Salerno. She read it and handed it back.

"I tol' 'em."

"You said he wore a mustard jacket, right?"

"Yeah."

"And black pants?"

"Right."

"You said it was a real dark Negro, didn't you?"

"Real dark? I don't think I said that."

"Here is the DD5 again. Will you read it?" She read the DD5 again.

"I told them that too."

"And all that is written down there, isn't it?"

"Yeah."

"And you also told the police that you didn't see the face of the man on the fire escape?"

"Yeah."

Sam was right. Ellis *had* prepared her to admit all the things in the DD5.

"And that was a lie to the police too?"

"Yeah."

"And did you have reason to lie to the police too?"

"Yeah."

"You wouldn't lie to this jury, would you?"

"No."

"But they have only your word for it?"

She studied Sandro. "So?"

"If you have a reason, you don't mind lying, do you?"

"I ain't lyin'."

"Detective Mullaly knows you're on relief, doesn't he?"

"Yeah."

"He told you he'd make sure you didn't get relief money any more if you didn't testify, didn't he?"

"I object, Your Honor," said Ellis, rising. "Unless the question is in good faith, unless there's some basis for it."

"Overruled. Mr. Luca may ask such questions, but is bound by the answer. He may not pursue it," said the judge. "You may answer, Mrs. Salerno."

"No."

"Detective Mullaly knows your husband's a junky, doesn't he, Mrs. Salerno?"

Her jaw muscles were twitching with anger. "Yeah."

"Did the police tell you your husband would go back to jail if you didn't cooperate?"

"No."

"That's your reason for lying to this jury, isn't it, Mrs. Salerno?"

"I object, Your Honor," Ellis said, leaping up.

"Sustained."

"You don't want your husband to go back to jail, do you?"

"I object, Your Honor."

"Sustained."

"I have no further questions," Sandro said, walking to his chair.

"Let's see what Ellis does now," Sam whispered as Sandro sat. "He'll have to let her explain why she lied to the police."

Ellis requestioned Mrs. Salerno. She testified that her reason for lying to the police on the day of the shooting was fear of "getting involved." That was the whole, the only, the easily testified reason. Ellis had no further questions. Siakos had none. Sandro rose.

"May I have one or two questions, Your Honor?"

"You may."

"Mrs. Salerno, you've told the jury you lied so many times because you didn't want to get involved?"

"That's right."

"And giving the police a positive statement, describing the man on the fire escape, his clothing, even the shoes he wore, going to the police station at night, speaking to the D.A., is not getting involved?"

"Objection as argumentative," Ellis said, half-rising.

"Sustained."

"Did you ever, Mrs. Salerno, tell the police you knew nothing about this case so you wouldn't get involved?"

"No."

"No further questions," Sandro returned to the counsel table.

"Your next witness, Mr. Ellis," said the judge.

Ellis called Roger Snider to the stand. As Snider was being sworn, Sandro looked toward the spectators. He saw Mike Rivera sitting in the front row. Mike nodded to Sandro.

Snider spoke very quietly, softly, wrapped in sorrow. The court was very still as he almost whispered his testimony. He testified that on July 3rd, 1967, he and Lauria were sent to investigate a reported prowler at 155 Stanton Street. He testified that a woman in 152 Rivington Street, the building directly across the rear yard from 153 Stanton Street, pointed to the roof. Snider said he had called to Lauria to go slowly while he, Snider, went into the building and up the interior stairs. When he reached approximately the second landing, Snider said, he heard a fusillade of shots. He dashed the rest of the way to the roof and found Lauria lying in a pool of blood.

The judge called a luncheon recess.

"Your Honor, may we again approach the bench?" asked Sam.

"Surely."

"Now, Your Honor, I want to renew my application to have the jury go to the scene of the crime to see the premises firsthand. I realize you initially denied this motion, but now, after Mrs. Salerno's testimony, I believe there's more reason to go there."

The judge looked at Ellis.

"Your Honor, I'm not generally in favor of such trips. However, since we seem to be getting more bogged down in what could and what couldn't be seen, perhaps it might serve some purpose to have the jurors see the area for themselves. It's up to you, of course, Judge."

"Let's go into chambers and discuss this, gentlemen," said Judge Porta, rising. The lawyers followed him through the side door into the rear corridor. A court officer opened the heavy door to the robing chambers.

Judge Porta sat at the desk. He lit a cigarette, inviting the attorneys

PART 35

to smoke if they wished. Sam and Siakos sat on a leather couch. Ellis sat on a chair next to the judge's desk. Sandro stood, leaning against a window that overlooked Columbus Park.

"I don't usually permit the jury to visit the scene of the crime," said the judge. "It's too hard to control what they see. It's almost impossible to show them the physical scene exactly as it was."

"We could restrict them to the hallway where Mrs. Santos said she saw Hernandez," Sam suggested. "She saw the pictures we took and said it appeared to be the same as when she saw Hernandez."

"We could do that," the judge nodded.

"Why not let them go into the backyard and see the rear facade of the building?" Sandro added. "The fire escape and the building are certainly still the same."

"That's pretty easily controlled, Judge," Sam said, lighting a cigar in a big billow of smoke.

"We'd better talk fast, before Sam fumigates this place," Judge Porta interjected. "What do you say, David?"

"If we can keep the situation controlled, staying in certain restricted areas, going to the scene could be beneficial. Frankly, I've never been there myself, and sometimes I get a little confused."

"Looking at that hallway where Mrs. Santos says she was seems all right," said the judge. "And the backyard. Maybe even the roof. However, I won't let them look out the window from which Mrs. Salerno said she saw the man on the fire escape. Who knows what the lighting conditions actually were that day? It's dangerous to try and re-create that. Could be very prejudicial one way or the other."

"But that's an essential element of Mrs. Salerno's testimony," Sandro protested.

"True, but we're simply not going to be able to duplicate what appeared on July third, 1967. We have no choice on that."

"Then we are definitely going there, Your Honor?" Ellis asked.

The judge nodded. "Unless there's some strong objection, David. I think we can obtain a salutary result. Do you agree, gentlemen?"

The attorneys nodded.

"I'll have to get the clerk to hire a bus so we can go there in some semblance of order. Maybe we can get a picnic lunch somewhere, and after we go to the scene, we'll go the Central Park and have a game of Softball." The judge was smiling.

"We'll have one defendant on each team," Siakos said. Ellis snorted. The others laughed.

"Let me work out the details with the clerk," said the judge, rising. "Perhaps we could go next Wednesday morning. We'll meet here, and take the bus to Stanton Street." Judge Porta crushed his cigarette in the ashtray and moved toward the door. "Lunchtime, gentlemen. We'll resume at two thirty."

For lunch, Sam, Sandro, and Mike went to Giambone's Italian Restaurant on Mulberry Street, directly across Columbus Park from the courthouse.

"Come on, let's tear off that sad puss of Snider's," Mike urged. "He's a phony. Now he says he was only at the second landing."

"I disagreed with you before," said Sam, "and I disagree even more now that Snider's testifying. You see how sad he is, how not one sound is heard in the courtroom when he speaks? The jury'd think it sacrilegious to attack him."

"Unless we could prove it," Sandro added.

"Right. Unless we could prove it. And we can't. And it won't help us to antagonize the jury. We've got a lot of really good stuff to use."

Mike was disappointed. "We'll get it. We'll get more," he assured them.

During the afternoon session, Snider was cross-examined without any forceful attack. Siakos and Sam each finished with him in short order, his version of the last few minutes before Lauria's death remaining unchanged.

The next witness for the people was Detective Thomas Mullaly. Sandro and Mike and Sam all perked up at the thought of Mullaly's having to stay in one place without slithering into the shadows. Mullaly, tall and broad, his thinning red hair combed neatly from a part an inch above his left ear across the top of his head, stood and was sworn.

Mullaly testified that he had been in the station house on July 3rd, 1967, when a call came in that a Patrolman Lauria had been shot. He and a Detective Johnson were the first detectives to respond. The only

PART 35

uniformed men at the scene before them were Snider and two other policemen from a radio car in the area.

Mullaly testified he arrived at the roof of 153 Stanton Street about 2:45 P.M. and saw Lauria lying face down in a pool of blood. Lauria appeared not be be breathing and was apparently dead. Mullaly saw personal property strewn about near the front of the roof—a radio, a television set, a purse, some tickets to an amusement park, and a woman's glove. Mullaly testified he helped remove Lauria's body from the roof to the hallway below to await the doctor. While Mullaly was there, he noticed the door to Apartment 5B was slightly ajar. The door jamb was broken and lying on the floor. With Detective Johnson, he entered Apartment 5B. It appeared to have been ransacked. After about five minutes of investigation there, Mullaly testified, he returned to the street. A 1961 Chevrolet, double-parked in front of 160 Stanton Street, was brought to his attention. It seemed suspicious that the car was left with the window on the driver's side wide open, despite the rain. Mullaly investigated and determined that the car belonged to a junky who lived on the top floor of 163 Stanton Street. Mullaly went to the apartment and there saw Hernandez for the first time.

Hernandez was fully dressed and was wearing a hat. He was sweating profusely. Hernandez told him he had not been out of the house and had not been driving the car; a friend had driven it. Mullaly said he had touched Hernandez's jacket. It was wet. He requested Hernandez to accompany him down to the street. Mullaly said that any lie at this point was highly suspicious, particularly since burglars often leave cars double-parked outside the site of their burglaries for a quick getaway. Mullaly testified that Hernandez had originally told him he had lent the car to a friend by the name of Lopez. Then, according to Mullaly, when asked if Lopez was Negro, Hernandez changed his story, saying that a white Puerto Rican borrowed the car. These suspicious statements caused Mullaly to be keenly interested in Hernandez.

Once in the street, Mullaly asked Hernandez to open the trunk of his car. It contained a cheap red valise filled with men's clothing. Also in the valise was a bankbook in the name of one José Arce. Mullaly said that Hernandez told him the clothing belonged to a friend, but he couldn't remember his name.

At about 3:50, Mullaly testified, he heard shouting from 161 Stanton Street. He ran there, leaving Hernandez in the custody of a uniformed policeman. In that building, under a staircase on the ground floor, he saw a revolver.

At the stairway, he saw that a door leading to the cellar was ajar. He said he went out and searched the cellar, but there was nothing or no one there. Mullaly said he returned to the street and took Hernandez to the station house. On the way, Mullaly said, Hernandez told him more about his activities that day.

Hernandez, once at the station house, reverted to the story about not having been out of the house all day. He said again that a person named Lopez had been driving his car. Hernandez said he could show the police where Lopez lived. Several policemen, including Mullaly, took Hernandez to Second Street where Hernandez pointed out a house. Lopez was not at home. Hernandez was returned to the station house and was again questioned. It was then about 5:10 P.M.

Ellis asked Mullaly to continue. Mullaly said that at about 5:30 P.M., Crispin Lopez, the person Hernandez had said was driving the car, was brought in. The police soon determined that Lopez had been at work all day. They showed him to Hernandez. Mullaly testified that at this point Hernandez was taken to a locker room on the third floor of the precinct because the crowd in the offices below was too great to continue the interrogation. In the locker room, Hernandez admitted lying about the car. He said that he had been driving the car and had met a friend.

"Your Honor," Ellis said, "I believe this is now the proper time for any voir dire relating to the defendant Hernandez."

"Very well." Judge Porta swiveled toward the jury. "Ladies and gentlemen, at this point we are going to have a voir dire, which will concern itself with the voluntariness, or lack of it, of any alleged statement made by the defendant Hernandez. Now, the term *voir dire*, although French, comes to us from English common law. Literally it means *to say true*. In modern practice, it refers to a procedure to determine the truth in a particular matter. The truth we are seeking here is whether any such statement is admissible as evidence. The voir dire is not concerned with the truth of such statement, but only with the methods of obtaining it. Our law is that even if a statement be true, but was involuntary, was coerced by force or fear or threat of force, it cannot be accepted as legal evidence. That is our law." The judge turned to Siakos and nodded. Siakos walked toward the witness stand.

"Detective Mullaly," he asked, "did you strike the defendant Hernandez in the face when you went into his apartment, when you first asked him about the car?"

"Did I hit him, Counselor? Certainly not."

"Did you strike the defendant at any time?"

"No, Counselor."

Mullaly testified in answer to Siakos's further questions that the third-floor locker room to which Hernandez had been taken was used exclusively by uniformed patrolmen. He said he had never asked Hernandez a specific question about the murder of the policeman or, except for the double-parked car, about anything that happened that day on Stanton Street. Everything Hernandez said, according to Mullaly, was voluntary, without prompting or questioning. In the locker room, Hernandez was sitting in a chair, without handcuffs, during the entire investigation. Mullaly testified that Detective Johnson, Detective Jablonsky, and Detective Tracy were also in the locker room, but that he personally conducted the proceedings and the taking of the statement. Lieutenant Garcia, in charge of detectives in the precinct, never entered the locker room.

By 6 P.M., Mullaly testified, Hernandez had made his entire statement. Mullaly then took Hernandez to the clerical office, next to Lieutenant Garcia's office, where he sat in a chair. Mullaly said that neither he nor anyone else questioned Hernandez after 6 P.M. At approximately 9 P.M., Mullaly and other detectives went to Brooklyn with Hernandez, looking for Alvarado. Alvarado was not there.

Siakos asked for the memorandum book in which Mullaly recorded his activities of the evening and early morning of the third and fourth of July. Ellis opened a red folder on his table and took a notebook from it. He handed it to Siakos. Ellis said that only the first eight pages of the pad contained the material at which Siakos now had the right to look. The judge nodded. A rubber band was inserted around the book so that only the first eight pages could be turned and read. Siakos began to read the notes.

"We'll recess for the day at this point," said the judge. "Remember, jurors, don't discuss this case. Ten fifteen."

When the judge and jury had left the courtroom, Sandro, Sam, and Siakos sat at the counsel table and read the first eight pages of Mullaly's memo book. Ellis hovered nearby to make sure that they did not turn to the ninth page. The memo book was not an official memo book of the police department. It was a secretary's dictation pad. It contained the same story Mullaly had just recited on the stand, almost verbatim.

CHAPTER IX

THE USUAL TABLES in the Two Steps Down Inn were filled. It was 6 P.M., and Sal Angeletti was seated in the back. Several men, some with faces now familiar to Sandro, were sitting at the table near the front door. Sitting with Sal were three men, engrossed in a quiet discussion. Sal winked and smiled momentarily at Sandro. He told the waiter to take care of him.

Sandro sat at a side table alone and ordered a drink. The jukebox was wafting Neapolitan songs into the air. Didn't anyone in Italy except the Neapolitans have any songs, Sandro wondered. He had never heard of anyone singing a romantic Genoese or Barese song. Sandro was halfway through his second drink when Sal finished his business. He motioned Sandro to join him.

"Hello, Sandro," Sal said, shaking hands. "Still lookin' great."

"Hello, Sal, how're you doing?"

"What's the use of kicking, right?" He shrugged and bit into his cigar. "All these guys come around, all in trouble. Sal, help me here. Sal, help me there. And no money, ya know what I mean? Nobody's got any money today. You read all these bullshit stories about this phony syndicate that they make up in the papers, even in books. Everybody, even he's not connected, the guy that goes for the pizza, is supposed to have a million bucks. I'll take half, they give it to me. The bullshit they sell people so they can get elected, those goddamn politician bastards. They put all this bullshit out to frighten the people out of their taxes." Sal puffed his cigar. "You got a problem, Sandro?"

"No problem, Sal. Just wanted to keep in touch about that case I have on the East Side."

Sal nodded. "You want a drink?"

"I've already got one, thanks." Sandro raised his glass. "*Salute.*"

"Drink hearty." Sal nodded his head to some unspoken thought. "You know, another thing, these goddamn politicians, they got no balls. They let the niggers push them all over the place. You go around this neighborhood, it used to be quiet. No trouble here. We won't let it. Women can walk the street at night. Now, you take these goddamn niggers, they carry knives, guns. If we carry guns, we get arrested. They carry guns, they get told to move on. The cops don't want no trouble with the niggers. That's the politicians' fault. Takin' the cops' balls away cause they ain't got none themself. Ah, what the hell. Let's make some money. The hell with the cops and the niggers."

Funsi, the owner of the Two Steps Down, walked quickly over to Sal's table.

"Sal," he said, "you remember that fellow Ferdinand Balsa? I told you he owes that money for a big tab he run up?"

"Yeah, right, Freddy Balsa. He's with Louie Bags from Brooklyn. He's okay."

"He's over here now. I just saw him go down the street. He keeps telling me he's got the shorts."

"Well, that's okay, Funsi. Some of these guys take a little time to get their money together, you know?"

"I know, Sal, but this guy's really been trying to con me out of it for six months now. I mean, six months? First he tells me he don't have it this week. Then I should charge less money. Then he says the food's not so good, so he don't want to pay. He's trying to stiff me."

"Oh, yeah, a wise guy? How much does he owe you?"

"Two hundred. The bill goes back six months."

"Hey, Tony, come here a minute," Sal called toward the front table.

PART 35

A tall, heavyset man with a stolid, fleshy face walked back. "Tony, go out in the street and get that kid from Brooklyn. Tell him I want to see him over here, right away. Tell him in a hurry, okay?"

"Right, Sal." Tony walked out.

"Come on, Sandro, have something to eat."

"Are you going to eat, Sal?"

"Yeah, I'll have something with you. Goddamn doctor won't let me eat anything that I like anyway." He motioned to the waiter. "Joey, take the counselor's order, and bring me a plate of that stuff that the chef makes for me. You in court on that case now, Sandro?"

"Right. We had a couple of cops from the Seventh Precinct today."

"Which ones? We know some of the cops over there."

"Snider and Mullaly. Mullaly is a detective."

"Snider, that's right. Frankie Sausage was telling me that Snider was the partner of the cop that was killed. I know him."

"You know Snider?" Sandro asked quickly. "How do you know him?"

The waiter brought Sal a plate of something very white and bland. He brought Sandro an antipasto. Sal looked at the antipasto hungrily.

"Just a second," Sal said, seeming to be searching his memory for something. "Mullaly, Mullaly. I think he was the guy that arrested Johnny Banjoes about three years ago. A name something like that. I think it was him."

"He's a big, tall Irishman, with red hair, getting bald now. His hair is thin and straight."

"I'll bet that was the same guy. I'll ask Banjoes when I see him."

"What about Snider?" Sandro asked. "He's more important."

"Snider. He was the one, he used to be on the narcotics squad. Then he got tossed off and is back in uniform again. Everybody got thrown off the narcotics squad that time. That was about the time when Don Vincenz', *Buon Anima*, was deported. Matter of fact, it was Don Vincenz's case that caused the whole shake-up in the goddamn narcotics squad."

"You mean, Snider was involved in Uncle Jim's deportation?"

"Not direct, no. But he was on narcotics, and they was investigatin' that funny business. Now, we don't do none of that stuff, never did. We get along without it, you know? But these cops are out to make a big score, they wanted to knock that funny business on its ass, once and for all for the twentieth time. So they start their investigation. And, like everything else, it comes around here to sit on our doorstep. They figured Don Vincenz'd be involved in the funny business too. They even was after me, had a guy folly'n me and Don Vincenz' around. And the phone was bugged, and they'd call and bother the wife, and my mother, God be good to her. That's part of the game. We had heat before that, and we got it again." He shrugged. "Even for somethin' we have nothin' to do with."

"What happened with Uncle Jim and this Snider?" Sandro asked impatiently.

"Nothing. He was just involved in the investigation, you know? They got some lousy tips from a stool pigeon, the whore bastard. Anyway, they come up with a whole barrel fulla bullshit information about us being in narcotics and everything, and with that, the cops get their indictments. And they go around arresting everybody. Me, I just on the way into the city, when they arrested Don Vincenz'. So I beat it. They didn't grab me. And they go to trial, and they convict everybody. And meanwhile, I'm in Philadelphia, laying low. I'm using another name. Nobody knows where I am."

"How long were you there?" asked Sandro.

"Oh, about eight months, about that. They convicted Don Vincenz' and a whole bunch of punks that he didn't even know. But what was he going to do—dog it, cry to the cops that he was framed? Anyway, he was convicted, and then the government started to deport him. While he's in jail, still the narcotics go on. We didn't have nothin' to do with it in the first place. And then he's deported, and the narcotics still go on. And then the brass in headquarters start to figure that either there was a fix, that some of the guys on that narcotics squad were on the take, or they had dumbbells. Either way they had trouble."

"You mean, the real reason all these cops were dropped from the narcotics squad was because they had done such a lousy job investigating Uncle Jim's case?"

"Sure. *After* the trial. Hey, they were interested in deporting Don Vincenz', and they didn't care too much how. But the cops are smart,

PART 35

too. They don't want a bunch of goofballs screwing everything up for them. So they dumped these guys later. Not Snider at first. He's still working for them after the first shake-up."

"Can I bring the rest of the food," asked Joey, standing discreetly away from the table.

"Yeah, come on, and bring some wine for the counselor, and some Vichy water for me."

"No wine, Sal?" asked Sandro.

"No, that goddamn doctor, I told you he don't leave me have anything I want, only the things I don't want."

"Do you know about how this Snider got dumped, Sal?"

"Like I said, later, after they figure that it was a lousy job, the cops dump a whole bunch of guys. But not Snider. Then, when the heat blows over, I come back. And one day, this guy Snider recognizes me, and he arrests me on this funny business bullshit. And he drags me down to the precinct. And they bust my hump for a while. They keep me there a few hours, and then let me go. Well, when they find out in narcotics that this guy arrested me on the same meatball charge that started all the trouble and didn't amount to anything, a coupla days after that, this guy Snider is walking the beat again."

"So it turns out," asked Sandro," that Snider isn't too much in the smarts department?"

"He's got the shorts in the smarts department, Sandro." Sal looked up. A well built, hard-faced young man had walked into the restaurant. "Speaking about the shorts, here's the guy that owes Funsi the money."

Tony walked back to Sal. "You want him now?"

"No, leave him sit over there and stew for a while," Sal replied. He ordered some dessert for Sandro and himself. They ate it in leisurely fashion, continuing to talk about the neighborhood. Sal lit up a fat cigar. Sandro thought that Sal and Sam Bemer could stink out any place smaller than Madison Square Garden if they were ever together in the same room.

"You want me to go so you can talk to this fellow Balsa?" Sandro asked.

"The hell with him. Let him sit there until we're ready. He ain't goin' nowhere."

Sal smoked his cigar, still chatting with Sandro about nothing in particular. Sandro could see Balsa, sitting at a table in the front, nervously watching them. Finally, Sal motioned to him. Balsa approached and stood at the far end of the table. Funsi hovered nearby.

"You know you people are always welcome here. Louis Bags's my friend for years. But this is where I stay. I like it here. You come here, you gotta respect that. You understand?"

Balsa nodded.

"I don't want Funsi upset. It spoils the sauce for the spaghetti." No one laughed. Sal wasn't making jokes. "Now Funsi tells me you're trying to stiff him."

"No, that's not it. I'm just a little broke right now. I ain't been in action for a while. I'm a little short. I'm going to pay him, sure." Balsa tried a smile.

"Sure you are, sure you are. That's what's I thought all the time. I tell you what I'm going to do. I'll pay Funsi for you. How much is it, Funsi?"

Sandro felt a little sorry for Balsa standing on the griddle.

"Two hundred, Sal."

"Okay, Freddy, I'll tell you what I'll do, then," said Sal, as he took a roll of bills from his pocket. He counted off two hundred dollars, handing it to Funsi. "I'll pay the restaurant. Now you owe me the money. When do I get my money?"

"Gee, Sal, I'm a little short. I mean, I'll try to get it for you . . ."

"I'll tell you what. You get the money for me by tomorrow afternoon, okay?" Sal leveled an emotionless look at Balsa.

The sweat stood in droplets on Balsa's upper lip. "Sure, Sal," he said, almost inaudibly, "sure. I'll get it for you. You don't have to worry about that. I'll get it for you."

"I ain't worryin'. If I was worried, I wouldn't have staked you. You just get it for me by tomorrow, okay?"

"Sure, Sal, sure."

"You won't forget, will you?" Sal asked.

"No, you'll have it. I'll get it somewhere."

"Good. I don't want to send nobody looking for you. Go ahead,

PART 35

now. And next time you come around here, don't be a deadbeat. You got it?" Sal pointed with his cigar.

"Sure, Sal, sure."

"Okay, go ahead."

Balsa practically ran out of the restaurant. Sal ordered another drink for Sandro, another Vichy water for himself.

"He's a good kid, that Freddy. Young yet, you know, but he'll be all right. Otherwise, I wouldn't even bother wasting time with him, you know?"

Sandro thought he did.

"I'm going to ask Banjoes about that Irish detective when I see him, Sandro."

Sandro nodded and stood. "Okay. I'd like to know more about these policemen, Sal. Both of them."

CHAPTER X

Friday, April 5th, 1968

SIAKOS CROSS-EXAMINED MULLALY all of the next morning. Mullaly said that he had been in charge of the case at the local precinct level, with Detective Tracy of the Manhattan South Homicide Squad. He himself had filed only two DD5's in the investigation. One involved an attempt to trace the telephone call that had summoned the two patrolmen, and the other reported an interview on July 10th with two residents of Stanton Street. He had not testified in the grand jury hearing.

"Notice how this guy has no DD5's or grand jury testimony," Sam whispered to Sandro. "This way he can't be trapped by any prior versions of the story. He can testify to anything they need."

Sandro nodded.

Mullaly was perfectly calm through Siakos's interrogation. Sam busily made notations in his book. Sandro listened, moving his chair to have an unobstructed view as the detective testified. The two defendants sat quietly, watching. The guards behind them were motionless.

Mullaly testified that approximately seventy-five members of the police department had been assigned to the case, besides hundreds of others who came to help after they got off duty in other precincts. The police commissioner himself was in the station house, along with the chief of detectives and many inspectors and captains from all over the city.

No prisoner before Hernandez, Mullaly said, had ever been questioned in the third-floor locker room. It was necessary on this occasion because of the overflow of police personnel, reporters, and television newsmen. There had not, he said, been room to interrogate Hernandez in the lieutenant's office or the clerical area within the squad office.

While Hernandez was being questioned about the car, he was also searched. He had no wallet, but approximately twelve pawn tickets were found in his pockets, as well as about two dollars in change.

Mullaly stated calmly but emphatically that no one had struck or abused Hernandez in his presence, nor did anyone call him a spic or any other names. Siakos checked his notes again and began a new tack.

"This goddamn Mullaly is as cool and calm as any witness I've ever seen," said Sam.

"Siakos isn't touching him," Sandro agreed.

Mullaly testified that Hernandez was taken to Brooklyn about 9 P.M., when they first went to get Alvarado, and returned to the station house about 11:30. He was then left alone in the clerical office. At 1:30 A.M, Alvarado was brought in. On two occasions thereafter, Hernandez was taken from the lieutenant's office to the third-floor locker room, where Alvarado was then being interviewed. The next morning they were both taken to headquarters to be photographed.

During all the time Hernandez was being interviewed and making his statement, Mullaly said, he was calm and cooperative. Siakos had no further questions. The court recessed for lunch.

In the afternoon, Siakos called Hernandez as his own first witness on the voir dire.

The interpreter stood next to Hernandez. He hunched forward, his elbows on the arms of the witness chair, his hands clasped, staring blankly at Siakos.

Siakos questioned Hernandez about his past police record, to beat Ellis to the punch. There was larceny and narcotics in his past, but no crimes of violence. Hernandez testified that he was in his apartment on the afternoon of July 3rd, eating a sandwich, when the police came to his door. As soon as he opened the door, Mullaly grabbed him by the throat and shoved him against a wall. He was taken down to his car and made to open the trunk. Then he was taken to the police station, where he was questioned. They took him to Crispin Lopez's house and then returned. When he arrived back in the office, Hernandez testified, a big policeman punched him. Hernandez demonstrated the punch for the jury, a hammer blow down on the top of the head.

Sandro glanced at the jurors. Some of them looked shocked.

After that, Hernandez testified, Lopez was brought in, and then he was taken to the locker room. His hands were handcuffed behind his back. He was surrounded by detectives, he said, and was set upon with fists and questions. Five or six detectives stood around him, asking about the roof on Stanton Street, about the murder, punctuating their questions with punches in the stomach and chest. He said he was knocked into the lockers several times and even fell to the floor.

"May the defendant step down and demonstrate, Your Honor?" Siakos asked.

The judge nodded.

Hernandez stepped down and stood next to the witness stand. Suddenly he threw himself to the floor. The crunch of flesh and bone on the wooden floor caused a wince through the jury. They looked at the judge, who did not move, then back to Hernandez.

Hernandez returned to the witness chair, answering Siakos's questions in passionate, rapid-fire Spanish. The stenographer, one of the old-timers who preferred pen to machine, was rapidly noting the interpreter's words. He was one of three who alternated in recording and typing the minutes to make them available for the next morning. Each recorded for twenty minutes, typed for another twenty, and then took a twenty-minute break.

Hernandez testified that the beating increased and that his pain mounted. He couldn't stand it any more. Finally he told the police: "Yes, I'm the one who killed him." But, he said, the police refused his confession.

"No! Not you! Someone else! The one who killed him was a big, tough colored fellow," they insisted. They were sure it was a very tough colored fellow because he had disarmed the officer and knocked him to the ground.

PART 35

Hernandez indicated that a Lieutenant Garcia, a detective who could speak Spanish, was translating the questions and answers in the locker room.

Hernandez showed how, while his hands were handcuffed behind him, two detectives had stood on either side, holding his arms while the others punched him. At one point, he said, when he fell to the floor, they kicked him twice.

With the court's permission, Siakos had Hernandez stand, remove his shirt, and uncover his thin, pale chest. There were two scar discolorations on the left side below the breastbone. The judge allowed Hernandez to step down and show the jury. He walked slowly before the jury box holding up his undershirt. The jury raned forward.

As Hernandez was displaying his chest, Sandro noticed Ellis taking some photographs from an envelope in one of his files. He could see that some were black and white, some in color. Ellis studied them a moment, then slipped them back into the envelope.

"And then what happened, if anything?" Siakos asked Hernandez.

"The detectives pulled me up to my feet and asked me again about, the roof. I told them I did it. It wasn't true, but I couldn't stand being hit more."

"Did the police stop hitting you?"

"No. They insisted it was another," the interpreter translated.

"When you said you did it, was that true?"

"I had fear. They were striking me. I wanted them to stop beating me."

This was of no use to him, however, Hernandez testified, for the police insisted he tell them the name of the man who had been with him on the roof. They beat him more, severely. Hernandez testified that not only did the police punch and kick him, but they were also striking him violently on the top of the head with a Manhattan telephone directory.

In desperation, for self-preservation, not able to think of anyone else, he mentioned Luis Alvarado, a friend he knew from the street. He said the only reason he gave Alvarado's name or that he confessed any knowledge of the crime was that he thought they were going to kill him.

Hernandez said that he was taken to Brooklyn later that night to point out Alvarado's house. Alvarado was not home. Later, when Alvarado was brought in, the police twice took Hernandez up to the locker room. He said he spoke quickly in Spanish to Alvarado, asking forgiveness, saying that they had been beating him and he could not help himself. He said he told Alvarado to cooperate or they would kill him, and that later they could straighten it out in court.

The assistant district attorney came to the station house later and questioned him. Before he saw Brennan, Hernandez testified, the police instructed him that if he didn't repeat the same story to the D.A. they would take his private parts and crush them.

Siakos was satisfied. He sat down.

Some of the jurors whispered to one another. Sam Bemer rose and faced Hernandez.

"Did you see Alvarado at any time on July third, 1967, until he was brought to the station house the next morning?"

"No."

"When you gave his name to the police, was that the truth?"

"No."

"Why did you mention Alvarado's name?"

"They beat me almost to death."

"When was the first time you mentioned the name of Alvarado to the police?"

"About eleven of the evening, something like that."

Sam walked back to the counsel table. "Hear what he said?" Sam whispered to Sandro. "He didn't give Alvarado's name until eleven P.M. That means they're lying even about going to Brooklyn at nine. They're trying to make it seem like a voluntary, quick thing, instead of an inquisition of several hours. Anything else I should go into with this fellow?"

"Maybe you should lead him through the beating again so the jury is sure to have all the details. Ask him what the police did to make him tell the name of Alvarado," suggested Sandro.

Sam asked. Hernandez described the beating again. He also testified that the police had brought in a small black radio. When asked what color it was, Hernandez said it was black. They told him the radio

PART 35

taken from the apartment, which was then being dusted for fingerprints, was actually red. They punched him several times until he said that the radio that looked exactly like the black one they were holding was actually red. They brought in a woman's purse. It was black, and they insisted it was white. Finally, Hernandez admitted that the black purse was actually white.

Hernandez said in response to Sam's questions that when he had been taken back upstairs in the early morning hours, Alvarado was standing against some lockers bleeding at the nose. His hands were handcuffed behind him, and policemens surrounded him.

At this point, Sam had no further questions. Ellis stood, wrinkled his nose and began to cross-examine. Ellis asked about Hernandez's narcotics habit. It cost six dollars a day to support, Hernandez replied. He admitted to not having worked from March to July of 1967. Hernandez repeated that he hadn't seen Alvarado the entire day of July 3rd, and the last time he had seen him was perhaps two or three days before that. He testified that he had left his house about 8:30 that morning, accompanied by his wife.

"Ellis's starting to go into the alibi," Sandro said apprehensively.

"Nick, object to this," Sam leaned over and whispered hurriedly.

Siakos motioned for them to be still, as he sat listening intently to the answers, not bothering with the import of the question.

"If they get to it now," whispered Sandro, "then they can go out and screw up the alibi, sink him. If he's sunk, we'll get sunk. Object, Sam. Think of something."

Sam stood. "Your Honor, Mr. Ellis's question has nothing to do with the activities of the police at the station house after Hernandez's arrest. It is, therefore, a collateral matter, and is not proper for this voir dire."

"Your Honor, I believe this goes to the issue of credibility," Ellis suggested.

"I'll allow it, Mr. Bemer. Credibility is never collateral. It is always an issue."

Ellis continued to question, and Hernandez told how he drove his wife to work the morning of July 3rd and then burglarized the apartment in El Barrio. The jurors sat upright.

Now, finally, Siakos stood to object, realizing where the D.A. had led Hernandez. The judge overruled. And now Siakos's entire defense was going to be revealed, not when he wanted and as he wanted, but leaked out here in the early stages of the trial, to be buried under the words and days the jury would yet endure.

"All right," Sam whispered to Sandro, who sat seething. "Take it easy." Sam pretended to be reading papers on the counsel table. "Don't let the jury see you carry on."

They listened to Hernandez describe how he broke into the apartment in El Barrio, put clothing, a portable radio, and a bankbook into a suitcase he found there, and put the suitcase in the trunk of his car. He told of driving back to meet his wife for lunch, and getting a dollar from her to buy gasoline. Then he told of his efforts to pawn the suits and radio under the name Antonio Cruz. He described his buying of narcotics and then driving home, desperate to take a fix. He testified that when he got to Stanton Street, it was blocked with an ambulance and many police cars. He left his car double-parked and ran to his apartment, where, a short time later, Mullaly arrived.

Ellis now produced a full-length black-and-white photograph of the defendants in the nude, taken at police headquarters the morning of July 4th. Hernandez said he remembered the picture's being taken. Ellis offered it into evidence. It was shown to defense counsel.

There, side by side, stood Hernandez and Alvarado, naked, forlorn, and embarrassed.

"You see how Ellis slowly, effectively cuts you down," said Sam. "And look how careful they were. I've never seen a photo like this. I guess they figured somebody'd complain of beating, and they got prepared in advance. I don't see any bruises here. Do you?"

"I can't see them either," agreed Siakos.

"But the doctor in the Tombs found scars," said Sandro. "The Department of Correction gave us the medical records."

"Pictures can be doctored," said Siakos. "I'm not going to object to the picture. I'll show the jury the medical records, even bring the doctor in to say what he noted on Hernandez's medical charts. Then in summation, I'll talk about how they doctored the pictures and who knows what else."

PART 35

Sam nodded. Siakos had his moments.

"Are there any black and blue on me in that picture?" Alvarado whispered to Sandro.

Sandro turned toward Alvarado. "Now, how in hell could I see black and blue on you?"

Alvarado put his hand to his mouth to hide his smile. He rubbed his lip and looked up at the jury soberly.

Since the picture was offered only against Hernandez, the judge had the clerk scissor it in half, and returned Alvarado's picture to Ellis.

"Now, Hernandez," Ellis asked, "you said you told Alvarado in Spanish, up in the locker room, that he should admit the crime to the police so they wouldn't kill him, and you could straighten it all out in court?"

"Right, right."

"Well, when you got to court for the arraignment, that very morning, did you say anything to the judge about the police beating you?"

There was tense expectancy in the courtroom as the interpreter translated the question, Hernandez replied in Spanish, and the interpreter spoke again:

"No, I don't believe so."

Two of the jurors exchanged glances.

"Did your lawyer say anything about a beating to the judge?"

"I hardly spoke to him. I didn't tell him nothing. I was in pain."

"Did you say anything to the doctor in the Tombs?"

"He saw it."

"Did you say anything, is the question."

"No."

"To any official in the prison?"

"No."

"No further questions."

Neither Sam nor Sandro said anything. Their faces were calm. Sam continued writing. Any juror looking at them would have thought that nothing at all had just happened.

Siakos rose. In answer to his question, Hernandez testified that the doctor's examination in the Tombs had been so cursory that he didn't have a chance to tell him anything.

"What did the doctor do for you?" Siakos asked.

"He put some bandages all around my chest, from the armpits to the waist."

"Jesus Christ, that's good stuff if we can support it," said Sam.

"It's here in the medical cards." Sandro slid the blue medical cards from the Tombs across the table.

"If he had that done, then it won't mean a thing that he's stupid and didn't say anything to anyone," Sam added.

Siakos took the medical cards and read them. He had Hernandez describe the doctor's step-by-step procedure in strapping his chest. Hernandez stood and showed the jury from where to where the bandages had been placed.

"I offer these medical cards in evidence, Your Honor," said Siakos.

"Objection, Your Honor. The doctor from the Tombs should be here to explain these notes before these cards are admitted into evidence."

"Yes, Mr. Siakos, you can introduce these cards when the doctor from the Tombs takes the stand."

"Very well, Your Honor."

Siakos asked the judge to have the detectives in the witness room brought into the court so that Hernandez might try to identify the men who hit him in the police station. The judge granted the application.

Five detectives stood side by side just behind the rail separating the spectators from the bench: Johnson, Negro, bull-like, bald; Jablonsky, tall, heavy, and potbellied; Tracy, tall, sleek; Mullaly, tall, emotionless; Garcia, the lieutenant, somewhat embarrassed and annoyed to be in a lineup. Hernandez was allowed to leave the stand and walk toward them. As he neared the rail, Hernandez visibly cringed. He pointed to Mullaly and Johnson, and returned quickly to the distant witness chair. The detectives turned and left through the side door.

Siakos, now that he had allowed the alibi to seep into the case, had no choice but to develop the entire story. He questioned Hernandez about his activities on July 3rd. Hernandez repeated what he had told Ellis about the burglary, lunch, and the pawnshops. Herandez said that he had not arrived at the first pawnshop until approximately 2 P.M. He

PART 35

said he arrived at Stanton Street at approximately 2:45 P.M. The police cars and ambulance were already there.

Hernandez testified he had never told the police of the pawnshops or of his activities because they had never asked him where he was. They had never asked him anything. They had just accused him and wouldn't hear anything from him except a confession. They did know, as Mullaly testified, about the pawn tickets, but they had ignored them.

Siakos had no further questions.

"Let the witness step down," said the judge. "We'll adjourn now. Members of the jury, do not discuss this case. Good night." The judge and jury left.

"Well," said Sam as he packed his briefcase. "At least, we didn't end on total failure today."

"I thought we were going to for a minute," said Sandro.

"So did I, but those medical cards are going to be awfully hard to explain. He was strapped from top to bottom."

"What do you think?" asked Siakos.

"I think you pulled it out," Sam said.

Siakos smiled.

CHAPTER XI

SANDRO AND MIKE SAT OPPOSITE DR. JOHN RIDER, director of the Metropolitan Hospital narcotics ward. Sandro sounded him out on the points that would convince a court that he was an eminent authority in his field. Dr. Rider treated perhaps fifteen hundred addict-patients a year. He also taught nurses and other doctors about narcotics, the withdrawal syndrome, and detoxification. He was a consultant on the staff of many other New York hospitals as well. Sandro was quite satisfied.

"Doctor, as I told you on the phone, my problem is that I need some expert medical advice on narcotics and withdrawal."

"I'll try and help," said the doctor. He was young, round-faced, with dark hair. "What are the facts?"

"As I explained, I have a client who is accused of murder. I'm not going to ask you to tell me that he wasn't responsible for any of his acts because of drugs, or anything like that. He had a seizure in prison, six days after he got there. I want to know if heroin could cause a clonic seizure, Cheyne-Stokes breathing, tachycardia, and various other things."

"Where did you get the diagnosis?" the doctor asked.

"This is a report from a Dr. Maish, who was on duty in the prison that night. It's his diagnosis."

Dr. Rider read. "How long did you say this man had been in prison?"

"From the morning of July fourth, 1967."

"And could he get any drugs there?"

"No. Certainly there's no one who would ever admit giving a prisoner drugs. For all practical purposes, we can assume that there were no drugs after he was incarcerated."

"And this seizure occurred six days later?" The doctor pursed his lips. "No, it could not have been caused by addiction to heroin, in my opinion. Do you know the size of his habit?"

"He said two three-dollar bags a day," Sandro replied.

"That's not much of a habit."

"And you'd say such a habit would not cause a convulsion six days after withdrawal?"

"I've never seen anyone have any kind of seizure—I've never even heard of it—at any time after withdrawal from heroin."

"Does it matter about dosage, Doctor?" Sandro asked.

"No, that wouldn't even be a factor. Heroin just doesn't cause convulsions. And, I'll tell you, with the quality of heroin that is sold in New York, it's even more unlikely."

"You mean the way it's cut down?" asked Mike.

"Exactly."

Mike looked at Sandro and smiled. "That's a nice start on the medical question, isn't it?"

"Does that help you?" the doctor asked.

"Sure does. Doctor, I don't know all the medical aspects of this. Where can I get myself trapped? What could the D.A. come up with to show that the convulsion resulted from withdrawal and not from trauma, from a beating?" asked Sandro.

"Barbiturates! Barbiturates can be far deadlier than heroin, if you can imagine that. We expect convulsions with barbiturates."

Sandro tried to remember if Alvarado had ever mentioned barbiturates.

"A lot of addicts want a change of pace and take barbiturates for a while, then heroin," the doctor continued. "They get their kicks different ways—so their bodies don't get tired of the same old destruction."

"How do we get around that?" Mike asked.

"I doubt we have to," said Sandro. "Alvarado says he had a heroin habit. That's all there was; that's all he'll testify to. How can Ellis dispute that?" Sandro paused a minute. "Unless, of course, he can offer some junky a break for testifying that he saw Alvarado taking pills."

"Barbiturates didn't cause this convulsion either," said the doctor, matter-of-factly. "The period of separation from drugs was much too long."

"You trying to get me old before my time?" asked Sandro, smiling.

The doctor grinned. "A barbiturate convulsion, which is very common—and more often than not it causes death—occurs after withdrawal, within, say forty-eight to seventy-two hours, two or three days. Then the danger subsides. Six days later is just too late, too remote for drugs to have caused this convulsion."

"Doctor, I'd like you to testify in court just as you've explained it to us here."

"When?"

"I'm not quite sure, yet. Perhaps the end of next week. Thursday or Friday?"

"Make it the following Monday, and you've got a deal. I've got to teach on Thursday, and Friday's out too."

"Okay," agreed Sandro. "I'll call you in advance and let you know exactly when."

"And, of course, you'll have to compensate me for the time I have to spend in court."

"Of course, Doctor. I'll get the judge to sign an order for it. It may take a couple of weeks for the comptroller's office to make out a check, but I'll get it for you."

"Fine." The doctor rose.

Sandro and Mike rose and shook hands with him.

"Thank you, Doctor. Talk to you at the beginning of the week."

Mike and Sandro left and drove across town to the office of Dr. Arthur Fulton, a well-known neurologist.

Dr. Fulton, a tall, well-tanned man with steel-gray hair, ushered them into his office and listened attentively while Sandro summarized the symptoms that Alvarado had had, and the history leading up to his seizure. He explained about the beating in the police station, how Alvarado's head had hit the lockers, and the convulsion six days later.

"Could this beating have caused the convulsion Dr. Maish found on July tenth?" Sandro asked.

"Certainly," Dr. Fulton said in a soft, firm voice. "Trauma can easily cause such a reaction. But I'm not too sure about the effects of narcotics."

"I've got a narcotics expert who will come into court and testify that narcotics did not cause the seizure. Heroin never causes convulsions, and he says too much time had elapsed for barbiturate convulsions."

Mike nodded.

The doctor smiled. "Very well, if you have an expert in the field who says that there is no cause of convulsion there, then I can safely testify that an injury such as the beating you've described could easily be the cause of a convulsion."

"What about the time factor?" Sandro asked. "Couldn't the beating also be too remote from the convulsion to be causally connected?"

"Not really. There's no great significance in that. A seizure following a brain injury can occur abruptly, or it may be delayed for days, weeks, even months or years. Post-traumatic seizures have been reported as long as twenty years after an injury. Most of them, however, follow immediately after, within two or three months."

"Well, that keeps us in the ball game. What about the fact that there have been no more seizures since that first one?" Sandro asked, trying to anticipate Ellis.

"A seizure doesn't have to be recurrent. A patient can have single or periodic post-traumatic seizure. There's no way of telling if they'll recur until they do."

"Doctor, would a week from Monday be a good day for you to testify?" Sandro asked.

"Monday? I have office hours that day. From two thirty to five. Can you fit me in before then? I'll be at the hospital in the morning, and then go to my office. But if you can squeeze me in around lunchtime, I'll do it."

"How about if I work it out with your secretary? I'll talk to the judge and see what time schedule we can get. I'd like you to go on the stand right after the narcotics expert, and then we can let you get right back to your practice."

"Fine. You call her and tell her where you want me, and I'll be there. Of course . . ."

"I know, you will get a check from the City of New York. It'll take a couple of weeks after I get the order signed."

"Fine. Good seeing you." Dr. Fulton stood and shook hands with Sandro and Mike.

"That's quite a nice piece of work, Sandro," said Mike. "I got a little hung up in the middle on some of that stuff, but it comes out in the end sounding great for our side."

"That's what it's got to do for the jury too, end up creating the impression Alvarado was seriously injured. That's all. Once we do that, Ellis has to prove the police didn't injure him. And he can't possibly do it."

"Why do you say Ellis can't possibly show that Alvarado wasn't injured by the cops?" Mike asked.

"First, he doesn't have anything except what we have, Dr. Maish's report from the Tombs. Second, for anything else he'd have to get a physical examination of Alvarado. The United States Constitution guarantees that no person can be forced to be a witness against himself. Alvarado can't be forced to submit to a physical examination."

Mike nodded, impressed.

CHAPTER XII

Monday, April 8th, 1968

THE COURT SESSION did not begin until eleven. At ten forty-five, Siakos entered the courtroom accompanied by Mrs. Hernandez. She sat alone in the first row of the spectator's section until the jury was polled and the judge sat on the bench. Siakos called her to the witness stand. The eyes of the jurors followed her with curiosity, watching as she was sworn. She stood tall, her strong, firm body accented by a clinging red and black silk dress.

Mrs. Hernandez testified, through the interpreter, that at about 8:30 the morning of July 3rd her husband drove her to the factory on East 121st Street where she worked. She next saw him about noontime; they ate in a nearby luncheonette. Some of her fellow workers, she said, were there at that time. At about 1 P.M. she went back to work and gave Hernandez a dollar to buy gas. The next time she saw her husband, he was under arrest, charged with murder.

At the station house, where she arrived at approximately 6 P.M. that day, the police kept her in a side room on the second floor. She was under constant observation and was not allowed to go to the ladies' room or anywhere else. At one time, the police moved her to a bench in the hallway near the stairs. After a while, she saw Hernandez coming down the stairs with some detectives. He had no shoes on, his hair was disheveled, and he was wearing only his undershirt, trousers, and socks. He looked quite racked.

When the detectives walking with Hernandez realized who the woman was who was sitting in the hall, they immediately had her moved back into the small room, where she was watched by two policemen. Mrs. Hernandez testified that she remained there for many hours. When Alvarado was brought into the station house about 1:30 A.M., he was taken into that room. Much later, about 4:30 A.M., she was taken into another room, the office of detectives. There was a large steel cage in the corner. In the cage, on the floor, moaning and groaning, holding his stomach, was Hernandez. Alvarado was on a chair in the middle of the room, his hands handcuffed behind his back. Mrs. Hernandez said that except when the police took her home to search her apartment, she was kept in the police station until 9 o'clock the next morning.

Siakos had no further questions. Sam stood to cross-examine. Mrs. Hernandez testified that when Alvarado was brought into the small room where she had been detained, one of the detectives hit him across the left side of the face with a vertical karate chop. Alvarado's nose began to bleed.

"Could you identify the man you say hit Alvarado if you saw him again?" Sam asked.

"I believe so," the interpreter said.

Sam had the five detectives brought into the courtroom again. Mrs. Hernandez studied them a moment. She stepped off the stand, on her firm, taut legs. Her dark eyes were narrowed. She walked to the railing on the other side of which the officers were lined up. She walked past each, her eyes looking straight into theirs: Garcia, Johnson, Tracy, Jablonsky, Mullay. Mullay was looking over her head at the wall. She poked her finger out at him, almost puncturing his chest.

"Him!"

"Let the record show she has pointed to Detective Mullaly," said the judge.

The detectives left the courtroom, and Mrs. Hernandez took the stand again. Sam had no further questions.

PART 35

Ellis stood in place, rolling a pencil between his hands.

"Have you ever seen your husband sick from want of drugs?"

"Yes."

"By the way, did you ever give him money to pay for drugs?"

"I paid for food and the rent, never for drugs," she answered firmly.

"When Hernandez was sick for lack of drugs, did he moan and groan."

"Yes."

"And when you saw him in the cage, on the morning of July fourth, when he was moaning and groaning, was it the same as when you had seen him sick from want of drugs?"

"Yes," she said softly, without hesitation. Her honesty was compelling.

"I have no further questions."

"Look at that jury," Sam whispered. "They respect her."

Sandro looked at the jury box. The jurors continued to watch Mrs. Hernandez, seeming to admire her spirit and fearlessness.

"She sank her own husband a little just now. As the jury sees it, she's got to be telling the truth," Sam continued. "And if she's telling the truth, then what she saw Mullaly do to Alvarado must be true. We got some great mileage out of that."

"Ellis doesn't even dare ask her about that karate chop," said Sandro.

Siakos called as the next witness on the voir dire, Dr. Joseph Waters, the Tombs doctor who had examined Hernandez on July 3rd, 1967.

Dr. Waters was short and graying and wore glasses and a white, knee-length medical coat. Somehow the coat made him look more like a butcher than a doctor. He took the stand and was sworn. Siakos handed him Hernandez's medical cards. He read them.

"Did you give this man a physical examination, Doctor?"

He read the cards. "Yes, yes. There was the usual examination upon commitment. I don't remember the man." The doctor looked up to study the counsel table. He didn't know which man was Hernandez. He shook his head.

"What sort of physical was it, Doctor, gross or detailed? Can you tell from those records?"

"We observe the men, mostly observe, to determine their condition."

"What were the results of this examination?"

The doctor looked at the cards. "Nothing remarkable. Nothing on the heart, no venereal history. He was an addict."

"Do you have his blood-pressure reading?"

"No, that wasn't done."

"Or heart evaluation?"

"No."

"Those cards say no marks on the man's body, do they not?"

"Yes, right here. No marks."

"And if there were any unnatural or unusual marks you would have noted that fact?"

"Yes."

"Does it note there any puncture holes and scar tissue on each arm from constant injection of heroin?"

The doctor studied the card again. He shook his head.

"Don't shake your head, Doctor," the judge admonished. "The reporter must hear your answers, and unfortunately he can't hear your head shake." The judge twisted and winked toward Sandro.

"No."

"Doctor, will you look at this man's arms? May we, Your Honor?"

"Certainly."

Hernandez was brought forward. The doctor examined his arms.

"Are there scars and marks that were not recorded on these cards?"

"Yes."

"Old scars and marks?"

"They do not appear to be recent."

Siakos nodded. "Does the card indicate anything else, Doctor?"

"Yes, there's a diagnosis of traumatic pleuradynia, here."

"What is pleuradynia, Doctor?"

"An inflammation or difficulty with the pleura."

"Where is the pleura, Doctor?"

"Behind the ribs, by the lungs." He pointed to the middle of his own chest.

"You point to the middle of your own chest, Doctor?"

PART 35

"Objection."

"Overruled."

The jury was alert and fascinated.

"It can be in there, yes," the doctor answered.

"And what does the word *traumatic* before pleuradynia signify?"

"The pleuradynia resulted from some trauma."

"What is a trauma, Doctor?"

The doctor rubbed his chin. "It means something to do with an injury."

"Actually, doesn't trauma mean injury caused by an external force, an external shock or blow?"

"Objection."

"Overruled."

"Yes, it can mean from a blow."

"In other words being struck by something or someone."

The doctor hesitated. He looked at Siakos steadily. He nodded. "Yes."

"What treatment did you give Hernandez for this traumatic pleuradynia, Doctor?"

The doctor studied the card. "Two aspirins," he replied.

"Just like the lousy Army," Sam whispered, not breaking the flow of his note-taking. "I wouldn't let this guy take care of my bunion."

"Do the cards indicate anything else, Doctor?" Siakos asked.

"A contusion of the left chest near the breastbone."

Two of the jurors edged forward to listen.

"What is a contusion, Doctor?"

"A bruise, a discoloration without a break of the surface."

"And do you diagnose a contusion objectively, by feeling and seeing, or by being told by the patient?"

"You can see it."

"And if it says contusion, is it a reasonable assumption that you actually saw and felt a contusion, and it wasn't just something the patient complained about?"

"Yes."

"Doctor, will you look at this man's chest now, particularly at two marks on the left side near the breastbone?"

327

The judge allowed the guards to bring Hernandez forward again. The doctor examined Hernandez.

"Can you see anything there?"

"Yes. Two slight discolorations."

"Could that be the remnants of the contusion you noted almost a year ago?"

The doctor scratched his head, rubbed his chin. "It's in the right place. It could be, I suppose, but I don't know for sure."

"Anything else done for this man, Doctor?"

"Yes. His chest was strapped."

"What with, Doctor?"

"Bandages. All around."

"When you say all around, Doctor, tell the jury where, if you will?"

"Well, from about the top of his chest, around the armpits, down to his waist."

"What does strapping do, why is it done?"

"Usually it's to relieve pain. Holds the chest and eases pain."

"And this strapping was of the whole chest?"

"Objection sustained, repetitious," the judge said without benefit of Ellis.

"How many times was this man treated by the doctors in the Tombs?"

"Since the beginning?" The doctor read and then counted ponderously. "Sixty-two times."

"I have no further questions."

"Let's take a short recess," said the judge. He admonished the jury and returned to his chambers.

When court resumed, Ellis, wrinkling his nose, began to question the doctor. Most of Hernandez's sixty-two clinic visits after the chest-strapping appeared to be complaints of the prisoner, and there did not appear to be any further indication of objective findings of contusions. Ellis had the doctor re-examine the scars on Hernandez's chest.

"It's an old scar," the doctor said. Although not displaying it to the jury, Ellis was ebullient. "About six months to a year old, perhaps," added the doctor. Ellis could almost be heard to deflate.

PART 35

The doctor testified that the marks came from some abrasion or contusion in the skin. Ellis sat while he was ahead.

Siakos had no further questions. He rested Hernandez's evidence on the voir dire.

"Your Honor, on the basis of this evidence, I move to exclude any alleged statement made by the defendant Hernandez on the ground that it could not be voluntary beyond a reasonable doubt."

"Your Honor," Ellis said, rising. "I have some evidence on the voir dire which I'd like to present."

"Yes, we'll hear Mr. Ellis's evidence."

For his first witness on the voir dire, Ellis called Lieutenant Garcia of the Seventh Squad. Garcia was about fifty years of age. He did not look Spanish. He looked like a cop.

Garcia testified he was never in the third-floor locker room on the evening of July 3rd, 1967, or the early morning of July 4th. He recalled that the first time he saw Hernandez was in the detectives' squad room on the second floor shortly after 5 P.M., July 3rd. From there, Hernandez had been taken upstairs and Garcia did not see him again until he was brought down about 6 P.M. At that time, Garcia had been tied up with an inspector and did not speak to Mullaly or any other detective who had been upstairs. Hernandez was placed in the clerical office, connected by a door with his own office.

"Lieutenant Garcia, did you ever hit, strike, kick, or in any way physically abuse this defendant?"

"Certainly not."

"Did you ever say anything to insult or abuse the defendant, his race, religion, or anything like that?"

"Certainly not."

"Did you see any other person or policeman or detective do any of these things in your presence?"

"No, never."

"I have no further questions, Your Honor."

"Proceed, Mr. Siakos."

Siakos asked Garcia how many policemen had been working on the case. The lieutenant answered it was a huge manhunt, perhaps four hundred policemen. He further testified that he was in charge of the investigation because he was commander of the precinct detectives. He said he spoke to Hernandez after he was brought down from the locker room at 6 P.M.

"Did he tell you anything about this case."

"Yes, off and on."

"And for how long, would you say, did he tell you things?"

"Well, on and off for several hours. As we needed information."

"Did he deny to you sometime after 6 P.M. that he had anything to do with this crime?"

"In the beginning he did. He made no admissions."

Siakos continued, not changing his tone or delivery. Sandro moved to the edge of his chair. Sam stopped writing notes and looked up.

"How many times would you say that, after six o'clock, he denied flatly having had anything to do with this crime?"

"Once or twice, perhaps three times."

Siakos continued, trying to open a bigger hole in the prosecution case. Mullaly had said there was never a denial by Hernandez, and by 6 P.M. the confession was complete. Now the lieutenant testified there were still denials on and off for several hours after 6 P.M.

At this point, the judge recessed the jury and the court for lunch.

Siakos walked over to Sam and Sandro, keeping his back to the jury as they filed out.

"You got him now," Sandro exclaimed.

"Sure," said Siakos, smiling.

"Mullaly and friends were probably afraid to prep the lieutenant and tell him what to say," added Sam. "Too bad we had to go to lunch before finishing him. Wait and see if his whole story isn't straightened out over lunch."

After lunch, Siakos questioned Lieutenant Garcia about all his activities after 6 P.M. on July 3rd, 1967. Garcia testified that Hernandez stayed in the clerical office until 9 P.M., when he was taken to Brooklyn to point out Alvarado's house. On his return, Hernandez was put in the cage in the squad room while awaiting the D.A., who was to take a formal statement. Garcia testified they had returned from Brooklyn about 11 P.M. He said he saw Mrs. Hernandez at the station house that night, but only once, about 8 P.M.

PART 35

Garcia testified that at no time did he see the prisoner manhandled; nor did he ever see the prisoner when he looked as if he had been manhandled. He never saw the prisoner without all his clothing.

Siakos was looking now for a strong point upon which to end the examination.

"How many times all together would you say the defendant Hernandez, when in your office after six P.M., denied to you any guilt in this case?"

"I object, Your Honor, there's no such testimony in the record," said Ellis.

"He made a mistake trying to bring him back over this," Sam whispered. "He's going to lose all his points right now."

"I'm afraid the district attorney's memory is conveniently faulty," said Siakos.

"Wait a minute. Your Honor, I don't think such remarks are proper. Mr. Siakos knows better than that."

"Gentlemen, let's not argue amongst ourselves. Rephrase your question, Mr. Siakos."

"Lieutenant, I believe you stated previously that you questioned Hernandez intermittently from six P.M. to nine P.M. IS that right?"

"Yes, sir."

"And I believe you further stated that Hernandez denied any participation in this crime?"

The lieutenant tilted his head a bit and crossed his legs. "What I meant to say, sir, is that he denied shooting the patrolman."

"Lieutenant, didn't you testify before you went to lunch that Hernandez denied at least twice, after six P.M., any part in the crime?"

"I didn't understand your question."

Sandro and Sam both knew Siakos was enraged. His face was impassive, however, projecting only calm to the jury.

"How many times have you testified in court, on any cases, Lieutenant?"

"I'd say approximately two hundred times."

"You're not nervous here, then, are you?"

"Not nervous, no."

"And if I ask you whether a man denied *any* part in the crime, and you say, yes, he denied *any* part in the crime, what would you mean by that?"

The lieutenant puckered his mouth. "Well, I understand your question to be—from what I understand, the part that he denied was the shooting of the patrolman."

"I told you the sons of bitches would straighten him out over lunch," Sam whispered to Sandro, not taking notes, just watching.

Siakos tried to recall the exact words of the question he asked the lieutenant before lunch. Ellis objected that Siakos's paraphrase was not exact. The judge called a recess, so that the stenographer who had recorded the morning's session could type the relevant passage and bring it to the court forthwith. The lieutenant went back to the witness room. Ellis followed him as soon as the jury had retired.

"You can't fight that," Sam said, watching Ellis.

"It's so goddamn obvious," said Sandro. "I hope the jury gets the byplay."

They walked outside. Sam relighted a cigar. One of the courtroom buffs, a tall, lean, gray-haired Irishman, came over to them.

"You're doing all right now," he said. "I wouldn't believe a station house confession on a bet. Now the lieutenant is spilling the beans on them."

"Not after he comes out again," added a gray-haired woman, another of the buffs, who was standing next to the Irishman. Sam smiled and nodded. "They'll fix him up good before he comes back." Sandro returned to the courtroom.

The stenographer from the morning session was in court within twenty minutes with the typed testimony. He gave copies to all counsel and the judge. Lieutenant Garcia again took the stand. Siakos rose to face him. He asked the lieutenant where he had been just before getting back on the stand.

"In the witness room, right outside."

"Was anyone in there with you?"

"Other detectives."

"Did Mr. Ellis walk into the room?"

"I don't recall."

"Mr. Ellis, will you rise, please." Ellis was reluctant. He looked at the judge. The judge nodded. Ellis was annoyed as he rose. "This is Mr. Ellis. Was he in the witness room with you just now?"

The lieutenant pursed his lips, uncrossed and recrossed his legs. "He might have been."

"Thank you, Mr. Ellis." Siakos stared incredulously at the lieutenant.

"Lieutenant, this morning I asked you the following question." Siakos read from the typed minutes, "'How many times would you say that, after six o'clock, he denied flatly having had anything to do with this crime?' You answered: 'Once or twice, perhaps three times.' Do you recall that?"

"Yes."

"And do you now tell this court and jury that you meant that he had denied only having shot the patrolman?"

"That's correct, sir." Garcia cleared his throat.

"Lieutenant, I'll ask you now the same question I asked you this morning. Did he deny to you flatly that he had anything to do with this crime?"

"What he denied to me, sir, was the killing of the policeman—"

"Yes or no, please, to my question."

Ellis objected to restricting the lieutenant to yes or no. He suggested the lieutenant might not be able to answer completely by just yes or no.

"Objection," said Sam, rising. "The witness hasn't indicated any problem in answering. Mr. Ellis should not prompt the witness into confusion."

"If the lieutenant can't answer yes or no, he should give a full answer," the judge allowed.

"Your Honor, will you ask the lieutenant whether he can answer yes or no," Siakos suggested.

"No, sir," replied the lieutenant, who was Ellis's quick student.

"You may give a full answer."

"Officer, do you mean you do not understand my question?" said Siakos.

"Your Honor," said Ellis, jumping to his feet, "the court has said the lieutenant may give a full answer."

"That's right. The lieutenant hasn't answered your first question yet, Mr. Siakos."

"Will you give the full answer as directed by the court, Lieutenant?" Ellis, still standing, directed the witness.

"I withdraw the question, Your Honor," Siakos interrupted. He stood staring at Ellis. Ellis sat.

"Officer, did you understand the last question I asked about the denials?"

"My understanding of the last question, sir, the way you put it to me—"

"No. Did you understand it, is all I would like to know."

The lieutenant sat quietly, studying Siakos. "I understood your last question."

"I'll ask it again. You don't have to answer. I just want to know whether you understand this question. Did he, Hernandez, deny to you sometimes that he had anything to do with this crime? Is there anything you do not understand in that question?"

"There is nothing that I don't understand in that question."

"You understand every word?"

"That is correct."

"Do you understand the whole import of the sentence?"

"Yes, sir."

"The thought?"

"Yes, sir."

Siakos looked at his notes momentarily.

"The lieutenant's ready for him now," Sam said.

"No further questions," Siakos said, turning to his seat.

Sandro sighed in relief.

Ellis stood. He asked the lieutenant to repeat the questions he had asked Hernandez. He was going to rehabilitate his witness.

Sam objected. "Your Honor, this is not proper in the voir dire. The voir dire would have no purpose if the lieutenant were allowed now to tell what he elicited from Hernandez when we've objected to any statements as involuntary. That's why you granted this voir dire—to determine the admissibility of such statements."

"I join in the objection, Your Honor," said Siakos.

PART 35

"And I grant your application. It is not part of the voir dire. Any other questions, Mr. Ellis?"

Ellis unwrinkled his nose and looked a little flustered. "None, Your Honor." He returned to his seat.

The judge recessed court until the morning. Siakos, Sam, and Sandro were pleased with their day.

CHAPTER XIII

MIKE AND SANDRO stood before Alvarado's rooming house. Even as the bright sun began to descend into the evening sky, birds were chirping joyfully for the coming spring. Sandro wondered if the birds that rested in the coping of the surrounding buildings realized that this was a shabby, drab neighborhood. It made him think of Christ's parable of the birds of the field. God took care of them and saw to it that they did not hunger.

"Let's ring the super's bell. Jenny said she'd be here about this time," said Sandro as Mike preceded him down the three steps to the door beneath the stoop. Shortly, Jenny came to the door.

"Oh, hello." She opened the gate and asked them in. Inside were the usual walls without pictures, the linoleum floor, the flowered couch. A votive lamp flickered at the feet of a Madonna.

"I was glad you called, Jenny. Can we talk to Jorge?" Sandro asked.

She shook her head. "I spoke to my father, and I can't help it, but he says there's no way that Jorge can help you."

"Well, perhaps we can just talk to him, even by telephone."

"No, my father said that that's impossible. Look, Jorge's got his own trouble."

"What happened?" asked Mike.

"It wasn't his fault, really, but it doesn't matter whose fault it was, I guess. See, my brother and his wife don't live together, you know?"

"Your brother Jorge?"

"No, my other brother, Philip. He's younger. Anyway, my brother's got this girl friend."

"Where does your brother live?" Mike asked.

"I can't tell you those things. I'm trying to help you all I can, but I just can't tell you some things."

"That's okay, Jenny. You don't have to tell us anything if you don't want," said Sandro. He motioned to Mike to take it easy.

"No, that's all right. At least I can tell why I can't get Jorge to help you. I mean, you're a lawyer, right?"

"Right."

"Anyway, this girl friend is a tramp, if you ask me. She's nothing, ugly too. But my brother likes her. And she's got some other guy seeing her, and one day Philip goes there and finds this out, and he starts yelling and arguing, and this guy hits Philip with a lead pipe and makes his head bleed. Well, Jorge has always protected Philip, and when he heard what happened, he went over to the girl's apartment and gave her a good beating."

"Jorge can't just be running from an assault charge. I mean, the most that could happen is that a judge would warn him not to go near the girl again."

"No, her other boy friend. Jorge killed him," Jenny said, shrugging.

Sandro exchanged glances with Mike.

"How'd he do that?" Mike queried.

"After he gave the girl a beating, this other guy comes looking for Jorge. Jorge tells him he don't have any argument with him. The girl wanted him, and he could have her. But this guy starts a fight. He pulls a knife. Jorge had a gun. And he tells the guy, 'Don't come any closer, I don't want to use this thing.' And the guy says: 'You won't use that on a man. All you can do is beat up on women.' And he comes closer. And Jorge tells him to keep away. And this guy says, 'You ain't usin' that on me, baby.' And he's shaking this knife, moving closer. And Jorge tells him, 'I'm warning you, don't come any closer.' And the guy does, and Jorge shoots one shot, and hits him in the heart. And then he has to run away. The cops are still looking for him. The cops come around maybe once a week, twice a week. They ask me for him. I tell them I don't know where he is. But you know," she shrugged.

"It doesn't sound like murder," said Sandro.

"Yeah, but Jorge's got a record. Not for killing. But, well, he got some trouble from before, and that won't help him."

"I guess that's it then," said Mike.

"If we can help Jorge out, just give us a ring, Jenny," Sandro said.

"Sure. But what can you do, you know?" She smiled bitterly and shrugged. And what was there to do, Sandro wondered.

Sandro and Mike rode the elevator to the twenty-second floor. The building was the middle-income cooperative where Mike lived.

Mike's wife, Rose, met them at the door.

"So you're the one who kidnapped Mike."

"See, I told you it wasn't a blonde," Mike said to her as they entered the apartment.

"There must be some mistake," Sandro was unable to suppress a grin. "I never saw this man before he dragged me here and said his wife would kill him unless he produced an alibi for a lot of late nights."

Mike fixed a Scotch for Sandro and himself. They talked easily for a few minutes until Mike's wife excused herself to go back to the kitchen. Sandro stood by the picture window in the living room, looking downtown along the East River.

"Can you see Williamsburg from here?" he asked.

"I've seen enough of it." Mike was sitting in a green upholstered wing chair.

"This is a lovely apartment," Sandro said, settling himself on the couch. He placed his glass on a coaster on the coffee table and looked around at the wallpaper that had been chosen to blend with the draperies and the upholstery, at the pastoral prints on the wall behind Mike.

"Thanks," Mike said, with some pride. "Rose is my decorator. For my usual ten percent I'll let her tell you what to do with your place."

"Daddy." A girl of about seventeen came into the room, with an armload of books.

"Linda, say hello to Mr. Luca."

Mike's daughter smiled shyly. "Hello. You working on that case again tonight?"

"You know about it, too?" Sandro smiled back.

"That's all Daddy talks about—Alvarado, Mullaly, Snider." She turned to Mike. "Daddy, do you mind if I go down to Margie's house tonight to study? We want to get some review work done."

"Sure, if you've had your dinner, and your mother says it's okay." He beamed at her as she gathered her coat.

"I don't want to sound like a boasting father, or anything," he said after she left, "but she's going to Marymount next year, on a scholarship."

"She takes after Rose, I imagine."

"Very funny. She really is bright, though."

"That's a great school."

"Supposed to be one of the best," Mike agreed. "It was funny, you know. They had a social, all the families and the new students got together. She was so happy, so proud. I felt a little strange, though. You know, we kid about it and all, but there are still a lot of people around who think that Puerto Ricans are just one species of monkey. I mean, the kids don't feel it. They're all friends. But their parents are another thing. We're introduced and we look at each other, and we know—if it wasn't for the kids, we wouldn't even be speaking. And the kids, they get along so great. They don't even know it's going on."

"Don't worry about it, Mike. Nobody'll push you around."

"You kidding? I've been pushed around plenty. I paid the dues."

"Forty years ago," Sandro said, sipping at his drink, "the Italians and the Jews went through it. Some still are going through it. And before them the Irish, and the Germans. We were all greenhorns when we got here."

"Not to hear some people. Now that they've been here thirty, forty years, they act like it never happened, like the other guy on the way up is a freak."

"Well, the next guy on the way up will probably get a tough time from some very American Puerto Rican."

"Yeah, guys like Soto, who forget where it all came from."

"Dinner is served," Rose Rivera announced, coming back into the living room.

"Let's see what that fine tailored suit looks like when you've got your stomach all full of some great paella," said Mike. They sat down at the dining room table, absorbing the pungent aroma.

CHAPTER XIV

Tuesday, April 9th, 1968

ELLIS CALLED MULLALY BACK TO THE STAND as his second witness on the voir dire. Mullaly testified that at no time did he strike, beat, punch, kick, or hit Hernandez or see anyone else doing so. He denied that Hernandez ever admitted having shot Lauria. He acknowledged that he saw Mrs. Hernandez in the station house about 6:30 P.M. on July 3rd. He testified that the last time he saw her was when he took her home about 12:30 A.M. He said he left her there.

"Detective Mullaly," Siakos asked as his first question on cross-examination, "you realize, of course, that you are under oath to tell the truth?"

"Of course."

"And you never asked Hernandez a question in relation to the crime?"

"No, Counselor. He told me."

Siakos started through the prosecution story that Hernandez had made a voluntary statement. He cut it short, however, rather than continue pounding the story into the jury. Siakos turned the witness over to Sam Bemer.

"Would you ever strike a prisoner, Officer?" Bemer inquired.

"Only in defense of my life, Counselor," Mullaly answered placidly.

"Is it a crime of assault even for a policeman to unjustifiably strike a prisoner?"

"Yes, sir, I believe it is."

"And would you admit committing this crime, if in fact you did assault Mr. Hernandez or Mr. Alvarado?"

"I've sworn to tell the truth, Counselor. I would have to."

Sam stared at Mullaly. Mullaly stared back. Sam had no further questions.

Ellis next called the bullnecked Detective Johnson to the stand. Johnson sat sheathed in all his muscled bulk, the whites of his eyes contrasting against his black skin as his eyes studied the lawyers and the jury. Both defendants watched him curiously, cautiously.

Johnson testified he saw Hernandez on four separate occasions at the station house, but saw no one strike, beat, punch, kick, or hit Hernandez. Nor, certainly, had he done any such thing. Siakos cross-examined briefly.

Ellis next called the tall, beer-bellied Detective Jablonsky. If Johnson was a bull of a man, Jablonsky was an elephant. He was uncomely, but great strength lay beneath that bulk. His testimony echoed Johnson's and Mullaly's verbatim. They could have testified together, in harmony. The judge recessed for lunch after Jablonsky left the stand.

During lunch, Mike joined Sam and Sandro at Happy's Café. He told them how he had just gone to the apartment on 119th Street where Hernandez had pulled the burglary job on July 3rd, to interview the two men who lived there. They had not been at home, although the names on the mailboxes showed that they still lived there. Mike had left a note asking them to call him at his office.

"Have something to eat, Mike," said Sam.

"No, thanks, Sam. I'll just have a drink. I had something to eat uptown."

"I guess Ellis'll finish up his voir dire this afternoon, Sam," said Sandro. "He'll finish up with the detectives."

"Yeah, then he'll start right in again with the direct evidence leading up to Alvarado's statement."

"Did anything come out about the cops taking Hernandez's wife home that night in the station house? And that bit about the two squad cars and the gang-bang?" Mike asked.

"No," replied Sandro. "As a matter of fact, Mullaly was on the stand this morning and testified he took her home about twelve thirty, the early morning of July fourth. He said he searched the apartment and left her there."

Mike laughed. "Well, he's been getting into everything else in this case. Why not Mrs. Hernandez too?"

Sam laughed. "No, she's testified they just brought her home to have the apartment searched and brought her right back to the station house in time to see Mullaly give Alvarado a karate chop in the face."

"Those are two different stories. Why should somebody lie about something like that?" asked Mike.

"Because the cops want to place her in her apartment at one thirty so she couldn't have seen any karate chop, that's why," Sam said.

Mike nodded. "Oh well, too bad we haven't come up with the gang-bang between the Anglo-Saxons and the Puerto Ricans." He shrugged. "It's a racy theory, though. You know what I mean?"

"One more crummy joke like that and I'll have Happy cut you off from the firewater," Sandro said.

In the afternoon, Ellis called Detective John Tracy of the Manhattan South Homicide Squad. Tracy was tall and thin, his features sharp-lined and alert. According to Alvarado, it had been Tracy who tried to stop the other detectives from continuing to beat him.

Ellis again posed his perfunctory questions about whether, at any time, Tracy or anyone in his presence had punched, kicked, or hit Hernandez. Tracy said he had seen nothing of the sort. Tracy testified that he had helped interview Hernandez, but at no time did he or anyone else ask Hernandez questions relating to the crime.

While Tracy was on the stand, Sandro located the DD5 reports the detective had filed on July 3rd and 4th. He handed one of them to Siakos. Siakos read it, nodded absently, and continued to listen to the testimony.

"Even when he reads, he doesn't read," Sandro whispered hopelessly. "He could tear Tracy apart with that DD5."

"If he doesn't, you get up and do it," said Sam.

"But it has nothing to do with our client. It only relates to Hernandez."

"Everything in this trial relates to our client, and the judge can't say it doesn't." Sam continued making notes.

As he cross-examined, Siakos held Tracy's DD5 in his hand. He rolled it lengthwise and used it as a pointer.

Tracy testified that Mullaly had been Hernandez's main interviewer.

"Don't you love that word *interviewer?*" Sandro whispered to Sam.

Siakos unrolled the DD5 and asked Tracy if the signature on it was his. He said it was. Siakos offered it into evidence.

"Show it to Mr. Ellis," said the judge. The court officer did.

"You thought he'd screw it up. He's all right," whispered Sam, putting his pen down for the moment. "Look at Ellis, studying the DD5 like he never saw it before. If he doesn't have copies of every one of them in his file, I'll eat every bench in this courtroom."

"No objection, Your Honor," said Ellis.

"Received."

Siakos took the DD5 and walked to the jury box. "May I read this to the jury, Your Honor?"

"Surely."

Siakos read aloud:

Subject: Investigation of Ramon Hernandez—male, white PR, twenty-eight years, of One sixty-three Stanton Street, Apartment Sixteen, under this department as G265327:

1. On this date the assigned with Detective Mullaly, Shield 7316, and Detective Johnson, Shield 7268, of the Seventh Squad interrogated the above-named subject at the Seventh Detective Squad relative to this case and the ownership of a 1961 Chevrolet.

2. As a result of this interrogation, the assigned took a statement.

3. Request this case be marked Active.

PART 35

Siakos finished reading, then looked up at the jury for a moment. "No further questions," he said.

Sandro looked at Sam.

"Don't carry on. The jury's right in front of you," Sam said without turning. "If you want to use it, get up on your feet."

Sandro strode toward the jury-box shelf where Siakos had left the DD5.

"Is it your testimony, sir, that during the time you were on the third floor, the defendant Hernandez was not questioned about this case?"

"About the perpetration? No, sir. He volunteered."

"No questions from yourself?"

"Correct, sir."

"And no questions from Detective Mullaly."

"About the death of Lauria? No, sir."

"May I see counsel, for a moment," the judge requested. All counsel approached the bench. "I'm never the one to stop a cross-examination, especially in a capital case, but this detective hasn't testified about your man at all, Sandro. I hardly see any point to this interrogation." He turned to Sam. "Maybe you can tell me, Sam."

"There's a purpose, Judge. Sandro has a purpose."

"All right, but let's get on with it," the judge insisted.

"God love you, Judge," Sam said smiling. The judge smiled back indulgently. As they walked away from the bench, Sam whispered, "Don't let the judge stop you if you've got something."

Sandro picked up the DD5 again and studied it. "Now, sir, you know what the word *interrogated* means, as far as police work is concerned?"

"Yes, sir."

"And, sir, when you said on this DD5 that you interrogated Ramon Hernandez relative to this case—and the DD5 was filed in relation to the death of Fortune Lauria—did that mean that you interrogated Hernandez relative to the death of Lauria?"

"I haven't read the DD5 in a while. I don't know."

"If I say that this says the three of you interrogated the above-named relative to this case, would that mean to you in the ordinary circumstance of a DD5 that the defendant was questioned about the case?"

"Your Honor, I respectfully object to the form of the question," Ellis said. "Mr. Luca is not reading the entire content of the sentence put down by the detective."

"I am not hiding it, Your Honor," said Sandro. "I am going at it piece by piece, if I may."

"If it is taken out of context, I will sustain the objection. Let me see it," said the judge. He read the DD5. "I will allow it. Overruled."

"When you said on this DD5 *interrogated the above-named*—and the above-named is Hernandez—*relative to this case*—and the case is the death of Fortune Lauria—did that not mean at the time you made this report, Detective Tracy, that Hernandez had been interrogated about the death of Lauria?"

"It would."

"That would mean, in other words, he was asked questions about the death of Fortune Lauria?"

"Yes."

"And questions were asked because Hernandez hadn't given all the answers the detectives wanted, isn't that right?"

"I'm not sure I understand what you mean, Counselor."

"You weren't asking him questions to waste time, were you?"

"No, sir."

"You asked them because he hadn't supplied certain information and he had to be interrogated, isn't that right?"

"Yes."

"I have no further questions," said Sandro.

"That's using it, kid," Sam said as Sandro sat at the counsel table.

"At this point, Your Honor," Ellis said, rising, "the people rest their case on the voir dire relating to the statement made by Hernandez."

"Very well." The judge looked to Siakos.

"Your Honor, I move, on behalf of the defendant Hernandez, to suppress any statement allegedly made by the defendant on the ground that the people have failed in their burden of proving thai any alleged statement was free of coercion, or was not the result of physical brutality."

"I'm going to deny that application, Mr. Siakos. I am going to leave the question of the voluntariness of the alleged statement up to the jury for their deliberation. Therefore, the district attorney may continue with the orderly presentation of evidence, including any statement that he may have in which he believes the defendant Hernandez incriminated himself."

"Thank you, Your Honor," said Ellis. "I wonder if we might adjourn a little early this afternoon. The next evidence I'll present is Hernandez's statement, and since the direct and cross-examination shall be lengthy, I think an adjournment at this time would be beneficial to an orderly presentation."

"You're not forgetting we're scheduled to take the jury to the scene of the crime tomorrow, are you, Mr. Ellis?"

"Not at all, Your Honor. However, it would be more orderly not to start the testimony now and have to cut it short today and have the trip tomorrow separate it further."

"I grant your application. We'll meet here tomorrow morning at ten thirty, members of the jury. Do not discuss this case."

CHAPTER XV

Wednesday, April 10th, 1968

THE LARGE BUS, its motor idling, stood at the curb in front of the courthouse. The jurors, accompanied by the court officers, were already seated at the back. The clerk counted heads, then returned to the lobby, where Judge Porta was standing with the attorneys. The judge, in a gray striped suit and a fedora, was smoking a cigarette. Siakos and Sam also wore fedoras. Ellis was without a hat, as was Sandro.

"They're all in the bus, Your Honor," said the clerk.

"Okay. Is the stenographer in there?"

"Here he comes now, Judge."

One of the stenographers came out of the elevator, carrying a stenographic machine. He nodded to the judge, moving quickly toward the bus.

"Tell the captain to bring the defendants out," the judge instructed. The clerk disappeared through a door that led to a private elevator, usually reserved for the judges. Alvarado and Hernandez, handcuffed to each other, emerged into the lobby. They looked about them unfamiliarly, curiously. This was the first time they had been in the outside world since July 3rd, 1967. People walking through the lobby saw the handcuffed pair, paused momentarily, then continued on their

PART 35

way. Prisoners and defendants are everyday business in the Criminal Courts Building.

"Let's get on the bus, shall we, gentlemen," said the judge, starting out through the revolving door. He waited while the defendants entered the bus and were seated about half a dozen rows from the front. Each defendant sat in a separate row, on the window side of the seat, handcuffed to the armrest with a guard next to him. The judge and the attorneys sat in the first rows; the stenographer moved close behind the judge.

The driver shut the door. In a burst of compressed air, the brakes were released, and the bus moved slowly from the curb.

The clerk polled the jury for the official record and noted the presence of both defendants and their attorneys.

"All right, ladies and gentlemen," said the judge, standing in the aisle, still wearing his fedora, "although it might not seem so, the court is as much in session as if we were inside the courthouse. So you will listen to my instructions as carefully, follow my directions, and comport yourselves as if in the courtroom. As soon as we've finished our tour of the Stanton Street building, we'll come back to the courthouse, but we will not have a courtroom session this afternoon. As you know, I have other cases, and I've scheduled some unfinished matters this afternoon. Is is okay with everybody if you take off a little early today?" He asked smiling.

Most of the jurors smiled back. The letter carrier and the young telephone repairman cheered. The judge motioned them silent with his hands.

The bus turned east on Canal Street, then north on the Bowery. The riders were silent, watching the city slide by the windows. On the sidewalk, three drunks, bearded and tattered, were passing around a pint of wine, their hungry eyes watching that no one took too much. Another derelict was curled up on a doorstep, asleep. One of his shoes was missing. A younger but equally tattered man stooped next to the sleeping derelict and rifled through his pockets. The sleeper roused himself and yelled coarsely, drunkenly as the younger man fled.

"You see that?" Sam asked Sandro.

Sandro nodded.

"What a way to live, if it is living," Sam added.

"One compensation, Sam. You ever see a bald bum?"

Sam thought, then shrugged as he lifted his hat and scratched his head. "What a price for a head of hair, though."

Two Negro derelicts were fighting, throwing weak punches at each other, staggering, but not from the punches.

They passed Sid Goodman's Pawnshop. Sandro looked, but could not see anything through the display window as the bus moved on.

They turned east again on Houston Street. On the corner stood some men who had retained slightly more of their humanity than those on the Bowery. These men were waiting for trucks that might stop, with drivers offering a day's pay for a helper.

"A couple of blocks from Suffolk and Stanton streets," announced the judge in his best tour-guide voice, "is Katz's Delicatessen. If you wish, we can stop there and the officers can take our orders, and we can have a kosher lunch. The menu features frankfurters, knishes, and celery tonic. This reminds me of my younger days, when I was running for Congress." He turned to see the jurors.

"Everybody seems to go for that, Your Honor," Haverly, the foreman, answered.

The bus turned into Suffolk Street, and then into Stanton Street. The police from the Seventh Precinct had been notified, and they had reserved a large parking spot directly in front of the building. A small crowd stood on the sidewalk, watching as the bus pulled up. Women came to their windows to watch, some leaning on pillows. With equal curiosity, the jurors and officers in the bus gazed out at the people on the sidewalks and at the windows.

"Ladies and gentlemen of the jury," the judge said, standing. "I've already indicated this is as much a courtroom as if we were back at One hundred Centre Street. Actually, even stricter compliance with my instructions and the directions of the court officers is necessary here in order to insure these defendants of a fair trial. Now we will see some of the physical features of this building we've heard about in the courtroom. There may be other features that you want to see, but I'm allowing you to view only what I believe shall be fair and nonprejudicial. I direct you to follow instructions exactly. And no one—I repeat, no one—is allowed to return here on his own, just out of curiosity, even well-intentioned curiosity. Does everyone understand?"

The jurors nodded. Alvarado and Hernandez were studying the onlookers, particularly the women. A Spanish song was coming out of loudspeakers in front of a record store near Norfolk Street.

The defendants were led from the bus and up the stoop of 153 Stanton Street. The stenographer and the clerk followed. The judge and the attorneys entered, and stood on the stairs leading to the second floor. Each of the jurors was allowed to enter the hallway, and walk back to stand at the spot where Mrs. Santos said she had stood when she saw Hernandez. A court officer stood on the steps where Hernandez was supposed to have been.

"Your Honor," asked Ellis, "will you permit the jurors to move from side to side as they stand there?"

Neither Sam nor Sandro objected.

"Very well," said the judge, "but they may not move forward."

When all of the jurors had viewed the spot, the entourage made its way slowly up steps worn rounded by generations of immigrants, through the dim hallways, to the roof.

"Let the record reflect," Judge Porta instructed the stenographer, "that all of the jurors are present upon the roof, approximately at its center, and are viewing the rooftop. To all intents and purposes, the roof appears to be in exactly the same condition as in the Police Department photographs taken July tenth, 1967. Is that correct, gentlemen?"

The lawyers nodded. The jurors were allowed to look, but no discussion or questions were permitted.

This odd procession made its way down to the street again, where the jurors lined up two by two in front of the building. The court officers led the way through an alley to the rear yards.

"That's where the Italian woman lives," Sandro said, motioning with his head.

"You mean, the Italian woman who turned out not to be *the* Italian woman," Sam corrected.

"Don't rub it in."

Some of the jurors appeared surprised at the refuse and debris over which they had to walk. They stood next to the one-story extension and looked up, studying the building and the fire escape. Again, no discussion was allowed.

It was 12:15 by the time they had finished with the rear yard. Everyone was brought out to the street again, and they took their seats as before.

"Well," the judge said, turning as the bus began to move away, "are you ready for a little lunch?"

Katz's capped the holiday mood. The judge pointed out the sign that said, "Send a Salami to your boy in the Army." Many of the huge delicatessen's patrons looked up from the hot tea they were drinking out of water glasses to scrutinize this strangely assorted party. The busboys, hats firmly in place as they cleaned off the tables, barely gave a second glance.

Finally, the holiday mood still prevailing, the bus returned to the Criminal Courts Building. Judge Porta admonished the jurors not to discuss the case, and sent them home. The defendants once again returned to the Tombs.

CHAPTER XVI

Thursday, April 11th, 1968

ELLIS RECALLED DETECTIVE MULLALY. The jurors edged forward. The courtroom grew still.

"Now, Detective Mullaly, you were about to tell us of a statement Hernandez made to you. Will you tell the court and jury what, if anything, you said to the defendant Hernandez at that point and what, if anything, he said to you?"

"I said, 'Now, you saw Crispin Lopez. Now, do you believe we have him?'"

"He said, 'Yeah.'"

"I said, 'Now, tell me again. Did you lend Lopez your car today?' He said, 'Yeah.' And I said, 'You're lying. You heard what Lopez said. He was at work. Now, tell me the truth. Tell me what happened today.'

"And he said, 'Okay, okay. I'll tell you what happened. I didn't loan Crispin my car. I was in the car today. And I met a friend, named Luis.' And I asked him what Luis's name was, and he said he did not know.

"I said, 'What time did you meet him?' He said, 'About nine o'clock this morning.' I said, 'Where did you meet him?' He said, 'The Hotel Ascot.' I said, 'Where is the Hotel Ascot?' He said, 'That's at Allen and Delancey Street.'

"I said, 'What did you do at the hotel?' He said, 'I met Luis, and we went into the hotel, and we went into the bathroom. And we talked about going to steal. Then we left the bathroom, and we got into my car, and we drove uptown to El Barrio.'

"And I said, 'What time was that that you were in El Barrio?' He said, 'That was around eleven A.M.'

"I said, 'What did you do then?' He said, 'We got back into the car and we drove around some more. And in the early afternoon I parked my car on my block, across the street, but near my house.'"

Sam Bemer rose. "Your Honor, I move that you explain to the jury that any alleged statement made by the defendant Hernandez can only be used as evidence against Hernandez. It is not evidence which can be used against Alvarado, and must not be considered by the jury as evidence against him."

"Mr. Bemer's recitation of the law is quite correct, members of the jury. You may not consider this evidence against Hernandez in any way binding upon or affecting the defendant Alvarado. You may continue, Mr. Ellis."

Ellis nodded to Mullaly. "Please continue, Detective Mullaly."

"I said, 'Go on. Then what happened?' He said, 'We had decided to do a robbery in a building near my house.' I said, 'What building?' He said, 'I don't know the number, but it was the building a couple of doors away, across from the factory.'

"I said, 'Then what happened?' He said, 'We broke the door of an apartment on the top floor of that building.' I said, 'What apartment was that?' He said, 'I don't know the apartment number.'

"I said, 'Why did you pick that apartment?' He said, 'We picked that apartment because we thought that nobody was home in it.'

"Then I asked him how he got into the apartment. He said, 'Luis used the jimmy on the door, and we both pressed on the door with the shoulders, and that's how we got into the apartment.'

"And then I said, 'Then what happened?' He said, 'We went into the apartment, and Luis took a TV set and a ladies pocketbook.' And I asked him what color the pocketbook was, and he said, 'White.'

"And he said, 'Luis gave me a small radio and the jimmy to take.' And I asked him what color the radio was, and he said it was red.

PART 35

"Then I said, 'Then what did you do?' And he said, 'I carried the red radio and the jimmy. And we put the stuff on the roof. And then Luis went down the fire escape, from the roof, to get back into the apartment again.'

"I said, 'Why did he go down the fire escape?' He said, 'Because there was another television set near the window, in the apartment.'

"Then I said, 'Then what happened?' He said, 'Luis came back up the fire escape and said to me he couldn't get in the window because of the bars on the window.'

"Then he said that he and Luis lifted the TV set to the high wall, and Luis walked over to the back of the roof and looked down the fire escape and said to him, 'The cops! The cops!'

"'Then what happened?' I asked. He said, 'I stood on the roof next to the TV set, and I saw the cop come over the roof, from the fire escape. And he had his hand out, with a gun in it. And I was afraid.' And he said, 'Luis hid behind the stairway wall,' and he demonstrated a crouching position. And he said, 'As the cop passed Luis and said to me, "Hold it, hold it," Luis jumped on the cop from behind and put his left arm around his neck. And the cop fell forward and fell down.' And he said, 'Luis grabbed the gun from the cop's hand, and he shot him in the back.'

"I said, 'How many times did he shoot him?' He said, 'I don't know, but it was many times.'

"So then what happened?' I asked. He said, 'I was afraid. I cut out for my apartment. I ran over the roof, and I threw the jimmy away on the way over to the apartment.'

"Then Detectives Johnson and Jablonsky brought the television set, the red radio, and the white pocketbook that had been recovered from the roof of One fifty-three Stanton Street into the room. And Hernandez identified the property.

"Then I again asked Hernandez if he knew the last name of this Luis. He said he didn't know. I asked him where he lived. He said that he lived in Brooklyn. He thought it was on South Ninth Street because he had been up there about a week before at about three or four in the morning. He said he thought that he could point out the house to us."

Mullaly testified that Hernandez's entire statement was made by

6 P.M. After the police had the statement, they undertook an investigation of their files to find the last name of the person Hernandez called Luis. At approximately 9 P.M., the police discovered it was one Luis Alvarado for whom they were looking. A squad was then sent to the rooming house in Brooklyn where Hernandez had said Alvarado lived.

Ellis had the radio, the television set, and the other goods found on the Stanton Street roof brought into court. Mullaly identified them. He testified further that he saw Luis Alvarado for the first time about 1:30 A.M. on the morning of July 4th, when he was brought in by Detective Johnson. Ellis turned the witness over to Siakos.

Siakos was now permitted to read beyond the first eight pages in the notes Mullaly made on July 4th, but only up to page 14. Beyond that page was the alleged confession made by Alvarado.

Mullaly repeated his testimony on Siakos's cross-examination with the same aplomb he had displayed earlier in the trial.

Mullaly was not only a relentless detective, Sandro thought watching him, but a superb witness as well. He might have been chosen to testify at the trial because of his ability to talk with a straight face.

Mullaly admitted that when he searched Hernandez at the station house he found ten or twelve pawn tickets. However, Mullaly said he no longer had them nor did he know who, if anyone, on the police force now had them. Mullaly said that he had looked at the pawn tickets when he obtained them, but that he had made no notes concerning them. He said Hernandez had no wallet.

Siakos started to attack vehemently. He questioned whether any investigation had been undertaken after Hernandez allegedly said he could point out the house where Luis lived. Mullaly testified that no one had been detailed to Brooklyn until 9 P.M., when the last name of the man Luis was known.

"Officer, you wanted to avoid a possible flight out of the state if this man Luis was the actual culprit, did you not?"

"It is possible, I don't know."

"You say you don't know?"

"That's right, Counselor."

Siakos studied Mullaly. He questioned Mullaly intensely about the

PART 35

time Hernandez's alleged statement had been obtained. Siakos suggested that it was not before 11 P.M. Mullaly insisted the statement was obtained by 6 P.M. Siakos turned the witness over to Alvarado's defense.

"He did nothing to him," Sandro whispered.

"What did you expect, for Christ's sake? This guy is a great witness, and what is there to question him about. Let me try my luck." Sam stood and walked toward the witness.

Sam showed Mullaly photographs which had previously been introduced into evidence. One, a police photo, showed that the broken door jamb of Soto's apartment was not in the place where Mullaly said he found it. Another was a photo which showed the window in the Chevrolet closed, not open as Mullaly said he found it. Sam was attempting to cast some doubt on the evidence that the police were relying upon. Perhaps small sticks, but enough small sticks might beat the prosecution down.

Sam showed Mullaly the picture previously identified by Loughlin, the engineer, showing the rear yard behind the Stanton Street buildings and the alley leading to Suffolk Street. Mullaly said that the yard had been different on July 3rd, that there had been a fence across that backyard, blocking the way to Suffolk Street. Sam walked over to the counsel table to shuffle his notes.

"What do you make of that?" Sam asked Sandro. "He just built a fence!"

"He's a liar. We'll prove it," said Sandro. "Try and get something on that Brooklyn investigation. The time is still all up in the air."

Mullaly testified that between 6 and 9 P.M., while Luis's last name was being searched out, nothing was done.

"There were many policemen working on this case, weren't there?" Sam asked.

"Yes, Counselor."

"And there were many police personnel crowding the station house, waiting for assignment during the hours between six and nine P.M.?"

"Yes, I would say so."

"That was the reason Hernandez was questioned in the third-floor locker room—the precinct was crowded, right?"

"Yes."

"And not one of those unassigned men was sent to Brooklyn between six and nine P.M.—three hours—just on the chance that Hernandez could point out Alvarado's house?"

"No."

"In Brooklyn there's a station house near South Ninth Street, isn't there?"

"Yes, Counselor. I think it's the Sixty-third Precinct."

"Did you call the Sixty-third Precinct and ask them to go over to South Ninth Street and search for Alvarado?"

"No."

"Were you saving the cost of the gas or telephone calls? Is that why nothing was done?"

"Objection," said Ellis.

"Sustained."

"Wasn't it actually that you didn't get any information from Hernandez until after nine or ten or even eleven P.M.?"

"No, he gave the information by six P.M. We were investigating."

"You had to work him over until nine o'clock before you got what you wanted, didn't you?"

"No. We never touched him, Counselor."

Their eyes locked, as if looking down would show weakness.

"Aren't you just saying you got a statement by six o'clock so it won't look as if you gave him the third degree?"

"I object, Your Honor," said Ellis.

"The detective may answer. Mr. Bemer is bound by that answer."

"No, Counselor."

Sam had no further questions.

Ellis stood and asked Mullaly some questions on redirect. Mullaly described the fence he saw in the rear yard behind the buildings on Stanton Street. It was between ten and twelve feet high, he said, with wide horizontal planking.

Ellis called Detective Johnson to the stand, this time to continue the direct case. Johnson testified he had been one of the detectives who remained in Brooklyn in the rooming house Hernandez had pointed out, awaiting Alvarado's return. He and the other two detectives awaited Alvarado in the vestibule of the rooming house, at the top of the stoop, just behind the front door, which was half wood and half frosted glass.

The detectives remained there until they heard loud voices in Spanish conversation outside in the street. Johnson testified he opened the front door and discovered Alvarado standing directly in front of the steps leading into the building, speaking to the superintendent. Johnson testified he drew his revolver and arrested Alvarado, searched and handcuffed him, and started walking east on South 9th Street. Johnson said Alvarado had turned to him while they were walking and asked what he was being arrested for. Alvarado had had a newspaper in his hand and said to Johnson, "Not about the cop who was killed on Stanton Street!" In reply, Johnson said he had asked Alvarado why he mentioned that crime when he, Johnson, had said nothing about any particular crime.

At the station house, Johnson released custody of the prisoner to Detective Mullaly. Alvarado was then taken to the third-floor locker room. Johnson testified he went there later on two occasions. Both times it was to accompany Hernandez. Ellis had no further questions.

Sam rose and walked toward Johnson to cross-examine. Johnson's mind seemed like his body, hard to move.

"Did he at any time say to you, 'What's this all about?'" Sam asked.

"No, he did not."

"He didn't ask you what's this all about after you arrested him?"

"All he said to me was, 'Is this about the cop who was killed on Stanton Street?' And I said to him, 'Why do you ask me a question like that?' And he says to me, 'Because I read it in the newspapers.'"

Sandro walked over to Sam. "Ask about the arrest. They didn't know Alvarado was there until after they heard the conversation in Spanish," Sandro whispered in Sam's ear as they bent close together to avoid having the jury hear. "Show Alvarado could have escaped without their knowing he was there. And ask him about any resistance to arrest. He'll go along with you. He's too stubborn to change the story."

"This door behind which you were standing in the vestibule, before you arrested Alvarado, it was half wood and half frosted glass. Is that right?"

"This is correct."

"And you couldn't see through that frosted glass?"

"Only when I opened the door." With each answer, Johnson had to hunch his hulk of muscle forward toward the microphone. Then he would sit back.

"But before you opened the door to arrest Alvarado, you only heard his Spanish conversation."

"This is correct."

"And you didn't know he was there until then?"

"That is correct."

"And at that time he was talking to the superintendent?"

"That is correct."

"And the superintendent was in the building prior to Alvarado's arriving? You saw him in the building earlier in the evening?"

"That is correct."

"He didn't arrive with Alvarado?"

"He was in the building earlier."

"When you first saw Alvarado, where was he?"

"He was just starting up the stoop."

"Did you identify yourself to Alvarado?"

"Yes, I did."

"Did he run away?"

"No, he did not."

"Did he pull out a gun?"

"No, he did not."

"Did he fight you?"

"No, he did not."

"Did he resist you?"

"No, he did not."

"Did he identify himself?"

"Yes, he did."

"Did he attempt to give a false name?"

"No, he did not."

"Did he yell at you?"

"No, he did not."

"Did he curse you?"

"No, he did not."

PART 35

"Your witness," Sam said as he returned to the counsel table.

Ellis had no further questions. He recalled Detective Mullaly to continue the narration of events after Alvarado was taken to the locker room for interrogation.

In his calm, assured way, Mullaly testified that he brought Alvarado up to the third floor because all the offices were still too crowded downstairs.

Sam rose and made an application that any statement Alvarado allegedly made to the police be excluded from evidence as being coerced by violence or fear. Ellis indicated to the court that this was not the point at which any voir dire was necessary. The judge allowed Ellis to continue.

Mullaly testified that Alvarado had given his name, age, and the fact that he did not have a job. Alvarado allegedly also told Mullaly that he had been alone in the movies on 42nd Street on the day of the murder, although he wasn't able to recall the title of the movie. Alvarado said he couldn't remember the name of the picture because he was "on the nod"—a state of sleepy, narcotic euphoria—having taken a shot of heroin in the men's room. Alvarado denied being with Hernandez that day.

Mullaly testified that Hernandez was then brought up to the locker room to confront Alvarado. According to Mullaly, after some urging to repeat what he had said earlier, Hernandez had said to Alvarado, "You killed the cop, you killed the cop." Alvarado jumped from his chair and said, "You killed the cop, you killed the cop." Mullaly had had Hernandez removed at that point. Mullaly testified that Alvarado then admitted seeing Hernandez on July 3rd, that Hernandez had driven to Brooklyn to show Alvarado his new car, that they rode around the block in Brooklyn, and that Hernandez had then left.

Mullaly testified that Alvarado had denied being in the car any longer than a few minutes, an hour at the most, and all that while in Brooklyn.

Mullaly had Hernandez brought into the locker room again, and asked him to repeat again what he had said to Alvarado. Hernandez said to Alvarado, "You shoot the cop, you shoot the cop on the roof." At that point, Mullaly said, Alvarado jumped up and screamed curses in Spanish at Hernandez. Hernandez screamed Spanish curses right back. They lunged for each other and had to be restrained. Hernandez was removed, and, Mullaly testified, he attempted to calm Alvarado down. He said he asked Alvarado if he wanted to tell what really happened the afternoon before. Alvarado said he wanted to talk.

"All right, Your Honor. At this point, I think it is time for the voir dire," Ellis announced to the court.

"You may inquire, Mr. Bemer. And again, I trust the jury understands the procedure the court is adopting in this case. The voir dire is to determine the voluntariness of the alleged confession of Alvarado. Not what was said, but the methods of obtaining the statement, if any."

Sam interrogated Mullaly, who testified that Alvarado had not been asked any, not one, question directly concerning the death of the policeman. Without being asked a question, after the two confrontations with Hernandez, Mullaly testified, Alvarado freely and openly told the entire story of Lauria's death.

Mullaly denied taking movie-ticket stubs or anything else from Alvarado's pocket. Alvarado had about two dollars in loose change, Mullaly said.

"We'll recess for lunch at this time, members of the jury. Do not, however, discuss this case," intoned the judge. The jury filed out; the prisoners were returned to the detention cells. All the spectators and lawyers and court officers left the courtroom.

"Any further questions of the witness, Mr. Bemer?" the judge asked, as court resumed.

"No, Your Honor."

"Please proceed. Call your first witness on the voir dire, Mr. Bemer."

"May I approach the bench, Your Honor?"

"All counsel, please." The lawyers stepped to the bench.

"Your Honor, we are willing to put the defendant Alvarado on the stand, although we are certainly not obliged to do so," said Sam. "However, I want it strictly understood that Alvarado's being on the stand now does not open the door for the district attorney to delve into portions of the defense at this time."

"Now, Your Honor," Ellis protested, "once the defendant is on the stand, I can ask him about anything relating to his credibility."

PART 35

"He can delve into all the immorality, past record, viciousness, if any, he wishes, Your Honor," replied Sam. "Anything which deals with credibility. However, I object to any invasion of the defense prior to our being able to present it in its proper order, because that would be so prejudicial as to deny the defendant a fair trial."

"All right. You'll go along with this, won't you, Dave?" the judge insisted.

"If you say so, Judge."

"Proceed."

Alvarado was called to the stand. The jurors watched as this man, described as a cold-blooded murderer, was sworn as a witness. They sat, waiting. Alvarado testified, in response to Sam's questions, that he had, on three separate occasions, been convicted of using narcotics, and that he had served three jail sentences. He said that he had never been arrested for any charge of violence before.

Alvarado was calm and courteous on the stand. He answered questions directly, and in English. He testified that Mullaly had removed the handcuffs after Johnson brought him into the station house; that they then proceeded directly up to the locker room. While on the stairs, Alvarado stated, Mullaly had hit him in the face. Alvarado was taken into the locker room. There, he testified, he was surrounded by eight or ten policemen who began to fire questions at him. He told them he didn't know what they were talking about, knew nothing about the death of Lauria. One of them drove a short, ramrod punch into Alvarado's stomach. Alvarado said that two detectives intertwined their arms in his, one on each side. They also each hooked a leg inside Alvarado's ankles, thus holding him spread-eagled in a standing position.

Sam had Alvarado step off the stand and demonstrate, with the aid of two court officers, how he was vertically spread-eagled. The jurors moved to the edge of their chairs.

Alvarado resumed the witness chair and testified that the police kept punching him in the chest and hammering him with questions about the roof and the dead officer. At one point, he said, he tried to drop down low enough so that the punch he was about to receive in the stomach would hit him in the face. He wanted to be cut or bleed, so that the evidence of his beating would be obvious. The policemen holding his arms jerked him up quickly.

Alvarado testified that one of the cops, a tall, nearly bald one, with some red hair, had said, "Listen, you black spic, you better talk to me and tell me the way you jump this police on the roof, because if you don't do it, I am going to kill you." Alvarado said he had then cried because he was "ascared" of this man. The cops continued to punch him. When he was punched in the chest, he testified, his head was thrown back and struck against the metal lockers behind him. One time, he said, his head hit so hard that he fell to the floor dazed and groggy. He came to and began to pray to God in Spanish. He heard a voice in Spanish inquire, "You want to talk to me?" It was Lieutenant Garcia. He replied in Spanish to Garcia that he did not want to talk to him but he knew nothing about the case. Alvarado testified that Garcia then said: "Round Two. Kick him in the balls." Alvarado said two detectives lifted him into the air by the legs, and spread one of his legs forward, the other to the rear. Alvarado testified he screamed and pleaded that he had had an operation in his groin area when in Sing Sing, and he'd die if they kicked him there. The detectives put him down and continued the stomach punches.

Alvarado testified that Detective Tracy then came into the room and announced: "Stop hitting that man. Let me talk to him." Tracy took Alvarado away from the others and said that Alvarado should not be afraid, that he should tell the truth. Tracy said even though he himself had a gun and badge, it was still sometimes difficult to enter a place to go after a man with a gun. And so, if Alvarado had been on the roof, it was certainly understandable that he'd be frightened by the policeman with a drawn gun. Perhaps he panicked. That wouldn't be murder in the first degree, not for having panicked. Maybe manslaughter.

Alvarado testified he replied to Tracy that a cop was killed, and he knew that whoever shot the cop would get the chair, but he didn't do it.

Alvarado further testified that when he had returned home that night at about 1 A.M., he observed the lights on in the superintendent Jorge's apartment. He knocked on Jorge's door. Jorge opened the door and immediately said to him, "Luis, you kill a cop?" And Alvarado

PART 35

replied, "Jorge, you crazy?" And Jorge told him there were three detectives upstairs waiting to see him about the cop-killing. Alvarado testified he had had a newspaper with him that contained a story that a policeman had been killed, and the police were looking for the killer, a five-foot-ten Negro. Alvarado testified he said to Jorge: "I don't have anything to do with this, I don't have anything to hide. I'm going up to talk to them." Alvarado then walked outside, talking to Jorge in Spanish, and started up the stoop to where he was told the detectives were waiting. A Negro detective, now known to be Detective Johnson, rushed out from behind the door at the top of the stoop, his gun drawn.

Alvarado testified that the detectives searched him in the station house and took from him the stubs of the movie tickets and $141 in cash, which he had in a money clip in his pocket.

Alvarado told the jury that he had that money as a result of receiving three one-hundred-dollar bills from someone who wanted Alvarado to buy heroin for him.

He had spent some of it, since part of the money was to be for his services.

While in the station house, Alvarado explained, he was brought down from the locker room to the detectives' office, where there was a door with a two-way mirror. A woman, whom he could not see, was on the other side of the mirror, trying to identify him. After that, Alvarado said, he was taken out into the detective squad room, where he was handcuffed to a steam pipe. After some while, he was taken back into the lieutenant's private office, and one of the detectives said to him that he should confess because the property taken from the apartment, which had been abandoned on the roof, had his fingerprints all over them. Alvarado testified that he had replied to the detective that whatever prints they found could not be his, since he was never near that property.

The detective, in fury, told Alvarado that they were going to bury him.

Another detective entered the room and told Alvarado that the district attorney had arrived, and that if Alvarado didn't confess to the district attorney, he didn't yet know what a beating was.

Sometime afterward, he spoke to the district attorney and, he said, told the D.A. that he did not commit the crime. Alvarado said he told the D.A. that anything about the case that the police might say, connecting him to the crime, was a lie. He told the district attorney that the police beat and punched him. Sam had no further questions.

The judge called a short recess before Ellis started his cross-examination of Alvarado.

Ellis stood to cross-examine. He studied Alvarado; Alvarado watched Ellis.

"Now, Alvarado, On July third, 1967, where were you employed?"

Sandro's eyes narrowed as he too watched Ellis cross-examine. He was struck by Ellis's addressing the witness as Alvarado. People might be indirectly referred to or spoken about in court, but a lawyer did not address a witness by his surname only.

During cross-examination, Alvarado testified he had not worked from August, 1965, to July 3rd, 1967. During that time, he helped the superintendent in his building in exchange for his room. In addition, he hustled, sometimes lending a hypodermic needle to a needy junky, occasionally helping a junky to locate drugs. He was paid in cash or in a donation of heroin, so that his habit and spending money were cared for at the same time.

Alvarado replied to Ellis that it was *The Daily News* he had had in his hand when Johnson arrested him, and that he had read about the cop being killed and the five-foot-ten Negro suspect in that paper.

Alvarado testified he saw Mrs. Hernandez in the station house after he was brought in at 1:30 A.M. He said she was nearby when Mullaly accompanied him to the third-floor locker room and, while ascending, hit Alvarado in the face with the edge of his hand.

After he was inside the locker room, Alvarado testified, he was dripping a little blood from his nose. He repeated that, at one point, when his head snapped back and hit the lockers, he lost consciousness. It was then that Lieutenant Garcia spoke to him in Spanish.

The judge recessed the court until the morning.

CHAPTER XVII

SANDRO WALKED ALONG ST. MARK'S PLACE, past shops displaying bell-bottom pants, embroidered vests, beads hanging from wires in the windows, granny glasses with clear lenses, psychedelic colored scarfs, felt hats, shirts.

Almost all the people he passed on the street were dressed like the shop windows—men and women, boys and girls, with long, stringy hair, beads, flowing clothes, capes, ponchos, colored kerchiefs tied around their legs or heads. These people, Sandro thought, had dropped out of one establishment into another, abandoned one world's conventions for another's. They were descended in a line of generations that went from the bohemian to the beat to the hip to the stoned.

Sandro entered the coffeeshop-bar called POT-tery. It was dark and smoky. The room rocked and throbbed with a loud, rhythmic sound that eliminated all other sounds; people's mouths moved, but no one could hear what they said; people walked, but they had no footsteps. Red, yellow, blue, and green lights were swaying across the room, moving and twisting as the patrons of POT-tery did.

Charlie D'Andrea, dressed in bell-bottoms and sporting dark

glasses and a chain with a large, cross-shaped pendant around his neck, was sitting at a table near the door.

Sandro approached, he, too, wearing bell-bottoms, with a dark turtleneck sweater.

"Out of sight, baby," Charlie smiled, as Sandro sat. "Watch some fuzz don't bust you before you get home tonight."

"That's what I worry about when I go into places like this," said Sandro. "No matter how way-out my clients may be, I've got a suit of armor and I ride a white horse. Once I get arrested, I'm just some guy standing around in his underwear."

"You don't have to worry tonight. I'll tell them you're okay. Want something?"

A girl in a suede miniskirt, with beads around her neck, an Indian headband at her forehead, her hair hanging long and straight, walked to the table.

"Peace."

"Peace," said Sandro. "A cup of coffee."

She nodded and walked away.

"I'm sorry you had to come down here to meet me, Sandro, but I just couldn't get away. I've got something big coming up."

"That's all right. It gives me a chance to get away from the neighborhoods I've been in lately and enjoy some real class." Sandro looked around.

"I checked this fellow Snider out for you," said Charlie. "You were right about the reason he was thrown off the squad a few years ago. Some big investigation, when they ended up deporting Jimmie Pearl. But the traffic and the doping kept going. I checked a couple of guys who know Snider. He's not too bright. Honest, though. When I say honest, I mean he's okay, you know, a little natural larceny here and there, but no way-out graft. He's not on anybody's payroll. He's supposed to be a good cop, just got caught up over his head in that investigation, and they dumped him."

"Are you telling me the guy's not a doper himself."

"He may be a dope, but he's not a doper," replied Charlie. "At least the way I get the story. It's pretty reliable information. Matter of fact, I understand he busted some guys a couple of months ago, they were pretty big dealers. He arrested them with twenty-eight thousand dollars in cash. And he turned the twenty-eight over to the property clerk." D'Andrea's head nodded. "Most guys would have turned in two or three, kept the rest. This guy turns in the cash. That's what I mean, he's a little dopey." He smiled. "You can't get straighter than that, can you?"

"Guess not."

A tall, lean, blond young man walked over to the table. His hair was long enough to be tied in a ponytail, which it was. He wore a purple shirt with a huge collar and bell-bottom jeans. He had a thick, jeweled bracelet on his left wrist.

"Peace, brother," said Charlie.

"Peace," the young man said. He looked at Sandro.

"This is a buddy of mine," Charlie said. "Sandro, I'd like you to meet Raymond. Sit down, Raymond."

Raymond shook hands with Sandro.

"Hey, Raymond, telephone," called the bartender.

"Be right back," said Raymond. He walked to a booth near the bar.

"This is my man for tonight," said Charlie. "You want to come to a little party with us?"

"Am I going to get busted?"

"If you leave when I tell you to, you won't. I'm going to get busted though."

"You're going to get busted? For what?"

"This guy is a little dealer. But we want his supplier. So I'm trying to flush them out. If I get busted with him, I'll be in a little tighter."

"You guys have to go through a lot."

Charlie shrugged. He looked up and smiled. "Sometimes it's not so bad."

A young girl came over to the table. She wore a silky blouse and pants. Her eyes were heavily made up. She wore no bra, and pronounced nipples pressed through the silk.

"I'm hip," said Sandro, watching the girl slide her arm around Charlie's neck. She gazed absently down at Sandro. Her eyes were vague, floating circles of blue-green.

"Baby, say hello to Sandro. This is Iris."

She smiled wanly. "Charlie, Charlie, I'm getting all strung out. All way-out all over this place. You have anything for me tonight?"

"I told you, baby. Things are kind of tough. There's a lot of heat lately."

"Come on, Charlie. Give me something. I'll treat you good. Just something."

"Not tonight. I can't help you tonight."

"Charlie, go get something and bring it over to my pad. Bring your friend too," she said, looking at Sandro. "Just bring something with you. Let's get out of here for a while."

"Okay, baby. I'll try."

"Don't hang me up, Charlie. Don't hang me up." She started rubbing the sides of her head with both hands. It made her breasts jiggle.

"I'll take care of it, baby. Just go ahead now and wait for me."

Iris walked slowly toward the door. She turned and made an appeal with her mouth and arms.

"She must have been a nice-looking girl, Charlie," Sandro said. "What's she on?"

"Heroin. She's all fucked up. Nice kid. What can I do? She can't help herself. I throw her some stuff once in a while."

Raymond returned. He sat at the table.

"What's happening? Are we going?" Charlie asked.

"Yeah, baby." Raymond studied Sandro, then looked at Charlie.

"Don't worry about Sandro. He's with me."

"Let's go then."

They walked out into the street and started toward Second Avenue. Just before the corner, Raymond led the way into a tenement. They followed him up three flights of stairs. Raymond knocked on a door.

"Who is it?" a voice on the other side whispered.

"Raymond and a couple of friends."

The door opened. Within, the room was dark, except for a wash of color that a revolving light played upon the ceiling. Sitar music stroked the thick air, made thicker by the heavy incense smoking near the door to mask odors of burning hashish or marijuana. Sandro's eyes fought through the dark. On the floor, sitting around a table, was a

PART 35

group of people, all with long hair, all dressed in levis and sheepskin jackets, with chains and beads around their necks. They were passing a small white pipe from hand to hand. Each person around the table was taking long drags on it.

Charlie led Sandro to a couch, a short distance from the table.

"Come on, man, let's sit down and float," Raymond suggested to Charlie.

"Okay, go ahead, you sit in there. I'll sit here."

"What are they smoking?" Sandro whispered.

"Hash."

Someone rose and offered the pipe to Charlie. He declined, taking a gnarled thin cigarette from his pocket. He gave another one to Sandro.

"Don't worry," Charlie assured him. "It just smells bad. This stuff is straight oregano."

Two of the longhairs around the table rose.

"I'm going out to take a ride on my bike," one announced. He was high out of his mind. The other turned out to be a girl. Sandro couldn't tell until he saw she had breasts.

Charlie smiled, nodded. He was studying the room, clocking the faces. He wasn't going to forget anyone.

"I'm going too," said the girl. She was as high as the motorcyclist.

They walked to the door. "Peace and love," the girl announced.

"*Et cum spiritu tuo*," Sandro added softly.

"You were an altar boy, too," said Charlie.

"What's a nice Italian kid like you doing, working in a place like this?" Sandro asked.

"If you ask the Wasp bastards from Westbury or Greenwich, they'll tell you all the Italians are in the Mafia selling junk to their kids."

"Charlie, they couldn't out-navigate, out-think, out-paint, out-sculpt, out-sing, or out-fuck us, so they have to knock it. They were still living in caves in Saxonia when Giulio Caesar sat in a palace in Roma."

Charlie nodded. "You better start making your move. This joint is going to be busted in about fifteen minutes."

"How do I get out of here?"

"Say you're going down for something. Nobody'll be here when you get back."

Sandro stood. "Thanks, Charlie."

"You blow my mind, man. You fit right in, you know?"

"Peace."

"Peace," said Charlie. He smiled as Sandro made his way to the door.

CHAPTER XVIII

Friday, April 12nd, 1968

ALVARADO RESUMED THE WITNESS CHAIR the next morning. After the jury was polled and the judge entered the courtroom, Ellis rose and began to chip away at Alvarado.

Ellis questioned Alvarado's testimony that Lieutenant Garcia was in the locker room and spoke to Alvarado in Spanish. Alvarado repeated the story, testifying that when the two detectives held him aloft by the legs, the lieutenant said, "Kick him in the nuts."

"Did he say 'Kick him in the nuts' or 'Kick him in the balls?'"

Alvarado thought momentarily. "He said, 'Kick him in the balls.'"

"Well, which was it now? You testified in answer to Mr. Bemer, the lieutenant said, 'Kick him in the balls.' Today you said, 'Kick him in the nuts.'"

"I see too many ladies today in the courtroom," Alvarado said, pointing to the spectators. "I don't want to be without respect."

"Isn't this a fine state of affairs and a fine cross-examination?" Sam whispered. "Ellis is compiling a glossary of scatology, while Alvarado is on trial for his life."

Alvarado testified that at no time did he make an incriminating statement to the police, despite the vicious beatings he had received.

He said that when he spoke to the district attorney the morning of July 4th, 1967, he told the D.A. the police beat him. He said he even showed D.A. Brennan the places where the handcuffs had cut into his wrist. He testified he told the district attorney that he had had nothing to do with the crime.

Alvarado responded to Ellis's cross-examination that he had been assigned legal counsel when he was first arraigned in court. However, he did not even speak to this lawyer at that time. The lawyer merely stood beside him and had the case adjourned. Alvarado said he had never had an opportunity to speak to the lawyer. He admitted he did not complain to the lawyer about the police beatings.

"And when you were in court on July fourth, did you tell the judge you had been beaten by the police."

"No, I didn't tell that."

"When you were brought to the Tombs, did you receive a medical examination?"

"Yes, sir."

"Did you tell the doctor who examined you that you had been beaten?"

"I don't think I have a chance to tell him that."

"Did anyone stop you from speaking when the doctor was examining you?"

"No, sir."

"And didn't the doctor ask you questions?"

"I believe so."

Ellis took out Alvarado's blue medical record cards, which had been subpoenaed from the Tombs. He introduced these into evidence, then stood before Alvarado, reading them.

"Didn't you tell the doctor you were an addict?"

"I believe so."

"Is there any doubt about that?"

"No, sir."

"And didn't he give you pills for your withdrawal pains?"

"I was a little sick then, but it was pain from the beating."

"But you didn't tell the doctor about the beating, did you?"

"No, sir."

"You didn't tell anyone about the beating when you were in court or when you were first brought into the Tombs, did you?"

"No, sir."

"You didn't tell anyone about this beating until after you were in the Tombs six days and had a chance to realize the tough position you were in?"

"Objection."

"Sustained."

"I have no further questions."

Sandro rose and walked to Alvarado.

Alvarado testified that while in the Tombs, a few days after first being committed there, he had to be sent to Bellevue after suffering some sort of attack where he couldn't breathe and from which he had passed out on the floor in his cell. A doctor from the Tombs treated him with oxygen, and then an ambulance rushed him to Bellevue where he underwent various examinations. He was returned to the Tombs sometime the next morning.

Sandro questioned Alvarado about any previous history of fits, seizures, epilepsy, or the like. He had had none, nor had anyone in his family.

Alvarado testified that his heroin habit cost about six dollars a day. Although he had been taking narcotics for eight years, his habit was small, and it had been broken by three visits to prison, one lasting as long as two and a half years. He had also been on self-imposed withdrawal from time to time.

Sandro had no further questions.

Sandro and Sam were pleased. Alvarado had held up well under cross-examination. Suddenly, they turned as Siakos stood and began to ask Alvarado questions.

"Now, Mr. Alvarado, when you were in court with Hernandez, did you speak to your lawyer?"

"No, sir."

"Did Hernandez?"

"I'm not sure. I don't think he did."

"Was there some reason for this?"

"I wasn't feeling too good."

"What the hell's he doing? That's *our* defendant on the stand," Sandro said. "Every question is potential dynamite. He might open doors we can never close."

"What the hell can we do?" Sam whispered. "Go up there, and tell him to sit down."

Sandro stood, walked to Siakos, and whispered the message as firmly as possible while yet maintaining his outward calm before the jury. Siakos nodded, then asked Alvarado if he had seen Hernandez at any time on July 3rd. Alvarado said no. Siakos asked if he had ever been in Hernandez's apartment. Sandro was just starting to his feet again as Alvarado answered "No," and Siakos quit.

Sandro called for a doctor from the Tombs as his next voir dire witness. It was Dr. Joseph Waters, who had examined Hernandez, again. Sandro wanted him to decipher Alvarado's medical records from the Tombs. The doctor, looking just as much like a butcher as before, testified that Alvarado had been given an examination prior to his being put into a cell in the Tombs on July 4th, 1967, and that examination revealed a man who had been a drug addict for eight years and who was suffering at the time of his commitment from withdrawal symptoms relating to narcotics.

The doctor admitted that at no place on the chart of that first physical examination was there an indication of a pulse rate, a heart rate, an evaluation or report of the patient's head, lungs, chest, abdomen, or anything else. No X-rays had been taken. The doctor indicated that the examination was more or less a gross-inspection examination, where the doctor stands some distance from the patient and merely observes him.

Dr. Waters acknowledged that the doctor who had made this cursory initial examination of Alvarado had already obtained from Alvarado the information that he was an addict, and so might have attributed the poor appearance and condition of the prisoner to withdrawal symptoms.

Sandro questioned the doctor concerning the reports of the illness which caused Alvarado to be transferred to Bellevue on July 9th, 1967. Ellis objected. He wanted Dr. Maish, the doctor who had actually examined Alvarado in his cell and sent him to Bellevue, to testify.

PART 35

Sandro said that he had subpoenaed Dr. Maish, but he had not as yet arrived.

The judge called recess for lunch, telling Sam to call the doctor's office to be sure he would arrive after lunch.

In the afternoon, Dr. Edward Maish, took the stand. He was tall, bald, gaunt. He testified that he had found Alvarado on the floor of his cell on July 9th, 1967, and as a result of his diagnosis, had sent him to Bellevue for further examination. The doctor said he did not recall all the circumstances of that evening, but he was sure he could refresh his memory from his charts. Sandro introduced Alvarado's medical card, relating to that night, into evidence. He had the doctor read it aloud to the jury.

> Patient was found unconscious on floor. An apparent clonic seizure, Cheyne-Stokes breathing, spasmodic shaking, tachycardia, rapid pulse, exquisite tenderness in the epigastrium. In lucid moments, patient stated he was beaten in police station.

The doctor described the apparent clonic seizure as a condition where the extremities were all twitching and shaking. In addition, Alvarado's eyes were rolled back, and he was salivating. Cheyne-Stokes breathing was a special kind of abnormal breathing, the doctor explained, where first the patient breathed deeper and deeper, then stopped completely, then started in again with shallow breaths. Tachycardia was fast heartbeat.

The doctor said that he had also found Alvarado to have marked tenderness of the epigastrium. Sandro had the doctor point out the region of the epigastrium. The doctor pointed to the center of his chest, just beneath the rib cage, the very place where Alvarado said he had been punched by the police.

"There was also guarding and rigidity of the abdomen," the doctor added.

"And what did that mean to you, Doctor?"

"That meant the prisoner might have been bleeding internally. That's why I sent him to Bellevue. When there's internal bleeding, there's also rigidity. From what he said about a beating, I wasn't taking chances. But the report from Bellevue was negative. No internal bleeding," the doctor added with apparent pleasure.

Although the doctor's testimony was sliding smoothly into the minutes of the trial, Sandro could feel the doctor's reluctance, a hostility growing with each question. The doctor didn't appreciate being subpoenaed into court, away from his practice, and now, it apparently seemed to him, having his medical opinion questioned.

"Doctor, does the fact that there was no internal bleeding mean that Mr. Alvarado did not have a clonic seizure?"

The doctor studied Sandro. "No."

"Does it mean he didn't have Cheyne-Stokes breathing?"

"No."

"In other words, all the other things you diagnosed did not change, even though Bellevue ruled out internal bleeding?"

"Right. That's right."

"When you use the words *apparent clonic seizure*, does that mean, as far as you could diagnose, that he was actually having a clonic seizure?"

"That's what I saw. It appeared that way to me."

"What causes a clonic seizure, Doctor?"

"It's from the brain—brain disorder, something like that. He was having a fit."

"Doctor, can you have a clonic seizure resulting from brain damage?"

"That's what I said."

"A person could get hit in the head, and it might cause such damage. Isn't that right, Doctor?"

"No, not just a blow to the head."

"How about if he was hit really hard, Doctor?"

"It would have to be very hard."

"Suppose instead of something's hitting a person's head, his head banged into something hard, several times."

"I'm not a neurologist. I can't tell you all the possibilities."

"It could happen, couldn't it, Doctor?"

"I don't know. I guess so."

Sandro studied the July 10th diagnosis sheet again.

PART 35

"Doctor, how did you determine this exquisite tenderness in the area of Alvarado's epigastrium?"

"By palpating, touching the patient. He grimaced with pain."

"And when you touched the epigastrium and there was a wincing on the face, that was an objective finding, was it not?"

"Yes."

"Even while he was unconscious?"

"Yes."

"Would that indicate to you that this objective finding was a severe injury?"

"It would indicate an injury."

"You have certain medical tests, do you not, Doctor, to determine whether a person is conscious or not?"

"There are ways, and there are ways that addicts can fake these things. I've been in prisons for four years—"

"Doctor, I don't mean to interrupt you," Sandro interrupted, "but I'd like to follow the questions chronologically. We'll save time if you will answer my questions, all right?"

"All right." The doctor glanced at the judge.

"No one has mentioned anything about narcotics since you've been on the stand, isn't that right, Doctor?"

"No, but I'm telling you. You asked me."

"I understand that, but we have to restrict ourselves to this case. Would you answer my questions, sir? I don't mean to cut you short, but I would like to keep a chronological order."

"I did not know at seven o'clock this morning when I was served that I was going to become an expert. Otherwise I would have studied."

"I understand that, sir."

"I don't even remember the case, to tell the truth. I am trying my best. I did not come here to be cross-examined. I'm not on trial."

"Doctor," the judge intervened, "you're here as a witness to try to help the jury as best you can. Now, just do your best to respond to the questions. I'll try and get you back to your office quickly."

The doctor nodded. "I certainly will."

The judge nodded to Sandro.

"Doctor, are there certain tests to determine a person's consciousness?" Sandro asked.

"Yes."

"What are the tests, Doctor?"

"Various things. Tactile stimuli, pinpricks, various things."

"And when you said before that addicts can fake these things, you were aware, at the time you examined this defendant Alvarado, that certain illnesses or conditions, even unconsciousness, can be simulated by a prisoner."

"I sure was. I've seen it."

"And to be sure a prisoner is not simulating, Doctor, do you administer these tests carefully?"

"Sure."

"And did you use these tests to determine consciousness on the defendant when you found him on the floor that night?"

"Evidently I did."

"And the man was unconscious?"

"According to my report."

"Is there any question about it in your mind, Doctor?"

The doctor read. "No. He was unconscious."

"And that determination was made by you, being careful to account for a prisoner's being able to fake things."

The doctor hesitated. "Right."

"And, Doctor, can the other conditions you found, the clonic movements, the twitching of all the extremities, Cheyne-Stokes breathing, salivation, rolled eyes, be simulated?"

"In my opinion, yes. I've seen addicts do a lot of things."

"Can any of these symptoms be simulated by an unconscious person, Doctor?"

The doctor stared at Sandro. "No," he said, at last.

"Your witness, Mr. Ellis," said Sandro, turning to the counsel table. Sam was looking down at his notebook, crowing softly.

Ellis questioned the doctor about his experience with addicts and the ability of addicts to simulate any sort of infection, disease, discomfort, or complaint in order to get out of prison and get to Bellevue or someplace where they might be able to get narcotics. The doctor

PART 35

indicated that anything could be simulated, even the clonic movements, the salivation, the rolled eyes, the Cheyne-Stokes breathing. He testified that he had sent the defendant to Bellevue as a precaution, for he wasn't sure what the defendant might have had, and he didn't want to take a chance.

"In other words, Doctor, you had some doubts about this patient, and you wanted him rechecked at Bellevue. Isn't that right?"

"Well, I must have had doubts. I didn't want him bleeding internally. Mind you, I don't recall the patient at all, but according to my report, I must have had doubts, otherwise I wouldn't have had him re-examined. Bellevue found he was not bleeding internally."

"I have no further questions," said Ellis, turning, resuming his seat.

Sandro stood in place, not moving toward the jury box or the witness stand.

"Doctor, did Bellevue do anything relating to the defendant's head? X-ray his head or run neurological tests?"

"Not from what it says in the reports."

"And from what you see on those diagnosis sheets, you cannot rule out a head injury causing these reactions in the defendant, can you?"

"No."

"One further question, Doctor. This person that you sent to Bellevue Hospital on July ninth, 1967—taking into consideration your knowledge of the ability of addicts to simulate—you had determined medically, clinically, objectively, that he was unconscious. Is that correct?"

"Yes."

"Thank you very much, Doctor. That's all."

"No further questions," said Ellis.

"We'll adjourn until tomorrow morning, members of the jury. Do not discuss this case with anyone or with each other." The judge rose and left the bench. Sandro gathered his papers.

"Well, another round, another good round," said Sam.

CHAPTER XIX

MIKE STOPPED THE CAR at the curb in front Of the American Broadcasting Company's studios on 66th Street. Sandro had called ahead and spoken to the city editor in the news department, asking if he might be allowed to come and view any news films covering the shooting of Lauria. He told Sandro to speak to Richard Sanford, head of their film-editing department. If any of the footage was still in the library, Sandro could view it.

Sandro and Mike identified themselves to the uniformed guard at the door, and took the elevator. From there, they were directed to the film section, where the daily film and videotape were processed, edited, and then spliced for the news broadcasts.

"I'm not sure that we still have any of that film," said Sanford. He was a man of medium height, with thinning dark hair. He wore a striped shirt with no tie, and his sleeves were rolled up. "But we'll look in the cans for that day and see what there is."

Surrounding them, in all the rooms through which they walked, men were walking quickly, talking quickly, typing, timing their copy; teletype machines were clacking, phones ringing, voices calling questions across the rooms. All the while the electric clock on the wall was counting down to broadcast time.

PART 35

Sanford led them into an editing booth. A young Negro was sorting out cans of film, looking for those marked July 3rd, 1967.

"That's all there seems to be, Sandy," the young man said, turning. "I don't find anything else."

"Okay, Frank. If anyone wants me, I'll be in here."

Sanford took the film from the first can and rolled it onto a larger reel. He fed the film through an editing machine that had a small viewing screen attached. "This segment must have been taken at the U.N. that day. You don't want that." He was hand-cranking the film through the machine.

Sandro and Mike stood just behind him, viewing the images on the small screen over his shoulder.

Here's some of it," Sanford said, still cranking. "The stuff you want might be anywhere in these three cans," he explained. "At the end of the day, when we finish taking what we need for the shows, we splice the rest of that day's exposed footage together and put it in storage. It isn't necessarily in sequence."

"Can we look at all of it, just to make sure?" Sandro asked.

"Hell, yes. It'll only take a couple of minutes longer. If we've got it, you've got it." He smiled and turned back to the viewing screen. He was the truly professional, technical man, whose behind-the-scenes work was precise, unglamorous, and essential. He was also very pleasant.

On the small screen were crowds of people huddled in the rain, standing on stoops, or on the sidewalk, outside 153 Stanton Street. There were ambulances and police cars, and policemen were moving into all the buildings. The camera panned toward and then focused in on a stretcher being carried out the doorway and down the stoop. It was placed in an ambulance, which then drove away. The camera panned the rooftops, then the crowd. There was a shot of Hernandez's double-parked car, guarded by a policeman.

"If you want me to turn the sound on for this stuff, I can," said Sanford.

"Not yet. When we get to a part where somebody is saying something, turn it on," Sandro replied.

The scene shifted suddenly to an interview with a city official who was explaining a parade planned for the next day, July 4th.

"This hasn't anything to do with your case. That's the end of this reel," said Sanford. "I'll put the next one on."

The next images on the screen were dark. It was the interior of the police station, as Hernandez and Alvarado stood in front of the main desk of the Seventh Precinct on the morning of July 4th, 1967. They were surrounded by detectives, who in turn were surrounded by newsmen. Flashbulbs kept popping all around the room, illuminating it with momentary intensity.

"Is there any sound on this segment?" Sandro asked.

Sanford nipped a switch.

"No. This must have been so noisy that they didn't even get a sound track on it." He kept cranking.

"This is a good shot to see what condition they were in just before they left the precinct," Mike suggested.

The images on the screen were now in close-up. Hernandez and Alvarado looked around them, confused and disturbed.

"Hold it right there. Can I look at that close-up of Alvarado again?" Sandro asked.

"Sure. I'll wind it back a little for you." He started the close-up segment through the machine again. The camera moved in on Alvarado and Hernandez, who were facing the desk sergeant. The camera moved in closer, then skirted to Alvarado's side. It stopped in front of the two men, close-up, watching them.

"This is great," said Sandro. "Could you rewind the film back a bit, to where the camera just comes alongside of Alvarado. See the side of Alvarado's head," Sandro said to Mike Rivera. "Okay, stop it right there."

Alvarado was suspended in profile as he looked at the desk sergeant.

"That's a great shot," said Mike. The arch formed by Alvarado's hair around the ear, the line at the bottom of his sideburn, and the hairline at the back of his neck were perfect, as if they had just been trimmed by a barber.

"Now wind it forward a little, please," said Sandro. On the screen Alvarado's face now appeared in three-quarter view. Alvarado turned toward the camera, peering quizzically, directly into the lens.

PART 35

"And look at that moustache," said Mike. "Perfect trim."

"Could you cut a couple of the frames from this film and blow them up to eight-by-ten still photos?" Sandro asked. "I'd take the film and do it myself if you'd let me, except it would destroy some of the punch of the evidence if I have it in my possession."

"Sure, I guess we can. I doubt that we'll be using this stuff again. Besides, one frame isn't going to make any difference. Of course, the still picture we get from this negative won't be as sharp as an ordinary still picture."

"That's okay," said Sandro. "If it's not as sharp as it should be, and it still shows a perfect hair and moustache trim, I can ask the jury to imagine what a really sharp-focus shot might have shown. Perhaps you can come to court and testify and explain all this stuff. And explain about the fuzziness."

Sanford shrugged. "Sure. But maybe you'd be better off with one of the newspaper photo files. They must have still shots."

"But here we can select the exact frame and angle that we need. Those newspaper shots are whatever they've got, and they may not have exactly what we need."

"Sure. The company'll let me come to court. As long as it's in the morning. I've got to be here in the afternoon. Let's pick out frames when a flashbulb was going off, if we can. Those are the ones where there'll be plenty of light."

Sanford found a full-face shot of Alvarado at the moment when a flashbulb went off. He couldn't find a side view so well lit.

"Pick out the best one you can find for the side view," said Sandro. "I hate to be putting you to all this trouble."

"It's no trouble. It's ABC's policy. Do you think you'll want any of the moving film?" Sanford asked. "If you do, I have a small projector and screen I can bring with me to court."

"That'd be fabulous. You sure I'm not imposing?"

"The city editor said if we have it, you got it. You got it!"

"Can we roll the rest of the film?"

Sanford continued the film. The crowd now moved out of the station house. Another camera outside picked up figures coming through the doors. First came the defendants, then the detectives,

385

then more policemen. A captain made a statement for the camera. He said that it was police effort and teamwork that had captured the killers so quickly. The camera picked up more figures coming out.

"Hey," said Mike, "there's Mrs. Hernandez."

Mrs. Hernandez, assisted by a man they didn't recognize, emerged and walked quickly down the steps.

"We'll need that, too," said Sandro. "That'll prove she was there all night."

"Okay. That's the end of this reel. One more reel."

Sanford set up the last reel and started cranking. On the viewer, Hernandez and Alvarado were leaving the basement of police headquarters and were being led to a waiting police van. The camera moved closer. A microphone was thrust into Alvarado's face.

"Can you get any sound on this?"

"Let's see." Sanford snapped on a toggle switch.

"Did you kill the policeman?" a voice synchronized with the lips of the interviewer on screen asked.

"That's Ron Roman interviewing your man," said Sanford.

"No, no," said Alvarado on screen. "I didn't."

"Do you know who did?"

"No, no."

"Okay, come on. Get up there," said an offscreen voice, as Alvarado stepped up into the van.

Hernandez moved into the picture next. He didn't understand the questions. He just looked blankly at the camera. When both defendants were in the van, the doors shut, and they were driven off.

"That's it," said Sanford, as the last of the film went through the viewer.

"I'll need this entire last segment," said Sandro. "And the segment when Mrs. Hernandez, the woman at the end of the second reel, came out of the police station."

"Okay. I'll put two stills together and two segments of the film. And I'll bring a projector and a screen. And then you'll want Ron Roman to come to court too, won't you?" Sanford asked.

"You been to law school?" Mike Rivera interjected.

PART 35

"No, but we've been through this kind of thing before. When do you need all this?"

"Let's see," said Sandro. "It should be about ten days. I'll have to call you when I know for sure."

"Okay. Just give us twenty-four hours' notice, and we'll be there."

"If there are any changes, I'll call you," Sandro said. "If there are any difficulties, I'd appreciate your calling me."

Sanford nodded agreement as he put the film back in the can.

CHAPTER XX

Monday, April 15th, 1968

DR. JOHN RIDER RAISED HIS HAND and was sworn by the clerk. Sandro walked to the jury box. He went over the doctor's credentials as an expert in narcotic toxicity by having him tell the court and jury of his training and experience with addicts, stressing his position as medical director of the detoxification clinic at Metropolitan Hospital.

"Doctor, I am going to ask a hypothetical question. I am going to recite certain facts for you. I want you to listen to these facts and, after hearing them, I want you to assume that they are true, so that we may have your opinion within a reasonable degree of medical certainty."

Sandro then described Alvarado's lack of past history of seizures or fits. He also mentioned Alvarado's history of narcotics, the amount and type he had been taking before his arrest.

Sandro asked the doctor to assume as true Alvarado's story about the third-floor locker room, the punches in the chest, and the constant hitting of his head against the lockers, his falling unconscious. He included the objective, medical facts as diagnosed by Dr. Maish on July 9th, 1967—clonic seizure, Cheyne-Stokes breathing, unconsciousness.

"Now, Doctor, I want to ask you if you would have an opinion,

PART 35

with a reasonable degree of medical certitude, as to whether or not the heroin addiction as described could be the competent producing cause of the clonic seizure and the other symptoms that were found by Dr. Maish on July ninth?"

"In my opinion, the seizure and the unconsciousness could *not* have been caused by heroin addiction."

"Doctor, do you have an opinion within a reasonable degree of medical certainty whether any narcotics could have been the competent producing cause of the clonic seizure on July ninth, 1967?"

"Six days after going to prison?"

"Yes."

"In my opinion, no."

"Can you explain your opinion to the court and jury?"

Heroin, Dr. Rider said, would not cause a seizure under any circumstances, no matter what the amount taken. Nor would any other narcotic cause a seizure after four days. Six days was too long for the seizure to have anything to do with narcotics.

"I have no further questions." Sandro returned to the counsel table. Sam leaned toward him.

"That's great. Now what is Ellis going to blame Alvarado's condition on?"

"I don't know. But if he goes after this too much, he's going to dig a deep hole, for himself."

Ellis began to cross-examine.

"Dr. Rider, is it your medical opinion that narcotics—I will specify, heroin addiction—could not have been the competent producing cause of these medical symptoms that were described to you in the hypothetical question?"

"Yes, sir, that's my opinion."

"Is that on account of the passage of six days before the seizure, Doctor?"

"Partly on account of the passage of time, but also, on account of other factors."

"What other factors, Doctor?"

"Well, primarily, during withdrawal from heroin, patients just don't have convulsions."

"You have never seen a patient who was addicted to heroin having convulsions in a stage of withdrawal?"

"Pure heroin addiction, by itself, doesn't produce convulsions."

"Well, you've indicated several years of experience in connection with drug addiction, Doctor. Would you describe the typical heroin addict when he is going through withdrawal? What happens to him?"

"Objection, Your Honor," said Sandro, "unless there is a qualification as to the extent of the habit."

"I'll ask the doctor to predicate his answer upon the habit described in the hypothetical question," Judge Porta said.

"This habit we're speaking about, I believe, is a six-dollar-a-day habit?" the doctor asked.

"Yes," said the judge.

"Well, that's not considered a very large habit. Some of the patients refer to it as a Pepsi-Cola or a Mickey Mouse habit. With a thing like that, the patients have, first, the usual restlessness and nervousness. Their eyes tear, they sweat, their pupils may be dilated. If they have a rough time of it, they may have some abdominal cramps. With a habit of this size, there wouldn't be severe diarrhea or anything like that. All this reaches its peak within forty-eight or seventy-two hours after withdrawal, and after seventy-two hours the patient would begin to recover.

"Now, six days later," the doctor continued, "one might expect him to have insomnia—that's a very persistent complaint. Many of them complain for weeks that they can't sleep. Some of them say that they have a poor appetite, and they may be a bit restless. But there wouldn't be anything dramatic, like a seizure, six days later."

"If the addict actually had a larger habit, in your opinion, would that make a difference in the withdrawal symptoms?" Ellis asked.

"Not very much. With the quality of heroin in New York City today, it is very rare that one sees more than grade-two symptoms."

"Grade two, Doctor?"

"Withdrawal symptoms are classified in four grades, one through four, four being the most dramatic. In grade one, watering of the eyes appears, as well as sniffling nose. That's about all. In grade two, you can usually see restlessness, perhaps vomiting, together with the watering eyes and the sniffling. In grade three, there is diarrhea and insomnia in addition. In grade four, there may also be an occasional involuntary movement of the extremities. That's where the expression 'kicking the habit' comes from. However, all the rolling on the floor and the climbing of the walls that is popular on television and the like is purely the psychological reaction, not the medical reaction. In other words, it looks good, or it seems that it looks good. However, in New York, I have never seen anyone, in thousands of cases, have more than grade-two withdrawal symptoms, even with the heaviest habits."

"Is there anything else besides addiction, besides a beating or brain damage, that might cause a clonic seizure, Doctor?"

"Well, something similar, but not exactly, would be like hysteria or hyperventilation syndrome."

"Hysteria? Can you explain how this happens, Doctor?" said Ellis voraciously.

"Well, hysteria is a mental condition, a mental disorder, and there is a form of it which is called conversion hysteria, in which the patient can show almost any kind of physical changes. Some patients have paralysis, some patients have twitches, whatever you like. It's not based on anything physical. It's based on the patient's idea of what he thinks he should have and, a patient, let's say, who had had clonic seizures or knew what clonic contractions were, might produce that kind of a picture by hysteria."

"And that could be faked or simulated, you say?"

"Well, that's not simulated. If it's hysteria, then it really isn't simulated. The patient is not completely in control of what he's doing."

"But it's not really a clonic seizure resulting from anything except the patient's imagination?"

"That's about it."

"I have no further questions, Doctor. Thank you."

"Have you any other questions?" the judge asked Sandro.

"Yes, Your Honor."

"Doctor, in order for a patient to have a seizure from hysteria, he imagines the symptoms he should have, and his mind thereafter causes him almost to attain them?"

"Yes, it's something like that."

"Well, Doctor, let me ask you this. Once a patient is or becomes unconscious—clinically, objectively unconscious—can a hysterical convulsion exist thereafter?"

"No. It's not really a medical symptom. Without his mind working to maintain the symptom, the symptom ceases."

"In other words, an unconscious man would cease to have a hysterical seizure?"

"That's right."

"And if it continued after that, you'd discount the hysteria and consider it a real, objective, medical seizure?"

"I'd have to."

"No further questions."

"No questions," said Ellis.

"We've got him grabbing for the ropes now," Sam whispered. "You knocked out the only thing he could blame the seizure on."

Dr. Fulton took the stand and was sworn in as a witness. He gave a long list of qualifications, including special consultation work for the district attorney of Kings County. Sandro then posed his hypothetical question again, asking now if Dr. Fulton had an opinion on whether the alleged police beating could have been the competent producing cause of the seizure.

"Yes. In my opinion, the described beating and the hitting of the head against the lockers could have been the cause of the convulsive seizure which the patient had six days later."

Sandro asked the doctor to explain his opinion. The doctor told what a seizure was, how it emanated from the brain, and how the hitting of Alvarado's head against the locker could have caused a convulsive reaction.

"Doctor, can an individual who is unconscious simulate a clonic seizure, with Cheyne-Stokes breathing, tachycardia, rapid pulse of one twenty per minute, rolled eyes, acute or exquisite tenderness in the epigastrium, and guarding and rigidity in the abdominal area?"

"A patient who is unconscious cannot simulate anything."

"Thank you, Doctor. I have no further questions."

Ellis stood and walked to the jury box.

"Let me ask you, Dr. Fulton, assuming that this person with whom we are concerned in the hypothetical question did not sustain the blows to the epigastrium and the blows to the head as recited in the hypothetical question, would the answer that you gave be different?"

"Why, of course. It would have to be."

"And would you then have to look for some other reason to explain this apparent clonic seizure that was included in the hypothetical question?"

"I would say so, yes."

"Is there any question about it?"

"No, no, I would have to try to find the cause of any clonic seizure occurring in a patient without a history of a head injury."

"Now, Doctor, would you be good enough to tell us in your medical opinion, with reasonable certainty, what other causes would there be for an apparent clonic seizure as described in the hypothetical question."

"Well, there are multiple causes of clonic seizures. Tumors or neoplasms of the brain can cause seizures. Second, infections, inflammation of the brain, such as encephalitis or meningitis. A third cause is trauma, or injuries to the brain. A fourth is toxic or metabolic causes for seizures. These can be toxic reactions to illnesses, such as diphtheria or some forms of polio, or toxic reactions to drugs, or the withdrawal symptoms from certain types of drugs."

"You say, Doctor, a clonic seizure can be caused by any of these things, including drugs?"

"Yes, it can."

"And, Doctor, your speciality is the brain and its function, or dysfunction, not narcotics, isn't that right?"

"That's correct."

"No further questions."

Sandro rose.

"Doctor, you mentioned that addiction can cause seizures in some cases. Is that possibility significant in this case?"

"Well, convulsion is not something that occurs from withdrawal from heroin under any condition. That would seem to eliminate this convulsion right there. Other drugs could produce seizure, barbiturates for instance. However, the withdrawal seizure would occur as soon as the blood level of the drug drops to the level where the brain cortex becomes irritated, and this usually takes place in less than forty-eight to seventy-two hours. So that most withdrawal symptoms, as far as seizures are concerned, take place within the first day, second day, or third day of withdrawal. A seizure that occurs six days after withdrawal would not be caused by the withdrawal."

"Are you saying, Doctor, that this clonic seizure in your opinion couldn't have occurred from any narcotic addiction?"

"From the information you have given me, yes."

"Doctor, from the facts given to you either by the district attorney or myself, can you point to any other cause for the clonic seizure diagnosed July ninth, 1967, other than a beating by the police on July fourth, 1967?"

"Objection, Your Honor."

"I will allow it in that form. Can you, Doctor, attribute this seizure to any other cause or causes?"

"No. I have stated that the beating described could be the cause of a seizure occurring six days later. I haven't been given any other facts to make me exclude this in favor of any other cause for the seizure. The beating, therefore, is the most logical cause of the seizure."

"Your witness." Sandro sat at the counsel table.

Ellis had no further questions.

Sam rested Alvarado's case on the voir dire.

"Members of the jury," the judge said, "we'll break now for lunch. Don't discuss the case."

"Sandro, you really put Ellis in a bind. If he can't dig up a doctor who can eliminate that beating as a possible cause, he'd better fold his tent," said Sam.

"The judge didn't buy it on the Huntley hearing, and he's obviously going to leave it to the jury to decide here," Sandro replied. "Maybe the jury won't buy it either."

"Well, you got it in here, even if it just turns out to be an escape route for appeal."

After lunch, Ellis started calling people's witnesses on the voir dire. He began by recalling Lieutenant Garcia, who emphatically denied that he had ever struck, beat, punched, kicked, or hit Alvarado on the

PART 35

early morning of July 4th, 1967. He also denied ever seeing anyone else abuse Alvarado. Ellis had no further questions.

Sam stood and walked toward the lieutenant. Garcia testified that he was alone in his office at 11 P.M., July 3rd, 1967, when Hernandez was returned from Brooklyn and placed in the adjoining office. He said he never left his room to see Alvarado or to inquire about the interrogation, nor did anyone inform him of its progress until the detectives brought Alvarado down after a statement had allegedly been obtained.

Lieutenant Garcia said, in answer to Sam's question, that he had never had anyone interrogated in that third-floor locker room other than the two defendants in this case. Sam had no further questions.

Ellis called Detective Mullaly to the stand. Calm as ever, Mullaly watched Ellis walk toward him.

"He must have rehearsed in front of a mirror for months," said Sam, looking up from his notes momentarily.

Just as before, when Hernandez was under discussion, Mullaly testified that he had not laid a hand on Alvarado, nor had he seen anyone else do so. Ellis asked no further questions.

In answer to Sam's cross-examination, Mullaly said that he had never before testified in a homicide case, nor had he ever been in charge of one. He said that he had not been under any particular pressure the night of July 3rd to 4th when he was interrogating the prisoners, despite the fact that this was the death of a policeman, and despite the fact that the commissioner of police and the chief of detectives and a great many other superior officers were in the station house.

Mullaly admitted that he was the main interviewer of Alvarado. Johnson and Tracy, according to Mullaly, only asked an occasional question.

Mullaly further said that from the beginning of the interview, at approximately 1:40 A.M., July 4th, 1967, until it was over at 2:15 A.M., Alvarado was asked no questions concerning his guilt or his participation in the crime which resulted in the death of Lauria. Rather, Mullaly testified, Alvarado was asked only questions like where he had been that day and whether he knew Ramon Hernandez. After twice being confronted with Hernandez, with whom he exchanged shouts and curses in Spanish, Alvarado began to tell the entire story.

Mullaly testified further that at no time during the interview did he send word down to his superiors about any progress they were making. Sam had no further questions.

Siakos stood and inquired of Mullaly about the Spanish words that Hernandez used. Mullaly said, although he knew only a little Spanish, that they were curse words. Mullaly couldn't remember the actual words used. Siakos had no further questions.

Ellis called Detective Jablonsky to the stand. Jablonsky denied hitting or insulting Alvarado or witnessing such actions. Ellis had no further questions.

"Officer, Alvarado was beaten in that third-floor locker room by your brother officers, wasn't he?" Sam asked suddenly, to throw Jablonsky off balance.

"No, sir," he answered. He was perplexed by the sudden attack.

"Assaulting any prisoner is, like any other assault on a private citizen, a crime?"

"Yes, sir."

"If you had seen a fellow officer strike Alvarado, would you have arrested him?"

Jablonsky hesitated, uncomfortable. "I hope so, sir."

"Is there any question, Officer?"

"As I said, Counselor, I hope I would do my duty."

"Thank you. No further questions." Sam was satisfied with Jablonsky's hesitation; it spoke loud and clear to the jury.

Ellis called Detective Johnson to the stand. Johnson told about taking Hernandez from the squad office to the locker room. He recalled the Spanish confrontation between Alvarado and Hernandez, but did not know what was said because he did not understand Spanish. He made the usual disclaimer about not having touched Alvarado.

"These cops stick together like glue," said Sam. "I just hope the jury can see through this crappy veil of sanctity."

"Don't worry, Tracy is up next. He's the only cop on the case who did any goddamn work, and it's all sticking to his fingers now that they've changed the story. He's going to get another DD5 shoved right down his throat."

"Why don't you take him then," Sam suggested.

PART 35

"Okay," said Sandro. Detective Tracy walked to the stand. He glanced at Ellis, then to Sam and Sandro. Tracy, too, said that he had never struck, beat, punched, kicked, hit, or in any way manhandled Alvarado. He testified that he did not stop any other officers from hitting or punching Alvarado, nor did he see any such thing. He said he never had a conversation with Alvarado where he advised him to say he shot the policeman in panic. Ellis sat down.

Sandro stood and walked toward Tracy.

"It was you who personally interrogated and took the statement from Alvarado, is that not so, sir?"

"I object, Your Honor. I'm not sure the witness understands the question," said Ellis.

"Your Honor, it is Mr. Ellis who has suggested that the witness does not understand. The witness said nothing about not understanding. Will you direct Mr. Ellis to refrain from testifying or suggesting testimony to the witness?" retorted Sandro.

"Reframe your question," instructed the judge.

"It was you who personally took the statement of Luis Alvarado?"

Ellis stood and objected again. "What does that mean, Your Honor. I object to the form of the question."

"You may answer it, sir, if you understand it."

"No, sir."

"Did you say, sir, you did not personally take a statement?"

"That's right, sir. I did not."

Sandro took out another DD5. He handed it to Tracy, who identified his signature at the bottom. Sandro offered it, and it was received in evidence.

"Detective Tracy, at paragraph three, this report states: 'As a result of this interrogation, the assigned personally took a statement from the above-named subject at the Seventh Squad detectives office relative to this case.' Does it not state that?"

Tracy read. "Yes, sir."

"You do understand what that means?"

"Yes, sir."

"You wrote it?"

"Yes, sir."

"And this means that you took the statement from the defendant Alvarado, does it not?"

Tracy was red now on the sides of his neck between his shirt and his ears. He swallowed hard. "As representative of the homicide squad, yes, sir."

"I see. It doesn't say that here?"

"No, sir."

"Nor does it say that you interrogated him in the third-floor locker room, does it?"

"May I read it again, sir?"

"Surely." Sandro handed Tracy the DD5.

Tracy read it slowly, carefully. The red on his neck deepened, now shading onto his face. "It says 'Seventh Squad detectives office, sir.'"

"And the reason you wrote the squad office in your official report was that you were covering up the fact that the precinct cops took Alvarado to the locker room on the top floor of the station house, where no one could see or hear what really happened?"

"Objection," Ellis exclaimed, rising abruptly.

"Sustained."

Sandro watched Tracy's eyes. Tracy looked at Sandro. Sandro was sure the jury could see the color in Tracy's face now.

"I have no further questions," said Sandro, turning back to his seat.

"At this point, gentlemen and ladies of the jury, we will adjourn for the day. Do not discuss this case. We'll resume at two o'clock tomorrow. We won't have a morning session because I have several cases which I have not been able to attend to, due to the length of this trial."

CHAPTER XXI

Tuesday, April 16th, 1968

THE COURTHOUSE LOOMED AGAINST THE BLUE, afternoon sky, its massive form of staged concrete symbolizing its function. Sam and Sandro walked slowly toward another day in court.

"Ellis'll start with Mullaly," said Sam. "After the judge denies our motion to suppress the alleged confession, that is. He's going to testify to Alvarado's confession. I don't know what the hell there is to cross-examine. He'll say he heard Alvarado confess. What are we going to say, his ears need cleaning?"

"We know what he's going to say," said Sandro.

"Sure, it's a simple confession, period, no frills, nothing. And Mullaly's cool enough to stick to his story and not get flustered. I think you should cross-examine him, Sandro."

"Why me?"

"This will have a lot to do with the roof and Alvarado crouching down and all that." Sam looked straight ahead, aware that Sandro was studying him. "You know the area and the scene better than I do."

"This son-of-a-bitch Mullaly is tough, Sam. And he's testifying to the goddamn confession. If we don't kick him around, Alvarado is well on his way to the chair. I'm not sure I can handle it, Sam. I'm really not."

"You won't do any worse than I will, Sandro."

"It's Alvarado's life, Sam."

"We can't do anything about that. Whatever you do is better than he'd get anyplace else. You take him, Sandro, okay?"

They entered the elevator to ascend. Sam stared straight ahead as the door closed.

As the session began, Sam made the obligatory motion to suppress the confession. The judge, as expected, denied it. Ellis then asked Mullaly to resume describing what had occurred in the third-floor locker room after the second confrontation between Alvarado and Hernandez.

"I said to Alvarado, 'Now, calm down. Sit down, Luis. Relax. You want to tell me what happened today? You want to tell me the truth?' And he said, 'Yes.' I said, 'Now, what happened today? Did you meet Ramon?'

"He said, 'I met Ramon.' 'Where did you meet him?' I asked. He said, 'I met him at the Hotel Ascot. It's on Allen and Delancey Street.' I said, 'What time was that?' He said, 'Around nine o'clock this morning.' I said, 'What did you do then?' He said, 'We went into the men's room in the hotel, and we shot up.' I said, 'What do you mean, shot up?' He said, 'We both shot up with heroin.'

"'Then what happened?' I said. He said, 'We talked about doing a robbery. And then we left the hotel, and we got into Ramon's car, and we drove uptown.' I said, 'Where did you go uptown?' He said, 'It was somewhere in El Barrio.' I said, 'Then what happened?' He said, 'Then we drove downtown. And Ramon had asked me to do a robbery on a building in his block.' I said, 'What block was that?' He said, 'Stanton Street, near Suffolk.'"

"Your Honor," said Siakos, rising, "may I at this time most respectfully interrupt the witness and ask the court to instruct the jury as to the effect of any alleged statement made by the codefendant, Alvarado."

"And I grant your application. I state again to you, members of the jury, that any statement made by Alvarado is binding only on Alvarado. Any matter which may be deemed incriminatory in respect to his codefendant, Hernandez, must be disregarded by you. Proceed, Detective Mullaly."

PART 35

"I said, 'How do you know that's Ramon's block?' He said, 'Because I have been there before.' And I said, 'Then what happened?' And he said, 'We double-parked the car on Ramon's block.' Then he said they went to a building across the street from the factory.

"I asked him what the number of the building was. He said he did not know. I told him to go on. He said they pushed open the door of an apartment on the top floor of that building. I asked him what the apartment number was. He said he did not know. I asked him how they got into the apartment. He said that Ramon had a jimmy and gave it to him, and he used the jimmy on the door."

The jury was transfixed as Mullaly spoke. So was Alvarado.

"I said, 'Then what happened?' And he said they went into the apartment and looked to see if they could get something to sell. I said, 'What do you mean, sell?' He said, 'We had to get money to buy drugs for our habit.'"

Mullaly was cool, telling a simple story.

"Then Luis said he took a TV set from a bedroom and a white pocketbook. He said that Ramon took a small radio. I asked him what color the radio was. He said he thought it was either black or red. Then he said they carried this stuff up to the roof. He carried the TV set and the pocketbook, and Ramon carried the radio and the jimmy. I asked him why they carried the stuff to the roof. He said because they were going to take the stuff across the roofs and down into Ramon's apartment.

"I said, 'Then what happened?' He said they put the property—the stuff—on the roof; and that he went down the fire escape, and he wanted to get into the apartment. I asked him why he wanted to get into the apartment. He said he wanted to get some of the stuff that was near the window. He opened the window, but he couldn't get in because the gate on the inside of the window was locked. He came back up the fire escape. He and Ramon started to lift the TV set over the roof when he heard a noise on the fire escape. He walked over to the edge of the roof, and he looked down the fire escape, and he saw a police officer coming up the fire-escape. And he said to Ramon, '*Los camarones! Los camarones!*' I asked him what that meant. He said, 'The cops! The cops!'

"I said, 'Then what happened?' He said he hid and crouched down behind the stairway wall, and he saw the cop go by him. The cop had his gun in his hand, and he was pointing it at Ramon. And he said that he was afraid, he saw the gun. And at this point Luis put his hands over his face, and he said '*Dios mio! Dios mio!* I did it! I did it!'"

The courtroom was deathly silent. Juror number six, the insurance salesman named Anthony Fresci, stole a glance at Alvarado, as if he were studying some wild beast.

"And I said, 'What did you do?' He said, 'I shot the officer. I shot him in the back.'

"And he was crying at this point, and sobbing. And I said, 'Tell me how it happened. Tell me.'

"He said, 'I saw him with the gun in his hand, and I was afraid. And he was pointing it at Ramon. He said, "Hold it! Hold it!" And when he passed me, I jumped on him from behind, and I put my left arm around his neck, and he fell down to the ground. And I struggled with him, with my right hand, and I pulled the gun out of his hand. And as the officer started to get up on his hands and his knees, I stepped back and shot him in the back.'"

Two other jurors, the retired buyer for Saks and the import-export man, looked quickly at Alvarado.

"I said to him, 'How many times did you shoot him?' He said he did not know but he thought it was more than three times. I said, 'Did you shoot him with your own gun?' And he said, 'No. I didn't have a gun.' I said, 'Then what happened?' He said, 'I ran over the rooftop, and I ran down one of the buildings.' I said, 'What happened to the officer's gun?' He said, 'I still had it with me.'

"I asked him what building he ran down, and he said he did not know the number of the building. I asked him if he passed anybody as he ran down the stairs. He said as he ran down he passed a Spanish lady and a little girl who were coming up the stairs. I said, 'Go on.' He said he ran down to the first floor, and he threw the officer's gun on the floor, next to the staircase. And he saw a door under the staircase. And he pulled an old radiator away from in front of it, and opened the door, and he ran out the steps to the backyard, and he hid there. And then he said later he went out another building and went to the front, to Stanton

PART 35

Street. And then he walked to Suffolk Street. And then he said he went to his room in Brooklyn, and he shot up again with heroin. And then he went down to the movies on 42nd Street, and he stayed there until he took the train home, and the detectives grabbed him."

Ellis asked Mullaly if he had had Alvarado demonstrate how he attacked the policeman. Mullaly said he had. He stepped off the witness chair and demonstrated for the jury. He crouched next to the witness stand and sprang out as the imaginary Lauria walked by. Ellis described the motions for the stenographer to record. Ellis then had the property that was taken from the roof brought into the courtroom. Mullaly said Alvarado identified these items as the ones he took from Soto's apartment. Alvarado, he said, also identified the policeman's revolver. Ellis had no further questions. Mullaly sat calmly waiting for the cross-examination.

Sandro rose and walked to face Mullaly. He still felt at a loss. The detective had only testified to a conversation he had with Alvarado; how could he be shaken from that? Sandro had ammunition for every witness except the most important one.

"Now, Detective Mullaly, you say that after a few preliminary questions to Alvarado about his name and address, and after confronting him with Hernandez twice, sometime about two A.M., you asked Alvarado to calm down and he told you a story, is that right?"

"He made a statement, yes, sir."

"And that was not a story that you obtained piece by piece in response to questions?"

"Well, I would say, 'Then what happened?' or 'Go on.'"

"You didn't have to pry it out of him, in other words?"

"Oh, no, sir. No, sir."

Sandro felt sure the D.A.'s case was swelling with strength with each of his ineffectual inquiries.

"You just had to say, 'Well, what happened then?' and then he went on for a little bit, is that correct?"

"Yes, sir."

Sandro thought he might as well go into the minor discrepancies, little sticks. But Mullaly's testimony was a whole forest.

"Now, you say that the defendant indicated that he had been with Ramon during the day, is that correct?"

"Yes, sir."

"And you indicated that Alvarado stated that, after they had ridden in Ramon's automobile, they drove to Stanton Street to burglarize an apartment?"

"Yes, sir."

"And between them they discussed the burglary on the particular apartment?"

"He said, Alvarado said, that he asked, Ramon asked him to do a robbery in a building on his block."

"Was it a specific building that Ramon asked him about?"

"Yes, I believe you could say that. It is hard—"

"I don't want to say it. I am asking you."

"In my opinion?"

"No, I am not asking your opinion. I am asking you what the statement said exactly that Ramon had said. 'Come to this apartment; I have already cased it,' or something like that?"

"Alvarado said to me, 'Ramon asked me to do a robbery in a building on his block,' and I asked him what Ramon's block was; and he said, 'Stanton Street, between Suffolk and Norfolk.' And I asked him how he knew that. He said he had been there before."

"Now, did you ask the defendant at that point, 'Well, what apartment were you going to go into?'"

"I asked him what the apartment number was, and he said he didn't know. He said they went to a building across the street from a factory."

"Now, you indicated that Hernandez had a jimmy?"

"Alvarado said that, yes, sir."

"And then you indicated that Hernandez allegedly gave the jimmy to Alvarado?"

"Yes, sir."

"And Alvarado jimmied the door open, and then they went inside, is that right?"

"Yes, sir."

"Now, after the goods were on the roof, you say the defendant Alvarado said to you that he went down the fire escape in the back so that he could take some property out the window, is that right?"

"He said some stuff that was near the window, yes, sir."

"Now, did he say that he was going to take the television set out of the window?"

"No, sir."

"Did he tell you to which window he went when he was going to take these things out?"

"He just said 'the window.'"

"There were two windows on the fire escape, weren't there?"

"Yes, sir. I assumed it was the window—"

"Let's just get what he said."

"He didn't say, Counselor; no, sir."

"At any rate, when he got down on the fire escape, he found that the gate and window were locked?"

"On the inside; yes, sir."

Why would anyone who had been in the apartment go out on the fire escape without first opening the locks? Sandro was building for the summation, but the jury didn't look impressed.

"Now, after this, you say, while the defendant was on the roof, you say he said he heard a noise on the fire escape?"

"From the fire escape," Mullaly corrected. "Yes, sir."

"Now, did he say where he was at the time he heard that noise?"

"He said Ramon and he were lifting the TV set over the dividing wall."

"And you say he said that he went from where they were lifting the goods over the dividing wall to look over the fire escape, is that correct?"

"He said he went to the back edge of the roof and looked over the fire escape, yes, sir."

"Now, do you know where the fire escape is on the building One fifty-three Stanton Street?"

"Yes, sir."

"It overhangs the rear end of the building?"

"Yes, sir; the back of the building; yes, sir."

"And this point, sir, where you say the property was found by the police, is almost at the frontmost part of the building, is that not right?"

"Yes."

"Now, the defendant Alvarado, you say, said he saw the policeman coming up; is that correct?"

"Yes, sir."

"Now, did the defendant then say that he went to Hernandez and told him '*Los camarones,*' or 'The cops are coming?'"

"This is what he said, Counselor: 'I told Ramon, *Los camarones! Los camarones!*'"

"Did he say, 'I yelled to him?'"

"I just told you what he said, Counselor."

"He told him?"

"Yes, sir."

"And that was the word he used to you?"

"He said he told Ramon, '*Los camarones! Los camarones!*'"

"And then you say that the defendant took this position which you later described for us, and you assumed for us; is that correct? He took this position behind the wall?"

"Yes. That is what he told me. He said he crouched down behind the wall. As a matter of course, Counsel, he demonstrated the position for me later. But at this time he only told me he crouched down."

"While you were up on that roof, you observed the bulkhead, or stairway wall, didn't you?"

"Yes, sir."

"The bulkhead is the covering over the stairwell, is that correct?"

"Yes, sir."

"Now, you say he said he crouched behind the stairway wall?"

"Yes, sir."

"Would that mean inside the stairway?"

"Your Honor, I object. He is asking the detective to interpret the language of this defendant, and I object to it," said Ellis.

"Objection sustained because of the form of the question."

Sandro easily envisioned the bulkhead on the roof. He couldn't believe that Lauria would not have seen his assailant if the assailant was outside, kneeling behind the bulkhead. And if the assailant was inside the bulkhead, he would have had to open the door to come out. And the door opened toward the rear. *The cop would have seen it opening.*

PART 35

"Did you ask him, 'Well, were you inside the stairway, Luis?' or, 'Were you outside the stairway, Luis?'"

"Did I ask him that, sir?"

Suddenly, Sandro realized that Mullaly didn't know the answer. He had been continually repeating the exact wording of the alleged confession. And he couldn't go beyond those words. The confession was something a high school boy could have surmised after seeing the roof and the dead Lauria. But there were gaping holes in it, whole areas unknown. Areas the police would have dug into with a man as voluntary, as cooperative as they said Alvarado was that night. The questions unasked and unanswered made Mullaly's recitation foolish.

"Now, was that outside, sir? Did he say he was outside, on the stairway wall?"

"He didn't say outside, but he was on the rooftop."

"I am going to object to this answer as not being responsive," said Sandro.

"Objection sustained. Strike it out."

"Did he say he was outside?"

"No, he didn't, Counselor."

"Did he say he was inside?"

"No, he didn't, Counselor."

"Did you ask him where he was?"

"He told me where he was."

"Well, did he say he was outside or inside?"

"Your Honor, I object to this. That has been answered."

"Objection sustained."

Mullaly looked at Sandro. His eyes showed that he knew what Sandro now realized.

"You say that the defendant Alvarado described how he grabbed the policeman when the policeman went past him?"

"As he passed him; yes, sir."

"Well, did he say how far from where he was standing the policeman passed?"

"No."

"Did you ask him how far the policeman was?"

"No."

"And as you sit here now you do not know that detail?"

"No."

"Did you ask him, 'Well, did you take a step and grab the cop?'"

"No, Counselor, I didn't."

Sandro's questions were more rapid, staccato now.

"Did you ask him, 'Well, did you have to run five steps and grab the cop?'"

"No."

"Did he say he just reached out and the cop was right there?"

"He didn't say that."

"Did you ask him, 'Did you open the door of the roof to go out and grab the cop?'"

"No, sir."

"Did you ask him, 'Were you hiding behind the door when you grabbed the cop?'"

"No, sir."

"And as you sit here now, you do not know that detail, do you?"

"No."

"Wasn't it something you thought important to know?"

"Objection, Your Honor."

"Overruled. You may answer."

Mullaly studied Sandro. "I wanted him to tell his story without prompting, to let him tell it without my telling him facts."

"I move the answer be stricken, Your Honor," Sandro moved.

"Strike it out."

"It was more important that the statement was voluntary," Mullaly answered.

"Did the defendant Alvarado tell you that he jumped on the cop from behind?"

"Yes, sir."

"Did he tell you how far he jumped?"

"No, sir, he didn't."

"Did he tell you from what he jumped?"

"From what he jumped?"

"From what? Did he tell you he was standing on the step when he jumped?"

PART 35

"No, sir."
"You don't know from where he jumped?"
"From behind the stairway wall."
"But we don't know where that stairway wall was, do we?"
"I know where the stairway wall is, yes, sir."
"All right, tell me."
"Are you asking me—"
"Yes, which stairway wall was it that the defendant Alvarado said he was behind?"
"You asked me if I knew—will you repeat the question, sir? I am sorry."

Mullaly had just staggered. Sandro had staggered the Mullaly talking machine. He took two steps closer. The jurors were on the edge of their chairs.

"I will withdraw the question and rephrase it, Your Honor," said Sandro.

"When the defendant Alvarado said he jumped onto the policeman, did he say from which spot he jumped?"

"No, sir."

"Well, now, was it a jump where he was actually in the air or was it just a reaching out, a lunging?" Sandro demonstrated a grab from behind as he questioned.

"I don't know, Counselor."
"And you didn't ask him that?"
"No, sir. I didn't."
"Not then, not later? Not at any time?"
"That's right."
"And as you sit here now, you don't know that detail?"
"No, sir."
"You say Alvarado said he grabbed the cop around the neck?"
"He said he grabbed the officer around the neck, with his left arm."
"And then you say he said he reached around and grabbed the policeman's right hand?"
"No, I said the cop fell down."
"The policeman fell first?"
"Fell down, falling forward."

"And then?"

"And he was grabbing at his gun."

"When the defendant Alvarado said to you that he knocked the cop down, he said the cop fell forward; is that correct?"

"He didn't say he knocked him down. He said the cop fell down, falling forward."

"All right. Did the defendant Alvarado say that when he had his arm around the neck of the cop and the cop fell forward that he, Alvarado, fell forward with him?"

"He didn't say."

"Did you ask him that, at any time, then or later?"

"I didn't ask him, no, sir."

"At any rate, the defendant Alvarado was taking the gun, fighting for the gun?"

"He was grabbing at the gun with his right hand."

"You didn't ask him whether he fell down with Lauria, right?"

"No, sir."

"Did you ask him if he was still standing?"

"I didn't, no, sir."

"Do you know as you sit here right now whether Alvarado fell down with Lauria or was standing?"

"I assume—"

"Not what you assume, Officer. Do you know?"

"I wasn't there."

"You're telling us the voluntary details, Officer. Was he on the ground or standing."

"I can't answer that."

Sandro studied Mullaly now. "You say he told you voluntarily that he grabbed for the gun with his right hand; is that correct?"

"I object to the form, Your Honor," said Ellis.

"Sustained."

"This statement of Alvarado's was totally voluntary, wasn't it, Officer?"

"Yes, sir."

"And you say Alvarado voluntarily told you he grabbed for the gun?"

"Yes, sir."

"And then he got the gun, finally?"
"Yes, sir."
"Did he tell you that he had to fight for it?"
"He said he struggled for the gun."
"Was he on the floor struggling, do you know?"
"I don't know, Counselor."
"Did you ask him that?"
"I didn't ask him that, no, sir."
"And you don't know that detail either?"
"No, sir."
"At any rate, he got the gun finally, is that correct?"
"Got the revolver, yes, sir."
"And you say he said he stepped back at that point, is that correct?"
"As the officer got up on his hands and knees."
"He stepped back?"
"Yes, sir."
"Did he say how far he stepped back?"
"He just said he stepped back."
"Where was he when he started to step back? Did you ask him that?"
"No, sir, I didn't."
"Did you ask him at what point he finally stopped—how far from the cop he was when he stopped?"
"I don't understand you, Counselor."
"Well, you say he started to step back. I assume he stopped stepping back at one point." Sandro stepped backward several paces, physically accompanying the tempo of his questions.
"He told me he stepped back."
"Did you ask him, 'How many steps did you take, Luis?'"
"No, sir, I didn't."
"Did you ask him, 'How far away were you from the policeman when you shot, Luis?'"
"No, sir."
"Did you ask him, 'At what point was the gun held, Luis?'"
"No."
"Well, did you ask him if he held it up high?"

"No."
"Down low?"
"No."
"You don't know where the gun was held even now?"
"No, sir."
"Did you ask him that?"
"No, sir."
"And you don't know that detail, do you?"
"No, sir."
"Now, did you ask him, 'Were you standing still when you shot?'"
"No, sir."
"Did you ask him if he was moving when he was shooting?"
"No, sir."
"Did you ask him if he shot all the bullets from the same position?"
"No, sir."
"Did he tell you, 'I shot all the bullets from the same position?'"
"No, sir."
"He didn't tell you how he shot the gun?"
"You mean how—what position?"
"What position it was in."
"No, sir."
"And you didn't ask him?"
"No, sir, I didn't."
"You did ask him, 'Well, how many shots?' And he said to you, 'Three or four'; is that correct?"
"He said, 'More than three.'"
"More than three?"
"He thought it was more than three. He didn't know, but he thought it was more than three."
"Did he tell you, 'I shot them in one burst, rapid-fire?'"
"That is all he said."
"Well, did you ask him, 'Were they all at once, or did you take your time and then shoot again after you thought a second?'"
"No, sir, I didn't ask him that."
"Didn't you ask him, 'Well, didn't you really fire the gun five times, Luis?'"

"No."

"Did you say, 'Well, do you think you might have fired five times instead of three, Luis?'"

"No."

"Did you ask him if he emptied the gun into the cop?"

"No, sir, I didn't."

"Well, did he tell you that he emptied the gun into the cop?"

"He said—"

"I am asking you a question."

"No, sir."

There was not one sound or movement in the courtroom.

"After that, you say, the defendant Alvarado said that he ran down another building?"

"He ran over the roof and down another building."

"Now, did he tell you if he ran over the front end of the wall at One fifty-three or if he ran over the rear end of the wall of One fifty-three?"

"He didn't."

Sandro walked next to the diagram of the rooftops, pointing. "Did you ask him, 'Luis, did you climb over this front wall that is *seven feet high?*' Did you ask him that?"

"No."

"Did he tell you that he climbed over a *seven-foot wall?*"

"He told me he just ran over the roof. That is all."

"Did you ask him if he leaped over the rear courtyard that is six feet in space between buildings One fifty-three and One fifty-five"—pointing to people's exhibit 1—"Did you ask him if he jumped over that?"

"If he jumped over the courtyard?"

"Yes, Sir."

"I wouldn't ask him that."

"You weren't interested?"

"I wouldn't ask him."

"Didn't you want details from the man you say said he was there, details to prove unequivocally that he was the man who was there?"

"Yes, sir."

"Did he or did he not leap over the open courtyard—five stories deep—when he ran?"

"I don't know, Counselor."

"He wasn't volunteering anything, was he?"

"Yes, he was."

"He didn't know anything to volunteer until he was worked over, did he?"

"Nobody worked anybody over, Counselor."

"Did Alvarado refuse to answer any questions?"

"No, sir."

"Did he hold back, reluctant to answer?"

"No, sir."

"Are you telling this jury that it never dawned on you to ask how he jumped on the cop, where he was when he shot, how he shot, how many times he shot, how he ran away—those details?"

Mullaly stared at Sandro. "Would you repeat that, Counselor?"

"Can we have the reporter read the question," Sandro said disdainfully.

"Read it," said the judge. The stenographer read the question to Mullaly.

"I thought of it, Counselor."

"What are the answers?"

"Objection to form, Your Honor," said Ellis.

"Sustained as to form."

"Give me any one of those details, Detective Mullaly, one, any one you want first."

"I didn't ask him those things, Counselor."

"Your witness, Mr. Ellis," Sandro said, turning toward the counsel table. Sam was bent over his notebook.

"That was the finest cross-examination I ever had the pleasure of hearing in my life," Sam whispered. He squeezed Sandro's arm tightly.

Ellis got up and began asking Mullaly questions to buttress his testimony about the confession. Sandro just sat, exhausted.

"You kill that bastard," Alvarado whispered, leaning to Sandro. "You're my man, for sure. You kill him good."

When Ellis finished, the defense didn't have any further questions for Mullaly. The judge recessed until morning.

CHAPTER XXII

"WE'LL TAKE THEM in the order of their importance," Sandro said to Mike as they drove across the Williamsburg Bridge toward Brooklyn. Below, the East River glistened white, reflecting the thousands of still-lighted office windows of the financial district. "Moreno is the most important of our witnesses, so we'll see him first."

"And then the guy from the restaurant, and then Annie Mae Cooper, and then Phil Gruberger, right?"

"Right. But not all of them today."

Francisco Moreno was not in the barber shop. The barbers who were there told Mike to try the Savoia Pool Hall, around the corner. The address they had been given looked like the rear entrance to a factory. There was no sign outside, no elevator, nothing but a drab steel door.

"This can't be a pool hall," said Sandro. "There's nothing here."

"This is the address," said Mike, lighting a match. "Come on. As long as we're here, let's go inside, walk up a couple of flights. Maybe it's upstairs."

They began climbing. At first, the stairs were not only dark but also tomb-silent. They could hear their own breathing. As they ascended higher into the building, they could faintly hear talking. It grew louder. As they opened the door at the third-floor landing, the noise exploded into full-scale charivari—chatter, pool balls clicking, laughter. Four pool tables, side by side, lay directly across their path. The air was smoky, and the swirls undulated in the lights suspended over the green-felt-covered tables. Men surrounded the tables and lined the walls. They were all Puerto Rican, a full spectrum from white to black, a full range of sizes. A radio was blaring a Spanish pop song.

As Sandro and Mike entered, the noise suddenly diminished. Men holding pool cues paused, watching them. They walked deeper into the room. The noise was still abating, although some men kept talking as they watched.

"There he is," Mike said, seeing Moreno bent over a table, drawing a bead on a fourteen ball near the far side pocket. He hit the cue ball, and the fourteen ball clicked perfectly and rolled in. Moreno stood straight, smiling, chalking his cue. He turned to see what had quieted the room. He smiled when he saw Sandro, and then he understood the sudden hush.

"*Esta buen'. No son camarones. Son amigos,*" Moreno announced to the room. He shook hands with Sandro, then Mike.

"He just told them we were friends, not cops," Mike said.

Noise immediately sprang back into the room, and Sandro and Mike were ignored.

"Tell him we want to talk to him. Let's go someplace a little more quiet," said Sandro.

Mike spoke to Moreno. He nodded and handed someone his pool cue. They descended the steps and walked two blocks to a tenement. At the top of the second flight of stairs, Moreno unlocked a door. The first room they entered was a kitchen. It was dark, with a little light spilling over from a hall beyond. Linoleum glistened in the reflection. Moreno led them to a room at the end of the hall. He unlocked the door.

Mike and Moreno spoke in Spanish.

"He rents a room here," Mike explained. "He says there are three other people who live here—the woman whose apartment it is and two guys who pay her rent to stay in the other rooms."

PART 35

Moreno pulled a cord hanging from the ceiling. A bare bulb glared over them. He motioned to Sandro to sit in the lone chair. He and Mike sat on the bed.

"Ask him to repeat to you the story of what happened on the third of July," Sandro suggested.

Mike spoke and Moreno answered.

"It's the same as he told us before. Alvarado came in about two twenty-five or two thirty and got a haircut. He was in the store for maybe twenty-five minutes, and left before three."

"Okay. Now tell him that we're here because we have to help him to get ready to go to court."

Mike translated.

"And tell him that I want to start asking him questions the way the district attorney will."

"He says that that's good because he's a little nervous about being a witness."

"Tell him that if he can get past me, he'll be able to get past any district attorney. I know the whole story, and all the traps to set for him." Mike translated. Moreno nodded and smiled.

"First of all, has he ever been convicted of a crime?" Sandro asked.

Mike asked him. "He says he was playing dice in the street once, and he had to pay two bucks fine."

"That's not a crime," said Sandro. "Anything else?"

"He said he was arrested once for having a fight. He said he was drunk and had a fight with his sister's boy friend. When everybody sobered up, they dropped the charges."

"What happened when he went to court?" Sandro asked.

Mike asked. "He said they threw the case out."

"Is he sure?"

"Sure. He said he had to know that when he went for his barber's license."

"Fine. Tell him that if Ellis asks him if he has ever been convicted of a crime, he should tell him about the dice playing. It's no crime, so there's no trouble. If he's asked if he's been convicted of any other crime, he should say no. Tell him that."

Mike translated.

"And also tell him that if anyone asks him whether he ever assaulted anyone, he should say *no*. It wasn't a conviction, and he can't be asked if he was arrested," Sandro added. Mike informed Moreno.

"Now, what time did Alvarado come into the store?" Sandro asked.

"He must have come in around two thirty," Mike translated.

"There's no clock in the store. He doesn't wear a watch. How does he know what time it was?"

"His friend came in," Mike translated.

"How does he know what time it was when his friend came in? He still didn't have a watch or clock."

"His friend always comes in around four o'clock. And this day, his friend came in early, and they kidded about it. He remembered they were kidding."

"How does he know what time it was when his friend came in?" Sandro insisted.

"His friend had a watch, and he looked at his friend's watch, and then they kidded about his friend working half a day."

"What day was it, does he know the date?"

"He says he doesn't know the date. It was the day before the holiday."

"Tell him it was July third. The holiday is July fourth."

Mike continued to translate the questions and answers. Moreno was a serious student. He listened to every word.

"Now, what day was it that Alvarado came into his store?"

"It was July third. The day before the holiday."

Sandro smiled and winked at Moreno. Moreno smiled, pleased.

"How does he remember that it was July third and not some other day in June or May?"

"Because the next day was the holiday. He didn't go to work."

"And wasn't there something unusual that he saw in the paper the next morning?" Sandro suggested.

Mike asked Moreno. Moreno nodded. "He says he saw Alvarado's picture in the paper the next day."

"Now, again, how does he remember that the day the man came into his store was July third?"

Mike asked the question. "Because the next day was a holiday.

He didn't work. And he saw Alvarado's picture in the paper the next morning."

Sandro nodded. "And what did he think when he saw the paper the next day?"

"He thought that he had given Alvarado a haircut the day before about two thirty in the afternoon."

"How does he know what time it was that Alvarado came into his store?"

"He said that his friend came in about two fifteen. His friend usually comes in much later. So he looked at his friend's watch, and they kidded about his friend working only a half a day. Alvarado came in about fifteen minutes later."

"Are you sure about that time?" Sandro shouted, standing suddenly.

Moreno studied Sandro, his body tensing.

"What time was it when Alvarado came in?" Sandro demanded.

"About two twenty-five, two thirty," Mike translated.

"How do you know what time it was? Did you look at a clock?"

"No."

"Did you have a watch?"

"No."

"How do you know what time it was?"

"My friend came in about two fifteen. He had a watch. I looked at it, and we kidded about what time it was and that he only worked half a day."

"This friend of yours comes in every day, doesn't he?"

"Almost."

"How do you know it was July third and that he came in early and not some other day?"

"Because the next day was a holiday. I didn't work. That's why my friend came in early. He got off early because of the holiday."

"Maybe it was Memorial Day, maybe it was another holiday. How does he know Alvarado came in on July third?"

"Because the next day was a holiday, and when he was off the next day, he saw Alvarado's picture in the paper, and he remembered having given him a haircut and trimmed his moustache the day before."

Sandro smiled. Moreno smiled.

"What time was it that Alvarado came into your shop?" Sandro said suddenly.

"About two twenty-five, two thirty."

"How do you know what time it was?"

"My friend came in about two fifteen. Alvarado came in about fifteen minutes later."

"Have you ever been convicted of a crime?"

"I played dice once and paid a two-dollar fine."

"Did you ever assault anyone?"

"No."

"What day was it that Alvarado came into your shop?"

"July third, because the next day was a holiday, and I remember seeing his picture in the paper. I remember his face and that I gave him a haircut."

"Okay, now explain this to him. I only want him to answer the questions the district attorney asks. Make the D.A. work. He should not volunteer anything."

Mike translated.

"So that if he's asked, 'Was it raining when he came in?' he should answer, 'No.' He should not answer 'No, the sun was out.' If he's only asked about the rain, that's what he should answer. This is like a game to see how few words you can use to answer. Little words, little sentences. See if he understands."

Mike explained. Moreno studied Mike as he listened. He nodded.

"Is it raining now?"

"No." He smiled.

"Wrong," Sandro said sharply. "How does he know what's happened outside since we came in here? If he doesn't know something, he should say so."

Mike repeated what Sandro had said. Moreno nodded sheepishly.

"Is it raining outside?"

"Now?"

"Now."

"I don't know for sure."

"Was it raining when you came in here?"

PART 35

"No."

"Was the sun out?"

"Yes." Moreno looked at Sandro. Sandro nodded.

"What time did Alvarado come into the barber shop?"

"Two twenty-five, two thirty."

"Did you look at a clock?"

"No."

Sandro nodded.

"Were you wearing a watch?"

"No."

"How do you know what time it was?"

"My friend came in at two fifteen. I looked at his watch."

"Do you always look at your friend's watch?"

"Just this day. He was in early, and we kidded about it, and I looked at his watch."

"How do you know when Alvarado came in?"

"He came in about fifteen minutes later."

"Are you sure?"

"Pretty sure."

"You mean it could have been later?"

"Maybe five minutes, more or less."

"Could it have been later than that?"

"I don't think so."

"Mike, tell him that he should use positive statements, not I don't think so, or maybe. He must say, 'Yes, I am sure. It was two thirty.' If he gives positive times, positive statements, the D.A. can't trap him. If he says I think so, or maybe, that leads to more questions. He'll be asked, 'Well, then you're not sure?' Or, 'It might have been later?' And then, 'How much later?' He'll avoid all that if he says positively, 'It was two twenty-five, two thirty.' If the D.A. asks, 'Could it have been later?' He should answer, 'No!' Explain that."

Mike translated.

"How long after your friend came in, did Alvarado come in?"

"About fifteen minutes."

"Are you sure?"

"Yes."

"Could it have been later?"

"No."

"Perhaps he came in at two forty-five."

"No!"

"What time did he come in?"

"About two twenty-five, two thirty."

"Is he sure?"

"Yes."

"What day was it when the man Alvarado came in?"

"July third."

"How does he know?"

"The next day was a holiday. He didn't work. And while he was off that day, he saw Alvarado's picture in the paper, and he remembered him from the day before."

"Is he sure?"

"Sure," Moreno said himself in English.

Sandro smiled. Moreno and Mike smiled.

CHAPTER XXIII

Wednesday, April 17th, 1968

"CALL YOUR NEXT WITNESS," the judge directed Ellis.

"Josefina Ramirez," Ellis announced. "We will need the interpreter for this witness, Your Honor."

The judge nodded to the interpreter sitting beside Hernandez. She rose and walked to the witness stand. From the side door, a small, frail-looking woman of indeterminate age—she might have been twenty-five or forty-five—entered the courtroom.

"Who is she, Sandro?" Sam asked.

"I don't know. I haven't come across her name before."

Sam shrugged. "I'm sure she's going to identify the defendants somehow."

Mrs. Ramirez testified that she was married and had six children. On the day of the murder, she was living at 161 Stanton Street. About 2:15 P.M. that day, she went to pick up her youngest daughter at the child-care center.

"She's the woman who was on the stairs with the kid when the killer ran down," Sam said flatly.

Mrs. Ramirez testified that after picking up her daughter, she walked home. She had been in front of 153 Stanton Street at 2:30 and heard explosive noises coming from an upper floor. These she learned later were the shots on the roof that killed Lauria. As she and her child were climbing the stairs of 161 Stanton Street, Mrs. Ramirez said, first she heard someone running down, then she saw a Negro coming down toward them.

"Here we go," said Sam, not looking up from his notes.

Sandro watched the witness.

The interpreter indicated that the man Mrs. Ramirez saw had bad hair. He was dressed in gray and had something she could not identify concealed in his right hand. He was running quickly and breathing very hard, as if fatigued. He said nothing to Mrs. Ramirez or the child, but just kept running.

"Did you get a good look at his face?" Ellis asked.

"I couldn't see him very well because he was going very fast. I saw him in a moment like this," she replied, waving her arm through the air.

Sam looked up. "Did she just say what I thought she said?"

"I'm sure I heard it, but I don't believe it."

Ellis asked Mrs. Ramirez what she did after the man ran past her. She said she went to her apartment, and sometime later the police came and asked her questions, and she told them about the man in the gray suit.

"That's where they got the description of a Negro in a gray suit," said Sandro.

Ellis had no further questions.

Neither did Siakos.

"She's not going to identify Alvarado," Sam said in amazement.

"Maybe I should have him stand, and ask her if this is the man she saw." Sandro suggested. "She won't identify him and that will be strong in our favor."

"Maybe it's a trap. She didn't identify him. Leave it at that. Don't ask her about Alvarado. Just about the guy on the stairs."

Sandro rose and walked to the jury box. The judge looked at Sandro as if to say, "The witness hasn't touched your man; why bother?"

"Mrs. Ramirez, this man you saw, how was he dressed?"

"In gray, like a suit," the interpreter translated.

"And his hair, you said was 'bad hair?'"

"It's not like our hair. It is crispy."

"When you say our hair, you mean yours, mine, whose?"

"Well, my hair is straight and smooth."

"You mean it's not like a Puerto Rican's hair?"

"Objection."

"Sustained."

"When you say our hair, whom do you mean?"

"It is not like my hair. It is curly hair. All plastered down."

"Was this man you saw tall?"

"No, he wasn't very tall."

"Was he as tall as I am?"

"More or less, but fatter. He was taller than I am," Mrs. Ramirez replied.

"How tall are you, Mrs. Ramirez?"

"I don't know exactly."

"Your Honor, may we have Mrs. Ramirez stand and be measured."

"Yes."

Mrs. Ramirez stood and was measured by one of the court officers. She was five feet four inches in her heels. She returned to the witness chair.

"Mrs. Ramirez, you saw me standing next to you just now. Was the man you saw as tall as I am?"

"More or less, but fatter."

"Your Honor, will you accept for the record that I am five feet ten inches?"

"We will accept that. Anything further?"

"No, Your Honor."

"Step down. At this time, we will have a short recess."

The jury began to file out. Sam stood and was placing his papers in his briefcase.

"You figure she was supposed to identify Alvarado?" Sandro wondered.

"I'm not sure that she balked on the stand. Ellis seemed too calm. He must have known she wouldn't identify our guy, but he needed her to support that confession. The police obviously based part of it on her description."

"You know, Sam, she actually helped us. She gave the guy 'bad hair' and made him five foot ten."

"Yeah, that helps. Not much, but it helps."

Ellis next called Claudia Lauria, sister of the dead patrolman. She testified that she went to the morgue the day after the shooting and identified the body as that of her brother Fortune Lauria.

There was no cross-examination.

Ellis next called Robert Soto.

"Here's the little bastard that led us down the garden path for Mullaly," Sandro whispered to Sam.

Sam nodded. "I'm glad he did. It gave you a chance to plant that story about not having any alibi witnesses. I still can't believe Ellis hasn't asked for a list of them."

"Maybe he will."

"Too late for that now. He would have done it before this. If those witnesses stand up the way you say they will, Ellis is going to have the shock of his life." Sam smiled slightly, his face still in the notes before him.

Sandro watched Soto take the stand. Soto was uneasy. He looked down at Sandro furtively, then looked away.

Ellis had Soto describe his old apartment at 153 Stanton Street. Soto testified that on the day of the shooting he had had three television sets there. He identified the property that had been found on the roof. Soto testified that he left for work early the morning of July 3rd and was not let back into his apartment until 8 o'clock that evening. Ellis had Soto inspect photographs taken by the police of the ransacked apartment.

Soto told the jury that there was a fire escape outside one of the windows in the living room extending over to the window of his children's bedroom. On all the windows he had installed folding iron gates. Soto indicated that these gates were effectively locked against intruders. He testified he had special screw locks on the windows. Ellis had no further questions.

Siakos cross-examined Soto. Soto testified that there were ordinary window locks on each window as well as the extra screw locks. Siakos had no further questions.

PART 35

"You want to take him?" asked Sam.

"No, you take him," Sandro replied. "You know what conversations I had with him. I think I'd jump right down his lying throat."

Sam walked to the jury box and faced Soto. Soto denied ever having told Sandro that a junky named Salerno, on one of the lower floors, might have been the person who burglarized his apartment. He denied that Mrs. Salerno had become friendly with his own wife after the burglary. Soto denied telling Sandro that Mullaly told him everything about the case. Soto denied calling Sandro's office and offering to go interview witnesses with him.

Sandro was restive. Soto never looked toward him. Sam had no further questions. Soto walked off the stand. His eyes met Sandro's for an instant; he saw the fury there, looked away, walking quickly to the witness room.

The judge recessed for lunch.

Mike and Sandro, talking quietly, turned from the main corridor on their way to the elevator. They stopped short. There, alone, waiting for an elevator were Robert and Alma Soto.

"There's that lying little spic," Mike muttered, loudly enough to be heard.

"Hey, you can't call me that." Soto didn't seem certain whether Mike could or couldn't. His wife remained silent. Sandro held onto Mike's arm.

"I already did, you lousy liar."

"I'm not any spic. I'm an American just like you and him."

"You're a fink. You think that's what America's about? People trying to hide what they are or where they're from?"

"I ain't hidin' nothing."

"You're damn right. Everybody can see what you're really like." Mike drew his right foot back slightly. Soto studied him.

"Mr. Luca," Soto said, "your friend's getting all excited. I don't want to fight him." The elevator bell rang.

"Go ahead, Soto. Get on," Sandro said, still holding Mike by the arm. Soto nodded and pushed his wife in ahead of him. The doors closed.

"Why didn't you let me smack him one?" asked Mike.

"Why get your hands dirty?"

Sandro and Mike took the next down elevator to the lobby. Soto and his wife were already gone.

In the afternoon, Ellis called a detective from the ballistics squad. He testified that the bullets found on the roof and in the slain officer's body were fired from Lauria's own pistol. The pistol was a Smith and Wesson .38, which could be fired single action, or double action, shot after shot.

Siakos had no questions. Sam stood and asked the detective how long it would take to fire all the shells in the gun double action. The detective answered it would take very few seconds. Sam had no further questions. The detective was excused.

At this point, Ellis turned to the judge. "The people rest, Your Honor."

Sandro looked at Sam. "What about the statements the defendants gave to the D.A. at the station house? They're supposedly confessions, too? Isn't he going to use them?" asked Sandro.

"I can't figure this. Unless they're not confessions!" said Sam. "But just let him not use them. We'll shove them right down his throat in summation. Their absence will destroy his case. Not much of a case either, if our witnesses stand up."

The judge excused the jury early, explaining that the lawyers and he had some legal matters to discuss. When the jury had retired, Siakos and Sam each made the customary motions to dismiss the indictment for failure to establish a prima facie case. After legal discussions and argument, the judge denied the motions and told Siakos to have his witnesses on the stand in the morning.

"You have your witnesses ready, Nick?" Sandro asked as they were gathering their papers.

"Oh, sure, sure. I'll have somebody go and get them tonight."

"You've spoken with them, haven't you?"

"Not personally. One of my men has, though. They'll be fine. I only have to talk to them for a few minutes before they go on the stand."

Sandro and Sam left the courtroom, hoping Siakos was right.

CHAPTER XXIV

MIKE'S CAR WAS SPEEDING across the Williamsburg Bridge again.

"What time did Moreno call?" Sandro asked.

"About four fifteen. He found Julio, the guy from the school, who was in the shop that day. But Julio's moving tonight, and if we don't see him now, we could lose him again for good."

"This case isn't going to be over until the last minute, is it?"

Mike pulled the car up to the barber shop. Moreno was inside giving a haircut.

"What day was it that Alvarado came into your barber shop?" Sandro flung at him quickly. Mike translated.

Moreno studied Sandro momentarily, smiling slightly, "It was on July third."

"How do you know?"

"The next day was a holiday, and I didn't work. I saw that guy's picture in the paper when I wasn't working."

"Is there any question in your mind it was July third?"

"No question in my mind."

"What time was it when he came into the store?"

"About two twenty-five, two thirty."

"Perhaps it was later, two forty-five?"

"It was two twenty-five, two thirty."

Sandro smiled and shook hands with Moreno. His customer was looking dumbfounded at everyone. Moreno spoke to him in Spanish, and he returned to the girlie magazine while Moreno turned back to Mike.

"He said if we wait for him to finish this customer, he'll come with us to the place where Julio is staying tonight, and we can speak to him."

"Okay, tell him we'll wait in the car."

While Sandro waited in the car, Mike went into a Cuchifritos, which is the up-and-coming Puerto Rican Howard Johnson's. He came out with something golden fried, which he told Sandro was pork.

The three of them drove through short, dark Brooklyn streets until Moreno told Mike to stop the car. They got out and entered a building. It was dimly lighted inside. A bicycle stood under the stairs next to a baby carriage. Moreno walked to the rear apartment on the first floor and knocked. A man, obviously a friend of Moreno's, answered. They spoke and then turned to look at Sandro. The man waved, asking them to come in.

The kitchen table was in disarray, covered with empty plates from the evening meal. In a corner was a sink. Another man stood at the sink, peering into a mirror at his soap-lathered face. He had a razor in his hand. He appeared to be in his thirties and was very light-skinned.

"That's Julio," Mike said.

The man at the sink looked in the mirror, meeting Sandro's eyes there. He nodded.

"Does he speak English?"

"Sure, I speak."

"Do you remember being in Francisco's barber shop on July third?" Sandro asked.

"I'm there all the time. I don't know the days."

"Well, this was a day before a holiday. Maybe you got off from work early that day?"

"No, I don't remember." He was slicing the foam off his face now.

"Do you remember seeing this fellow in the shop at any time?" Sandro asked, handing the newspaper clippings to Mike. Mike

PART 35

held them in front of Julio. Julio turned from the mirror, wiped his hands on the towel hung across his shoulders, and studied the pictures.

"No, I don't remember." He resumed shaving.

"Did someone give you a dollar to let him take your place in the barber shop? It would be a day before a holiday. Do you remember that?"

"You know, I can't remember that. I'm in there all the time. But no guy give me a dollar. If a guy wants my place, and I not in a hurry, I let him take it. Go ahead. No, I never get a dollar. And I don't remember that guy anyway."

"Are you saying, Julio, that you were there but you didn't see this fellow, or just that you don't remember whether you were there or not?"

"I don't remember if I was there or not. Maybe I was. Maybe I wasn't."

"In other words, maybe it happened. You just don't remember?"

"That's right."

Sandro looked at Mike. "At least we won't get hurt with this. You think of anything else?"

"Why don't we let Moreno talk to him, try to remind him?" Mike suggested.

"Okay with me."

Mike spoke to Moreno, and Moreno spoke to Julio. They had an involved conversation in Spanish, Moreno explaining, Julio shaking his head. Moreno finally turned and spoke to Mike.

"He just doesn't remember," Mike translated.

"Okay. Thank him for us, and let's go and see if we can find Pablo Torres before it gets too late." They turned and left the building and got back in the car.

"Do you think we should have taken a statement from him?" asked Mike.

"Probably we should get a negative statement, but I'm too tired. He doesn't know anything anyway."

Mike drove Moreno home, and then they continued to where Pablo Torres lived.

"This is the restaurant. We want his house," said Sandro as Mike parked at the curb.

"This is the address he gave," said Mike. "Maybe he lives above the store. There's an entrance over here."

They got out of the car and entered the building. Mike searched the mailboxes and bells. "Here it is. It's marked Basement."

"So give a little ring and we'll see," Sandro mugged. Mike rang the bell. They waited to hear a door open.

"*Quién es?*" asked a voice from the rear of the building.

"Rivera," Mike announced as they walked to the back. There was a stairway leading down, and at the bottom stood Pablo Torres in a white T-shirt, blue polka-dot shorts, and black ankle socks. He smiled and nodded, waving them to come down.

"My mama wanted me to be a professional man," Sandro said. "Do you think she knew about nights like this?"

Mike laughed as they walked down. They entered the cellar of the building, which served as the storage area for the restaurant. There were cases of beer and soda, large burlap bags containing beans, cardboard cases of canned tomatoes. Torres walked toward the back. In one corner, a wire was strung across the ceiling, and on it was a curtain that separated his quarters from the bottles and cans and beans. Behind the curtain was a bed, unmade. Torres had obviously just risen from it to open the door. His clothes were on hangers, suspended from the walls around the bed. There was a cigarette in an ashtray on the bed, curling smoke ceilingward. An open can of beer was next to the bed.

Torres respectfully motioned Sandro to sit on the bed. He moved two cases of tomato cans close for Mike and himself. Sandro noticed that he was a little red-eyed. If you could get used to the restricted view, Sandro reflected, it was easier than having to stagger home from a bar. Besides, he had an unlimited supply of free beer.

"Tell him it's coming time—"

"*Tell him it's coming time?*" Mike repeated, laughing. "You hardly speak English better than he does. Or are you being condescending, you bastard?"

Sandro laughed. "Tell him that we'll be needing him in court soon,

PART 35

and we wanted to get him prepared. Give him the whole thing—tell him to answer only what he's asked and give positive answers."

Mike explained it to Torres, who sipped his beer, listening. He nodded and looked to Sandro.

"Do you remember the man you now know as Alvarado?" Sandro asked.

"Yes," Mike translated.

"Do you remember what day it was that he was in the restaurant?"

"Yes, it was the day before the holiday. He came in to eat."

"Tell him only to answer the question and not give information I didn't ask for," said Sandro.

Mike explained it again.

"Do you remember what day he came in?"

"Yes, it was the day before the holiday."

"Which holiday?"

"I don't know which holiday," Mike translated. "I know I didn't work that day."

"Tell him the holiday was July fourth. That Alvarado was therefore in on July third."

Mike explained it to Torres. Then Mike turned to Sandro. "I don't think we should try to be too tricky. He's a simple little guy."

"That's okay. The witnesses shouldn't sound exactly alike. But we have to make sure he knows what the hell he's talking about. Tell him I'm going to ask him questions as if I were the D.A."

Mike told Torres, who nodded, then rose. He offered Mike and Sandro a beer. They refused. He started to open a new can. Sandro took the beer can out of his hand.

"Tell him to drink the place dry when we're gone. But right now he should pay attention."

Mike did.

"Do you remember what day Alvarado came into the restaurant?"

"Yes. It was the day before the holiday."

"What holiday?" Sandro asked, a bit exasperated.

"I don't know," Torres shrugged. "But I saw the man's picture in the Spanish paper the next day, and it said he killed the policeman."

"Fine, fine," said Sandro. "We'll tie him down that way. Tell him that that's the way he should answer the questions. He remembers the day because it was a day before the holiday, and he saw Alvarado's picture the next day."

Mike explained. Torres nodded, smiling.

"What time did Alvarado come into the restaurant?"

"He says he doesn't know exactly what time it was."

"He told us the first time we spoke that it was after the lunch rush, one forty-five to two. See if that helps him."

Mike spoke to him. He nodded.

"What time did Alvarado come into the restaurant?"

"After lunch was over. It must have been near two o'clock."

Sandro was learning not to argue with Torres. If *he* couldn't make any headway with him, neither would Ellis.

"How long did Alvarado stay in the restaurant?"

"About fifteen minutes."

"What time did he leave, then?"

Torres thought a moment and answered in Spanish.

"He says it was about five after two, something like that."

"Is he sure about the time?"

"He says it must have been five after two, maybe ten after."

"Could it have been three o'clock?"

"No, because Alvarado was there before Pablo ate his lunch that day."

"What day was it that Alvarado came into the restaurant?"

"He said it was the day before the holiday."

"Does he know the day of the month?"

"He says he doesn't. But the next day, he saw Alvarado's picture in the papers about killing the policeman."

"Ask him if he's sure that it was the next day that he saw Alvarado's picture."

"He says sure, because he was off that day, and he was right in this bed reading the paper. He sat up and said to himself, 'I gave that guy beefsteak yesterday.'"

"And what time was it that Alvarado came in?"

"He said it was after the lunch rush was over."

"What time? Approximately."

"It was a little before two o'clock."

"Could it have been one o'clock?"

"No, that's lunch rush. This was after."

"Could it have been three o'clock?"

"No. He says it was before he ate, so it had to be just after the lunch rush. About two, a little before perhaps."

"How long was Alvarado in the restaurant?"

"About fifteen minutes."

"And what time does he say Alvarado came in?"

"About a little before two."

Sandro rose to his feet suddenly. He thrust his head close to Torres's. "Are you sure it was two o'clock?"

Torres shrank back, frightened. He spoke to Mike in Spanish.

"He wants to know if you're crazy?"

"Tell him I want an answer."

Mike translated. Sandro's face was angry.

"He says he's sure."

"Is there any question in his mind that it was two o'clock?"

"He says it was after the lunch rush, about a few minutes before two o'clock."

"Is he sure?"

"He's sure."

Sandro smiled, patting Torres on the back. Torres smiled, obviously not sure of what was going on.

"Tell him he did fine," Sandro said, opening another can of cold beer for Torres. He handed it to him. He opened a can for Mike and one for himself.

"*Salute!*" said Sandro.

"*Salute!*" the others answered.

CHAPTER XXV

Thursday, April 18th, 1968

THE NEXT MORNING, as Sandro arrived in the corridor outside the courtroom, he saw Siakos surrounded by five highly vocal Puerto Rican women. They all seemed to be talking quickly at once. Sandro felt more relaxed than he had in several weeks, knowing he could take it easy for the next couple of days as Siakos presented his defense. He also knew that he had to use his evenings to finish preparing his witnesses. Sandro made his way to a telephone booth to make sure Mike Rivera was ready for work that evening. Mike said he would come to court in an hour or so.

As his first witness, Siakos called Josefina Cortez. Mrs. Cortez testified that she worked in the factory with Mrs. Hernandez. She remembered July 3rd, 1967, because it was the day before the holiday, and she did not work the next day. She said that because the next day was a holiday, she was paid one day early. She testified she received her check about noon, and went to the bank, which was on the corner of 125th Street and Park Avenue.

At this point, Siakos had Hernandez stand up. Mrs. Cortez said she recognized him, had seen him before July 3rd, 1967, when he came to the factory to pick up his wife. She testified she saw him in the bank

PART 35

at about 12:15 P.M. on July 3rd. He was waiting for his wife, who was on line to cash her paycheck. At the time, Mrs. Cortez testified, she was with three other women. Siakos turned the witness over to Ellis.

Mrs. Cortez testified, in reply to Ellis's questions, that she had not noticed a Chevrolet nearby, nor had she seen any man with Hernandez. She said she had no idea what Hernandez was doing between 2 and 3 P.M. that day. Ellis had no further questions.

Siakos next called Nela Alvarez. Mrs. Alvarez also worked at the factory where Mrs. Hernandez worked. She testified that on the morning of July 3rd, 1967, about 8:50, she saw Mrs. Hernandez arrive at the factory in a car driven by Mr. Hernandez. She could not identify the car, even when shown a picture of it. She said there were so many cars that look alike, and she didn't pay much attention to the type of car it was. There was no other man with them.

Ellis had no cross-examination.

Siakos called Marcelina Ortiz. Ortiz also worked with Mrs. Hernandez. Mrs. Ortiz testified she had seen Hernandez on several occasions before July 3rd, 1967. On July 3rd, she saw him on the corner near the bank at about 12:30 P.M. She was just going to cash her paycheck. Hernandez's wife came out of the bank and joined him on the corner, and then they went to a luncheonette or something like that. Siakos had no further questions.

Ellis asked Mrs. Ortiz to describe, if she could, what Hernandez was wearing on July 3rd when she saw him. She didn't remember exactly what he was wearing, except he wore a straw hat, and he carried a portable radio. She said she didn't see any car, nor did she see him standing with another man.

Siakos next called German Ortega. Ortega said he worked in the same building as Mrs. Hernandez, although for another company. He said he had seen Hernandez on only two occasions, both on July 3rd, 1967. He said the first time was when Mrs. Hernandez introduced him. It was about 12:15, and he was on his way to lunch. Later, as he returned, after lunch, he saw them again as Hernandez walked his wife back to the building. He testified the second time he saw Hernandez was about 1 P.M. Ortega indicated that he was not a friend of Hernandez, as he had never seen him before July 3rd, 1967. Ellis asked Ortega if he had ever been convicted of a crime. Ortega said no. Ellis had no further questions.

The judge called for a short recess.

Mike joined Sandro and Sam in the corridor.

"Listen," Mike said. "I came in earlier and saw some blond guy. Looked like a cop. He was sitting in the audience taking notes when the witnesses were on the stand. When the recess was called, he got up and went through that side door."

"That's the door that leads to the witness room," Sandro said.

"Probably a spotter for Ellis," Sam remarked. "He'll get information from the witnesses and feed it to Mullaly for the cops to check on, since Mullaly can't be in court."

"Is that proper?" asked Mike.

Sam shrugged. "How can you stop him? It's a public proceeding."

Siakos called Mullaly back to the stand as his next witness. He questioned Mullaly about the pawnshop tickets taken from Hernandez at the station house. Mullaly produced two of them. He testified, however, that he didn't know where the other tickets were or what shop they were from. Mullaly said that he had checked the pawn book at Sid Goodman's Pawnshop, from which one of the two available tickets came. A portable radio had been pawned there. Mullaly testified he had taken from the pawnshop the signature card which belonged to that pledged item. He later took the property from the pawnshop, in about the first week of April, just before this trial. Mullaly said also that he had been at Excelsior Pawn Brokers on Delancey Street, to which the other available pawn ticket belonged. There he also investigated the pawn book, the signature card, and the property pawned, two suits.

Siakos called for the production of the valise which had been taken from the trunk of Hernandez's car on July 3rd. Ellis had it brought in from the witness room. Siakos also called for the two suits that had been at Excelsior Pawn Brokers and the radio from Sid Goodman's. Ellis had these produced. Siakos had Mullaly identify all of them, and they were offered into evidence.

Mullaly testified further that he never investigated or telephoned the pawnshops on July 3rd or 4th. He did not investigate them until a week later, July 9th, 1967, much after Hernandez had allegedly confessed. On July 3rd, Mullaly indicated, he did not think the pawn tickets had any significance.

Siakos searched through the photostatted police records to find the one relating to the burglary on 119th Street. He asked Mullaly if he had ever spoken to Antonio Quiñones or Jose Arce, the two men who lived in the apartment on 119th Street that Hernandez had broken into on July 3rd, 1967. Mullaly said he had spoken to them on July 9th. He said they identified the suits from the pawnshop, the portable radio, and the property in the valise. Mullaly testified he never interrogated Hernandez about the pawn tickets on the evening of July 3rd.

The thin, tall blond man Mike had remarked about returned to the courtroom. He walked up to the bar and handed a piece of paper to Ellis.

"I have no further questions of this witness," said Siakos.

"I have no questions," Ellis said. Mullaly stepped down. "Your Honor, with your permission," said Ellis. "I see German Ortega, the previous witness, now sitting in the courtroom as a spectator. May I recall him for a short examination?"

"You may, sir."

"Bet Ellis has a yellow sheet on him," said Sam. "See what we're up against. We have to send out a subpoena and wait two or three days. Ellis has it in twenty minutes."

Ortega took the stand again.

"A few minutes ago you were asked if you had ever been convicted of a crime, do you remember that?"

"Yes."

"And what was your answer?"

"No."

"Was that the truth?"

"Yes, sir."

"Isn't it so that on August seventeenth, 1963, you were convicted of policy and fined fifty dollars."

"Yes."

"So that you lied on the stand when you had sworn to tell the truth."

"If numbers is a crime when you get fined, then I guess I did."

"You lied on the stand?"

"I already said I guess I did."

"No further questions, Your Honor."

"Isn't this something," said Sandro. "Nonsense."

"Cheer up, Sandro. Ellis wouldn't be fooling with trash if he had real bombs. He's worried."

Siakos called Carmelita Delfino as his next witness. She testified that she had been working in the same shop as Mrs. Hernandez on July 3rd. She said she saw Hernandez there on July 3rd. She was not a friend of his. She said at about 12:20 P.M., when she went downstairs, she saw Hernandez by himself in front of the building. Siakos had no further questions of Mrs. Delfino.

Ellis had no cross-examination.

The judge called the lunch recess.

Sandro stood after the jury left. "Siakos's case is going in," he said, "but what does it all add up to?"

"He's got more. He's got those people that you saw from the pawnshop. That's the important stuff, not this. He's just laying the groundwork now."

"I hope you're right," said Sandro.

"We can't do everything. Just sit there and worry about your own case."

In the afternoon, Siakos called Willie Morales, the manager of Sid Goodman's Pawnshop. Morales carried a large book with him. When he saw Sandro sitting at the counsel table, he smiled slightly. Siakos approached and began his direct examination.

Morales said he remembered July 3rd, and he remembered Hernanadez coming into the pawnshop on that day and pawning a portable radio. He said that Hernandez used the name Antonio Cruz when he pawned the radio. Morales opened the big book and showed the name Antonio Cruz as pledge No. 4 on July 3rd. Morales testified that he had seen the man who called himself Antonio Cruz on several occasions before July 3rd. He had also seen Hernandez's picture in the newspaper on July 4th, and now, seeing Hernandez sitting in court at the counsel table, he was positive that Hernandez was the man who as Antonio Cruz came into the shop to pawn the radio.

Morales showed Siakos the signature card. There was no question that it was Hernandez's handwriting. Morales testified that the radio was pawned sometime in the afternoon of July 3rd. He wasn't positive of the exact time, but it had to be after 1:50 P.M. and could have been anytime between 1:50 and 3:30. It had to be after 1:50, Morales said, because he hadn't returned from lunch until 1:45 and from the handwriting in the book, he knew that he had taken care of the transaction.

Siakos offered the portable radio, the signature card, and the pawn book into evidence. Morales testified further that he was able to recall the particular transaction because he saw Hernandez's picture in the newspapers the next day and had recognized Hernandez as the man who had been in the pawnshop the day before. He testified that the police had come into the pawnshop sometime in the middle of July and he had told them the same story he had just testified to. He said that Detective Mullaly had taken all the information, and put a stop on the radio so that it could not be redeemed.

To Ellis's cross-examination Morales replied that he couldn't recall the exact dates when Hernandez had been in the pawnshop before July 3rd, but he knew that it had been two or three times. He said he could not remember the time of day when the other transactions had taken place either, nor whether they had been before or after his lunch break. Morales admitted that his memory of what happened on July 3rd, 1967, was better on July 9th, 1967, when the detective was at the pawnshop, than now while he was on the stand.

Ellis asked Morales if he remembered telling the detective that Hernandez had been waiting for him to come back from lunch. He said he remembered and that it was the truth. Ellis asked him if he recalled telling the detective that he didn't remember what time it had been when he came back from lunch. Morales sat up a little straighter in the witness chair.

"I remember telling him that I went out after one, sir, and that I came back before two o'clock."

Ellis had the answer stricken. He asked Morales whether or not he remembered saying that to the detective. Morales said he didn't remember it too clearly. He said he knew that the time was not written in the book, but it had to be after 1:45 P.M.

Ellis asked Morales if he had spoken to Mr. Siakos about this case. He said he had and that he had also spoken to Mr. Luca. Ellis was surprised by that. Morales said that Sandro was the first person after the police to whom he had spoken. Ellis asked Morales if Sandro had written down what he had said. Morales said he had.

The judge called a conference of counsel when Ellis asked to see the signed statement of the witness. The judge explained, out of the hearing of the jury, that the defense had no obligation to give to the district attorney copies of signed statements. Sandro volunteered to give the statement to Ellis in the interests of justice, knowing that the statement would best serve the interests of the defense. Sandro handed the statement to Ellis. Ellis read it.

"Read it and weep, Mr. Ellis," Sandro whispered. Sam, keeping his notes, smiled softly. He made his smile disappear, and he looked up to watch Ellis read the statement.

Morales testified he remembered speaking with Mr. Luca and that there had been another man with him who wrote down what he said. After the other man finished writing the statement, Morales said, he signed it. He identified his signature.

"Did you tell Mr. Luca what time it was you went to lunch on July third?"

"Not the exact time. I said sometime after one o'clock."

"You remember saying it was sometime after one o'clock?"

"Yes, sir."

"Ellis is digging a hole for himself now," said Sam, reading from a photostatic copy of the Morales statement which was in their file.

"Let him nibble at this nonsense. It'll make the prosecution look ridiculous," replied Sandro.

"Your Honor, I offer this statement into evidence," said Ellis.

"No objection," said all defense counsel, without even looking at the paper.

Ellis read it to the jury. The statement was the same as the testimony Morales had just given, about identifying Antonio Cruz as Hernandez, about the radio, about reading the story in the paper. As to the time, the signed statement said:

> On that day, July 3rd, 1967, I do not remember the exact time, but it was in the afternoon, I accepted a portable radio and case...

The jurors, who had edged forward in their seats to hear Ellis topple Morales's testimony, eased back. Some looked at their fellow jurors. Juror number seven, the bearded music teacher, lifted his eyebrows, surprised that there was nothing significant in what Ellis had just read. He shrugged, put his hand to his chin, and continued to listen.

"Let him go. He's doing very well for us. He's strengthening our witness," said Sam.

"Do you remember telling Mr. Luca that you did not remember the exact time, but it was in the afternoon?"

"That is correct."

Sandro rose quickly. "Your Honor, I object to this type of examination. There is no discrepancy whatever in what the witness has said on the stand and what is contained in that statement, concerning the time. It was after one P.M., exactly the same."

"It is not exactly what he just said," retorted Ellis, angry at Sandra's re-emphasis of the point.

"Don't raise your voice to me, sir," said Sandro.

"Gentlemen, let's continue with the trial," admonished the judge. "You may answer the question."

"I don't remember the question," said Morales.

Ellis had the reporter read back the question.

"I did so, but I didn't say—I said after one o'clock in the afternoon."

Ellis asked Morales about the pledge book. He testified he handled the transaction, took the radio in pawn; the transaction took about five or ten minutes. He said he didn't notice if Hernandez went back into an automobile or not when he left the store, nor had he noticed anyone waiting for Hernandez while the transaction was going on. Ellis had no further questions and returned to his seat. He jotted some notes, and let his pencil drop to the table.

The judge ordered a short recess for the jurors. Sandro, Sam, and Siakos walked outside.

Siakos was smiling from ear to ear. "That was beautiful," he said. "Ellis was dying out there."

"That statement of Sandro's didn't hurt you too much," said Sam.

"Not at all, not at all. You know, I think we can do all right here. These fellows may actually be innocent, and the cops actually might have the wrong fellows."

"Really?" said Sam. "I'm going to the men's room."

As his next witness, Siakos called Albert Rojas. Rojas worked for Excelsior Pawn Brokers on Delancey Street, where Antonio Cruz had pawned two suits. Rojas had with him the store's pledge book. He identified the signature of Antonio Cruz, testifying that he had personally entered the transaction in the pledge book. He testified, however, that the person who had actually negotiated with Antonio Cruz was the pawnshop's proprietor, Artie Horowitz. Rojas said that he did not know exactly the time of the negotiation but that he had a rough idea. Ellis objected to Rojas's rough ideas. Sandro and Sam were watching silently as Siakos floundered because he hadn't even talked to his own witness before putting him on the stand.

Ellis further objected to all of Rojas's testimony since there was no connection between the Antonio Cruz on the books at Excelsior and Hernandez. The judge allowed him to continue, subject to the jury's determination if the man who signed the pledge book at Goodman's had been the same as the one who signed at Excelsior. Rojas said that there had been eighty-four transactions on July 3rd, 1967, and the Antonio Cruz transactions were numbers 57 and 58.

"The handwriting is exactly the same in the Excelsior books as in Sid Goodman's. The jury can see that right from the pledge book," Sandro whispered to Sam.

Rojas further identified the signature of a friend of his, Ishmael Perez, in the Excelsior book. This was a transaction that Rojas had handled. Rojas said Perez had been in the pawnshop at about 1:15 P.M. on July 3rd, 1967. Perez's signature was six signatures above Antonio Cruz.

Siakos had no further questions of his witness. Ellis cross-examined

PART 35

only enough to establish clearly that Artie Horowitz was the person who had taken in the pledge, and that he, if anyone, was the one who would know the exact time of the transaction. He had Rojas testify that he had not seen Hernandez or Alvarado at any time on that day. Ellis had no further questions.

Siakos called Rosalinda Estevez. Miss Estevez testified that she had been in Sid Goodman's Pawnshop on July 3rd, 1967. She pointed out her signature in the pledge book that Willie Morales had brought in with him. Her name appeared ten signatures above Antonio Cruz. She testified she had been in the store at about 1:30 P.M. on July 3rd, 1967.

Ellis asked her if she had seen either Hernandez or Alvarado at that time or at any time on that day. She said she had not. Ellis had no further questions.

The judge decided not to start a new witness at that time. He recessed the jury until the following day.

"Hey, Mr. Luca," said Alvarado, as the jury filed out. "Can you do somesing about the food we getting in that bullpens?"

"What do you mean? What's wrong with the food?"

"What's wrong? Mr. Luca, how you feel, every day you eat that stinky jelly sandwiches and tea what's more like water?"

"You mean they don't send over hot lunch or anything special for you on a long trial like this?"

"Special? You kidding, right, Mr. Luca?" Hernandez was watching. "We get two pieces of bread with some jellies in between every day, every day. We can't eat that no more. Believe me this thing, I getting the chits. Him too." He nodded toward Hernandez.

Sandro stood. "May I approach the bench, Your Honor?"

"Yes."

Sandro walked to the bench. Ellis also approached. "Your Honor, it seems we have a complaint about the Department of Correction menu."

Ellis frowned and returned to his table.

"I can't do anything about the Department of Correction, Sandro. You have to talk to their commissioner. What's the matter, are they leaving the truffles out of the pâté?"

"They send these inmates jelly sandwiches, every day. They're starting to get dysentery. Can't we get them some substantial food?"

"I have no authority to do anything about that. Unless you can arrange with the court captain to bring them a sandwich yourself after lunch. Go over on Mulberry Street and get them a hero." The judge smiled.

"Will you tell the guard it's all right?"

"Surely. Captain," he called.

The officer in charge of the court approached the bench. Sandro returned to his counsel table, thinking that now, in addition to worrying about things like the law, the witnesses, and the direction of his questions, he was in charge of the mustards and jellies.

CHAPTER XXVI

"DO YOU REMEMBER what time Alvarado came into the store?" Sandro asked Annie Mae Cooper.

"Well, it was after my break, a few minutes after, which is one to one fifteen, my break. I figure it was about one twenty."

"Is there any question in your mind that Alvarado was the man who was in the store that day, Annie?"

"No. I seen him before, cause he changed another hundred-dollar bill here a few days before."

"And what day did he come in the second time?" Sandro continued.

"July the third, 1967."

"How do you know it was July third?"

"How come you askin' me all these questions? I tol' you all this already."

"I know, I just want to be sure I have it down right," Sandro said.

"Well, for one thing I was off the next day. It was July fourth. And when I was off, I seen his picture in the papers, and I say to my husband, 'That man was in my store yesterday.' And the next day, when I come here to work, I showed the newspaper to Phil and told him too."

"Are you sure about the time you saw Alvarado come in?" Sandro asked.

"Sure. I always take my break the same time cause there's another girl who has to take a break soon's I get back. She goes at one fifteen."

"That's fine," said Sandro.

"I don't mind helping you out, mister, but I don't want to go to no court. I mean, I just ain't goin'. I got other things to do."

"But Annie Mae, it's as easy as that. You'll be in and out in a couple of minutes," said Mike.

"I ain't goin', so don't start foolin' round. I don't want to go to no court."

"Let's not argue about it now," Sandro said. "Where's Phil?"

"He's round here somewhere." She went to find him.

"What the hell good is she to us if she won't come to court?" Mike asked.

"Let's talk to Gruberger first. Maybe he can get her to come to court. If not, we can always subpoena her if we have to."

"We could do that," Mike agreed.

"I'd rather not, though," said Sandro. "It's not good to bring in a reluctant witness. She could just be mean when she's up on the stand, and we'd be stuck with her."

Phil Gruberger walked toward Sandro and Mike. He shook hands.

"Phil, do you remember the day the hundred-dollar bill was changed?"

"There were two of them. Which one are you talking about?"

"The second one. Do you remember what day it was cashed on?"

"Sure. July third. The day before July fourth."

"You're sure of that?"

"Sure. I'm the one who brings the deposits to the bank, and I know the second one was July third. The only other deposit I made of a hundred-dollar bill was a few days before."

"Did you see the man who cashed the hundred-dollar bill on July third?" Sandro asked.

"No. I was downstairs. Annie Mae came down and asked me if I'd approve her cashing this bill she had in her hands. I looked at it, and it looked all right. So I told her it was okay. She told me it was the same guy who had cashed the first one."

"Did you see the fellow who cashed the *first* bill?"

"Yes. That time I was upstairs, and I saw the guy. It was your Alvarado."

"How do you remember now that it was Alvarado who came in here to cash the hundred-dollar bill the first time?"

"Well, when Annie Mae came to work the day after July fourth," said Gruberger, "on July fifth, she said, 'Remember that hundred-dollar bill that I cashed for some guy on July third? Well, look, here's his picture in the paper.' So I looked at the paper and saw this fellow Alvarado. I recognized him to be the fellow from several days before who had cashed the first hundred-dollar bill."

"Are you sure it was Alvarado who cashed the first bill?"

"Sure."

"Because of the rules of evidence, Phil, you wouldn't be able to tell the jury what Annie Mae told you when she came to work on July fifth . . ."

"That'd be hearsay, right?"

"That's right."

"Are you a law student or something?" Mike wondered.

"No, I went to law school for a year, but I didn't finish. I had to get a job and support my wife. And then a kid came along, so here we are." He shrugged without bitterness.

"I could use your help now, Phil," Sandro said in a confiding tone.

"How's that?"

"Annie Mae doesn't want to come to court. She tells me that she'll help out here, talk, tell me what happened, but she won't go to court to testify. Now you know that her story isn't worth a damn if she doesn't testify to it in court."

Gruberger nodded knowingly. "I'll talk to her when you go. When do you need us?"

"Today is Thursday. Tomorrow Hernandez's defense'll probably wind up. The way it looks now, I'll need you Monday."

"Let me talk to her."

"You won't even have to go to any trouble to get there. Mike can pick you up here and drop you off again. Before you know it, it'll all be over. And, of course, you'll both be paid for any time you lose from the job."

"That's not necessary. She won't lose any time. I'm in charge of the time cards. Okay, I'll talk to her. Anything else? I've got to get back to the floor."

"No. You'll be helping a great deal if you can straighten her out. I may serve her with a subpoena anyway, just to cover myself," said Sandro. "Maybe that'll make it easier for you too. You can explain all the trouble she'll get in if she doesn't obey the subpoena."

"You play it any way you want, and I'll do what I can on this end, okay, Counselor?" Phil smiled.

"Right." Sandro and Mike turned and left the store. They got back in the car.

"Aren't we going to serve her with a subpoena first?" asked Mike.

"No, I want to get one signed by the judge, so it's a court order, not just a lawyer's subpoena."

"Where to now?"

"Let's go see that superintendent for the buildings on Stanton Street. The ones behind which Ellis says Alvarado hid because there was a big fence blocking the rear yard."

Mike started the car and headed out into the traffic, toward the bridge.

"At least you can be sure of one thing," Mike said.

"What's that?"

"She sure isn't a friend of Alvarado's who's trying to tell a phony story to help him out. She doesn't even want to help him out."

"That's true. I guess we can take some consolation in that. Except that if we don't get her to court, Alvarado's going to have to take that consolation while he's doing time, maybe waiting for the electric chair."

"Yeah, that won't do a hell of a lot for him, will it?"

"Not much."

Sandro and Mike walked down the back stairs of the tenement, into the rubbish-strewn rear yard that they had come to know and hate so well. It didn't seem half so bad at night, in the dark, when you couldn't see most of the filth stagnating there.

"Where did his wife say he'd be?" Sandro asked.

"She said she thought he was in the boiler room of One sixty-one. I guess that's over this way."

PART 35

They walked toward the rear of 161. Out of the dark, suddenly, the bulky figure of a Negro stepped toward them.

"Roosevelt?" Sandro asked quickly.

"Yeah, who is it?" He stood facing them, the light over the door shining on him.

"My name is Luca. I'm an attorney. This is Mike Rivera. We're working on the case where the policeman was killed on the roof last July. Remember?"

"Yeah, I remember. The cops was runnin' all over my yards. Still comes around, one of them. But I don't know nothin' 'bout that case. I told that to the cop what came to see me couple days ago." Roosevelt Jackson spoke slowly, thickly.

"A cop came to see you a couple of days ago?" asked Sandro. "Do you know his name?"

"No, I don't pay no 'tention to his name. He's the same one use come aroun' here all the time. He don't come round much no more. He don't have no uniform."

"What does he look like, this cop? A tall guy, with red hair, thin on top, like he's going bald?" asked Mike.

"Somethin' like that," Jackson replied.

"He asked you about the fence in the back, didn't he?" Sandro said.

"That's right. All you fellows come round askin' the same things, don't you? Seem you save a lot of time only one of you come round and he tell the rest."

"I think you've got a good idea there, Roosevelt, but they don't talk too much to us, so we have to do it ourselves," Sandro replied.

"That don't make no sense, does it? Nope, no sense at all. I got to pull my barrels now. You want to talk to me, better talk fast now, cause I got to pull my barrels. I'm not rushin' you or nothin', but those barrels don't pull themself, you know?"

"Just tell me about the fence, Roosevelt."

"Nothin' to tell, cause there wasn't no fence. They ain't been no fence back there cuttin' across my yards for a long time. They cut behind my buildings, the long way, you know." He looked out toward the back. "Well, you can't see them now."

"We know what the yard looks like, Roosevelt."

"Well, then you know. The fence separates this here side of the block from that other block. But they ain't no fence that keeps me from walkin' from one to the other of my buildings on Stanton Street. Got a alley, all the way to Suffolk Street. Been that way a long time, too. Used to be a fence though," Roosevelt rambled on. Sandro wanted to listen. "Yep, used to be one up by Suffolk Street, but the kids tore that down, too. Maybe two, three years ago. Ain't been none there since then. Hey, I got to get my barrels pulled."

"One thing, Roosevelt: how long have you been the super here?" asked Sandro.

"Oh, 'bout, lemme see. Maybe five years, just about five years."

"Can you come to court, Roosevelt? I'll have Mike pick you up in the car, and he'll drive you to court and drive you right back?"

"I got to take care of my buildin's. Who's going to do that if I go to court? You goin' to come here and take the buildin's when I'm in court?"

"We'll do it quickly, so you won't be gone, no more than, say, one hour. How's that? And of course, I'll compensate you. I'll pay you for any time you lose from the job. Double time."

"That's okay, then." He smiled now. "Now you talkin'. Where is this court, anyways."

"Mike'll pick you up Monday morning. About ten o'clock."

"No, better make it later, 'leven. I got to pull the barrels early. I'll be here 'leven."

"On Monday morning, at eleven."

"Right, Monday," Jackson repeated. "At 'leven."

CHAPTER XXVII

Friday April 19th, 1968

SIAKOS BEGAN THE DAY by recalling Mrs. Hernandez. As she walked to the stand, Sandro glanced at Hernandez, whose eyes longed after her. She was twice the woman Hernandez deserved, Sandro thought. She was even twice the man he was.

She testified through the interpreter that after Hernandez had dropped her off at her place of employment, the morning of July 3rd, he drove away. He returned a little after noon. They walked to the bank, where Mrs. Hernandez cashed her paycheck. She said she was paid on July rd because of the holiday, the fiesta, the next day. They went to have lunch, walking back to her building at about five minutes before 1. They met German Ortega in front of the building, and they had all laughed because Mrs. Hernandez had introduced her husband to Ortega at the very spot when they were going out to lunch. At 1 P.M., Mrs. Hernandez testified, she gave Hernandez a dollar to buy gas, and returned to work.

On the way home that night, she testified, there were crowds milling about Stanton Street, and many policemen were near her car. Upon telling the police who she was, she was taken to the station house. She testified that no one else had been with Hernandez in the car or anyplace else when she was with him that morning and early afternoon. Siakos turned the witness over to Ellis.

Responding to Ellis's questions, Mrs. Hernandez testified that she had waited for Hernandez to pick her up after work that day, but he had never arrived. She went home by herself on the subway. When she reached Stanton Street, and had identified herself, the police searched her purse, and took her to the precinct house. There, detectives asked her where she had been, where she worked.

"He's getting ready to impeach her credibility with this statement," Sandro said, handing Sam a photostat of a police DD5. According to the report, Mrs. Hernandez had told a detective on July 3rd that she had left Hernandez in their apartment that morning.

"If the cops can perjure themselves on the stand, what's to stop them from writing out a phony DD5?" said Sam. "But she handles herself all right. Let's wait and see."

Ellis asked Mrs. Hernandez if she had said to any policeman that she had left Hernandez at the apartment when she went to work on July 3rd. Certainly not, she replied firmly. He asked her, as he read from the DD5, whether she actually lived at 163 Stanton Street. She said she did. He asked whether it was true she and Hernandez had a child, and if he was in a day-care center while she worked. All that he read from the DD5 was the truth, Mrs. Hernandez said, except for her having left Hernandez in the apartment that morning.

"All they asked me was where was I, where was I," she said through the interpreter. "That is all. They wanted to know where had I been that day, and I kept saying I was working, I was working, I was working. They didn't ask about when I went to work."

Ellis had no further questions. Sam rose and asked Mrs. Hernandez if she had been in that station house all night, except when the police took her home briefly to search her apartment.

"Yes," she replied. She said she had even fainted from fatigue on the station house steps as she left there the morning of July 4th. Sam had no further questions.

Siakos stood. "Ramon Hernandez," he called. Hernandez, tall, lean, dark, rose and walked to the stand. The jury watched him intently.

PART 35

He looked out at Siakos as a player looks at his coach. He was totally uneasy.

Through the interpreter, Hernandez testified that he did not see Luis Alvarado at all on July 3rd, 1967; that he did not plan a burglary with Alvarado; that he was never in or on the building where the policeman was killed. He said that he had, in fact, broken into an apartment on 119th Street in El Barrio at approximately 11 A.M. that day. He testified that he pulled the job alone. Once again, he repeated that he met his wife for lunch, got a dollar for gasoline, left her at about 1 P.M., and drove to the pawnshops.

Siakos had Hernandez identify the suits and the radio he had pawned. He also identified the signature cards from the pawnshops. He said he had had identification in a wallet which belonged to one Antonio Cruz, who had lent him the wallet in return for a bag of heroin. Hernandez said that after leaving Sid Goodman's at about 2:15, he had gone to 387 Essex Street to buy heroin from a man called Angel Belmonte. He then drove to his house on Stanton Street, arriving about 2:35 or 2:40.

The street was filled with policemen, and there was an ambulance. He double-parked and ran up to his apartment. As soon as he got inside, he prepared a hypodermic and injected himself. Calmer, he began to fix a sandwich. In a few minutes, the police arrived. He remembered the stolen goods in the trunk, and wanted to allay their suspicions, never realizing they were looking, not for a double-parking violator but for a murderer. He told them that someone else had had the car all day. One of the officers grabbed him by the neck, he testified, pulled him close, shouted that Hernandez's jacket was wet, that he was lying about not being out. The cops dragged him out the door and down the stairs.

Hernandez denied having anything to do with the burglary or murder at 153 Stanton Street. He lifted his hand to God and swore he did not participate in the crime. Siakos had no further questions.

Sam Bemer rose. He asked if Hernandez had ever told the police that he had, in fact, participated in the crime. Hernandez replied he had told them many things, but these things were not true. He testified that he told them what he had told them because he was afraid, because he was being beaten. Hernandez said that the only reason he gave the name of Luis Alvarado to the police was that they were beating him, insisting that another man was involved with him in the shooting, and that this other man was a Negro. Hernandez testified that the only man dark enough that he could think of was Alvarado. He said that they refused to believe that he shot the cop himself, insisting it was a tough Negro who shot the cop. Sam had no further questions. Ellis rose to cross-examine.

A court officer whispered to Siakos that Artie Horowitz, proprietor of Excelsior Pawn Brokers, was in court. Siakos asked the judge if it would be possible before Ellis began the cross-examination of Hernandez, to have Horowitz take the stand. The judge permitted the interruption.

Horowitz, whose slick hair and uncooperative attitude Sandro remembered very well, said that there had been a total of eighty-four transactions on July 3rd. The pledges of Antonio Cruz were numbers 57 and 58. Horowitz said that Antonio Cruz could *not* have pledged the suits in the morning. There was no question whatever that the transaction took place in the afternoon. He could not say at exactly what time. Siakos had no further questions.

On cross-examination, Horowitz said that he himself had taken these pledges, but that he could not recognize the man who pledged the articles. He only knew that he took the transaction because the pledge tickets were in his handwriting. He remembered Detective Mullaly's coming into the shop months before the trial and asking questions. Ellis asked him if his memory was better when Detective Mullaly was in the shop or now when he was on the stand. He said his memory was exactly the same. Ellis asked him if he remembered telling Detective Mullaly that the pledges could have been transacted any time between 11 A.M. and 3 P.M. Horowitz replied that he might have said that, the afternoon certainly being after 11 A.M. Ellis asked no further questions.

"Let's recess for lunch now," said the judge.

Sandro had arranged to share the lunch-pail duties with Siakos. Sandro took the first day. He brought four hot dogs and two apple turnovers for the defendants. They wolfed it all down just before the afternoon session began.

PART 35

In the afternoon, Hernandez resumed the witness chair. Ellis began his cross-examination. Hernandez repeated the story about the burglary on 119th Street. He said he had gained access to the apartment by swinging from a fire escape and through a partly open window. He said he never mentioned the uptown burglary to the detectives questioning him at the police station because they didn't want to know that. They just kept beating him, hounding him to confess to the murder. He said that he had burglarized the apartment on 119th Street because he was desperate for money for heroin. He said that after the pawnshops, he had bought two bags of heroin from Angel Belmonte. Ellis asked Hernandez to describe Belmonte.

Sam leaned over to Sandro. "You watch the blond guy that's been spotting for Ellis. As soon as Ellis gets all the information about this guy Belmonte, the spotter is going to take off, and the police'll have Belmonte in this court as sure as we're sitting here."

Sandro turned slowly and looked out at the spectators. Sure enough, after Ellis had exhausted Hernandez's memory of Belmonte, the spotter stood and walked out.

Hernandez testified that Mullaly and several other policemen came into his apartment on the afternoon of July 3rd and wanted to search it. He was then wearing his jacket and hat. He said he was not breathing hard and was not sweating profusely, even though he had just taken a shot of heroin.

"He full of chit, man," said Alvarado, leaning over to Sandro and Sam. "When he take that shot, he sweat for sure."

"Well, he's trying to be cute with Ellis," said Sam. "Watch Ellis tear his head off. When you get on the stand, just answer the questions you're asked, nothing more, nothing less. Don't try to be smarter than Ellis."

"I'll be okay," Alvarado assured them.

Hernandez testified that after being beaten horribly, he had admitted certain things concerning the murder to the police. But these admissions, he insisted, were based on information that the police supplied.

Ellis dug into his file and removed some typewritten papers. He handed a copy of the typed pages to Siakos. It was the typed question-

and-answer statement that Assistant D.A. Brennan obtained from Hernandez the morning of July 4th.

"So this is the way he's going to get the Q. and A. in," said Sam. "I knew he couldn't risk not using it."

Siakos asked for a few moments to read the document. The court granted a short recess.

Upon resumption, Ellis questioned Hernandez about the assistant D.A.'s examination of him in the station house on July 4th. He was trying to establish that Hernandez's testimony did not agree with his statement to Brennan. Hernandez said he didn't remember either the questions or the answers because they were beaten into him. The judge struck out his answer as not responsive.

In the statement Hernandez had allegedly told Brennan that he had met Alvarado at the Hotel Ascot the morning of July 3rd. Hernandez now testified that he had said that to the D.A. but that he had lied.

Siakos rose. "Your Honor, I object to having the statement read since it is not in evidence. Further, I would like to request that the voir dire be reopened to question the validity of this statement because Mr. Ellis is attempting to use it as an additional confession. The beating that the defendant Hernandez said he received is the continuing cause of this statement. I object further that there is no proof of the accuracy of the statement, the method of its being taken, or the ability of the stenographer or interpreter who recorded it."

"This is not being used as a confession," said Judge Porta. "It is not being used for the truth contained therein, but merely to impeach the witness's credibility by a prior inconsistent statement. Overruled, Mr. Siakos, except that I direct Mr. Ellis to produce the D.A. who took this statement, the stenographer, and interpreter at the proper time."

"This is the proper time, Your Honor," Siakos persisted. "If it's not done now and the statement is later found to be inadmissible, the damage would have already been done, and it would be grounds for a mistrial."

"Overruled. Continue, Mr. Ellis."

"Hernandez, do you remember the following questions asked of you on the morning of July fourth, 1967, and these answers? Question: 'Now, my name is William E. Brennan. I am an assistant district

PART 35

attorney in Manhattan. Do you understand? Answer: Yes. Question: Now, in this room are Detectives Tracy and Mullaly, Mr. La Fontana, an interpreter, and Mr. Connors, a stenotypist. Do you understand that so far?'"

Ellis read on. Brennan had explained the defendant's rights to him. Brennan then asked Hernandez for his name and address and about his background. He asked questions about the hotel on the morning of July 3rd, about meeting Alvarado, about talking with Alvarado, about stealing, about the size of his habit. The answers were the same as those Mullaly had testified to.

"Do you remember being asked those questions, Hernandez, and giving those answers?"

"Some of them," the interpreter said.

"Will Mr. Siakos concede that I'm reading the statement accurately?" Ellis asked.

"Without conceding anything as to the truth of this alleged statement, Mr. Ellis is reading what is here correctly."

"Perhaps further questions will refresh your recollection, Hernandez: Question: How long were you riding around? Was it one hour, two hours, or three hours? Answer: Minutes. Question: How long were you talking to him in the hotel? Answer: Until about ten o'clock. Question: Do you know what time it was when the shooting took place? Answer: No. Question: Was it in the morning or the afternoon? Answer: I believe it was in the afternoon. Question: If you left the hotel around ten o'clock, weren't you driving around for a few hours before you came to Stanton Street? Answer: Yes, sir.'

"Now, do you remember those questions and your answers?" Ellis asked.

"Some."

"This Hernandez is so dumb," Sandro said, "he didn't even remember what the cops beat into him. He's fouling up the confession for them."

"That's a break for us. It makes the confession look ridiculous if the man who was there doesn't know what happened."

"And do you now deny that these things you said are true?"

"I was beaten. I was afraid."

"Did you say that to the D.A.? Did you tell him that?"

"I was going to save it for my lawyer."

Ellis stared at Hernandez. "Perhaps these questions will refresh your memory: 'Question: Where did you go when you went into the building? Answer: Went to break the door. Question: What floor did you go to? Answer: Second floor.'"

"It was the fifth floor," Sandro whispered to Sam.

"The jury knows it, too. Look at number five." Sandro saw Youngerman, the telephone repairman, frowning with confusion. "This is going to help us."

Ellis went on. "'Question: How did you open the door? Answer: I open with a crowbar. Question: Who had the crowbar? Answer: Luis. Question: Well, then, did you open the door with a crowbar? Answer: Luis opened the door. Question: So you didn't use the jimmy? Answer: No. Detective Tracy: Did you use your shoulder? Question: Did you push the door open? Answer: No, sir. Question: Luis used the jimmy? Answer: Yes, sir.'"

"Did you say those things to the D.A., Hernandez?"

"Some of them."

"But now, after you've had almost a year to think about it, you say these things aren't true?"

"They were a lie then, too."

"Did you tell that to the D.A.?"

"No."

"Perhaps these questions will help your memory. 'Question: Well, did you go into the apartment to take the radio out? Answer: No, he brought me the radio. Question: What color was the radio? Answer: Black. Question: You sure it wasn't red? Answer: No, sir. (At this point, Detective Johnson left the room and brought back a red radio.)

"'Question: Is this the radio? Answer: Yes. (Mr. Brennan then said, Let the record indicate this is a red radio.) Question: Was it red? Answer: Yes, that's the radio. Question: So when you said black, were you mistaken? Answer: Yes, I was mistaken.'"

"Jesus Christ," said Sam, "this is beautiful."

"Why the hell is Ellis using this stuff? It can't be helping."

"Just think what we could do on summation if he didn't use it.

PART 35

We'd be able to say that they never confessed to the D.A., that they denied the crime, and Ellis was afraid to reveal it. He's stuck, and it's beautiful."

Ellis repeated Brennan's questions. They were about the TV set and the roof and the policeman coming onto the roof. Hernandez's answers still followed Mullaly's version.

"'Question: Is that true, Luis grabbed the cop from behind? Answer: Yes. Question: Did Luis knock the cop down? Answer: He shot him.'"

"He's not reading the whole statement," Sandro whispered quickly. "He's skipping whole sections."

"They must hurt him," Sam replied. "We'll read them for him."

"Siakos should read the rest of this to the jury."

Sam nodded and leaned over to whisper to Siakos. Siakos nodded.

Ellis finished reading. He pointed out that at no time had Hernandez made a complaint, not even in reply to the D.A.'s direct questions about being ill-treated.

"Your Honor," said Ellis, "that completes what I intend to read from this statement. Now with Your Honor's permission, I'd like to bring someone into the court for Hernandez to identify."

"You may, sir."

"Angel Belmonte," called Ellis. A court officer went through the side door to the witness room. He returned with a dark-haired man in a white shirt, tieless.

"Did I tell you or not?" asked Sam.

"Is this Angel Belmonte who you bought drugs from on the afternoon of July third?" Ellis asked Hernandez.

Hernandez nodded. The interpreter said it was.

"Twenty-five dollars says Belmonte denies it when Ellis puts him on the stand," said Sam. "Belmonte probably has charges against him or he will next week, and they'll give him a break for this testimony."

"I have no further questions," said Ellis.

"We'll take our luncheon recess now." The judge retired from the bench.

After lunch, Siakos rose. Hernandez testified that Detective Johnson had taken him to the washroom before he saw the D.A., and Johnson told him that if he didn't say the right things to the D.A., they'd take him back to the third floor and break his balls. He said that he believed they would. Siakos took the question-and-answer statement.

"Mr. Hernandez, do you recall these questions and answers?"

"Objection, Your Honor. That document is not in evidence. It can only be used as a prior inconsistent statement, and defense counsel may not impeach his own witness."

"Quite true. Sustained."

Siakos's disappointment was obvious. He asked Hernandez if the story he had told the D.A. were true and, if not, why he had told such a story. Hernandez said that he had made up much of the story because he couldn't remember the things the police had said to him. He had thought that if he told the D.A. something, anything, the police wouldn't hit him.

"Mr. Hernandez," Siakos asked dramatically, "did you have anything to do with the crime which occurred July third, 1967—the murder, that is?"

"I swear to God, no."

"I have no further questions," said Siakos.

"No questions," said Ellis.

"No questions," said Sam.

"Call your next witness," the judge intoned.

"Antonio Quiñones," Siakos said. A court officer stood to go out to the corridor. "He's sitting on the windowsill by the elevator," Siakos said.

Shortly, a tall, thin man entered the courtroom. He was sworn and sat in the witness chair.

"Mr. Quiñones," said Siakos. "Was your apartment burglarized sometime last year?"

"Yes, on July third."

"What time did you leave your apartment that day?"

"About eight thirty in the morning."

"Was anyone then in your apartment?"

"No, it was empty."

"What time was it that you came home that day?"

"Five thirty."

"And you found your apartment had been burglarized?"

PART 35

"Yes."

"Do you recognize these things, Mr. Quiñones?" Siakos showed him the portable radio and the suits.

"These are my things."

"Will you put on one of the jackets, please?"

He did. It fitted him.

"May we have for the record that the black suit fits the witness perfectly?"

"It fits him," said Judge Porta. "That's enough."

"I have no further questions," said Siakos.

None of the other attorneys had questions.

"At this time, Your Honor, the defendant Hernandez rests."

The judge nodded. "Very well. We'll adjourn until Monday at ten fifteen. Be prompt, and do not discuss this case with anyone," the judge admonished. The jury filed out.

CHAPTER XXVIII

"NO, NO, I TOL' YOU. I am not testifyin' in no court," Annie Mae Cooper insisted angrily. "I tol' you the other day, an' I'm tellin' you again."

"Don't get excited, Annie Mae," said Sandro. "I only want you to help a man accused of a crime he couldn't have committed. You know that; you saw him here. He was supposed to have killed a cop over in Manhattan a couple of minutes after he was here with you. Now, how would your conscience feel if you let a man like that get convicted without even trying to help him? He could go to the electric chair."

"That's not my fault. Besides, that's your job, not mine. I already tol' you he was here. You go to court and tell them what I said."

"That's not the way it can be done, Annie. You have to go to court."

"I don't have to nothin'."

Sandro reached into his inside jacket pocket and took out the buff-colored subpoena that Judge Porta had signed, ordering Annie Mae Cooper to appear in court on Monday, April 22nd, 1968.

"Annie, I didn't want to have to do this, but I've got to serve you with a subpoena," Sandro said. He took a dollar bill from his pocket. "Here. Here's a subpoena and a dollar. That's the mileage fee that I have to give you to travel to court."

PART 35

"I don't want none of that. I tol' you I don' want that," she insisted. She took the paper and the bill out of Sandro's hand and threw them both on the floor. She turned and stormed toward the back of the store.

"What the hell are we going to do with her?" Mike asked.

"Who knows? If she doesn't cooperate, we're stuck. I won't put her on the stand if she's hostile. I thought the subpoena would loosen her up a bit. Do you see Phil around?"

"Yeah, there he is," said Mike. Gruberger was walking toward them.

"What the hell did you do to Annie? She's all upset, crying. What happened?"

"I told you I was going to serve her with a subpoena. Now it's up to you to see if you can get her to court. Explain to her that she'll get herself in trouble if she doesn't honor the subpoena. Try and calm her down."

"Okay, leave it with me," Gruberger assured Sandro. "I'll see if I can do something with her. Don't worry about it. She'll be there. I can't lose my first big witness, can I?"

"You want me to talk to her again?" Sandro asked.

"I don't think you'd better. She'll listen to me. Where do we have to go?"

"I'll have Mike pick you up about eleven Monday morning. Right in front of the store."

"That's fine."

Sandro and Mike got back into the car. "Where to now?" Mike asked.

"Drive down to Spring Street, between Mulberry and Mott," Sandro replied.

"What are we going to do down there?"

"I got a call today from a fellow who wants to see me."

Mike parked the car directly in front of the Two Steps Down Inn.

"Come on in," said Sandro.

"Who do you know hangs around in an old beat-up place like this?" Mike asked.

"Just an old fellow I know."

They entered. One of the men at the front table saw Sandro and recognized him. He whispered something to the other men. Their interest was piqued, however, by the stranger who walked in behind Sandro. Sandro turned to Mike and said, "Come on," so that they would know Mike was with him. They watched Mike carefully, their wariness only somewhat allayed by Sandro's presence.

Sandro walked toward Sal who was sitting in the back by himself, chomping his cigar, reading a racing form.

"Hiya, kid," said Sal. He looked to Mike.

"Sal, this is Mike Rivera. He's my number-one man on this murder case."

Sal put out his hand and shook Mike's, nodding. "Sit down, sit down. Have a drink. Joey," Sal called. "Bring something to the counselor and his friend." Sal had not taken notice of Mike's name.

"No, thanks," said Mike.

"Come on, have a drink."

"I'll have a Scotch on the rocks," Sandro said.

"I'll take the same," said Mike. He looked at Sal, then the waiter. His eyes scanned as much of the room as he could see without turning his head.

"The reason I had Tony call you, Sandro," said Sal, "I talked to Banjoes. Remember I thought that detective you told me about arrested Banjoes a couple a years ago? Well, I talked to Banjoes, and it was true. What's his name?"

"Mullaly."

Mike sat up straight.

"Right. That's the guy that arrested Banjoes about three years ago. It was a meatball case, all taken care of, one, two, three."

Sandro nodded.

"But that's not the reason I want to talk to you." Sal looked at Mike, then back to Sandro.

"Mike's all right, Sal," Sandro assured him. "We were just out investigating. That's why I brought him along. I thought you might have some news for me."

"Banjoes tells me that he's seen this guy, this detective Mullaly around that East Side neighborhood lately, which ain't no surprise since that's his precinct. But Banjoes tells me that one night, must be about three in the morning, right, and Banjoes's just cruising around—

PART 35

he had someone to meet—he sees this guy Mullaly comin' out of a gin mill with some Puerto Rican dish."

"You mean a woman?" Mike asked.

Sal looked at Mike, hesitated, then turned to Sandro.

"Yeah, he said he saw Mullaly with some tall, real good-lookin' spic. No offense," Sal said, looking to Mike. "A Puerto Rican."

Sandro looked to Mike, their eyes exchanging a question.

"I wonder if that might be who I think it is," said Sandro.

"If her initials are Mrs. Hernandez, it's the same one I'm thinking of," said Mike.

"I don't know who it is," said Sal. "I just thought you'd be interested."

Two men entered the restaurant.

"I'll be right with you," Sal called to them. "You want another drink, something?"

"No, we've got some more investigating to do tonight," Sandro pretended, realizing Sal was busy. "We're going to run, Sal. Thanks for the drink. And thanks for the information."

"Are you kiddin'? What are you thankin' me for? Come on, get outa here." Smiling, Sal shook hands with Sandro. "You're with a good man there," he said to Mike. "Pay attention, and he'll learn you to be a lawyer." He winked at Sandro.

"Thanks, Sal," Sandro said as they left.

"Good night, Counselor," said the waiter, as Sandro handed him a folded dollar bill.

Mike was unlocking the car, watching Sandro move around to the passenger's side.

"Where the hell do you know those people from?" Mike asked. "Sal, Banjoes, Tony. Where the hell did you get in with that group?"

"What group are you talking about?"

"You know exactly what I'm talking about."

"No, I don't. Sal was a boyhood friend of my family, and he knows a lot of people on the East Side. I asked him to see if he could get any information that might help us. He called and said he had some. That's about the long and the short of it." Sandro gave it a sound of finality. "What do you think about your buddy Mullaly, running around town with a tall, good-looking, Puerto Rican woman?"

"Yeah. I can count all the tall, good-looking, Puerto Rican women I know on one finger."

"Me too," said Sandro. "That must be how that story started. Mullaly took her home from the station house that night, and he's probably been banging her. And by the time the story got back to Hernandez in the Tombs, it was a gang-bang."

"Yeah, but what about Mrs. Hernandez? She denied it."

"She denied the gang-bang," Sandro replied. "We didn't ask about Detective Mullaly alone."

"Why don't we ask her—like right now?" Mike suggested.

"No, I've got to get ready for our witnesses Monday morning. I want to read through the file tonight, at home, alone, with a cigar, a drink, quiet."

"Hey, don't give me a big story, will you. You got some tall broad of your own stashed in your apartment. That's why you want to get home."

"Well, somebody's got to cook for me. I don't have a lovely wife like you do."

"Don't rub it in, you bastard."

Sandro laughed as Mike headed the car north to drop him off.

CHAPTER XXIX

Monday, April 22nd, 1968

THE NEXT MORNING, after the jury had been polled and the judge took his place at the top of the bench, Sandro rose to begin Alvarado's defense.

"Your Honor, in accordance with my understanding of Your Honor's previous suggestion, last night I gave to the district attorney a list of police personnel who made DD5 reports in this case whom I wish to call as witnesses, witnesses that the district attorney has failed to produce."

"Your Honor, I object vehemently to such a remark in front of the jury. Mr. Luca knows better than that. I have no obligation to produce any particular witnesses. If Mr. Luca wants to put these men on as witnesses, he's free to do so. I've even brought the men he's requested to court for him this morning. They're in the witness room."

"Very well, proceed."

"I call Detective Frank Ryan," said Sandro. He turned to watch the door to the witness room. Detective Ryan emerged, looked around the courtroom as he walked to the witness chair. He was tall, with a crew cut.

In response to Sandro's question, Detective Ryan testified that he was a member of the police laboratory. He said that he had responded to a call to the scene of the shooting in the late afternoon of July 3rd, 1967, and had been part of the team that searched for fingerprints in the Soto apartment, on Lauria's revolver, on the stolen articles, and in the double-parked car.

In addition to uncovering and developing fingerprints, Ryan testified, he and the other lab men investigated and processed all physical evidence at the scene of the crime. The Bureau of Criminal Identification evaluated and attempted to compare the fingerprints with prints on file. Ryan testified that he had also investigated a shoeprint that had been found on the stairs leading to the roof. Sandro showed Ryan a copy of a laboratory report. Ryan identified it as his own. Sandro introduced it into evidence without objection.

"Now, Detective Ryan, as a result of your investigation, did you not state in your report that the entry to Apartment number five-B at One fifty-three Stanton Street had been effected by a force *other* than a jimmy?"

Ryan read his report. "That is exactly what it says, sir. That's right. May I explain that?"

Sandro wasn't about to loosen his grip.

"No. Mr. Ellis can help you explain anything on your report later. I just want to know whether you stated in this official lab report, filed July third, 1967, that the force which opened the door was *other than a jimmy*?"

"Yes, sir. Yes, sir. Probably a kick-in." Ryan looked up and glanced at Ellis. Ellis, his face blank, was looking straight ahead.

"And when you say in this official report, force other than a jimmy, does that indicate that the force used to open the door *was not* a jimmy?"

"No, sir, it does not."

"I see. But your report, filed July third, 1967, does say force *other* than a jimmy?"

"May I explain it?"

"I would like an answer to my question first," said Sandro.

Ellis rose. "Your Honor, I submit the witness should be allowed to explain it."

PART 35

"No, it's a question which lends itself to a simple answer. I think that any clarification can be brought out and be the subject of your examination of the witness, if you wish." The judge nodded to the witness to answer.

"As I see it here, sir, yes."

"And this report was one of the laboratory's official written reports to be made part of the file in this case?"

"Yes, sir, that is correct."

Sandro studied the report, nodding, allowing the gaping wound in Ellis's case to bleed by itself.

"And, sir," Sandro continued. "Did you dust the revolver, with which the officer was shot, for fingerprints?"

"Yes, sir."

"And were there any fingerprints found there?" Sandro knew he was on safe ground.

"No, sir, only some ridges but not enough to identify."

"When you say ridges, you mean the papillary ridges that every person in the world has on his fingers and palms."

"And feet. Yes, sir," Ryan answered.

"And the ridges on the gun could have been left, as far as you know, by anyone in the world, even Mr. Ellis or the judge?"

"I object," said Ellis quickly, annoyed.

"All right, Detective, leave Mr. Ellis out of this."

The jury laughed.

"Yes, sir," Ryan answered. "They could not be identified."

Ryan's report also contained the fingerprint findings of the Bureau of Criminal Investigation. It identified from the Soto apartment the prints of Robert Soto, his wife, Alma, his mother-in-law, and an aunt.

"And were there *any* prints found *anywhere* in that apartment that belonged to the defendant Luis Alvarado or the defendant Ramon Hernandez?"

"No, sir. I have no report from the BCI stating such." Ellis squirmed quietly as Sandro questioned Ryan further.

"Were *any* fingerprints found in Hernandez's automobile double-parked in the street that day?"

"Yes, sir, there were."

"To whom did they belong?"

Ryan read the report to himself. He looked up. "To Ramon Hernandez. Three prints—one on the rear-view mirror, one on the steering wheel, one on the dashboard. All belonged to Hernandez."

"Is there *anything, anywhere* in your report which indicated that there were *any* prints *whatever* found in that automobile which are identifiable with and connected to the defendant Luis Alvarado?"

"No, sir, there is not."

"I have no further questions." Sam winked as Sandro returned to the counsel table.

Siakos rose. "And, Officer, you didn't find any fingerprints, except in his own car, which belonged to Hernandez, did you?"

"No, sir."

"No further questions, thank you."

Ellis rose. He asked Ryan what he had wanted to explain concerning his findings about the break-in and his report. Ryan testified that when he had said that the door had been opened by something other than a jimmy in his report, he did not mean that no jimmy had been used. From marks on the door, he had concluded that the first intrusion had been made by a jimmy. But ultimately, the door had been kicked in.

Ellis had no further questions.

Sandro rose. "Detective Ryan, you didn't include any mention of any jimmy marks in your report, did you?"

"No."

"And these jimmy marks you now recall clearly from memory?"

"Not clearly, but I do remember them."

"And these jimmy marks, what were they? What did they look like?"

"Marks, scratches around the locks."

"Could they have been made by a key as it's inserted in the door? In other words, usual wear and tear?"

"Perhaps. It's possible, but I don't think so."

"Do you know when these marks were made on that door? Were they fresh marks at the time that you saw them?"

"I couldn't say exactly."

PART 35

"In other words, these jimmy marks that were there may have been there before July third, 1967?"

"Perhaps so, Counselor."

"And when you made your report, indicating that the door was opened by means other than a jimmy, probably a kick-in, it was because you didn't feel that a jimmy was significant in this break-in?"

Ryan was reluctant now. "Basically."

"And one of the reasons for that is that those marks that you say were there might have been there an hour, a day, or a week?"

"I can't say exactly how long they were there."

"No further questions."

"Score that round for us in a big way," said Sam.

"Should we call another officer from the police lab?" asked Sandro. "I asked Ellis to bring him, but I think we have enough from the lab men already."

"Don't bother to call him," said Sam. "We'll save some time."

Sandro rose and expressed his intention to save time and not to clutter the record with cumulative police-laboratory testimony. He told the judge he would not call the other detective from the police lab. Ellis was indignant. He insisted. Sandro acceded.

"Detective Joseph Sullivan," Sandro said to the court officer, who went out to the witness room. "Ellis must be going nuts to insist on this," he whispered to Sam.

"Listen, if he wants you to buttress your case and underscore his own weakness, let him," said Sam.

Sullivan was a fingerprint-comparison man at the Bureau of Criminal Investigation. Sandro showed him a copy of a laboratory report filed July 3rd, 1967. Sullivan identified it as his own, and it was received in evidence. Ellis sat very still.

Sullivan testified that, after careful comparison, all the identifiable prints found in the Soto apartment belonged to Soto or some member of his family. No prints of any value had been found on the articles taken in the burglary. Nor were there prints of any value on the revolver. The only prints found in Hernandez's car belonged to Hernandez and his wife. There were no prints of Alvarado anywhere.

Sandro had no further questions.

"If that's what Ellis wants, give it to him," Sam gloated.

Siakos had no questions.

Ellis rose to cross-examine. He asked Sullivan what it meant that there were no fingerprints found on the stolen articles in the apartment.

"Objection, Your Honor," Sam rose. "That question is totally irrelevant and calls for speculation and conjecture."

"Overruled."

Sullivan testified that many times prints are found at the scene of a crime that cannot be processed because they are too fragmentary, smudged, or unclear. Ellis asked if the fact that there were no prints eliminated the possibility that Alvarado was in the Soto apartment or at the scene of the crime. Sullivan said it did not. Ellis sat.

Sandro rose immediately, standing in place.

"Officer, does the mere failure of your finding his fingerprints in the car, or fingerprints in other places, or on the property connected with this crime eliminate the possibility that David Ellis could have been in that apartment or in that car?"

Ellis jumped up to object, red and angry. The judge overruled. The jury laughed.

"No, sir, it doesn't eliminate it. It doesn't do anything."

Sandro had no further questions. Ellis was fuming. Sam smiled just at the corner of his mouth, so the jury couldn't see.

Sandro called for Detective Anthony Panetta next. Panetta was the officer who had interviewed Carmen Salerno on July 3rd, 1967, at 153 Stanton Street. Sandro showed Panetta a copy of a DD5. The detective acknowledged it as his own, and it was received in evidence.

Panetta said that Mrs. Salerno had given him certain information concerning the prowler she had seen on the fire escape before the shooting. After reading the DD5, Panetta testified that she had described the prowler as a male Negro.

"Did she say the man was tall?"

"It says so here. She must have."

"And did she describe the Negro as real dark."

"I don't think she did."

"Will you look at the report again."

PART 35

He read and looked up. "Yes, she did."

"What did she say he was wearing?"

"His clothes were a shabby, yellow, waist-length jacket, black pants."

"Did she describe his hair?"

Panetta read. "She said it was kinky and close-cropped."

"And did she also say to you that she did not see the man's face?"

"That is correct. That's what she said."

"Thank you very much, Officer." Sandro had no further questions. Siakos had no questions.

Ellis sat still as a statue. "I have no questions."

Sandro called Randolph Torrance to the stand. Torrance was with the Department of Correction, and been chosen to come over with the financial record books of the Tombs. He testified that whenever a prisoner was brought in, all the property and money on his person was taken into custody. Everything but money was placed in envelopes bearing the prisoner's number. The money was put into an account against which the prisoner could charge items from the commissary at the Tombs.

"If the defendant Alvarado had any money with him when he first arrived in the Tombs, would that fact be recorded in the record book you brought with you?"

"Yes, sir. It has to be."

"Is there any entry there stating that the defendant Alvarado had $141 with him when he arrived?"

Torrance studied the book. "No, sir."

"Is there an entry for *any* money Alvarado had with him when he arrived? Even $2?"

"No, sir."

"I have no further questions." Sandro walked back to the counsel table.

"Now they're even beating him out of the two bucks in change Mullaly said he had," Sam whispered.

"I'll bet you thought you couldn't get screwed for two bucks in New York anymore," Sandro whispered back.

Siakos asked Torrance about any money Hernandez had with him when he first arrived. Torrance said that Hernandez, too, had had nothing with him.

Ellis had no questions.

"We'll take our luncheon recess now. Do not discuss this case," said Judge Porta.

As they walked out of court, Sandro made his way to the north elevator bank where Mike was sitting with the alibi witnesses on the windowsills. They all smiled and nodded, but they were getting weary.

"Say, this is really charming," said Mike, looking around the hallway. "Who decorated your witness room for you?"

"Otis Brothers," Sandro smiled. "Let's go to lunch. We'll take all the witnesses with us." They took the elevator down and went to Happy's. Sam and Sandro were involved in a discussion of the coming defense strategy during lunch. Since Francisco Moreno and Pablo Torres didn't speak English, they didn't feel left out. Mike chatted with Annie Mae Cooper and Phil Gruberger. Only once did Sandro turn his attention from Sam, when he heard Pablo Torres talking about *camarones*. He knew from reading menus that *camarones* is the word for *shrimp*, but his recent education in Delancey gave it a more sinister meaning.

"Did he say the cops were bothering him?" Sandro asked Mike.

"No, he said his lunch was delicious," Mike laughed. Torres, unaware, continued eating his shrimp salad. Sandro laughed and turned back to Sam.

"Call your next witness," the judge said.

"Annie Mae Cooper," said Sandro. One of the uniformed officers walked out to the public corridor. Annie Mae Cooper entered the courtroom and walked to the witness chair.

She testified that she worked at the Associated Five & Ten on Broadway and Roebling Street in Brooklyn, and was working there on July 3rd, 1967. She said she recalled an incident with a hundred-dollar bill that took place on that day, involving the man sitting at the counsel table. She pointed to Alvarado. Sandro asked her to step off the witness stand and walk over to him. She walked directly to Alvarado and pointed at him. She resumed the stand.

"Is there any question in your mind that that's the man who was in your store with a hundred-dollar bill on July third, 1967?"

"That's him, all right."

She testified that when Alvarado asked her to change the bill, she had said: 'Gee, another hundred-dollar bill. I haven't seen one in a long time. Are you making these things?' She said she had told Alvarado to wait while she went to the assistant manager to okay her changing it. She had seen Alvarado only once in her life before then, and that was two or three days earlier. On that occasion also, Alvarado had come into the store to change a hundred-dollar bill.

She had seen Alvarado between 1:15 P.M. and 1:20 P.M. She said she fixed the time because she had her coffee break at 1 each day and had to be back on the floor at 1:15 so that another girl could go for her break. She had just returned when Alvarado came in.

There was no doubt in her mind that it was Alvarado and that the day was July 3rd. She remembered the rain and the holiday the next day, when she saw television newscasts about the murder. She also saw Alvarado's picture in the newspapers. Sandro had no further questions.

Siakos asked one question. She testified that Alvarado was alone when he entered the store and she had never seen Hernandez before coming into court this afternoon.

Ellis began to question. She said she couldn't describe what Alvarado was wearing on July 3rd, except he was wearing a hat. She said she did not notice where he went when he left the store. She again fixed the time between 1:15 and 1:20. When asked if she was a friend of Alvarado's, she said she wasn't. She said she had certainly been subpoenaed to come into court. She wouldn't have come any other way. Ellis had no further questions.

Sandro called for Philip Gruberger. Gruberger, small and alert, his eyes passing across the defendants, sat on the stand, waiting for the questions. He identified himself as the assistant manager of the store in which Annie Mae Cooper was working on July 3rd, 1967. He recalled that she had come to him, asking if she could change a hundred-dollar bill. He said he had studied the bill and okayed it. He testified that he had not seen the person who cashed the bill, but one was unquestionably cashed on July 3rd. Gruberger said that he had approved her cashing another hundred-dollar bill the Wednesday before July 3rd. He remembered both bills specifically because they were the only hundred-dollar bills cashed in that store that year. This he knew, since he was the person who made all the bank deposits at the store. Gruberger testified he didn't recall the exact time the bill was cashed on July 3rd, but it was definitely after 1 P.M.

He said he had seen the man who cashed the first hundred-dollar bill. He identified Alvarado. Sandro asked Gruberger to get out of the witness chair and walk over to the man he was identifying. Gruberger walked over to the counsel table and again identified Alvarado as the man who had cashed the hundred-dollar bill. Gruberger stated that he was not a friend of Alvarado, nor had he known or ever spoken to him.

Siakos asked Gruberger if he had ever seen Hernandez before. He said he had not.

Ellis asked Gruberger only if he had seen the person who cashed the hundred-dollar bill on July 3rd. Gruberger said he hadn't. Ellis had no further questions.

Sandro called Pablo Torres. As he was waiting, Sandro thought to himself that the defense was going in like greased glass so far. Ellis hadn't caught the drift of the current yet, but he was about to get flooded. Torres took the stand. He was the typical rustic immigrant, shy and uncomfortable on the stand, wearing his Sunday-go-to-*iglesia* best.

Through the interpreter, Torres identified himself as the cook in the Velez Restaurant on Roebling Street, a half block from the Associated Five & Ten on Broadway in Brooklyn. He said that on July 3rd, 1967, he served Luis Alvarado lunch in the restaurant. He said he hadn't known Alvarado by name at the time, but he had learned the name afterward when he saw Alvarado's picture in the newspaper. He testified he couldn't say exactly what time it was when he saw Alvarado in the restaurant, but it was a few minutes before 2 o'clock because the lunch rush hour had been over about fifteen minutes when Alvarado came in.

Torres testified that he remembered the exact date because he was off the next day for the fiesta of independence. He said he remembered this one man, Alvarado, because the next morning he saw the pictures of Alvarado on the front page of *El Diario*, one of New York's two major Spanish newspapers. He testified it was not often that a man he recognized was accused of killing someone, especially a policeman. Sandro had no further questions.

Siakos asked Torres if he had ever seen Hernandez before. He said he had not.

Ellis asked Torres if he had ever seen Alvarado before July 3rd. He testified he had seen him pass the store once before. Torres testified that on July 3rd, Alvarado had actually come into the store with another man. Ellis had Hernandez rise. He was not the man, Torres said firmly. The man who was with Alvarado was very dark-skinned, as dark as Alvarado. Torres believed that Alvarado was wearing a blue suit and a hat when he was in the restaurant.

Torres testified that Alvarado had stayed in the restaurant about fifteen or twenty minutes while eating a steak, and then left.

Ellis had no further questions.

"We'll take our recess now," said the judge.

Out in the corridor they found Mike. He had the barber Francisco Moreno sitting in a courtroom across the way.

After recess, Moreno took the stand. He sat quietly, composed, watching Sandro walk to his position by the witness chair. He testified that he was working in the Imperial Barber Shop on Roebling Street on July 3rd, 1967. The barber shop was about a block from the associated Five & Ten and a block in the other direction from the Velez Restaurant. Sandro asked Moreno if he could identify in the courtroom anyone who was in his shop on July 3rd, 1967. Moreno nodded, rose, walked toward Alvarado, and pointed directly at him. He then resumed the witness chair. He testified that Alvarado came into the shop on July 3rd, about 2:25 or 2:30, waited while Moreno worked on another customer. Moreno stated that there was one man, a friend of his, ahead of Alvarado, but the man had not been in a hurry, and he allowed Alvarado to go first. Moreno testified he cut Alvarado's hair and trimmed his moustache.

Moreno testified that Alvarado had remained in the shop about twenty-five minutes, leaving before 3. Sandro asked him how close Moreno was to Alvarado when he worked on him. Moreno grinned. "Close," he said, moving his hands with an imaginary scissors and comb.

Moreno testified that he did not know Alvarado before July 3rd, 1967. He said he saw Alvarado's picture in the newspapers the morning of July 4th, and remembered that he had been cutting the man's hair in Brooklyn at the time the newspapers said Alvarado had killed Lauria in Manhattan. Moreno stated he couldn't very well forget something as unusual as that. Sandro had no further questions.

Siakos had Hernandez rise, then asked Moreno if he had ever seen Hernandez before in his life. Moreno said he had not.

Ellis rose. "Have you, Mr. Moreno, ever been convicted of a crime?"

"I was caught playing dice, and I paid two dollars fine once," the interpreter translated.

Juror number twelve, the retired newsman, nudged juror eleven, the textiles man, and smiled. He must have been a craps shooter too. Sam rose and asked that the answer be stricken since Moreno had not been convicted of a crime when he paid a two-dollar fine. The judge struck the answer.

Moreno testified in answer to Ellis that he was sure he had cut Alvarado's hair on July 3rd because the next day was a holiday and he didn't work, and especially because he recognized Alvarado's pictures in the papers. He said Alvarado had been wearing some kind of a blue sweater when he came into the barber shop. He said he had given him a medium haircut, not too close. Alvarado had a thin-line moustache at the time.

Moreno testified that he remembered the time as being 2:25 or 2:30 because a friend of his who worked at a nearby school playground always came over after his job. He usually arrived about 4 P.M. But this day, on July 3rd, because of the holiday the next day, Moreno said his friend got off from his job early, and when his friend arrived they kidded and remarked about the friend's working only half a day. Moreno testified that his friend had arrived at 2:15 P.M. Alvarado entered the shop about ten minutes later.

Ellis asked Moreno what the name of his friend from the school was. Moreno said he called him Julio, and that was the only name he knew the man by. Ellis asked where this Julio worked.

"You can bet Ellis's spotter is busy back there now," Sam whispered.

"Let's hope Moreno doesn't make it too easy for him."

PART 35

"What's so difficult for the cops to find a guy called Julio who works at a playground near the barber shop? How many playgrounds you think there are near there?"

Ellis asked Moreno to describe Julio. He described him as a light-complexioned Puerto Rican, about thirty-five years old. He said he didn't know exactly where Julio was living now, but it was somewhere in the Williamsburg section.

Ellis asked Moreno if Alvarado had been with another man when he came into the barber shop. Moreno said that Alvarado *had* been with another man, but that it had definitely not been Hernandez. The man with Alvarado was Negro. Moreno told the jury he had not see Alvarado since he gave him a haircut on July 3rd, except for his picture in the newspaper. He was positive, however, that this was the man who had entered the barber shop on July 3rd at 2:25 or 2:30 P.M.

Ellis asked Moreno if anyone had spoken to him about the case. He nodded, and said yes, pointing to Sandro. He acknowledged that Sandro had had someone write down what was said when they first spoke. Moreno testified that there had always been an interpreter present. He said that when Sandro questioned him, he immediately remembered about cutting Alvarado's hair. Ellis asked Moreno to tell the jury of the conversation he had the first time he spoke to Sandro. Moreno repeated what he had said on the stand a few minutes before. Ellis asked if Moreno had told Sandro the first time he spoke to him that Alvarado came into the shop at 2:25 or 2:30 P.M. Moreno said he had.

Ellis turned and asked Sandro if he could look at the statement signed by Moreno.

"Your Honor, are you directing me to show the statement to Mr. Ellis?" Sandro asked, rising, wanting to whet the jury's appetite.

"I'm just asking if I can see it, Mr. Luca," Ellis said.

"I do not believe I'm required to show this to the district attorney, Your Honor," said Sandro.

"Your view of the law is correct, sir," replied Judge Porta.

"However, the defense at least is interested in making all the evidence available to the jury," said Sandro.

"I object to such statements, Your Honor," said Ellis.

"Sustained. Strike it out. Don't make speeches, Mr. Luca. Sum up at the proper time. Do you want to show Mr. Ellis the witness's statement or not?"

Sandro fished out a sealed envelope from his file and slit it open. He handed the envelope to Ellis without looking at its contents.

"May I note for the record," said Sandro, "that this statement was written in Spanish, and the signature of this witness appears thereunder. However, I have supplied to Mr. Ellis, on the same page, beneath the Spanish, what I have been informed is an accurate translation."

The judge nodded.

Ellis stood, reading the statement. He handed it to Moreno, who identified his signature. Ellis's face suddenly showed he tasted blood. Sandro wondered what Ellis had hooked into. He took a photostatic copy of the same statement from the file. Siakos came over, and the three defense lawyers read the statement.

"Did you say to Mr. Luca that around two thirty *or* three o'clock, two thirty *or* three o'clock, about that time, Alvarado was in your shop?"

"Yes. Well, it was about two twenty-five, but I started to cut his hair about two thirty."

"But did you tell Mr. Luca it was about two thirty *or* three o'clock when Alvarado was in your shop?" Ellis asked, reading directly from the English translation.

"I object, Your Honor," said Siakos, rising.

"Overruled," said the judge impatiently.

"May I explain my objection, Your Honor, on the record?"

"You may, sir."

Siakos held the copy of the statement in his hand. "This statement in Spanish, which is the one signed by the witness, says 'between two thirty *and* three o'clock.' In Spanish, the word appears *y—and—*three o'clock, not *or* three o'clock."

Ellis, his back to the jury, glared at Siakos. "Did you see this statement?" Ellis asked. He handed the paper to Siakos.

"I saw it," replied Siakos. "I saw a copy of it, and I challenge the translation."

"You can't challenge my translation because this is the translation supplied to me by Mr. Luca," Ellis fumed.

PART 35

"Mr. Luca is not a good translator," said Siakos. "Let's have it translated now. Let's have the official interpreter here do it."

Sandro rose, "I am not any kind of a translator."

Siakos smiled and winked at Sandro.

"If he pulls this off, he's made up for everything else during the trial," Sam whispered.

Sandro nodded.

"I submit, Your Honor," said Siakos, "the word *or* in English is written in Spanish *o*, meaning exactly the same; the word here in Spanish is *y* meaning *and*—between two thirty *and* three, not *or*."

"I heard the point. We will recess for a few minutes to let the interpreter look at it," said the judge.

Everyone filed out of the courtroom.

When the trial resumed, Sandro asked to have the interpreter translate the entire statement, so that there would be no further mistakes. She did, including the phrase "and between the hours of two thirty *and* three, about that time, Luis Alvarado was in my shop."

"Your Honor," Sandro requested, "may I at this time correct the English translation contained on that statement to read two thirty *and* three?"

"Deem it corrected. The interpreter has said so."

"Thank you, Your Honor." Sandro sat and leaned over to look at Sam's notes. Sam squeezed his arm.

"Don't smile," Sam cautioned.

Ellis tried to pick up the pieces. He questioned Moreno about how many other times he had spoken to Sandro. Moreno said he had seen Sandro many times, and each time he had said the same things to him. Ellis handed Moreno a two-by-two photograph taken of Alvarado the morning of July 4th at police headquarters. He asked if the photo fairly depicted the haircut he had given to Alvarado on July 3rd. Moreno studied the picture and said it looked like it.

Sam objected to the picture, since it was not in evidence, and since the conditions of its taking or developing were unknown. In addition, the photo was too small to show anything more than a general impression of a haircut.

Ellis offered the picture into evidence.

Even though the photograph was small, the line around Alvarado's ear and neck was straight and clean. His moustache was perfectly trimmed. The judge allowed the picture into evidence.

"Don't worry about it," Sandro assured Sam. "I'll have motion pictures and eight-by-ten glossies Tuesday."

The clerk gave the jury a magnifying glass, and each of the jurors studied the picture.

The police spotter returned to the courtroom and whispered something to Ellis.

"Mr. Moreno," Ellis asked, "in August of 1964, were you living at Eighteen-ten Broadway, in Brooklyn?"

"Yes."

"Did you assault someone with a bottle in that month?"

"No."

Ellis looked at Moreno, then turned toward his chair. He looked at Sandro. "No further questions, Your Honor."

Sandro asked no further questions of Moreno.

"Your next witness, please," said the judge.

"In our orderly procedure, Your Honor, our next witnesses will be from the American Broadcasting Company, but they cannot be in court until tomorrow. Our only available witness is the defendant Alvarado. Since the hour is late, and his testimony shall be lengthy, may we adjourn until tomorrow?" asked Sam.

"Yes. We stand adjourned until tomorrow morning, members of the jury. Do not discuss this case amongst yourselves or with anyone else."

The judge and jury left the courtroom.

"It's always best to leave the jury with a strong point to think about overnight. And we were strong!" said Sam.

CHAPTER XXX

"WHAT THE HELL did Roosevelt say when you finally found him?" Sandro asked.

"He said he was too busy, that he didn't have time to go to court," Mike answered.

"Well, we'll get him tonight. Either he goes to court, or, goddamn it, I'll get the judge to send a court officer after him. I'm tired of having to beg these witnesses to help us. Not only do we have to know the law, be able to plead the case, and sway the jury, but we've also got to wet-nurse a bunch of people who think they're doing us a favor."

"I'd love to see some of them if they were ever in trouble," said Mike. "They'd sing a different tune if they needed someone to testify for them."

Sandro grunted.

Mike parked the car on Stanton Street.

"While we're here," said Sandro, "we might as well talk to Hernandez's wife, and see if we can get to the bottom of this story Sal Angeletti told us."

"Why bother? At the bottom of it, is the beast with two backs," Mike said as he wheeled the car into the tight space.

Mike knocked on the door to Roosevelt Jackson's apartment. Music was coming from within. Mike knocked again. A small Negro boy opened the door.

"Is your daddy home?" asked Sandro.

Mike looked impatiently at Sandro. "Is Roosevelt in?" Mike asked. The boy disappeared inside. "He might disappear forever if you want him to find his daddy. Let's just get to Roosevelt."

The boy returned and waved them to enter. They found themselves in the kitchen. The sink was piled with dishes. The rest of the apartment was dark except for a small night-light in the bedroom. The boy pointed that way.

"Can you see anything in there?" asked Mike.

Sandro peered into the darkness. He could see a dark mass on what seemed to be the bed.

"There's our Roosevelt, if I'm not mistaken," said Sandro. He entered the room cautiously. Mike was a step behind him. As they got closer, the air became thick with the smell of cheap wine. Jackson was in his shorts, sprawled face up on the bed.

"Roosevelt," Sandro called.

There was a grunt.

"Roosevelt, it's Mr. Luca, the lawyer." Sandro crouched next to the bed, inhaling reluctantly.

A groan, and Jackson shifted position.

"What happened to you today, Roosevelt? You know we needed you in court. I even sent a car here to pick you up."

"I jus' di'n't have no time today to go to no court. I was busy."

"Roosevelt, you've got to go to court tomorrow," Sandro said, wishing that he didn't need him.

"Maybe I can make it, 'n maybe I be too busy again."

"No, tomorrow you've got to make it, Roosevelt. Where's your hand," Sandro groped in the dark. "Where's your goddamn hand?" He found Roosevelt's hand and put a subpoena and a dollar into it. "That in your hand is a subpoena. If you don't come to court tomorrow, I'll have the judge send a court officer after you."

"You gon' get me in trouble? You gon' do that to your friend, Roosevelt?"

PART 35

"I don't want you to get in trouble, Roosevelt. That's why I'm going to send the car for you again." Sandro peered into the dark, still not able to make out if Jackson's eyes were open or closed.

"You gon' send car?"

"That's right. At ten o'clock this time. And you'd better be there. And you'd better be sober, Roosevelt. I don't want to tell the judge that his friend Roosevelt is not behaving himself."

"You tell that judge Roosevelt is behavin'. You tell the judge I be there tomorrow."

"I'm going to send the car for you, at ten," Sandro said. "You be sure to be ready."

"I'll be there. Don' you worry none. I'll be all ready."

"Come on, let's get out of here. He doesn't even know what the hell we're talking about tonight. But tomorrow morning, you come here, and if he's not ready, you get him dressed. He'll wake up with that subpoena. It's no joke. You tell him that."

"I'll get him there if I have to carry him," Mike replied. "No, I take that back."

"You may just have to." They started out of the apartment.

They walked over to 163 Stanton Street and climbed the stairs. Mike knocked. Mrs. Hernandez came to the door and smiled. She began chatting with Mike in Spanish as they entered. She nodded and smiled at Sandro. She offered them a cup of coffee. Mike accepted. Sandro said he didn't feel like coffee.

She and Mike continued to talk, and Sandro let Mike dispose of all the amenities.

"She's asking me about how the case is going, what I think, and all that."

"And are you telling her what a wonderful job you're doing for her husband?"

"Right. I might as well make some points too."

"Tell her that I'm still investigating, and I'm trying to track down something that has to do with the police in the case."

Mike translated.

"And tell her that I want to talk to her about Detective Mullaly."

Her eyes reacted to the sound of his name in English. She looked at Sandro, then back to Mike as he translated.

"Tell her that I'm interested only in the truth, so I can save my man, and her husband too, and I'm not interested in what she does with her time, or where she goes."

She was watching Sandro's face. Now she watched Mike as he spoke.

She shrugged.

"Ask her if Mullaly has been coming around here to see her."

Her face grew into a bitter, resigned frown as Mike asked the question. She answered him.

"She says he was coming around investigating, and she spoke to him."

"Tell her I'm not interested in that, and she knows it." Sandro looked at Mrs. Hernandez as Mike spoke. Her eyes slid over to Sandro. He nodded knowingly.

"She says that he came over, and they went out to have dinner one night."

"Would you tell her I'm a lawyer, not a priest, nor the D.A., nor her husband. I'm not interested in her private life, except as it affects the defense of this case."

Mike spoke Spanish to her. She replied.

"She says she saw him hit Alvarado in the station house, this Mullaly, and he seemed to be running things."

"Go ahead, get the rest of it."

"I am, I am. She doesn't like the idea of telling me. She doesn't mind you so much. You're like the official, an American. But she's embarrassed in front of me."

"Well, when I learn Spanish, she can tell it to me directly. Right now, ask her to explain it to you for me."

Mike spoke to her again. She responded, slowly. Her voice was getting softer and slower.

"And he took her home from the station house," Mike translated. "She figured that he was the law, that he could help her husband if he wanted to. Dumb bitch! The next time he came around, a few days later, she asked him in for coffee."

"When did they go for dinner?"

Mike asked. "She says about two weeks later. He was being nice to her, seemed to be trying to help. She didn't know what the hell was going on or where to turn," Mike said with irritation. "Every time she'd go to the jail or the station house, they'd give her the runaround. So she tried to make friends with the police through Mullaly. She sure picked a beaut."

"Whose version of this am I getting, hers or yours?"

"Both." Mike was about to say more when Mrs. Hernandez started speaking again without any questions to prompt her this time. Her voice rose suddenly. She let the coffee cup she had been drying with a towel drop shatteringly to the floor. She started walking around the room, talking loudly.

"What the hell is going on now?" Sandro asked.

"She said they went to dinner a couple of times. They couldn't communicate too well, each spoke only a little of the other's language."

"Come on, get down to the gory details."

"Wait a minute, will you. She's telling this story like it's the Chinese water torture. Son-of-a-bitch Mullaly's telling her all sorts of bullshit about helping her husband, and she's eating it up." Mike was openly angry now.

"Listen, Mike, if you don't want to go through with this, we don't need it. I don't think Mrs. Hernandez's peccadilloes affect the case that much."

"No, let's find out what kind of real scum this Mullaly is."

Mike spoke to her again. She responded as she bent over the broken coffee cup picking at the fragments.

"She says they started seeing each other here. The fucking sport Mullaly used to bring Chinese food here, and she'd let her kid stay over at her girl friend's house while she's trying to do her husband some good over here. Can you imagine these goddamn greenhorns? They discussed it, her girl friend and her, and they figured it was a good move." Mike shook his head.

Mrs. Hernandez continued speaking.

"He used to come over here two or three nights a week," Mike translated, "telling her he was trying to *help* her husband. Helping himself is what he meant."

"Hey, Mike. Will you stop the bullshit. Just tell me what she's saying and stop adding confusion to the story."

"Sorry. It just burns me up, this flatfoot bastard, taking what he can get from her, to help her husband, and meanwhile he's giving us every screwing in the book to sink not only Hernandez but Alvarado too."

"Go ahead with her story."

"That's about all there was to it. When the time for trial came around, she was asking him, you know, how come they were going to trial. She figured he had it all fixed up. I can't help it, Sandro, that son of a bitch really burns me up, handing her that line and slipping it to her at the same time."

"She knew what she was doing. I mean, she thought she was bribing him for his help. She was wrong. Don't get carried away."

"These people just off the plane, they don't know what the hell is going on here. Mullaly should have left her alone."

"And if you were in his position?"

"Yeah, but I'm her own kind." Mike smiled ruefully.

"What happened then, after the trial started?"

"They had a big fight, because he was stalling her, coming over, saying the judge insisted on the trial, even though he was trying to put in a good word, and all that kind of bullshit. And then she figured it out. The reason she didn't tell you is she figured you might make trouble for Mullaly and that'd only make it worse for Hernandez. She's still afraid."

Mrs. Hernandez was watching the conversation between Mike and Sandro. Sandro looked over at her. She shrugged with resignation and tiredness. Tears seemed to be welling up at her eyes.

"Has she been seeing him since the trial began?" Sandro asked.

Mike relayed the question.

"She says she didn't see him again until she saw him in court and pointed him out."

Sandro looked at her again. The tears were unmistakable now. Sandro nodded, trying to convey understanding. He reached out and touched her hand. She sobbed and put her head down on the kitchen table.

"I'm going," Sandro said, standing.

"You're not leaving me here," said Mike. He rose.

PART 35

Hearing the scrape of their chairs, she looked up. She started to speak again to Mike, wiping at her eyes.

"She says she was only trying to help."

"Tell her everything is fine."

Mike spoke to her again. She replied.

"She's saying something about some guy who owns a factory in a building right behind this house," said Mike. "He came over one day and told her that he and one of his men saw the whole thing from a fire escape, but they didn't want to go to the police. They didn't know who to speak to."

"He said he saw what whole thing?" Sandro asked.

Mike inquired. "He told her he saw the cop going up to the roof and all that."

"Did he say that he saw the shooting?"

"She says he didn't say."

"Does she have this guy's name and address?"

Mrs. Hernandez went to a pad on the windowsill. Something was scribbled on the top sheet. Mike read it. "Abdul Safi, One sixty-two Rivington Street."

Sandro looked at his watch. It was 8:30. "Let's try it."

"There's probably nobody left in the factory now," Mike suggested.

"Then we'll have to see this guy first thing tomorrow after court."

"I'm ready," said Mike.

"Tell her everything is going great. Tell her we're doing fine. Tell her anything you want."

Mike spoke to her. She looked at Sandro and tried to smile. It turned sour, as the tears started down her cheeks again. Sandro walked out into the hall. Mike followed, and shut the door behind them. They could hear her sobbing as they went down the stairs.

"That shoots a hole in the great Mullaly-Snider conspiracy," Sandro said as they descended.

"What do you mean? How does that change anything?"

"You figured Mullaly was protecting a cop—Snider. Well, it turns out he was protecting a cop, but the cop he was protecting was himself. It explains what he was doing here all the time, why he seemed to be working overtime on this case."

"What about all the other things that are suspicious, that haven't been cleared up?" asked Mike. "How about Salerno—feeding us that story through Soto that Salerno was involved? How about putting a stop on the pawnshop stuff?"

"Well, the pawnshop stuff stayed where it was. He didn't take it out and destroy it. He could have. But he left it there, and it ultimately ended up in court, didn't it?"

"Yes," Mike agreed reluctantly.

"So, what else did he do?"

"What about the Salerno bit? Doesn't it seem to you he was trying too hard to get Hernandez convicted?"

"That's like saying there's something wrong if we work hard doing our job. Even if he was screwing Hernandez's wife, he was still doing his job, and he wasn't anxious to help us acquit Alvarado and Hernandez. He wasn't about to let two cop-killers go just for a piece of tail, but he wasn't letting a good piece get away either. Neither of those things has anything to do with covering up his own involvement in the murder. Or Snider's involvement for that matter."

"That whole story of Snider's stinks. And you know it. Tell me it doesn't."

"I still can't explain the time discrepancy, but your ideas about Mullaly don't seem to hold so much water anymore."

"Hold on a minute! There's still Snider, and Mullaly knows it. And is covering for him. That's what he's been doing. He's been protecting his piece of ass and Snider at the same time. That makes sense—doesn't it?"

"I can't say it's not possible."

"You bet your ass."

CHAPTER XXXI

Tuesday, April 23rd, 1968

"CALL YOUR FIRST WITNESS, Mr. Bemer. Bring in the jury," said the judge. The jury was brought in and polled by the clerk.

"I'd like to recall Detective Mullaly for a moment, if Your Honor please," said Sam.

"If he's still here. Mr. Ellis, is Detective Mullaly still here?"

"Yes, Your Honor," Ellis replied.

"Very well. Ask Detective Mullaly to step in here from the witness room."

A court officer opened the side door and called. Mullaly walked into the courtroom, looking at Ellis. He sat on the witness chair.

"All right, Detective, you are still under oath," said the judge. "Proceed."

"Detective Mullaly, you were with the defendant Alvarado when he was in the station house, isn't that so?" asked Sam.

"Everyone knows he was, Mr. Bemer. Get to the point," said the judge.

"Did the defendant speak to anyone other than police personnel and the district attorney while he was in the station house?"

"No, sir. No one."

"After he left the station house to go to headquarters, did he speak to anyone other than officials?"

"No, sir."

"When was the first time that he spoke to anyone other than officials, if you can remember?"

"I imagine when he left headquarters on his way to court for arraignment. Reporters were able to get near when they were being loaded into the van."

"Those were the first civilians he spoke to after being arrested?"

"Yes, sir."

"No further questions."

Siakos stood. "And, Detective, the same is true for the defendant Hernandez?"

"Yes, sir."

"No further questions."

Ellis, looking mystified, said, "No questions."

"Now bring in your news photos and newsreels," Sam whispered, as he again sat at the counsel table.

"Your next witness, please."

"Richard Sanford," said Sandro. He looked to the back of the courtroom. Sanford was in the public corridor, peering in through the glass panels in the courtroom door. Sandro motioned for him to enter. He swung the door open and took the witness chair to be sworn.

Sanford testified that he was employed by television station WABC-TV as a film editor in the news department. He indicated that he had been doing such work for the last fifteen years. He testified that on July 4th, 1967, certain film was brought to the studio from police headquarters by motorcycle. The film contained footage taken at the Seventh Precinct in the early morning and at police headquarters later that same morning. This film related to the investigation of the death of Patrolman Fortune Lauria. Ron Roman was the interviewer and had been in charge of the assignment.

Sanford testified that, at Sandro's direction, he had taken two frames from the motion-picture film and had eight-by-ten blow-up stills made from them. Other than that, he said the films were intact, just as they had been taken from the film containers and developed.

PART 35

"I am going to show these to you and ask you if you recognize them," Sandro said, showing the two eight-by-ten still pictures.

"Yes, I blew these up from the motion-picture film."

"And in developing these, did you in any fashion change, alter, or modify the negative or the positive print?"

"No, sir. That's just the way it came from the negative."

"I offer these into evidence."

"Show them to the district attorney," the judge instructed.

Ellis looked at the still pictures of Alvarado taken in the station house early on July 4th, 1967. He saw the neatly trimmed sideburns and the neat are up and over the ears. He saw the neat, trim, pencil-line moustache. "I have no objection," he said calmly.

"Received in evidence."

Sandro had no further questions.

Siakos had no questions.

Ellis had no questions.

"Thank you, sir," said the judge. "Your next witness."

"Your Honor, in connection with the next witness, I'll need the assistance of Mr. Sanford, the last witness. May he stay in the courtroom now that he has completed his testimony?"

"He may."

"I call Ron Roman," said Sandro. The familiar face of the newscaster came in through the rear door of the courtroom. "Your Honor, while Mr. Sanford sets up the screen and the projector for the next witness, may I show these still pictures of the defendant Alvarado taken the early morning of July fourth in the Seventh Precinct station house to the jury?"

"I object, Your Honor. He doesn't have to make a speech every time he stands up. If he wants to testify, let Mr. Luca take the stand."

"Is there any question that that's where these pictures were taken, Mr. Ellis?" Sandro asked quickly.

"Gentlemen, please. Let me make the speeches. Let me run my own courtroom. Show the pictures to the jury."

Sandro handed the photos to the court officer, who handed them to the jury. The jurors scrutinized the photos, two at a time. Some of them pointed to Alvarado's sideburns, some to his moustache.

"Perhaps," Sam said, rising, "the clerk can provide the jurors with his magnifying glass."

"If any of the jurors can't see these pictures without a magnifying glass, he should be disqualified from duty and given a Seeing Eye dog," the judge said. The jurors laughed. "However, the magnifying glass is available for anyone who wants it."

All during this, Sanford was setting up a projector and screen. Roman sat in the witness chair. When the jurors had finished with the pictures, Sandro began.

Roman gave his background with the WABC-TV news department, and his experience with filming and taping stories. He testified that nothing had been done to the film, and no technique had been used to make the events they recorded appear any different from the way they had happened. He said that the film of the Alvarado investigation had been made at his direction and under his supervision. He described the scene at police headquarters, the throng of reporters and cameramen. When Alvarado and Hernandez came out to get into the police van, he asked them questions.

"Were you the first reporter to speak to him, do you know?" asked Sandro.

"There were a lot of men, but I think I was first. There were a couple of the people from other networks right there with me at the time. No one was before us."

"Did you ask Alvarado if he had killed the officer?"

"I did."

"What did he say?"

"He said he didn't."

"Did you ask him anything else?"

"I think I asked him if he knew who did do it."

"What did he answer?"

"He said he didn't know, he didn't do it."

"Your Honor, I would like to have this film Mr. Sanford has set up screened for the jury as Mr. Roman explains what is taking place."

"Very well."

The film rolled. There, depicted for the jury, was the scene as the men came out of police headquarters. Hernandez was first. Then came

PART 35

Alvarado. Mullaly and Johnson had Alvarado, one at each elbow. Roman asked him questions. Alvarado, appearing dazed, answered. The questions and answers were those Roman had just testified to. Sanford stopped the projector.

"Your Honor," said Sandro, "there is another section of this film which I would like to have the jury see, which is most germane to this trial."

"Very well, I accept your representation. Proceed."

Sandro went over and spoke to Sanford. He nodded, then let the film run on the projector without turning on the light so that no image appeared on the screen. He nodded again to Sandro.

"Mr. Roman, did you take films of other events related to this investigation."

"Yes, sir."

"Did you take films at the station house, the morning of July fourth before you went to headquarters?"

"Yes, sir."

"As a matter of fact, wasn't it from some of that film at the Seventh Precinct station house that the still photos of Alvarado were taken?"

"Yes, that's right."

"Is this next segment of film exactly what occurred that morning?" Sandro nodded to Sanford, who snapped on the projector light. On the screen, Mrs. Hernandez suddenly emerged through the doors of the station house, accompanied by policemen, down the steps and into a patrol car. Sanford stopped the projector.

"Yes, sir, that occurred there."

"What time of day was that film taken?"

"I'd say about nine A.M., maybe nine thirty on July fourth, 1967."

"Your witness, Mr. Ellis."

Ellis had no questions.

The judge indicated that the jury should now take a lunch recess. Everyone filed out of court.

After the lunch recess, Sandro saw that Roosevelt Jackson had finally arrived. He was sitting on the radiator outside the courtroom next to Mike Rivera. Sandro called him as his first witness. Jackson walked with his slow gait to the stand. He was sworn and sat in the witness chair.

He testified that he was the superintendent for the buildings 155 to 161 Stanton Street, had been for more than five years. He testified that on July 3rd, 1967, there had been no fences separating the yards behind his buildings from one another or, for that mater, from a free, unhindered passage all the way to Suffolk Street. In fact, he testified, there had been none such for more than five years. Age and the kids had destroyed whatever fences there had been years before.

His stolid manner made it impossible to think that his mind could conceive of lying about his fences.

Sandro had no further questions.

Ellis stood to cross-examine. Jackson was too slow to be caught in a trap of cross-examination. Ellis asked him if he had not, in fact, told the detective who had spoken to him just a short time before the beginning of the trial that there had been a fence but that it was taken down about "watermelon time." Jackson replied he told a detective who questioned him at his home only one week ago that that fence was not behind the buildings, but rather at Suffolk Street. There was no fence behind the buildings which would have frustrated an attempt to walk down the alley behind the buildings all the way to Suffolk Street.

"So they knew there was no fence, too, but they just kept it to themselves," said Sam. "Ellis must know that this case of his doesn't add up to a row of beans. I can't believe that he doesn't."

"So what's he going to do, throw it all up in the air and go home?" said Sandro. Sam studied him and smiled as he looked down to his notes.

Ellis was finished with the superintendent.

Sandro called Luis Alvarado. Alvarado walked to the stand, followed by his guard. He sat, folded his hands in his lap, and looked out to Sandro.

Alvarado testified that in the very early morning of July 3rd, 1967, he went to sleep in his room on South Ninth Street. It was about 2:30 A.M. He awakened around 1 o'clock the next afternoon, dressed, and went out. It was raining lightly. On the corner of Broadway and Roebling Street, he met a friend, Eugene, and stopped for about five minutes for conversation. He and Eugene then went to the Associated Five & Ten to cash a hundred-dollar bill. There he saw Annie Mae

PART 35

Cooper. He left the five-and-ten about 1:30 P.M. Then he went to the Velez Restaurant and had something to eat. Eugene declined to join him and waited outside. He testified he was in the restaurant about 2 P.M. From there they went to the Del Gato Haberdashery, where he bought a belt for $1.25. Still with Eugene, he went to the Imperial Barber Shop on Roebling Street at about 2:15.

Alvarado testified that one man was "taking" a haircut and another was waiting. He testified that he gave the man waiting a dollar to let him go next. After leaving the barber shop at about ten minutes to three, he returned to his room on South Ninth Street, bathed, dressed, and went back downstairs, where he met Jorge the superintendent.

Alvarado told the jury he was in his room for twenty or twenty-five minutes before meeting Jorge. Alvarado had a bottle of whiskey, which he sold to Jorge for two dollars. He asked Jorge to credit the two dollars to his week's rent. Alvarado left the house and took a subway to Manhattan. It was 3:40 P.M. He said he was wearing a green shirt, gray pants with stripes, and a blue cardigan sweater.

Alvarado said he took the BMT to Times Square. Once at Times Square he walked around 42nd Street, looking into the shop windows. He bought a cigarette lighter. Finally, he entered a movie theater. He saw two pictures, *It Happened at the World's Fair* with Elvis Presley and *The Son of Spartacus* with Steve Reeves. He fell asleep for a while in the theater, left sometime around midnight, bought a newspaper, and went home.

Alvarado testified that when he walked home, he saw Jorge's lights on. He stopped at Jorge's apartment, and Jorge told him about the three detectives waiting upstairs. He said that when arrested he had had $141 in his pocket, what remained from the two hundred-dollar bills he had changed within a week. Sandro had Alvarado explain to the jury how he had obtained three hundred-dollar bills, two of which he had changed.

Alvarado was asked about and denied each and every statement that Mullaly had attributed to him. He not only denied having said these things, but he also flatly denied having done any of them. He swore that he had had nothing to do with the crime and that he had not been on Stanton Street on July 3rd, 1967.

He said that, although he had been arrested for narcotics, he had never been arrested for a crime of violence in his life, nor had he ever committed any. For a last question, Sandro asked Alvarado if he had shot Fortune Lauria. With emotion almost spilling over, Alvarado shook his head.

"No, sir."

The jury was motionless.

Ellis stood to cross-examine. His first question was whether Alvarado was aware of the charge against him and the possible attendant consequences. Alvarado said he was. Ellis asked him, as Siakos and Sam had asked the police, whether, if he had committed the crime, he would admit it.

Alvarado answered that he would be truthful.

"Is that answer as true as all the answers you gave to Mr. Luca when he questioned you?"

"Yes, sir."

Ellis questioned Alvarado's ability to remember the specific times he had been in each place he said he had visited on July 3rd. Alvarado answered that he had had a long time and nothing else to think about since he was arrested.

Ellis asked if Alvarado's memory was as good on July 3rd, 1967, and, if so, why hadn't he told anyone in the station house of all these places to which he had been. Alvarado said no one had asked him about where he had been; they only told him where he had been, that he had killed the officer.

"Well, did you try to tell somebody where you had been?"

"No, sir. They don't give me a chance to talk to nobody."

"Did anybody put any adhesive tape over your mouth to keep you from talking?"

"They put punches in my stomach."

Alvarado testified he had never said anything to the police in the station house about where he had been.

"Good thing he didn't," Sandro whispered to Sam, "or our alibi would have disappeared a long time ago."

Sam nodded.

Ellis questioned Alvarado about his friend Eugene. What did he

PART 35

look like? What was his last name? Where did he live? Sandro could almost hear the point of the spotter's pencil touching the paper in the back of the courtroom. Alvarado said he didn't know anything about him except that his first name was Eugene. He couldn't tell where he lived or where he hung out. He could say, however, that Eugene had a dark complexion similar to his own.

"How old is he?"

"I can't tell you how old he is. He is jung," said Alvarado.

Ellis jumped on that. "A junky?"

"Jung—not old."

Alvarado said he didn't know if Eugene was a junky. Ellis asked him to repeat his chronology of July 3rd, 1967, which Alvarado did, almost word for word. He explained that the reason he was in a hurry in the barber shop was that he had an appointment to meet a girl at 4 P.M. in the subway.

Sandro looked up in amazement. Would Alvarado never stop recalling new details about that day?

The girl's name was Maria, Alvarado continued. He had met her the night before. She never showed up. He went to the movies by himself. He testified he didn't remember the name of the movie house, but it was on the south side of 42nd Street between 7th and 8th Avenue.

Ellis started to hammer at Alvarado with questions about the confession Mullaly had testified to. Alvarado denied ever saying anything to Mullaly about the movies.

Alvarado admitted having seen Hernandez at the Ascot Hotel on several occasions, but definitely not on July 3rd.

"Let him screw around with this insignificant crap," said Sam. "He's finished if this is all he can come up with."

Ellis continued. Alvarado denied having shot up in the men's room of the hotel with Hernandez at any time.

Alvarado also denied he ever made a confession to the police, despite the beatings. Ellis asked Alvarado if he remembered having made a statement to the district attorney in the station house.

"Here comes the sixty-four-dollar question," said Sam. "Ellis is opening up now."

Sandro watched Ellis fish a typewritten question-and-answer statement from his file. Ellis handed Sam a copy. The judge refused to permit a short recess to allow Sam and Sandro to read the statement. He said they could follow along and would have time later.

Sandro started to read into the meat of the statement, while Ellis asked some preliminary questions concerning whether or not Alvarado remembered the statement's being taken.

Alvarado testified there were only two or three questions asked. That was all.

Sandro's eyes lighted up as he read. "This is great, Sam, great." He pointed to some questions and answers.

"No wonder Ellis didn't want to put this in evidence."

Sandro read rapidly through the document, marking passages.

Ellis asked Alvarado about the introduction D.A. Brennan made, of the preliminary questions. Alvarado denied that such took place. Each denial gave Ellis more reason to read further into the document, attempting to refresh Alvarado's recollection and, at the same time, drive home the inculpatory statements.

"Now, Alvarado," Ellis said, "do you remember District Attorney Brennan asking you these questions, and your giving these answers? 'Question: Didn't you tell the police that you panicked and went after the cop and took his gun away from him? Answer: I said that. Question: Did you tell that to the police. Answer: Yes.' Do you remember those questions and answers?"

"No, sir. I don't say that."

Ellis looked blankly at Alvarado.

"Well, do you remember these questions and these answers? 'Question: Did you tell the police that you shot the cop? Answer: Yes. Question: Was that the truth? Answer: Yes, that's the truth. Question: That is the truth? Answer: Yes, that's the truth.' Do you remember those questions and answers?"

"I don't say that. He don't ask me those things."

"He's not reading all of it," said Sandro.

"What did you expect?"

Alvarado insisted that the D.A. had asked him three questions at most. He said he had denied being on the roof to Brennan, denied

PART 35

having anything to do with the crime, and denied shooting the cop. That was the extent of the examination by the D.A.

Ellis kept reading questions from the document. Even where the answers were helpful, Alvarado steadfastly denied having been asked the questions, having given the answer.

"Why the hell would a guilty man deny a statement like this? It's a repudiation. Why would he deny it?" Sam asked rhetorically.

"I don't know. Except it seems that he really believes he didn't make it. I can't believe that the D.A. would fake a statement, and if he did that he'd make up one like this. Alvarado might have been groggy from the beating and didn't remember all the questions that were asked."

Alvarado continued to insist that he had never made any statement to the D.A. Ellis eased away from the statement, embarking upon the subject of the hundred-dollar bills. Ellis wanted information about the man who gave the money to Alvarado. But Alvarado was cagy. He said the man's name as far as he knew was Paco, but he didn't know if it was his real name, or where he lived.

Alvarado testified that he was supposed to buy one ounce of heroin for Paco and meet him on Allen Street near Delancey the night after the day he received the money. He said he showed up to tell Paco he hadn't made contact yet, but Paco never appeared, and Alvarado had not been able to catch up with him thereafter.

Ellis had no further questions.

Sandro rose, in his hand the question-and-answer statement that Ellis had been reading.

"Mr. Alvarado, do you remember District Attorney Brennan asking you these questions and your answering as follows—"

"I object, Your Honor. Same objection as that to reading Hernandez's statement. This statement is not in evidence and can only be read as a prior inconsistent statement. Defense counsel, however, cannot impeach his own defendant. I object."

"I'll hear you on that, Mr. Luca."

"Rather than respond to the argument, Your Honor, I'll offer the document in evidence, in toto." He looked at Ellis. Ellis couldn't object to his own statement.

"Received," said Judge Porta, nodding.

"I would also like to offer into evidence the statement allegedly made by Mr. Hernandez that Mr. Ellis referred to before."

The judge looked at Ellis. Ellis just looked back at the judge for his reaction.

"Received," said the judge.

The jurors were moving to the edges of their seats again.

"May I first read the portions of Mr. Hernandez's statement that Mr. Ellis left out."

"Objection, Your Honor. First of all I don't have to read the entire document. I can use any part I need for my cross-examination. And Mr. Luca knows it. Second, he's defending Alvarado, if he remembers it or not."

"First of all, Your Honor, I didn't say Mr. Ellis had to read the entire document. I just want to read what he left out. Second, anything that will show Hernandez not guilty also helps the defendant Alvarado. This is a joint trial."

"Proceed."

Sandro turned to the jury and began to read from the Hernandez statement:

Question: Did you see the policeman come onto the roof?

Answer: Yes.

Question: Did he have his gun in his hand?

Answer: No.

Question: He didn't? You say, he didn't?

Answer: He had his club.

Question: His nightstick?

Answer: Right.

PART 35

Question: Did you see Alvarado jump on the cop?

Answer: He got scared and ran away.

Question: Alvarado, you say, ran away?

Answer: Yes, he was climbing the wall to go away. The policeman grabbed him and pulled him back off the wall.

Question: Did you see Alvarado fight with the policeman?

Answer: Yes, then he fight for the club. The cop fell to the ground. Alvarado got the gun then.

Sandro looked up at the jury. The jury looked confused.
"Now, Your Honor, I'd like to read those portions of the alleged question-and-answer statement relating to the defendant Alvarado that Mr. Ellis left out."
"Your Honor, I object to this insistence by Mr. Luca that I left portions out. I do not have to read in its entirety a document I am only using as a prior inconsistent statement."
"Your Honor, I think Mr. Ellis protests too much. He didn't read the entire document. I want to read the portions he left out, the ones he did not read. That is a fair statement."
"Proceed, without speeches, please."
"I'll start with the top of page three."
Sandro read aloud:

Question: Didn't you tell the police that you went into the building with Hernandez and went to the apartment and broke into the apartment?

Answer: Yes, sir.

Question: And was that the truth?

Answer: No, sir.

Question: You're saying it wasn't the truth?

Answer: No, sir.

Question: It was a lie?

Answer: Yes.

Question: Who made it up?

Answer: I do.

"At the bottom of page six now," said Sandro. He continued reading to a completely hushed courtroom:

Question: Didn't you tell the police that you panicked and went after the cop and you took his gun away from him?

Answer: I said that.

Question: Was that the truth?

Answer: No, sir.

Question: Did anybody tell you to say these things? You're shaking your head.

Answer: You don't know what happens with those kind of persons over there.

Question: What kind of persons?

Answer: Prison.

PART 35

Question: The prison?

Answer: The prison. See my hands from having cuffs.

Question: Did you tell the police that you shot the cop?

Answer: Yes.

Question: Was that the truth?

Answer: Yes, that's the truth.

Question: That is the truth?

Answer: Yes, that's the truth.

Question: That you did shoot the policeman?

Answer: Yes, sir. I know they're going to break my ass over there, that's why I said that.

Question: Pardon?

Answer: I know they're going—

Question: Was that the truth?

No response.

Question: How many times did you shoot?

No response.

Question: How many times did you shoot the policeman?

No response.

Question: What happened to you in the station house? You're shaking your head.

No response.

Question: Did the police tell you to say these things?

Answer: Why don't you take me out of here?

Question: Pardon?

Answer: Don't leave me here.

Question: In this room?

Answer: In this building at all.

Question: Now Mr. Alvarado, did you tell me, is that correct, just a short time ago that it was the truth when you said you shot the cop? Now is that the truth?

Answer: I wish to answer you outside of here.

Question: You wish to answer me. You would talk to me in some other room?

Answer: Not here in this building.

Question: Well, what is it, Luis? Why can't you tell me here? What is it?

Answer: Because I'm afraid.

Question: What are you afraid of?

Answer: I'm afraid they'll kill me back there.

PART 35

Question: Who is going to kill you?

Answer: All these guys here.

Question: You mean the police?

No response.

Question: What would they want to kill you for?

Answer: I don't know. I'm going to catch TB or something. I can't hold my chest too much.

Sandro paused. There was now a slight movement in the courtroom, as if everyone present were taking the opportunity to draw a breath again.

"And the final passage, on page twelve, Mr. Ellis." Sandro resumed:

Question: Did the police ask you questions about the shooting that took place on the roof of One fifty-three Stanton Street?

Answer: Yes.

Question: And you told them certain things, is that correct?

Answer: Yes.

Question: Before, and on the record, you told me, with the exception of one thing, that what you told the police wasn't true. Right?

Answer: Yes.

Question: Now, although you don't have to answer my questions because you have a right to be advised by a lawyer, is what you told the police the truth?

Answer: It wasn't the truth.

Question: It was not the truth or it was?

Answer: It wasn't.

Question: But you did say, am I correct, when I asked if you shot the cop, you did say, yes, that was the truth. Is that correct?

Answer: I was afraid.

Question: You were afraid of what?

No response.

Question: You don't have to answer any of my questions. Now, if after you have been advised by a lawyer, after you have talked to a lawyer about this case, you still wish to talk to me—

Answer: Yes, I want to talk to you, yes.

Question: All right, one last question. Do you have any complaints against the police department as to how you were treated?

Answer: I don't answer that question.

Question: You can't answer that question, or you don't want to answer the question?

Answer: I don't want to.

"I have no further questions." Sandro walked back to the counsel table.

PART 35

Ellis had no further questions.

"At this point, Your Honor, the defendant Alvarado rests," Sandro announced.

The judge nodded. "Does the district attorney have anything further."

"Yes, Your Honor," said Ellis.

"All right, we'll recess for today. Do not discuss this case, members of the jury."

As the jurors filed out, they stole furtive glances at the counsel table.

"That's a good sign," said Sam. "They never look at you if they're against you."

CHAPTER XXXII

SANDRO AND MIKE entered the building where Abdul Safi had his dress factory. They walked up four flights of steps and entered the loft. It was a long, open floor, with cutting machines and sewing machines spotted between long low tables at which men and women worked on the garments. A man was standing at one of the tables, cutting material. Many women, talking rapid Spanish, were sliding material under the dancing needles. Some women looked up, studying the two strangers. They started whispering and smiling among themselves.

A small, dark man approached them. He spoke Spanish.

"This is Abdul Safi," said Mike.

"Spanish?"

"All the people who work here are Spanish. He has to speak Spanish, too."

"Tell him I'm the attorney for the fellow accused of killing the cop on the roof. Tell him that Mrs. Hernandez told us he saw what was going on. She told us to get in touch with him."

Mike spoke to him again. Safi answered, then motioned for them to follow him. He called one of the men who worked for him to accompany them.

"This other fellow and Safi were here the day that Lauria was killed. One of the broads on the sewing machines happened to be looking out the window and saw the cops in the yard. Safi and this guy went to the back, on the fire-escape platform, and were just watching. They saw the cop going up to the roof, heard the shots. The whole bit."

Safi opened the rear door, and Sandro, Mike, Safi, and the other worker, who was introduced as Pete Sanchez, stepped onto the platform. It faced the rear of the buildings on Stanton Street. Safi started to describe the scene in Spanish. Occasionally, Sanchez contributed something. Mike listened, nodding.

"What's the story?" Sandro asked.

"The woman saw the cops in the yard over there," Mike said, pointing toward the back of 153 Stanton Street. "And then they saw one cop go up the fire escape, and the other run around to the front. When the first cop was almost to the top, Safi saw him draw his pistol and then go over the top. A few minutes later, they heard shots."

"Did he see anyone besides the policeman on the roof?" Sandro suggested.

Mike asked. Safi and Sanchez both replied.

"No. They just saw the cop go up, and then they heard the shots. They couldn't see anyone up there at any time."

"While the cop was going up, did they see anyone looking over the top down toward the cop?"

Mike asked. "No," he finally translated.

"After they heard the shots, did they stay on the fire escape?" Sandro asked.

"They said they stayed."

Sandro nodded. "Ask Safi about the other cop, the one who didn't go up on the fire escape. Did he run? Did he walk? Or just what did he do when he left the yard?"

Mike asked, and they replied. Mike asked something more, surprised. They answered.

"He says Snider didn't go through the alley next to One fifty-three when he went through to the street! He apparently bolted, and ran behind two buildings, One fifty-three and One fifty-five Stanton Street, then ran to the street."

"Are they sure?"

"That's what *I* asked them, and they said they were positive. Both of them said the same thing. Snider ran too far out of the way, and had to go all the way behind two buildings, around One fifty-five to the street."

"Did they ever see the men who were supposed to have done this thing in their neighborhood, either that day, or some other day?"

"Never."

"Thank them for me," said Sandro. He turned back into the shop. Mike followed. Safi shut the platform door behind them. As Mike and Sandro were descending the stairs, Sandro turned.

"You know what this bit about Snider means, don't you, Mike?"

"If I'm reading you right, it means that it took Snider time to go the extra distance down to One fifty-five and then out to the street and then back to One fifty-three, and that's why he got up to the roof so much later than he should have."

"That's it, Mike, exactly. That seems to kick that idea in the stomach for good."

"I'll be a son of a bitch."

"All that worrying, working, for nothing, Mike? You even have to give up on Mullaly with this. Mullaly couldn't very well be protecting Snider, if the only thing Snider did was to goof again."

"We can still use it," Mike exclaimed. "Mullaly's been around making it with Mrs. Hernandez, Snider doesn't even know where he ran the day of the murder. Why can't we put this guy and Mrs. Hernandez up to testify about these things? Okay, so it's not because Mullaly and Snider are involved in the killing, but because they're liars and fuck-ups. We can undermine the whole case, shake their credibility with the proof we have about them. The jury'll have to buy that."

Sandro shook his head as they reached the front entrance and walked out to the street. "No, Mike. I agree, you've finally come up with the way to use this evidence against Mullaly and Snider. And we could still put it into the rebuttal. But I'm not going to use that evidence or these witnesses."

"Why not? We've got them cold."

"Mike, we're representing Alvarado, and whatever we do has to function around Alvarado."

"Right, and this'll undermine Ellis's main witness, Mullaly, and also Snider."

"It'll destroy them, all right, in their jobs, with their families. What will it do for Alvarado? What does the fact that—in addition to other things—Mullaly's been fooling around with Mrs. Hernandez do for our defense? What does the fact that Snider is dumb do for our defense? Snider hasn't even testified to anything that hurts Alvarado."

"That's true, but it's one of those straws Sam is always talking about. Add it to the load, maybe it'll help."

"If we haven't already done it with our alibi, our destruction of their eyewitnesses, the inconsistencies, then character assassination isn't going to help us. Why bother destroying two men, no better, no worse than the average, just for the sake of destroying them? One is dumb, the other's horny. Isn't everybody?"

"You think Mullay'd let up on you if he had you in his sights the way you've got him?" Mike asked.

"I don't base my decisions on what Mullaly might do, Mike. I'm doing what I think is right."

"Couldn't we bang just Mullaly's ass around then, and leave Snider out?"

"Mike, Alvarado's life is on the line, not our pride. Or whether we look good or Mullaly looks bad on any given day."

"Ah, you're a pain in the ass," said Mike, as they walked to the car.

CHAPTER XXXIII

Wednesday, April 24th, 1968

ELLIS STARTED HIS REBUTTAL with Francis Connors, the stenotypist who recorded the statements taken by D.A. Brennan on July 4th, 1967. Tall, blond, and pockmarked, he sat on the witness chair watching Ellis shuffle through his notes. Connors described the persons present and their relative positions at the time the defendants' statements were taken. He testified that he had accurately transcribed the questions of the district attorney and the answers.

Sandro questioned Connors about what had taken place in the room when Alvarado said to the D.A., "See my hands from having cuffs." Did Alvarado, he asked, display his hands? What, if anything, appeared on the wrists? Connors said there was nothing in the record. He didn't know.

Sandro asked Connors about the point where Alvarado referred to his chest and said that he couldn't hold it any longer. Connors was unable to say whether Alvarado had been holding his chest in pain. He admitted that it would appear in the transcript only if the D.A. had told him to record it. Sandro had no further questions.

Ellis next recalled Assistant D.A. Brennan to the stand. Brennan testified in answer to Ellis's questions that there had been no off-the-record conversations with either defendant before or while the statements were taken. Brennan said that Alvarado had shown him his wrists, but he had not seen any cuts or bruises. During the statement, he said, Alvarado had watery eyes, and he was sniffling. He also kept his arms crossed over his chest, and every once in a while would bend forward, then sit back. Ellis asked Brennan if, in his official capacity, he had ever had occasion to observe drug addicts in the throes of withdrawal. Sam objected to Brennan's expertise in diagnosing a medical symptom. The judge sustained the objection, but Ellis had already conveyed the idea to the jury.

"You know, Sam," said Sandro, "I was just looking at these nude pictures of Alvarado taken at police headquarters, to see if we could actually get a look at the cut wrist."

"We *know* his wrist was cut. We saw it the first time we talked to Alvarado in the Tombs," said Sam. "Do you have any pictures that show it?"

"No. But, you know, when Siakos was examining Hernandez, about two weeks ago—must have been on his voir dire—I saw Ellis with some color pictures in his hand. He looked at them and put them back in his file."

"You saw pictures that Ellis didn't give us?" asked Sam.

Sandro nodded. "I didn't even think of them until now. I'm going to ask about them."

Siakos rose to cross-examine Brennan. Brennan said that the police had outlined to him the alleged confessions before he had taken the statements. He said, however, that he did not speak to the prisoners off the record at any time. Siakos asked Brennan if he had taken any notes while he spoke to the police. He said he had. Siakos was given the notes. He read them, and showed them to Sam and Sandro. The notes indicated that Brennan had been told that Hernandez had been interrogated intermittently by Mullaly, Tracy, Johnson, Jablonsky, Garcia, and others. No one had told Brennan, however, that pawnshop tickets had been taken from Hernandez, or that any goods had been found in the trunk of his car. Siakos had no further questions.

Sandro approached Brennan.

"Now, Mr. Brennan, you mentioned that Alvarado's eyes were watery and he was sniffling and holding his arms across his chest. Is that correct?"

"Yes."

"Did you ever see anyone cry?"

"Yes."

"And when you say his eyes were watery, were they similar to those of someone who had been crying?"

"No!"

Sandro hadn't really expected Brennan to cooperate.

"When you indicate they were different, in what way were his eyes different?"

"Well, he was sniffling and watery..."

"I am asking you about the eyes."

"His eyes were watery, but the water was not running down. It wasn't running down his cheek."

"No, but we are talking about the eyes. Were they watery in the same way they might have been had someone been crying, other than the fact that tears were not rolling down his cheeks?"

"Yes." Brennan was angry.

"And, sir, at those times when you have observed people crying, have you ever observed any of them also sniffling?"

"Yes."

"And have you ever observed simultaneous sniffling and crying?"

"Yes."

"Very fine. Now, the arms folded across the chest, where were they folded? Do you recall?"

"Right here." Brennan demonstrated.

"Around the middle of the chest?" Sandro asked.

"Yes."

"Also called the epigastrium?"

Reluctantly he said, "Yes."

Sandro just nodded.

"At this time, Your Honor, I am going to call upon the district attorney to turn over to defense counsel all photographs of these defendants, *in color* as well as in black and white. I have reason to believe

PART 35

that there are photographs available which have not as yet been shown to counsel."

Ellis looked at Sandro, then at the judge.

"Do you have any photographs, black and white, or color, which you have not yet shown to counsel, Mr. Ellis?"

Ellis rose. He began to untie a string on his cardboard file portfolio. He reached inside and removed an envelope. There *were* color photos!

"I am turning five color photographs over to counsel," said Ellis. He handed the pictures to Sandro.

"May we have a few moments to look at these, Your Honor?" asked Sandro.

"Yes. We'll take a short recess now while you look at those photographs. Do not discuss this case, members of the jury."

"Look at these, Sam," said Sandro. "Here's one of Alvarado that we can use." It was a side view. Alvarado was naked, shown from just above the knee to the top of his head. "Look at his wrist. There's the laceration on it in living color."

"And Ellis didn't even give us these before," said Sam.

"He's just protecting his case. Part of the game, right, Sam?"

Sam grunted.

When court resumed, Brennan was still on the witness chair. Sandro offered the color photo of Alvarado into evidence. It was received without objection from Ellis, except that a small square of white paper was stapled to the picture to cover Alvarado's genitalia.

"Now, Mr. Brennan, I show you this exhibit, defendant's exhibit triple B, which the district attorney failed to turn over to counsel before, and—"

"Mr. Luca," Judge Porta admonished, "no more speeches, please."

"Very well, Your Honor," Sandro returned his attention to the witness. "Do you recognize what this is a picture of?"

"Yes, of course. It's the defendant Alvarado."

"What is that mark that appears on the right wrist, on the underside."

Brennan studied the picture.

"Do you want the magnifying glass?" asked Sandro.

"No, that's not necessary. It looks like a scrape of some sort."

"It looks more like a laceration, doesn't it, Mr. Brennan?"

"I'm not an expert on medical things, as you know."

"Very well. May we show this photograph to the jury, Your Honor?"

"You may."

"One further question. Do you recall seeing this mark now that you see the picture?"

"No."

"I have no further questions."

No one had further questions of Brennan. The court officer handed the photograph to the jury as Brennan walked toward the witness room.

Ellis next called William John Cesar, the Puerto Rican police buff who had interpreted for Hernandez and the district attorney when Hernandez made his formal statement to Brennan. Cesar testified to his education, his ability to speak Spanish, and the correctness of his translation. Ellis had no further questions.

Siakos stood to cross-examine. He gave Cesar a whole string of words from Hernandez's statement for translation into Spanish. Cesar responded, although not a juror, nor the judge, nor the other counsel knew what he was talking about. He was shaking his head, talking to himself in Spanish as he wrote.

After this Spanish lesson, the court was recessed for lunch.

Sandro brought the defendants two pastrami sandwiches on rye and two pieces of chocolate cake. They smiled happily as they unwrapped their delicacies.

In the afternoon, Ellis called Detective Lawrence Reilly, who testified that he had interviewed Mrs. Hernandez on July 3rd, 1967, in the Seventh Precinct station house. He testified that she had spoken English to him and had said to him that she last saw Hernandez when she had left him at home at 8:30 A.M.

On cross-examination, Reilly told Siakos that he had used no interpreter, since Mrs. Hernandez spoke English clearly.

"Now that's a lie, out and out," Sandro whispered to Sam. "I've been with that woman plenty of times, and she couldn't communicate with me. I always had to have Mike as an interpreter, even for the simplest thing."

PART 35

Siakos had no further questions. There was nothing to question. It was only Reilly's oath of truth against Mrs. Hernandez's.

Ellis now called the name Angel Belmonte. The courtroom stirred. Hernandez watched Belmonte every step of the way up to the witness chair. Belmonte did not look at Hernandez. Ellis immediately started to develop Belmonte's criminal record, which was extensive.

Belmonte testified that he had *not* seen Hernandez at any time on July 3rd, 1967. He also testified that sometime after the shooting, in September, 1967, he had been arrested and, while detained in the Tombs, he met Hernandez, who then suggested that Belmonte be a favorable alibi witness for him in this trial. Belmonte said that he refused Hernandez because he didn't want to get caught in perjury and get five years. He said that Hernandez asked him to say that he, Hernandez, had been at Belmonte's home on July 3rd, at about 3 P.M.

Ellis went on to establish that Belmonte, at the moment, did not have any cases or charges pending against him. Belmonte testified he had been picked up by the police and brought to the D.A.'s office a few days ago, but he did not know the D.A., nor had the D.A. offered him any benefit for testifying. Ellis had no further questions.

Siakos launched an offensive of questions against Belmonte.

"Mr. Belmonte, are you married?"

"Yes."

"Legally married?"

"No."

"Where does your wife live?"

"I don't know. In New York somewheres."

"Does she live on welfare?"

"I don't know."

"How is she supported?"

"She's living with some guy, okay?"

"How about your children, Mr. Belmonte?"

"He supports them, too."

These were questions Sam or Sandro might never have asked; they were subjects too accusatory for proper cross-examination. But Siakos knew people like Belmonte and how they lived, and to them this was not accusation but a way of life.

Siakos inquired about Belmonte's criminal record. It ran from petty larceny at seventeen, to indecent exposure, narcotics on seven different occasions, and assault. He had been a junky for approximately seven years. Siakos badgered him, intentionally angered him.

"Have you ever worked with the police, helped them with information?"

"I don't understand you."

"Do you work with the police, help them in court?" Siakos insisted.

"You think I'm a stool pigeon?" Belmonte raged.

"I only want to know if you work with the police, so you can get consideration on your own record?"

"I ain't got no charges. I ain't no stoolie."

"I see that even with a record like this, you've received three suspended sentences, one quite recently. Was that because you're more valuable to the police out in the street?"

"I made no deals with nobody—nobody." Belmonte looked at Hernandez now.

Belmonte testified that he had worked honestly for four out of the twelve years since he had been in New York. He indicated that his narcotics habit, at its worst, cost him twenty dollars a day, or one hundred and forty dollars a week. He admitted that he had stolen to support the habit.

Siakos asked Belmonte if it weren't true that when he met Hernandez in prison, Hernandez had simply reminded him of their meeting on July 3rd.

"No."

"And isn't it true you refused to tell what happened on July third because you didn't want the D.A. to put you in prison for ten years as a narcotics pusher?"

"No."

Siakos asked him if he were aware that Hernandez had testified that he had bought heroin from Belmonte on July 3rd. Belmonte said it was a lie. He insisted he had told Hernandez that he would not perjure himself.

"And now you want this jury to believe that after you told Hernandez that you would not come to court to testify because you didn't want to commit perjury, Hernandez still came here, where he is on trial for his life, and told a false story despite the fact that you had warned him you wouldn't back him up?"

Ellis objected. The judge sustained the objection. It was improper surely, but it had its effect. Siakos had no further questions.

Belmonte walked off the stand. Hernandez glared at him. Belmonte did not look at Hernandez.

The next name Ellis called was Julio Maldonado. Sam looked at Sandro. Sandro shrugged. From the witness room came a Puerto Rican in his thirties. He looked around unfamiliarly. The court officer showed him to the witness chair.

"That's the barber's friend," Sandro exclaimed.

"That's great," replied Sam. "Let's hope he hasn't suddenly remembered too much."

Julio testified that he worked for the Board of Education of the City of New York. He was a cook in the lunchroom at Public School 17, and during the summer he took care of the kids whose mothers went to work. It was the neighborhood day-care center, and the kids spent their time in the school playground. He testified that he had been so employed by the city for eleven years. His working hours were 7:30 A.M. to 3:30 P.M. He testified that he knew the barber Francisco Moreno, and dropped into his shop very often to talk and kid around. He said he usually got there about 4 P.M.

Julio testified that July 3rd, 1967, was a workday like any other, and he didn't leave his job until 3:30 P.M. He said he did go to the barber shop, and he arrived there the usual time, about 4 P.M. He got a haircut that day.

"He remembers too much, all right," said Sam.

Sandro didn't turn or speak.

Julio testified, after Ellis had Alvarado stand up, that he didn't recognize Alvarado. He said Alvarado might have been in the barber shop, but he didn't remember him. He said no one gave him any money, nor did he let anyone take his turn to get a haircut.

Julio said that there was no doubt in his mind that he had left work at 3:30 P.M. on July 3rd, 1967.

Ellis had no further questions.

Sandro rose and walked to the jury box. Julio testified that he signed a time card every day when he started and when he finished work. He said he signed out on July 3rd at 3:30P.M. He testified that he signed the card by hand, that there was no time clock to punch or superior to sign him in or out. He said that at the end of each week, the school superintendent had to sign the completed card so he could be paid.

"Mr. Maldonado, if you did leave your job early on a particular day, say around two P.M., you could still write three thirty P.M. down on your time card, couldn't you?"

"But I don't do this."

"You *could* do it though, couldn't you?"

"Maybe so, but I don't do this."

"The superintendent isn't there to check you out each day, is he?"

"No."

"You sign yourself out, right?"

"That's right."

"And at the end of the week, when the superintendent signs your time card, he doesn't know for sure that you've really been there every hour, does he?"

"Sure he does."

"You mean he has to take your word for it. He has to rely on the time you filled in on your card."

"Right."

"Suppose, Mr. Maldonado, you had left your job early on July third, 1967, say around two P.M. and you put three thirty down on your time card instead, what would happen to your job if you admitted here in court that you put the wrong time on your card?"

"Objection, Your Honor."

"Sustained."

"Mr. Maldonado, if you put more time down on your card than you really worked, would you be fired?"

"I don't do this."

"If you did, would you be fired?"

"I believe so."

PART 35

"I have no further questions."

Ellis rose. "Mr. Maldonado, did you put the proper quitting time on your card on July third, 1967?"

"Yes, I do."

"What time was that?"

"Three thirty in the afternoon."

"No question in your mind?"

"No."

"No further questions."

Sandro rose. "Mr. Maldonado, you're employed by the City of New York, are you not?"

"Yes, sir."

"The same employer as the police?"

"Objection, Your Honor."

"If he knows, he may answer. Do you know, Mr. Maldonado?"

"I guess so," said Maldonado.

"No further questions."

Maldonado was excused. Ellis next called Edward Steinberger to the stand. Steinberger was in the controller's office of the Board of Education. He produced Maldonado's time card for July 3rd, 1967, and testified that it indicated Maldonado had left work at 3:30 P.M. Ellis offered the card into evidence. It was received. Ellis had no further questions.

Sandro asked Steinberger if he knew whether Maldonado had actually worked until 3:30 P.M. on July 3rd, 1967. Steinberger replied he knew only what was written on the card, that he worked in the office. He said Maldonado had been paid for a full day on July 3rd. Sandro had no further questions.

Ellis rested the people's rebuttal. The judge recessed the court until the morning.

"Not so strong today," said Sam.

"There's tomorrow, Sam. Tomorrow is our day."

"We'll need it."

CHAPTER XXXIV

SANDRO GOT ONTO THE DOWN ELEVATOR at the tenth floor. It was empty. After the court session, he had gone to the clerk's office to check a file, and he was now heading for the street and, ultimately, his office. The elevator stopped again on the sixth floor, one of the district attorney's floors. Mullaly stepped in.

"Good evening, Counselor." Mullaly smiled his aloof, cool smile.

"Hello, Detective Mullaly," Sandro replied.

Both men gazed forward, watching the numbers on the panel above the door light up as they descended.

"Guess we'll be winding up soon," Mullaly said.

"Finally. Another ten days of this, and they'd have to bury me."

"You really work, Counselor, I'll say that for you."

"From you, that's a compliment."

Mullaly's thin lips squeaked out a half-smile, half-snort.

The elevator door opened at the ground level. They made their way out to the street. The sun had already descended, and the Civil Court Building across the street was lighted up.

"Let me ask you this," said Mullaly. "As a lawyer, a man dedicated to the law, doesn't it bother you, even a little, trying to get these guilty crumbs off?"

"If that's what I was doing, it might."

"I mean, you're one of the people out in the street," Mullaly continued. "Some night when one of these niggers or spics comes up behind you to mug you, you think it's going to make a hell of a lot of difference to them that you're a lawyer who's always breaking his hump to get punks off and back into the street?"

"He'd probably roll me harder, thinking I had a lot of money."

"So, how come you do-gooders are always bleeding all over these punks? I don't understand it."

"The opposite of do-gooder, Mullaly, is do-badder. Should I be a do-badder instead?"

"Come on, you know what I mean. These punks go around abusing everybody, demonstrations, disrupting schools, and the Supreme Court is tying our hands so we can't even arrest anybody. Black bastards are getting away with murder. It wouldn't be so bad, if they were only murdering each other. And then you guys with the bleeding hearts go out and save them because they had three hundred tough years."

"Wait a minute, Mullaly, you've got me a little wrong. First of all, I'm not in this thing because one of these guys is black or white. I couldn't care less that Alvarado is Negro and has a rough three hundred years behind him, or that he's Puerto Rican, or any of that sort of thing. The only color they have, as far as I'm concerned, is prison pallor. I'm their lawyer, and while I am, I'll do my job. And that job, in case you don't know it, isn't getting them off."

"You sure could have fooled me, pal. What are you trying to do then? These guys are guilty. I was there. I saw Alvarado on his knees, crying, 'I did it, I did it.' You're trying to get a guilty guy off!"

They had now walked to the corner of Centre and Leonard Streets. The lights in the State Building were burning brightly, not for the workers—they had already departed—but for the cleaning crew.

"Apparently, what you don't understand is my function and probably your own function, Detective. You're a gatherer of evidence. You turn it over to the D.A. He's the prosecuting attorney, I'm the defense attorney."

"Thanks for the tour—"

"Let me finish," said Sandro.

"Let me ask you this, Counselor," Mullaly continued. "If you knew your guy was as guilty as sin, wouldn't you still try to get him off?"

"Yes."

Mullaly shrugged. "My conscience'd haunt me if I did that. I couldn't sleep at night."

"You keep using the phrase 'get him off.' I'm not trying to get anyone off. You know there's a great difference between being not guilty and being innocent?"

"What's the difference?" Mullaly asked.

"Innocent is where a man absolutely didn't do an act. He's innocent. Not guilty means only that under the law, a defendant hasn't been proven guilty. Even if he *did* do the act, he must be set free."

"That's what I mean, you want to get guilty crumbs off to roam the street."

"Look, Detective Mullaly, I'm not God, and whether you know it or not, neither is the D.A., nor are the men in Albany who make the laws. Once drinking was illegal, and a lot of people probably died in jail because they were guilty of breaking that law. Now, drinking is legal, and what a goddamn waste all the death and suffering about Prohibition was."

"Murder isn't ever going to be written off the books, believe me, pal."

"I believe you. And morally speaking, taking life is repugnant, evil. But the ingredients of murder under the Penal Code, the five elements, or four elements, were thought up by men. Maybe God has seventeen elements to determine guilt of murder, maybe only one. But while I'm in a courtroom, I'm going to make the D.A. prove every single facet of the elements required by the law. Suppose the defendant is guilty only of manslaughter. You want him punished for murder anyway?"

"I guess not," Mullaly allowed.

"Why not? Lives were taken in both instances. Who said they're different?"

"It's in the code."

"Who put it in the code?"

"In Albany, those fakers in Albany."

"And if they wrote into the law that several ingredients are necessary to make an act murder instead of manslaughter, what's wrong with my going in and fighting cheek to jowl to make them prove all of it?"

"You fight to get the guy off, that's the difference. You want the jury to go all the way with you."

"Can I do a half-ass job, with hounds like you and Ellis on my back? Are you doing half a job trying to convict the man of murder?"

"No, the guy is guilty."

"That's where you make your mistake, Detective. You think you're in a moral court, to punish for evil. You're not. I don't know if the man is guilty, nor does anyone else. And I'm talking about legal, not moral guilt. And the jury has to make that determination, not you, and not me. Don't you realize I'm as much a representative of the people as the D.A.?"

"Hey, Counselor, what are you giving me now, a flaming liberal snow job?"

"No, a little lesson in the law. In the adversary system, the D.A. brings in everything he can against the defendant. Defense counsel brings in everything he can in favor of the defendant. And when both lawyers are finished, it's up to the jury. Whatever the jury says—guilty, not guilty, murder, manslaughter—that's it. Not morally, but according to what we poor, dumb men have written into books. It's the best system we have. It may not be infallible in your eyes, but it's the best we've got."

"When it lets guilty crumbs out into the streets, it stinks."

"You know something, Mullaly. You're thickheaded. I'll go in and fight whether you think a man is guilty or not. My job is to make the D.A. go through his paces and prove what the law says he must. If he doesn't, he doesn't deserve to win his case. And don't worry about it. If there's a God in heaven, as I'm sure there must be somewhere, he really doesn't need your help. He'll give out perfect punishment someday, to everybody for everything."

Mullaly's face cooled with a smug smile. "You guys are really something."

"Oh, by the way, Detective Mullaly, talking about that conscience that wouldn't let you sleep—does it keep you up much when you go around screwing the wives of defendants?"

Mullaly's face uncurled its smile as he stared blankly after Sandro.

CHAPTER XXXV

Thursday, April 25th, 1968

"SAM," SANDRO SAID, walking into court excitedly. "You won't believe the phone call I just got from Siakos in the office."

"What was it?" Sam was unpacking his briefcase.

"Josefina Ramirez, the woman the guy ran past on the stairs?"

"What about her?"

"She called Siakos up. She wants to come back to court to testify."

"Let her tell it to Ellis. What's she going to do this time—identify Alvarado?"

"No, she says she wants to testify for us."

"What?" Sam stared at him. "What's she want to testify to."

"Alvarado was not the guy."

"Are you kidding me?"

"Not about something like that."

"Ellis'll go nuts. Where is she?"

"Siakos is bringing her here."

Sandro called Josefina Ramirez to the stand. Ellis turned his head quickly. His face grew stern when he saw Mrs. Ramirez enter the courtroom.

She took the stand and was informed through the interpreter that she was still under oath.

"Mrs. Ramirez," Sandro started. "Did you call Mr. Siakos and talk to him in Spanish?"

"Yes."

"And is that why you have returned to court today?"

"Yes."

"Now, on July third, 1967, the day the policeman was killed, did you tell the police that the man you saw on the stairs was dressed in a gray suit?"

"Yes."

"Pants and jacket matched?"

"Yes."

"Your Honor," said Ellis, rising. "This is repetitious."

"I am going into new matter, Your Honor. I just wanted to pick up the train of thought," said Sandro.

"Proceed."

"Did the police tell you the man was wearing a yellow jacket?"

"I didn't tell them that."

"But did they tell you that the man from the roof was not wearing a gray suit?"

"They told me he was wearing a different color."

"How did they tell you the man was dressed?"

"I think it was yellow pants. No—yellow jacket and black pants. But he was not dressed like that."

"Did you see the defendant Alvarado in the station house on the early morning of July fourth?"

"Yes, the police brought me there, and I told them that I did not recognize that man."

"Your Honor, may I have the defendant Alvarado come closer to the witness?" Sandro asked.

"You may."

Alvarado rose, and the guard accompanied him toward the witness stand. He stood directly before Mrs. Ramirez.

"Mrs. Ramirez, look at this man. Is this the man you saw on the stairway on July third?"

"No, sir. That's not the man I saw running. No."

The jurors were looking at one another. A whisper swept through the spectators.

PART 35

"Any further questions of this witness?" the judge asked.

"No, Your Honor."

"Any questions, Mr. Ellis?"

"Your Honor, in view of the unusual aspect of this last witness's appearance here this morning, I'd like a recess for a short while."

"Your application is granted," said the judge. "Members of the jury, we'll have a recess at this time. Do not discuss the case."

The jury filed out. Ellis had not waited for them to leave. He had already left the courtroom, his face etched with anger.

The recess ended, Ellis, cold and as hard as steel, faced Mrs. Ramirez.

"Mrs. Ramirez, when you appeared here before at this trial, did you not testify that you did not get a good look at the man on the stairs?" Ellis asked.

"Objection, Your Honor. Mr. Ellis is trying to impeach his own witness," said Sam. "Mrs. Ramirez is still the prosecution's witness."

"Not anymore," Ellis said.

"Overruled."

"That's true. I cannot tell you exactly what the man looked like, but this is not the man. No. No," insisted Mrs. Ramirez.

"Did you not describe the man you saw to the court, the last time, as a colored man with pushed-back hair?"

"He's not colored!" she said, pointing to Alvarado.

Ellis looked around at Alvarado. He studied him. The Negro guard behind Alvarado, whose skin was lighter than Alvarado's, was leaning forward to get a better look.

"You say the defendant Alvarado is not colored?" Ellis wondered. "How would you describe him?"

"He's white, like I am," said Mrs. Ramirez.

Ellis stared blankly at Mrs. Ramirez, his mind totally stalled. Mrs. Ramirez was white. Alvarado was almost black.

"Are you now telling this court and jury that the defendant Alvarado is not the man you saw, even though you don't know what the man looked like?" Ellis asked, starting forward again.

"This man is Puerto Rican. The other man on the stairs was colored. The other man had the 'bad' hair. I can't tell what the colored man looked like, but this cannot be that man."

"Did the lawyers for Alvarado call you after you were in court the last time?"

"No, I called. I wanted to be sure my conscience would not bother me. I may not have said the things right. These people should know," she said, pointing to the jury.

"You were at the station house the night of the shooting, weren't you?"

"Yes."

"And didn't you see the defendant Alvarado there at that time?"

"Yes. The police showed him to me through a glass."

"Do you remember there were other women in the station house at that time?"

"Yes, I remember."

"And do you remember a woman there named Carmen Salerno, a short, young woman?" Ellis asked.

"I don't know the name. I don't know," Mrs. Ramirez replied, shrugging.

"As a matter of fact, when you saw this defendant Alvarado in the station house the morning of July fourth, did you not tell one of those women at the station house that you recognized Alvarado as the man you saw running down the steps, but you wouldn't tell the police that?"

"No, sir, I never said that to anyone."

Sam whispered, "You can bet your ass he's got Mrs. Salerno ready to swear up and down to that."

"Ellis must have had one of the detectives go and get her during the recess."

"Do you remember coming into my office about a month ago, Mrs. Ramirez?" Ellis continued.

"Yes."

"And I showed you a picture of Alvarado?"

"Yes. You showed me a picture of this gentleman," the interpreter translated.

"And did I ask you if you could recognize that man as the man who ran past you on the stairway on July third?"

"No, that is not the man," she replied.

PART 35

"I move that the answer be stricken as not responsive."

"Strike it out," the judge ordered.

"Ellis is going deeper and deeper into the hole," Sandro whispered, watching intently.

"And did you not at the time tell me that you did not see the man well enough to recognize him?" Ellis asked.

"I couldn't tell from the photograph. But seeing the man now, in person, I know he is not the man!"

"I move that that answer be stricken as not responsive. I ask Your Honor to instruct the witness to answer the questions asked."

"Yes. Please tell Mrs. Ramirez to answer only the questions asked," the judge told the interpreter. She complied.

"Did you not say in my office that you didn't know what the man who ran past you looked like?" Ellis pressed.

"It is true. I cannot say what the man looked like, but I can say that this could not be the man."

"Did you say that in my office?"

"Yes. I said that the man in the photograph does not look like the man."

"After you testified the last time, did anyone, a friend or relative of the defendants, speak to you concerning this case?"

"No, no. I talked only to my conscience."

"No further questions," Ellis said with control. His anger was strangling him.

"Anything further, gentlemen?" the judge asked Sam and Sandro.

"No, if Your Honor please. The defendant Alvarado rests."

"Do you have anything further, Mr. Ellis?"

"Yes, Your Honor, the people recall Mrs. Carmen Salerno."

Mrs. Salerno came into the courtroom, her face as unemotional as ever. She took the witness stand and was advised that she was still under oath.

"Mrs. Salerno, do you remember being in the station house of the Seventh Precinct on the morning of July fourth, 1967?"

"Yeah."

"And when you were in the precinct, where were you?"

"Upstairs," she answered.

"Is that the detectives' room, the squad room?"

"That's right."

"And were you standing or seated?"

"Sitting down."

"Did you see the defendant Alvarado?"

"When I walked in, I seen him."

"Where was he?" Ellis asked.

"He was sitting in a chair in the room there."

"Did there come a time when someone else came in and sat down near you?"

"Yes," Mrs. Salerno replied. "A woman came in."

"Do you know that woman's name?"

"Ramirez, Josefina Ramirez."

"Where was she sitting?"

"Right next to me."

"Did she say anything to you?"

"Objection."

"Overruled. You may answer, Mrs. Salerno," the judge instructed.

"She told me in Spanish that that was the guy that she saw, but she wasn't going to say anything because she was afraid," Mrs. Salerno testified.

"Did you thereafter look at the defendant Alvarado through a mirror?"

"Yes."

"And did Mrs. Ramirez look through that same mirror?"

"She was standing right next to me."

"And did she say anything to the police at that time?" Ellis asked.

"She told them she wasn't sure if it was the man."

"Did you, some weeks ago, come to my office with a policeman?"

"Yes."

"And was anyone else with you?"

"Yeah. Detective Mullaly brought Mrs. Ramirez and me in his car down here together."

"You were in the room with Mrs. Ramirez when I spoke to her?" Ellis asked.

"Yes."

"And did she say at any time, after looking at a photograph of the defendant Alvarado, that he was not the man on the stairs?"

"No."

"I have no further questions." Ellis returned to his chair.

Sandro rose slowly and walked to the jury box.

"Mrs. Salerno, when you were in the station house the early morning of July fourth, you spoke to the district attorney there, didn't you?"

"Yes."

"And you told him certain things, didn't you?"

"That's right."

"And at that time, you didn't want to get involved, did you?"

"That's right." She was snapping her answers, curt and fast.

"And although you didn't want to get involved, you described an entire incident, didn't you?"

"I don't know what you mean."

"You told the D.A. what the man allegedly wore, didn't you?" Sandro asked.

"Yeah."

"And what he did, how he moved?"

"Yeah."

"And you told him that you didn't see the man's face well?"

"That's right. I lied," Mrs. Salerno said spitefully.

"And you lied to the police too, didn't you?"

"That's right."

"You also told them you didn't see the man's face?"

"That's right."

"And you lied to me, too, didn't you?"

"I didn't have to say nothing to you, did I?"

"Mrs. Salerno, when I'm on the witness chair, and you're down here, I'll answer your questions. Would you mind answering my questions now."

"Objection, Your Honor."

"Yes, Mr. Luca, I'll run the courtroom," Judge Porta intoned mildly. "Proceed."

"Mrs. Salerno, you lied to me, did you not?"

"Yeah, you too."

"Did Mrs. Ramirez ever say to anyone else that Alvarado was the man she saw?" Sandro asked.

"No."

"She told the police she wasn't sure, didn't she? And she said the same thing to the district attorney?"

"Yeah."

"And the only time, you say, that Mrs. Ramirez said to you that Alvarado was the man on the stairs was when you two were alone. No one else heard?"

"That's right."

"And this jury has only your word for that?"

"I ain't lyin'!"

"No further questions, Your Honor," Sandro said. He turned back to the counsel table.

"The people rest, if Your Honor please," Ellis said, rising.

"Both sides rest?" the judge asked.

Sam looked at Sandro, brows upraised.

"That's all there is. There ain't no more," Sandro murmured.

"The defendant Alvarado rests, Your Honor," said Sam.

"The defendant Hernandez rests," said Siakos.

"Very well. Ladies and gentlemen, we will have summations tomorrow morning. I want you here promptly at nine forty-five. The lawyers and I have some legal business to take care of now, so I'll excuse you at this time. Do not discuss this case."

The jury began to file out. When they were gone, Siakos first, then Sam, made several motions to dismiss the indictment on grounds of legal insufficiencies and judicial errors. The judge denied the motions and directed all the attorneys to be prepared to sum up in the morning.

"How long will you require, Mr. Bemer?"

"Mr. Luca is going to sum up for the defendant Alvarado, if Your Honor please." Sam turned toward Sandro and winked. Sandro took a quick breath.

"Very well. Mr. Luca?" The judge's eyes were smiling.

Sandro hesitated a moment. "Two hours, if Your Honor please."

The judge nodded. "Mr. Siakos?"

PART 35

"The same, Your Honor."

"Mr. Ellis?"

"I'll require about the same, Judge," said Ellis.

"Very well. Tomorrow at nine forty-five. Good day, gentlemen." The judge left the courtroom.

CHAPTER XXXVI

Friday, April 26th, 1968, A.M.

ELLIS WAS SITTING, drumming his fingers on the prosecution counsel table. Siakos, Sam, and Sandro sat at their table. Sandro was reading some notes. Alvarado and Hernandez were in their places, staring straight ahead; the guards behind them were talking about a pay raise. Sandro looked around. The courtroom was crowded. The buffs, a number of the witnesses, many of the policemen who had been on the case, including Mullaly, all were out there.

"Put it all together for the jury, Sandro," said Sam. "And anticipate Ellis. We won't get another chance to answer him."

"Don't worry, Sam. It's all together."

The judge was announced. The jurors filed in and took their places. They sat gazing about, ready to listen, needing to be romanced, swayed, convinced.

"You may proceed, Mr. Luca," the judge said.

Sandro stood and walked to the jury box, facing the jurors. He put his notes before him on the shelf.

"If it please this honorable court, Mr. Ellis, Mr. Siakos, Mr. Bemer, Mr. Hernandez, Mr. Alvarado, Mr. foreman, ladies and gentlemen of the jury. As you know, this part of the trial is called the summation. It is not a preview of what is to come, as the opening was, but a recapitulation of what has passed before you during the trial."

The jurors were all solemn, most of them looking straight ahead, not at Sandro.

"I am not going to try to persuade you, to sway you with fiery oratory, as some of you might have anticipated from courtroom dramas in the movies or on television. Rather, I am going to attempt merely to highlight some of the facts, the evidence in this case. And it is upon those facts, without prejudice or sympathy, that you must decide this case.

"Before I go into those facts, however, I'd like to extend my appreciation to you on behalf of the defendant Alvarado for your patience and attention during this long and sometimes tedious trial.

"My summation is not part of the evidence. Nor is anything the district attorney says, nor anything the court says. And if anything I say disagrees with your recollection of the evidence, just forget what I say, throw it away as if I had never spoken. The same goes for what the district attorney says, or what the judge says. For you, the jury, are the exclusive judges of the facts, just as His Honor is the exclusive judge of the law in this case. And so it is your recollection of the evidence that must reign here, that is supreme here. If there are parts of the testimony or the evidence that you wish to have read again, to refresh your recollection, I am sure the judge will accommodate you."

The majority of the jurors were still gazing calmly ahead, looking at Sandro occasionally. Sandro moved to the far end of the jury box now, near the alternates.

"In this role as the exclusive judges of the facts, you are, each of you, shortly to assume a role similar to that of the ancient kings, whose word was law, who decided questions of life or death."

"Now, Your Honor," Ellis said, rising. "I hate to interrupt a summation, but the intrusion of the concept of death has no place in this trial. It is totally improper. This jury has nothing whatever to do with death penalties or punishment."

Sandro had hoped Ellis would leap to the bait. He wanted the thought of the death penalty planted firmly in the jurors' minds.

"Yes, Mr. Luca, do not get involved in matters not in issue," said the judge.

"Very well, Your Honor. Ladies and gentlemen, as you were informed when you were picked as jurors, there may be what seem discrepancies in the law. Now, none of you, of course, would be sitting here today if you had any moral scruples against capital punishment in the proper case—I emphasize that, in the proper case. Yet I am not allowed to mention death penalties.

"Murder, the taking of human life, is the supreme human' passion. And to be a part of a jury to determine questions relating to murder is a supreme responsibility. I, too, *had* a responsibility—had, past tense. For with each word that I utter, my responsibility here decreases and, in direct proportion, yours increases. And soon my task shall be completed, and you will have the full responsibility of fulfilling your oaths as jurors to try the issues here well and truly.

"Now, the district attorney will tell you that he represents the people of the State of New York. And so he does. But my mandate from the selfsame people of the State of New York is no less clear and no less powerful than his. Our system of law, called the adversary system, requires that a lawyer representing one side gather all the information he possibly can to support his position, and that a lawyer on the opposite side gather all the information he possibly can to support the opposite position. And when all this information has been brought forth, at a trial, in the form of legal evidence, the jury becomes the scale upon which that evidence is weighed.

"Now the people of this state in their majesty and wisdom demand that a person charged with a crime have the strongest and boldest defense possible, just as the people want the boldest and ablest possible prosecution, so that truth may be discovered and there will be no miscarriage of justice rendered in the name of the people. Mr. Bemer and I have been appointed by the Supreme Court of this state, therefore, to represent not merely the defendant Alvarado but, more important, the people, just as truly as Mr. Ellis represents the people.

"The result of this trial, either conviction or acquittal, is immaterial to the people of the State of New York, for the people and the district attorney are victorious not when a man is convicted, not when one of their citizens goes to jail, but when justice is done. Even an acquittal, if it is just and true, is a victory for the people. And that is what your oath requires of you—justice, truth, not conviction, not even acquittal.

"And the people of the state again in their majesty and wisdom have legislated that the district attorney must prove all the elements of the crime charged to your satisfaction *beyond a reasonable doubt* or there can be no conviction. Reasonable doubt. There's a common phrase you've heard hundreds of times. Idle words before, perhaps, but they are not idle words here. The defendant needn't say a word in his own defense. Rather, the defendant is cloaked in a mantle—he is presumed to be as innocent of this crime as you are. And that mantle of presumed innocence cannot be taken from him until and only until the district attorney can remove from your minds *all* reasonable doubt about *all* the elements of the crimes charged.

"Remember, you do not have to be convinced that the defendant is innocent beyond a reasonable doubt. You are required under your oath to pronounce the word guilty *only* if you are convinced beyond *all* reasonable doubt that he is guilty of *all* elements of the crime. Anything short of that, whatever suspicions you might harbor, *requires* an acquittal."

Sandro kept his delivery slow, suiting it to the solemnity of his words.

"To do otherwise would be a violation of your oath; it would be a violation of your sacred duty. You would be doing something the people neither want nor appreciate."

His eyes scanned the jury. That got through, thought Sandro, as he strode slowly toward the number four juror, the shoe company man who had marched to Washington. They were watching him now.

"I am not going to explain to you what reasonable doubt is. That's the judge's province. But so that we have a basis for speaking, reasonable doubt is doubt which is based on reason. Easy! It is a doubt for which you can point to a reason. I *don't believe the witness; there's not enough proof.* Those are reasons. And they don't have to be Einstein's reasons, but your reasons. What makes sense to you counts here.

"The court will advise you what the elements of the crimes are, and, however many of them there are, the district attorney must remove all reasonable doubt from your minds about each and every one of them, or he has failed in his burden of proof. And you would be required to acquit."

Sandro wanted to get into the meat and potatoes before the jurors' attention waned. He still had them looking. He walked toward the foreman, Richard Haverly, the advertising man they had battled to get so many weeks ago. All eyes followed Sandro.

"Now, just what evidence did Mr. Ellis present here to convince you beyond a doubt that the defendant Alvarado committed this crime?

"There was Mrs. Santos. Mrs. Santos who just happened to be everywhere, to see everything. On the stoop she saw the car and the defendants. Inside the hallway coming out of the toilet closet, she saw Hernandez. In her child's room, looking out the window, she saw Alvarado. She saw just everywhere, and she saw . . . Well, you heard what she saw. On the stoop, five months pregnant, in the rain, bending over, her head turned toward the *bodega* to look for her girl friend, she saw men in a car. She didn't know what they were doing. Couldn't tell if they were looking at her, or up, down, around. Or if they were talking. But she said she saw the defendants. Even saw their eyes were open. Through the rain, through the wet windshield of a car ninety feet away. Then in the hallway she saw Hernandez going up the stairs. She could see Hernandez on a stairway where a camera couldn't photograph a person. Here's the picture," said Sandro, raising the picture to the jury. "Here's the hallway, here's a hand, but where's the body of the person who belongs to that hand? It isn't there because a person on that stairway can't be seen from where Mrs. Santos was. And she told us where she was. She put an 'X' on another photograph showing where she was. She stood at the very spot where the photographer took this picture of a hand. And all of you stood there yourselves and saw what she could see.

"And then she was in the bedroom, looking out the window, seeing Alvarado standing on the fire escape—remember the position—standing, looking at her, face-to-face level. Remember that motion I made with my arm. Face-to-face level."

Sandro was warm now and he was starting to move.

"And for how long did she see this man? For the snap of a finger. Remember that, for the snap of a finger, face-to-face level. And I

PART 35

asked, 'Mrs. Santos, where was that fire escape outside your window? Did it start at the floor level of your apartment?' And then Mrs. Santos thought, and then she remembered that the fire escape started at the windowsill, three feet above the floor on which she stood. And the man *standing* on the fire escape couldn't be face-to-face level with her. 'Oh, he was higher,' she recalled. 'You mean, not face-to-face level?' 'No, now that I think of it, he was higher.' 'How much higher?' 'I don't know.' 'Four inches?' 'I don't know.' 'Two feet?' 'I don't know.' 'Ten feet?' 'I don't know.'

"And remember how accurate Mrs. Santos's testimony was about the car that was double-parked? One day she testified it was parked on the south side of the street. Remember, Mr. Siakos questioned her carefully about that. The next day, when she returned, the car had moved to the north side of the street. Just a slight mistake, just a slight error in recollection.

"And remember the accuracy of this witness in describing that door to the toilet closet. She insisted that it opened from the back of the hallway toward the front. If it had, it would have blocked her view of the front hallway completely. And we showed her the picture, showing her that it opened just the opposite way. And even after she saw the picture, she insisted it opened the other way. Even looking at what was there, the physical facts, she didn't know what she was looking at. And it wasn't almost a year later, either. But at that moment, as she was looking at the photograph, she couldn't testify about what she was looking at. And you were there. You saw it for yourselves."

Juror number seven, the bearded music teacher, was nodding agreement. Sandro wanted them all. He was going to get them all.

"And didn't Mrs. Santos tell the police on the day of the murder and for many days thereafter that she knew nothing about the killing, had no knowledge of it whatever? She told them day after day. After that, she moved to another building. And one day, just before this trial started, someone came to her and told her they wanted her to tell her story to the jury. What story? She had told the police she didn't know anything! Who wanted, needed, this fascinating information of hers?"

Sandro moved toward the foreman of the jury slowly.

"Or was it that Mrs. Santos was an easy prey because she blames the ones responsible for the death of the policeman, somehow, for the death of the child she was carrying at the time. Someone, perhaps some policeman, in need of a witness, convinced this woman of simple memory that these were the terrible fellows who committed this crime." Sandro pointed at the defendants. "And she believed them. Weren't they the police? Shouldn't they know?

"But we're not here to convict on what someone said to Mrs. Santos. That's not evidence. Only what Mrs. Santos said to you, what she testified to, is. And did she convince you beyond a reasonable doubt that Alvarado committed this crime?

"Let me ask it this way." Sandro's voice grew soft. He leaned toward the jurors. "You have an important financial decision to make. You have to decide whether to invest, say, ten thousand dollars of your hard-earned money to buy a business."

Sandro's eyes picked out the import-export executive, Magnusson, and the textiles man, Apfel.

"And a woman came along and gave you information about that business you were going to buy. And the woman was Mrs. Santos. And she was telling you all about this marvelous business she was selling you"—his eyes caught the salesmen's—"and she described where the property was that she was selling. But you found out that the property was really across the street from where she said it was." He looked at Hanrahan, the ex-newsman. "And then she described how some of the machinery operated. But you found that it was physically impossible for that machinery to operate the way she said." Sandro looked straight at the young telephone repairman, Arthur Youngerman, whose attention he knew he had at this point. "And then she told you about one product and just how it looked after it was off the assembly line. And then you found out that it didn't look like that at all. Tell me, on the basis of that information, would you invest your money? Don't tell your neighbor. It's not his vote I'm talking about. It's yours."

Sandro moved toward the middle of the jury. They knew they wouldn't sink ten thousand dollars into that business.

"Would you invest? Would you be convinced beyond a reasonable doubt that this was a good risk? I'm not asking you to take a flyer." Sandro's voice rang out now. "You have sworn to go into the business

PART 35

on your solemn oath *only* if you are convinced, *beyond* a reasonable doubt, that it's a good investment."

Sandro's voice grew soft again. "Is it? Would you plunk down ten thousand of your bucks? If you wouldn't, you can't vote to convict the defendants on Mrs. Santos's information. If you had to be convinced beyond a reasonable doubt, would you even hang a dog on that testimony? Be honest. Would you?"

Sandro walked to the end of the jury box, returning the stare of the jurors. He had them thinking now.

"And then Mr. Ellis presented Mrs. Salerno to convince you beyond a reasonable doubt. Mrs. Salerno, who only lied to the police, lied to the district attorney, lied to me, and then came in here to say that she was telling *you* the truth. How do you know? I wonder. It's the same mouth that's told so many stories, that admitted she'd lied to protect herself when she said she didn't want to get involved.

"Mrs. Salerno was so worried about being involved, about being bothered by the police, that she described the entire event, even down to the clothing of the person on the fire escape. And remember that clothing, we'll come across that again in a moment. Yellow jacket and black pants, she said the fellow wore. And she told the police that *she didn't see the man's face.* And that's the way it was! She couldn't see the man's face. We brought in pictures of the same fire escape on which she said she saw the man, and she looked at the picture and said, 'This looks like it, except *those things* weren't on the fire escape when I was looking up.' Here's the picture," Sandro said, holding up the photograph.

"Sure those things weren't there. Those *things* were the feet of a man standing on that fire escape, and that's how a man appears if you're beneath him and you're looking up through the slats of that fire escape. That's why she told the police that she didn't see the man's face! She couldn't!

"But, oh, now Mrs. Salerno said the man looked over the rail right down at her. He looked over the rail, saw a woman looking back up at him. Then, suddenly, she disappeared, and the burglar turned back and calmly continued to break into the apartment, without a care that the woman who had been looking up might, just might be calling the police."

Sandro was picking up the tempo.

"But there's one thing more about that fellow leaning over the rail. He'd be in silhouette. He'd be in dark profile against the uninterrupted backdrop of sky, and Mrs. Salerno wouldn't be able to see the man, not a dark shadow of a dark Negro two stories above her.

"And did you wonder about the weather? Mrs. Salerno testified that the sun was coming out and going in all day. But that's not what the Weather Bureau says. It was raining all day, according to the United States Weather Bureau. You know why Mrs. Salerno testified to that? Well, did you ever try looking directly up into rain? What happens? Of course. Your eyes close when drops come down into them. And you can't see when your eyes are closed, can you?"

The woman in the number three jury seat, the widow of the railroad man, nodded.

"Well, we now have another witness who can see the impossible. But the impossible is not unusual here. It had better not be, for Mr. Ellis's sake. In order to convict the defendant Alvarado you're going to have to accept an awful lot of impossible things.

"Just before we leave Mrs. Salerno, that paragon of veracity, should we wonder if she was prompted to come here because she's on relief, because her husband is a junky, and he's spent about twenty of their twenty-four married months in jail? Do you think it too harsh of us to think that Mrs. Salerno might lie to protect her family, her husband?"—Sandro's eyes sought out the civil service employees from the post office and the housing authority; they were the two black jurors, and they'd know—"Do you think that such a thought could even be contemplated by such a fine lady? Well, of course it could! She already told us she lied to everyone under the sun to protect herself!

"Would you invest in that business we were talking about, not just gamble, would you be convinced beyond a reasonable doubt about every element of that business now that we've the added assurance of a woman who lied to one of your partners about that business, lied to another of your partners, told again another lie to a third partner, although she assures you that to you, to you now, because she just happens to like you, to you she's telling the absolute truth?" Sandro's voice grew soft again. "Oh, you also just happen to find out that if you buy this business, Mrs. Salerno's husband won't go to jail, they won't lose their welfare income.

"Are you convinced beyond a reasonable doubt? Remember, you can't gamble or take a chance here.

"Well, to buttress all of this marvelous testimony, you have several policemen, especially Detective Thomas Mullaly, who came here and gave you an exhibition of magic the likes of which has hardly ever been seen . . . outside of a circus.

"May I say that if ever you need any repairs or any carpentry done around your house, you should call Detective Thomas Mullaly."

Sandro turned and pointed at Mullaly sitting among the spectators. Mullaly stared back coldly.

"There he is. Give him a call, because he is probably the fastest carpenter you've ever seen. Didn't he erect a fence for you, right here, in front of your eyes—a ten- or twelve-foot fence, made of heavy horizontal planking? Yes, indeed.

"Of course, Roosevelt Jackson, the superintendent in the buildings behind which the fence was supposed to stand, said there was no fence. But that's no problem for the talented Detective Mullaly. He'll whip one up for you lickety-split."

Juror number ten, the letter carrier Clarence Noble, was smiling.

"Another impossible thing, a fence that wasn't there, and suddenly it was there. Or at least you'd have to believe it was there in order to accept the alleged confession to hiding in the yard.

"And what did the police testify to in order to remove all reasonable doubt that Alvarado committed this crime. They told you that Alvarado was brought into the station house about one thirty in the morning. I won't go into Hernandez's story, or any of the facts that relate to Hernandez. Mr. Siakos will do that for you.

"But let's go back just a little, after Hernandez allegedly named Alvarado. Where were the police between, say six and nine P.M.? They knew Alvarado's first name. Hernandez said he could point out the house. Did the police waste a drop of gas, a dime for the phone, to apprehend this killer in Brooklyn? No! Why not? Hernandez said he knew the house! Was it that they really hadn't finished torturing the defendant Hernandez by that time, they hadn't beaten it out of him?

The police want it to seem that Hernandez's confession was voluntary, easy, fast. That's why Hernandez's chest was strapped with adhesive tape from top to bottom. All that voluntary talking wore out his chest.

"Well, when Alvarado did finally arrive home, that desperate killer, the police didn't even know he was there until he walked out of Jorge's apartment and into the street, holding a loud conversation in Spanish. He walked into their arms to face them, because, he testified, he had nothing to hide. He could have run away. They didn't know he had arrived, and he could have left still unknown to them.

"And they took him to the station house, and of course they didn't lay a finger on him. It was a very nice conversation, a social *chat*." Sandro fired a look at Mullaly.

"Well, before you accept that alleged confession, you have to look at three things: one, the confession was totally inaccurate, a hasty concoction that could have been thrown together by high-school boys; two, Alvarado told the district attorney, the first person he saw after the police, and the newscaster, the second person he saw after the police, that he didn't do it; and, three, for a guy who wasn't beaten, Alvarado had to simulate the best unconscious seizure in medical history.

"Wait a minute," said Sandro, whispering now, "did Dr. Maish say Alvarado was unconscious? He *was* unconscious, wasn't he?" Sandro looked to the foreman, to the ex-fighter, to the ex-GI. "Why, that would mean that Alvarado wasn't faking it, that he really had a seizure. But how did that happen?

"Let's ask the doctors, not the police, not Alvarado. Doctors. And the first doctor tells you that narcotics or the lack of them couldn't have caused the seizure. The next doctor says a beating is the most logical explanation for Alvarado's seizure.

"And did you see Mr. Ellis knocking down the door with any other explanation for the seizure. Did Mr. Ellis justify, account for that seizure? The pages of medical testimony on behalf of the people in this case are hopelessly blank.

"No suspect had ever been questioned in that third-floor locker room before. But then, this night, it was so crowded in the station house that there wasn't any room to interview Alvarado, except in that third-floor locker room. Of course, the lieutenant was alone in his office, and Hernandez was *alone* in the clerical office when Alvarado was brought in. And there wasn't room to interrogate the chief suspect and object of all the work being done in the station house? Is that what they're telling us? There wasn't room? No one ever thought of moving Hernandez. The lieutenant was too busy to move. He was working on this case. Now what more important work do you think there might be on this case than interviewing Alvarado, the accused killer? And the police tell you they didn't bring Alvarado to that third floor to work him over. Like a Greek chorus they come in, one after the other, and tell you Alvarado's interview was very calm, very voluntary.

"Of course, Detective Tracy put his foot in his mouth here a couple of times because his original reports, filed on July third and fourth, 1967, came back to haunt him. The only efficient cop here, the only one who bothered to file correct reports, wound up choking on them, because the other cops decided to change this whole story, including the alleged confession, in order to convict the defendants.

"You say that that's not possible. That the police wouldn't strip a man of his rights so brazenly? Well, what happened right here in this court, before your very eyes, when the defendant Alvarado got on the stand to testify. Was his dignity not stripped from him? Mr. Ellis didn't address the defendant Alvarado as he did everyone else— Mister so and so, Detective such and such, Officer, Doctor, Mrs. No. For Alvarado, it was Alvarado. Hey you, Alvarado. Why not just call him boy?" Sandro gave a quick glance to Roscoe Anderson to see how that sat. "And that was done inadvertently by a district attorney in this temple of justice. Just imagine how much dignity, what rights were reserved for the defendant Alvarado by the police in that third-floor locker room. Just imagine.

"In their haste to solve this crime, as Mr. Bemer told you in his opening statement, the police picked Alvarado to be the dupe. They forced upon him a confession the details of which they hadn't quite figured out, a confession their own laboratory was going to show to be a lie.

"Alvarado allegedly confessed, early on the morning of July fourth, that he had jimmied open the Soto apartment door. But the door was not jimmied open, the police lab men reported. Three or four days after the formal statement was made to the D.A., on paper, the cops found out that their theory of the break-in was wrong. But it was too late then. Too late. And you're being asked to accept a man's confession to jimmying open a door that in fact *wasn't* jimmied.

"Is this convincing you beyond a reasonable doubt? Doesn't it give you a moment of pause? How could there be a valid confession by the man who was there that he jimmied open a door when the door wasn't jimmied? Remember, I said I'd just go over the facts, and you decide. Well, these are facts, not my facts. Police laboratory facts.

"Let's go further then. The district attorney brought Mrs. Ramirez here to testify. And she testified that a man in a gray suit ran past her holding something in his hand. That was to bolster the alleged confession that Alvarado ran past a woman and child. What was that?" Sandro whispered. "*A gray suit?* Not a yellow jacket and black pants? But Mrs. Salerno said the fellow had a yellow jacket and black pants.

"Aha, this fellow Alvarado is tricky. As he was running across the roofs, he changed clothes just to fool people. Like Clark Kent turning into Superman, he changed from his yellow jacket into his gray suit as he ran down the stairs.

"But listen to this. Even better. Mrs. Ramirez, the people's own witness, the woman who was to bolster the alleged confession, came back here and told you that Alvarado *is definitely not the man she saw running down the stairs*. She can't describe the man who ran past her exactly, can't tell you what he did look like. But she knows that Alvarado *isn't* the man.

"Do you think that could mean that Alvarado was *not the man who was there?*"

Sandro felt a soaring sensation. His voice, his words, his movements embraced, caressed the jury. Their eyes followed his every gesture. The weeks and months of investigation and trial were caught up in these moments. Everything was together now.

"And this fellow, who is running and changing his clothes as he runs, does something to top it all off. He changes his face so that Mrs. Ramirez sees a man completely different from Alvarado.

"Now," Sandro asked, looking directly at the Italian insurance salesman, juror number six. "Wasn't that a good trick?" Sandro addressed

PART 35

Clarence Noble, number ten. "Aren't you maybe, just maybe, a bit confused? Doubtful? You're not alone.

"You know this would be a joke if a man's life weren't at stake."

"Your Honor," Ellis said, rising from his chair to take the bait. "I hate to object, but this reference to life or death is improper."

"All right, Your Honor. I withdraw that last remark. Ladies and gentlemen of the jury, Alvarado's life is not at stake here."

"Your Honor, this is totally improper."

"Yes, Mr. Luca, please refrain from that."

Sandro paced slowly before the jury box; sixteen pairs of eyes followed him as if he were a swaying cobra preparing to strike.

"Are we being insulted here? Is this one of the guys from the office playing a trick on us?

"Alvarado confessed? He wasn't beaten? Well, let's see what he said to the D.A. And, remember, this is the first person he spoke to other than the police. 'They're going to break my ass over here.' I said those things, but they're lies.' I told them because I was afraid.' 'You don't know what happens with those kind of people there.' Terror, ladies and gentlemen, sheer, undisguised terror leaps off the pages." Sandro held up the question-and-answer statement. 'I put this in evidence so you could read it. I had to put their confession into evidence. Just as I had to put in their lab reports, their fingerprint reports. Facts. That's what we're after. And the truth is going to set Alvarado free.

"He said he was afraid. He said he couldn't hold his chest any more. And he said that his wrist was cut from the handcuffs. And he showed it to the district attorney! Of course, the district attorney never saw anything on this wrist. Not until we demanded, *we demanded*, the additional color photographs that hadn't been given to defense counsel. And, lo and behold, the scar that never was appeared. Another impossible thing accomplished by the extraordinary Alvarado. A picture showing a scar that didn't exist. This Alvarado can even play games with the police cameras. Or at least that's what you would have to believe in order to convict him.

"Now, there were other people who came here," Sandro said, matter-of-factly, "who said that Alvarado couldn't have been the man because he was in Brooklyn at the very time Lauria met his death in Manhattan. People like Annie Mae Cooper and Phil Gruberger and Pablo Torres and Francisco Moreno.

"Do you think it's possible to get much closer physically to a person than a barber gets when giving a haircut or trimming a moustache. That's closer than eighty feet away, or two stories away, isn't it?

"And the barber Moreno says Alvarado was in his shop getting a haircut and moustache trim at the very time, *the very time* the officer was being killed in Manhattan. And the pictures, taken by ABC, show Alvarado as he appeared early on the morning of July fourth, moustache and haircut perfect. *Perfect.* And Annie Mae Cooper tells you Alvarado was in Brooklyn changing a hundred-dollar bill; and Phil Gruberger supports that story. But the police will have you believe Alvarado needed money for a fix. And there was Pablo Torres, who also tells you that Alvarado was in Brooklyn.

"Can you dismiss these people? Did Mr. Ellis discredit them in the least on cross-examination? Well, I know that Moreno was once fined two dollars for shooting dice. A wonder he wasn't hanged for such a crime. But other than that, did Mr. Ellis show that these witnesses were unworthy of belief?

"Doesn't that testimony create some doubt in your mind? Maybe Mrs. Santos and Mrs. Salerno are wrong. Maybe Moreno is correct. Maybe. That is reasonable, isn't it? There are reasons to support such belief. Well, that's all I'm asking you to think about. Reasonable doubt."

Sandro stood still before the center of the jury box.

"Now the district attorney might tell you that Julio, the barber's friend, is the key to Alvarado's alibi, that Julio didn't get to the barber shop until after four P.M. and not two P.M., and therefore Alvarado wasn't there at two twenty-five. Well, you saw Julio here, and you heard him testify on the public record that if he had signed out early on July third and put down a false time he would be fired, fired by the City of New York, the same city for which the police work, the same city that pays the bills around this courtroom. Do you think he was going to admit here that he left the job early on July third?

"Nobody checked Julio out that day, no clock punched his time out. He just wrote something down in pencil and left. It was July third.

PART 35

The next day was a holiday. People were leaving early, preparing to go away for the weekend. I'm not saying Julio is a liar and a cheat. He's just a normal person, doing something that is repeated in thousands of places of work on every holiday weekend. You get out a little early so you don't get caught up in the crowd.

"With all the evidence in this trial—the medical evidence, the testimony of Mrs. Hernandez, the doctors, the witnesses who saw Alvarado in Brooklyn at the time the policeman was killed—all that evidence pointing to Alvarado's innocence, is that going to be outweighed by Julio's protesting that he didn't sign his time card out early on July third?"

Sandro was starting to move up toward the foreman again. He was starting to speed the tempo again. The jurors were tuned perfectly.

"Are all the inconsistencies—the jimmy that never was, the yellow jacket and black pants, the gray suit, the face that Mrs. Salerno didn't see, then did see, the face Mrs. Ramirez said was definitely not Alvarado's, Mrs. Santos seeing face-to-face level, which turned out not to be anything like face-to-face level, Mrs. Santos seeing impossible things in that hallway, testifying to the double-parked car on the wrong side of the street—are all these inconsistencies, taken with the proof in Alvarado's favor, going to be outweighed because Julio couldn't possibly have signed out early on July third?

"How many of you have wanted to leave early on a holiday weekend? How many of you *have* actually left your job early on a holiday weekend? Is it so unusual for a fellow to think of, to do, when no one else is around? The job is finished for the day, and you have nothing to do except wait for the clock to move around so you can check out.

"Are Alvarado's own activities on that night when he was captured to be outweighed by Julio's denial? Did Alvarado ever, *ever*, except for what the police say occurred behind the closed doors of that third-floor locker room, did Alvarado ever once do anything that would be the act of a guilty man? Think about it!"

Sandro stood still, searching the eyes of the jurors.

"If Alvarado were guilty, why did he go back to that rooming house in Brooklyn? If Alvarado were guilty, once he did get there unnoticed, why didn't he run away when the super told him the cops were waiting there? And if he were guilty, why didn't he fight, try to get away, give a false name?

"And if he were guilty, when he was here in court, why did he reject that statement he supposedly made to the D.A.? The statement where the terror leaps from the pages? Wouldn't a guilty man grab that to his bosom, wouldn't he hold on to that repudiation for dear life?

"But, no! Alvarado says he didn't make such a statement. He denies the denial. Would a guilty man do that? Is this the act of a guilty man? I ask you again, has Alvarado ever once in this case acted as a guilty man might, other than what the police say happened in that third-floor locker room? I ask only that you use your senses. That's all your oath calls for."

Sandro had moved back a couple of steps now.

"Now, the death of Fortune Lauria was a crime—indeed, a heinous crime. And no one is saying it didn't happen. The question you have to answer is, are you convinced beyond a reasonable doubt that it was Alvarado who did it? Because the crime was committed doesn't mean that Alvarado was there. Because some of the elements of the crime exist doesn't mean that Alvarado was responsible for them.

"We are here for justice, for truth—not vengeance. *Vengeance is mine*, saith the Lord. *I shall revenge*. He doesn't need you to help Him.

"There's something that bothers me," Sandro's eyes were searching out each of the jurors intently. "Perhaps it shouldn't, but it does. It bothers me when people in the street, people on television, newspaper accounts, even law-enforcement officials—people who should know better—it bothers me when I hear them say that the rights of the ordinary citizens are being stepped upon, that the courts are letting criminals get away with murder.

"When the rights of a defendant, a man on trial, are being protected, the rights of citizens *are* being protected. For criminals are citizens before they are criminals. And if we decide, arbitrarily, that the only rights to be protected are the rights of those who are *not* arrested, and anyone who is arrested be damned, then what happens in a case where an innocent man is arrested? What happens the night, God forbid, when you are coming home from the movies, a newspaper under your arm, and you find yourself looking into the business end of a .38

caliber Police Special. You are innocent, but you are arrested nonetheless. Would you want to lose your rights at the moment you are arrested? Should you? And if *you* shouldn't, why should anyone else?

"Didn't all of you say that you understood a man to be innocent until proven guilty? Well, if that is so—and it is—then the Supreme Court of the United States is not coddling criminals when it provides protection for accused citizens who must stand trial. Until convicted, Luis Alvarado and all defendants on trial are citizens presumed innocent of crime. To protect them is to protect citizens. To protect Luis Alvarado is to protect yourself."

Sandro still hadn't moved a muscle in his body except for his hands, which occasionally gave full shape to his words.

"Oh, yes, you might think that you are different from Alvarado, that you could never be where he is today. Let me tell you just how close you, *you*, came to being the defendant in this case, gentlemen. How far, really are most of us removed from where Alvarado stands? Supposing it was a white man with red hair who had been seen on the fire escape, and the police badgered and burdened Hernandez until he gave them the name of a white man with red hair instead of the name Luis Alvarado. Then someone else would be on trial here, not because he was any more guilty or innocent than Luis Alvarado, but because he fit the new description as Luis Alvarado fitted the old. Didn't Hernandez say Alvarado was the first Negro he could think of, and he gave this name because he thought they'd kill him in that station house if he didn't give them any?

"And if a white man with black hair had been described to Hernandez, someone else would be here today.

"And suppose Hernandez worked with you, had delivered something to your home, saw you in a store somewhere, and as punches were being rained upon his head, as he was being beaten and badgered, prodded, shoved, a name was demanded of him, and suppose he said, as a vision came before his mind, the repairman who came around to my house the other day is the white man with red hair, the man in the store on Sixty-eighth Street and Second Avenue is the white man with black hair, the letter carrier from around the corner is the colored guy you're looking for.

"And that person he named turned out to be you. Think about it for a moment. He mentioned you. Just think that somewhere in this city right now someone may be giving your name to the authorities. And just suppose when you go home, you are told there are policemen waiting for you, and you go to see them, because you have nothing to fear or hide, because you are innocent. Then see how different you are from Luis Alvarado.

"Ladies and gentlemen, what has happened here, as Mr. Bemer suggested in his opening statement, is that the police have put a patch-quilt story together. They had to fit the accused into the available facts, and they did it with no more skill than a high-school boy might have if he saw the roof and the dead patrolman, his gun missing. They patched this surmise together because someone saw a Negro on the fire escape, and someone else saw a Negro running down the stairs several buildings away.

"Why else would it be necessary, as the alleged confessions indicate, for a burglar to see the gates and the locks on the window from the inside and not *know* the windows were locked until he came down the fire escape?

"Why else would they need that fence in the rear yard?

"And don't forget that story about the jimmy.

"In their haste to fasten the blame on someone, the police patch-worked these defendants into this courtroom today.

"Have you at any point stopped to consider what story the police would have told if Hernandez were Negro? The police did not need two men. They would have accepted Hernandez's confession of the crime—if he had only been Negro. He would have fitted the available facts. And there would be only one defendant here today.

"Think about these things, ladies and gentlemen. Think about them, citizens."

Sandro wheeled and pointed to the defendant.

"Look at yourself, citizens, sitting there, wondering how you, who might be sitting where Alvarado is sitting now, ever got here. And it's as easy as that. As easy as that. Alvarado was arrested only because he fit a description. Maybe next time, it will be your description.

"And don't tell me that you'll be able to prove with whom you were. Don't tell me, unless you constantly associate with police officials, legislators, bank presidents, financiers, priests, and the like. Don't just be in a five-and-ten, a luncheonette, a barber shop getting a haircut. Do important things, always. Because juries disregard common citizens doing common things, things that each of us, you and I, do, day in and day out. Sure, change it to a beauty shop, change it to a grocery store. Do you think that if the people who know that you were in such a shop came in here to say you were there, it would make any difference to a jury?

"Well, we'll see here. You'll give that answer.

"Or will your answer be that once you're arrested, once you're sitting at that table as Luis Alvarado is at this moment, you have no rights, you have no dignity, you are a criminal, you should be flogged, you should be cut into bits, you should be drawn and quartered, torn apart by horses?"

Some of the jurors looked frightened. Sandro started again, more quietly.

"Or should you be judged by men who accept you as a stranger who should be pronounced a criminal only after the district attorney has presented enough evidence to convince those jurors beyond all reasonable doubt about all the elements of the crime charged?

"The law, ladies and gentlemen, is the foundation stone of all culture; it is the bedrock upon which we can move freely as human beings, rather than as animals in a jungle who can be struck down at random and by whim. And the law says that Luis Alvarado is presumed to be innocent. The facts in this case show him to be innocent. But it is you who must pronounce him innocent.

"When you go into the jury room, decide the fate of Luis Alvarado as if your verdict affected you personally. Believe me, it does.

"Thank you."

Sandro walked back to the defense table. Sam reached up and shook his hand.

"That was fabulous, kid. Fabulous."

Sandro smiled.

"Don't smile," Sam cautioned, ever the watchdog.

"We'll take a few minutes recess before Mr. Siakos begins his summation," said the judge. The jury filed out of the courtroom. The attorneys went out into the corridor.

CHAPTER XXXVII

Friday, April 26th, 1968, P.M.

ELLIS AND HIS DETECTIVES had retired to the witness room. The defense lawyers walked into the public corridor, where a crowd of spectators milled around them, buzzing with comments and questions. Sandro smiled, nodded, continuing to walk with Sam until they got clear of the crowd.

Sandro leaned against the wall. "My mind is starting to close down for the season."

Mike walked over to join them. He was smiling. "You got them. You really got them with that." He grabbed Sandro in an embrace, twirling him around.

Siakos came over. He clapped Sandro on the back. "You know, Sandro, I think we may really have something here. We may have a real bombshell on our hands here with these fellows. You showed that to the jury. These men may be innocent."

"*May* be?" asked Mike.

"Sure," said Siakos, heading toward the men's room at the far end of the corridor.

Sandro's eyes followed Siakos.

PART 35

The break lasted about ten minutes. Finally, a court officer entered the corridor.

"Case on trial," he called out. The crowd started back in. The lawyers followed.

Now Siakos began his summation, facing the jury. Sandro watched his back. Passages, sentences, words drifted occasionally into his consciousness. Fortunately, Sam was there as the ever-vigilant guardian of the legal concepts, the objections, and the arguments. Sandro's mind floated off on thoughts of long aquamarine waves rolling "*—over Hernandez's taped chest.*" Sandro gave a start and relaxed back into the white foam, and saw the sand and colorful cabanas beneath the sun "*—of El Barrio on a rainy morning where the defendant Hernandez broke into—*" And so it went, station house, pawnshops, and medical records fusing into small, single-sail boats far off on the horizon, long strips of beach, long, firm, beautiful legs, and brief bikinis.

When Siakos had summed up the entire Hernandez case to the jury, Judge Porta declared a lunch recess.

Sandro, though tired, remembered the defendants' lunch. He bought four hot dogs at the orange-and-blue umbrellaed wagon just outside the courthouse. The defendants didn't have much appetite, however, as they awaited Ellis's summation.

Now the courtroom was filling up again, waiting for Ellis to begin. After the morning session, with its two summations, and the lunch recess, the atmosphere had become quiet, almost exhausted. Ellis sat at his counsel table looking at some papers. The defense counsel and the defendants sat waiting. The drone of the central air-conditioner could be heard vibrating in the silence. The jurors were brought out. The judge entered the courtroom. He too now seemed quiet, slow, as if ready to relax after the long, hard struggle.

"Mr. Ellis, you may begin," the judge said.

Ellis rose and walked to the jury box. He put his notes down on the shelf and viewed the jury quietly for a moment. His stony face was emotionless.

"Your Honor, defense counsel, Mr. foreman, ladies and gentlemen of the jury. I am frank to say, after listening to the summations for the defense this morning, that when I went to my office after lunch, I had to reread the indictment to make sure the defendants—not the policemen, not the witnesses—were on trial here. Mr. Luca seems to want us all to believe that everyone who came here, including plain ordinary citizens who have nothing to do with the police, who just happen to live on the block where Patrolman Fortune Lauria met his death, were involved in some monstrous conspiracy against the defendants. Mr. Luca would have you believe that everyone who came here lied, everyone except the defendants.

"Now, as I see it, there are only two aspects of importance in this case, the alibi defense and the confessions by the defendants. I'd like to address myself to the alibis and then to the confessions, for if you apply your common sense to the facts—not to the fireworks and smoke screens we have seen here—those alibis fall apart. And when the alibis, on which the defendants lean so heavily, fall apart, these defendants are left standing nakedly and confessedly guilty before you.

"I'd like to make just a quick aside. You know, I heard Mr. Luca tell you that he wasn't going in for any emotional, fist-pounding oratory. And then he proceeded to make a totally emotional, fist-pounding oration. Do you know why? It was because he had to shout to drown out the facts that speak against the defendants.

"Let's look at some of those facts.

"Of all the alibi witnesses who have come here, we need concern ourselves with only two. The others are smoke screens to distract you. But these two are the keystones, without whom the alibis are worthless. For Hernandez, the keystone is Angel Belmonte; for Alvarado, it's Julio Maldonado.

"Hernandez told us about committing a burglary on the morning of July third in El Barrio. Well, maybe he did. He also said he pawned some of the things he burglarized. Maybe he did that too. But the time when he left that last pawnshop, according to his own admission and witnesses, was about two o'clock, perhaps a couple of minutes later. Now, Hernandez himself made Angel Belmonte the keystone of his alibi, for Hernandez said that he went to buy some drugs from Belmonte *after* he was in the pawnshops. He said he was with Angel Belmonte at two thirty, the very time when Patrolman Lauria was killed.

PART 35

"Remember, those pawnshops Hernandez mentioned were only a few short blocks from Stanton Street, and even if Hernandez did everything else he told us he did, he could still have gone home and gone onto the roof with Alvarado. And the patrolman could have come, and he and Alvarado could have killed him. *Unless, of course, he was actually someplace else buying heroin from Angel Belmonte.*

"Let's look at that last crucial piece of evidence in Hernandez's alibi, the only crucial piece of evidence in it. We didn't even know Angel Belmonte existed until Hernandez dropped his name here at the trial. I know Mr. Luca likes to believe in conspiracies, but this isn't someone the police planted, someone we planned on as a witness. Hernandez himself brought him up. And we found Belmonte and brought him here. No lawyer for the defense went to see Angel Belmonte, the keystone of Hernandez's alibi. Oh sure, the defense brought the smoke screen, the people who saw Hernandez in the morning in El Barrio, the people in the pawnshops, the names, the lists of pledges, the estimated times of going to the bank, of going to lunch. I urge you to accept all of that as true. And still Hernandez admitted having time to get back to Stanton Street, to invade the Soto apartment, and to aid in killing the patrolman—*unless he was actually with Angel Belmonte.*

"What does Angel Belmonte say? He says he *was not* with Hernandez on July third. He says not only that, but he says also that later, in the Tombs, Hernandez solicited him to lie, to say that Hernandez *had* been with him at two thirty on that afternoon of July third. Belmonte, Hernandez's own alibi key, says Hernandez asked him to perjure himself. Because that was the only way Hernandez's alibi could hold together.

"You may say: How can we believe Belmonte? Just look at him, look at what he is. But this is the defendant's friend, this is the man *he* named, the type that *he* associated with.

"Mr. Luca has suggested that as part of this conspiracy we arranged some sort of deal with Belmonte. But Belmonte is a citizen, not a criminal, a distinction that has been made so eloquently clear for you. He has no charges pending against him. He can't benefit from any deal.

"And Belmonte, on whom Hernandez depended so heavily, has

branded Hernandez's alibi an unmitigated lie. Hernandez has not, cannot, account for himself at the time Patrolman Lauria was killed. And why not? Because Hernandez was there, he was at the scene, just as he described it to Detective Mullaly. Is that an unreasonable interpretation of the facts?"

If the jury's attention had wandered as Sandro's had during Siakos's summation, there was no question that Ellis had brought it back.

"What about Alvarado's alibi? I'd be insulting your intelligence, as well as those good citizens who came here to testify, if I were to say that all those plain, ordinary people were lying. But I don't say that. *I* don't have to invent a conspiracy. What time was it that Alvarado changed that hundred-dollar bill? What time was it that he ate? Mrs. Cooper said it was about one fifteen on July third when she changed the bill. Mr. Gruberger, the assistant store manager, agreed with her, although he said he didn't even see Alvarado. I urge you to accept all of that as true also. There was still plenty of time for Alvarado to get to Manhattan. Remember, Williamsburg in Brooklyn is just a bridgespan away from the Delancey area, and Stanton Street is just three or four short blocks from that bridge.

"So at one fifteen in the afternoon, Alvarado was just a few scant minutes from the building where Patrolman Lauria met his death. Pablo Torres, who worked in the restaurant, said he served Alvarado food on that afternoon. He didn't know exactly what time it was except that the lunch crowd had thinned out, and it must have been somewhere around one forty-five. Well, that's not an exact time, but even if it were, at one forty-five, forty-five minutes before the time when Patrolman Lauria was killed, Alvarado was only minutes away in Brooklyn. I think it's reasonable to say that Alvarado's alibi really depends on the barber Moreno. The others are leading up to Moreno, but they do not exclude the possibility that Alvarado could have done all the things they described and still have had more than enough time to come to Manhattan, go to the roof on Stanton Street, take the patrolman's revolver, and shoot him five times in the back.

"If you look at the keystone of Alvarado's alibi as Alvarado testified to it, you'll find that it's not stone at all. It's mush, it's chicanery, it's false, it's a lie, and it brands Alvarado as the cold-blooded murderer that he is."

PART 35

Sandro's face was becalmed, but he felt Ellis's emotionless hammer blows.

"Well, the barber, Moreno, said that he knew that Alvarado came into the store about two twenty-five or two thirty. He said he knew what time it was because his friend, Julio Maldonado, came into the shop. He said Julio usually came in later, but this day he was early, and they kidded about it, and that's how Moreno knew what time it was.

"*We* didn't mention Julio. We didn't even know his name. He was another witness the defense brought into this. Now, Moreno didn't look at a watch or a clock on the wall. He said he looked at Julio's watch.

"But Julio testified he didn't leave work until after three thirty on July third. That's what he said. It was after three thirty that he left work, and he worked several blocks from the barber shop. That would mean that Julio did not get to the barber shop until about four o'clock, not two o'clock.

"And if Julio didn't get to the barber shop until four o'clock, and Moreno is basing the time of Alvarado's arrival on Julio's arrival, then maybe Alvarado arrived in that barber shop about four twenty-five or four thirty, and not, as Alvarado would like you to believe, at two twenty-five or two thirty.

"That would mean that the pictures from ABC are correct. We don't have to find some motive for the ABC witnesses to have lied. Alvarado *did* have a haircut, he *did* have his moustache trimmed on July third. But in between the time he ate and the time he was trying to establish his alibi by getting a haircut in his own neighborhood, Alvarado snuffed out the life of a New York City patrolman by shooting him five times in the back."

The eyes of the jurors showed all too clearly that they were by now sure of nothing.

"Is it unreasonable to suggest to you that a man who killed a patrolman might try to establish an alibi for himself?

"Oh, I'm sure some of you are thinking that Mr. Luca managed to shake Julio a bit with his questions. *Not* with the answers, mind you—with the questions. Julio insisted that he left his job at three thirty. Now, Mr. Luca would have you believe that Julio was goofing off and left early that day. But Mr. Luca's questions are not evidence, and Mr. Luca would be the first to point that out. *Julio didn't leave the job until three thirty.*

"Well, if that's so, we see the other alibi crumble, shattered as an absolute lie by this slip of paper. The time card Julio made out is here, and it is marked very plainly. He checked out at three thirty P.M. on July third." Ellis raised the time card in one hand. Every juror's eyes studied it.

"Now, I'm not saying any of those alibi witnesses were lying, and yet the alibis are gone. They've evaporated into the nothingness they were and are. The defendants are lying here, the defendants want to lie about the time to convince you they were not at the scene of the crime. But their own words, their own alibis have backfired. Angel Belmonte brands Hernandez a liar. Julio brands Alvarado a liar. I don't have to invent a monstrous conspiracy. I don't have to smear every one of those independent witnesses as liars, accuse them of all sorts of insidious acts in order to destroy the alibis. The alibis destroy themselves. Does it now abuse your common sense to look more carefully at the other evidence?

"The people presented Mrs. Santos. It seems ages now since she was here, but you recall her and the manner in which she testified, the kind of person she was. And she said she saw the defendants, both of them, in the car outside, and Hernandez in the building on the stairs, and Alvarado on the fire escape.

"Now, what motive, what possible motive would that woman have for coming here and testifying falsely? She may not have had much education, but what reason would she have for testifying falsely?

"Mr. Luca argues that she is not telling the truth because she didn't tell the police anything when she was first questioned. Now, ladies and gentlemen, here again is where I ask you to use your common sense. Does the fact that Mrs. Santos, in her pregnancy, concerned about her unborn child, did not rush to disclose what she saw to the police—does that brand her a liar? What possible motive would she have to come into this court and expose herself to the blistering cross-examination that she was subjected to for two days?

"Is there any indication that she has anything against these defen-

PART 35

dants? The ridiculous argument was advanced that she has a grudge against the defendants, that in some unexplained—and unexplainable—manner she blames them for having caused her miscarriage.

"Now, if this were all a part of a monstrous conspiracy on the part of Detective Mullaly and the other detectives, as the defendants want you to believe, I submit the detectives could have done a much better job in framing the defendants. Mrs. Santos did not accuse either defendant of doing anything. All she said was that she saw them in the car, saw Hernandez on the stairs, saw Alvarado on the fire escape. If this is a frame-up, why did Mrs. Santos stop there?

"And there was Mrs. Salerno, who testified that she saw the defendant Alvarado on the fire escape, bending down, near the window. And you were shown photographs that supposedly prove she couldn't have seen the face of the man on the fire escape. Do you think that you would have difficulty seeing a face at a distance the engineer Loughlin described as thirty feet? You were in that rear yard. You saw how near that was.

"And what possible motive would Mrs. Salerno have to come into this courtroom and testify falsely? It has been not too subtly suggested that Detective Mullaly, the archconspirator, and the other policemen were putting pressure on Mrs. Salerno because her husband is an addict and she is on relief.

"You know, it's staggering when you consider the charges and accusations that have been leveled against these detectives. The defendants would have you believe that these detectives are so depraved, so conscienceless, that they would stoop to anything to frame two innocent men.

"But you heard the frightening cross-examination that Mrs. Santos and Mrs. Salerno endured. Do you think there is any pleasure for two women like these to be pulled away from their normal household routines, to be brought down here to court, and be subjected to the kind of cross-examination and abuse you witnessed? Is there any wonder then that citizens, knowing what goes on at these trials, the way a witness is attacked and cross-examined, is it any wonder that they are reluctant to come forward and speak to the police, to be witnesses at a trial to the commission of a crime?

"Mrs. Salerno said she saw Alvarado on the fire escape, not doing anything particular. She did not accuse him of anything. She just saw him up there, and a short time later Patrolman Lauria was shot. If this were that monstrous conspiracy the defendants are trying to convince you of, I'm sure Detective Mullaly could have done a much better job with Mrs. Salerno too. He could have had her testify to something far more incriminating. But no, these witnesses, plain women, uneducated women, just came here and testified to what they saw. Nothing technical, nothing fancy. Just the faces of two men they saw a few minutes before the patrolman was shot.

"And then Detective Mullaly testified. You have seen the detectives in this case, and you have seen the defendants. I ask you to use your common sense in evaluating their conflicting testimony, compare their demeanor, their possible self-interest in the outcome, the manner of testifying. Who was the more credible, who had more of a motive to lie? Remember, you have no alibi to save the defendants now! I ask you, are my thoughts and ideas unreasonable, insulting to your intelligence? Or do they begin to ring true for you?

"The defendants want you to believe that the name of a Negro was beaten out of Hernandez. Didn't Mrs. Ramirez come here, the woman Mr. Luca called a people's witness, didn't she come here originally and tell you that she told the police about the man running down the stairs? And didn't Alvarado confess to that?

"Simply, Detective Mullaly became suspicious when Hernandez gave all sorts of untrue, evasive answers about the double-parked car. They were suspicious, and you don't have to be a trained detective to find them suspicious. So Hernandez was brought to the station house, where he continued to lie about the car, and about driving the car that day. That is, until his friend who he said had the car was brought in, and Hernandez was again shown to be a liar because his friend was at work all day. And then, trapped, he said, okay, I'll tell you where I was today, I met a friend.

"Isn't it reasonable that Hernandez, realizing he was trapped, knowing that he didn't actually shoot and kill the patrolman, understood that he'd be better off telling the police everything he knew?

"There's been a great deal made of the fact that the defendants were questioned in the third-floor locker room. All I can say is that you heard the detectives. The police station was a madhouse, police personnel, brass, reporters everywhere. Certainly, when a police officer is killed, there is an intensive effort to find the perpetrator. But does it necessarily follow that in their anxiety to find the killer or killers, the police would get hold of an innocent man and beat him into such a state of submission that he would implicate himself and another innocent man?

"Does it abuse your common sense to say that the defendants are making a desperate attempt to escape their responsibility for the death of Patrolman Lauria? They have had nothing else to do in the Tombs except think about this case, and they had plenty of time to concoct what I call a vicious tissue of lies. But is it so difficult to see it as a desperate attempt to escape the consequences of a brutal and vicious crime? Surely, lies are as nothing to a man who has already shot a fellow human being five times in the back.

"You've been told about all the time it took before going over to Brooklyn to look for Alvarado, and you've been told that was a sure sign Hernandez was being beaten. Well, what were the police to do without an identification of Alvarado, without a picture? Were they to hold the defendant Hernandez in Brooklyn for hours, waiting in a hallway in case Alvarado came back? Or should the policemen who were left there on a stakeout go running out of the building every time a man went past or came into the building, because they didn't know who they were looking for? Isn't it reasonable to think that the police might wait until they knew who they were looking for, until they had a picture?

"I say, ladies and gentlemen, that this is typical of the confusion, the smoke screens, that were thrown at you during this trial to keep you from learning the truth. These fine police officers, who did their job, have also had to bear the brunt of some vicious accusations here.

"The police asked Alvarado where he was, and he said in the movies. Although to hear him tell it, he didn't get a chance to move before he was being beaten. Who would you believe, the defendants or the police? Who has reason to lie? Who has a motive to lie? Who has already lied about the alibi?

"And when Alvarado started in with this story about being in the movies, Detective Mullaly brought up Hernandez, and Hernandez accused Alvarado. The thieves fell apart, and they went for each other's throats.

"And Hernandez was taken away, and Alvarado started talking about the movies again. And Hernandez was brought back a second time, and they started cursing and lunging at each other again. Oh, I know there was something about the detectives not speaking Spanish, so how did they know they were cursing? Does it abuse your common sense to think that these detectives, working where they do in a Spanish-speaking neighborhood, would have some knowledge of the language of the street? And Hernandez was taken away the second time, and then Alvarado knew the jig was up. And he said, okay, I'll tell you where I was.

"Now, does it abuse your common sense to accept that version of the events which occurred as Detective Mullaly described Alvarado's confession? Is there anything that violates your sense of logic there?

"Of course, by the time the district attorney arrived, Alvarado—and you saw him here, not a stupid man, uneducated but clever—realized he had to get out of this somehow. So he started pulling away from the statement he made to the police. But I'll hold that for a moment.

"While we're on the subject of this frame-up, if these detectives were in desperation to frame these defendants, does it abuse your common sense to suggest that the detectives could have really done a job on them? They could have concocted a far better story for the witnesses to lie about. And they had all the opportunity in the world to get hold of both these defendants and plaster their fingerprints all over the TV set and all over the radio, and make sure they got the ideal conditions that the expert on fingerprints described for us here. If these policemen are the type that the defendants would have you believe, that would have been easy, and that would have been the best, the strongest evidence in the world. They wouldn't have to be bothered questioning these defendants at all. They wouldn't have to bother with confessions that a smart defense lawyer could say were beaten out. If they were setting out to frame this defendant Alvarado, they allegedly had Alvarado completely at their mercy. Why bother with his statements? Just wrap his hands in the correct fashion around that gun and obtain identifiable fingerprints, and the rest of this case would be over. If the detectives were out to do what they were accused of trying to do here, does it abuse your common sense to say they would have done a far, far better job?

"And then Detective Mullaly tells you that Alvarado told him that he was scared when he saw the cop on the roof. Do you think that Mullaly would throw in something like that—that Alvarado said he got scared? Mullaly would make it as vicious and as desperate and as cold-blooded as he possibly could if he was framing Alvarado. Does it abuse your common sense to think that Detective Mullaly is telling you just what the defendant told him, the way it happened?

"Now, what about this Mrs. Ramirez, the witness who returned, she said, because her conscience bothered her? Rather than being unhappy that Mrs. Ramirez returned, I was grateful for the opportunity to produce Mrs. Salerno, who testified about what she heard Mrs. Ramirez say in the station house. Now, I couldn't have done that otherwise. With Mrs. Ramirez here as the people's witness telling us she couldn't say what the man looked like, I was stuck. But when she returned, when her conscience bothered her so much that she didn't get in touch with the district attorney, but with Mr. Siakos, and she came here and said that Alvarado was definitely not the man, why then I was able to put Mrs. Salerno on the stand and tell exactly what Mrs. Ramirez said in the police station on the early morning of July fourth.

"Now, I don't think I need remind you, ladies and gentlemen, that a crucial question in this case is whether or not those confessions are voluntary. For, if you find that they are true and voluntary, then I don't think it's unreasonable to suggest to you that you have practically finished your job.

"Now, what evidence do we have that these confessions are involuntary? Well, Hernandez tells you that he was beaten so badly, so viciously, that he insisted in his delirium that he had killed the police officer. And then he said he changed that story at the suggestion of the detectives. The detectives contradict Hernandez, and the credibility of the witnesses is a question for you to decide. Hernandez against these detectives—who can you believe? Who has the motive to lie?

"Now that the alibi has been eliminated as we discussed before, it's as simple as that. Hernandez against the policemen—who has the most to gain by a lie?

"What guideposts can you use in helping you to determine who is telling the truth? Well, Hernandez told you of the viciousness of the beating. Yet he never mentioned anything to his lawyer at the first arraignment on July fourth, nor to the judge in court on the very same day, nor to the doctor who examined him in the Tombs that day.

"And you saw a picture of Hernandez without his clothing, taken in police headquarters by the detectives just for this purpose on July fourth. And did you see any marks? You look at the photographs—they're in evidence—and see if there are any marks.

"Alvarado, in his defense, denied saying anything to the D.A., and he said he even told the D.A. that he hadn't confessed to the police. Alvarado also testified that he told the D.A. that he was beaten. Well, this statement is in evidence, ladies and gentlemen, and you have a right to take it into the jury room with you. Read it, and see if Alvarado didn't again damn himself as a liar.

"He was even asked by the D.A., do you have any complaint, and he said *no*. Now doesn't that brand his testimony here a total lie?

"Now when Alvarado's lies start backing him into a corner, because what he testified he said to the D.A. was different from this typewritten statement, well then, in keeping with the vicious plan he's been concocting for months, he starts bringing the D.A. into the monstrous conspiracy. He has the audacity to imply the D.A. and his staff were part of some frame-up. Does it abuse your common sense that he protests too much? Doesn't he unmask himself as a liar?

"Sure, Alvarado said to the D.A., get me out of here, and I'll talk to you. That wasn't because he had been beaten, as he wants you to believe. I suggest to you as a matter of common sense, anybody who was being questioned in connection with the killing of a police officer would be afraid if he knew he was involved. But His Honor will tell you that just because he was afraid doesn't destroy the admissibility of the confession. It has to be fear from physical threat or violence, not fear because of his own guilty conscience.

"The police officers got on the stand, and they testified they never

PART 35

touched Alvarado. Need I go any further to make out the fact that Alvarado is a liar? Need I go any further to show which witnesses are more credible?

"And after this alleged vicious beating, did Alvarado say one word to anyone—to a doctor, to a lawyer, to a judge?

"Oh, sure, six days later, he says he started to spit blood, he started to have an attack. The doctor from the Tombs told you that he has seen people in the Tombs fake anything, just to get a fix, to get drugs. The doctor said that Alvarado appeared unconscious. Perhaps Alvarado was so good he fooled the doctor. Well, let's not just suppose. Let's be reasonable. If Alvarado had been unconscious, could he have described what the doctor in the Tombs did for him? When he was here testifying, didn't he tell you about being on the floor, about the doctor putting the oxygen mask on his face, about all the details of that evening?

"How unconscious was he, this cunning killer?

"And doesn't that testimony finally and completely brand him as the liar he is—and being that, also the killer he is?

"I know I don't have to remind you of the theory of the people's case. I ask you to consider the evidence calmly, coolly, dispassionately, without prejudice or sympathy. Your only task at the present time is to decide the guilt or innocence of these defendants, and nothing else.

"You promised me that you would accept the law from the court. I ask you to be faithful to your oaths, and based upon them and the credible evidence, and the law, in the interest of justice, and in the name of the people of the State of New York, I ask you to find both of these defendants guilty of murder in the first degree. Thank you very much."

Ellis sat. The courtroom was silent. The judge adjourned until Monday morning, when he would charge the jury.

CHAPTER XXXVIII

Wednesday, May 1st, 1968

IT WAS 9:15 P.M. Sandro, Sam, and Mike were sitting in the jury box. Ellis, Mullaly, and Tracy were in the spectators' seats. The rest of the courtroom was empty, as it had been since shortly after Judge Porta had sent the jurors out for deliberation. The jury had had the case more than two days—53 hours and 15 minutes all told. And, as usual, the lawyers had not been able to leave the vicinity of the courtroom for any length of time except during lunch break or at night, when the jury, together with several of the court's uniformed officers, was sent in a private bus to a midtown hotel for the night. The jury was returned to the courtroom about 10 A.M. and was sent to bed by the judge at 11:30 P.M. During the long vigil, the lawyers talked, read, played cards, and did anything else they could devise to kill time. Now that it was over, Ellis was a fellow lawyer and not merely an adversary. He was three dollars ahead in the poker game.

"Now you know what I meant about Ellis," Sam said to Sandro, "a bear trap that looks harmless, without a lot of pizzazz, but he's effective. He pieced a damned strong summation together. Of course, he didn't get around the medical evidence with that bit about unconsciousness. The report itself said Alvarado had lucid moments. But he sure was strong on those alibis."

Sandro nodded.

"I don't buy it anyway," Mike said, shaking his head. "With all we know about this case, how could these guys be guilty?"

"Remember, Mike," Sandro cautioned, "the jury wasn't with us. Everything that we saw didn't and couldn't go into the record. They don't know about the witnesses, the Sotos, the Salernos, all about Mullaly—all those things we know from our investigation. They only know what happened during the trial days here in court."

"That's right," agreed Sam. "The rules of evidence are part of the system, and a lot of your stuff just couldn't be introduced. Go and read the minutes of the trial, Mike, day by day, and then you'd see what the jury knows, nothing more. And Ellis built a nice, solid case. Not as good as ours," he added hastily.

"It couldn't be," said Mike. "That phony stuff Ellis put in the summation is just bullshit. How can they come back with any verdict except not guilty?"

Sam shrugged. "Who ever knows what a jury will do? The only way you can tell anything is when they come out of the jury room. If they look at us, we've won. If they avoid our eyes, we've lost."

"What do you say?" Mike asked, turning to Sandro.

"Only two people know what actually happened on that roof, Mike, and one of them is dead. Frankly, I want to walk out of here with Alvarado. But if we lose, I can accept that too."

Mike looked incredulous.

There was a commotion at the side of the courtroom, near the clerk's desk. Judge Porta entered the courtroom and ascended the bench.

"I believe we may have a verdict," the judge said. The sound echoed through the silent room. A couple of the buffs, still waiting for word, entered the back of the courtroom.

Sandro saw the tension in the defendants' faces as they were brought back in. They sat at the counsel table.

"Bring in the jury," the judge instructed.

The jurors filed in. The first three—Haverly, Roscoe Anderson, and the railroad man's widow—didn't look toward the defendants' table. But the fourth man, the shoe salesman who had marched with Dr. King, did. As did the fifth, Arthur Youngerman, the Vietnam veteran. The sixth man—the insurance salesman Fresci—didn't. Seven and eight—the bearded music teacher and the retired buyer—did. It was hard to tell about the rest. They took their places in the jury box.

"Let the prisoners rise," said the judge. "Mr. foreman, look upon the defendants. Defendants, look upon the jury."

The foreman stood.

"Have you reached a verdict?" Judge Porta asked.

"Your Honor," Haverly said, "the jury is unable to agree upon a verdict. We've deliberated for many hours, and we still cannot agree."

Alvarado's hand was on Sandro's arm, squeezing. Sandro motioned him to remain still.

The judge nodded. "Do you feel, Mr. foreman, that if the jury returned to the jury room, you would be able to deliberate and possibly reach a verdict?"

"Your Honor," Haverly replied, the weariness obvious in his face and voice, "we've been deadlocked for about sixteen hours. It is my opinion, and that of the others, that if we stayed in the jury room another week, our opinions would not change. It has gotten to that point."

The judge looked at the lawyers. He studied their faces, then turned back to the jury. "Very well. I am going to dismiss you from service at this time with the thanks of the court. You may return to . . ."

Sandro wasn't listening any more. It was all over. They had started so long ago with the impossible, and they had gotten a hung jury. Wasn't that a victory in itself?

"Remand the prisoners," the judge said.

"You still my man, Mr. Luca," said Alvarado as the guard led him away. "We going to get them. We really going to get them next time. You my dynamite." Sandro watched the defendants being led back to the bullpen. They had been in jail ten months, and they would stay there now until a new trial.

The jurors filed out. Ellis shook hands with Sam. Then with Siakos. Finally with Sandro.

PART 35

"Great job, Sandro," said Ellis, still stony-faced.

Sandro smiled briefly.

"Mr. Luca, would you step up to the bench, please," Judge Porta asked. Sandro walked up to the bench. Judge Porta leaned forward and said in a whisper: "You are one beautiful lawyer. *Bravo!*" He shook hands with Sandro.

"Thanks, Judge," Sandro said, hearing his own voice coming as if from a great distance.

Sandro started out of the courtroom with Sam and Mike. "It's all over, and I'm tired. But at least I know I put everything I had to give into this trial."

"That's fine, kid," said Sam, "but winning would have been the icing on the cake."

"No, Sam, for me the icing on the cake is that I did it the way I did. No matter what the jury says or what other people think about it, I did my job the best I knew how."

Sam snorted.

"Could I have done more, Sam?"

"No, Sandro, you couldn't. In fact, I don't think I ever saw anyone do as much."

Sandro smiled. "They sure knew they were in a fight though, didn't they?"

"That they did, kid. You really earned your spurs. But me, I want them all to count. I don't have time for moral victories. This case is all yours now, Sandro. I'm finished."

"What do you mean? You can't desert the ship now."

"It's your case. You know more about it than anyone in the goddamn world."

"If it's tried again, I need you with me, Sam."

"You don't need me. You'll handle it fine. I can't take this kind of strain again, not so soon."

The three of them stood facing the elevator door. They could hear the cables whining around the pulleys.

Mike finally broke his thoughtful silence." Do you *really* think they might have done it?"

"God knows." Sandro shrugged wearily. "It doesn't matter."

"Yeah, yeah. You did all you can. I heard all that."

"It's true. We've got enough just doing what we have to do, guarding the legal concept of guilty or not guilty. God's responsible for moral guilt or moral innocence. It's all part of the system, right, Sam?"

Sam looked at him, not speaking. He took a cigar from his breast pocket and unwrapped it.

"Come the millennium, it's going to be better, right, Sam?"

Sam bit off the end of the cigar and blew the bit of tobacco off his tongue. He grunted as he lit up.

The elevator arrived, and they entered.

"How long before we go back to trial?" asked Mike.

"Could be any time, but we'll have a couple of months, I'm sure," Sandro replied.

"Good. Cause I've been figuring. Somewhere out there is a colored guy about five nine or ten—"

"Hold it," said Sandro. "Right now, all we're going to look for is a drink. Maybe in a couple of months we'll talk about it."

"You guinea bastard, just because these guys are spics, you don't give a damn about them, is that it?"

Anyone watching the three men leaving the elevator and making their way out into Centre Street might have thought they were laughing happily.

CPSIA information can be obtained
at www.ICGtesting.com
Printed in the USA
LVHW092330260420
654483LV00001B/51

9 781480 476875